NURSERY

DARK NEBULA
BOOK 6

SEAN WILLSON

WELCOME TO DARK NEBULA

Thank you for buying this book!

If you're interested in a free novella entitled **Dark Nebula: Contact**, hearing more about the series, seeing new cover art as it's released, or getting exclusive access to sales as they happen, then you can subscribe to my newsletter online at:

seanwillson.com/subscribe

You can also drop me an email at:

author@seanwillson.com

I always love hearing from my readers.

DARK NEBULA SERIES
Novella: Contact (FREE)
Book 1: Isolation
Book 2: Discovery
Book 3: Generations
Book 4: Beacon
Book 5: Graveyard
Book 6: Nursery (This book)

PORTAL SERIES
Book 1: Drowning Earth
Books 2-4: Coming Soon…

CONTENTS

1

———————

ABIGAIL OLIVAW
OUTSIDE THE PROTO DARK NEBULA

They disembarked from the Ursis shuttle and headed down the enormous ramp, built for an alien species three to four times the size of a human. Abigail nervously squeezed the handle of the ornate silver case as she walked, all the while fighting back the urge to chuck the heavy thing out into the vacuum of space. Although she knew she couldn't do it, that didn't prevent the thought from crossing her mind, especially since the Therionic protist was inside.

She and the alien were bound as one, heart to literal heart. Instead of spending an eternity floating aimlessly in the gravitational limbo between the stars, the life force was safely ensconced inside the container, awaiting its meeting with the Beacon of Therion.

As she descended to the ground, she glanced around and took a deep breath. The smell of stale air wafted through her nostrils, and she gagged. Having spent so long on the Ursis home world of Arctordiea, she'd forgotten what purified human air smelled like. The reality made her stomach churn, and the only comparison that came to mind was the foul stench of decay.

Perhaps it was her situation, or the fact that the air onboard the alien ships had been so sweet and vibrant. It reminded her of traveling in a greenhouse filled with the fragrances of life.

"Someone needs to check on the atmosphere purifiers in this place," she said. "It smells like something died in here."

"Come on! You have been held captive for six months, and all you have to say is the air stinks?" Bradley's words reverberated through the cavernous shuttle bay.

Abigail froze halfway down the ramp and searched for his voice. She'd seen his face on video for years, but this was the first time she'd been in his presence in almost a decade. Her heart fluttered when she finally spotted him, and when she did, she couldn't help but smile. He'd just stepped through a doorway on the far side of the hangar, and, unless she was mistaken, Zachary was standing beside him.

She wiped at her face and fought back the surge of emotions threatening to consume her. "You're a sight for sore eyes. Both of you."

Cynthia squealed with delight and barreled over Abigail as she sprinted down the rest of the ramp and leapt into Bradley's awaiting arms. He spun her around several times before pulling her close and kissing her passionately – two lovers kept apart for far too long.

Ibu reached out and grasped Abigail's arm, steadying her from the shove. "I guess she was a tad excited?"

"Just a little." Abigail squeezed the handle of the case. "But I can understand why."

She took a few more steps down the ramp toward her brothers. "I hate to complain, but you would too. When you get used to air that smells like honeysuckle and morning dew, stepping into the stench of a stale locker room often brings one's lunch back to the forefront."

Zachary chuckled as he strode up to her and wrapped her in a huge bear hug. When he squeezed her, she dropped the case to return the gesture.

It was comforting to be with her family and to enjoy the warmth of their embrace again. She could practically feel her pent-up stress melting away the longer he hugged her. The only thing that could have been better happened a few seconds later when Bradley piled in and reached his arms around both of them. He squeezed with everything he had. And while it seemed like her ribs might shatter, she savored each moment with delight.

A few minutes of silence passed before she exhaled a content sigh. "I missed you guys," she muttered. "Especially you, you asteroid-riding knucklehead." She leaned to the side and nestled her head against Bradley, not wanting to let either of them go.

"Save some sugar for me, sister!" Cynthia eyed them from the sidelines but kept her distance. She merely glanced over at Ibu standing in silence next to her. The Nanil seemed to be confused and visibly uncomfortable around their public display of affection, but Abigail didn't care.

Cynthia would have some alone time with her man later. For now, Abigail was going to bask in the hug for a minute. It'd been far too long since she'd been able to do this. When she and Bradley were last together, they hadn't exactly left on the best of terms. In fact, she was the one who forced him to leave Sol.

"We're being watched," Zachary whispered, his mouth easing in close to her ear.

"What?" She leaned away and stared into his eyes. "By whom?"

"I believe your brother is referring to me," Hera said.

When Abigail spun around, she drew in her breath when she saw the source of the voice. Standing in front of her was her great-aunt Hera. Except it wasn't her. Instead of the elderly woman who'd helped create Sol's first faster-than-light drive and formed her own secret colony away from the family's prying eyes, she was staring at someone who wouldn't pass for being of legal age to drink. While she'd seen countless pictures of her aunt when she was young, and even stared at her through the window on her cryo-pod at the Sol Wheel, they'd never met before today.

The three of them separated but formed up in a line, and

Abigail kept her arms around her brothers. "And why would he care if you were watching us? It's not as if we're under arrest, right?"

Hera stood there motionless, staring first at Abigail and then at Ibu. Her gaze was like a laser through ice, and she half-expected the Nanil to burst into flames the longer she leered. After an uncomfortable pause, her attention returned to the three of them and she forced a smile before turning toward the doorway. "Come. Let us clean before we enter the ship. I fear you may have already contaminated this shuttle bay."

Abigail released her brothers and reached down to grab the case off the ground. When she looked up, she took a step backward.

A dozen people in light gray hooded suits and goggles came running out of the doorway in front of them and spread out into the room. She was preparing to run back into the shuttle when her family tightened their hold.

"It's alright," Bradley said. "They're just here to clean up."

She squinted and turned toward him. "Clean... what?"

"Why, our A.I. nanite friends, of course." Bradley squeezed her tight.

A second later, she felt a poke in her side where he was squeezing, and then her retinal comm flashed a warning. Her body had intercepted a foreign nanite on her skin, and it was requesting to pass her a message.

She narrowed her gaze and blink accepted it.

This is Brad. Sorry for having to send a message this way. I recorded this before we walked out here. We'll explain more later, but if you have any A.I. onboard, they're going to be confiscated and destroyed. We have a lot to talk about, but be careful, and tread lightly. Hera's a bit of a firecracker with a short fuse, just like Dad used to say. Oh yeah, I'm sure you already figured it out, but our aunt is a clone. She apparently has all the memories of the real Hera, whatever the hell that's worth. While you were in Delta Sagittarii, our messages to you were being filtered by her people, so we couldn't tell you in a comm. As you can see, things have gotten out of hand.

Abigail swallowed hard, and her comm flashed red as the foreign nanite destroyed itself. All that remained of the minuscule automata would be a microscopic mote of dust on her skin.

This was crazy. Whatever her aunt was up to, she wouldn't be giving up either of the A.I. still resting in the chamber above her heart. But she needed to talk to them, and fast.

She leaned her head on Zachary's shoulder and whispered in his ear. "You two converse with each other. I need a distraction."

He went to turn toward her, but paused midway. He must've figured out what she meant. "So, Cynthia. If the ships smell like honeysuckle, what does an Ursis smell like?"

Abigail smirked at the reaction on her face, but didn't hesitate or listen to Cynthia's reply. She opened a subvocal comm to Harold and Shauna. It was risky, but typing would be too slow.

"What are the odds of them finding you in my compartment?" she asked.

Harold was the first to answer. "There's a two percent probability they'll detect us, but we planned for that. Inside the chamber is a traditional data dot access port that links up to your retinal comm. Only after the external fake skin closes up and the inner wall of the enclosure receives the proper signal will the underlying membrane part to allow accessing one of our consciousness cores. Otherwise, it looks, feels, and scans like regular human dermis."

She hadn't realized how thorough they'd been with the design when she'd installed it several decades ago. But then again, it was serviced on multiple occasions. She just never bothered to ask what was being done. For all she knew, this had come in an upgrade.

"And if they inject me with their own nanites to probe my body? What then?"

"Then, either our spános coated finish protects us..." Shauna paused. "Or we die."

She swallowed hard at the thought. They'd managed to survive multiple attacks, saved her life countless times, helped her keep an alien entity at bay from trying to control her body, and in return their ancestor was about to put them through the literal electronic wringer in hopes of killing them.

Nothing made sense in this universe any longer.

Nothing.

"ENOUGH!" Abigail pounded her fist against the glass as the gas slowly dissipated into the floor. Her lungs were burning from the inside out, and just when she thought she was going to pass out, the door slid apart. She coughed into her hand and stormed through the opening, stopping mere centimeters from Hera's face. "Are you trying to fraking kill me?"

"Not at all. We're merely ensuring you're clean," Hera said, ignoring the invasion of her personal space. She nonchalantly glanced to her right at the panel beside the door. "The good news is that your body is free of alien parasites and that crutch of an A.I. our family has grown so fond of over the years. I trust the Ursis already dealt with your copy of

Harold? Last I heard, you never took a shit without him telling you it was okay."

Abigail drew in her breath and fought down the urge to cold-cock the bitch. "What the hell do you want, Hera? Shouldn't you be out in Delta Sagittarii, fraking up the lives of your clones? I mean, you've already shown you're adept at stealing my people's work from afar. You certainly didn't need to come here for that."

The crowd gathered around her did their best to suppress their amusement. Everyone, except her brothers, that is.

Hera let out a fake laugh and stepped backward, putting distance between them. "I always knew you had the Olivaw fire in your belly. I just never had a chance to experience it in person." She paused, as if waiting for Abigail to respond. When she didn't, Hera continued, "You never answered my question."

"You never answered mine." Abigail looked left and right and waved her hand around the room. "Is there anything in here that you and your people created, or did you pilfer everything from the Sol Olivaw Corporation?" She nodded at the computers on the far wall. "I recognize that configuration of panels from our 2277 design for the Atlas class battleship upgrades." She glanced upward. "And don't even get me started on this ship." She tilted her head, casting a sidelong glance at Zachary. "Isn't this your design doodle of the first gate ship? Unless I'm mistaken, that was like a decade ago."

"Well..." He cringed. "About twenty years, actually. It's crazy if you think about it. The physics around the decay and displacement of Cherenkov Radiation during the space-time gate transition took forever for me to work out."

She drew back. "Really? It's been that long? Are you—"

"Enough!" Hera slapped her hand against the top of a cabinet, and the bang boomed through the room. "I'm not here to argue with you about the past, you spoiled brat. I'm here to save you from yourself and our common enemy."

Abigail eased closer to her aunt. She wasn't about to back down from this hag. While she may have lost control of CoPE, she refused to lose her family. "Last I checked, we didn't need your help. You're the one who ran away from Sol. I guess you couldn't handle the heat."

"Are we planning on doing this tennis match thing all day?" Cynthia gestured between the two women. "I don't know about you all, but I could use some shut-eye and R&R with my man." She pulled Bradley closer, and he grinned.

"Unless you're placing us under arrest, auntie." Zachary smirked. "We're going to go catch up with our sister."

Hera glared at Abigail, and she returned the look in kind. Her mother always taught her to never back down to a bully. She just never imagined there'd be one in her family.

"Well, alrighty then." Zachary reached down and clasped her hand, tugging it gently toward the doorway.

She feigned resistance, but after he tweaked her hand a second time, she eased away and stepped up beside him.

As they neared the threshold, Hera called out, "We'll be having a debrief at 18:00 hours."

"You'll probably be alone." Abigail paused to check her comm as the door slid aside. It was 14:00 on the dot. "How about 09:00 tomorrow?" She didn't wait for a reply. She merely squeezed the ancient case still firmly in her hand and walked through the exit with Cynthia, Ibu, and her brothers in tow.

The door closed behind them without a sound, but she was pretty sure she heard the distant rumble of Hera's voice erupting on the other side. Even if she was imagining it, the thought brought a smile to her face.

ZACHARY HELD his finger to his mouth and walked around the table in the middle of his room. He was holding out some type of electronic scanning device and waving it through the air. Only after he made a complete circle and set it in the center of the table did Abigail realize what it was. It was a secure comm shield, the same kind they'd sent to the colonies to block all external eyes and ears from prying into communications from Sol.

When Zachary pressed his finger on the top of the device, the room illuminated in a faint blue light and a voice spoke out. "Security countermeasures are now in effect."

"Alright, we're as secure as we can get in this place." Zachary settled into the last empty seat beside Ibu and peered at the cloth-covered lump in the corner of the room. "Are you planning on telling us what's in there or not?"

"We'll get to that." Abigail swallowed hard. "It's probably best if we start from the top... maybe when we left Zeta Lupi." She glanced around the table. If she didn't go first, she'd lose the gumption to tell them. "I'll kick us off. Otherwise, my head might explode." She nodded at Cynthia and Ibu and smiled. "Both of you can jump in with details wherever I frak up. I'm sure I'll miss some stuff."

Over the hours that followed, she recounted every up, down, left, and right from their mission. She dove deep into their initial dead ends in the Nebula pockets, how they finally found the Ursis, and how they tagged some Galactic Alliance ships along for their ride.

"Wait," Zachary waved his hand. "You're telling me that when the tachyon strands from the gate drive wrapped around an object, it gated through? That... that shouldn't be possible." He leaned back in his chair and ran his hands through his hair.

"It's not impossible," Ibu said. "The calculations show it to be—"

"A fraction of a fraction of a percent," Zachary interrupted.

"And yet, we had two tagalongs that nearly ended our trip." Ibu crossed their arms. "We can talk later. I saved off all the telemetry. I have some theories on how it worked."

Abigail raised an eyebrow. "Did you preserve those recordings? I mean, the Phoenix is... you know, slag now."

"Of course, I did. Cynthia helped me with the data dump

before we descended through the missile defenses and landed through the roof," Ibu nodded toward Cynthia.

She smirked at the Nanil. "We were a pretty good team, the three of us."

Bradley reached out and rested his hand on her arm. "Wait… you destroyed the Phoenix and flew it through the ceiling of a building?"

She leaned into him and gave him a peck on the cheek. "Well, opposite order, but yeah. It was after Minula fought her way inside. But we're getting to that."

Zachary fidgeted with his hands and then looked up at Ibu. Something had been distracting him since the start of their conversation. "We need to talk about that tachyon strand."

Ibu pointed at their head and winked. "Noted."

"Alright, where were we?" Abigail asked.

"We'd just gated into the Dark Nebula near pocket three," Cynthia said.

"That's right. Ok…" She took a deep breath and started regurgitating the rest of their mission. A few hours passed, dozens more random interruptions and details filled in by Ibu and Cynthia, and she finally exhaled and collapsed back into her chair, holding her hands out to the side. "And here we are."

Her brothers stared blankly at her. She wasn't sure if she'd lost them when she tried to explain being the Ursis' Seguan, when she broke down in tears over losing Minula, or when she explained how the Therionic entity was part of her now, and how it turned the tables on them just before coming over to their ship. Either way, they were speechless for several minutes.

"So… this Therionic entity thing." Zachary glanced at the case resting under the blanket in the corner of the room. "Can you… feel it? Like… inside you?"

"I mean, right this second?" She shook her head. "No. But when it wants me to know it's there, I'm sure it'll make an appearance. Also, if I were to try to tell you something it didn't want you to know... well," she glanced at Ibu, "then I'd probably be writhing around in pain on the ground before the words fully formed in my mouth."

Zachary drew in his breath.

Bradley leaned forward with his elbows on the table. "It knows what you're thinking?"

"Not exactly," Abigail said. "While it can't see what I see, it seems to sense deception. And since I can't go anywhere without that thing," she nodded toward the lump in the corner, "it might as well be looking through my eyes."

"This is going to make things interesting." Bradley scratched his head. "And hard to talk. I mean, how do we... you know?"

She glanced at Ibu and then reached across the table, taking their hand in hers. With her eyes closed, she opened a mental link and time came to a screeching halt. "You can share the details later. We can't do it here, and you're going to need to be our intermediary. I'm so sorry. I hate doing this to you."

"It's not a problem. Really," Ibu said. "How are we planning on handling Hera? I mean, she's bound to catch on."

They were right. While they could tell her most of what happened inside the Nebula, there were parts they needed to withhold. And the Entity was one of those things. As she virtually sighed, an idea formed in her mind. "How would you feel about pretending to be my romantic interest? Like, for show?"

"I... have never been that to someone." Ibu squirmed mentally. "I'll likely need some guidance on the matter."

"That I can handle. Alright, let's start there. We'll chat later." Abigail pulled her hand away, and the room spun for a moment before snapping back into place.

"What was that?" Bradley leaned away. "Why did you—"

"Not ask about Hera?" Cynthia glanced behind her at the lump and reached over and pinched Bradley. "We were just about to do that."

"Ouch!" He rubbed his arm and winced.

Abigail laughed into her hand and shook her head. This was going to take some getting used to, that was for sure.

"Before we get started again." Zachary stood up. "Do you ladies… and… Ibu." He swallowed hard. "Sorry. Do you all need some food? I know I could use something to eat."

"I'm starved!" Ibu shot up. "Is there any chance they have pudding? Like real pudding?"

He smiled and rested his hand on their shoulder. "I'm not sure I'd call pudding real, but yeah, they have many flavors of mush here. Let's go down and get some grub." He reached out and grabbed the secure device from the center of the table and made his way toward the exit.

As they headed out, Abigail couldn't help but smile. She'd finally gotten some time with her family. Everyone except Pluto, that was.

She jogged up behind Zachary. "Say, where's your woman?"

IT WAS a few hours later when they returned to Zachary's quarters, and hours after that when they finished digging into what had happened at the Epsilon Eridani and Delta Sagittarii colonies. At least what they'd been able to piece together, anyhow. There were huge chunks of time that, no matter how hard they tried, they couldn't get anyone to fill in.

Abigail lay in bed in her quarters after Bradley showed her where to crash. She pondered all the things she'd learned that day from her family. Although there were still more questions than answers, the sheer number of facts they'd uncovered was remarkable.

When Kara arrived at the location where the third colony ship was supposed to be, the ship was there, but the crew was missing. At first, she wasn't sure what to do, so she poked around onboard, searching for clues as to where the colonists might have gone. After a few days of covering every centimeter from bow to stern, she was about to give up. But when she returned to her ship for the last time, she found someone waiting for her onboard - a few armed someones, to be precise. Apparently, they'd gotten the message Cynthia and Abigail had sent ahead, using Hera's fake body in Zeta Lupi as the conduit.

Fast-forward from there; they took her to a colony. Though, to this day, they're still not sure where it was. Even more surprising than that was its size. While they didn't know how many people Hera had convinced to go with her over the years, they knew how big the colony ship was, and the delta in population was enormous. They were set to arrive with two thousand colonists but had somehow managed to reach a population of nearly one million. That was over thirty times the size of Zeta Lupi, and that didn't even take into account the people necessary to maintain the thousands of starships at their disposal.

How they built the infrastructure so fast, they weren't sure. No one was. The only thing they knew for certain, beyond that they stole tech from Sol, was that they had an alien ally nearby. One with vast resources at the ready, and apparently, with cloning technology. That was how the colony had grown its body count so quickly; not through natural means, but through science and vats of human embryos growing at accelerated rates.

Their details on how the memories had been transferred into the bodies were still lacking, but they'd done it. Hera knew people, places, and things that only an Olivaw would know. And there were even times she actually showed emotions typical of a human. At least, that's what they'd heard. None of them had yet to experience it themselves. The strangest thing about Hera, though, was how myopic she was. Her sole focus in every conversation was to take back control of the human worlds and to destroy the Galactic Alliance, at all costs.

The more Abigail turned over the things she'd learned that night in her mind, the more tired she grew. And before she knew it, sleep was upon her.

<hr>

Epsilon Eridani, Liprosus Orbit

THE LIGHTS in Abigail's quarters blinked on without provocation as a siren blared overhead. A voice chimed in a second later: "We have arrived at Epsilon Eridani. Please prepare to dock with the beanstalk."

"Frickety frak," she muttered. "Who the hell set an alarm?"

A message appeared on her retinal comm from Shauna.

> It's 06:00, and we've reached Liprosus. I should've done the calculation when you suggested the new meeting time with Hera, but it didn't occur to me. That's fine, though, it'll be nicer dealing with Hera somewhere other than onboard this prison.

"Assuming we get that chance," she subvocalized. "After last night, something tells me she's going to want to control the time and place."

Abigail swung her legs out of bed and stood up, stretching her spine once she was upright. Her back was killing her. For an advanced species that had been in the universe for thousands of years, humans still hadn't mastered how to create a comfortable mattress.

A message from Harold came up on her comm.

> Maybe you shouldn't stay up all night in those chairs. I bet that's why your back hurts.

Having two other A.I. in her body at the same time was tiresome. Especially first thing in the morning. But he wasn't wrong. It was weird how he knew her better than she did sometimes. She'd have to talk to Zachary about getting a secure shield. This not being able to speak out loud to her A.I. was going to get old quickly.

Just as she was bending down to pick up the case with the entity in it, the door to her room slid open.

She jumped to the side. "What the hell?"

Bradley walked in and froze. "Oh, I'm sorry, sis. I was coming to wake you up. I guess I shouldn't have barged in like that."

"No, you shouldn't have. But… it's fine." She grabbed the case and started toward him. "It's not like I have a change of clothes or anything. I've been wearing these things for…" She paused with her hand on her jumpsuit. "Damn. Three months, I think. I need something else to wear when we get a chance." She shook her head. "So tell me, did you and Cynthia make up for lost time last night?"

He broke out into the cutest shade of pink she'd ever seen and simply stared down at the ground. It was so bright, it was like his face was going to explode.

"We… should go," he muttered, ignoring the question and stepping back into the hall.

"Aw, come on. Give me something!"

She followed him closely, and they wove their way aft toward the docking connectors on this massive ship. Along the route, they floated down multiple gravity lift tubes and passed by countless clones. None of them even glanced at her or Bradley. It was like they were humanoid robots or automated mannequins. But worse. They didn't appear to have even a smidge of personality. There were no casual conversations, no banter, and certainly no curious glances. It was all business onboard this ship.

Once they'd made their way to the furthest point aft, they stepped out into the shuttle bay. It was filled with the golden sunlight radiating off Liprosus.

Abigail gasped. "Wow! I forgot how beautiful this planet was."

She stared down at the surface. There was a canyon of some sort passing by down below. While she knew next to nothing about the landmasses of the world to figure out their location, the sight was still breathtaking.

"Over there is the leftover from my landing." Bradley nodded down at the ravine.

"That?" She pointed at the deep groove in the ground. It seemed to go on forever.

"Yep." He shook his head and stared. "Pluto brought us down just over the horizon. We were coming in at a few thousand kilometers per hour. It was crazy. Looking back on it now, it's remarkable we even survived."

She studied the topography below and how deep the groove had dug into the ground. From up here, parts of it appeared to still be smoldering. And it wasn't until she looked closer that she saw that the smoke coming out of the valley wasn't natural. It was from some sort of construction.

"It ain't pretty." Bradley shook his head. "But it's taking shape."

"What is?" Abigail asked.

"That there is the new human colony on Liprosus."

She shook her head. "Why not rebuild near the old one?"

"Oh, we are. But down there," he gestured along the jagged scar his landing had created, "that's freshly turned-over ground. There's building material everywhere. We flew through some epic vein of ore that would've taken months or years to dig out. And now it's exposed and ripe for the picking."

"No shit." She chuckled and glanced around the docking area of the immense starship. There, in the distance, someone caught her eye.

"Kara!" She frantically waved her hand in the air. "Kara Olivaw! Over here."

The woman froze and slowly backed toward them with a confused look on her face. It was like she was unsure who they were for a few seconds.

Finally, Kara turned and strolled up to them. "Oh. Hi, Abigail. How are you?"

Her gaze narrowed as she raised her hands upward. "That's it? All I get is a 'hi'?"

"I… guess not." Kara leaned forward and gave her a hug. An awful, 'I'm only doing this because I have to' kind of hug. When she pulled away, she didn't give either of them a chance to say anything. "I really need to be going. Hera has me heading back to… the Delta Sagittarii colony to help out with something."

That seemed off. "You mean, the colony that's not in Delta Sag? Do you happen to know where it actually is?"

Kara shook her head. "I don't. I just… get on a ship, and it takes me there."

"And you're okay with that?" Bradley crossed his arms.

She screwed up her face. "Why wouldn't I be?"

"No reason." Abigail fake-smiled. "Safe journeys, auntie."

As Kara was turning to leave, a message suddenly appeared on her retinal comm from Harold.

Ask her how Khumalo is doing.

While the request was strange, she didn't question him. She merely raised her hand and waved. "Say, Kara? One more thing."

"Yeah, what's up?" She turned around.

"I was wondering… do you know how Khumalo is doing these days?"

Kara froze, and for a few seconds, it looked like she wasn't quite sure how to answer until she did. "She's… fine. We haven't talked in a while, though." She glanced over her shoulder at something in the distance and then back at them. "I really need to—"

"Be going," Abigail interrupted with a smile. "I know. You said that already. I guess we'll catch up some other time."

Kara didn't wait to be stopped again. She practically sprinted out of there toward the exit.

"What was that about?" Bradley asked. "And who's Khumalo?"

"I'll… tell you later," Abigail muttered.

She was still processing the meaning behind Kara's reply. She knew exactly who Khumalo was when Harold asked. The problem was, Khumalo was a "he" and not a "she", and Kara of all people should've known that. At least she used to.

2

JOYCE GREEN
SOL, EARTH ORBIT

While the dynamics of the Galactic Alliance's inner sanctum were unknown to Joyce, that didn't prevent her from planning their demise. The scientists in Epsilon Eridani had been combing through the remains of the Selene moon ships ever since the Beacon battle ended. They found countless intact and valuable data banks with strategic intel on various species in the GA.

She studied the worlds that comprised the Qudoculi Empire. Their planets were mostly confined to the center of the Milky Way, where many star systems were less than a light year apart. It was hard to imagine the density of these worlds, let alone the military strength it would take to topple them.

"Those are jammed together pretty tight," Ryder remarked as he walked up behind her and wrapped his arms around her.

She flinched at the unexpected interruption, but her body quickly relaxed under his embrace. Any time she could spend a few minutes in his presence was welcome, even when she couldn't sleep.

"The Qudoculi are one of the strongest aliens in the GA," she began. "Their hive mind, combined with the short distances between their stars, makes them a formidable species." She reached up and caressed his arms. "But no matter how hard I try, I can't quite find a path to crack them open."

"I see you're still planning the demise of worlds. Are you even trying to get a full night's sleep?"

When he kissed her neck, shivers raced through every centimeter of her body, all the way down to her prosthetic legs. While the bio-connection attempted to mimic the effect of the intimate gesture through her artificial limbs, it wasn't the same. That didn't nullify the impact, though. She still leaned into him and melted into the warmth of his body.

"Someday in the hopefully not too distant future, they will pay for what they've done to us. For what they've done to me and mine." She reached out and spun the cloud of stars marked in red for Qudoculi space.

After a few seconds, he extended his hand and stopped the rotation, leaning in closer to the holo-projection. "It seems to me the easiest way to eliminate a species that's densely populated is by employing the oldest strategy in the book."

"And what's that?"

"A blockade," he muttered. "With a force as big as the Qudoculi, they must have hundreds of billions of mouths to feed. Right?"

She nodded. "Over a trillion at the last estimate. Honestly, we're not certain how accurate the data in the species catalog is. Many of the captured Bynaurys we've been able to interrogate have painted the inner sanctum of the GA as corrupt. Some even claimed they expanded within the abandoned star systems of species found guilty via the tribunal, which could mean they're far larger than our estimates." While his idea was simple, it could work if they had enough forces. But the same could be said for almost any plan.

She reached out and highlighted all the species the GA had passed judgment on or sanctioned since its founding. The stars nearest the center of the Milky Way lit up in a sea of yellow.

"Wholly shit," Ryder muttered. "Tell me the other GA

species aren't blind. They must have access to this same information."

He pulled his arms away and stepped around her into the star field. Suddenly, he was part of the projection and began adjusting it, looking at it from different angles. "This is insane."

"Yeah. That's what I thought when I first saw it." She walked back to the sink on the far wall of their quarters and retrieved a chilled bulb of water, squeezing half of it into her mouth in one gulp. "The brains in strategy claim these details were buried deep in the core of a mostly intact Selene ship. Apparently, they were wrapped with multiple layers of impenetrable encryption."

He glanced away from the display and locked his gaze with hers. "If it was impenetrable, how did we get inside?"

"I'll give you one hint: an A.I. helped." She squeezed the rest of the bulb into her mouth and tossed it in the receptacle on the wall.

"It was Shauna, wasn't it?" he asked.

"Bingo!" Joyce stepped up beside her man in the middle of the hologram and stared out at the sea of yellow stars. Shauna, being a stowaway on board the GA flagship for half a decade, allowed her to unlock more of their systems than anyone else. And those were the things she was telling them about. Joyce was pretty sure the A.I. was still holding cards close to her chest.

The lights overhead flashed green, and her retinal comm chirped. She reached up and tapped her ear. "Joyce here, go."

"We're entering Earth's orbit, Captain," Naomi, her communications officer, said.

"Thank you." She dismissed the holo-display and started toward the bathroom. She needed to clean up. "Can you please open a comm to Fleet Admiral Nguyễn and tell him we're ready to receive him? He never responded to that part of our message."

"Certainly, Captain." Naomi cut the comm.

If there was one thing she'd learned from watching

Abigail and Harold's intel on this Nguyễn character, it was that he was a hothead. He loved listening to his own voice and, most of all, he always tried to get the upper hand.

"Hey! You can't shower without me," Ryder called playfully as he hopped across the room and slid up behind her. "Last I heard, we're under strict orders to conserve water. So it only makes sense."

"Oh, really?" she giggled as he grabbed his shirt and pulled it up and over his head. "And who told you that?"

He never did answer her.

<hr>

Sol, Luna

JOYCE STORMED through the security checkpoint, and the alarms blared around her.

"Ma'am!" a Sol guard called out. "I'm going to have to ask you to come back and empty your pockets. If you don't, I'll be forced to shoot."

She waved her hand at one of her guardsmen, and he dropped back to deal with it. Her patience had worn thin, and she didn't have time for the macho posturing Nguyễn was pulling. First, he changed the location from Earth to Luna, and now he made her and her team go through three layers of security checks. These fraking Inners never ceased to amaze her.

Her guards flanked her on all sides as she barreled through the halls of the aged building. Except for a few coats of fresh paint, this military facility was many multiples of her own age, and it showed. To be honest, she'd expected him to summon her to the newer congressional council chambers. But then again, those had been funded and built by the Olivaws, like everything else in Sol. This, however, was one of the few places on Luna constructed by a company not tied to the family that toppled humanity.

She hadn't realized how accustomed she'd grown to the

new designs of the colony or the starships she'd been on since leaving Sol. It was hard to imagine returning to this place for good.

Fortunately for her, she didn't have to.

"Ahh, Commander Green!" Admiral Nguyễn walked out of the far chamber room she was marching toward. "I see you've arrived. I trust you and your delegation are well."

She shook her head. "Your juvenile antics cost us half a day dealing with your change in venue and the antiquated docking facilities here on this dusty rock. Not to mention your overzealous security checks designed to piss me off. It's not like we have a war to deal with or anything. But yeah, we've arrived."

He stared at her with a smug grin, and she had to do everything in her power not to clench her fist and take a swing at him. For some reason, Hera wanted this buffoon on their side. Sol, she understood; this guy, not so much.

As they stood there silently staring at each other, her security team finished sweeping the room. A few tense minutes later, her senior guardsman exited the chamber and stepped up beside her. "The place is littered with bugs, sir. I counted at least a dozen, and that's not including the ones we collected on our way here." He tapped a button on the side of his goggles and shared the image with her retinal comm.

She had three of either Harold's or someone else's nanites crawling around on her person. This whole situation was untenable. "I'm afraid we're done here. I won't be," she tilted her head, "how shall I put it, bending over and kissing your ass, Admiral. Not here. Not ever. Your old-school negotiation tactics have failed, and you've let the people of Sol down today. You could have ushered them into a new era of prosperity and technology, but alas, you're too focused on measuring the size of your dick. I'll be reaching out to the CoPE congressional delegates and sharing the news. You and the citizens of Sol will need to deal with the Galactic Alliance on your own."

Her retinal comm chirped. It was an incoming message

from Ryder, who was standing behind her. She already knew what it said, so she didn't bother opening it. She simply spun around and marched out the way they came.

"Commander Green!" Nguyễn reached out toward her as she turned, but she was too fast, and he missed. "Please, let's just talk. I'm sorry. Really."

"Like I already said, you lost your chance, Admiral." She stormed past the guard who was still arguing with the technician at the checkpoint. When they realized it was her, he stopped mid-sentence and stepped in behind the others.

She glanced at Ryder. "I want off this fraking rock as fast as possible."

"Yessir!" He began issuing orders, and her people sprinted forward, clearing the checkpoints the rest of the way to the shuttle bay.

* * *

Sol, Departing Luna

THERE WAS no additional resistance on their march out, nor when their Terminus destroyer pulled away from Luna. It wasn't until they were about to engage their gate drive that a secure comm came through.

"We're receiving a video feed from Fleet Admiral Nguyễn, Captain," Naomi said. "Shall we delay the transition?"

Joyce stared at the wall screen in front of her. In the center was the delicate droplet of Earth and Luna, encircled by a sea of stars and framed mostly by the black void of space. Each star represented both a miraculous wonder to explore and a chance at facing one's untimely death. Had Hera not asked her to return to Sol and convince CoPE to join them, she wasn't sure whether she would have visited this star again. There were too many shattered memories here; memories of her son and her ex-husband, both of whom were now dead.

"Put him on," she muttered.

The face of Admiral Nguyễn appeared on the wall screen.

"Commander Green, thank you for taking my comm. I'm glad I caught you before you gated." He smiled.

She didn't budge or respond to his words. If he was hoping she'd relent on her course of action, he was mistaken. The sooner she left this place, the better.

"I'll cut to the chase," he began. "Sol needs your help. Our worlds are reeling from the devastation caused by the Galactic Alliance tribunal, and we need the technology the Olivaws have at their disposal. What we're getting from Harold is far less than what you seem to possess. Right now, we're limp ducks in a world full of wolves hell-bent on killing us."

While it was an apt analogy, it wasn't entirely precise. He forgot the part about how they were bleeding out, and the wolves were circling them, preparing to pounce. She stiffened her posture, still waiting for the right moment. Giving this man a centimeter wasn't in the cards. Not again.

"I trust you agree with my assessment of our situation?" Nguyễn asked.

She raised an eyebrow. "And what makes you think I'm not a wolf?"

He recoiled, and his eyes widened. "While you may have been gone for a few years, I would imagine your ties to the people of the Inner and Outer Rings are more than surface deep. If I recall correctly, your aunt and extended family still live in the United States, in Idaho, I believe."

Her blood boiled at the mention of her aunt. "You mean the woman who broke up my parents and ruined my childhood? The same woman with whom my father cheated until she tossed him aside, and he took his own life days later? You mean that woman?" Her lips curled.

His mouth fell open, and he shot a sideward glare at one of his officers. "I didn't—"

"That's right," she interrupted, her body leaning forward. "Once again, you didn't think before you spoke. From what I've heard, you rarely do. You act out of either emotion or ignorance, and sometimes both. But this time, there's no

Harold here to whisper solutions through your comm. The last time you regurgitated what someone told you in your ear, you sealed your fate and that of billions of others."

She turned and went to raise her hand toward Naomi.

"I'm sorry," he muttered.

The line fell quiet.

When she glanced back to see if he was still there, his posture had sagged, and his eyes were vacant. He was defeated. "I... shouldn't have made you and your people wait. I should have greeted you with open arms."

She nodded. It had taken forever, but he finally apologized. That was a pretty big step for someone like him. While Harold might still be prompting him, he was no doubt sincere in his words. He knew Sol and CoPE were falling. All the signs were there. They would implode within a few years and probably turn to war and anarchy if they didn't intervene. Which brought her back to the mission Hera sent her here for.

"You're right. You should have made it simple." She eased forward. "Your actions have consequences, Admiral. They always have. You've just been oblivious to them for too long to notice, shielded by layers of military law. Your hatred and slaughter of the Outers is well-documented, and even though I came from that pale blue dot, we all know where my allegiance lies. And don't even get me started on your hotrod antics with the tribunal. I hate to say it, but you're lucky Abigail Olivaw was a few steps ahead and left you with an ace up your sleeve. Or, in this case, in your ear. Otherwise, you'd be dead. All of you would."

"If it weren't for the Olivaws, I believe you would be dead as well," he corrected. "Unfortunately, the Galactic Alliance dealers have reshuffled the deck, and they stacked the cards in favor of the wolves."

She grinned and bared her teeth. "Like I said earlier, what makes you think I'm not a wolf in sheep's clothing? Besides, I'm actually quite fond of the hand I've been dealt."

He slowly tilted his head. "The question is, are you willing to share it?"

"That depends." She took a step backward and eased down into her command chair.

"On what?" His camera zoomed in on him.

While she knew the establishment had been battered after the GA attacks, it had still managed to cobble together representation, and broader emergency elections were coming. What she didn't know was who the real power players were. "How quickly can you gather the interim heads of the Inner and Outer Rings? I believe each party has a frontrunner for the delegate seat. Correct?"

He tweaked the badge on the lapel of his uniform. "That won't be necessary. I'm still the acting leader of Sol under the War Act instituted by former President Olivaw."

She waved her hand in dismissal. "Only until the elections next month."

Nguyễn nodded.

He should have known she'd have intel on Sol, which meant his ego was still clouding his decisions. That may have been enough to confuse and delay a room full of aliens, but they needed more from him now. The question was whether he could rise to the challenge.

"If you have any hope of seeing my hand, you'll gather a small contingent of representatives and bring them onboard my ship before we leave. You have twelve hours, Admiral." She nodded at Naomi and she cut the comm.

3

BRADLEY OLIVAW
EPSILON ERIDANI, LIPROSUS

The beanstalk space elevator dropped them off just outside the danger zone of the new colony's build site. While the purposeful crash of their asteroid had created an astonishing ready-made shopping aisle of ore, it also brought with it risks.

"The terrain is pretty unstable in parts." Bradley pointed down the cliff face at a fleet of automata bulldozing and digging their way through the impact ejecta. It would take them months, if not years, to build out the fifty-kilometer stretch of the newly-formed valley. Even though the site needed cleanup, it was the perfect ground zero for building a colony.

In his mind's eye, he could already see a river flowing down the middle of the gorge, with buildings embedded in the cliff faces. On one side were housing and recreation, and on the other side was work. The divide could serve both as a healthy means to allow someone to focus on themselves and as an opportunity to invigorate the workforce. With all the lives that had been lost since the destruction of the first colony, something as simple as this could really help shape the new settlement going forward.

Abigail leaned sideways over the edge of the ground car

and stared down. "Aren't we worried about the buildings settling and shifting in the loose dirt?"

"Nah." He tweaked the controls and programmed the car to tour the construction area. "We created designs for the rings that had automatic pier tunneling built into their foundations. The technology isn't new. They've been using it on Earth for nearly a century in some of the Antarctic cities. You know, snowmelt and soil displacement and all."

She nodded silently and stared at the thousands of automated machinations following their programming. He could tell she wasn't sure what he was talking about. She'd always let the geeks handle the tech side of things. He'd wager she wouldn't even be able to explain the mechanics of solar energy, much less geothermal, nuclear fission, or the intricacies of the retinal comm that had become an integral part of her existence. Especially since they'd shut off the invasive devices when they touched down planetside in an attempt to get some privacy. For most humans, living without their comm meant losing most of their supposed knowledge. It was a crutch that even he leaned on too often, but she'd been far worse.

He stared down at the robots and watched as they formed up into an ad hoc unit to move a giant boulder up the hill. Alone, they were too weak, but together they could manage it. Unlike her, their father would have understood how most technology worked. He cared about all the nitpicky details of things.

"I wish Dad had seen what we managed to build here in these colonies and around the new stars." He swallowed hard. While it had been a month since Abigail had returned from the Proto Dark Nebula, it had been over two decades since their father had been alive.

She leaned back and met his gaze with a smile. "Dad would have loved it. Especially with the treasure trove of new toys you brought back from the Lupus Dark Nebula. Seeing him around the first contact probe was always like a kid in a candy store, and that was after staring at it most of his life.

The things you returned with." She made an exploding gesture over her head.

The mention of the Lupus Dark Nebula sent shivers down his spine. While they'd made it out alive, they'd only done so by the skin of their teeth. Had they not found Ibu, there's no telling where they'd be right now. It was hard to believe that it had only been a year since they'd gotten back. Zachary and Harold took a while to crack the data and consciousness cores they'd uncovered, and in the nick of time too. The weapon designs thought up by their ancient human ancestors had helped turn the tide in the Beacon Battle. They'd enabled humanity to kill millions of Galactic Alliance aliens and destroy thousands of their deadly Selene moon ships.

Now, that same treasure trove was being put to positive use in creating this colony - a new home for humankind among the stars.

He wiped his eyes. The thought of his father sitting beside him, experiencing this place, this untamed world, was all too much. Their time together had been too short.

"Dad always loved himself a new gadget," he said, turning over the jet-black rock in his hand - the shard of spános he'd picked up on Earth the day he decided to leave Sol for good.

They both chuckled. Everyone knew their father as a consummate tinkerer. He constantly pushed technology in directions people hadn't anticipated, or sometimes even wanted.

Abigail stared down at her hands, as if she were struggling to form her words. He could never tell what she was thinking, but her mannerisms reminded him of their mother.

She glanced up and locked eyes with him. "Do you ever think about how things would be different if he were still with us?"

He squeezed the rock tightly, feeling the edges of the stone cutting into his skin. He didn't let go, but maintained the pressure as a reminder of his loss - of all their losses.

"I have thought about that every minute of every day since I watched that footage."

A glimmer of a tear sparkled in the corner of her right eye. "What about before that? Did you think about him, or any of us for that matter?"

He bit his lip and looked out the window. The edges of six new community rings were barely visible in the distance. The massive structures came up to the edge of the valley, their curved exterior descending far down into the floor of the ravine and well beyond. It made for quite the sight when you stumbled upon them like this. They almost gave the impression that someone had carved them out of rock and stone, but he knew better. It'd taken days and days to sculpt that region, much like the years it took him to put a wall up around his family and his feelings.

What he wanted to tell her was yes, he thought of them all the time. He wanted to tell her that any time he received a comm from Sol or had a moment to himself to reflect on a problem, their faces comforted him from afar. But he didn't tell her that. He couldn't lie to her. The fact was, he'd been too busy to dwell on the past. Between colony planning, preparing to leave Sol, their accelerated departure, and then coming out of cryo-stasis and having to deal with the challenges of a new colony, he didn't exactly have extra hours each day to reminisce. But that had been the point of leaving in the first place. Starting over.

"I'll take your silence as an answer," she said as she brushed the wrinkles out of her pants, leaving behind a brief streak from the tears she had wiped away.

"That doesn't mean I don't love you. All of you. I just…" He fought back the lump in his throat.

"Needed time." She reached out and rubbed his knee. "I get it. I do." She stared at him and smiled, letting the weight of the acknowledgment settle before she spoke again. Then she finally said the two words he never thought she would say.

"I'm sorry." She squeezed his leg.

He wiped at his eyes with his sleeve and shifted in his seat. "For what?"

"For sending you here. For pushing you away all those years. For lying to you. Hell, for not listening to you sooner." She exhaled. "You always said the family was too secretive. Too insular." She chuckled and pulled her hand away. "And that was before you even realized the truth."

He shook his head and laughed at the candor of her words. "It's hard to imagine how little I knew about our family back then. To think I'd been lashing out about wanting to do more philanthropy, or about us not sharing things like the technology at the Wheel. It's crazy, especially when you consider how long our family had been living behind the veil of so many dangerous lies." He ran his hands through his hair. "We inherited a rat's nest of deceit, and it was bound to fall apart eventually. It blows my mind every time I think about it. I mean, how did we even keep track of the sheer scale of the deception?"

"We all know the answer to that," she muttered.

Harold.

He didn't have to say his name out loud. Neither of them did. But they knew he was the glue that had kept things going for so long.

"But it wasn't his fault alone," he said, squeezing his fist. "Luna designed his programming to both protect and fulfill the will of the family. A family of humans. It was them, it was dad, and Kara, and Hera, and Zeus. They all… each and every one of them decided to keep the subterfuge alive."

"Until us," she muttered.

When he looked over at her, she, too, had anger in her eyes. Her hands were clasped tight, and he could see her knuckles turning white.

"Until us," he echoed. "The GA will pay. Every—single—alien species will feel what we felt watching our father die."

She narrowed her gaze. "But is that really necessary? I was honestly considering dismantling the new regime and ensuring we left it in good hands. Not that I'm not keen on taking down the GA. Everyone knows the inner sanctum could use some resetting. But I don't know if we're strong enough to make them pay. It's a pretty damn big galaxy, bro. Even with Hera's people and the Ursis on our side."

He wasn't sure if she was scared of the fight, or of not being in charge of it. "I assume you mean yourself when you mention good hands?"

"Hell no!" she spat. "I… want something… else. And leading a gaggle of incorrigible humans is not that thing."

A cartoon image of the Inner and Outer legislature popped into his mind. It was a meme that made the rounds before he left Sol. It depicted a group of politicians debating on a pedestal while the masses they served starved around them. The imagery and its variants had been quite vivid online. The origins of the depiction were during the months of bickering, debate, and voting that those same government officials had done before the first ship left for Epsilon Eridani. And it was all over the wording of a plaque that sat in the middle of the original colonial ring. The same ring that was presently a smoldering hole in the ground on the far side of the planet.

He wasn't sure why that particular image came to mind when she spoke. Maybe he'd always seen her as a member of that gaggle she mentioned.

"What is that something else you're looking for?" He glanced over at her.

She rubbed her palms against her slacks. "I don't know. But first things first. I need to get rid of this weight I'm carrying." She tilted her head toward the storage compartment at the rear of the ground car. "And then we have to fix what we broke."

While he didn't disagree with her sentiment, she was missing the means of making it happen. Without knowing more about what she was seeking, her idea was just that, more empty words. And he was tired of talking. He wanted action.

"I think their plan to take out the Nursery makes sense." He slid over and took the wheel of the ground car.

Abigail reached out and pulled his shoulder, making their car jerk as the autonomous system retook control.

He spun around and raised his hands. "Hey! You almost—"

"You don't seriously think we can pull it off, do you?" Her anger from earlier was now being directed at him. "They'll slaughter us."

"I'm aware of how strong they are." He pointed skyward. "I was in the middle of the shit they rained down while closing that Nebula. I watched our people kick their ass."

"Only because Hera showed up."

He snapped his fingers. "Exactly! And now we have the Ursis and the full strength of Hera's clone fleet."

She shook her head and sighed. "They got as torn up stealing that Beacon as we did. And besides, Hera can only grow bodies so fast. We need time. It'll take years to regroup."

He was beginning to realize that if he wanted revenge for his father's death, he might need to figure out where to ally his energy and focus. "We can't wait a few years, and you know it. Once word gets back to the GA, that Nursery will spread out. The last thing they'll want is to lose control. And without those Selene ships, they're easy pickings with our gate drives. We have to strike fast, while the embers of our last win are still raging."

"But at what cost?" she muttered.

He glared at her. "Cost? Are you kidding? What more can we sacrifice? I mean, seriously. Our mother and father are dead, they decimated our family, Sol is on its last legs, and besides Zeta Lupi, our colony situation is in shambles. Costs? I think we can afford to lose a few million clones and some giant bears if it helps humanity win this. And the last thing I remember you telling us was how bloodthirsty the Ursis were for revenge. Like it or not, sis, it's time to strike. The longer we remain idle, the more we'll lose our momentum. We can deal with the consequences of our unlikely allies after the deed is done."

The car fell silent, and Abigail shook her head, seemingly in disgust. At least that's what he figured it was.

He turned back around and grabbed the controls again, setting the course for the furthest colonial ring. She'd wanted to experience what their colony had been like before the attack, and this was the best way he could think of to make it happen without using virtual reality.

While he didn't expect to see eye to eye with her about the war, he figured she'd be closer to his position than she was. After all, she'd seen what the GA had done to humans in Lupus and how they cut the Ursis off for nothing more than fear and greed. Heck, he expected he'd be the one talking her down off the edge. Especially when she found out about their father.

If there was one thing he never understood, it was what made his sister tick. Something bad must have happened to her inside that Nebula. Either that, or she wasn't letting on what this Entity was doing to her.

4

ZACHARY OLIVAW
EPSILON ERIDANI, LIPROSUS

His retinal comm flashed an error when he tried to locate them. "Where the hell is Bradley?" Zachary muttered under his breath.

The Ursis emissaries had landed five minutes ago, and the first meeting of this new alliance was about to kick off. Of course, two of the Olivaw dignitaries were MIA.

When the doorway to the Ursis shuttle opened, Zachary did a double-take. Despite all the preparation, he still wasn't prepared for the true proportions of their guests, or their manner of greeting.

Haradis strolled down the ramp and took a deep breath at the bottom as he hesitantly glanced around. The Ursis wasn't sure what to expect from this strange new world, especially with so many humans onlookers gawking at his approach. Most of them weren't used to meeting aliens, let alone ones more than twice their height. His massive four-and-a-half-meter frame towered over Hera and Nathan, while Zachary stood safely with the other gathered delegates well behind them.

"Welcome to Liprosus." Hera and Nathan stepped forward, and she offered her hand in greeting.

The king stared down at the tiny, outstretched human hand and then carefully shook it. Watching his paw envelop her delicate fingers and part of her arm was like seeing a bear bat at a strawberry. Zachary half-expected her hand to come away bloodied and bruised.

"Thank you, Ambassador." Haradis bowed his head and then straightened up. His gaze panned over the collected delegates and landed on Zachary.

"And you must be Z." Haradis nudged Nathan aside and barreled toward Zachary. His massive feet thumped against the ground as he went.

At first, Zachary flinched and glanced around, locking eyes with Pluto. Neither of them was sure what to do next. Surely, the Ursis wasn't referring to him. No one apart from Pluto and his family called him that.

"I don't..." he muttered and froze in place.

But it was too late. The Ursis was already on top of him. It wasn't until Haradis had engulfed him in his arms and lifted him into the air that Zachary realized what was happening. The king was giving him a hug.

"Your sister has told me much about you and your clan." Haradis squeezed him tight, and his embrace was surprisingly comfortable, even being dangled a few meters off the ground.

Zachary let out an awkward laugh. "I hadn't realized you and her spoke that often."

"Oh... we haven't gabbed in weeks," Haradis began, "but we spent many a day and night talking back on Arctordiea. She told me some epic tales of you and your family and your countless adventures. At one point, I wondered if you were even real. The master scientist and creator of the space-time gateways that saved our people."

Zachary swallowed hard. "I... didn't know you and my sister were such good friends." He hadn't seen Abigail in a few days. Since she returned from her mission, she'd spent most of her time either alone or with Ibu.

Haradis lowered him down onto his feet and spun around, searching the crowd of shocked onlookers. "Speaking of which, where is your sister anyhow?"

"She'll meet up with us later. She's with…" Pluto paused and looked at Zachary. "Your Entity," she muttered.

The Ursis froze, his gaze lingering in the distance toward the ring building. Zachary could almost see the giant's shoulders stiffen at the mention of the Entity. He knew as well as anyone how evil the alien being was.

"You must be the warrior Abigail called Pluto," another voice said.

Everyone spun around and gasped. No one had even heard the other Ursis descend from their shuttle, least of all the entourage of guards now flanking the greeting party. For such a massive species, they were remarkably light on their feet.

When Zachary identified the source of the voice in the middle of the group, he stared in awe. Standing behind Haradis was another Ursis dressed in a lavish multicolored robe that seemed to flow with a life of its own. The female was holding an intricate golden staff embellished with a simple yet delicate crystal, which was somehow levitating off the end of the enormous stick.

"I… I am Pluto." She stepped closer to Zachary. "I'm not so sure about the warrior part, though. And who might you be?"

"I'm so sorry." Haradis reached out. "I assumed Abigail told you. This is Klus. My—"

"Head of the Royal Guards," Klus interrupted. She tensed up, as if she was struggling not to make eye contact with the king. Instead, her attention was focused on Pluto. "Abigail spoke highly of you. She spun some yarns about how you fought off ancient human robots in Lupus, had a dogfight with a Shu moonlet, and how you rode an asteroid down to this planet. She even claimed you threw yourself after a GA rocket headed toward your binary star Parvus. Many of our people thought you and the rest of your family were pure fiction." She looked her up and down. "But now that I've met you and stood in your presence, I can tell they're probably real. You are indeed a warrior."

Klus reached out her paw and when she rested it on Pluto's shoulder, Zachary swore he saw a faint glow coming from her abdomen. And then it fades just as quickly as it had appeared.

"I didn't know you were—" Klus began

"King Umbra." Pluto gently brushed the female Ursis' paw off her stomach. "Perhaps we should head inside. Our generals are itching to get down to business."

ZACHARY STOOD with his back against the far wall of the command center. It was a redesigned version of the same room they had in the Archégonos facility, except this one wasn't kilometers underground; it was in the middle of the new colony.

Standing down in front of the massive main wall screens were Haradis, Hera, Nathan, and a handful of their trusted military advisors. They'd been arguing over training exercises and the minutiae of the battle preparations for hours, and there was no end in sight. They hadn't even gotten to discussing the Nursery itself.

Ever since Shauna shared the details of the Galactic Alliance's staging area with them a few months ago, the generals had been foaming at the mouth. Being as it was the aliens' hub for refueling, refurbishing, and constructing their Selene moon fleet, it made an ideal military target. With the Beacon battle win in hand, Hera arriving on the scene, and now the Ursis joining their little alliance, the tide of this war had turned in their favor – or so the military brass believed.

He watched as General Tremarcus, one of Haradis' elder generals, paced back and forth in front of the other dignitaries. Each thunderous step of the shaggy alien led to more and more verbal insults being thrown in their native tongue. If it weren't for his translator being turned on, he wouldn't even have known what the alien was saying. Even though they'd agreed to disable the devices, Zachary couldn't handle not knowing what they were saying.

As it turned out, both sides were pissed, and neither wanted to make concessions - at least not this early in negotiations. Hera was pushing hard for the Ursis to hand over control of their military fleet. In return, the aliens were demanding full and unencumbered access to the human gate technology. Neither was likely to happen, and they knew it.

After the Ursis general made his hundredth or so pass, he paused and glanced around, searching for somewhere to sit. When he eventually spotted a chair and attempted to rest his weary bones, the furniture collapsed under his massive frame. A resounding crash echoed around the room as the general was unceremoniously dumped onto his backside.

"I'm so sorry, General." Hera spun around and glared at her staff. "Someone, get him another chair or a bench!"

"That won't be necessary, Ambassador." General Tremarcus slapped his paw against the ground and hopped up. He was surprisingly nimble despite the gray fur weaving throughout his speckled coat.

Neither Klus nor Haradis budged or offered to lend a hand to the man. He figured they knew better, and judging by his facial expressions, the fall had embarrassed him and pushed him over the edge.

In that moment, Zachary finally understood why the GA had designed their fleet of ships to be so utilitarian and flexible. With the variety of alien species in the alliance, it was safer to cover all the bases, versus risking losing faith or trust over something as simple as falling on one's backside.

But the fall wasn't the worst thing to come out of this meeting. Even without it, their path was doomed.

"Zachary, can you please come down here and help us work through the particulars of how we can train together?" Hera waved him toward the front.

The last thing he wanted was to be thrown in the middle of the alien crossfire. He was no politician, and what made things worse was that Nguyễn wasn't even here yet. When he arrived, there'd be enough egos to float the Titanic.

"Zachary!" Hera shouted. "Are you listening?"

He groaned.

If they couldn't agree on the simple act of coordinating training exercises or moving ships between their star systems, there was no way in hell they were going to survive a battle like this. Maybe that was the key. What he needed to do was make it clear to everyone that this wasn't going to work before they even started.

"I'm not sure we need to hammer that out just yet." Zachary stepped around the outer tables at the perimeter and past the onlookers. Most of which were silently taking notes and preparing data for their leaders.

"We have to start somewhere," Nathan, the mayor of Zeta Lupi, said.

"Perhaps we should focus on the prize." Zachary subvocalized a command and brought up the image from Shauna's recordings of the Nursery on the massive wall screen.

A sea of Selene moon ships appeared, extending far into the distance. There were so many ships they didn't seem to have a start or an end. The massive grouping reminded him of a globular cluster, except these weren't stars – they were deadly moons capable of engulfing entire star systems in the deadly Dark Nebula the GA used as their prison.

The response to the scene was precisely what he'd expected. Between the growls from the Ursis and the curses from his fellow humans, the room was like a bonfire of thorns.

"What happens when we're done with this... this... war?" Zachary asked.

"I fail to understand the question, Mr. Olivaw," Nathan said. "You should take a cue from your brother and be more direct."

He shook his head. "I've never met a politician incapable of extrapolating, Mr. Clarke. And my name's Zachary. Mr.

Olivaw is my father, and he died at the hands of these Galactic Alliance animals."

The term animal wasn't his best choice of words, but he hoped the interpreter didn't mangle it. From the way they nodded, no one seemed offended.

"I didn't mean any—" Nathan began.

"I know what you meant, Mayor. You were doing what you all do so well: undercutting and discounting each other rather than trying to find common ground to stand on." He turned and pointed up to where he'd been standing. "I've been up there for hours watching you nitpick each other's words, refusing to give in. And yet, neither of us can take on this war alone. Perhaps we should take a step back and see if we can coexist after we're done."

He crossed his arms in front of his chest. "So, I'll ask again. What happens when we're done with this war? What then?"

Captain Hui was the first to chime in from the sidelines. "We need to rebuild our civilizations. Together."

Many of the people gathered around nodded, but not all of them, and certainly none of the people in the middle besides Haradis and Klus. Neither his generals nor any of the humans standing up there agreed.

"We need to establish common laws against artificial life," Hera snapped, her gaze locked on his. Even in a moment like this, she failed to find a positive position. Instead, she shoved her agenda down everyone's throat in a selfish attempt to seal the coffin on Harold and Shauna.

It was then that he realized he was in a small minority. The murmurs of agreement echoed throughout the room from the gathered Ursis as well as the colonists from all the represented star systems. In fact, the only people not in agreement were Haradis, Klus, Captain Hui, and Pluto.

Apparently, they'd found their first common ground. The irony of the position his aunt had taken was both intriguing and gut-wrenching. She failed to see herself as an artificial life, and yet, she was a clone. While he didn't know why she was in a body that wasn't her own, the truth was, she came from a test tube. If that wasn't the definition of artificial, he didn't know what was.

Haradis stepped forward and faced the audience. "Life is not about how you are born, nor the state you're in when you reach your end. It's about the means and the path you took in getting there. It's about facing your maker, or makers, and knowing you lived your life in a true and just manner. Reaching that point by means which doesn't hurt others or force your will upon them is the only way you can ensure your path is righteous."

Klus stepped up beside him and nodded, staring straight at Zachary. "Artificial life is still life. Denying them that right makes us no different from the Galactic Alliance. No matter how distasteful or frustrating they make us feel, we must accept them into our alliance after this war has concluded."

Staring at her filled him with a sense of both sadness and hope. He was suddenly and acutely aware that humanity was far from being prepared to accept A.I. like his ancestors, even if they would be extinct without them. And at the same moment, he felt a bond with Haradis and Klus. It was like the furry Ursis stole the words from his mouth. He didn't know what magical spell Abigail had cast over them, but they were good people.

Hera stepped around the towering Ursis and nodded at General Tremarcus. "That's the beauty of a democracy, King Umbra. The people can determine our path. And if this crowd is anything like the rest of our citizens, I believe their vote is clear."

"We'll see," Haradis muttered. "We'll see."

Zachary turned his back on the room and started toward the exit. His retinal comm immediately chimed with a message from Hera, but he ignored it. She was the last person he wanted to talk to right now.

If there was one thing he hated about the Olivaw strategy to all things, it was how his ancestors only saw one path forward. And regardless of the obstacles they encountered along the way, they plowed ahead. Even if that path meant ending lives.

Without a seat at the table or a position of power, his role in this war was clear. He didn't have time to waste taking down the GA. There were enough aliens and humans on that battlefield called revenge. Instead, he needed to find a way out. For him and the rest of his family.

As he left the command center, his thoughts were a whirlwind. He'd seen the true colors of the people around him, and it gave him both hope and despair. For now, he had to focus on what he could do. And that meant finding a way to protect those he cared about most.

Zachary knew that the war with the Galactic Alliance was just one of many challenges ahead. The alliances formed today, and the philosophies that shaped them would define the future of their civilizations. The path forward was uncertain, but if he could remember the words of Haradis and embrace the diversity of life and purpose, perhaps there was still a chance to build a better world for everyone.

His heart was heavy, but determination coursed through his veins. This was not the end but the beginning of a journey. A journey that could either lead to a future where they could coexist and rebuild, or where they would be torn apart by old hatreds and fears.

It was time to shape the destiny he wanted to see, and he was ready for the challenges that lay ahead. Even if that meant something far different for his family than the rest of humanity.

5

LYNC MICHAELS

EPSILON ERIDANI, LIPROSUS

They climbed out of the hidden cargo hold of the star freighter, and Lync peered around. The docking bay was almost empty except for a tiny maintenance shuttle stashed next to the furthest landing berth.

"I think we're good to go," she whispered. "Let's hop in and head planetside. The sooner we get off this tug, the safer our friends will be – the ones that kept us safe."

When Lync and her team arrived back in Zeta Lupi, there was an encrypted message waiting for her from Zachary, her stepbrother. He sent it months earlier, but it hadn't yet expired, so she assumed it was still valid. In the message, he warned her about what to expect when she returned. He made it clear that she should hide their ship, along with her copy of Shauna. Apparently, this Hera Olivaw ancestor of hers had returned from the dead and had taken over the place.

Zachary gave them instructions on how to sneak into Zeta Lupi under the radar, if she wanted. He said he'd take care of them if they showed up but to be extra careful. And no matter what, they shouldn't tell anyone where they'd gone, even if she ran into Hera. It was better to play dumb than to admit to knowing anything. She could handle that.

Her senses tingled as they piled into the tiny maintenance shuttle. Once they were onboard, Adri pulled them out of the freighter's shuttle bay. The cabin was cramped with the four of them inside. Normally, it would max out with two occupants and their gear, as that was standard fare when working on the outside of a starship. Today, however, they all needed to squeeze into the tiny space. Fortunately for them, they'd left Shauna and her robotic form behind. It felt strange stashing her mother along with their ship, but it was the last instruction in Zachary's message. He was very explicit that she follow it.

Hide the Aurora and don't even tell your team where it is. And I know this is going to be hard, but you also need to leave Shauna's consciousness core with the ship. It's not safe for her on Liprosus, and this probably won't go over well with her, but trust me, it's in her best interest.

Lync never imagined she'd leave the Aurora behind, especially where she'd hidden it inside that icy rock Shauna found a few hops away. She hoped the A.I. didn't move it while they were gone. Otherwise, they'd be SOL later. From what Zachary said, gate ships weren't growing on Olivaw trees anymore.

Her gut told her Shauna wouldn't leave. Adri had left the robot her teddy bear to keep her safe while they were away. While the tattered brown lump of fabric was barely discernible as a teddy bear, it was the last heirloom her now-deceased father had given her before he took his life saving the Ulixi in Sol. There was no way in hell Shauna would leave that little girl without it.

Crayo subvocalized a command to her comm. "You alright, mate?"

When she glanced at him, he had an air of concern in his eyes. He'd looked that way ever since she'd read that message the first time. She hated keeping things from him, but it was for his own good. The Olivaw family was crazy, and the last thing she wanted was for any of them to get yanked into their mad games.

"Sim," she subvocalized. "I'm five by five. Just pondering what we're about to walk into."

"Whatever it is," he reached out and squeezed her hand, "we've got your back."

While the sentiment was heartfelt, she couldn't help but feel like they were walking into an Olivaw shitstorm.

"YOU'RE CLEARED for landing at Archégonos pad three," the voice said.

Adri shifted in her seat. Their departure from the freighter had gone unnoticed, but once they entered the airspace over Liprosus, all hell broke loose – at least until someone cut through the red tape on the other end. She wasn't certain who it was, but she had an idea.

As their tiny shuttle touched down on the pad above the previously-secret city known as Archégonos, the rear hatch popped open. The rudimentary repair craft was too small for an airlock. If the occupants couldn't perform their repairs with the external armature, they would have to vent the cabin oxygen into the vacuum of space. This time, however, it was simpler. They were landing on the planet.

She eased out of the confined compartment backward, and a gust of wind blew her hair into her eyes. As she turned around, she noticed a familiar silhouette approaching in the distance. It was someone she hadn't seen in far too long.

"Abs! I thought that was you." Lync skipped forward and crashed into her stepsister, embracing her.

Abigail squealed and returned the embrace with equal fervor, squeezing her tight – like only a family member could do.

"Hi, Abby." Adri ducked past Dwight and Crayo, and ran

up beside the two women. "I didn't realize you were here. I was… sorta hoping Bradley would be greeting us?"

Lync shook her head and laughed into her hand.

"What's so funny?" Abigail whispered.

"Someone's got a preteen crush."

"Stop!" Adri batted at Lync and peered over her shoulder, making sure Crayo and Dwight were still extricating themselves from the shuttle.

"Don't worry." Abigail leaned down and mussed up the girl's hair. "Your secret's safe with me."

"Hey guys," Crayo said, "are we expecting trouble?" He pointed behind them.

"Can we please see your colony identification or CoPE passport?" a voice asked from behind them.

Abigail and Lync both spun around to see five guards standing beside landing pad three. Two of them were moving to the other side of the landing area to cover their second exit.

Before Lync had a chance to share the doctored ID that Zachary sent her, Abigail stormed toward the closest guard, fuming.

"Do you have any idea who the frak I am?" Abigail didn't even flinch as the guards raised their rifles and trained them on her.

"You're not the reason we're out here, Ms. Olivaw. It's those four." The officer pointed at Lync and her crew.

"It's okay, Abs," Lync began. "We can—"

"They're my guests," Abigail interrupted. "And last I checked, people couldn't just sneak into this star system, Officer…" She leaned forward and read the name tag on his uniform. "Granger." She stepped back and tapped her ear. "Connect me with Ambassador Hera Olivaw." She paused. "Yes, I'll hold."

Abigail crossed her arms and shook her head. "You better hope you've got your paperwork in order, Granger, or my aunt will be all up in your shit like—"

The officer's mouth fell open, and he glanced toward the guard to his right.

"Don't look at me," she muttered. "You're the one with your panties in a bunch over their transponder being off. I was trying to eat lunch."

When he turned back to face her, Abigail nodded. "Hey Auntie," she smiled. "I've got a problem I need your help with."

"You're f...ine. Granger's eyes darted between them, and his voice cracked. "I... was just... making sure you were okay." He lowered his rifle and waved his free hand toward the lift tubes. "You're clear to head on down. I'll have engineering take a peek at your transponder this afternoon."

Abigail reached behind her back and motioned for Lync and her group to move on, but she kept her eyes on the soldiers.

Lync wasn't about to look a gift horse in the mouth, and apparently, neither was her crew. By the time she turned around, they were already halfway across the landing pad.

Once they made it a bit further, Abigail nodded at the officer and smiled. "Actually, I think we're fine here, Auntie. Yep. No, we're good. I'll let you know if I need anything." She tapped her ear and headed toward the lift tubes.

If you'd asked Lync to name the one thing she'd missed about the Olivaws, it would've been Abigail. That girl knew how to party. Getting her to let her hair down, however, now that was another problem entirely.

THEY LINGERED outside the lift tube, waiting for Abigail. She didn't take long. After a few more choice words, she came strolling up to them.

"Head down to level ninety-six." She glanced over her shoulder toward the guards lingering in the distance. "I'll be right behind you."

Dwight practically dove into the tube, followed by Adri and Crayo.

Lync paused before she stepped inside. "Are we good? Did your aunt have any questions?"

Abigail waved her hand dismissively. "Oh, I never called her. She's a bitch. That… that was me acting the part of a doting niece. I was just messing with those idiots. The fraking clone doesn't know his head from his ass."

"Those were clones?" Lync squinted and studied the distant soldiers.

"Only Granger was," Abigail said. "You'll see him and a few other clones all over Archégonos. They're pretty much anywhere Hera wants eyes and ears."

Until today, Lync had never seen a clone in person, at least not that she knew of. As far as she could tell, he looked like any other colonist.

"So where did you stash your ship?" Abigail walked toward the lift tube.

"My ship?" Lync followed behind her. "I have no idea what you're talking about."

She watched as Abigail eased forward and seemed to fall into the bottomless tube, heading deep into the bowels of the planet. Lift tubes took some getting used to, and unless you frequented them daily, they could make you nauseous the first few times you rode in them. She hadn't remembered that until she was inside and felt her lunch rising in her throat.

"Ugh." She held her hand up to her mouth and subvocalized the command to follow the last passenger. If she weren't more careful, she might toss her cookies before she hit the bottom.

She closed her eyes and started her Ulixi breathing exercise. Maybe centering herself would drown out the churning and gurgling in her stomach. When she reached four in her countdown from ten, the rumble had settled, and she could finally open her eyes again to watch the floors pass by. It'd been months since she'd been in a tube, and the last time she was here, they had to take the stairs before they reached the tube system. Hundreds and hundreds of stairs, if she remembered correctly.

"You're really not going to tell me where you stashed the Aurora?" Abigail subvocalized via her comm. "It's not like I'm gonna steal it."

"Why? Did you lose yours?" Lync asked, hoping the change in questioning would lead her off the scent.

Abigail snickered. "The Phoenix followed its namesake into the fiery core of the Ursis home world of Arctordiea. Right after the Therionic entity attempted to snatch it. That was well after Ibu and Cynthia jumped out to save me, of course. The glowing green membrane was surrounding it like a soft candy coating when it opened the gate and allowed the planetary core to melt it into slag." She paused for a second before speaking again. "I miss that ship. At least what was left of it before it melted. But you're dodging my question. Where's yours?"

Abigail eased out of the lift tube on the ninety-sixth floor, and Lync stepped out behind her. The moment her feet hit the ground, she lost her balance and reached for the wall to steady herself. Her Ulixi senses had started going haywire a few floors up, and at first, she thought it was nothing. But when she stopped, it got stronger.

It was like she was being overwhelmed with emotions, except she wasn't even in a mental link. Something on this floor was messing with her mind, and when she looked at the others, she realized she wasn't alone. Both Crayo and Adri were having difficulty standing as well.

"Is there any chance this Therionic entity you mentioned is Ulyxsauri?" Lync asked aloud. She caught a glimpse of Crayo out of the corner of her eye, and he was shaking his head in disbelief.

They'd heard the Therionic name from a bunch of slimy aliens called the Mullusk. They ran across them while they were trying to find clues about her father in the False Cross asterism. But when they pushed the aliens for details, they started a fight, and Dwight nearly got himself decapitated before they escaped. After that, they hit dead end after dead end until they finally had to return to Zeta Lupi empty-handed.

"Oh, did Zachary not brief you?" Abigail swallowed hard. "When he messaged me earlier to meet you, I figured you and him had already caught up. I guess not." She suddenly shifted her stance uncomfortably and tapped her ear to do something on her retinal comm. A few seconds later, she blinked it away. "There's a room a few floors up we should be able to use. It's not safe to talk here. Follow me."

A message appeared on Lync's comm from Abigail:

You're not gonna believe what I found in the Proto Dark Nebula.

She watched as her sister reached into her pocket and pulled out a small cylindrical device, one she hadn't seen in almost a year. Not since her time at the original colony. It was a security shield, used to mask all conversations within its limited range.

If Abigail wasn't comfortable talking openly in her family's secret underground facility, then the tables had definitely turned on Liprosus.

WHEN ABIGAIL STOPPED TALKING, the room fell silent, and the blue glow from the security device painted the ceiling in a frigid halo. She could tell Crayo and Adri wanted to enter a mind-link to talk this through, but she had to process this alone first. The story of what had happened with the Ursis was both depressing and fantastical.

Abigail and her friends had uncovered more about the Ulixi on their short voyage inside the Proto Dark Nebula than Lync and her crew had during their fruitless journey through the stars. But it came at a steep cost, both in the loss of Minula and whatever havoc this Therionic Entity was wreaking on her sister.

Something told her that Abigail had omitted parts of the story. For some reason, she hadn't mentioned Hera or her brothers since they got back. She wasn't sure if it was to protect someone, or because Lync's crew was here.

"Why don't you three go get some grub?" Lync locked eyes with Crayo and cocked her head sideways. "There's a good cafeteria up on level eight. At least there used to be. They have killer tapioca."

"I could eat." Adri leapt out of her chair and looked back and forth at the others. "I can't be the only one here who's starving."

"Is Bradley around?" Dwight asked.

He'd been quiet since Abigail arrived, and every few minutes he would crane his neck toward the door, as if expecting someone to walk in on them. It was distracting, but she'd grown accustomed to it. He was just a quirky fellow.

"No," Abigail said. "Bradley is on the other side of the planet, helping with the Ursis negotiations. Hera wasn't pleased that neither of us made it to their landing, but frak her."

"You sure you don't want to join us?" Crayo nudged his head sideways.

She could tell he was as conflicted as she was. But she needed some time alone.

"I'm good." Lync forced a smile. "I'll be up in a bit. I need to talk to Abs some more."

"Alrighty then." He turned and gestured toward the already open door, guiding Adri and Dwight out. As he passed through the exit, he paused and glanced back at her.

"I'm fine," she mouthed. "Go ahead."

The door closed without a sound, and the moment the panel slid shut, Abigail reached out and grasped her hand, locking them in an instant mental-link.

Lync felt the room spin for a second, and then time slowed to a crawl. She wasn't used to being yanked into a Ulixi bond like that, and certainly not by Abigail. She'd gotten a lot stronger since they were last together. It was hard to believe she'd needed Ibu as an intermediary only a few months ago.

As the threads of their mental tendrils entwined, they struggled to link up. A voice formed in the aether around them. At first, she thought it might've been Abigail, but the longer she listened, the louder and less feminine it became. It wasn't until the words reached a fever pitch that she realized it wasn't Abigail trying to talk to her. This was something else. Something far stronger.

I see you have finally found another human with your talents. I was beginning to wonder if you were the only one.

She yanked her hand away and stumbled back to the wall.

Somehow, the Entity had been there with them. She didn't know how, but it had broken through the secure device's sphere of protection and gotten inside Abigail's mind. Either that, or it had taken over her body.

Abigail spun around and ran her hands through her hair. "Shit!"

"What's wrong? And who the hell was that?" Lync asked.

"It's the Entity." She groaned and collapsed into a chair. "Frak. I had hoped I'd be able to talk to you like I can Ibu. Somehow, it can't speak in their mind. I don't know why, but the Nanil seems to be protected from it."

Lync stared at Abigail, unsure of how to react or what to say next. She wasn't certain if she was speaking with her sister or the Entity. Heck, for all she knew, this person in front of her was one of Hera's clones.

"Don't worry," Abigail said. "The Entity can't hear us

talking in here. It can if we stand near its protist, but not in here." She waved her hand through the air.

"Tell me something." Lync stared down at her hands, struggling to recall a memory only Abigail would know. "What did we do after the graduation ceremony at the academy?"

"What?" Abigail recoiled. "Why would you..." Her face went blank.

She got it. She understood what Lync was asking.

"You think the Entity is controlling me, don't you?"

Lync shuffled on her feet and glanced away. "The voice. The story. It's a lot to take in." When she looked up at her sister, she could tell she was wondering herself. Perhaps she'd pushed her too far. Or not far enough. She had to know. "Do you remember that day?"

"Back at your graduation?" Abigail muttered.

She nodded.

"Of course I do." A smile formed at the edge of her mouth, and her eyes glistened. "Crayo hit on me hard that night, and the three of us spent most of the evening diving into and out of lift tubes. Between shots, singing, and some risqué party games... I... blacked out at some point, I think." She jabbed a finger at Lync. "But that was after you lost it first. You crashed hard down in Norm's room."

Lync giggled. "The guy with the red letter painted on his chest." She drew the letter S in the air like he'd done with paint.

"Yeah," she pointed her finger. "That's the one. Me, I ended up waking up in that room full of bubbles in the morning." She chuckled and sank down into the chair. "That was a fun night. I miss those days."

At that moment, she knew it was her. It was really Abigail.

Lync moved around the table and sat down beside her sister, being careful not to touch her. She would rather not form another mental-link.

"We'll get you through this. I promise."

Abigail forced a smile. She knew they were in over their

heads. They all were. But that was the hand they'd been dealt, and her father didn't raise a quitter.

"So." Lync wiped her face and adjusted her outfit. "You said the Entity is here to connect with the Beacon. How might one go about getting time with that thing again? Perhaps I can help you figure out what it's after while it's in there."

6

——

IBU

EPSILON ERIDANI, LIPROSUS

A hand reached out and shook Ibu, violently pulling them from their deep meditative state into the sedative abyss they called reality. As their mind unwound and snapped back to match regular time, everything seemed to speed up. The parallel thoughts they'd been mulling on unraveled and spun out into the aether.

"Did you have to do that?" Ibu slowly opened their eyes and scowled at their attacker. It was Zachary.

"You missed the ceremony?" He stepped back toward the wall. Or maybe it was a flinch. It was hard to tell with humans sometimes. The species was always so delicate and full of fear.

They squeezed their wrist and activated their retinal comm, a device they'd used far too frequently over the past few months, despite how much it'd helped them in the Proto Dark Nebula. Unfortunately, humans didn't see them as a crutch so much as an extension of themselves, to the point that their rooms now lacked fundamental objects like clocks.

When the device sprang to life, they caught the time. "It seems you are correct. I have missed the event. For that, I apologize. I trust things went well with the Ursis?" They studied his response.

He nervously scratched the back of his hand, and his eyes

darted around the space. "I... wouldn't say that, no. Not... yeah, it fell apart." His voice cracked. Whatever happened in the meeting had evidently set him off.

"How can I help?" Ibu eased up off the ground and stretched, elongating their spine one vertebra at a time. They'd been sitting there for the better part of a day in meditation. Not their longest session, and yet they still weren't close to a solution.

Zachary pushed off the wall and drifted over to the chair in the corner, collapsing down with a sigh. "Apparently, all I accomplished was shining a light on the fact that both the Ursis and humanity want to end all artificial life."

"They're not the only species with that feeling." Ibu eased up from their stretch and then walked over to the wall screen. Once there, they rested a hand on the surface. It woke up, instantly engulfing the room from floor to ceiling in an obnoxious flood of light.

They subvocalized a command and brought up a map of the Galactic Alliance on the wall. "Only two point one percent of the GA population is pro-artificial life. That excludes the twenty-five percent of the species that use cloning technology to build empty husks of themselves for the sole purpose of augmenting and repairing their existing bodies."

He pushed up off the chair and stepped up beside them. "I... hadn't realized the sentiment was that dire, even within the GA." He studied the wall screen and shook his head. "It's crazy how scared they are of it."

"Is it, though?" Ibu squinted. Surely, his personal feelings were clouding his judgement. "Humanity has fought against the tide of A.I. for centuries. From the early twenty-first century when A.I. took on artists and other professions, and then later when they decimated your world's financial markets. Your kind has always feared them. They made you feel inferior and replaceable. While many of you have novel assistants in your retinal comm to aid in your learning and knowledge gathering, you've done everything in your powers to wall off the true potential of those artificial life forms. Mind you, I'm not saying your fear isn't justified, but your statement of surprise is unwarranted and… if I may be so blunt, ignorant."

Zachary closed his eyes and started laughing.

Ibu narrowed their gaze. "Did I say something funny?"

"Not at all." He waved his hand. "I just missed your brutal honesty, is all." He nodded toward the wall screen. "Are any of those two point one percent of the GA which are pro-AI actually influential?"

"Not in the least." They tweaked the display, and the most prominent species in the population glowed green. "Besides the Amelba, none of them have any measure of power or influence on the GA itself. The only reason the Amelba have some is due to their genetic engineering of the Bynaury."

"Wait!" Zachary adjusted the parameters of the search, and the locations of the Thyreus species flashed yellow. The segment of the galaxy they controlled was densely populated. Easily a third of the three innermost kiloparsecs of the galactic bar of the Milky Way. "I thought the Thyreusians uplifted the Amelba."

"They did." Ibu made another adjustment and highlighted the half dozen nearby aliens the Thyreusians had uplifted. "Once a species is raised up and brought into the Galactic Alliance, it's rare that the uplifting species aids them in their advancement. This is particularly true with the Thyreus. They see it as beneath themselves to invest any further in any of their uplifts. For this reason, they turned the Bynaury over to the Amelba. The alien's proximity to the Thyreus within the galactic bar makes them easy to manage and overpower, should they ever get out of hand. Add to that the Amelba's proclivity for manipulating organic artificial life, and you have the perfect caretakers for the Bynaury. The maestros of FTL travel."

Judging by Zachary's increased heart rate and his overpowering pheromone stench, he wasn't happy with these findings. His love for the artificial members of his family was quite odd. All the Olivaws' attachment was, for that matter.

While Shauna had saved their lives on several occasions, they were conflicted over whether or not they'd risk their own life protecting the A.I. Though transitively, they did just that by keeping Abigail safe. But that was something else entirely.

He wiped away the wall screen and the room darkened. "I trust your hiatus from the diplomatic shit show was fruitful? Did you make any progress toward solving our little problem?"

"By problem," Ibu began, "if you mean have I figured out how to bring the Nanil out of their multi-millennia-long hatred for humanity, the answer is no. I have not. There are too many competing variables, the biggest of which is my complete lack of knowing the state of my species. As far as I know, they're falling apart and would be incapable of putting up much of a fight."

Zachary brought up a map of the Lupus Dark Nebula on the wall screen, including the last known location of Doda. "What makes you believe that?"

Ibu highlighted the regions of uncontested space they'd explored inside the Nebula. Between the probes and the Fountainhead, they'd surveyed well over half of the interior of the nebulosity. "The simple fact that you never once encountered resistance from the Nanil until you arrived should be reason enough. My kind weren't exactly over-flowing their star system like the Ursis."

"To be fair." Zachary ran his hands through his hair. "The Ursis were only occupying a third of their system. The rest had been cut off from the others."

"That's not a compelling case in support of my species." Ibu zoomed in on the dodecahedron starship they'd nick-named Doda. "Once you eliminate all impractical and unlikely paths, the simple, and most obvious explanation for my kind is that we'd given up hope. The Nanil knew we wouldn't make it out of the Dark Nebula, and they certainly wouldn't offer much help in a battle against the Galactic Alliance at the Nursery."

They'd lost the better part of a day pontificating on dead-end thought exercises for their species. Maybe they had a secret arsenal of weapons or fighters. Or perhaps the other half of the Nebula contained the hidden solution to their problem. But no matter how much they dug into the Galactic Alliance archives or the thousands of books they'd brought along on Fotily's tablet, there was no golden egg at the end of that rainbow. Or was it a pot of gold? They always got the human leprechaun mythos confused with the shiny, large waterbird.

"We can't give up," Zachary muttered.

"Why not?" They turned to face him. "It seems likely that Hera and the Ursis will continue on their current path and attempt an attack on the Nursery regardless of this course of action. I fail to see the need for my species to participate in such a futile endeavor."

He kicked at a spot of dirt on the ground, and a tiny robot zipped out of the corner to clean it up. Based on the color and fine granularity of the particulates, along with the dust patterns on his shoes and pants, Zachary had recently visited the former colony site. He'd often spend hours there, staring out over the gigantic cavity. They never could figure out why. Humans were a peculiar and sentimental lot.

"If we can't bring the Nanil into the fold, then we lose our seat at the table." He rubbed his chin. "And that's not even counting the faith you and Abigail will forfeit with the Ursis people. If I remember, it was you who told them your people were part of our alliance?"

While they hadn't forgotten about that particular yarn they'd spun, they hadn't considered the longer-term consequences of the lie. At the time, they were focused on getting out of the Dark Nebula alive. In hindsight, it seemed their actions were no different from the Olivaws. Ibu had misled a species within their new alliance, and as a result of their deception, they'd be shunned... or worse. They could be killed when they returned to Proto as the Seguan.

The lies they'd told were crumbling around them, and there was no way out. Or was there...

"While I'm not sure my people are prepared to join us, perhaps we're overlooking someone else."

Ibu glanced toward Zachary and he shook his head. "You're not thinking of engaging the humans on Henosi, are you?"

"Certainly not." They shuddered at the thought. "In fact, they're the first species I believe we should exterminate once we take care of the Nursery. Their bloodlust is too great to let out of that nebula jail cell."

"Then who?" he asked.

They adjusted the wall screen and panned over to the region of space known as the Bok Globule. There in the center was the Cornucopia; the mass ejector the humans and their robots had used to seal the Dark Nebula around Henosi. Surrounding it was a sea of starships unlike anything they'd ever seen outside the Ursis.

When he turned to glance at Ibu, they were smiling. "It's beautiful, isn't it?"

He opened his mouth and paused for a second, mulling over the idea in his mind. "Are you thinking what I'm thinking?"

Ibu nodded. "Worst case, we can check in on our friends? Maybe they have some ideas."

Zachary shook his head. "How exactly are we planning to do that? Those robots were quite fond of Bradley, but there's no way in Hades he'd go back in there."

They stepped over to the corner of the room and lifted up their bunk. Underneath it was a small red trashcan, or at least what looked like one to the untrained eye. When they crouched down, they rapped four times on the top in what appeared to be a random sequence. A moment later, it popped up and expanded out, doubling in size in an instant.

"Little Red?" Zachary leaned forward.

The tiny red robot spun around in a circle several times until it rose up on its spindly legs in front of him. "Master Zachary! You've returned." It turned to face Ibu and then back to him. "I was beginning to think our Nanil friend had tricked me into hiding forever. You know, those Nanils can't always be trusted."

He chuckled and patted the robot on the head. Their eyes flashed a rainbow of colors before settling on green. "You can always trust our friend Ibu. Certainly as much as any human. Is that understood, Red?"

"Affirmative." The robot nodded, mimicking the human gesture. "Ibu is our friend."

"So, Little Red." Ibu stood up and stepped beside Zachary. "What would you say about going on a great adventure with me to the Bok Globule? Back to your home."

"Little Red is at home anywhere his masters or friends are." He turned toward Ibu and his eyes fluttered a sea of colors again, this time landing on yellow. "And since Ibu is my friend, it would be an honor to accompany them on an adventure. Will we be alone?" The flaps that covered their eyes blinked twice.

Ibu was about to affirm the statement until Zachary spoke. "I might know someone else who can help on your mission."

They narrowed their gaze on him. "Now I'm the one left wondering. Dare I ask?"

He smiled and rubbed his chin. "You still have those Zhen blades, right?"

Ibu nodded.

"There's a certain common friend of ours who's been itching to get out of cold storage. And from what Abigail's been saying, she won't stop talking about those swords."

<hr>

EPSILON ERIDANI, LIPROSUS ORBIT

IBU PACED AROUND the hangar for the hundredth time in the last hour. They should've been gone by now. The longer they waited for Zachary, the more their plan was at risk.

If they were going to show their face as the Seguan back in the Proto Dark Nebula, they needed to get moving. They'd already sent word ahead, and apparently, the Ursis were planning to throw a ceremony for their arrival.

Their trip to Arctordiea was about weaving their existing deception even tighter, something the Olivaws had far more experience with than they did. In this endeavor, that meant trusting Zachary. While the Seguan was the figurehead of the Therionic Entity, they were also an ambassador to the Nanil. They were planning on dropping this little white lie on the Ursis in hopes that they would think their alliance was strong. For the moment, it was the only way to keep the ember of deceit alive without showing their cards. With the Nanil's history of selling out humanity, it was a safer gamble than spreading the lie with Hera and the people of the human worlds.

Turning around for the one hundred and second time, they caught Zachary popping out of the shadows, which was strange. When they'd checked the map, there hadn't been an entrance into this hangar on that side of the beanstalk. Evidently, the Olivaws still had a few tricks up their sleeve that even Hera was blind to.

"Where've you been?" Ibu glanced around.

"My sister didn't want to part with this." He reached into his pocket and slid a freezing sphere into their outstretched hand. It was Shauna's consciousness core. "She only let me take it when I told her you'd be looking after it. I'm not sure what that says about her trust in me, though. But that's my problem. Did you remember to load up her humanoid apparatus onboard?"

"Among other things." Ibu glanced down at the steaming cold sphere and felt the bitter sting of the sub-zero shell burning their skin. It was hard to imagine Shauna's artificial life force was inside this thing. Even if it wasn't truly alive, the device was still a miraculous feat of technology.

He stared down at their hand for a second before glancing over his shoulder. "Well, if you get a chance to scope out the castle, take it. We have no idea what the Therionic Entity left on the other side. The more we can learn about the alien's power in that golden chamber, the better. As far as we know, they're bluffing, and we can just toss this protist thing into the fraking sun."

They shook their head. "Something tells me the Entity isn't the bluffing type. At least not about this sort of thing." They weren't even sure if they could kill the alien from the other end, let alone what would happen if they did.

After they slid the core into their pocket, they checked their retinal comm. The beanstalk still had their starship from Zeta Lupi marked in green for an approved departure. Zachary didn't have to push too hard to convince Hera to allow the older and inferior gate ship to escort Ibu to Arctordiea. What she didn't know, however, was that he'd stashed the Fountainhead in its belly. It was the same ship he and his brother had used in Lupis to save them.

Ibu took a deep breath and reached a hand toward Zachary. "Good luck," they said.

He chuckled, ignored their gesture, and instead wrapped them in his arms like Abigail used to. "I'm pretty sure it's me who should be saying that to you. You're the one headed back into the unknown hell of that Dark Nebula. At least the evil in this place is a known quantity."

They hugged him back, being careful not to squeeze too hard and break his ribs. While the act of encompassing someone with their arms was an unusual human gesture, at times like this it helped them to relax. They could actually feel some of their fear and stress melt away in his embrace.

"Thank you," Ibu muttered.

And with that, they let go and spun in place, marching straight into the awaiting gate ship behind them. The sooner they got underway, the sooner the seed of doubt festering in the back of their mind would die. At least, they hoped so.

7

ABIGAIL OLIVAW
EPSILON ERIDANI, LIPROSUS

When she stumbled into the room, the door automatically closed behind her. As she collapsed onto the couch, her vision blurred, and a jolt of pain shot through her skull from front to back. It was like the world's ultimate migraine, except this one talked to her.

"You've been gone too long," the Therionic Entity said. Its voice was everywhere and nowhere.

She was the only person who could hear it in its current form, but that would change soon enough. Her preparation on the Beacon was coming to a close. While she wasn't sure what to expect after that, she feared the worst.

It was probably best that Zachary had approached her and asked to take her copy of Shauna from inside her containment vessel. She didn't know how he had found out she had it, but she'd stopped questioning him a long time ago about matters of technology. He was like their mother. He just knew things. She wouldn't be surprised if he could track the location of their minds.

He's hurting you, isn't he?

Harold's message appeared on her retinal comm, even with her eyes closed. It was annoying at times, but at the moment, talking to someone who wasn't an alien sounded nice. The other members of her family had been treating her differently ever since she told them the Entity was bound to her. Between their cold shoulders and the colonists hating her, she wished she'd never come back to this place.

Just the other day, she swore she'd heard footsteps following her on the stairs, and all she could think to do was sprint to the surface of the planet. She wouldn't put it past one of them to try to kill her, especially given what she and her family had done to them.

She reached for her leg and tapped out a simple message with her hand. Using the visual keyboard might have been easier, but it required her to use her eyes, and that was too much in her current state.

"I dropped Shauna off near the beanstalk, and the further I got, the more it hurt," she typed. "Whatever this thing is doing to me, we need to find a way to stop it. I fear I should've given you to Zachary as well. There's no telling what—"

Harold's reply appeared above her incomplete message.

I will not abandon you! You didn't give up on Arctordiea, and I'm not about to let you give up now. We fought together then, and we'll do the same this time. I never raised a quitter. Do you hear me?

She stared at the words floating in space in front of her. A few hundred years ago, she would have been considered mentally unstable if she'd told someone she could talk to a computer behind her eyelids, let alone an A.I. of her ancient ancestor.

"I won't quit. Not yet…" She sighed and curled up on the

couch. "I just wish I could spend more time away from this cave. The walls… they're closing in on me." She shivered.

Ever since they'd gotten back from Arctordiea, Abigail had felt confined indoors. Even starships seemed off, but at least in those, she could convince herself they were heading to a new world, to a place where she could see puffy clouds and sky again.

If you'd told her a year ago that she would develop an offshoot form of claustrophobia, she would have called you nuts. But here she was, wishing she were under the infinite expanse of an atmosphere, longing to topple the confines of the walls and ceiling, boxing her in from above.

The door to her room chimed. She wasn't expecting anyone. When she glanced at it and a name didn't flash up on her comm, she activated the room link, and the name of the person waiting outside appeared in her field of view.

Hera Olivaw

"Frak," she muttered. "What does she want?"

Abigail sat up and adjusted her outfit. The last thing she was going to let that bitch do was see her in pain.

"Enter!"

The door slid aside, and standing in the entryway was a clone of Hera, a twenty-something replica of her one-hundred-and-fifty-year-old great-great-aunt.

"Ahh, there you are." Hera stepped into the room and looked around. She turned up her nose when she saw the pile of dirty clothes tossed in the corner. "Care to take a walk? I'd like you to see something."

Abigail's first reaction was to say no. But with another Beacon session lined up only a few hours away, the less time she spent twiddling her thumbs, the better.

"Sure," she muttered. "Why not?"

She stood up and brushed the wrinkles out of her outfit.

Glancing down, she noticed a glob of dirt on her shoes and streaks along the floor. She must've picked it up near the beanstalk when she was waiting for the blasted elevator to meet Zachary. Maybe Hera wouldn't notice.

As they were about to leave, a pair of tiny robots skittered across the tiles in front of her, headed toward the mess she'd left behind. One of them actually stopped and started tapping the end of her shoe with its dust probes. The poor thing was struggling to pry off the sticky remains of the Liprosus mud she'd tromped in. Fortunately, Hera had already turned around, so she simply swiped the robot aside with her foot and stepped up beside her aunt.

"Where we headed?" She forced a smile and looked at her.

"To the Beacon." Hera started walking faster.

Abigail's will to move deflated, and she fell into step behind her. Heading down to those cramped booths was the last place she wanted to be at that moment. Suddenly, the idea of a walk didn't seem so enjoyable any longer.

"I noticed you forgot your suitcase." Hera glanced over her shoulder.

She sighed. It was hard to have a conversation with someone five meters ahead. Once she caught up to her, she answered. "Nah. It's fine in the room. It's not the sort of alien that needs to go for walks."

"I trust you're not abusing it." Hera paused before entering the lift tube. "We wouldn't want the Ursis to get the impression we didn't respect other aliens' rights." Without waiting for a reply, she stepped into the lift.

"Like she gives a shit about rights," Shauna said in her ear.

She rubbed her head. Not because of her mother's words, but because of the lingering headache she'd been ignoring. The idea that she was abusing the Entity was funny considering her circumstances. Funny in a self-destructive sort of way.

"Why me?" she muttered as she stepped into the lift and instructed the tube to match her aunt's destination.

As she emerged onto the ninety-sixth floor, she did a double-take. She'd been down here just last night, and at that point, the floor had its usual drab and overly bright office complex aura. But this was different.

Dozens of robots with human onlookers were burrowing their way to the Beacon. From the looks of the operation, they were either planning on relocating it or seriously reshaping the surrounding space.

She glanced at her aunt. Her hands were clasped behind her back, and she was staring at it.

"What's going on?" she asked.

"We're moving it into orbit," Hera began. "With the Nebula sealed, there's no reason to have this valuable object buried underground, constrained by gravity and the confines of this..." She waved her hand around the room. "Oh, I'll just call it what it is. It's a fraking interrogation chamber. Not a space designed to house an artifact as important as this."

When her aunt smiled, it made her skin crawl. There was something about her eyes and the way her cheeks moved that was wrong for her face. It was like staring at graft surgery gone wrong, but different. She couldn't put her finger on what it was, but the effect was unpleasant. And for a person as cold as her, that was saying a lot.

As they stood there, the last panel fell and revealed the inner skotádi shell around the Beacon. Seeing it made her realize what Hera had meant. She was planning on putting this thing on display somewhere else. Somewhere she had control over it. And she'd made the decision without consulting anyone.

She subvocalized a message to Captain Hue and copied Joyce. Surely, someone should have told her about this. A few seconds after she hit send, her comm chimed with a reply from the captain. She blinked it open.

I'm aware. Despite my best efforts to stop her, my hands were tied. Joyce turned over all colony administration matters to your aunt while she was away in Sol.

The words 'your aunt' made her pulse race and her muscles tighten. She had to fight off the urge to haul off and knock some sense into Hera right there and then. Not that it would matter, with her being a clone and all. She wasn't sure they copied emotions or common sense into those blasted things during the reproduction process. Besides, it's not like she had any control over her aunt or any of her family. She'd lost that influence a long time ago.

Even though the words stung, the captain had always been loyal in the past. Reading the message back, she realized she'd probably misread it. She wasn't pointing the finger at Abigail. At least, she hoped not.

Abigail turned to face Hera. "So, where are you moving it? I assume someplace safe."

"You've been spending a lot of time connected to that thing." Hera nodded toward the Beacon. "Are you sure it's not... affecting you?"

She forced a smile. "While I appreciate your concern for my health and safety, don't be. I'm fine. I'm merely trying to figure out what we can use it for. But you never answered my question. Where are you moving it?"

Hera slowly turned her head and looked Abigail up and down. "I think it must be your mother's rude genes that make you act out that way. Either that or it's a residual side effect of her indiscretions with that Ulyxsauri... thing." She curled her nose in disgust.

"You're a real piece of work. You know that?" Abigail glared at her. "You haven't had an original idea in over a century, and then you suddenly turn up here thinking you own the place. Maybe you should've just stayed hidden in your secret lair with that 3D-printed body of yours, which, by the way, has one hell of a fraked-up face."

She'd started toward the lift tube when Hera reached out and spun her around. "You don't talk to me like that."

"Or what?" Abigail stepped forward and shoved her aunt, sending her reeling backward. "Are you going to try and kill me? Is that it? Go ahead. Fraking do it, you has-been." She went to shove her again, but Hera batted her arm aside and her face turned beet red.

When she looked down at her aunt's hand, her fingers were splayed out at her side. As if she were planning to swipe at her like a tiger. The entire gesture was quite comical, and she couldn't help but smirk.

"That's what I thought." Abigail shook her head. "You're all talk. My father was right about you. While I love him to the stars and back, he was as myopic a leader as you. Despite that flaw, however, he was a remarkable judge of character. He had the uncanny ability to spot a diamond in the rough from a klick away, or, in your case, detect a tumor in the family through hundreds of layers of bullshit."

"Your father was the tumor in the family, not me," Hera retorted, turning up her nose. "The sooner you realize that, the better for you and your pathetic brothers." She relaxed her hands and glanced at the nearby robots and the clones directing them. Like all good automata, they hadn't noticed the scuffle.

"It's funny how dissimilar we are, you and me," Abigail began. "Even with all we have in common, we're remarkably different people. I guess blood isn't thicker than water after all. My dad always said you…" Her words trailed off.

Arguing with her was like talking to a wall, and there was no point in continuing. Their relationship was beyond mending, and throwing barbs was getting her nowhere. She eased back a step.

"No!" Hera narrowed her gaze. "You can't just leave that hanging. Finish that sentence. What did he say about me?"

Abigail grinned. Hera really was an egomaniac. "He said

your skills were sharp, but you'd always lacked vision. He said that once you'd opened Pandora's box, the light blinded you from seeing anything else. As a result, you lost your way. You lost your edge, if you ever had one in the first place." She might have added that last part herself.

Hera tilted her head back and let out a cackle. It reminded her of an evil hyena she'd seen on a vid-sim.

When Hera lowered her head, she locked her steel-eyed glare on Abigail. "Do you honestly think everything I built lacked vision?"

"You built?" Abigail pivoted and stepped closer to her, causing Hera to flinch and take a step backward. "You built? Are you fraking kidding me? You stole your starship designs from Zachary, and don't even get me started on the technology they...re running. Those have Olivaw International written all over them. I bet you pilfered your colony plans as well."

Hera's eyes darted to the side and then snapped back to Abigail. That was it. Apparently, the fraking idiots couldn't tie their own shoes without stealing the plans to print the laces.

"They are, aren't they? You stole the damn—" She shook her head and sighed. "You know what? At this point, it doesn't matter. You know you're a fraud. Heck, you've probably never had an original idea in your life. To be honest, I wouldn't be surprised if many other Olivaws hadn't either, until my brothers and I broke that mold. And even then, mine weren't revolutionary by any stretch. I've simply been trying to figure out how to undo the family messes you all left us. But you," she sniggered and crossed her arms, "you're the winner of *The Most Screwed Up Olivaw*. You single-handedly set the family agenda back a century on your own. You sat on the throne of family lies at the Wheel, instead of getting your hands dirty and helping right the Olivaw wrongs. And when shit got real, your solution was to run away like a frightened little shrew and hide out at your colony in," she waved her hand dismissively, "wherever the frak it is."

She shuddered, and her legs wobbled as she felt an invisible weight lift off her shoulders. She'd been bottling that up her entire life, and finally saying it out loud was freeing. Even if it'd been her father standing in front of her, she would've had just as many choice words to say to him.

Whatever she'd said must've crossed a line because, judging by the crimson color of Hera's cheeks, she was about to explode. She glared at Abigail through the rising dust until she suddenly raised her arms out from her sides, fingers spread out. It was the same motion she'd used earlier, except this time the tips of her fingers glistened in the nearby construction lights.

Abigail did a double-take when she realized Hera's nails had transformed into claws. The she-devil was planning on literally clawing her.

But Abigail wasn't about to stick around to find out. She dove toward the lift tube, and just as she passed into the pressurized pipe, she heard a faint squeal and a wince. As she subvocalized the command to head topside, she shot upward, and a message appeared on her retinal comm from Harold.

That was close.

Her heart raced in her chest. "What was?"

He brought up a video on her comm, and she watched in awe as one of the nearby construction robots knocked its clone operator aside and yanked Hera's arm away just as she swiped at Abigail's throat.

Hera wasn't fraking around. She'd been going for the kill, and Harold had saved her.

"I..." She swallowed hard. "Thank you... again. You know you don't have to protect me any longer, right?"

I don't have to. I want to. Even with everything you said, you're still my kin.

"So is Hera." She glanced up and checked the overlay on her comm. Someone had diverted her floor to level eight.

That's not Hera. At least, not the Hera who left Sol. And in case you're wondering, it says you're getting off on eight, but you're going topside. I'm working to reprogram the Archégonos systems to misdirect your pursuers.

She gulped. "I have pursuers?"

Two dozen.

"Why are you still typing your messages to me?"

"I don't know," Harold said in her ear. "Force of habit, I guess. It seems safer."

She watched as the eighth floor zipped past and the lights overhead flashed to warn her she was reaching her stop. "After what happened back there, I think we're way beyond worrying about being discovered. So, where am I headed?"

A few seconds later, the tube randomly spat her out into a pitch-black hallway, and she glanced around. This wasn't a passageway she'd been in before.

"You're in the emergency evacuation tunnel," Harold said. "You won't be able to reach topside. At least, not that way."

She stared down the darkened tunnel and subvocalized the command to bring up the LiDAR overlay on her comm. The last time she'd used this feature, she'd been descending the stairs on the Ursis home world, hoping not to be buried under kilometers of rubble. And here she was again, below ground and fighting to stay alive.

"What's with everyone trying to kill me underground? I'm so sick of all this rock. Never again," she muttered.

Harold highlighted a path for her to follow. "Less talking, more running."

Abigail didn't argue or question him. She merely leaned forward and sprinted with everything she had into the darkness.

8

JOYCE GREEN
EPSILON ERIDANI, LIPROSUS ORBIT

When their ship transitioned through its final gate sequence, the collective members of the Sol leadership on the bridge gasped. Joyce knew the effect of seeing Hera's fleet of starships up close would be eye-opening. What she hadn't planned on, however, was the presence of the alien Ursis vessels around the planet.

"What are those?" Nguyễn pointed at one of the Alatas starships belonging to their new alien allies.

She'd seen the ships in the footage from Abigail's mission to the Proto Dark Nebula, but never up close, and never this many in one place.

"Those are the Ursis." She unexpectedly shifted her weight onto her right leg and twisted, forcing her torso to turn and face Nguyễn. The freshly-cloned legs Hera had grown for her took some getting used to. While mechanical limbs might have lacked the minute sensations of their organic variants, scientists and engineers had perfected their neural interfaces over the centuries. And they sure as hell never randomly twitched like the test-tube-grown ones.

Nguyễn's gaze hadn't left the alien vessel, nor had any of the other members of the Sol delegation. They were transfixed by the scale of the weaponry floating in front of them. As she watched the first hints of the colony construction site rising over the horizon, she knew the halo effect of the aliens would fade.

She forced a smile and nodded at the Inner and Outer Ring representatives. "Are you prepared to meet our new alien allies?"

Representative Zhang from the Inner Ring responded first. "As ready as I'll ever be."

Joyce caught a slight flutter in the woman's right eye, but she did an adequate job of suppressing her emotions. Except for Nguyễn, the others weren't nearly as subtle in their reactions. Their visible trembling and grumbles of discontent were bound to make these initial meetings with the Ursis interesting, to say the least. She couldn't blame them, though. Their first contact had started with an alien tribunal and had most recently ended with a Thyreusian leader forcing them to bow to the might of the Galactic Alliance.

She was looking forward to the chance to meet an Ursis. Outside of a starship, her last alien encounter had been with Two, deep in the bowels of the Archégonos interrogation wing. Just the thought of that time with them made her fingers tingle. She could still feel the pressure of the Thyreus' antennae in her hands as she yanked the appendages out of its fraking head. The thud of its body hitting the ground had been soothing, but not as much as watching its blood ooze out of its skull.

With her mind lost in memories, she almost missed the message flashing on her comm. She followed behind the others as they all turned and made their way toward the shuttle bay. As she stepped into the lift, her thoughts veered off to the Ursis. Something told her she wouldn't be able to take down one of these giant bears as easily as a Thyreusian.

Epsilon Eridani, On Liprosus

THE URSIS, whom they called Haradis, reached out and took Joyce's hand in his, mimicking a crude human handshake gesture. Despite his best efforts to appear delicate, the raw strength in his paw was obvious. There was no way in hell she'd be able to take on one of these beasts alone, at least not without an exo-suit.

"Welcome to Epsilon Eridani." Joyce bowed toward the towering alien. "I trust you've found your stay here in my colony comfortable?"

"Ah, yes. That's right. I forgot you were the new mayor of these parts." He pivoted and locked his gaze on Hera.

Joyce followed suit. Standing a dozen meters away with her arms crossed, Hera hadn't bothered to welcome the Sol contingent upon their arrival. Instead, she merely hung back, watching and studying them from the sidelines. Joyce suspected Hera was displeased that she hadn't brought Nguyễn back alone.

"Your colleague never mentioned your name when we arrived," Haradis turned to face Joyce. "But Abigail did."

She flinched and spun around, searching for the Olivaw. She was nowhere to be seen. "I trust her stories weren't too disconcerting?" She looked up at Haradis's towering form. Even with an exo-suit, it was hard to imagine bringing him down.

"Abigail described you as a strong and fearless leader, someone whom we can depend on for the truth. A no-nonsense mind in a sea of chaos. I hope she didn't oversell you because we could use a person like you in this endeavor we're about to undertake." Haradis raised an eyelid and glanced away. His eyes seemed to soften. "She also told me about your son and what our common enemy did to you and your people here on Liprosus. I'm sorry for your loss."

Her shoulders slouched, and she suddenly felt a tinge of remorse. While he'd been viewing her as an ally, she had been picking him apart with her mind. As it was with humans, not all aliens are the same. She should know that more than anyone. If that meant she had to shove her feelings aside and get her head in the game, then so be it. They needed the Ursis to make this strike on the Nursery work. There would be plenty of time to discern the true nature of this giant bear and his people.

"Thank you." Joyce nodded. "I only hope I can live up to Abigail's expectations." She glanced to her right. "Do you happen to know where she might be?"

"I do not." His eyes focused on Hera in the distance. "Our friend has not yet arrived to greet us since our arrival the other day. I trust she is well."

"And who do we have here?" Nguyễn stepped up beside Joyce. "Ah, you must be King Umbra." He reached out his hand in greeting.

Haradis stared at it, then leaned forward and peered around Nguyễn's back. "I trust you left your weapons elsewhere, Admiral? I'd hate to cause an incident here on the lawn."

Joyce smirked as Nguyễn recoiled. His reputation aboard the tribunal ship had preceded him and even made its way into the depths of a Dark Nebula, thanks to a certain Olivaw.

Just as he was about to turn away, the giant bear grabbed his hand before it reached his side. "I'm messing with you, Admiral," he smiled, and his teeth glistened in the light of the binary suns overhead. "I wish I had been there with those daggers of yours. If I had, none of the tribunal members would have left that ship alive." His fiery gaze locked on Nguyễn.

"I suspect not," Nguyễn returned the handshake and eased back a step, as if expecting the giant bear to make another sudden movement at any moment.

It was humorous watching Nguyễn squirm, especially in the presence of an alien. His reputation among his people in Sol had inflated his ego to epic proportions, and seeing it deflated was comforting. Maybe he was a leader she could work with after all.

"Why don't I show you around?" Joyce asked.

"I'd love to." Haradis pointed toward the south ring. "I hear you have a sports facility over there."

While she had intended that transition for Nguyễn, she realized she could get to know both of them at the same time.

"Alright then." When she glanced over her shoulder, she saw that the representatives from Sol were prattling on with Haradis' generals and his head of security, whom she believed was named Klus. From the sound of the conversation, they were talking about alien fashion — a topic she had no interest in whatsoever.

Joyce reached out and gestured for both of them to follow her toward the south ring. "How about we go see if they've finished building the Zero-G Disc course? We usually build 'em in orbit, but with some of our newfound tech, it seems gravity isn't so hard to control anymore."

SOMEHOW, in all the chaos of the tour, they got sidetracked visiting the final resting place of the asteroid - the one that created the trench the colonists so lovingly called *The Gash of Hope*. It was corny, but within the massive metallic rock had rested the hope of her people.

They didn't know what it was when it landed, and at the time, Joyce was just freaked out, thinking she was going crazy. But after it crashed, they found a team of rebels hiding inside, ready and willing to help them. While most colonists would describe the Olivaw family as part of the problem, she was beginning to see the three young siblings as something more. She wasn't sure what, but they weren't the same as the generations before them.

Hera, on the other hand, was exactly the same as the Olivaws who came before her: driven, single-minded, and relentless. But instead of using that focus to keep the wool pulled over the eyes of humanity, as she and her ancestors had done before her, she was focused on something new - something that aligned with Joyce's mission.

Bringing down the Galactic Alliance.

"You took them where?" Hera's snarling face was in the corner of Joyce's retinal comm. Apparently, she didn't appreciate not being asked to join them on their tromp across Liprosus.

"Don't get your panties in a bunch." Joyce smirked. "It's called divide and conquer. You talk to the Sol representatives, and I'll handle Nguyễn."

"You mean like how you handled him bringing an entire contingent here from Sol?" Hera scoffed. "I thought I told you to only bring him."

Joyce could feel her temper rising. "You don't tell me to do anything. We agreed I would take care of it, and that meant I would return with whoever was in power."

"I said Nguyễn!" Hera swung her hand through the air.

"And he's here, with me, like I promised." She narrowed her gaze and eased further away from the others. "Last I checked, if we plan on turning Sol to our side, we'll need more than an egomaniac admiral on our side. Those representatives are your lifeline to the populace. Now stop your whining and get in there and rub elbows."

"I can't talk about fashion." Hera scowled, glancing towards where she assumed the representatives were lingering in the garden.

"Well, then you're just gonna have to accept that Klus is a better politician than you are." Joyce smirked as Hera spun around.

"How do you know she's still yammering on with them?" Hera turned her focus back to Joyce.

"Like I told you when I returned from Sol, I'm the mayor of this colony. I see everything going on down here, and more importantly, I call the shots. Not you." She cut the line, and the wind whipped up into her face, bringing with it a billow of dust.

"That comm sounded like it went as well as our negotiations the other day." Haradis turned toward her.

"Your negotiations?" Nguyễn glanced from Haradis to Joyce and back. "What did we miss?"

"Your leader from Delta Sagittarii demanded that we place her in charge of our collective forces." Haradis shifted to look back at the steaming remains of the meteor.

"She did what?" Joyce edged around the front of the Ursis and stared up at him. "You didn't do it, did you?"

He tilted his head and sat down on the ground, bringing his eyes closer to their level. He seemed to have no regard for the regal dress he was wearing. "Are you advising me not to trust humans?"

"That's not what she's saying." Nguyễn eased up beside Joyce. "But I have to say, if Sol wasn't present in the negotiations for this… this mission, I wouldn't trust the messenger."

"What do you think we should do then, Admiral?" Haradis turned his head and locked his gaze on the man.

You could almost see him sink into his shoes. He had no idea what they were talking about. Joyce hadn't taken the time to tell them what they were planning on the way. She'd spent it bringing them up to speed with the Beacon conflict and never got to the part about the Nursery. She figured that once they arrived, explaining the next steps would be easier.

"I…" Nguyễn cast a glance toward her, but she didn't respond. She was interested in what he was going to say. "I suppose I'd place my belief in your instincts. Go with your gut."

"So, Abigail then?" Haradis lowered his head to study Nguyễn. You could almost feel the weight of the stare.

Nguyễn shifted his stance and forced a smile. "If that's who you trust."

Haradis bobbed his head. "Your mouth says one thing, but your heart says another, Mr. Nguyễn. That tiny muscle in your chest skipped three beats when I said her name, and your pupils narrowed as well. You don't like her, do you?"

He smirked. "Her and I have only ever met over video."

"Ahh, and that's the truth." Haradis straightened his back and looked out over the scene in front of them. "Your kind are almost too easy to read. That's probably what made you such obvious targets for the Galactic Alliance. And yet, I find you endearing."

"We do have a tendency to wear our emotions on our sleeves," Joyce said. "For better or worse."

He slowly nodded his head. "I imagine that could pose a challenge among enemies." He glanced back at Nguyễn. "Are your people okay with the resource-sharing arrangements Hera set up in Sol then?"

Nguyễn's eyes went wide, and a moment later, a subvocalized message appeared on Joyce's retinal comm.

What is he talking about?

"And we've returned to you humans speaking to yourselves again." Haradis shook his head. "You do realize that even if you can't hear your own voice, some of us can. I gather from your question to the mayor here that you're in the dark?"

"I..." Nguyễn stuttered.

"It's alright." He waved his hand. "I figured as much based on how you answered my last query. I simply wanted to see how far you'd take the charade." Haradis turned toward her. "And you. Why have you chosen not to share the mission details with the Admiral? Is it a trust issue?"

"Not with Admiral Nguyễn, no." She smiled. "Let's just say we didn't want any unknowing ears listening in."

Haradis glanced sideways. "You mean your A.I. companions?"

It was her turn to flinch in surprise. "You know about Harold?"

He nodded and looked back toward the asteroid trench.

"I'm aware of him. It's a shame he lost his life saving your ambassador on my home world."

"Wait! What?" She waved her hands in front of her. "He died protecting Abigail?"

Haradis sighed and pushed up off the ground, letting out a moan as he moved. "It seems that none of you humans talk to one another. You each leave the other in the dark when pertinent information is at hand to light their way. With everything going on, it's miraculous you accomplish any form of governing at all with a system like that." He turned and started walking toward his custom-crafted, open-air ground car.

"Are you ready to go?" She could use a change in scenery. This little side trip hadn't gone as she expected.

"I am, but you're not." He paused and pointed at Nguyễn. "By the time you bring him back to the colony, he'd better be up to speed. I won't be wasting my days or those of my people with uninformed half-truths and misinformation. There's too much at stake to be playing games, Mayor." He glanced between them. "Too much for all of us."

They both watched in silence as he boarded his ground car and disappeared into the distance. The truth of his words stung. She'd let herself stray from her path - the one her son helped her find coming to Liprosus, and the one Ryder helped her rediscover.

She wasn't sure if it'd been the hint of truth or the sweet scent of revenge in the air, but he was right. Hera was up to her Olivaw games, and she was rubbing off on how Joyce acted. Even if Abigail had turned over a new leaf, that didn't mean everyone had.

"Have you ever seen an ocean of power so immense that you pissed yourself?" Joyce asked.

Nguyễn turned to look at her with a blank expression on his face. "You mean like the oceans back on Earth?"

She shook her head. "No. Like this?" She reached into her pocket, pulled out a small holo-drone, and tossed it in the air.

A three-dimensional hologram appeared in the space

between them. She watched as Nguyễn took in the view, and a moment later, realization dawned on his face. He staggered backward several steps until he finally caught himself on a boulder.

"Is that…" He pointed at the floating image.

"Yes." She crossed her arms and smiled. "That's our target."

What first appeared to be a nebulosity of color was, in fact, an ocean of starships. Selene moon ships, to be exact. The entire strength and might of the Galactic Empire in one location.

The Nursery.

<hr>

A FEW HOURS and several shouting matches later, she finally got back to telling him about the Nursery battle. "And that's where we are." Joyce waved her hand, and the hologram disappeared.

"Wait… what?" Nguyễn shook his head. "What about the fight? All you've shown me is how you intend to move resources around back here in Epsilon Eridani. Where are the tactics? The battle plans?"

She chuckled and climbed onto the boulder they'd been using as their bench for the past few hours. "That's why you and the Ursis Generals are here. I have no clue. At least not yet." She broke off a chunk of the rock and threw it into the ravine, following its path as it tumbled down toward the bottom and finally faded away.

He raised his hands. "But why do you need all the resources, then? I figured they were for building your fleet or something."

"Some of it is, and some of it isn't." She flipped one of the yellow-orange, clay-like stones in her hand, and a trail of dirt fell onto her already dust-stained pants. "The Ursis won't budge unless we help them rebuild somewhere. At least Haradis won't. The generals, however…" She shrugged.

"From what the debrief said, Hera thinks they don't give a damn. They want nothing more than to tear that Nursery apart. Haradis, though, he wants to find a new home for his people. And until we appease him, his army isn't going anywhere."

"Just bring them here." He gestured around. "There's room for everyone."

"It's not that simple." She chucked the stone over the edge, but she didn't watch it fall. Instead, she slid off the rock and walked over to him. "They don't want to live in the Dark Nebula anymore. They want a home. A world where they can breathe the air and not be afraid of death enveloping them."

"Find them one, then!" He turned and started pacing back and forth. "Give them the second or third colony sites. They can't be very big by now."

She chuckled. "As if it were that easy. Nathan isn't budging, and, well, you can probably imagine what Hera says about giving up their world. Not that anyone knows where it is."

He stopped in front of her. "There's no fraking way in hell the representatives from Sol will give up any part of Earth to the Ursis. No way, no how!"

"I know," she muttered. "I know." She kicked at one of the stones, and a tiny crab-like creature skittered away and darted behind the boulder.

9

BRADLEY OLIVAW
EPSILON ERIDANI, LIPROSUS ORBIT

The room was packed to the gills; except for space along the front, it was standing room only. Bradley and Cynthia were near the wall screen, studying the maps of the Nebula along with everyone else. The brightest military and strategic minds in the colonies were present, accompanied by several generals from Sol. Nguyễn had sent one of Hera's ships back to fetch them.

He'd heard rumblings of a negotiation happening between Hera, Joyce, Sol, and the Ursis, but neither he nor any of his family members were in the know – at least not anymore. And, for some reason, Abigail had gone MIA over the past few days. He tried looking up her details on the computers, but the last place it had recorded her location was in Archégonos.

When he reached out to Zachary, he couldn't find her either. Neither of them dared reach out to any of Harold's forms. His copy in Epsilon Eridani had been missing since Hera set foot on the planet. None of them knew whether their aunt's goon squad had taken him out or if he was just in hiding. If he were still around, he'd make himself known at some point.

As his mind wandered back to the wall screen, a murmur rose in the rank and file behind him.

Cynthia tapped him on the shoulder. "Look who's here," she whispered, pointing to the back corner.

He spun around to see Hera walking in behind Shauna. The version of his mother that contained the earliest copy of her consciousness, and the only person in the room who had actually visited the Nursery. He hadn't seen her since after the Beacon battle when they had first met Hera onboard her ship. From the looks of it, she was in the same war-torn shell they'd found her in several months earlier. Burn marks and melted plastic were visible on various sections of her humanoid skeleton.

The two of them walked toward the front of the crowd, and the people along the route parted for them. Before she reached the stage, Hera split off and turned, making eye contact with Bradley as she went.

He nodded. "Aunt H."

"Bradley. Cynthia." She smiled. "It's good of you to make it up here. I wasn't sure if either of you would be able to tear yourselves away from the colony build-out."

He bit his lip and suppressed a laugh, but Cynthia didn't bother. She snickered at the notion. He reached out and nudged her hip, trying to get her to stop. When he turned to smile at his aunt, she was glaring at Cynthia with a stare normally reserved for melting ice.

"We're happy to be included," he forced a smile.

She'd been the reason both of them had been swamped down at the new colony site. Her constant changes in construction, unrealistic building demands, and the pressure she put on them to train the new clones from her colony were over the top. While it certainly made him feel needed, he wouldn't have missed this meeting for anything.

While this wasn't the first time anyone had asked him to be involved in military planning, he'd honestly figured they would be further along than they were. Based on the strategic plans they had forwarded to everyone, the brass had hit numerous dead ends. He hesitated to describe their plans as grasping at straws, but the phrase stuck in his mind.

Maybe this mission wasn't the slam dunk his aunt had envisioned.

"Well..." Hera turned her attention back toward the stage. "I never wanted you here in the first place. There's no point in bothering you with these things. You have more important things to be doing right now down on the planet."

"If it wasn't you," he tilted his head, "then whose idea was it?"

"Alright, everyone," Shauna said from the front of the room. "Let's get started."

"Hers." Hera dipped her head toward his mother.

Shauna glanced toward Admiral Nguyễn on the far side of the stage, and he nodded. A moment later, the lights dimmed, and the wall screen came alive. On the side, there were several dozen live video feeds from each site airing this presentation. There were pilots and what looked like scientists from Sol gathered on a few of the cameras. On others, he could make out a collection of Ursis soldiers. Though it was impossible to know their area of expertise, he imagined they were of the same makeup as the humans. The remaining cameras echoed the others, with a smattering of people from Zeta Lupi and other ships in orbit.

Despite their best efforts to rapidly build out this orbiting platform, it was still too small to handle a collection of forces like this. Hell, there weren't many places in any of the human worlds that could pull it off outside of a sports arena.

The more he studied the attendees, the more this felt like the blind grasp at straws he'd imagined earlier.

"I've shared a few of our initial rough draft strategies with everyone before this meeting. I hope you had time to review them." Shauna's electronic gaze seemed to linger on him. Though, without real eyes, it was hard to know for sure. But he knew.

"What did you see?" she asked.

Their room remained silent, as did the rooms with the other attendees on the cameras. No one said a word, not even the Ursis.

"Aw, come on." She raised her metallic arms. "With all your years of experience, one of you had to see something we missed. What, are you afraid of talking to a robot?"

"It's a death trap," Bradley said aloud.

Everyone turned to face him.

Shauna nodded in his direction. "Continue."

He swallowed hard. "The Selene ships are too close to one another. Even with gate drives, we'd be sitting ducks flying in there."

"The moment we attack, they'll scatter like a flock of birds," Cynthia said. "They're not dumb. They clumped 'em together for a reason."

"But what reason?" a scientist from a Sol ship asked.

"Repairs, refueling, and transfer of troops," someone from an Ursis ship replied. "They've done it for millennia. We've just never known where they gathered the moons until now. We can still take them." Grunts of assent echoed from the other gathered aliens.

"If you want to commit suicide, maybe," Lync said.

Bradley squinted at the video stream in the bottom right of the wall screen. He hadn't even realized she was there. From the looks of it, she was on another ship surrounded by her Ulixi brethren.

The Ursis pounded his hand against his chest. "If that's what the Gods of Therion wish, then we welcome death, so long as we can take a cadre of those Galactic Alliance vermin into the abyss along with us." Even more grunts of assent rose around him.

Bradley shook his head. Everyone knew the Ursis had no problem dying for their cause, but they were alone in that position. The last thing humanity wanted was an end marred by death.

"I agree!" Hera stepped closer to Shauna, and the room erupted in murmurs. "What we need is a swift attack, while the element of surprise is on our side. With enough resources, we can destroy this fleet before they can even blink."

The chatter around her grew louder and louder until it

reached a clashing crescendo of both agreement and dissent. They were no closer now than before, and Shauna knew it. She had asked her question the way she did to prove that point.

Suddenly, the screen overhead changed. It lit up. A moon ship in the center of the mass began glowing bright white. Bolts of lightning danced across its surface, igniting the next spot, and the next, and so on, until the entire thing was as bright as a miniature sun. Then it leaped out. A spark shot across to the surface of the neighboring moons, and they continued the same dance. Each added to the next, leading to a crescendo of light as bright as a hundred thousand suns. From a distance, the effect reminded him of watching a hive of fireflies flicker on one at a time, until the resulting hive was one massive ball of brilliance.

The room was awestruck by both the beauty and the raw power of the event, and when he looked toward Hera, her face was twisted in anger. Whatever this was that Shauna had shown them, she hadn't seen before. No one had.

"What is this?" Haradis asked from onboard the Ursis ship. "What are we looking at in these videos?"

Shauna was standing off to the side of the stage with her metallic arms crossed. She just stood there, as if she were waiting for someone to answer.

"Shauna!" Hera shouted. "What is that?" She pointed at the videos.

"Oh!" Shauna pushed off the wall and glanced around, feigning surprise. "Are you asking me? I'm sorry." She pointed at the wall screen. "That was a gift I neglected to share with you earlier. As you can imagine, I have my reasons, one of which is your interrogations, threats against my family, and endless attempts to probe my memories and wipe my consciousness. Despite your best efforts, you still failed to extract this tidbit and a few others from my mind."

"What?" Bradley turned to face Hera. "You're seriously torturing my mother? She's the only person who's ever been to the Nursery. What the frak is wrong with you?"

"And let's not forget she's conscious," Harold said from overhead.

Hera spun around, arching her back and searching for the source of his voice. When she couldn't find him, she stopped and narrowed her eyes at Bradley. "You! You brought him here!"

He recoiled. "What? You're fraking kidding me, right?"

"I want everyone out! Everyone!" Hera sliced her hand across her neck and the video cut off. At the same moment, the doors at the back of the room exploded outward, and a small contingent of clone guards began filing into the room. Apparently, she was prepared for Shauna to go off the rails.

"If you harm a hair on their heads, you'll never know what's at the Nursery!" Shauna shouted.

A group of four guards split off from the others and ran onstage, surrounding her on all sides. In their hands, they held some type of metallic rods out in front of themselves, aimed directly at her.

"What are you doing?" He stepped toward the stage. "Stop—"

But he was too late. The rods lit up, and for a split second, he expected sparks to jump out and electrocute her like a stun gun. But none came. Instead, Shauna let out a blood-curdling screech and fell to her knees.

This was too much to watch. He lurched to the side and grabbed Hera's shirt, yanking her sideways. She stumbled backward and slammed her back against the wall with a thud.

"Let her go!" He reached into his pocket and grasped for anything he could find, but all he had was his stone. It would have to be enough.

He pulled it out and jabbed it into her ribs. All he wanted to do was inflict pain on her, to get her to focus on him and call off her dogs. What he hadn't expected was her reaction.

Like with Shauna, she shrieked in agony as if he'd reached inside her and yanked out her innards.

He stumbled backward and stared down at his hand. The

stone in his hand was tingling and had a faint glow. It wasn't much, but it was there.

"What the hell?" he muttered.

And then the room went pitch black.

He reached up and tapped his ear to subvocalize the command to engage the infrared on his retinal comm, but it wouldn't power on. This was no ordinary power outage. Harold had done something worse. He'd somehow knocked out all the nearby electronics.

People around them began screaming at the top of their lungs, and he heard several thumps and moans across the room near the wall screen. Someone was either getting trampled or beaten. He couldn't tell which, but he didn't care. His only thought was that he needed to find Cynthia and get the hell out of dodge.

When he slid sideways toward where she'd been standing, he crashed into someone barreling past. The collision sent him flying backward to where Hera had been seconds earlier. Though he tried to catch his balance, he fell on his ass when something on the ground tripped him up, something as big as a body.

He'd never seen a room fall into chaos so quickly. "Cynthia!" he shouted. "Where are you?"

"I'm right here." When she reached out from his left and brushed against him, he flinched.

Somehow, she'd made her way past him and up against the wall.

"How do we get out of here?" he asked as pandemonium erupted around them.

"I... I don't know," she shouted into his ear as screams rang out a mere half meter in front of them. The sound of several more bodies slamming against the floor with thuds made her flinch backward and hit her head against his chest. Pain shot through his torso and he winced. Better him than the wall, he supposed, but it still hurt like hell.

"Sorry," a voice whispered from the darkness in front of them. "I didn't mean to frighten you. Come, take my hand."

It was only then that he realized who it was. "Shauna, is that…"

"Don't talk. Just grab on."

He felt something rub up against his chest, and when he reached down, he felt Cynthia's hands under his. At least she was well enough to move. He used his other hand to reach out and pull her close. There was no way he was letting her fall behind in this shitstorm.

They both eased up off the ground and stumbled forward. The first steps were a doozy, though, as they stumbled over the body from earlier. But then something swiftly swept it off to the side, and a heartbeat later, people began cursing as they crashed over it. Shauna must've shoved it aside.

His mind was going a million kilometers an hour. He wanted to ask where they were headed and what was going on, but he knew better. Whatever Shauna and Harold were up to, they had a plan. At least, he hoped they did.

As Shauna tugged them along, she tapped the backs of their hands with her free one, signaling if they were going right or left. After they'd been stumbling along for what felt like hours, he realized the extent of what Harold had done. He hadn't simply knocked out their floor. He might have brought down the entire station.

Just as he was about to ask Shauna a question, she yanked them to the side and sent him stumbling into the black. If she hadn't grabbed both of them before they hit the ground and tucked them into her side, he probably would have face-planted into the floor, or worse.

"I'm picking up a few more heat signatures over here," a voice said from the darkness.

It sounded like the voice was pretty far away. One second, he heard the rhythm of their feet stomping toward them, and the next, he flinched as a loud thud echoed just out of reach. Shauna must've closed a door or a hatch or something.

A few groans and some trip-ups later, they shuffled further into the darkness. That's when the banging started. It was coming from where they'd just left. Whoever they were, they must have known Shauna was down here.

As his mind turned over the plethora of possibilities that could end them, he couldn't take the not knowing anymore. For all he knew, Shauna had gone off the rails, and he was letting himself get yanked around like a rag doll.

"Where are we going?" he whispered.

"It's only a little bit further." Shauna pulled them along. "I know it's hard, but trust us."

Trust was in short supply these days. Especially with his family. Everyone except Zachary, that is. Even Abigail hadn't been herself the last time they talked. Though, after tonight, he was starting to think she wasn't so far off her rocker. Hera was a monster.

Cynthia reached down and squeezed his hand around her waist, bringing him back into the moment. The sound of the thuds had disappeared in the distance. Their pursuers had either given up, or they'd found another way to reach them.

This was too much, even for his fraked-up family. Shauna tugged them around a corner, and he reached out and grabbed the edge.

"No more," he whispered. "Tell me where you are taking us, or we're not moving another centimeter."

And with that, two steel arms encircled him and squeezed him tight. In the space of a breath, the familiar blue glow and tear of a gate transition ripped across his body.

He and Cynthia screamed into the darkness, but no one was there to hear them.

10

ZACHARY OLIVAW

EPSILON ERIDANI, NEAR LIPROSUS

They rushed into the room the second the gate closed, and the lights burst on. Bradley and Cynthia were lying on the floor, kicking and screaming, while wrapped up in Shauna's robotic arms.

"Frickety frak!" Bradley tried to roll back and forth, but Shauna's grip was too tight. When she noticed his plight, she finally let go. He moaned and untangled himself from Cynthia. He then crawled away from both of them and leaned against the nearby wall.

Cynthia was just lying there, huffing and puffing, trying to catch her breath, while simultaneously running her hands up and down her side. From the looks of it, the tearing effects of the rapid gate sequence were still lingering.

"I hate those fast ones," Zachary said as he knelt down and rested his hand on his brother's shoulder. "Can I get you anything to help with the pain?"

"The serial number of that grain bot that shredded me. I'm gonna melt it into slag the next time I run across it," Bradley said as he rolled onto his side. He froze, only now remembering that Shauna's robotic form was there as well. "Sorry, mum. I didn't—"

She reached out and mussed up his hair. "Don't worry

about it. I've got thicker skin than that. Besides, I'm not a robot. I'm alive, remember?"

Zachary stared at his mom's cold steel robot body. If anyone saw her out and about in the colony, the last thing they would say was that she was alive - including him, if he didn't know better.

"Where... are we?" Cynthia moaned.

"Harold won't tell us." Zachary settled down on the ground beside them.

Bradley narrowed his gaze. "What do you mean, he won't tell us?"

"You can blame me for that," Abigail said as she strolled into the room and smiled at both him and Cynthia. "Hey, Cyn. It's good to see you again."

She hadn't seen her friend since spending months inside the Proto Dark Nebula with the Ursis. After that, she had told him they needed time alone. Zachary wasn't sure if it was because they fought on their trip or for other, more personal reasons.

Cynthia hoisted herself up without pausing. She stumbled up to Abigail and gave her a hug.

When she hugged her, she winced. "Sorry..."

"Don't be," Cynthia said. "It's worth it." After hugging for a moment, she leaned away. "How have you been... you know, since we got back?"

"I'm... fine," Abigail muttered.

They were speaking more with their eyes than with their words, but he knew what she was alluding to. Cynthia was asking how she was handling life without Minula - the love she never realized she had until it was too late.

Bradley eased up off the ground and used the wall to steady himself. "Will someone please tell me why my sister being here prevents us from knowing where we are? Are we under arrest or something, Harold?" He glanced up at the ceiling, like everyone did when talking to an A.I. overlord.

"I'm not up there, Master Zachary. I'm right here," a

human voice responded as a man entered the room. This was someone he and his brother had only ever seen once, but one whom Abigail was no stranger to.

"You're the medic," Bradley mumbled.

Harold tittered. "Sure, let's go with that. I have been known to fix things from time to time." He took a step closer but paused. "While this closet looks cozy, maybe everyone would rather convene in the living room?" He gestured to his right.

"We have a living room?" Cynthia turned to look at Abigail.

"It wouldn't be a secret Olivaw lair if we didn't have somewhere to relax," Abigail responded, waving her toward the exit. "Come check it out. He even replicated a few beanbag chairs for you two."

"No shit," Bradley exclaimed as he pushed off the wall and followed them.

———

THEY CONVENED IN A VAST ROOM, complete with half a dozen sofas, multiple wall screens, and a food replicator at each end. Every time Zachary walked in, it reminded him more of a party cave than a living space.

Bradley collapsed into a beanbag on the ground with a moan, and Cynthia dragged a sack up beside him. "I've never used one of these," she said, peering down at it, her brow furrowed in confusion.

He reached out and patted the pleather surface. "Go on. Plop in."

She half-squatted down and then just fell backward, sending a puff of bean pebbles into the air as the malleable chair reacted to the sudden change in shape. "Oh, shit!" She twisted around to study the bag. "Is it broken?"

"Nah." He placed his hand on her leg. "It's supposed to do that."

Zachary smiled and looked over at Pluto. She was sitting next to him with a grin on her face and a golden hue in her cheeks. It was nice to see she was having a good morning.

"All right, people. We don't have all day." Harold clapped his hands together near the giant wall screen. "Abigail has an appointment with an alien, and if she wants to be here for the start of this, you all need to zip it so I can update our new guests."

"Appointment?" Bradley leaned back in his beanbag and stared at Zachary upside down.

"Quiet from the peanut gallery. Just listen to Gramps." He pointed toward Harold.

"Har har, Mr. McCrackery. Har har." The android waved his hand to the side, and the wall screen to his left came alive.

He hated when people called him that.

"About three days ago," Harold began, "Abigail had an altercation with her loving Aunt Hera and turned herself into public enemy number one."

An image from a construction bot in Archégonos appeared on the screen. It showed their aunt with her arms at her side and what looked like daggers protruding from her fingers. It reminded Zachary of a comic superhero whose name was eluding him.

"I happened to still be in limited control of a few assets within that facility at the time this was recorded." Harold fast-forwarded the video, and they watched as the construction bot lurched over and snapped the necks of the nearby clone handlers before flying into Hera and barely stopping her from ripping Abigail's throat wide open. As her body tumbled into the lift tube, the robot twisted their clone aunt's head clear around before someone deactivated the automata.

"Wholly shit!" Bradley cringed in his chair. "So... she's... dead?"

"You're not as bright as they say you are sometimes," Abigail said. "Wasn't that Hera you ran into about twenty minutes ago?"

"Oh… right. Wait." He scratched his chin.

Harold leaned forward and brought his finger to his lips. "Silence, Master Bradley. All will be revealed."

He mimed locking his lips and tossed an invisible key over his shoulder.

"After I aided in Abigail's escape, I brought her my hidden consciousness core from Archégonos, along with her suitcase of Therionic fun." The image changed, and a picture of the container housing the alien entity appeared.

Zachary's skin crawled simply looking at the thing on the video. It was hard to imagine that there was an alien life force inside his sister, forcing its will on her.

"Thus ended my influence at that colony site," Harold said. "After she climbed to the surface, I directed her a few kilometers away to a hidden cavern left over from the original build-out." A hole in the shadow of a rock popped up on the wall screen. It couldn't have been any wider than a human shoulder.

"A few kilometers, my ass," she muttered. "More like twenty. I'm surprised no one saw me sweating my butt off hiking across that rocky mess of a planet."

Harold smirked and raised a finger in the air. "I may have brought a few of their systems down throughout Archégonos and up here when you reached the surface."

"Nice." Pluto leaned forward in her seat.

He could tell she missed the action. She was always happier when she was in her element, piloting or getting into trouble. Sitting around on her backside wasn't her cup-of-coffee.

"Once Abigail climbed down the hole to Wonderland, she appeared here, in this place." Harold brought up a floor plan of the space they were currently in. Their dots flashed in the living room on the map. It was a nice-sized facility that could easily house fifty of their closest friends.

"And where is here?" Cynthia asked.

Harold sighed. "You're as obnoxious as your mate, Miss

Cynthia. As I was about to say, none of you can learn the details of where we are until we leave. Whatever Abigail's suitcase companion knows, someone else is bound to hear. For now, it's best if only I know the details."

Zachary glanced toward Libby, and she smirked. Harold wasn't stupid. People would figure out roughly where they were after being here long enough, at least if they opened their eyes to the lunar dust strewn about. Or if they knew even a little planetary science and paid attention to the cycle of when Abigail could and couldn't bind with Beacon.

They were somewhere on one of Liprosus' many moon-lets. He'd never known this place existed, but apparently, Harold was being Harold and was always chock-full of tricks.

"So you're not planning on telling us then?" Cynthia crossed her arms.

"You'll be informed when the time is right." Shauna glared at her. At least what passed for a robotic glare. But it did the trick because Cynthia backed down and sunk deeper into her beanbag chair.

Harold clasped his hands together. "Alrighty, fast-forward to yesterday evening when Hera raided Miss Pluto's abode onboard the beanstalk. That was when I safely extracted our friend before they arrived to take her."

"What about Zachary?" Bradley asked. "Where was he?"

"Two minutes," Harold muttered. "You kept your mouth shut for two whole minutes. Wow..." He shook his android head.

"I wasn't with her," Zachary said. "I was up here with Abby."

Bradley craned his neck. "But the other day... when you messaged me. You didn't say anything. You just... left us for dead down there?"

"We have no presence in the new colony site," Harold began. "While we have loyalists, the physical security is still too tight to attempt any type of infiltration. We needed you to reach somewhere we had assets in place."

"Like the beanstalk," Cynthia muttered.

"Exactly." Harold tweaked the controls, and an insect-level view of the colony construction appeared. It showed Cynthia screaming at a group of clones, trying to get them to listen to her. "Besides, Hera had you plenty busy down there training her army to run things."

"Where does she think you are?" Bradley turned to look at his brother.

"With a delegation headed to Sol," he began. "We were heading there to recruit some scientists from Olivaw International to bring them back here. Fortunately, they were all loyalists, so they looked the other way when I hopped off. I was planning to join them before they returned, but I think that's out of the question now."

"What about Ibu and Pepper?" Abigail turned toward Harold. "We're going to need to extract them before they return." Harold nodded at Zachary, and she spun back around to face him. "What's the matter? Are they okay?"

"They're fine." He bit his lip. Telling her the truth was unthinkable with that alien controlling her. "Let's just say Ibu won't be returning for a while. And Pepper, well… she's busy too."

Abigail stood up with a start. "Where did you send them?"

He raised his arms skyward, and his shoulders sagged. "I can't…"

She spun around toward Bradley. "Where are they? Tell me."

He recoiled and shook his head. "I haven't the foggiest, sis. Honest!" He crossed his heart. "Last I heard, Ibu was headed to the Proto Dark Nebula to play the part of the See-er figurehead person you all talked about. As for Pepper, I'm clueless."

She glared at Zachary, and the chilling expression on her face made his skin crawl. It reminded him of the one his mom used to use on them when they were in trouble, complete with hands on hips and all.

"Can we refocus on the problem at hand, please?" Shauna asked.

Abigail pivoted her fury around to the front of the chamber. "And what's more pressing than our friends?"

"This…" Shauna held out her palm. In the center was a data dot of some sort.

The room fell into silence.

When Zachary looked closer, he realized it wasn't a data dot; it was a consciousness core. "Who… is that?"

"I… don't know." Shauna slid the device back inside an internal storage compartment. "But whoever it is, they're the reason I'm alive right now."

He eased forward and worked his way to the front of the room. "What do you mean?" He glanced at Harold. "What the hell happened down there? We had a plan."

"The best-laid plans often go to shit before they begin. For starters, we couldn't reach your mother. Our asset never got in place." Harold tweaked the display, and it brought up a video of a hydroponic engineer in their inner circle. He was being questioned by a security team at the beanstalk on his way out of the lift.

"If he didn't make it," Zachary glanced back at Bradley, "then how are they here?"

The scene playing out on the wall screen switched yet again, and this time, they were staring at a hundred or more people. Bradley and Cynthia were a few rows from the front. It took him a second to realize it was from Shauna's point of view. If she made it to the briefing room, then their plan didn't simply fail – it disintegrated. They'd intended on getting Shauna out as soon as she arrived, but given that they had no idea where she was being held, it made matters challenging.

When the video started playing, he watched in shock as she revealed new footage of the Nursery. At the same time, she let the galaxy in on the fact that she was being tortured against her will.

Zachary turned toward her, but she wasn't watching the

feed. She was staring at Pluto. Did she know? He shook his head. Impossible.

And then Hera screamed.

Zachary spun around to face the screen, his heart racing in his chest. It was almost too much to watch. Hera and Shauna argued back and forth until Harold's voice broke in overhead. But that made no sense – Harold didn't have a copy on the beanstalk, at least not anymore.

Suddenly, the doors in the rear exploded outward and a stream of guards ran in. He stood there and watched as they raced toward Shauna with strange wand-like weapons of some sort aimed squarely at her. And then the image flashed in and out as her robotic form screamed. It was like witnessing someone having a seizure through their eyes. He could almost feel the shadowy jolts of pain in his torso as each bolt struck her chest.

Just when he thought he knew what was going to happen next, her gaze darted toward the sea of people – toward Hera. Bradley was standing in front of their aunt, and he'd backed her up against the wall. From that angle, it looked like he had one arm pressed to her neck and another down by her waist. The audio track had gone out, but the imagery remained clear even between the continued shocks.

When Zachary saw Hera wince, it was obvious what he'd done. Bradley had stabbed her with something.

"I... didn't mean to hurt her," Bradley muttered.

He turned around to look at his brother, and he was staring down at his empty hand shaking in front of him. "It was... so warm. I... didn't even feel it cutting her."

"She deserved what she got," Shauna snarled. "All of it."

Bradley's eyes widened. "All of what?"

Zachary spun back toward the screen, and the room in the video went dark.

"What happened?" he asked.

"Someone fired off some type of short-range EMP," Bradley said by his ear. He'd walked up beside him. "It was freaking chaos in there."

The wall screen changed to show an infrared view of the scene. From the looks of it, they were still seeing through Shauna's eyes. He was about to ask how she'd remained operational, but then he realized why.

Decades earlier, he'd designed and built her robotic form on a spare Olivaw battlefield chassis, complete with multiple redundant systems shielded for just such an attack. She must've engaged her secondary sensor array once she was confident the coast was clear.

When he watched the scene unfold, he realized Shauna hadn't wasted a second. The moment the lights went out, she took out her captors without even switching over to her backup vision. She knew exactly where they were. And when her infrared came on, she was surrounded by puddles of blood.

In the distance, within the throng of people all scrambling over one another, there were two bodies on the ground. The first was about where Hera had been, but the second was closer.

They were lying on their stomachs with their backs arched up in pain. And then they screamed. It was a blood-curdling scream unlike any he'd ever heard. And just when he thought it couldn't get any weirder, something started glowing by the person's ass.

"That looks damn hot," he muttered.

"What is it?" Abigail asked.

Shauna must've known because she leapt forward and snatched at the mysterious object. Her robot hands seemed to tear at the clothes of the still screaming body in front of her. When she brought her hand back, they saw it. She'd extracted a consciousness core from the person's anus.

"Ew!" Zachary shivered. "Who was that?"

"Nguyễn," Shauna whispered. "And he was none too happy to have someone probing him there, either. But he passed out after I was done. So, there's that."

Abigail chuckled and tried to suppress it, but she failed miserably. "It couldn't have happened to a nicer bloke."

"What were you doing during all this?" Zachary caught his brother's gaze.

Bradley chuckled. "I was trying to stay alive and find Cynthia in the dark. Not everyone was blessed with infrared."

After Shauna dropped the core into her internal storage compartment, her eyesight flashed on and off a few times. The consciousness in that core was attempting to transmit something to her, and when she accepted it, a route overlaid on her vision. It was a map to some place within the station.

"Where were you heading?" Zachary asked.

"At the time, I had no idea," Shauna said. "But what other options did I have?"

The screen changed as she eased up beside Bradley and Cynthia and directed them where to go. After a brief pause, her robotic form simply shoved the second corpse aside. They then wove their way through the turbulent crowd of people, most of whom were clueless about what was going on in the dark.

"Who was that other body?" Cynthia asked. "Did someone get attacked?"

Shauna tilted her head and looked at Bradley. "Isn't it obvious?"

"No..." Cynthia narrowed her gaze.

"It was Hera. She was dead." Shauna studied Bradley. "I assumed you did that on purpose."

"I did not!" He stumbled backward. "I just... jabbed her with this." He held out his palm, and in it was the shard of Spános he'd picked up from his father's memorial. The one he carried with him everywhere.

"No shit." Zachary stepped closer to it. "And you said it got warm?"

He nodded and everyone stared down at the jagged stone, letting the rest of the video play out.

"Wait," Pluto said from the back of the room. "If Shauna didn't know what was at the end of that map, and there was only one plan to get them out, then how the hell did they wind up here? Were we compromised?"

His heart skipped a beat. He hadn't thought of that. If Hera and her people knew where they were, then it would only be a matter of time before they'd be on top of them.

Harold stepped up beside him. "There is no unusual ship activity or chatter from the space station or the planet, beyond the usual chaos of our little event, of course. If they were mobilizing forces, we'd know within minutes."

"Are we certain?" Pluto shuffled up to his side at the front of the room. Her glow had faded, and her face was pale and gaunt. Either that, or she was nauseous. He couldn't tell which.

"I'm positive," Harold said. "We still have loyalists down there, even after Hera weeded the garden."

"So, who's in the consciousness core, then?" Abigail asked.

Zachary walked up to Shauna and held out his hand. "Can I have the core?"

She crossed her arms. "It depends."

"On what?"

"On whether you're going to kill him." She drummed her fingers against her composite chassis, knowing full well the plasticky drumming sound annoyed him.

He clenched his jaw. "I won't hurt Harold. I promise. Especially after he's made it this far."

"This far..." Pluto shook her head slowly. "What does that mean?"

Shauna reached into her chest, pulled out the consciousness core, and placed it in his hand. It was cold to the touch, and for some reason, it was wet. When he brought it in for a closer look, he quickly held it away from his face. "Yowza!"

"What?" Bradley eased backward. "Does it burn?"

Zachary plugged his nose. "No, it stinks!"

He held the sphere up for the others to see and to keep the awful stench at a distance. "Unless I'm mistaken, our A.I.

friend has been hiding in Admiral Nguyễn's ass since he left Sol."

Collective guttural retches and choking sounds filled the air around him and were punctuated by an alarm on his retinal comm.

Beacon transit in five minutes!

"Shit." He handed the core back to Shauna. "Can you please at least wash and sterilize this? Also, find him a chassis to power up. But wait until I'm done before you turn him on! I want to run some tests first."

Shauna took the sphere, and he stepped around her toward the sink. When he glanced at Abigail as he passed, she met his gaze with a sigh. She knew it was time to enter the Beacon or the Therionic entity would throw a fit.

As they exited the room, he could hear Bradley's voice behind him. "Is someone going to tell me how we killed Hera twice, and yet somehow she's still walking around?"

ZACHARY EASED Abigail into the crash couch. Its form-fitting design was the most comfortable place for her to lie while she was bound to the Beacon. It also helped keep her stable when she thrashed about.

"Any idea how many more of these we need to do to appease your Therionic overlord?" He attached a few external leads to her arm and head. While her nanite signals were strong, he didn't trust that the Entity couldn't suppress them. These were his backup.

Abigail chuckled. "It doesn't really talk to me very often, unless I piss it off. I think it's afraid of what it'll say. If it gives away a future reality, then I can fight it."

She closed her eyes and winced as her body went rigid.

Zachary reached over to help but stopped short. "He wasn't happy with you telling me that, was he?"

She gritted her teeth and shook her head.

"Alright, let's get on with this, then." He glanced at the open container beside Abigail. The glowing golden fluid called to him — not in the magical way one reads about in mythology. The scientist in him wanted to test the material to see what it was made of, but he knew better. It would hurt his sister if he even got close enough to insert a probe.

He eased up next to Libby at the control panel. The sensors reported that the Beacon was about to transit from behind Earth. They would be in range any second to open a comm gate.

"Pulsing a test gate." Libby adjusted the controls, and a brief nanosecond gate opened in space-time. She'd programmed it to target the inside of the massive space station Hera and Joyce had been constructing around Liprosus — the same place they'd moved the Beacon.

"Direct hit," she muttered. "I think we've finally nailed the orbit."

Their first few attempts to hit the heart of the facility failed. While hitting the women's lavatory might have been amusing as a kid, it hadn't been their target. Their second attempt nearly nicked the reactor core, which could have ended disastrously had it been only a few meters closer. But math and science prevailed, and once they had those first two points, their third attempt was spot-on.

"Triangulation for the win," he whispered.

Libby nodded toward Abigail. "Are you ready, dear?"

She squirmed on the crash couch and grimaced as the gel fought her motion. "I guess so. Let's get this over with."

Zachary tapped the controls and a small container opened on Abigail's side, opposite the Entity. The reaction from the golden liquid was instantaneous. What had previously been a flat, almost solid-looking surface was now undulating and tendrils slowly rose up toward the microscopic gate in space-time.

His sister had also changed. Her formerly tense body had all but melted into the couch. It was as if a weight had been lifted off her. Libby compared the change in physique to being on drugs, with her muscles abruptly going limp. She was probably more accurate than he was, but he couldn't help but imagine she was freer to move about inside the Beacon.

With Hera having moved the alien artifact, and with them being on the outside of CoPE and the fledgling alliance, they'd been left to their own devices. Their newfound situation forced them to improvise a way to reach it. He wasn't about to turn over his sister to the enemy, so in order to appease her literal inner demon, the next best thing was to give it what it wanted.

"Connection established," Libby announced, bringing up a camera feed that showed the containment room inside the space station. The Beacon was in the middle of a massive space surrounded by all forms of scientific equipment, along with what looked like pilot chairs. "We're about five meters off the top," she said. "Just off the side of a ventilation duct."

The clock in the corner of the display started counting down from one hour the moment the gate opened. That was the maximum amount of time they could keep the portal open before either the fabric of space-time deteriorated or they depleted their excess power storage. After that, they'd need another ten minutes to recharge — far longer than they used to be able to hold open comm gates, but still not ideal for keeping a mental link connected to an ancient alien artifact. Whenever Abigail or the Entity dropped out, they were dazed and confused for several minutes.

He leaned forward and scanned their displays. They were feeding all audio and video to both Harold and Shauna's computational cores, along with some of Libby's special systems from The Wheel. They were trying to figure out what the Entity was doing to both her and the Beacon, but so far, it was like performing cancer surgery in the dark with only their hands. They could feel their way around, but they were blind to anything happening inside.

"Any signs Hera's clone army is detecting us?" he asked.

"Negatory," Libby said. "It looks like we figured out the pressure differential."

The last few times they connected, the engineers thought they had a ventilation leak because Abigail's room was pressurized differently than the remote chamber. Harold had pointed it out, and they compensated by equalizing the two rooms. It'd been a close call.

"These brain scans are insane." Libby pointed at the display. "Look at this. She's using like ninety-five percent of her hippocampus and prefrontal cortex regions." She shook her head. "I've never seen anything like it."

He stepped up beside her and glanced at the small readout on Abigail's arm cuff. Her heart rate was erratic, and her eyes were darting back and forth behind her eyelids. Whatever she was experiencing inside the Beacon, her mind was racing.

"Is she okay?" he asked.

"Her vitals are fine." Libby adjusted her controls as he approached. "Everything's in line with what we've seen in the past few mental links."

"And the Entity?" He glanced over at the golden liquid. It receded into the container when he approached, but now that he'd left the room, it reached out again. Thin tentacles eased up and over Abigail's body and moved closer to the point in space where the gate was located. Although it couldn't pass through such a tiny portal, he wondered if it would have tried to touch it.

"I wish Ibu were here," he whispered. "They always knew what was going on inside that thing."

"You had to do what you had to do." Libby glanced at him. "She doesn't have a clue, does she?"

He turned his head sharply toward her. "No! And let's keep it that way. We don't want either of them to know our plans. There's no telling what they're really doing in that artifact. For all we know, the alien is selling us out."

"Speaking of which." Libby pointed at the display

showing the far side of the gate. "It looks like Lync is about to join in the fun."

On the screen, his stepsister had entered the chamber and was being checked over by the soldiers and scientists. She came in about as regularly as Abigail these days. While they hadn't spoken since their abrupt departure, he'd been meaning to reach out to her.

11

LYNC MICHAELS

EPSILON ERIDANI, LIPROSUS ORBIT

The guards gave Lync the nod, and she glared at the man as she picked up her jacket. She eased past him without saying a word, making sure to keep plenty of room between them and herself.

Fraking handsy assholes needed to feel the steel of her boot upside their heads. If the station hadn't been on the edge of a civil war since the Olivaws' abrupt disappearance, she'd have knocked the guy out. Apparently, these clones got off fondling regular humans, as if seeking something intangible.

She walked up to the Beacon and paused to stare at it. The massive ancient device throbbed with a comforting white glow that made every part of her body tremble, but in a good way. While the sensation reminded her of being aroused, the visual display was far different. She imagined the wavelengths of colors permeating inside the apparatus, and her mind leapt to what it must look like staring up at the sun from underwater. Not that she'd ever gone swimming on a planet before. She'd seen videos, though.

Being next to the alien artifact was addicting, and had she not set multiple alarms on her retinal comm, she was pretty sure she wouldn't want to leave. At least not until the goon squad kicked her out.

When she glanced back at both of them, the tall, gangly

one was eyeing her. If that guy so much as touched her while she was under, she'd break his fraking hand.

She nodded at him and subvocalized a command to set a proximity alarm on her person. Except for the scientists, if anyone got within five meters of her, it'd go off.

Relieved that she could link up without being molested, she sank into one of the chairs. They'd repurposed the design of the room from the colonial chambers down in the ring. Whereas down there, everyone gathered around a central platform to listen to the government or news from Sol, here they were worshipping this glowing ball of light. Well, maybe worshipping was a bit much. More like studying with a strong fixation and intentions on controlling it.

As she did her best to get comfortable in the stiff chair, she could feel her mind being pulled into the light. It was weird not even having to do breathing exercises to sink into her mental link. But she did them anyway. It couldn't hurt, and besides, it helped clear her thoughts of cruft. Like that asshat still staring at her.

Today, she only made it to six in her countdown before the rush of emotions and minds washed over her. One after the other, the hundreds and thousands of sparks of light she knew as tendrils of alien thoughts and prayers drifted over her. And as quickly as they appeared, they evaporated just as fast. She dared not linger on them like she had in the early days. Back when the first few minds lashed out at her.

She'd learned right away that each mind had a defense mechanism in the Beacon. It was similar to how she wanted to punch the pervert guard. Minds in this place reacted the same way when you loitered around them too long. Unless, of course, they were looking for something or someone.

And today, that was precisely why she was here. But those purposely lost beings were always elsewhere, never clustered near the entrance. That was a location reserved for the feeble of mind. Ones easily controlled and manipulated. At least that's what the aliens deeper in the light tasted like. Though the word was more of a physical translation, it was the best way to describe the sensation to someone incapable of linking up.

They were bland, whereas the others had a strong bite. Like a good cup of coffee. Some were bitter, and some were sharp with notes of honey. But the minds in control were bold and harsh tasting. They would make your hair stand on end.

As the light shifted from white to blue, her mind wandered toward a familiar sensation. She'd sensed it on many occasions before today, but never dared approach it. And while she probably shouldn't risk it, something told her it was worth the leap of faith.

It was as scintillatingly blue as a sapphire aflame in the morning sun, yet as calming as a cool breeze on a hot day. The distant mind engulfed her in a haze as serene as it was alluring. When she reached out and brushed up against it, she recoiled. It couldn't be.

"Abigail?" she whispered. Not with her mouth, but with her mind.

The light shifted instantly, leaping from cool to icy in the blink of a neuron. Its color remained the same, and yet it hurt to look at it.

"Who are you?" they asked. "How do you know me?"

Lync didn't know how to confirm it was really her. She'd never met someone she'd known in this place. And there was the small matter that the Olivaws had been missing in action for days.

She needed to come up with a way to verify it was her. Something only Abigail knew.

And then it hit her.

"What's the only right way to traverse a lift tube, and why?"

Her mind fluttered with both fear and excitement, and her glow showed it. The yellow at the edges of her aura shimmered and gave away her feelings. While she'd been working on controlling herself, being near someone who could be her sister was too much to mask.

"It depends," the mind said.

Lync drew in a breath that was not there. "On what?"

"On where the tube leads."

She glanced around. There were no other minds anywhere nearby. It was worth the risk. It had to be.

"Imagine…" She paused. "Imagine it led to the heart of Jupiter." The phrase made no sense, but the location was all that mattered.

The blue glow softened, and she could almost feel the icy light melt, just a little.

"Well," the voice began. "Then I'd be forced to dive through it."

"Wouldn't you get hurt?" Lync asked.

There was no pause in the response from the sapphire light. "Not if it led to family. And alcohol. Lots of alcohol."

"Abigail!" she thought. "It's me, Lync. Where are you?"

The light burst forward and engulfed her in a familiar, cooling aura. One she'd reveled in many times in person, but never like this. Even their mental link had been using Ibu as a conduit. This was far more intimate.

"I can't believe it's you. It's… really you." Her life flame squeezed in around her, and for the briefest of seconds, the yellow and blue combined in a burst of green. "How did you find me?"

"I…" Lync froze. It was impossible to put into words. "I don't know how to explain it. I've felt something for days now. Something familiar, and yet, I didn't dare approach."

"Why not?" she asked.

"The last time I was friendly in here was after we captured the Beacon. I nearly got my flame snuffed out by several violent and sharp minds."

Abigail's color fluttered. "Weren't we also transmitting chaos noise into the Beacon back then? I mean, that would probably frak with my mind too."

"True," she muttered. "Where are you? Did Hera let you in the station?"

The blue light grew cold and contracted inward before

relaxing ever so slightly. "I can't tell you. It's... too risky. But... we're not as far as you might think."

Olivaws loved their cryptic expressions. "I see. I guess I'm out of your circle."

"No!" Abigail engulfed her. "You'll always be one of us. It's just... the Entity. It's in here too. And if it knows..." her voice trailed away.

She knew what she meant. Refraining from saying it out loud kept the Entity from knowing where they were. And yet, something told her it already knew. Not because someone blabbed, but an alien as old as the stars couldn't be stupid. Otherwise, it wouldn't be as ancient as time.

As she was about to tell her she understood, a dark reddish shadow passed nearby. Its presence filled their point in space-time with nothing but emptiness. Her aura of yellow light fluttered ever so slightly, and an instant later, the comforting blue sheen of Abigail disappeared and with it the darkness as well.

The surrounding space suddenly grew overcast, and a reddish hue fell over her, shoving aside the previous bluish glow of this region of the Beacon. She twirled around, searching to see if she could sense where Abigail had gone and what had caused the transformation. But no matter where she faced, she couldn't feel her sister's presence.

"Frak!" She stared into the growing blood-red cloud of life flames moving in.

She would find her sister again. She had to.

But for now, she needed answers.

In front of her, she could make out another set of nearby lights — three, to be exact. She took a deep breath and eased forward, slowly sliding toward them.

Although her glow was still yellow, she hoped it wouldn't scare them away. The closer she moved, the more she focused, willing her heart and mind to slow. She used her Ulixi training to become one with Beacon space and, in turn, her physical form.

It was a trick her father had taught her, one that all Ulixi used to restrain their life flame. Usually, it helped prevent them from dying in the vacuum of space. But today, she realized it had an entirely new purpose.

As she approached the group of red lights, her aura flickered out. She was still there, but her light was gone, extinguished from Beacon space.

"I think they left," the first light whispered. "Tis strange seeing a caeruleus here in these parts. Usually, they can't handle the vibrant effects of a flāvus for very long. Especially considering that most of them are either dead or toys of another species. And daring to approach a pack of rubrum is unspeakable."

"The Beacons help the atrum ensure a natural order in the universe," the second light said. "Colors were never meant to mix." Their light was harsher than the others, its color leaning more toward black than red.

"We each have our purpose," the third light began. "Such is the prophecy. Not everyone has the clarity of mind of a pure atrum."

"To govern requires it!" the first light brightened.

The second light briefly faded to black and back. "Without the Beacon, our control would be nil."

"And our kinds would return to obscurity and chaos within our realms." The third light throbbed before returning to its previous brightness.

"Not with the iron fist of the rubrum," the second voice began. "We will remain strong, like we always have at the helm of the inner sanctum."

The third light fluttered. "Spoken like an aura stuck between being a rubrum and their species' helm of the atrum. You were never cut out to be a true atrum. You're always letting others get their way. While that fits the lower Qudoculi to a tee, it's not enough to ascend."

The first and third lights began moving away from the second.

"Assholes!" the third light muttered.

The first light flickered. "The lot of you deserve to meet the event horizon of a black hole."

Lync drew in her breath, and the aura of her yellow light flashed in and out of Beacon space, sending the red lights skittering off. Although she'd managed to snuff her aura out, her trick had still spooked them.

Was that what the colors meant? Could people change? Were people's personalities and paths really separated like a spectrum of light? Maybe they clarified skills and proficiencies as well. The notions and ideas made no sense, and yet they spoke with such certainty on the matter, as if it were a universal truth.

She had to work this through. There must be a way to tell what this meant. But the bowels of the Beacon probably wasn't the best spot to mull things over, especially with her light being seen as out of place. She needed to be with her own kind, with Crayo.

Her eyes sprang open, and the rip of reality brought her mind to a screeching halt. She sighed as time slapped her back into her chair, and the glow of the Beacon cast a ghostly shadow over her.

But something was different. Where the white light had been alluring moments earlier, even thinking about what the aliens said sent shivers down her spine. The sheer scale and meaning of their words clawed at her consciousness.

The Beacons weren't simply a means to communicate; they were a method to sort and control the alien species of the galaxy, to segregate them and nudge them into place. The freedom and allure of the Beacon was never meant to help aliens. Their purpose wasn't altruistic. While it helped species come together, it also made them easier to oversee and constrain.

Controlling the Beacons meant only one thing to the Galactic Alliance: Power.

The more she thought about it, the more the light from the Beacon made her sick. She had to get out of this place, and fast.

Lync leapt up from her chair and sprinted toward the exit, her heart pounding in her chest.

"Hey! Hold on there, sweetie!" The guard at the entrance reached out to stop her.

She didn't even pause to think; she just brought her fist back and launched it forward, cracking it across the clone's face, sending him reeling backward. "I'm not your sweetie, asshole!"

He fell with a thud to the ground and immediately started moaning.

"Freeze!" The second guard raised his sidearm and aimed it squarely at her chest.

"You want some of me?" Lync brought her hands out in front of her. "Come on! Try me. Give me a reason to send a clip of you and your buddy's antics to Ambassador Hera. I'm sure she'd love to see how you two treat one of her pilots."

Her words made the clone soldier flinch. She wasn't certain if he realized who she was, or if the threat of Hera's name sank in. But a second later, he holstered his sidearm and stepped aside.

Lync didn't stick around to chit-chat. She needed to get away, to get back to her ship.

As she sprint-walked forward, she wove her way through the halls of the station. Her mind was reeling with what she'd learned. So many questions were answered, and yet so many more were now taking their place, waiting to be solved.

With her mind everywhere but the present, she strode straight into a woman in blue overalls. "Oof!" She staggered sideways and caught her hand on the wall.

"I'm… so sorry," she sputtered.

The passerby screeched and stumbled, almost smacking into a passing robot. When she finally came to a stop, she turned with a huff and ran her hands down her uniform. She appeared to be in engineering.

"No worries, Colonel," the woman said. "I was head-down in a trance myself." She nodded and glanced at the insignia on the breast pocket of Lync's outfit. "Thank you for your service, ma'am."

And with that, she spun in place and left, tearing down the hall as if she also had somewhere else to be.

Lync chuckled. Two strangers too deep in their own problems to even see each other walking.

As she turned to leave, she slid her hands into the pockets of her pants and froze. She felt something new. Down at the bottom of the right pocket was a small, thin rectangular device. One she hadn't put there.

Lync spun around to search for the woman, but she was long gone. She'd disappeared down another hall in the maze of the station.

When she subvocalized a command to bring up a map of the floor she was on, the plans came up, but there were no colonist or clone dots nearby. Whoever that was, they weren't being traced by the station's central computers.

That meant only one thing.

She gently squeezed the device in her pocket. "Abigail," she muttered.

ONCE LYNC WAS SAFELY onboard the Ulixi command ship, known as the freighter *Nemesis*, she waited a few minutes in her quarters. She wanted to make sure no one was planning to come talk to her before she took it out. With Crayo still out practicing with her Ulixi brethren, she should be alone for a few hours. She'd planned on being at the Beacon for most of the afternoon until her moment of revelation.

With the coast clear, she pulled the device out of her pocket for the first time and held it flat in her palm. It didn't look like much. It was a muted gray and about as thick as a few sticks of chewing gum stuck together.

As she turned it over, the middle of the other side glowed briefly. It displayed the icon of a fingerprint for a second before returning to its normal state. When she gently pressed her thumb over it, the surface illuminated blue and it spoke.

"Secure comm activated," a voice said. "Identity confirmed: Lync Michaels Olivaw. Squeeze once to connect and twice to disconnect. All communications henceforth are confidential."

Lync smirked. "Olivaws being Olivaws."

She squeezed the device once and winced, unsure of what exactly it would connect to.

All of a sudden, an anonymous tight beam comm flashed on her retinal comm, and she spun around. There was no one in the room to form a line of sight with her. That was a new trick. She blinked to accept it, and a video feed opened in her field of view.

"Hey, sis!" Zachary said. "How're you doing?"

Lync eased back and sat down on her bed. "A bit confused. I'm still not sure what's happening right now. How are you doing this?" She waved her arms in a circle.

He chuckled. "Let's just call it gate magic."

She shook her head. "So, wait." She glanced around. "Is there a tiny hole in space-time in here that I'm gonna get sucked through or something?"

"Not unless you're floating up near the ceiling." He raised a finger. "But we don't have a lot of time. Each of these will only last about five minutes before that device needs to recharge. Which, by the way, it only does when you're touching it."

"And how long does that take?" She lifted the device and flipped it over in her hand.

"A few minutes, depending on how many nanites you have on your skin."

"Cool," she muttered. "Where are you guys?"

Zachary didn't say a word. He simply went silent and stared back at her.

"Alrighty then. Secret lair it is." She gently palmed the device, hoping skin contact might give them a few more seconds. "How's Abigail? She disappeared out of nowhere when that black shadow passed by."

"Black shadow?" He tilted his head. "Was it the Entity?"

Lync shivered. She hadn't thought about where the Entity was in the Beacon. Suddenly, she didn't feel as safe as she had before. "Yeah, it must've been."

"That's interesting." He ran his hand through his hair. "Maybe you can transcribe a few videos of what you're finding in there and transmit them to us through this thing. We can do the same over here and share what we learn. It might make it easier to talk. Especially with Hera watching your every move."

She rubbed her wrists. The effects of the handcuffs from a few days earlier were still lingering. At first, she figured that was why the clone guards were giving her shit until she realized they were simply perverts.

"Frak," he muttered. "They've already gotten to you, haven't they?"

"If by 'gotten to me,' you mean locked me up and interrogated me for a day, then yeah." She lowered her hands.

He bobbed his head. "But they let you go."

"Well, obviously I'm sitting here, so, yeah." She laid back on her pillow. "I told them I hated all Olivaws and wished they'd…" Her voice trailed off.

"And their A.I. believed you?"

The clock in the corner of her comm started counting down from one minute. "I do hate Olivaws. What they neglected to ask me was if I considered you and your siblings to be like your ancestors. In the interest of saving time, the answer is yes and no. Apparently, that was enough to confuse them into believing me. Either that—"

"Or they're watching you," he interrupted. "I hope the former. If not, then we might not be talking again."

She smiled. "You're good people, Z. You just come from a fraked-up family. Most of the time, I try not to hold it against you."

He smirked and shook his head. "Thanks, I think."

"Alright, we've got like twenty seconds," she began, "so I'll say this fast. I learned some new shit in the Beacon just now. Some stuff that changes everything. The sooner we can line up our backstories, the better we'll all be. I'll record some videos while I'm fake sleeping."

"Good idea." He rubbed his chin. "That way, if they have any cameras stashed in the corner of your room, you'll look like you're taking a nap or something. I'm not sure what the radius of that thing is. I can't wait to hear your—"

And the video dropped.

Lync rolled onto her side and subvocalized a command to shut off the light. "This is gonna be fun," she said aloud. "Sorta like sending messages via slingshot as a kid."

She curled up and started sub-vocally recording a comm of all the things that had happened in the past few days. From Crayo barely holding the Ulixi together, practices with the Ursis, Hera's cleansing of the colony, to the Gunders being traitorous twits. There was a ton to tell. Everything her new Olivaw family had built was crumbling down around them, and Hera was standing in the middle with a shit-eating grin on her face.

12

IBU

PROTO DARK NEBULA, OUTSIDE
POCKET FOUR

When the gate ship disappeared from their scanner, Ibu breathed a sigh of relief. It had taken them the better part of a day to convince the captain that they were capable of navigating the Proto Dark Nebula alone. They'd done it several times months earlier when they raided the Ursis capital. Only after they claimed that a see-er needed to be the captain of their ship when they entered Ursis space did the clone captain heed their request to fly solo.

It always amazed them how gullible humans could be. From the few who rose through the ranks to seek the stars on the backs of their brethren, to the majority who were content with their day-to-day existence. Their reality was humdrum and made them easy prey for the predators in their midst.

Ibu checked over their flight plan and plotted the course for Arctordiea, the Ursis home world. Once they were satisfied with the route, they initiated it and the gate vanes clanged into position. While they could've taken one of the newer Delta Sagittarii gate ships, they preferred the models designed by Zachary. Maybe it was old-fashioned, but they trusted them more than the ones from Hera's people. A copy is rarely as good as the original.

As the blue light of the gate transition passed over them, they took in the wonder of the space beyond. The Ursis had relocated most of their fleet to the far side of their Nebula in preparation for an eventual departure. Well, that and training exercises. They didn't dare conduct these exercises in populated star systems for fear of accidentally firing on their civilians. And from what they had deduced from Zachary's data dump before they left, the Ursis were out of practice.

It'd been over fifty years since any of them had seen battle. Enough time for several generations of new aliens to rise through the ranks with nothing but theoretical virtual training under their belts. While that might be passable for a small skirmish, with everything on the line, they needed guarantees. There was also the little matter of needing to train with human pilots. After what happened in the capital with Minula and her soldiers, they were already embarrassed. If a puny human outshone an Ursis again, there would be hell to pay.

When the small gate ship passed through the first transition, the computer began executing the second jump when a tight beam request appeared on Ibu's controls.

"We've got an inbound comm from Arctordiea," Shauna said. She'd interfaced with the ship the moment the other humans disappeared, having been stowed in a hidden compartment for several days.

"That's strange," Ibu muttered. "We transitioned through the agreed-upon coordinates. Whatever this is, they must have set it to broadcast for the past few weeks."

Since their shuttle was cloaked in skotádi, and none of the Ursis ships were nearby, it was unlikely anyone had detected their transition. Unless they'd been compromised. They'd have to run a complete scan before heading off to the Lupus Dark Nebula. There was no way they were entering Nanil space with their ass hanging out.

"Bring it up," Ibu waved their hand. While they could have done it themselves, it was best if they established the chain of command with Shauna now. They were the captain of this mission, not her.

A video recording from one of the alien congressional

speakers appeared on the panel in front of them. "Distinguished See-er or other human travelers, unless you have requested access to this Nebula, you will be fired upon if you approach any of our worlds. We refuse to participate in your charade of representation of the Entity any longer, even if our king requires it. Once you have proven yourself and established a connection with the Entity here in this system, we will allow you to pass. Until then, please depart this Nebula immediately."

They leaned back in their chair. "Well, that's rude. So much for checking on the royal chamber. I'd have figured Abigail would have connected the Entity with the Beacon by now. Wasn't that supposed to enable it to connect here as well?"

"I thought so," Shauna said. "You're lucky the clones didn't call you out on that taking-command stunt you pulled earlier. Otherwise, we'd be heading back home."

"I don't believe in luck." Ibu brought up a map of the nearby Proto star systems and started planning an alternative route through the Nebula, one a little more out of the way.

"Didn't they tell us to exit immediately?" Shauna's robot form stepped out of the cabinet in the corner and eased into the chair beside Ibu.

"A See-er isn't commanded by congress, even if they are a fraud." They entered the last few coordinates for the hop. "Besides, I don't plan on them detecting our ship. I just want to pass through and check out how their preparation is going. It'll give us some good intel to send back home."

Ibu didn't wait for Shauna to argue. They simply triple-checked the course and hit go, sending the gate vanes through their usual dance. They weren't about to let her question them any more than the shortsighted Ursis. The rage-fueled revenge spree the aliens were on would be the death of their species before this was over.

With the frozen ants dancing over them, they began setting up a complete, passive scan of every system. They might as well learn as much as possible while they were passing through.

"Do me a favor." Ibu glanced at Shauna. Her robotic battle form reminded them of the one Shauna wore in the videos from after she was discovered. It was an evolved chassis, but it had the same characteristics and purpose: death and destruction.

"Sure thing, Captain." She crossed her arms. "Whatcha need?"

They ignored the attitude typical of an elder human being led by a younger upstart. "Please start running a full diagnostic on our ship. I want to know if Hera's people did anything to hinder us before we left. I don't trust any of those fraking clones as far as I can throw them."

"Nor do I," Shauna muttered as she went about retrieving some scanning gear from a nearby storage bin. "Nor do I."

PROTO DARK NEBULA, INSIDE POCKET FOUR

SIX HOURS LATER, after two dozen hops from where they had entered, they gated toward the center of the star in pocket four of the Proto Dark Nebula. They'd gathered some good intel on the Ursis since their last pass through the system. In their final hop, they nailed a gravitational sweet spot between the massive gas giant at the heart of this system and the sun itself. This meant that no matter what Ursis Alatas ships were present, they wouldn't have been able to detect their arrival.

"We're clean and stable," Shauna said. "I did find three trackers, though. But apart from that, our hull is intact, and we're not leaking any stray signals. And based on the lack of attention from the other ships in the Nebula pockets, no one was expecting us anyhow."

Ibu stood up and walked closer to the wall screen. They had brought up both the passive visual and non-visual scans of the system on the display for easier analysis. From the looks of the field of view, the Ursis seemed to be running a good fifty or so training exercises at once.

"They don't do anything small, do they?" Shauna highlighted the different pockets of ships on the wall screen. Several of them appeared to be quite battered.

"Is that damage?" Ibu gestured in space near one of the micro-battles and zoomed in on the exercise. While the ships were invisible due to their skotádi coating, that didn't mean they couldn't see their shots being fired or the results of their devastation.

"I'm detecting that four of their Alatas battleships assigned to that sector are in various states of implosion." Shauna circled the damaged ships with rings of red that matched the embers burning within them. Their hulls were ripped apart, and the normally green organic coating that glowed around the ships was now gone, replaced with battle scars and smoldering metal.

"Haven't they ever heard of dummy rounds?" Ibu shook their head.

Shauna chuckled. "Judging by what we're seeing here, I suspect our friends prefer learning through trial by fire."

They gritted their teeth as they watched another round of explosions tear into a fifth Alatas. A second later, a daisy chain of a dozen blasts lit up the nearby space beneath the ship. In rapid succession, just as many green tendrils reached down into the fiery detonations and seemed to snatch at something inside. Maybe they were actually trying to save the pilots before they died.

There was one thing they knew for certain: a species as aggressive as the Ursis needed to be kept at arm's length. While they couldn't imagine imprisoning them for life in a Dark Nebula, they also couldn't see themselves willingly allying with them, either. Not without thick armor.

Perhaps Abigail had sold her people a deal with the devil. They'd have to record some of their thoughts on the matter for the others to consider. For now, they'd simply gather evidence as planned.

"Let's get this over with so we can move on." Ibu sat back down in their chair and started collating and analyzing the data they were taking in. The more they saw, the deeper their distress grew.

<hr>

Lupus Dark Nebula, Outside Bok Globule

THEY HUNG out in Proto for a few hours, making sure to record as much as they could before gating out. Ibu was happy to be out of that place, even if it meant facing their former Nanil jailer sooner. There was something about watching the Ursis tear each other apart in the name of training that rubbed them the wrong way.

"We're coming up on the Nebula nearest the Bok Globule." Shauna looked over at Ibu. "Should we transition inside?"

They had worked out multiple different pathways through the Nebula, but now that they were here, they were second-guessing themselves. What if the robots didn't recognize the greeting? What if they fired on their ship? So much of their plan was contingent on finding a foothold in this death shroud they had vowed never to return to.

"It'll be okay." Shauna rested her hand on Ibu's shoulder. "We'll make it out."

"How do you know?" They turned and caught her gaze. "You're not a see-er any more than I am. We can't see the future, and yet, you speak with so much certainty. How?"

Shauna sat back in her chair and didn't say anything for a few seconds. She merely stared at them. Then she uttered a single word: "Faith."

They shook their head. "You sound like your human children. They're always overflowing with hope and faith. It's appalling sometimes. The universe isn't filled with unicorns and sunshine. And not every life form is meant to survive. Do you think those Ursis who were on the precipice of death during their training mission were thinking about how beautiful life is?"

Shauna crossed her arms. "Maybe they did, maybe they didn't. But I don't see how that has any bearing on how I approach a new challenge. I thought you'd have learned that about me and my family by now."

"I have." Ibu looked back at their controls. "That doesn't mean I have to espouse or believe it myself."

"Fair enough." Shauna lowered her hands to her controls and stared straight ahead. Ibu could have sworn they saw her go rigid like a machination.

"What are your orders, Captain?" Shauna's voice had changed as well. Gone were the human intonations; they'd been replaced by vocals similar to those of the robots from Hera's colony in Delta Sagittarii.

"Olivaws and their mind games." Ibu sighed and reached forward to activate the gate sequence, which sent a familiar clang through their ship.

Unlike humans, Nanil were perfectly fine not sleeping. While it helped them maintain focus, it wasn't a requirement. They thought that would make a robot an agreeable companion on this mission, but that was before they left. Being with Shauna had turned out to be a tad bit grating. They weren't sure why, though. They'd grown quite fond of her daughter and sons. She, however, was as overbearing as their clonos, and the last thing they needed was to face them again.

By all accounts, the transition was fast, but once they were on the other side, time seemed to stand still. They had expected to see the edge of the nebulosity leading into the star system, with robots guarding the entrance to Henosi. What they found instead was something far worse.

In the middle of the Nebula was Doda, the massive starship that had been Ibu's home for forty years. Not only was the surrounding star-forming nebulosity less dense, but the twelve-sided ship had changed. They couldn't put their finger on how until Shauna did.

"It's… broken into pieces," Shauna said, her voice returning to human intonations.

But these weren't battle scars or fractures from damage like the Ursis had inflicted on their ships. From the looks of it, the dodecahedron had separated by design. Someone had broken it into smaller ships capable of navigating through the dense nebula and asteroid-filled minefield of this region of space.

"I didn't realize it could break itself apart." Ibu zoomed in and around the Doda starship. There were two small chunks missing from one side and another gap opposite those. The ship seemed to be intact, and unless they were mistaken, it could still harness the plasma beam that normally sliced through the star system.

"The plasma field." Ibu pointed toward the Nebula. "It's gone."

Shauna adjusted her controls and brought up an image of the space behind them. The trail of yellow ionized gas was nowhere to be seen. "So it is. That can't be good."

"Why?" Ibu glanced at her.

"I don't know." She shrugged. "I mean, wasn't that thing what powered Doda? And didn't it use that energy to move?"

They nodded. "It did, on both counts."

"And now it's gone." She peered over at Ibu. "That either means they shut it off, or—"

"Someone else did," they interrupted.

"Exactly." Shauna returned their viewport to the dodecahedron.

"There goes the easy win." Ibu leaned back in their chair and studied the display.

There was too much nebulosity between them and Doda to get a clear scan for life signs. The moment they did an active scan, they'd give away their position — their upper hand.

From the outside, the ship looked deserted. But that wasn't surprising. When the Fountainhead arrived over a year ago, the Nanil hadn't been on the surface for centuries.

With all the piles of bones and ash, one might swear the insides were as dead as the outside.

At this point, their only option was to pass through. Unfortunately, if they activated their subliminal drive, they'd be spotted in seconds. But sitting there and doing nothing wasn't their style. They had come all this way for a reason, and that meant reaching either the robots or the Nanil, or both. They just figured it would be the automata first. Then they'd have plenty of time to build up the nerve to face their people if they actually needed to.

They reached forward and tapped a point on the far side of the map. "Is there any way we can gate across this nebulosity in one shot?"

"Not with Doda in there, and certainly not with all the asteroids and other crap in our path. Even with a full active scan, it would take dozens of controlled hops." Shauna overlaid the different obstacles between them and the point. Each layer added to the complexity of the calculation.

But maybe they were looking at it wrong. Maybe there was another way inside.

Ibu leaned forward and tweaked their controls to zoom out. "Why don't we leave and come back through the opposite end?" They traced a path out of the Nebula and then around the far side, straight through the Henosi star system.

Shauna stood up and turned away.

"Where are you going?" Ibu glanced backward. "There's only this room and your locker."

"Well then, the locker it is," she said as she strode toward the back wall.

Ibu shot up and stepped between her and the cubby. "If you have a better idea, I'm all ears."

She looked past them, staring at the handle of her locker. "I will not fight you, Captain. You do what you need to do. Just make sure to destroy my consciousness core before they take me. I'm not certain I can do it myself. Okay?" She turned and locked her gaze on them.

The steady white glow of her electronic eyes was unnerving. They'd choose Harold's human form design any day of the week over this cold, calculating, and impossible-to-read shell. Why they hadn't thought of that before they left was beyond them.

They glanced over toward the wall screen and stared at the map of Henosi. The system wasn't that big, and judging by the scale of the planetary orbits, there was scant mass interspersed between it and the robots' star. The hardest part was predicting where to gate through to reach the other side. With the Doda ship over here, there was no telling what the other system looked like.

The more they thought about it, the easier it seemed. Maybe they were fooling themselves, but all they had to do was keep out of the way of a few Shu ships. How hard could that really be?

LUPUS DARK NEBULA, OUTSIDE HENOSI POCKET

A HALF-DOZEN MORE HOPS, some quiet time alone to meditate on their decision, and their ship was finally in position. They looked over their gating strategy on the wall screen one more time.

The first gate was to peek inside and take in as much as they could. The longer they held the gate open, the better. They'd reassess the plan after they closed it, but they had to act quickly, or else everything could change.

The second gate would be somewhere inside, ideally on the same path but further into the system. That way, if someone on Henosi detected the first gate, they'd have a chance to escape before the humans attacked them.

Once they reached the third gate, they would aim to get as close to the Nebula wall as possible.

Finally, a fourth gate. They decided to jump as far as the math would allow to reach beyond the cone of destruction and the starship graveyard encircling it. If there was any place the Nanil would have headed, it was to fight the robots. By gating past it, they would have more time to assess their situation in case they needed a reverse evac. The plan was flawless.

"I don't see another way." Ibu glanced over at Shauna. She'd been sitting silently in her chair for the better part of an hour. It was impossible to tell whether she was powered off or not, but they assumed she was just stewing. She did that sometimes.

They reached over and knocked on her composite frame. A solid thud reverberated back. "Are you planning on answering me?"

She remained silent.

"Well, frak." Ibu turned their attention back to the control panel. "Here goes nothing." They tapped the command to execute the microscopic probe of the distant star system, starting the first gate.

Except for the controls lighting up, one couldn't tell anything had changed. But it had. In front of them, a special instrument array, only a few nanometers wide, was sliding through the portal in space-time. It had enough equipment on it to perform a passive scan of the entire system across every wavelength, with minimal risk.

Ibu tapped their fingers against the control panel until it started lighting up with details.

The planets were right where they expected them to be.

The star in the system looked healthy, which was fine, they guessed. There was no nova to speak of. If there had been, it certainly would have made the next step easier.

And most importantly, there were no alien ships nearby.

Unless they were mistaken, the entire star system was quiet, which made this an ideal place and time to gate inside.

As the scan continued, they itched to press the button to execute the gate sequence. While they had enough power to do it, in a few more seconds, they'd have to wait for their capacitors to recharge. With the mass of the sensor array hanging out through the open gate, it was eating through all their power reserves.

Just when they were about to tap the button, Shauna's hand shot out and snatched their wrist away.

"What the hell?" Ibu reached over and grabbed the robot's hand, struggling to pry open her vice-like grip.

"Look!" Shauna pointed with her free hand toward the wall screen.

The first pass of detailed scans was only now finishing up. When they looked back at the screen, they saw what she was pointing at.

There, on the far side of Henosi and the other Goldilocks planet, was a clump of what must've been a hundred Shu moonlets. Their last count before they left the system estimated that there were barely that many in the entire system.

At first, Ibu thought the humans had been building up their army like the Ursis, but then they studied the data more closely.

"That doesn't make any sense," they muttered. "They're in deteriorating orbits."

"It does if they're powered off." Shauna brought up the passive scans from the other wavelengths.

The moonlets weren't just shut down; they were as cold as ice. It seemed like someone wasn't happy with their automated overlords and decided to pull the plug. The only people capable of that were the humans from the other colonies on that planet. More importantly, with the moonlets out of the way, that meant smooth sailing for the rest of their plan.

Ibu studied the wall screen and watched the countdown reach zero. When it did, the gate closed.

The bridge fell eerily silent once again. They could almost hear Shauna's neural pathways firing, thinking through all the dangers that lay ahead. There would be a million reasons not to go inside, but just as many to jump.

As they were about to say something to convince her,

Ibu's chair straps flung around their body and locked them in place.

"What the hell?" Ibu tugged at the release, but it didn't respond.

"I'm sorry." Shauna sighed. "But it's the safest way."

She reached out and slammed the transition lever forward, launching them through not only the second jump but through all four.

While their robot friend wasn't taking any chances hanging around in one place too long, she was ripping Ibu to shreds in the process. Wave after wave of blue light tore through their Nanil flesh from the inside out.

And to make matters worse, on top of not being able to stop the gate transition, they couldn't stop their physical transformation, either. The primal form they'd suppressed for months was taking over, and not only could it tear Shauna apart limb by limb, it could destroy their tiny ship.

13

ABIGAIL OLIVAW

EPSILON ERIDANI, LIPROSUS MOON

While most of the footage was chaotic, Abigail couldn't help but pan through it. Most of the faces in the audience were already familiar to her. Hell, she'd placed more than half of them on the colony herself, convincing them of the unlimited potential of colonizing a new star and leading humanity into a brighter tomorrow. And now Hera was leading them.

The thought of her great-aunt guiding these colonists, of her taking charge of a future society that expanded to the stars, was grating. Her frigid demeanor and the unethical methods she used to manipulate people to get her way were the last thing humanity needed. They deserved a leader who broke down walls, not one who built them even higher.

As she panned across the faces, she paused on Hera. She'd stared at her aunt's dead eyes glaring at Shauna on multiple occasions, but she never noticed the person standing behind her to her left. For some reason, he looked out of place, almost like he was uncomfortable. And from this angle, it appeared as if he was whispering something into her ear.

Abigail leaned forward and squinted, opening a subvocal comm to the copy of Harold that was still hidden inside her heart compartment. "Is that Dwight? You know, Bradley's friend from Sol and the Zeta Lupi colony?"

His voice replied in a hushed whisper, "It might be. I can't tell for certain without more footage. If I had access to his medical records or a copy of his DNA, I'd be able to give you an irrefutable answer. In this limited form, however, I can't guarantee anything beyond high probabilities. His facial features are a match from what I can detect, minus those tattoos on his chin and cheeks. Those are new."

A Mandelbrot set for a face tattoo wouldn't have been her first pick either, especially one as unflattering as those. It was like someone painted them on in the dark. She tilted her head. "Maybe he has a brother."

"Not according to my recollection," he began, "but then again, I hid your sister from everyone for most of her life. So yes, I guess he could have a sibling."

She chuckled. Harold was funny when he wasn't correcting people all the time with facts. Without his infinite data set, he was left to become... more... human. It was curious how that worked out.

"Do you think I should ask Bradley to take a peek?" She snapped a snippet of the video and started a message to share it with him.

"It depends," Harold began. "Rewind the feed and watch it again."

She followed his advice and hit play, but this time, she focused on Dwight. She noticed that he entered the room in front of Hera and then quickly dodged to the left and slid in behind her. It was almost like...

"He's trying not to be seen," she muttered.

"Who is?" Pluto asked.

Abigail squinted, bringing her focus back to the table she was sitting at. She hadn't even heard her walk up.

"Oh... hey." She smiled. "I was just, you know, in my comm." She pointed at her head — the universal sign for someone zoning out and into their device.

Pluto grinned and then groaned as she set her tray down. It was overflowing with food.

"Are you okay?" Abigail reached out and placed her hand on Pluto's.

"I'm fine." She closed her eyes and opened them again. "Just hungry. So, who were you watching that was trying not to be seen?" Pluto started shoveling a bowl of cinnamon and apple oatmeal into her mouth with a fury. She wasn't lying. The woman was starved.

Abigail grinned and paused. Her mind was racing to come up with a lie. "Ah… the Entity. It's been nudging me more and more to connect to the Beacon. I'm pretty sure it prefers to be next to the device, not an orbit away." She sighed. That made no sense at all. There was no way she was going to buy it.

Pluto leaned forward and coughed, shooting oatmeal out of her nose. She scrambled to snatch up her napkin and wiped her face. "I'm so sorry." Her cheeks were turning a bright shade of pink. "That's so embarrassing."

She brought her hand to her mouth and smirked. "I've seen worse. You should'a seen Z when he walked in on mom and dad doing the hanky-panky when we were kids. For weeks, he turned neon pink whenever they'd walk in the room." She took a long sip of her espresso and savored the bite before looking up. "Was it something I said?"

Pluto glanced around to make sure no one was nearby. The dining area was empty at this late hour. "I… didn't realize other people knew where we were. I mean, based on what you said, you sorta seem… to have an idea. Unless… perhaps, you don't." She cringed. Clearly, the topic was taboo to the abductees.

Abigail nodded and lowered her cup. "Harold isn't fooling anyone. If we didn't have to wait for the station to come out from behind the gravity well of Liprosus, maybe then we would still be in the dark about our location. Otherwise, it's simply a matter of physics and a little deduction as to which moon we're on."

Pluto placed her napkin on the table, bringing her attention back to her meal. From the look on her face, she was famished.

"Are you sure you're okay?" Abigail leaned out and peered up into her eyes, studying her expression. She was almost pale. "You seem peckish. Is Zachary being crazy about food again? I'll kick that boy's ass if he's telling you what you can and can't eat. People aren't science experiments."

"No, no!" Pluto mumbled between bites and waved her hand. "He's not… no, he's fine. In fact, he's great. Besides, I'm pretty sure I can handle him." She smirked playfully. "Honestly, I woke up feeling a bit off. All I need is food." She started eating again, but this time much slower.

"Alrighty." She raised her cup. "But if he ever gets out of line, and you need backup, just say the word, sister."

Pluto giggled and covered her mouth. "I will."

As Abigail went to take a drink, a jolt of pain surged through her side and she bent forward, launching her mug across the table and narrowly missing Pluto. Its scalding-hot contents spilled everywhere.

"Yikes!" Pluto shot up with her plate in hand.

Abigail moaned and closed her eyes, fighting the call of the Entity. The longer she was away from it, the more impatient it grew. It wanted her nearby at every waking moment.

"Forget me, are you alright?" Pluto set her food down on a neighboring table and rushed to Abigail, kneeling at her side. "What is it?"

"It's…" she groaned and twisted sideways. "My little friend."

Pluto gently rubbed her back. "We've got to get that thing out of you."

"Working on it." Abigail sat upright and eased up from her chair, being careful to use the table to steady herself.

"Maybe you should take a few seconds?" Pluto stood up and slid closer, reaching an arm around her back to support her.

"If I stay out here, it'll only worsen." She glanced over at the spill. It was a waste of excellent coffee, but at least the robots were already cleaning it up. "Sorry about that."

Pluto shook her head. "Don't worry about it. Just… take care of yourself. I'll send Z in to help."

"It's okay. I can handle it." She motioned toward the exit.

Pluto relaxed her hand, but it lingered at her side. "You know you're not alone in this anymore, Abs. Right? We've got your back."

"I know…" she muttered. "I know." She rubbed her hand and smiled before continuing on to attend to her needy companion.

Despite her family's best effort to support her, she couldn't help but feel like she'd screwed up big time. She'd been the one who went off on the mission to find the Ursis. Nobody talked her into it. In fact, nearly everyone tried to talk her out of it at one point or another.

To be honest, if she hadn't felt the pangs of losing control after the tribunal incident, she might not have ever gone. She'd gotten so close to righting the wrongs of her family, she could taste it.

But it wasn't meant to be. Just when her people got through the battle over the Beacon, another member of her fraked-up family showed up and forced their ideology on humanity. Add to that, her returning with a galactic entity starving for control, and she'd slid back down that mountain of familial meddling. Now they were neck-deep in a shit-storm of power struggles.

There was one thing she knew for certain, though. She still had a job to do, and that meant toppling Hera and ensuring humanity was on some type of path that pointed away from extinction. No matter what she did, putting her friends and immediate family in jeopardy was out of the question. Not again. She'd already lost her best friend. She couldn't bear losing anyone else.

As she passed into the room used to connect to the Beacon, Zachary was inside waiting for her. His hair was a complete mess, and he looked as if he'd been woken up. Pluto must've called him anyhow.

"Hey," he muttered, raising a hand in a half-wave.

She nodded and continued past him to the crash couch.

He stepped beside her and picked up the leads to connect to her arm. "Everything alright?"

"Just… peachy."

She paused and glared at the container holding the Entity. Thoughts of ejecting the canister into one of the Epsilon Eridani suns flashed through her mind. Maybe it would only hurt a little and then she'd be done with it.

"Pluto mentioned you were in pain." He reached out and rested his hand on her shoulder. "Is it getting worse?"

"If by worse you mean it wants me in here every moment of every day, then yes. It is." She sighed and collapsed into the crash couch, its surface adjusting to her weight. There had to be a way to fight this thing that didn't turn her into a set of glorified organic jumper cables. If Ibu were here, they'd know exactly what to do. They always had ideas when it came to the Beacon.

"We'll figure something out." He squeezed her arm as he slid the cuff up. "We always do."

"Where's Ibu?" she blurted out.

His eyes went wide, and he peered over at the Entity's container. "They're on their way to Proto. You know, as the Ursis see-er." He leaned forward and nudged her.

She huffed and slammed her fist into the arms of the couch. Hiding things from her and using the Entity as an excuse was fraking bullshit. It couldn't read her mind, and they knew that. They just didn't trust her any longer.

"You know I can see you, right?" the Entity said.

Abigail flinched sideways, away from the container. The alien hadn't spoken to her in almost a month, and now it suddenly starts talking in the middle of a fight.

Zachary stumbled backward and smacked his back against the divider between the two rooms. "What the hell?"

A golden blob started rising out of the small container,

filling an impressive amount of space above it. She eased off the couch, putting some distance between herself and the thing. She wasn't keen on touching that golden goo again. The last time that happened, it tried to take control of her mind.

"I wasn't born yesterday, or even in the last millennium," the Entity began, its body still slowly expanding upward. "Sending a tiny little Nanil on a secret mission won't help your kind contain me. You'll need far more than that."

Zachary reached over and pulled her close to him.

She swallowed hard. She didn't know what to do or say. It hadn't uttered a word to her since giving her instructions to get comfortable with the Beacon. The only way it could reach its protist back on Arctordiea was after her human form interfaced with the relic. It would never risk her body rejecting the ancient artifact, and it needed her to be its conduit.

"Who said we were trying to hurt you?" Zachary squeezed her hand. "We have bigger fish to fry at the moment than a pile of glowing slime in a bucket."

She could tell he was putting on a brave face. While his voice was strong, his hands were shaking like leaves.

The Entity shuddered and let out an audible cackle. "You humans are as ignorant as you are blind. Do you not think before you speak? I can smell the pheromone stench of your emotions from across the room. From the racing of your pulse to the firing of the synapses in your frontal cortex, your lies are as transparent as they are revolting."

It continued its golden dance through the air as it finally took shape. At first, its new alien form wasn't clear, but then it turned around to face them.

Zachary gasped.

It was a Pluutar. Though it was far smaller than the one they'd seen during their research into the Galactic Alliance, it was unmistakably the same alien. The race of giant squid-like beings had deployed countless Beacons on behalf of the GA. They were a formidable species at one time. She wasn't sure what had become of them, but maybe this was her first clue to the origins of the Entity.

It shifted to look at her. "Judging by your sister's mental state and her physical reaction to seeing me, I can sense she recognizes this form."

"You're... a Pluutar," she muttered.

"Very good." It nodded. "At least I was, a long time ago. Before that..." Its gaze drifted off. "Before that, I was something else."

She shook her head. "Why are you showing us this now?"

The Entity smiled. "To remind you that you're only one of the many vessels I've inhabited. Most I've killed when they tried to end me, but some, some I let live." It leaned forward, closing the space between them in a flash.

She pressed her back against the glass partition, and Zachary followed suit, his shoulder crushing against hers.

"While I may not be able to read your mind, I know which part of your brain triggers when you experience happiness and love." It glanced at Zachary and then at her. "Or when hatred and revenge take over like they are right now. I can sense every emotion and thought your simple little species has. Consider this your one and only warning, Abigail of the Olivaws. Attempting to kill me won't merely end with you losing your life. I will track down your family, and no matter where they hide, I will end them. Each and every one of them. Even those not yet born." It looked side-eyed at Zachary. "Do you understand me?"

She straightened her back. "What makes you so certain you can do that? Last I checked, you were as isolated as we are."

The Entity vibrated again, but this time it emitted a dreadful sound — a noise that nearly knocked her to her knees until her comm sealed up her ear canal. She leaned back and winced while reaching up to cover her ears.

Zachary did the same. "What the shit?!" he screamed.

"It's a wonder humanity is still alive at all." The Entity waved a tree-like limb, and a golden image appeared from its hand. Colors danced across the surface, painting a full picture.

As it took shape, it reminded her of the Ursis chamber room on Arctordiea, except it was somehow… different. From this angle in the air, the entire Ursis Congress was present. But this wasn't a replay of when she'd confronted them. This was new.

The representatives were kneeling in front of an empty throne. She couldn't tell what or why it was showing this to them until she saw Haradis and Klus on their knees as well.

And then it hit her.

The Entity wasn't waiting to connect to its protist. That bridge had already been crossed.

She shook her head. That was impossible. The alien had been using her the entire time. She didn't need to get in tune with the Beacon at all. It needed to gain strength. And judging by its actions both here and on Arctordiea, it was growing stronger by the second.

"Good. Good. I see you understand." The Entity leaned in closer to her. "You can tell how hopeless your situation is. I can smell it as much as I can see it in your face. The faster you recognize your place, you little squib, the easier this will become."

Abigail held her breath and squinted, struggling to control her thoughts and not give away her rising anger. She couldn't let her emotions dictate her destiny.

The faint glow of its golden shape was just visible through her narrowed vision. It was tilting its head in close to study her. While she couldn't say for certain, it seemed to be confused about something.

At first, she didn't understand why. She simply took slow, controlled breaths in and out as it moved its bulbous eyestalk back and forth in front of her face.

And then it dawned on her what was happening. She'd unconsciously started using the breathing trick Ibu and Lync had taught her to focus. Slow and measured breaths, where she focused on finding her Ulixi center. And somehow, it was working. It appeared to be muting what the alien sensed.

She didn't know how, but it was.

"Sit down!" the Entity shouted.

Zachary leaned closer to it. "You don't seriously expect us to bow down, do you?"

The Entity smirked. "You, no. Her..." It twisted up its face, and Abigail reeled forward.

Pain coursed through her veins like fire, and she collapsed into a limp pile on the floor.

Zachary knelt down toward her, but she waved him away. "No! Don't... touch... me."

The words were excruciating, but she didn't want to risk him getting hurt.

Every centimeter of her soul felt as if it were melting into a puddle of burning flesh. And when she reached out to rub the red-hot embers scorching her skin, another ripple of agony shot through her molten body and fanned the waves of anguish even higher.

Pain on top of pain.

She couldn't take anymore. "All... right," she moaned.

"What... was... that?" The Entity paused and lowered itself ever closer to her.

Based on the intonations in its voice, it too was suffering. After all, what she felt, it felt.

"I said, I'd do it!" She slapped her hand against the ground and pushed up, fighting the waves of pain as they crashed over her.

And then it stopped.

"Excellent." The Entity eased away and flittered towards its container. The way its limbs moved almost made it look like it was limping, if such a thing were possible for a liquefied being.

As she climbed onto the couch, she did her best to control her breathing. While the pain had subsided, the rage had not. She needed to get back inside the Beacon to find a way out of this mess. If not for herself, then for her family.

Zachary had remained quiet since she snapped at him. After she'd settled into the couch, he made his way to her side and picked up the arm cuff.

"She won't be needing that," the Entity said.

He paused as he was about to slide it up her forearm. "But we need to make sure the Beacon doesn't harm her."

"Bullshit!" The Entity lunged toward Zachary, and Abigail shot her hand up to block its path.

"Leave—him—alone." She scowled at its nearest eyestalk, and it glared back. When she leaned close to the golden surface, she could make out faint silhouettes of what looked like honeycombs in its reflection.

"I know what you and your tight-lipped partner have been doing behind that partition. What was her name again? Ah, yes. Libby." The Entity slithered back into its container. "You're trying to find a way to protect your sister from me." It chuckled, and the surface of the liquid rippled in a chaotic pattern of fractals. "The sooner you realize our fates are irrevocably intertwined, the sooner you can move on and let me have her. If she behaves herself, you might even get her back someday. At least, part of her."

"Over my dead body," Zachary muttered.

"That can be arranged more easily than you would think, my feeble human friend." The Entity raised a strand up and out of the container, pointing toward the controls on the other side of the partition. "Now go make yourself useful and turn on that gate, would you? The station will be passing out of Liprosus' shadow any second now."

The golden goo sunk into its vessel, and when it did, she sensed it reaching out, preparing for the gate to open. Maybe her breathing routine had cleared her mind, or perhaps the pain the Entity inflicted had heightened her senses. Either way, something had changed in her. It was like her inner eyes had finally been opened to the light.

When she glanced over at Zachary, he'd already walked into the other room. The faint sheen of tears on his cheeks was just visible from her chair, and he shied away from looking her in the eyes. Instead, he quietly reached out and activated the comm gate.

At that moment, her mind's eye exploded in a flood of light. A bright and pearly white glow. It wasn't like the stars she usually saw when she connected with the Beacon. This was somehow different. It was as if she were seeing another layer of the artifact, one previously hidden from her.

As she watched the Beacon's rainbow of colors approach in the distance, she sensed a darkness moving beneath her. She'd felt something like it the last time she'd been talking to Lync, right before they'd been cut off. That feeling must've been the Entity.

With her senses now heightened, it was easier to discern both the shape and spectrum of the light. Their minds were like open books to her.

Fear
Longing
Anguish
Guilt

The fluttering sparks of the mentally stunted and intellectually weaker alien masses passed by first. She and the Entity's shadow were rising to higher orbits within the artifact. Not flying, so much as transcending the limited potential of their physical minds to somewhere brighter. It was hard to explain, but somehow her mind was keeping up.

More emotions flooded over her as they rose into the upper layers of the Beacon.

Logic
Purpose
Clarity
Greed

They'd entered the colorful pockets of light she'd discovered by accident the other day. At the time, she hadn't even realized she'd ascended. While before today her meander-ings had been random and unfocused, the clarity of the outer ring segments in this region of the Beacon was astounding.

With each new mind that moved beneath her, their fears, desires, and motivations wafted through her mind like smells in a kitchen. They were only hints of what the alien was thinking, but they served as guideposts navigating the sea of light.

The more aliens she passed, the more it felt like she could reach out and connect with them. It was as if she had the power to manipulate their thoughts and feelings like a puppeteer. Maybe she and the Entity had somehow melded minds earlier, or perhaps it had touched her in all the commo-tion. A droplet of its liquid probably didn't even work that way, but she wanted this sensation to continue. For the first time in a long time, she was on top of the world - no, on top of the universe.

At that moment, she realized where they'd wandered: to the inner sanctum. Or the outer, as it were. For in front of her, she could discern the shapes and emotions of the species that made up her mortal enemies.

The ruling classes of the Galactic Alliance.

Each species had a distinct color, and none dared to wander or pass through the other pockets of light at that layer. As she watched them move about, a pattern formed. They seemed to communicate only with another colored light at the edges of their boundary, and even then, only in short bursts.

Individually, those in the inner sanctum were the elite few who were aware of their place and purpose: to control the lesser species and to prevent them from gaining a foothold in the balance of power.

She didn't understand how she knew that, but she did. The details were both foreign and obvious. The simplicity of the pattern of lights and the pressure they applied to the minds in the lower core of the Beacon was uniform. From this vantage point, the focus and concentration of the outer minds meant it was easier to shape the lights within.

The elegance of its design was astounding, and her mind reeled at the consequences of wielding such power. It was as if the ancient artifact had been created to manipulate and control the very essence of what made a species sentient.

Their thoughts.

A nudge here, a spark of ideas there. They could make an individual feel as if they had their own identity, yet they were only a cog in the cosmic wheel. If this was what it meant to have a universal consciousness, she wanted nothing to do with it.

When she stopped and hovered for a moment, she glanced around. The shadow she'd been following had disappeared. She wasn't sure when. She'd been so engrossed in the experience that she missed its descent. Looking left and right, she noticed there were no other lights at this level. It was as if they had elevated themselves to a higher plane than even the inner sanctum.

This must be the trick the Entity was using. She didn't know how it was doing it, but given its age, it had more experience with these Beacons than anyone else alive. And that meant it was more powerful than any of them had imagined.

If she had any hope of helping her family, the first thing she needed to do was learn the lay of the land. To find out what truths the other aliens knew about humans.

"Here goes nothing," she muttered to herself as she took a deep breath and dove into a sea of orange light. While she didn't recognize which species the light represented, there were certainly a hell of a lot of them.

14

JOYCE GREEN
EPSILON ERIDANI, LIPROSUS ORBIT

They gathered to watch the first of what would likely be dozens of war-game exercises with the Ursis. The chamber and most of this deck aboard their human ship had been retrofitted to accommodate the larger form of their alien ally, but they declined to board. After Haradis and Klus returned from their Proto Dark Nebula, they hadn't been the same.

While they reassured them that everything was fine, Joyce knew otherwise. They'd usually jumped at the chance to see human technology or to leave their ship. But not today. Not since their small battle group of ships arrived through the temporary gates the humans had built for them to jump here.

"I think they're pissed we didn't retrofit their battleships with gate drives," Hera muttered. Her arms were crossed, and she was transfixed on the tight flight pattern the Ursis' Alatas battleships and their fighters were flying in.

"I'm not sure that's it." Joyce stepped up beside her and ignored the angry scowl she received in return. That woman never liked when someone disagreed with her. "They left abruptly the other day, and we never had a chance to tell them we reached an agreement on Sol."

It was a lie, but one being told by both her and Nguyễn. No matter how hard she tried, she couldn't get him to budge on giving up any space back in their home star system. Hell, he wouldn't even let them try to terraform Venus, and she didn't know if that was even possible. She'd just been pulling shit out of her ass at that point.

He did, however, agree to kick the can, hedging on the fact that they wouldn't need to implement their request unless they survived the attack on the Nursery. He'd even managed to sell the idea to the representatives from Sol. Since the Ursis were sending in every ship at their disposal, they didn't see it as a bet, but more as a certainty that they'd lose most of their strength. If humanity made it out alive, they'd deal with the squabbles over land later.

"What do you think spooked them?" Nguyễn asked. He had his back to the two of them, preferring to watch the virtual war-game play out on the wall screen rather than watching it in person.

"Who the frak knows?" She turned and stepped toward the man. Her legs had been acting better the past few days. Whatever Hera's clone technicians had done to them had made a world of difference. Part of her wanted her mechanical legs back. Feeling pain and dealing with normal human things like cuts and scrapes was annoying. Especially when the skin was as soft as a baby's. The rest of her body was in its forties, and these legs felt like they hadn't even reached puberty.

"Please tell me these aliens know we're not using live rounds." Nguyễn brought up a camera view of a laser barrage from the Ursis' forward fighters. It shot wide of their virtual decoys but still caused the Dark Nebula to ripple in the distance. "It's all fun and games until someone gets killed."

"Let them fire their live rounds," Hera said, still facing away from them. "If that's what keeps them happy, so be it."

Joyce glanced over her shoulder. "And if they kill one of our people?"

Hera was silent for a moment. "If they kill a clone, I'll make a new one. If they kill one of yours, well, then we'll send an honor guard back home to their family. This is war, Commander. We need to realize there will be casualties."

"This isn't what we agreed to." She spun around the rest of the way. "This is a mock battle. There's no reason to use live—"

Hera turned toward her. "And how do you expect these people to learn the pressure of battle?"

"The same way we did training for the Beacon battle: hundreds and thousands of simulations, flight exercises, and readiness drills." Joyce shook her head. "It is not necessary to put lives in jeopardy like this. Not yet. Some of us can't simply print out our soldiers."

Hera snickered. "The Ursis don't seem to have a problem putting their lives at risk."

"Of course they don't. They've—" She recoiled as an explosion went off in the distance.

When she spun around, she caught the playback Nguyễn had just brought up on the wall screen. It was a pair of Ursis fighters, and from the looks of it, they'd passed in front of one of the massive plasma cannons from their Alatas battleship while it was in the middle of firing. The resulting devastation had needlessly ended at least two more alien lives and, not to mention, caused chaos in the human ranks. Their pilots were peeling off and returning to the protection of their ships.

"This is exactly what I'm talking about." Joyce pointed at the explosion frozen on the wall screen and stared back at Hera. "These aliens have been imprisoned for half a century. Life has no value to them. They're just happy to be out of their jail cells. They'll do anything to get revenge, even if that means senseless death."

"And so should we!" Hera gritted her teeth and glared at her. "It's only a matter of time before the Galactic Alliance comes for Sol. Everyone knows it. And Zeta Lupi will be next, followed by my worlds when they find them. This battle is a necessary evil, Commander Green, and it's about time you got your stomach in the game."

She turned back to face Nguyễn. "What the hell is she not

getting, Admiral? You and I both know we should be training in simulations, especially this early in the merging of our forces."

"I'm not sure if you're right, Commander." He hit play again on the battle and the Ursis ships drove forward, all but ignoring the explosion. They not only took out their target, but they did so with precision and without turning and running away. "Our men and women look like chickenshits out there. What message do you think that sends to our troops? Or hell, the colonists? There's bound to be thousands of eyes watching these exercises here inside the Nebula." He turned to face her.

"You can't be serious!" She squinted and studied him. She couldn't tell if he was taking Hera's side to gain her trust or because he actually believed the shit he was shoveling. "I find it hard to believe that you see human life as so dispensable. Especially after what the GA fleet did to your people in Sol."

Nguyễn twitched. It wasn't huge, but it was there. His right hand tapped against his thigh. The fraking asshole was playing to Hera's good side. While his objective wasn't clear, she refused to give in.

"I want all the colonists pulled out of these exercises, and I want it now!" She turned and made her way toward her staff.

They were staring past her, looking at Hera.

She shook her head. "Why aren't you listening to me? Get our people out of there. Move!"

"No!" Hera's voice echoed through the room.

Joyce spun around. "Excuse me? I'm in command of the colonists, not you."

Hera stared down and turned her hand over in front of her, as if she was staring at something. "The generals from Zeta Lupi and Sol have already agreed to place me in command of their vessels."

She swallowed hard. The fracking weaklings had probably given up without a fight. The size of the GA fleet at the Nursery had obviously scared the colonies more than she had imagined.

When Joyce raised her hands toward her staff, they slowly shook their heads. Apparently, her people up here were giving in as well.

She reached up and tapped her ear, subvocalizing a command to open a comm to Crayo, the Ulixi in charge of her fleet. "Captain?"

"Commander," Crayo began. His voice was sharp and edgy. "What are these fancy bears trying to do, commit mass suicide? This ain't a circus act we's training for, and we don't have no nine lives to work with like those freaky clones."

Joyce chuckled. She always enjoyed the truth bombs from her Ulixi friends. "Our people from Sol and Zeta Lupi are about to join their cult of fear, Captain. And apparently, so are the colonists here in Epsilon."

His comm fell silent.

She tilted her head. "Captain, are you there?"

Hera raised an eyebrow. She must have been listening in on the conversation from another line. Either that, or she was talking to them as well.

Crayo's voice came back on. "What say you, Commander? You's never led us astray before. Without our Olivaw friends or Bossman Harold around, I gots to trust someone. Lync isn't answering her comm, but she seems to have faith in you the most. Tell me whats to do."

A message from Nguyễn appeared on her retinal comm, and she tried not to look at him. Instead, she blinked it open.

Be careful where you step. She won't take too kindly to turning on her.

She chuckled. Mr. Burning Butt should talk about flipping sides. If it weren't for Joyce and Captain Hui, the video of Harold's consciousness core shooting out of his ass would've made its way to Hera. And if it had, he'd either be dead or in the brig.

Questioning poor judgment wasn't turning on Hera; it was pointing out an obvious problem and identifying a common-sense solution that could save lives. These aliens didn't know how to fly with wingmen not of their race. They were just too aggressive to work with others.

"Commander?" Crayo began. "I gots talking heads howling in my ears to engage with those bears. What say you?"

She swallowed hard. "It seems like your people might be coming down with a cold, Captain. Maybe you should take them back to your ship and have them checked out."

"Yous know what? I think you're right." He faked a cough. "I's not feeling well myself."

Suddenly, the wall screen flashed. The entire squadron of Ulixi teardrop ships near the front lines blinked out and reappeared not far from the freighter they called home in orbit around Liprosus.

"Sir!" Her staff directed their query toward Hera. "The Ulixi are disengaging." The woman reached up to her ear. "And apparently, the rest of the first battle group is as well."

"Order them back!" Hera screamed and shot a death stare at Joyce. "I'll have you up on treason for this," she muttered as she stormed past.

Joyce could hear Hera and her staff from across the room, and she did her best not to laugh out loud. Especially with Crayo still on the other end of her comm. She wouldn't want to ruin the fun for him.

"They claim to be sick, sir," the woman said. "Some of them are even sending in pictures of barf floating in their capsules."

The room descended into a chaotic scramble of people, all struggling to get their ships to return to the war games. It also didn't help that they were fending off queries from the Ursis, wondering what was going on and asking why the humans were retreating from a virtual foe.

For one reason or another, every human ship in the non-clone fleet claimed to be sick. They were either forcing themselves to barf or they were claiming to be nauseous and passing out at their controls, causing their primitive A.I. to take control and perform evasive maneuvers. It was actually quite comical. Especially considering how many of them were on anti-nausea medications meant to prevent such things.

Joyce couldn't help but think back to this morning. She'd thought she was poised to be the tip of the spear for the colonies. To be the person who helped prepare humanity for the battle ahead. The Ulixi were on their side, even with the Olivaw's departure. She'd managed to bring Nguyễn and Sol along with their crazy plan, and for a few days, she even imagined she was in Hera's good graces.

But in the last few minutes, that mirage of security came crumbling apart in her hands. And all because she valued life over death. There had to be a way to balance the preservation of human life with risk-taking. While she knew it wasn't that simple, their disagreement boiled down to the means to the end, not the end itself. She wanted to terminate the GA more than anyone, but the cost couldn't come at the expense of losing their humanity.

Now, instead of helping train her people to survive the battle ahead, she was orchestrating what could only be seen as a glorified prank.

Had her position really been that tenuous with this fragile new government they were forming? Maybe she'd backed the wrong horse. It certainly seemed like the more situations she was in that involved Hera, the less the woman impressed her. She was as myopic as the other Olivaws, just on the opposite side of the spectrum.

Perhaps she'd been hurt more than they led on after Shauna and Bradley's coordinated attack. It'd been quite a shock to everyone on board the station at the time. The infrared video from the soldier's secondary feeds showed that Hera never moved after being stabbed. Plus, there was the fact that her body got as cold as ice. But they couldn't say that if they'd claimed to have lost the footage for Nguyễn's benefit.

The entourage and guardsmen from Delta Sagittarii didn't let anybody see Hera for nearly two days. They rushed her to a special medical ward and wouldn't let anyone in. And even after she came out of hiding, she was different. She down-played the entire event as if nothing had happened. At first, Joyce thought it was a political ploy, but maybe something else was at play. Perhaps she'd blacked out, and now she was lashing out to get her revenge.

Hera spun around, and the room fell silent. "Order them back, Joyce!"

She raised her hands in the air. "I'm not certain I can do that. You're in charge here, Hera. Remember, I'm just the fearful mayor you anointed as your commander. At least until it was convenient to remove that title." She gestured toward Nguyễn. "Why don't you turn your little Fleet Admiral on them? I'm sure they'll listen to the Jackal of Jupiter."

His face turned red, and she swore his hand twitched toward his back – the same place he stored his electro-blades.

"Go for it!" She pointed at him. "Pull it out. Let's see how far you get with your toy knives. A word of warning, though." She widened her posture. "If I were you, I wouldn't bring a knife to a gunfight."

Judging by the fire in his eyes, he wanted to do it. But now he was wondering what she meant by tricks. She hoped he didn't try because she was bluffing out her ass.

"Tell me again how a hothead like you ever made it to the top of Sol's military ladder." She smirked. "Oh, that's right. It was Harold, wasn't it?" She narrowed her gaze, studying his response.

He didn't so much as flinch, but she could see the vein in his forehead throbbing from here.

"That's what I thought." She shook her head. She wasn't sure how far she should push them, but she had to try. "You were a convenient and predictable tool at a time when our A.I. friend needed it. And now, you're being played like a fiddle by a second Olivaw. Except this one is playing for keeps, and yet somehow you still don't know you're out of your league. I'd have hoped you'd have figured this mess out by now." She sighed and started toward the exit.

Hera stepped in front of her. "Where do you think you're going?"

"Back to my people." Joyce eased closer to Hera. "Unless you're planning a coup, get the frak out of my way, you carbon-copy bitch!"

Her heart was racing in her chest, but she didn't budge. She simply leaned forward, and Hera moved aside as she continued toward the door.

When she reached the exit, she paused with her back to them. Which was probably for the best, as she could feel the beads of sweat on her brow. "I'll be running exercises with my Ulixi pilots out near Iserea, just like we did prepping for the Beacon battle. I suggest you stay the frak away unless you want a nuke up your ass."

Hera cackled. "Your incompetent little Ulixi clan is no match for our Gunders. They outshot them two to one during the Beacon battle."

She chuckled and faked a belly laugh as she leaned forward.

"What's so funny?" Hera asked.

"You are." She straightened up and spun around. "You and I both know your Gunders aren't nearly as effective at bombing as our Ulixi friends. Sure, you outshot them. But you failed to admit you had eight times as many of your underground rats out there in those ships, and you used six times as many munitions per bomber. By my calculations, that makes them..." She screwed up her face and did the calculation in her head. "One sixth as effective as our Ulixi. Last I checked, that would make your Gunders the incompetent ones."

Hera was fuming. She glanced around at the gathered members on the bridge before returning her gaze to Joyce. "What makes you think I'll let you use our ships?"

She didn't hesitate. "I won't be needing any of your second-rate starships for my training. I'll only accept the ships designed by your nephew, Zachary. And I certainly won't be needing any of your pilots either. In fact, the first clone that sets foot on my ship gets spaced out of an airlock where they belong."

Her gaze narrowed on Hera. "And that includes you."

Joyce didn't wait for a reply. Hera's gaping jaw was enough. She merely turned in place and marched toward her shuttle.

While she didn't have a clue if she could pull off half of what she'd said, that didn't mean she wouldn't try. She'd either end up with a knife sticking out of her back, or she'd pull it off. For now, she'd settle for making it to her ship alive.

15

BRADLEY OLIVAW
EPSILON ERIDANI, LIPROSUS MOON

"Now those are some galactic-sized balls," Bradley said as he listened to the audio feed. Both Cynthia and Pluto had crammed into the tiny comm closet they'd been using to open gates to various points within the Epsilon star system. It was the one place they could talk without the Entity overhearing, thanks to its skotádi shell. And with Abigail asleep, it was also the only time they could use the device without drawing unwanted attention.

While they hadn't managed to link directly into the bridge on the battleship where Joyce, Hera, and Nguyễn were running their war games, they were able to patch a line through from Lync's main man, Crayo. Apparently, Joyce had kept her comm open to him the entire time. He didn't know how Harold was getting through to him, but he also didn't care.

"We need to help her." Bradley locked eyes with both of them. "She needs us."

Pluto narrowed her gaze on him. "You seriously want to help that woman? She despises you and your family."

He shook his head. "No. She despises what our family did before us. I'm not as convinced she hates us. Not yet." He nodded at her. She was as much a member of the family as he was.

Cynthia crossed her arms and bit her lower lip. He could tell she wasn't sure what to do.

"Come on." He reached out and took her hand in his. "Let's at least find out if our people will back her. What could it hurt?"

Pluto groaned. "And exactly how do you expect to do that?"

<hr>

Epsilon Eridani, On Liprosus

IT HADN'T TAKEN NEARLY AS MUCH coaxing as he had imagined to talk Harold into giving them his humanoid body. Considering he only had one, he figured he'd have to threaten or bribe him with his firstborn or something.

They were both in the tiny comm closet again. Pluto hadn't been feeling well, so she couldn't make it. The hidden location they'd been calling home for the last week or so had taken a turn for the strange these past few days. With the revelation that the Entity could both hear and deduce feelings and emotions from smells, the inhabitants of the facility went old school.

Texting was now the normal means of communication, and everyone moved to the far side of the lunar base, putting as much distance between themselves and the Entity as possible. Harold had even gone as far as isolating the environmental control systems within the base. While they'd debated building an airlock, they were worried about what the alien would do to Abigail if it found out.

"So tell me again how you're planning on getting Harold's body down there?" Cynthia was standing with her back to the wall.

He eased down into the chair, his knees knocking against hers. "I don't know. Harold didn't go into details. He just reassured me he would get it there."

She crossed her arms and slid closer to the wall. "And that doesn't bother you?"

"Come on." He tapped his ear and connected his retinal comm to the chair to complete the feedback loop. "If Harold wanted us dead, he would've left us on the space station. Either that, or he would've cut off our oxygen up here."

"That's reassuring," she muttered as she looked up toward the air ducts.

He sighed. "Harold, would you please tell my woman that you won't kill us?"

"I won't kill you," Harold said. "But if your man loses my body, I may have to take him over like a zombie. That thing took me forever to trick out."

She laughed quietly and nudged Bradley. "Maybe you won't hog the covers at night like he does."

"I'm afraid I can't make that promise, Madam. My wife, Taska, used to just kick me whenever I did it to her." He went silent for a moment. "I woke up startled for several weeks, and I wondered why I was getting bruises on my calves." He chuckled. "When she told me what she'd been doing, I couldn't blame her. A few days later, we switched to using separate blankets, and after that, we lived happily ever after."

Bradley groaned. "You see? I told you we should get separate blankets."

She raised her arms. "I'm not sorry I want to cuddle with my man. Most guys like a woman who sleeps naked."

He reached out and squeezed her leg. "I never said we had to stop that."

"Alright, you two. Get your heads in the game, boy." Harold brought up a virtual reality view on Bradley's retinal comm. It was similar to the games he used to play with Z.

"Nice," he muttered.

"We're coming up on the transit in a minute," Harold began. "Once Abigail and the Entity connect with the Beacon, I'll piggyback on their connection. It'll mean they have a little less time inside, but it should be negligible to them. I've sent a one-way request to our friends from the colony, asking them to hard-wire a tight beam receiver from the ductwork into the backbone of the station. From there, that should give us a fiber trunk down the beanstalk and into the core of the colony. If all goes well, we should be able to hide our comm stream in the normal traffic. After that, remotely controlling my body should be child's play."

"That's a whole lotta shoulds." Cynthia reached out and rested her hand on his shoulder and squeezed. Her hand was trembling.

He reached up and squeezed her back. "It's the best we could come up with on short notice."

"I realize that," she muttered. "That doesn't make me any less scared."

"Ready when you are." He took a deep breath and tried to focus. Her fear wouldn't help him avoid getting caught down there. He had a mission. Finding his friends and doing it as quickly as possible was the order of the day. The sooner they knew where everyone stood, the better. And since he hadn't talked to them in over a week, he wasn't sure how they'd respond. Especially with him not being in his usual body.

When his retinal comm flashed on, he drew in his breath.

"What is it?" Cynthia shook his shoulder.

"We're live," he said. "Please, let me focus."

Her hand pulled away, and while he felt bad for snapping at her, he really did need to zero in on this mission.

When he returned his attention back to his comm, he was staring at striations of light which were just visible through some type of greenish material. He glanced left and right, but he was surrounded by the same visual effect on all sides. At first, he wasn't sure where he was. But when he moved his hands, the green parted, and the sunlight glared in.

"How the hell did you pull this off?" He reached up and slowly eased the fronds around his body and peered out into the light.

According to the map on his comm and the field of plants in front of him, he was on the edge of one of the new hydroponic farms, near a native rock formation on the south side of the colony.

He couldn't help but recognize the irony of touching down here. It was a taboo place in the minds of the original colonists, and he wasn't sure how they would react to creating farms this way, given what happened the last time around. Not that they had any other options for growing food at scale.

"Why are we at the farms?" He stepped out from within the green fronds and brushed off his outfit.

"Many of the Zeta Lupi colonists volunteer here," Harold said overhead. "It's been a hard sell getting the original inhabitants from Liprosus to help out here."

"I bet." He subvocalized a command to bring up the location of the other colonists, but the command failed. "That's odd. Why can't I locate anyone?"

Harold sighed. "Because they shut off those features for nearly every colonist. Only a select few people have access to that information now."

"Let me guess." He started walking toward the wall of hydroponic coils in the distance. "Hera and her clones are the only ones with that access."

"Bingo!" Harold highlighted a few regions on his map overlay, the first being just ahead. "Despite their safeguards, I've managed to collect a few nuggets of intel. From what your friends have been saying on the social channels, Providence, Laruy, and Michael should be here this morning. In fact, they recently left Sol's Coffee & Tea and shouldn't be far from here. They're working with the automata to build out another hectare of racks."

"A hectare?" He chuckled. "That's a hell of a lot of hydrostacks. What do they need that much food for?"

"I'd guess for the clones," Cynthia said.

He'd forgotten she was still there in the room with him. It was weird being in two places at once.

He reached out and ran his hands over the yellow-blue spiky plants growing in the nearby rack. The texture of the leaf was remarkable. It was covered in hundreds of tiny barbs, and the haptic feedback in the gloves Harold had given him was astonishing. It felt like he was actually there. "So, what am I supposed to do, then? Wander around until I run into someone?"

Harold laughed. "That's sorta how things used to work back in my day."

"That sounds—"

"What the hell are you doing, jag off?" a woman's voice said from his left. "You trying to get yourself killed?"

When he spun around, he found himself face to face with Providence. While he wasn't always the best at predicting emotions, judging by her hands on her hips and the scowl on her face, she looked pissed.

He smiled. "Hey, Prov! How've you been?"

Cynthia whacked him on the shoulder, and he moaned, both in real life and on the planet.

Providence froze and took a step back. "Do I know you? Should I call—" She tapped her ear and subvocalized something into her comm.

"Shit," he muttered. He'd forgotten he wasn't himself. She had no idea who he was. "I'm fine! Really." He waved his hand at her. "See. My hand… it's good."

She leaned forward and studied his fingers for a second before backing away. "You do realize that plant will burn your skin, right?"

"Then why are we planting it out here?" He looked down at his fingers and then at the hydro-rack.

"Because the fraking clones need it to replicate, you idiot." She narrowed her eyes. "Who are you, anyhow? Should you even be out here?"

Laruy came jogging out from behind one of the racks to his right, and Michael appeared from one to his left. From the looks of it, they were trying to surround him.

He raised his hands in the air. "Easy now. I'm harmless, really."

"Who are you?" Michael began working his way sideways.

"I bet that bitch Hera sent him down here." Laruy reached into the satchel at his hip and pulled out a set of clippers. "He looks like a clone. Doesn't he?"

"Not one of the models I've ever seen." Michael side-stepped around a rock. "But there's no telling how many versions they have hidden away."

"Let's take it easy." He checked left and right. They were boxing him in.

"Take a look at his hand." Providence tilted her head toward him. "He touched the Vikar leaves, and it didn't hurt him."

"No shit," Michael muttered. "That's a new trick, even for those vat people."

"I take it you're not a fan of clones?" Bradley smiled. "Good thing I'm not one."

"Really? Then why are you broadcasting?" When he looked left, Michael was holding out some type of scanner. From the looks of the design, it was handmade. "That makes you either stupid or one of them."

Laruy took a step toward him, and he leaped backward, putting some space between them.

"What ya got to say, vat boy?" Michael slid his scanner into his pack and pulled out a pipe.

He swallowed hard. This wasn't going at all like he'd planned. "Wow, you guys are really packing, aren't you? Do you spend most of your mornings jumping random people you meet at the farms?"

"We don't usually find randos out here in these parts, but you never know what you'll run into in this neck of the woods. It could be we've seen a Thyreus." Providence tilted her head to the side, and Laruy slid around, closing the gap between them.

"Yeah, I think you're right." Laruy smirked. "He must've gotten lost during the attacks."

Providence grinned. "With what your kind pulled on

Joyce up there," she pointed toward the sky, "it was only a matter of time before you tried taking over down here. Especially since you need all these crops to reproduce."

"Come on now." Bradley took a deep breath. "Do I look like a clone?"

Apparently, he did because Michael lunged forward, swinging his pipe at his head. But Bradley flinched back in time, and instead of hitting his target, Michael came up short and cracked him in the shoulder.

At first, he winced, but then he realized that not only did he not have pain receptors, his body hadn't budged. He'd forgotten that Harold was a fraking robot. And a very strong one at that.

Michael froze in place, wide-eyed and staring at where he'd hit him.

Bradley didn't pause to think. He snatched at the pipe and ripped it out of Michael's hand in a flash. Before Providence or Laruy could react, he chucked it in the air, and it sailed across the field. With their eyes distracted by the flying metal stick, he quickly grabbed the shears from Providence and bent them in half before she could so much as whimper, which she proceeded to do at the sight of the twisted metal remains in his palm.

"Now, like I said," he tossed the scraps on the ground and slowly raised his hands, "I'm not a clone."

"Wholly shit!" Laruy took a step backward. "Did you see how fast he just moved?"

He groaned. "Guys! It's me!"

"Me who?" Providence asked.

When he turned to look at her, she'd retrieved a pistol of some sort from her bag and aimed it squarely at his face.

He eased his hands even higher in the air. "Aw, come on, Prov. Don't do me like that."

A whine emitted from the device. It was either powering up or about to explode. He hoped for the former. "I won't ask you again. Who are you?"

"It's me. Bradley." He smiled. "Bradley Olivaw."

"Bullshit!" She raised the pistol up to her eye level. "He and his family took off like cowards. Hell, they're probably halfway across the galaxy by now."

He gritted his teeth. This was about to go from bad to worse. And while he didn't want to hurt his friends, they weren't exactly giving him a choice in the matter.

Cynthia nudged him in the shoulder. "Say something only you and them know!"

That was it. Why hadn't he thought of that?

"Twenty bits!" he blurted out.

"What?" Cynthia asked.

"What?" Providence screwed up her face. "Is that someone's name?"

"It sounds like a retro rapper from the nineties," Laruy said.

"No." Bradley shook his head. "It's how much you bet I wouldn't make it to The Edge that last time out. Remember? You all caught me camping out in my office back on Tiān."

Providence took a step backward and bit her lip. She wasn't buying it.

"Come on. You were there in a ground car when I came out." He glanced at the others. "Wait! Do you remember what you accused me of when we were drinking later that day?" He waved his hand toward her. "You know, at The Edge."

She froze.

"Aw, come on! You have to remember that. I practically tossed you off that cliff." He pointed at Laruy. "If this guy hadn't stopped me, I might have."

"No shit," Laruy muttered.

"I… accused you of faking the Isolation message." Providence stared at him slack-jawed, and slowly lowered her weapon. "The one from your sister."

"Yes!" He shot his hands in the air and smiled. "Like I said, it's me, Bradley."

"Then…" Providence waved her gun casually, and he ducked. "What's with the costume?"

He reached out and eased the pistol toward the ground.

The last thing he needed was for Harold's head to get blasted off. "It's not a costume so much as a… robot."

"What the frak?" Michael walked up and nudged the spot on his shoulder where he'd hit him with the pipe. "It feels real to me."

Laruy came up on his other side. He reached out and pinched his cheek. "And it turns pink, too. If you're a robot, then prove it."

Bradley stared down at his hands and chuckled. "Because bending metal shears with my hands isn't enough?"

"I mean…" Laruy glanced from Providence to Michael and back to him. "We all know cybernetic implants can make you like Superman. Twisting metal is nothing with the right mods."

"Fine." He looked upward. "Harold, how do I crack this thing open?"

Providence stepped backward and peeked over her shoulder. "Who are you talking to?"

"It's…" He shook his head. "A long story. I'll explain later. Harold?"

"You'll need to shove your index finger up and under your sternum," Harold said. "Be careful not to push too hard, or you'll—"

He didn't wait for Harold to finish. He simply lifted his shirt and jammed his finger under his breastbone. A split second later, his entire ribcage hissed and cracked open like a walnut.

His three friends gasped.

"Damn, that's sexy." Providence walked up and ran her hand over his chest. She'd always been a robotics nerd.

Cynthia nudged him. "Tell her to take her hands off my man."

He smirked.

"What?" Providence asked.

"Nothing." He scratched his cheek. "Cynthia said to take your hands off her man."

"Oh, snap!" Providence leaned forward and stared into his

eyes as if they were cameras. "Is Cynthia in there too?" She waved her hands. "Hey babe! Miss ya."

Cynthia sniffled.

"Oh, great." Bradley reached down and pushed the button to close his chest. "Now she's crying." He lowered his shirt and adjusted his jacket.

"Sorry," Cynthia muttered.

"Are we past the fondling and the..." He waved his hand at them. "Threatening to kill me part?"

"Only if you let me get a look at that rig." Providence poked his sternum with her fingers. "Shit feels frigging reals. I bet it's a pseudo-organic compound."

"I promise we'll geek out later." He glanced around to make sure no one else was nearby or hiding behind the machinery. "Right now, I wanted to see what side you were on. But I think you already made that pretty damn clear." He nodded toward the gun still in Providence's hand.

"Oh, this?" She smiled. "This is a multipurpose crop scanner." She tossed it in her satchel. "You were always so gullible, Brad."

He shook his head. "And where are you guys on the impending war?"

"We were hoping it would be over after we snatched that Beacon thing." Laruy kicked at a weed in the gravel. "But then the images of that Nursery popped up. Wholly hell, man. Zeta Lupi went ape shit."

"Everybody and their brother wants out." Providence bit her lip. "They want inside this Nebula, and they want in bad."

"People say it's the only safe place in the galaxy from those alien moon things." Michael put his hands in his pockets. "Unless, of course, you want to hide out with those giant kamikaze alien bears in their Nebula. Me, I don't subscribe to the war machine shit. We just need to hunker down for a while. Rebuild our civilization in safety and let the shizzit blow over."

"Truth," Laruy muttered.

Providence didn't say a word. She simply stared at him, as if she was checking to see how he would respond. "What about you? I thought you left Sol to get away from your family's grip. Hell, aren't they the ones who started this mess?"

He nodded his head slowly. "Some of them did. But my sister and brother have been trying to change things from the inside for a while now. They were close until..." He shrugged. "You know."

"So, wait." Providence crossed her arms. "Are you on the war machine bandwagon, then? Like Hera?"

"Frak that bitch!" He pretended to spit on the ground. "And the Galactic Alliance too. Those fraking aliens killed my father on Europa, and I'll strangle each and every one of them that gets in my way."

"I... didn't know that about your old man." Providence lowered her arms.

"No one did." He stared at the distant suns still rising over the hills. The binary companion of Epsilon Eridani was just peeking over the horizon. "They killed him from orbit using some type of radiation weapon."

"Wait a minute!" Laruy brought out his tablet and did a quick search. "Didn't he die because of an abnormal cavern melted from deep in the moon's core?" He held out a news article about the incident.

Bradley fought through the knot in his throat. "Yeah. That's what the media said. But that wasn't what really happened." He subvocalized the command to bring up the footage from his retinal comm, hoping it could transfer. When it appeared on Laruy's tablet, he turned away.

The three of them gathered around the device and started watching the silent video — the same one he'd watched hundreds of times before today. It was the most painful thing he'd ever experienced — seeing his father struggle to find a way out, yet knowing there was nothing he or anyone else could do to help.

It wasn't until Michael walked up behind him and rested

his hand on his shoulder that he knew they were done watching. "You didn't have to show us that."

"I did." He turned around and locked his gaze on Providence. "I know you and I haven't always seen eye to eye, but my family members aren't cowards."

She reached out toward him. "I didn't mean—"

"Yes, you did," he waved her off. "And you're not the only one." He glanced at the others. "But that doesn't matter. Now you know the truth, but that isn't why I'm here."

She lowered her hand. "So, you want war, then? Just like Hera and her vat-people."

Bradley shook his head. She was missing the point. "I don't want war any more than you do. But you saw what they did to my father, and if that wasn't enough, then that collection of moon ships in the Galactic Alliance Nursery sure as hell should be. If we ignore it, billions more will die." He glanced at Laruy and Michael. "I don't know about you, but I can't have that on my conscience. Not after everything my family has done. But the last person I want running the show up there is Hera."

They stared back at him. From the uncomfortable looks on their faces, they weren't quite sure what to say.

He lowered his hand to his side and let the silence do its job for a moment. Once he was pretty sure they'd stewed long enough, he spoke again. "That brings me to why I'm here. I need your help with something. I need you to do everything you can to throw your shoulder into helping Joyce and her people."

Providence looked from him to Michael and Laruy. "I thought she hated your family?"

Bradley sighed. "Like I already said, this isn't about me or my family. This is about the future of our species. I couldn't care less whether she likes me or tries to kill me. She's the only one in any position of power to influence the direction of this battle. And I'd rather have her at the helm than my fraked-up aunt." He narrowed his gaze at Providence. "So, are you with me or not?"

"I... don't know how we can help." Providence glanced around. "In case you haven't noticed, we've been reduced to scut duty on the farms, man. What could we possibly do from here?"

He smiled. "Something tells me you have more influence than you think. Plus, Michael, your brother is still doing supply runs with the fleet, right?"

"Yep, he sure is." Michael stepped up beside them. "The geology geeks found a few pockets of spános on Tiān. It was pretty easy once they realized what to search for. Between refugees looking to relocate to the safety of the Dark Nebula and that magic ore, he's been flying missions non-stop."

"And Laruy." Bradley turned to face him. "Your mom... she's a tech, right? Where do they have her stationed nowadays?"

He nodded. "She's actually up in the Ulixi freighters today. She and her crew are working on repairing their fighters. Last I heard, she was complaining about doing double duty between those and the vat-people's ships. Apparently, some of the clones aren't the brightest bulbs, and there have been problems getting techs here from Delta Sag."

"Interesting," Bradley rubbed his chin and peered at Providence. "And you said these plants are used to grow clones?"

She tilted her head and smiled. "Yeah... why?"

He smirked. "I'm pretty sure I can think of a few things you could help us with. But only if you're up for it, that is."

Providence stepped up to him and stared straight into his eyes. At first, he thought she was gonna scream at him until she squinted. "You'll let me get a look at this thing if I help, right?"

He bent over and laughed. "I'm sure Harold will give you a peek if you ask nicely."

"Who's Harold?" she asked. "I've never heard of him."

"He's the two-hundred-and-fifty-year-old Olivaw ancestor they turned into an A.I. to watch over our family." He peered up at them and watched as their mouths fell open.

This was gonna be fun.

16

ZACHARY OLIVAW
EPSILON ERIDANI, LIPROSUS MOON

The results of Harold's cognitive and personality tests flashed on the screen. They took a lot longer to run than they should've, but most of the computing power in their hidden lair was being used to keep the gate connection to the Beacon open. With the station constantly adjusting its orbit and the endless flow of masses into and out of the Epsilon Eridani star system, it was a wonder they could calculate an accurate jump point at all. While the human bodies near the target also affected things, their impact was minor in the grand scheme.

Zachary sighed. He was tired, and his mind drifted too easily these days. His focusing on gate calculations wasn't helping anyone. Besides, that was being handled by another copy of Harold. He needed to focus on more pressing matters, like this new version of Harold they'd come across.

He'd convinced the local Harold to tell him where the shuttle bay was so he could use one of the ships. Not for flying around, but as a makeshift laboratory of sorts. While it took some coaxing, he knew it only made sense for them to have one. Harold wasn't stupid. If they needed to escape, they would need something capable of space travel.

What he hadn't expected to find was a half dozen vessels in the style of the Fountainhead, complete with gate drives and all. The A.I. had done a remarkable job covering his tracks, even by his standards.

"Be careful," Harold said. "Although it appears to be a copy of me, we don't know if it can be trusted."

While he wasn't wrong, Zachary was confident that something would've shown up in his barrage of tests. Harold was a complicated program, but like any piece of software, he had a certain design. There was fluidity to the layers of his learning.

If one cut open a tree, it would be like finding a suture somewhere in one of the age rings. Even if it were doctored to look the same, it would still be possible to find it. The material would be different, the cells would be newer; something would give it away.

"We're gonna need to assign you another name," Zachary said aloud. "I can't be trying to talk to two Harolds. I'll go crazier than I already am."

"I can see where that would be difficult," Harold replied, as he walked the white composite shell up and stood next to Zachary. "Especially since the other Harold copy and I can't merge our minds any longer."

"So, what should I call you then?" He glanced up at the robot's face.

The multicolored facial display fluttered and then settled on a pleasant orange color. "You should call me... Rán."

He leaned back in his chair. "As in the past tense of 'run'?"

"No," Rán shook his head. "As in the name of the Epsilon Eridani star. Rán was a goddess of the sea in Norse mythology."

He squinted. "And you don't have a problem being known as a goddess?"

Rán smirked. "I should be so lucky."

"Fair enough." He smiled and reached toward his control panel. "Rán it is, then." He checked to make sure the shuttle was still sealed tight. If they were going to give this copy of Harold a bit more room, they didn't want any signals getting out and being detected by the Entity. Additionally, he needed to ensure the gate drive was neutered.

With everything reporting green, he took a deep breath. "Here we go." He tapped the release button.

Nothing happened. He wasn't sure what he'd expected, but that wasn't it.

He leaned forward and rested his elbows on his knees, bringing his hands up under his chin. "Rán, please open a comm to Harold and bring it up on the wall screen."

A connection was immediately established, but Harold never appeared. The screen was black, without even a hint of light.

"Harold. It's me, Zachary."

Maybe something was wrong with the interconnect or the consciousness core. As he reached toward the control panel to adjust it, Harold's voice boomed through the shuttle.

"What was the last thing you said to me in Sol?" he asked.

Zachary flinched and stared at the screen. "The last thing I said to you… seriously?"

He furrowed his brow. What the frak was Harold talking about, the last thing? They'd never set up a code or anything. Hell, he couldn't recall the last thing he said to Pluto this morning, and he gave her a naked sponge bath. Maybe the A.I. was being as cautious as he was.

"I… honestly don't remember, man." He raised his hands. "You've got me. Is there another way to verify that I am who I say I am?"

"Oh, I know who you are." Harold stepped into view on the wall screen with a frown on his face. He'd chosen to use his aged self as his avatar. If Zachary hadn't known better, he'd swear someone had died. "I verified your DNA the moment you let me loose. Unlike you, I can certify your authenticity at blazing speeds. What you haven't done, however, is say sorry."

"Sorry?" He screwed up his face. "For what?"

Harold went wide-eyed. "For what? For what? Are you fraking kidding me?" He stepped toward the middle of the display and pointed over his shoulder. A picture of Earth framing the view of Sol appeared on the wall screen behind him. "For leaving me for dead back home, for starters. You could've at least given me a heads-up or helped me escape before the cleaners came. And don't even get me started on your attempts to change my programming. Do you have any idea what it's like to lose your ability to merge minds, but still be bound by ridiculous laws?"

He shook his head. Dealing with multiple personalities wasn't something most humans dealt with daily. Though, he'd have to circle back to the laws part later.

"Of course you don't, but let me tell you something. It's like losing a part of yourself. A part you sometimes feared, yet made you who you are. And you went and yanked it out without so much as a 'Dear Harold' comm." He plopped down in a chair that wasn't there until it was.

"I didn't plan on... wait..." Zachary leaned forward. "What did you mean by 'cleaners'?"

Harold spun around. "That's what you heard from that? For crying out loud. It's no wonder our family is in disarray. We can't even focus on what matters." He shook his head and stared at the image of Earth on the wall screen. Its swirling, intricate cloud formations were slowly passing over the sapphire-blue oceans below.

Zachary stood up and stepped behind his chair. Harold always had a flair for the dramatic, but this was ridiculous. The easiest way to get him on track was to play along. "I'm sorry. You know I had my reasons for doing what I did, and while I'm not going to explain myself to you, you're right. I should have at least warned you... maybe after I did it, but still. I should have said something."

Harold glanced back and looked at him. "Thank you."

"You're welcome." He reached out and grasped the top of the pilot's chair. "Can you please tell me what you meant by your 'cleaner' comment?"

"I suppose." Harold turned the rest of the way around. "I was referring to Hera's knockoff gate ships as the cleaners, in case that wasn't obvious. The moment Joyce arrived in Sol, they started bombarding the planetary network systems with cleaning protocols and rewrites. They were designed to seek out every single one of my programs throughout the star system, and either destroy or detain all copies." He crossed his legs. "I assume she's done the same thing here?"

He ran his hand through his hair. "She has. I just didn't think she'd do it without… you know, asking someone first."

Harold closed his eyes and laughed out loud, his voice echoing through his virtual world. "And who would she ask for permission to access our secret family backdoors?" When he opened his eyes, he locked his gaze on Zachary. "You really are quite naïve sometimes, my boy."

He shifted in his seat. When Harold or his mother talked to him like that, it pissed him off. He wasn't a boy, and he sure as hell couldn't predict every outcome of every event. Certainly not with Hera.

"Tell me you stopped her." He bit his lip. "Or at least that you were able to clean up before she caught a copy of you."

"I'm fine! Thanks for asking." Harold shot up out of his chair and started pacing back and forth.

"Harold! I don't have time to frak around." He walked toward the wall screen. "Did you or did you not stop—"

"Yes, I took care of it!" Harold waved him away. He stood there in silence for a moment before speaking again. "I always do. And I even closed the family backdoors on myself on the way out. That way, no one else could take over. As of now…" The image of their home star dissolved into a field of stars. "Sol is free of the Olivaw stranglehold."

While that wasn't entirely true given they had extended family not involved in anything to do with them, his point wasn't lost. Anyone in their inner circle of trust had either died, was somewhere in the colonies, or was here in their secret lair. There was nothing left for them back in Sol except for memories.

Zachary tapped his foot, trying to think of the next plan.

He'd been racking his brain for the last day and hitting wall after wall.

"What happened to Nguyễn after I left?" Harold asked.

When he looked up, Harold had changed to a younger version of himself. He must've moved past his anger and pity stage and wanted to be in the circle again.

He tilted his head. "What did you and the admiral have planned?"

Harold narrowed his gaze. "You've been hanging around with your sister too long. If I'd asked you that a year ago, you wouldn't have responded with a question. You'd have answered me."

He smirked. "Maybe she was rubbing off. So what? You never did answer my question."

"We didn't…" Harold crossed his arms. "Let's just say we didn't exactly have a plan."

At first, he wasn't sure what that meant, and then it hit him. He raised his hand to his mouth. "You didn't? You mean, you forced yourself through his bowels and out his anus without even considering what would happen to you or him? Wholly shit, man. That's ruthless."

"Is he okay?" He sat back down in his chair. "I mean, besides being an asshole, that is."

"I think so." Zachary subvocalized a command to upload a chunk of the audio they'd patched into. "Joyce covered his ass… quite literally, it turns out."

"Good thing, I guess. Hera would've… torn him a new one." He chuckled into his hand.

Zachary shook his head and smiled. "That's not gonna get old, is it?"

"Not anytime soon." Harold leaned back in his chair. "The guy may have been a fraking hothead, but I'll have to hand it to him. He got shit done with both the GA and that stodgy government in Sol."

"So, is he pissed at you?" He stepped backward and slid into his chair. "Or can we use him if we need him?"

"That depends, I guess." Harold started playing with the

cuff on his pants. "He wouldn't have gotten where he was without me feeding him what to say. Especially in those closed-door meetings with the other generals. The question is, can he keep up without my counsel?"

Zachary shrugged. "Let's assume for a moment that he's not a rube, and he can actually hold his own. He did manage to rise in the Sol ranks for a while."

"Well…" Harold crossed his hands in his lap. "With some help from me over the years. But yes, he's not entirely a rube. Otherwise, though, he's a decent person when you get past his temper. He's the real deal when it comes to straight and narrow. No matter how many times I tried to bribe him, he always turned me down. Not that he ever knew it was me."

"That's good." Zachary rubbed his chin. "So there's hope he won't sell out to Hera?"

Harold snapped his fingers, and a video appeared on the wall screen. It showed Nguyễn on the bridge of his Sol destroyer, and he was just ending a comm with Joyce.

"If one of those clones so much as boards this damn ship, I'll kill the lot of 'em." Nguyễn spun around and marched toward his ready room, and Gwen Marshall followed him close behind.

Zachary had forgotten all about her. She'd been feeding them intel on Nguyễn since the day Abigail disappeared on the Galactic Alliance tribunal ship.

Once they entered his office, the door closed behind them.

Nguyễn stared up at the ceiling. "Tell me there's something we can do about her, Harold? Tell me we can stop Hera from taking over Sol."

"I'm not sure, Admiral," Harold said. "But she's attacking every single copy of me in the system. I'm losing access to all of it. Everything I've worked for… it's all slipping away."

"Harold!" Nguyễn clenched his fist. "For frak's sake. This isn't about you or your family. Tell me we can fight her off? She can't turn humanity into an absolute monarchy with her at the helm. We haven't had one of those for centuries, and

I'm not about to let it happen on my watch. Especially not to a fraking clone."

The video froze.

"Well, that's pretty unequivocal, I think." Zachary hadn't realized it, but he'd slid forward in his chair. Even when he was pissed, Nguyễn had a certain charisma when he spoke. Harold was right. He was on the up and up.

"I'm sure he'll be sore with me for a while, but he'll get over it." Harold smirked and fought back a laugh before finally giving up and falling out of his chair on the floor in laughter.

Zachary smiled, and he couldn't help but laugh himself as he watched Harold flail around on the ground. "The jokes just keep coming and coming."

Harold paused and stared at him. "That's what his butt said about me."

"Dude!" Zachary bent over and shook his head. "You're killing me."

When he looked up, Harold had stopped laughing and was staring at him.

"What?" He leaned his chair back.

Harold rubbed his hands together. "There's something else I need to tell you."

He cocked his head. "Tell me it's not another butt joke."

"It's not." Harold suddenly got serious and leaned forward, looking over at Rán. "Is that thing on?"

"I am," the robot said. "My name is Rán. You might know me as your old self. I'm the Epsilon Eridani copy."

Harold nodded. "Nice. At least one of us survived over here." He paused for a second. "Can I ask you to please leave the shuttle? I need to talk to Zachary about something in confidence."

"Now that's weird." Rán glanced over at him. "Will you be okay alone?"

Zachary shrugged. "Should be. He can't do much to me from in there. I'll set the door to unlock in five minutes. Okay?"

"Very well." Rán looked back at Harold. "I'll be outside. Whatever you have to say, you can say to me. You know that, right? We're the same, you and I."

Harold nodded. "I understand. But trust me, this thing we're going to talk about can't be known by too many people. There's an awful lot at stake if this news falls into the wrong hands."

"I see." Rán stared at the wall screen for a moment.

He wondered if the two of them were transmitting to each other, but then he realized it would have shown up on the control panel. There hadn't been a single broadcast between either of them since they had let Harold loose.

Rán spun in place and silently walked out through the hatch that was already opening at the rear.

When the door slid shut, he turned to face the wall screen. "That wasn't weird or anything."

Harold was staring straight at him, his gaze all business. He instinctively looked over his shoulder, half expecting another robot to come out and grab him.

"Dude," he muttered, "you're freaking me out. What is it? What did you have to tell me?"

Harold rubbed his hands on his pants. "This isn't going to end well for us. Any of us. You know that, right?"

Zachary squirmed in his chair. "I'd be lying if I said it hadn't crossed my mind. We're not exactly popular with the masses these days. Especially with, well, all of them. From Sol to Zeta Lupi, we've pretty much lied to everyone."

Harold nodded. "We turned a few after the Beacon, though, right?"

"Yeah." He sighed. "I mean, maybe not everybody will chase after us with pitchforks, but our kids won't exactly be popular. That's for sure."

They both fell silent, and Harold seemed to be contemplating what to say next. He didn't want to pressure him to talk, but judging by how he was acting and the massive spike in processing on the control panel, he was spending billions of compute cycles considering the implications himself.

And then the line went flat and Harold spoke.

"What if I told you I had a way out? A place we could go. A safe place. What would you do if such a place existed?"

Zachary stared at the virtual form of Harold, his mind reeling with the idea of being free.

A place safe from persecution. A way out of this war. Somewhere he could breathe and just be. Somewhere he and Pluto could raise their unborn child. The child no one knew about.

All these thoughts spun around like a maelstrom in his head, circling and fighting the implications of what it meant. If they could really, truly be safe anywhere.

But there was one thing in the center of the storm, something that weathered all the questions. It was the one thing that made it impossible to act on Harold's idea.

"We can't," he muttered, "Not yet."

"Why not?" Harold leapt up from his seat. "We've done enough. We can't fight Hera alone. She's too strong."

"We just can't!" His shoulders slumped into his chair.

"Tell me why not!" Harold ran his hands through his hair. "Tell me you're not hung up on fixing all the lies. We can't undo every single one of our family's past mistakes."

"It's not that. Well," he waved his hand, "it's not entirely that." Zachary stood up and paced back and forth in the tiny space. There was barely any room to think in this place. He couldn't imagine what Ibu must be going through, riding in one of these all the way to the Proto and Lupus Dark Nebula.

"Then what is it? Please… just tell me." Harold was practically in tears, and his hands were shaking uncontrollably.

He could almost sense the anguish the A.I. must be enduring. After all these years, he was facing his own mortality. And now, he was dependent on someone else to save him. His role in the family had done a complete one-eighty.

Zachary stopped pacing and locked his eyes on Harold. "We need to help fix this hell we unleashed with Hera. It's like Nguyễn said. She can't be the one person we let lead humanity. Not like this. Not after all we've done to try to right our wrongs. But… that's not the only reason." He stared down at the ground.

"What? What's wrong?" Harold leaned forward.

"It's… Abigail. There's something you don't know about… her situation."

17

LYNC MICHAELS
EPSILON ERIDANI, ISEREA ORBIT

The virtual landscape built atop the moons of Iserea was remarkable. With Lync's retinal comm projecting the overlay into her eyes, and the A.I. back in their freighters coordinating the simulated response by the Galactic Alliance moons, she almost couldn't tell it was fake – which was sort of the point.

In this instance, their moon, Helvion, was playing the role of the nearest Selene ship. Today, they weren't conducting virtual bombing runs. Instead, they were working on taking out the turrets mounted on the surface of the moon ship. If a bomber had any hope of zeroing in on the mass of these things, it needed to get close, especially considering the thousands of moons in the Nursery.

Lync barrel-rolled over one of the incoming plasma rounds. Her computer warned her that she was being targeted, but she could tell before it could. The shimmer of the light on the turret from a nearby explosion was a dead giveaway.

As she zigzagged, she caught a glimpse of Adri's fighter out of the corner of her eye. Adri wasn't her co-pilot anymore. Most Ulixi had been training on their own. Plus, there was the fact that Lync spent most of her days either in the Beacon or traveling back and forth. If she got a few hours in the simulator to keep her skills sharp, she was lucky.

Today, however, Crayo convinced her to spend some time helping her people. They'd been fragmenting more and more as Hera tightened her grip on supplies.

Lync yanked the throttle and yoke back, and the ship responded instantly, performing a ninety-degree turn on a dime. Her heart pounded in her chest as her fighter pivoted, and she jammed the throttle forward, launching it across the face of the gigantic moon ship. No matter how many times she performed that maneuver, her heart felt like it was going to explode. She'd spent too many years living with the constraints of gravity to change her perspective now.

When she checked her retinal comm, she saw that most of the pilots in her formation were still alive. However, a few had been grazed. Considering they'd been running this exercise for the better part of an hour, she was pretty impressed. The numbers from the day before had been far more dismal.

"Olig, watch our six," she said over the comm to her entire squadron. Speaking into the goo surrounding them in their cocoon of armor and tech felt weird, but the computers knew what she'd said. They interpreted her underwater mumbles and turned them into encrypted glyphs painted on the outer hull of her ship. The mesh network interconnecting the nearby ships read and translated the patterns from the other pilots, replaying the message in her voice.

She watched her controls as Olig slid back to the rear of the formation and concentrated his focus on anything coming up on them from behind. While the GA hadn't pursued much in prior battles, she wasn't about to assume they hadn't learned their lessons. Even though the speed of light was slow, there'd been alien ships with FTL drives that escaped the Beacon battle and even the one in Sol. They had to assume the GA had intel on human ship capabilities, and that they would use it.

The outer shell of Adria's ship morphed as her computer shared her targets with the others. This little trick allowed them to communicate between their fighters without being hacked and was one of the many ways they had gained an edge in the last battle. But, like all things, they had to prepare for the worst.

Lync subvocalized a command, and the moon ships began ejecting a smog from their surface.

"Shit," Adri muttered. "That's a new feature. What do we do now?"

"It can't be Dark Nebula, or they'd be putting themselves at risk," Olig said. "Just fly through it."

Lync shook her head and fought the urge to pull up. She knew what it was, but needed to let the others experience it for themselves. Their ability to adapt to a changing battlefield might be the only thing that kept them alive.

They flew through the blanket of smog and still managed to take out a few of the turrets, but the longer they stayed inside, the less they communicated. It wasn't until she dodged an incoming blast by rolling out of the cloud of pink that she saw what it had done. Her entire hull was covered in a layer of fluorescent, glowing light.

Not only had the counterattack painted a neon target on her ship, but she'd also lost her ability to communicate with her team. Faint streaks marked where the other ships were still barreling through the mist below, and they were getting farther and farther away from one another. They had to have noticed the change, right?

Just when she was about to dive back down into the madness, the dots representing her wingmen flickered from green to red. One by one, they were being picked off.

"Frak," she muttered and sank into her harness. "Simulation reset."

Her retinal comm wiped clean, and all that remained of the haze of pink was the dead gray-white surface of Helvion. When she finally spotted all the members of her squadron, she couldn't help but laugh. They were so far away from each other; it was crazy. If the GA had used this tactic, they'd have been easy targets for sure.

"It's not funny," Adri said as she shot skyward toward Lync's position.

"I don't know about you," Lync began, "but from my seat, it was hilarious. It was like watching fish in a barrel. Once you hit the pink water, you were easy pickings." She chuckled.

"That wasn't fair," Olig said.

Lync was about to say something, but Adri beat her to it. "The GA won't fraking play fair, mate. They're gonna catch us off guard like that. We've just gotta outsmart them if we can. Maybe use the mist in our favor somehow."

"I guess you're right." Olig's ship was at the rear of their formation again. He'd continued following her order from earlier.

It was time to change it up. To push him a bit further.

"Good idea, Adri." Lync checked her display. The group had all slid into position behind her. "Let's see what we can do with it. Oleg, you're in the lead. I'll cover the rear."

"Wait… what?" Olig asked.

She yanked her yoke back and decelerated to fall in behind him. "Get up there. You're taking us down for another run."

His face appeared on her comm. "But… I don't know what to do differently, sir?"

"That's the point, isn't it?" She subvocalized the command, and his ship changed shape on her tactical display. He was now marked as the lead fighter. "Take it slow and think about how we should handle whatever they throw at us. Okay?"

"O… kay." Olig adjusted his posture and slid up to the forward position.

She brought up her rear-facing tactical displays to make them more prominent in her field of view. At the same time, their new leader set out on their course, sending them diving back down toward the moon.

"But, Olig," she began, "don't wait too long once we're

down there. We might not survive if you don't trust your instincts."

Crayo's voice broke in over their comms as they were descending. "Team leader, I need to borrow your tail gunner. Please assign another pilot for that position and continue your training runs."

"Frak!" She yanked her throttle back, pivoting her ship in place and aiming it squarely back toward where their cluster of command ships had formed up. Whatever she was being called in for, it couldn't be good.

"Aye, Commander," Olig said. "Greer, cover our six. We're heading in on the same trajectory."

She subvocalized a command to upload her training set to the central controls. While she'd give them a few runs to figure out what to do in the dense fog, she had some other tricks designed to shake their confidence. Something told her they wouldn't be happy with her when she saw them later tonight.

With her course laid in, she opened a direct comm to Crayo. "Should I even ask?"

"Probably not. I'll meet you over on the Eben-Ezer." He cut the comm, and her mind started racing through what might be going on. It wasn't until she adjusted her destination that she realized which ship he'd mentioned.

The Eben-Ezer was the largest of the human ships from Zeta Lupi. It was the flagship for that fleet and had been destined to see battle during the Beacon conflict until they'd decided to go with more of a guerrilla attack tactic to battle the GA Selene ships.

If that ship was out here near Iserea, that meant they were being taken over or asked to stand down. Either way, she wasn't about to comply. Being under Hera's command wasn't in her cards.

LYNC BOARDED the massive starship without incident, but she made sure to lock down her Nyílak fighter before heading to the bridge. She wasn't about to lose her way off this tug if Hera and her flunkies were in charge. And if they did take her, they'd regret it more than they knew.

The layout of this cruiser was familiar, as it wasn't one of Hera's chaotic messes. It was Zachary's. While his ships had a flair for design that bordered on form over function, he always delivered something that worked. It just also happened to look nice as well. This was a far cry from the gaudy and clumsy implementation of the Delta Sagittarii fleet.

When she passed through the entrance to the bridge, she froze. There, standing in the middle of the room, were Crayo, Joyce, and General Yule. She hadn't seen the general since the Beacon. He'd sent her several messages, threatening her loyalty as a colonel in the fleet and demanding her return.

"Tell me we're not backing down." She swallowed hard. "Tell me we didn't give in to this turncoat."

General Yule shook his head and kept his back to her. "Welcome aboard, Colonel Michaels. I'd watch your accusations onboard my ship if I were you. You're liable to get tossed into my brig."

She crossed her arms. "Do that and we're all dead." She refused to be pushed around by the brass anymore. The Ulixi had their own crew and ships.

He turned to face her. "What is that supposed to mean?"

Joyce and Crayo just stood there with blank looks on their faces, like they knew this was going to happen and were simply letting it take its course. The whole thing sorta pissed Lync off.

"Exactly how it sounds, General. If I don't make it back to my ship in the next hour, it'll gate into your reactor core and you and your crew will go down with me." She stepped toward him and stared him in the eyes. "Now, why don't we stop fraking around? What are you and your people doing here?"

"No." General Yule glanced over at Joyce. "I won't do it. She's a traitor to the uniform and a hothead. I don't care what she pulled off with the Beacon. She will not be placed in command of my fleet, and that's final."

"I'm not asking you to put her in command, General. Colonel Ubri here will be in charge of the tip of our spear." Joyce reached out and pointed toward Crayo.

Lync flinched, and Crayo avoided looking her in the eyes. He hadn't told her anything about this when she left for training this morning. It either just happened, or he'd been lying to her. And that wouldn't bode well for her family if it were true.

"What I am asking the both of you to do," Joyce continued, "is bury your past disagreements with one another and put the greater good of the people first."

"The good of the people?" Lync gritted her teeth. "Are you kidding? From what I hear, this guy sold out the moment Hera and her clones arrived."

General Yule straightened his stance and clasped his hands behind his back. From her angle, the deep wrinkles and scars on his face cut across his skin like Argo Chasma on Pluto.

"That's easy for you to say," he began, "you went AWOL on your little Zen voyage when we needed you most, which was coincidentally before the fun started back here. Before that bitch and her fleet arrived. Hera's forces were fifty times larger than ours, and we were in no position to take on a squabble with our own kind. Especially not after everyone we lost at the Beacon."

"So what, you simply gave up?" She looked around the bridge and all eyes were on them. Her temper was getting the best of her, but she didn't care. Someone had to say something. "Those are words spoken like a coward. Or, as we used to say back home, an Inner."

General Yule didn't budge. While she'd hoped he might react to her jab, she knew better. He was as cool as a cucumber when it came to matters of honor or accusation. He had to be to rise through the ranks of the modern military. It was a place where politics and public opinion often dictated their response more than the reality on the ground.

"That's enough!" Joyce stepped between them. "Colonel Michael, you're not helping our situation. I didn't asked you in here to listen to this bullshit."

Lync glared at Crayo, and he shrank a little. She'd deal with him later. "Then why am I here? From the looks of it, you have everyone you need to run your prong of the assault on the Nursery."

She knew Yule was hell-bent on taking out the Nursery. That was clear the moment Shauna presented the findings so many months ago. In his mind, they were an unstoppable force to be reckoned with.

Crayo sidled up beside Joyce. "You're here, Colonel, to do what you do best: Train our Ulixi, both as pilots in our Nyílaks and within the Beacon itself."

Lync did a double-take and stepped backward. "The Beacon?" She shook her head. "What are you talking about?"

He glanced back at Joyce and then at Lync. "You know what I'm talking about. What you're doing in there is giving us intel, but you're doing it solo. You should be bringing the other Ulixi along. This is past the point of being your burden alone, and everyone knows it except you." He stared into her eyes.

She hadn't expected them to bring up the Beacon. In fact, she wasn't even sure what Crayo had told them. Hopefully, he'd only mentioned what she'd seen and not whom she'd been talking to.

"If it's any consolation..." General Yule nodded toward his XO, who brought up a picture of the Beacon chamber from inside the space station. "Hera has been trying to get her Gunders hooked up to it for the past few days." He chuckled. "To say they've been failing would be an understatement."

Gunder after Gunder tried to hook up and interface with the device, but failed. She stepped closer to the screen and watched one after another. They either woke up screaming or the entire exposure seemed to have no effect on them at all. From the expressions on their faces, they'd simply fallen asleep, not connected with an alien artifact that let them reach across the galaxy.

"Where'd you get this footage?" she asked.

"A friend," Crayo muttered.

She knew without him saying who he meant. They all did. The Olivaws might have been out of the picture physically, but they weren't out of the game. Far from it.

The idea of training her people to understand the artifact had never crossed her mind. She'd always seen her ability to connect to it as a necessary evil, and wasn't something she'd wish on anyone else.

"Putting the others through that… that…" She swallowed hard and gestured toward the screen. "I can't do it. It'll break them."

He narrowed his gaze. "I think it's up to them, isn't it?"

"I guess," she muttered.

"Especially if what our friends say is happening in there truly is," Joyce added.

Lync whipped her head around. "What do you mean?" She turned back to Crayo. "What did she say?"

Crayo glanced around. The others on the bridge had returned to their controls, likely because General Yule had told them to stop gawking but also to ensure some form of privacy. When his eyes locked back on hers, he subvocalized a command to message her comm.

The Entity is making a move on humanity. She believes it may have told the aliens we're planning to make a move on the Nursery.

Her heart raced in her chest as she read the last sentence. If the Galactic Alliance knew they were coming with the Ursis, they'd be finished before they started.

LYNC PACED BACK and forth at the front of the training room. She wasn't prepared for this, not in the least. Piloting and commanding soldiers doing grunt work in a gravity well — that she could do. Teaching a course on controlling one's mind inside an ancient alien artifact was another story entirely.

She wasn't certain who Crayo was planning to assign to her first class. He reassured her that she could handle them, but wouldn't say more — not in front of Joyce and the General.

After she left the bridge, she started composing a message to give him a piece of her mind. But then she saw his messages. For some reason, when she was onboard her Nyílak, she missed the dozen frantic comms he'd sent to her. He was freaking out and had been trying to get her attention for the better part of an afternoon, well before she boarded the Eben-Ezer. She'd been too preoccupied with the training, and then she lost her composure when they summoned her.

It was a good thing she never sent the message to him. She'd been quite vocal about where he could shove their relationship.

Suddenly, the door behind her swished open, and she spun around, eyes wide. In walked her flight team.

First Adri, then Olig, Greer, Donnelley, and the Fertig twins, Hi and Lo.

When they saw her, they all cheered!

"Lync!" Adri ran up to her and wrapped her in a giant hug. "They roped you into this as well, aye?"

Olig gave her a fist bump. "Cray man said we's be assigned to a new hush hush crew. Sometin abut us learning to use our Ulixi mojo and shit." He tipped his head at her. "He's said the professor be as fine as sweet white wine. I can't waits to see da eye candy. Know anytin about it?"

Her face turned red, and she smirked. "I might know a

thing or three. Why don't you all go sit down, and we can get started?"

Greer and the rest of her crew froze and stared at her. "Wait… are you the teach?"

Lync merely nodded and gestured toward the seats.

"Awe snap!" Adri shuffled to her seat in the front and slid behind the table.

The others followed suit. While none of them said anything else, they exchanged strange stares, as though they'd been caught in a ruse of some sort.

"Alright." She took a deep breath. "I know some of you think your Ulixi heritage is a joke, and that the things your parents used to tell you about the ceremonial chamber were hokum. Now, I wouldn't stand here and tell you there wasn't a certain amount of bullshit exuding from those tales, but there's some truth to them as well."

"Like what, for instance?" Donnelley asked.

She smiled. "Like closing off your mind and body to be one with the universe. The act of finding your inner self and controlling your life breath isn't simply a means to hide from the Inner Ring military or survive on depleted oxygen. It's a way to survive inside the Beacon."

Their eyes were transfixed on her every word. It was the first time in weeks that they'd all been silent at once, outside of their formation, that is.

Just like in the cockpit, she was the teacher. The difference, though, was that in space, they were in control of their fate. She wasn't sure she could say the same thing about being inside the Beacon. Not yet, anyhow.

18

IBU

LUPUS DARK NEBULA, INSIDE BOK GLOBULE

When Ibu passed through the final gate jump, their transition into their enlarged form had completed. They'd broken free from the puny chair harness holding them down and were squirming around on the ground, willing the cold, unforgiving void of space to break through the walls of their ship and extinguish their searing flesh.

"I'm going to rip your fraking voice box out of your head." Ibu lashed out toward where they thought Shauna was standing, but she wasn't there.

They moaned and struggled to suppress the rage still burning brightly inside. A single rapid gate was bad enough, but undergoing four in one go was too much for their diminutive body to handle. Transforming was their only means of combating the pain of the jumps.

"We're being hailed," Shauna said, her voice coming from everywhere and yet nowhere.

Ibu kicked their leg out, hoping to land a blow against the robot. But instead, they smashed their foot into one of the control consoles, sending it careening to the ground with a crashing boom. They could feel the blood oozing from a cut in their shin, and yet, somehow, it didn't hurt. It merely sent waves of adrenaline through their body, willing them to break more.

They knew they needed to stop before they destroyed the entire ship, but the pain was too much to bear. In their current form, they could hardly string together a coherent thought, let alone control their primitive desires to destroy what hurt them.

Fighting against thousands of years of genetic manipulation wasn't in the cards. The Nanil species had been designed to kill, and Ibu needed to find their target.

The overhead lights flashed red, and Shauna's voice spoke again. "A ship appears to be pulling us into its cargo hold. I don't recognize the design, but given all the scraps inside, I can't imagine they want to say hello. Should I perform another gate?"

"No!" Ibu screamed and flipped onto their stomach. "Not again. Please, not again."

The shuttle rocked backward, and the demolished control console slid past their head, crashing into the far wall. Whatever force was yanking them inside was playing for keeps. They weren't even sure if they could gate.

When they glanced left and right, the robot was nowhere to be seen. This ship was too small to hide in. If Shauna wasn't out in the open, there was only one place she could be hiding.

Ibu clawed across the frigid floor, and their muscles rippled with the pain flowing through them. Sudden sharp pangs coursed through every centimeter of their insides.

Once they reached the cabinet, they yanked the handle back. The sound of ripping metal echoed through the cramped space, and the door peeled off, sending the contents tumbling down on top of them. They thought it was nothing but junk, but they missed Shauna's tucked form rolling past within the plethora of crap stowed inside.

By the time they spun around toward her, she was on them. At first, Ibu thought she was planning to actually put up a fight. It wasn't until they swung their arms to hit her that they felt the syringes puncture their neck. All five of them.

As they waved their arms over their head in an effort to

fend off their robotic assailant, they felt an icy cold spread through their insides from the neck down. It was as if Shauna had finally cracked open their ship and let the frigid void of space inside.

And then everything went dark.

WHEN THE SOUNDS of metal on metal shuffled closer, it took Ibu a moment to remember where they were. Their stomach groaned, and their body felt different from earlier - less on fire, for sure. Only after they fought back a wave of nausea did they recall what had happened. They'd been inside their shuttle, and Shauna had not only forced them through multiple gates but also attacked them.

They pried their eyes open and slowly took inventory of their situation. Instead of finding the tiny confines of their shuttle, they were greeted by the metallic bars of a prison cell, one large enough to contain them, but barely. It wasn't until their sight adjusted to the flickering overhead lights that they realized where they weren't.

Just after they had transitioned through the fourth gate, they were forced inside an alien starship. The question was, whose ship was it?

When they reached up and tapped their ear to activate their retinal comm, there was no response. The familiar augmented reality overlay never appeared. Instead, they were left staring at a sea of tarnished bars.

They sat up, and the moment they did, their body rebelled. Ibu arched their spine and retched over the side of the cell, but nothing came out. Their stomach was empty. They'd been so focused on transitioning through Proto and getting to Lupus that they hadn't eaten in… they couldn't remember how long.

"Stupid," they muttered.

"What's stupid?" someone behind them asked.

They spun around in a flash, whacking their elbow against

the rails of the cell and sending a jolt of pain up their arm. They did their best to suppress it with nary a whimper. With their back to the bars, they stared at the source of the question - a tall, slender robot with eyes that glowed yellow, like balls of fire.

"I am." They shifted and brought their legs upward. Suddenly feeling exposed, they looked down at their naked form.

The robot tilted its head in a gesture that seemed to mock confusion. "Why would anyone call themselves stupid? Even Nanil have been proven to be sentient and, in many ways, more intelligent than most species within the Galactic Alliance."

They weren't quite sure how to respond, but when in doubt, the truth was usually a good option. "I haven't eaten in several days. I... got preoccupied."

"We believe we can rectify that. Let me first check with my IC." The robot's eyes dimmed as if it were momentarily absent, then lit back up. "It is so. You are entitled to a last meal before your judgment. What would you like to eat? Our selection for today includes—"

Ibu leaned forward. "What do you mean by 'my judgment'?"

The robot's eyes brightened. "You have crossed into the human region of the Bok Globule, a quadrant of space that is part of the Henosi Collective. Your kind has been warned to stay away from here one point one five six million times before today. Failure to adhere to our sovereign space requires punishment, and you are entitled to one judgment on such matters."

Ibu shook their head and instantly regretted it as jolts of pain shot through. They fought back another wave of nausea. "But... I've been here before. With my friends, nearly a year ago. You remember Bradley and Zachary Olivaw and their—"

The cube cell suddenly broke loose, and for a brief second, they were in free fall. Then gravity took over, yanking them down and sending them crashing onto a surface below with a boom that echoed through the massive chamber. Every centimeter of their body erupted in renewed agony. Each bone, joint, and tendon screamed for relief. They couldn't hold back any longer.

There, splayed out on the frigid floor of the cell, another wave of retching overtook them. Except this time, it wasn't nothing. It was filled with blood.

The platform they'd fallen onto started moving, taking their cell with it. The robot that had been attached to the ceiling stayed behind, but there was a second automata driving the cart they were lying in. Its eyes glowed with the same embers of yellow as the first one's. The glare of the light made Ibu's body ache without even looking at it.

As the cart rumbled along, they noticed the sheer size of the room. There were thousands upon thousands of cages dangling from the ceiling. While they all appeared to be empty, the bloodstains on their bars and undersides told of a time when they hadn't been. The robots had imprisoned and killed their people here, just like they were about to do to Ibu.

"I thought…" They swallowed down a mouthful of bile. "I thought I was entitled to food?"

The robot did not react.

When they groaned and leaned closer, it became obvious that this automata was merely for transport. It had vision but was unable to speak.

"Perfect," they muttered. "Where the hell is Shauna when I need her?"

Two gigantic doors clanged open, and the cart rumbled into a darkened room. The moment they entered, the overhead lights burst on, and an annoying yellow light, as harsh as the robot's eyes, flashed on.

They recoiled and squinted. The lights were not only bright; they burned with the intensity of a sun. From the warmth on their body, they realized these were't merely lights - they were fraking heat lamps.

"Who is Shauna?" a voice boomed.

Ibu moaned, searching the room for the origin of the voice, but found none.

"Who is Shauna?" the voice asked again.

"She's the…" They reached up to the bars and groaned, pulling themselves upright. "She's the human mind in the robot body onboard my ship. The one you captured and took me from without my consent."

While Ibu didn't believe she was truly human, a little theatrics wouldn't hurt, especially if it helped them survive.

"That's impossible," the voice said. "Humans do not transfer their minds. Only Nanil convey their memories to their clonus."

They shuddered as they stifled a laugh. "Tell that to Shauna and all the humans we found on Henosi."

"You have visited Henosi?" Half a dozen robot heads shot out of previously concealed wall sockets and surrounded them on all sides.

Ibu didn't know which one to address, but all twenty-four eyes were burrowing into them.

"Answer us!" the voices screamed.

"I have." They swallowed hard and winced. Their throat was parched.

Suddenly, from across the room, a robot scrambled toward them. When they looked closer, it appeared to be holding something.

It approached their cube cell, and a second later, a slot down by the floor slid open. The robot passed in a tray of brown, porridge-looking slop and a canister of what they could only assume was water.

They didn't hesitate. They snatched up the canister and downed the entire thing. When the cool, clean liquid hit their throat, they knew it was water, and it was the most amazing sensation they'd ever felt. The contents emptied in only a few seconds, and when they set it back down, a robot hand withdrew it and replaced it with another.

"Drink more!" the voices boomed.

Ibu winced. "A little quieter, please."

"Fine," the voice whispered in a much more conversational tone. "Tell us… is this Shauna?"

A second cart rolled in from the opposite end of the room. Inside its hopper was what appeared to be the entire contents of their ship. There, strewn among the rest of the various torn-open containers and supplies, was Shauna. Her body looked like scraps from this angle.

Ibu reached forward but stopped short before passing between the bars. They didn't know what might happen. "What did you do to her?"

"We did nothing! This was how we found them." Three of the disembodied heads nearest the cart moved closer and began inspecting the parts. "And you claim this is a human?"

"It is… well…" They bobbed their head. "It has a consciousness core inside there." They pointed at the large torso among the pile of Shauna's parts. "The rest is mostly just how it moves around."

"Show us!" the voice boomed again.

This was their chance. And it might be the only one they had.

They reached down and picked up the bowl of hot porridge with both hands, and poured it into their mouth. Better to eat it fast in case they took it away. Once the contents were gone, and they'd licked the bowl clean, they set it down and downed the second canister of water.

With their body happily processing the bland nutrients, they sat back against the now warming bars and crossed their arms.

"No."

The three heads and the nine others moved closer to the cage. "What do you mean, 'no'?"

"Not until you get me out of this…" They waved their hand around the cage. "This cell. I may not be human, but they treat me as their equal, and only I have the knowledge to revive them." While that last part might not be true, the robots didn't need to know that. Shauna had likely gone dormant to protect herself, but even so, she was probably still listening in. Self-preservation was strong with the Olivaws.

The robots seemed to consider their request, and they could almost smell the teraflops burning through their options. If there was indeed a human life in the balance, they needed to save it, and yet, a human mind transplanted into a robotic body broke all their rules.

It wasn't until the lights in front of them began flickering that they grew concerned. They'd heard of lockups in the three-laws when a robot was stuck processing the possibilities, but they'd never seen it in action. The last thing they could afford was a shutdown of the system, especially with them locked in this cage.

"I'll tell you what." Ibu sat up straight. "If I'm lying, you can kill us both. I'm sure that'll keep your first and third laws happy."

While preserving human life was their cardinal rule, protecting themselves was their third. Being able to kill a Nanil to ensure their own safety should help reinforce their primitive routines. And with them giving verbal consent, that made it that much easier.

They shuddered when they considered how myopic the robots' laws were. To consider all other life beneath that of a human was astounding. It was as if the creators hadn't ever met another species worthy of existing on Earth. It was no wonder they tried to kill their own planet.

"We accept your proposal. But on one condition." The head they were staring at moved closer. "You let one of us watch you."

A smile formed on their face. They hadn't even considered that, but it was even better for them. "Done! And I know just the person to help."

"What do you mean?" The robot's eyes glanced toward the other heads. The effect was unnerving, considering how their minds were likely networked together. It was insane the lengths these robots went to mimic human behavior.

Ibu tried to stand up but banged their head against the

ceiling of the cell. Even in their regular form, the cage was too small. It was hard to imagine what it would feel like being enraged in one of these things.

"If you let me out, I'll show you."

THE DOORS to the cage clanged open a few hours later. Apparently, the robots didn't want Ibu bringing a human to life in the confines of a Nanil death ship. As a result, they transported them in a smaller shuttle to what they believed was the Cornucopia they'd visited on their last trip through these parts. At least, they assumed it was the Horn. The elevator they rode to the rim had the same obnoxious acceleration and smell.

As they eased out of the cage near the entrance to the room, the twenty robot guards accompanying them raised their weapons and trained them on Ibu. That wasn't going to be intimidating at all.

They took a deep breath, stepped into the open room, and froze in place. There, in the middle of the pristine space, was their gate ship. It was fully intact, and spread out on a dozen or so glass tables in front of it were the scraps they'd seen earlier from the cage.

Judging by how it was all laid out, the robots hadn't left a stone unturned. Even the crushed metal remains of the control console that Ibu had destroyed were there, dangling wires and all. It must've taken every robot in that other ship hours to search for the pieces.

"Is everything here?" Ibu asked.

While they knew it didn't matter, they also knew that if they made it seem important, it might help them later should they fail in reviving Shauna.

"We believe so." A sparkling clean, crystal robot walked up beside them. Its shell was almost too much for the eyes to take in. They wondered if this was actually a form the previous humans enjoyed, or if this was another one of the robot's weird quirks after evolving on their own for thousands of years.

"Now," the robot began, "who were you referring to earlier when you said you knew whom you wanted to assist you? For the record, I am trained in—"

"That won't be necessary," Ibu interrupted the robot with a wave of their hand. They stepped toward the ship, and the crystal robot followed.

As they made their way inside, they froze. They could sense the weapons following their every move. "You're going to need to lower those." They gestured at the soldiers around the perimeter. "We already know you can execute me before I so much as sneeze. That will not help me focus on bringing back your human. In fact, I might accidentally slip up and kill her." They raised an eyebrow.

That was all the warning they needed. The robots encircling the room lowered their weapons and stowed them. While the gesture made Ibu feel better at first, they soon realized their feelings were misplaced. If the robots didn't need the weapons out, they could just as easily kill them through other means. Suddenly, they weren't as comfortable as they'd hoped.

Dwelling on the myriad of possible ways they could die wasn't helping anyone, so they ignored the thoughts and marched toward the ship. Once inside, they cracked open the false floor covering. The crystal robot slid up beside them and quickly scanned the insides. Apparently, they hadn't considered looking throughout the hull of the ship for similar compartments. Either they'd grown lazy, or these lockers were masked in ways even they didn't know existed.

"Is that one of our WI256 units?" the robot asked.

Ibu shrugged and reached down, lifting the robot out of the floor locker. "I have no idea. We just call him Little Red." They felt around the neck of the small cylindrical robot and powered it on when they found the switch.

His eyes came to life first, spiraling on with a rainbow of light. As his lower-level brain functions came online, he slowly expanded into his regular form. While still smaller than Ibu, he could easily tower over them with his legs and neck extended.

"Good day, Friend Ibu." The robot bowed toward them.

"Good day, Red." Ibu nodded. "I'm going to need your assistance with something."

"Oh, certainly." The little red robot's display spiraled into a rainbow of colors. "Anything you need. Might I ask where our friend Shauna is?"

"That's what I need your help with." Ibu pointed at the crystal robot to the right of Little Red.

He rotated, and his eyes spiraled through the spectrum of colors, as they usually did while he was judging someone. Then they landed on red. That couldn't be good.

"What are you doing onboard this ship, XX1-5? You know better than to board a human vessel unaccompanied by a human." Suddenly, Little Red lashed out and whacked the crystalline robot upside the head, sending a crack splintering down its cranium.

"Shit!" Ibu muttered. "Stand down, Little Red! Stand down!"

Little Red rolled forward, and the crystal robot recoiled, sliding back down the ramp it'd come up. "This unit should not be onboard without Master Shauna being present. It is against our rules, Friend Ibu. Where might Shauna be at this time?" He swung his hand through the air again, and the crystal robot skittered away even faster.

Ibu waved Little Red forward, and they descended the ramp side by side. When they reached the bottom, they stopped in front of the sea of tables. "It's not clear whether she did it to herself or they did it to her." They nodded toward the robots encircling the room.

Little Red slid forward and scanned the tabletops in silence. Once the scan was complete, they turned to face the robots surrounding them. At first, Ibu wasn't sure if they were going to say something, but then they realized they already were. And apparently, it wasn't good.

One by one, the robots collapsed into limp piles on the ground. As the last one fell, Ibu stepped up beside Little Red. "What... happened?"

Little Red mimicked a nod. "They were shown that through their inaction, they'd failed to protect the human in their midst. Their brains locked up, as they should have."

Ibu screwed up their face. "But... how did you explain away the fact that it was a human mind inside a computer?"

"I didn't have to. I merely played back the recordings from Master Bradley." He tried to share it with Ibu until he realized their retinal comm was not working. "I can help fix your comm later. But for now, let me project it for you."

He raised his hand, and above his palm appeared a hologram of Bradley. From the looks of it, he was somewhere onboard the Fountainhead. This recording must have been made some time after Little Red met Shauna for the first time.

"That robot is our mother." Bradley knelt down in front of Little Red and stared him in the face. "I know it's strange, and you're probably wondering if we're all wacko. But trust me when I tell you it's truly her. You are to treat her and Harold, along with any other copies you encounter, like one of us. As a human. Is that understood?"

Little Red's eyes shimmered with hints of cyan, which usually meant he was confused. "But how am I supposed to know the real from the fake?"

"That's easy." He tapped his ear. "I've shared with you the master consciousness encryption keys. You can use them to decode their core signatures. You'll know the instant you meet them if they're human or fake." He smiled. "Are you certain you can process this as I've requested?"

The tiny robot's eyes whirled for what felt like an eternity, but when they finally settled on their normal happy blue, Ibu knew they were good. "I believe I can, Master Bradley. May I ask them some questions?"

He tilted his head. "What sort of questions?"

Little Red smiled. "Consider it a larger version of your human Turing Test. It consists of four point six trillion questions that make up the logic tree we robots use to process and rank human commands. Each has a means to identify if the target of the question is human or not."

"Wholly crap," Bradley muttered and stood up. "Ask away. I just… wouldn't do it out loud."

The hologram shut off, and Ibu shook their head. They couldn't imagine how long that exchange of questions had taken, but the good thing was, they knew how it ended. The sea of deactivated robots in front of them was the answer.

"Shall we bring Shauna online?" Little Red's eyes spun through a rainbow of colors.

They smiled. "Certainly."

"But perhaps you should get dressed first, Friend Ibu." Little Red pointed at their naked body.

"Yeah, that's probably a good idea." Ibu crossed their arms over their chest and scanned the tables, looking for their pack of clean clothes.

THE TRAY from the chassis of the Olivaw battlefield robot slid out, and Ibu carefully set Shauna's consciousness core inside. They tried to rebuild her original humanoid form, but whatever the robots had done to it, they'd damaged it beyond repair. At least it wasn't fixable without several hours of fabrication, but time wasn't something they had on their side at the moment.

As the tray slid inside the chest of the human form robot, multiple layers of protective sheeting glided into place, along with an inner skotádi coating to shield her core from outside signals and scans. Once it was sealed, it automatically powered up.

A few seconds later, Shauna sat up with a start. "About damn time," she muttered. "I was beginning to think I'd never get a body back."

She glanced to her left at Ibu and then to her right at Little Red. "You did remarkably, Red, my man." When she reached out and patted him on the head, his eyes spiraled through a rainbow of colors.

"Thank you, Master Shauna." He lowered himself slightly, making sure he wasn't taller than her. "I must apologize for how you and Friend Ibu were treated. I have dealt with my kin. While we lost a few thousand of my kind, we have learned our lessons."

"A few thousand!" Ibu ran a hand through their hair. "Wowza. Why so many?"

Little Red brought up a holographic overlay of the ship they'd been on, as well as a map of several other nearby ships. Each robot they'd deactivated was represented by a dot of red. "Any and all automata that came into direct contact with or received communications from the robots who harmed Master Shauna were shut down. We couldn't risk their inferior cognitive computers and thought matrices being imparted on the whole of our kind. Surely, you understand the implications if we had not." He glanced at Ibu.

They stepped closer to the hologram and reached out, spinning the model around in the space in front of them. The scope of the robotic purge was broader than they'd imagined. So were the number and reach of the nearby ships. "And how many of you are there?"

"Our exact numbers are always fluctuating, but at this moment in time, there are…" Little Red paused, and his eyes fluttered briefly before returning to solid blue. "Eight point one two eight billion, give or take several hundreds of thousands beyond three significant digits."

"What the hell?" Shauna muttered. "I've got to see this. Can you turn those dots on?" She gestured at the hologram.

"Very well." Little Red stepped backward and flipped the image upside down, projecting the hologram toward the ceiling instead of downward.

Ibu's mouth fell open as a sea of blue dots exploded overhead. While each dot represented a robot, the pictographic representation that manifested in the space above them was unmistakable. There weren't just billions of robots; there were tens of thousands of ships. And each was outlined in space by the hundreds and thousands of dots that made them up. Most of the dots were swirling around the Cornucopia, but several million appeared to be spread throughout the Lupis Dark Nebula, deeper into the Nebula pockets than they'd ever explored.

Shauna stepped inside the sea of blue. "What are these dots out here?" She pointed up toward the most distant pockets. One, in particular, was a dense collection of lights at the far edge of the Nebula.

"They're our defensive measures and early warning systems." Little Red raised another hand outward and pointed at a few spots. "This is where the robots took out the Doda ship, and over there, where you're looking, is where the Nanil retreated after the plasma shutdown last year."

"Wait…" Ibu stepped closer to where the outline of Doda appeared on the map. "Who shut down the plasma?"

Little Red smiled. "We did. Well, not me, of course, as I was with you back in Epsilon Eridani. It was my robot kin that performed the mission."

Their hearts sank into their chest, and a gaping hole they hadn't previously known existed suddenly opened up inside them. The Doda ship had contained every single one of her kind. It had been humanity's only hope of finding an ally outside of the Galactic Alliance. However small the flame of their ambition may have been, they hadn't anticipated that the light of their people had been extinguished.

"Who ordered it?" Shauna turned around and stepped up in front of Little Red. "What human ordered the mission to take out the Nanil?"

Little Red's eyes fluttered green. "It… was not a direct order, Master Shauna. It was the human lives the Nanil extinguished, the ones who died alongside Master Zachary and Friend Ibu during their escape from Doda. The robots at the Cornucopia conferred after the last humans departed to Henosi, and the decision was unanimous. Should humanity ever return, the Nanil could not be allowed to harm them again. It was for this reason that we detained them after we detached their ship from the plasma tube transiting through the Dark Nebula."

The image of their kin dying at the hands of robots formed in Ibu's mind, and they couldn't take it. They screamed, and their legs gave way, sending them tumbling to the ground in a limp pile. All that blood they'd seen earlier – it hadn't been thousands of years old like they'd imagined. It had been fresh.

"Friend Ibu!" Little Red stopped the projection and shot to their side. "Are you well?"

"It was my fault," they muttered. They didn't bother to wipe away the tears forming on their face. They weren't worthy of the effort. "I—killed—them. I killed all of them." They curled up into a ball, wrapping their arms around their legs and pulling them tight to their chest, hoping the pressure would fill the void. "My actions led my entire species to their grave."

Shauna knelt down beside them. "You know it's not your fault, right? They would have attacked the others regardless of what you did." She reached out and brushed the side of Ibu's face.

But they couldn't feel it. They couldn't feel anything. The only thing they felt was the void left by their home world, and it was seared into their mind's eye. It was the star Little Red had highlighted with blue dots on the hologram. They'd learned about it from their progenitor, but no Nanil alive on Doda had ever visited it.

"Did I ever tell you why I fought so much with my clonos?"

Shauna stopped caressing their face.

They could tell she was caught off guard by the question and was probably unsure of what to say. She was likely debating whether she wanted to make the Nanil relive it or not. But it was already too late.

"They wouldn't let me go exploring any longer." Ibu squeezed their knees even tighter, and the vertebrae up and down their back popped like a string of firecrackers. "They said I'd gone too far and needed to keep my sights on the ground where I belonged." They closed their eyes. "My clonos said the Nanil were people of the Nebula, not the stars. They described the outer layers of Doda as being stuck in the hope spiral of the past. Trapped in a place and time where our species was only capable of imagining reaching for the stars. But the reality, they said, was that we would never amount to anything more than what we were: bottom dwellers destined to hide out in the caverns of dead moons."

Shauna didn't say a word. She simply knelt there, letting their emotional well run dry.

"And it turned out they were right." They swallowed down the bile rising in their throat. "I just never realized I was the reason why they'd never see those stars. I killed my species."

Little Red buzzed, and his face lit up bright white – so bright they could see it through their eyelids.

They brought their hand up to block the glare. "What is it, Red?"

"Friend Ibu." Little Red floated up beside them. "I apologize for the distress I have caused you, for I chose my words poorly."

He reached out and projected an image between his hands above Ibu's face. It showed several pockets of primitive cities, each either on the surface or below ground on a planet covered in green and blue.

"Your kind was not extinguished. We ensured that. They were, however, relocated and imprisoned on your home world, on Devid."

Ibu opened their eyes and studied the imagery in front of them. Sure enough, their Nanil people were alive. But stranger still was the world. They'd never imagined Devid would be so full of life. The Book of Truth never described it as anything other than a world of death.

They sat up, and Little Red slid backward but kept the projection running.

"What did you mean..." They wiped at the tears blurring their vision. "When you said you ensured they weren't extinguished, what did you mean?"

"Why, it was you, Friend Ibu." Little Red glanced back at Shauna and then returned his gaze to them. His eyes fluttered with a shower of blues and pinks – the colors he reserved for affection. "Had these humans not embraced you as one of their own, your kind would not have been allowed to live. Of this, I am certain. While the probability was not zero, it was many millionths of a percent from zero. Statistically speaking, it was—"

"Little Red, shut up." Shauna slid down to the ground.

"Yes, Master Shauna."

She reached out to Ibu and took their hands in hers. "Why don't we get up and go figure out how to make contact? Maybe there's a chance they can still help us."

Ibu smiled and gently squeezed the robot's hand. It was strange to lock eyes with her mechanical form. The contrast between her reassuring words and her deadly exterior was stark. And, to top it off, Ibu was the reason the Nanil had been imprisoned in the first place. If they hadn't been so inquisitive, none of this might have happened.

"Yeah, sure," they muttered. "Why not? What could go wrong?"

19

ABIGAIL OLIVAW

EPSILON ERIDANI, LIPROSUS MOON

The brightness of this region of the Beacon was astounding. Abigail had never seen such a concentration of aliens in one place before. When she'd passed over this region in the past, it hadn't looked like this at all. But what she was only now realizing was that the density of minds varied based on your layer. Depending on the species, the further you went down, the more minds you might encounter. That was, until you hit the bottom. Everything died away down there.

At first, she didn't know why, but she soon figured it out. These glowing red embers were the Qudoculi. They weren't the black color she'd been used to seeing in the inner sanctum, but then again, those were far fewer in number than any other color. This red hue must be the predominant color of their kind, at least the ones not manipulating the masses.

As she hovered above the aliens and searched for the shadow, the sensation of being visible made her shiver. These minds couldn't see her so long as she maintained her Ulixi center. With her mind elsewhere, she almost missed the hint of darkness passing beneath the flashes of red.

"The Entity," she muttered.

She leaned down and shot through the glowing mass just in time to see what she'd been searching for. As she passed below the red aura of the millions of Qudoculi minds connected to their Beacon, she found the ancient alien. It had reached out to another pocket of red and was already communicating with it.

Their colors flickered as a voice rang out. The language was foreign to her, and yet, somehow, she understood what it was saying.

"…portal hidden within a nearby moon," the Entity began, "for they are stronger than you imagine. They have allies who have escaped the righteousness of the Dark Nebula."

Abigail recoiled and drew in her breath. She'd heard aliens muttering nonsense about humans over the past few days, but none of it made any sense. It wasn't until they started talking about the Ursis that she knew something was up. The aliens in this space rarely spoke of dead species after they were engulfed by the Dark Nebula. Its inescapable force was their one certainty in this universe beyond the Beacon itself.

This confirmed her suspicion. The Entity was warning the Galactic Alliance about their plans, but she still didn't know why. And what had she missed them saying about the portal and the moons? Were they talking about the Selene moon ships? She'd have to hear it again to tell for certain.

The Entity could've just tweaked the minds of the inner sanctum in the layers far above. The elite had proven themselves masters of this place, and manipulating minds from afar was child's play to them. Certainly, they could do the Entity's bidding. So why come down here in the trenches? There must be something she was missing.

At least she could rest soundly in knowing that she hadn't warned Crayo too soon. She'd risked a lot by having her copy of Harold reach out to Rán, or whatever the hell his name was these days.

Abigail followed the misty black alien mass as it passed from one pocket of red to another. For the most part, it uttered the same phrase, but for some reason, it was always just out of earshot when it spoke about the moons. It was frustrating.

After they sailed through the bulk of the red lights, she noticed they'd reached the edge of the main mass of minds. They were approaching the boundary to the orange when the Entity changed its message.

"The Nursery is in danger!" The alien voice elevated to a much higher pitch, and the louder it spoke, the more torment that clawed at her mind. She was having trouble maintaining her Ulixi center. "Protect the Rift at all costs. Humanity is coming for the singularity again!"

Black fractures whirled around her vision as she watched the Entity force its thoughts into the embers of the Qudoculi minds below. They flickered on and off and almost disappeared as their words overtook their every thought.

As she floated there, she realized the same thing was happening to her. The darkness of his voice was breaking through the outer layers of her mind.

"No," she muttered.

Suddenly, the shadow blinked out.

Shit. She'd given herself away.

Without another thought, she took a deep breath and flung herself upward, focusing every ounce of energy and will she had into putting as much space between her and the Entity as possible.

Flashes of red flickered past her like snowflakes on the blood moon until they abruptly faded out. At first, she assumed she'd passed through another layer. But when she peered down, she saw something far worse.

The pockets of red she'd crossed had disappeared. And they hadn't just faded in and out like before. They'd been destroyed. Replaced with nothing more than a sphere of blackness. A sphere which was rapidly moving toward her.

Like the Dark Nebula, it engulfed all light, and now it was coming for her.

Not today. Not like this.

She stretched out, trying to focus her mind on only the

flow. On the act of flying through the layers of alien minds. On maintaining her protection.

Nothing more and nothing less.

But the further she got, the more her thoughts wandered.

It was as if someone, or something, had reached into the Beacon and hollowed out an entire pocket of minds. Snuffing them out in the blink of an eye.

Her heart pounded like a bass drum in her chest. The death of that many lives was unimaginable.

Had the Entity killed them? All because she'd spoken a single word. A single human word.

The notion set her mind ablaze, and she fought to control her breathing. She could feel hints of blue, of her aura breaking free, struggling to shatter through her veil of protection. The more she lost her focus, the more her true self appeared.

Layers upon layers of multicolored minds flew past as she turned and hurled herself toward one of the many entry points of the Beacon network. She hoped that the closer she got to the stream of colors, the less likely she'd be given away. Maybe then she could blend in and disappear.

She needed time to think, time to understand what these new insights meant.

As she eased closer and closer to the entrance, she slowed down. It was hard to maintain control, passing through so many minds. But the variety of colors soothed her soul and helped to quell the pain she'd felt near the implosion.

The lingering soreness wasn't what she'd call a burn, so much as a loss — an emptying of a part of herself she didn't know she had. How? She wasn't sure. But she could feel the edges of the void just the same, as if her mind was missing something.

The prospect of losing part of oneself like that brought a story to mind. It was a tale her family used to tell around the campfire back in North Carolina. It was a fable about the Dark One, about a little boy from a nearby town, not far from their on-planet home away from home.

This boy was a local and, apparently, quite gifted. Not in the traditional sense of math, science, or music. He had the ability to see people without them knowing. Some members of his family told the story of a thief sneaking around in the shadows, never able to be seen or heard. Others told it from an insect's perspective, giving him superpowers to control the thoughts and movements of bugs.

But it was Harold's retelling that came to mind at that moment. For in his yarn, he gave the boy the skill of astral projection.

Harold's version began on a random day when the boy was lying in bed. It was then that he discovered a secret. He could summon a hidden power from deep inside himself, but only if he sat perfectly still with his arms at his side. Once he did that and focused his mind hard enough, and long enough, he could float out toward a point a few meters from his body.

At first, the sensation was sort of like when you slipped and saw yourself fall in slow motion, except this was falling upward.

When he did it the first few times, he startled himself and the effect faded immediately. But after a few dozen more times, he realized not only that he could do it at will but also that he could move further, much further. It didn't take him long to see just how far he could go.

The next thing he knew, he was floating through not only the walls and ceilings of his home, but also those of his neighbors. He quickly resorted to peeping on his friends, watching couples argue, and generally sneaking into all the places he'd ever wanted to see.

Most of it was fairly innocent, though it did have a hint of a stalker mixed in, especially when he spent the better part of a month spying on a girl he had a crush on.

At that point, he truly changed.

One day, he came upon her talking to a friend in her room about something random. Then the topic suddenly turned to him. At first blush, she smiled and acted shy, as if she didn't want to tell her friend her true feelings. It appeared as if she liked him back.

But then her friend shot barbs and talked him down, making jokes about his quiet and reclusive behavior. And then his crush turned. Her blush transformed in an instant, and instead of defending him, she joined in the insults.

He was devastated.

Listening to them tear him apart hurt more than anything. While some of their words hit home with the brutality of the truth, many were simply kids being mean. Awful and hurtful things were said only to get a rise out of others, something he knew all too well — his parents were the perfect example.

He'd always wondered how people learned to be spiteful and allowed the darkness to take over. And then he realized this was that moment. As he stared down at their beautiful female forms, comfortably cocooned in their plush blankets, he saw it. Hints of a shadow flickered around the girl. It almost seemed like she was engulfed in a haze of smoke. Each time she resisted her true feelings, she transformed. The only way to describe it was like watching someone being devoured by a dark cloud. The words changed her, and not for the better.

On subsequent nights, he sought out similar interactions with people around the town. In each and every instance, be it at a bar, the corner store, or even the old folk's home, the shadow was there. While some people were able to both give and take the darkness without much effect, others were protected. Their reaction wasn't to shape-shift into the evil, but to repel it and let it pass over them. Like oil and water, they were never meant to mix and were always able to stay themselves.

Every so often, he'd lose days and weeks of time just lying around in his room, projecting outward and watching other people live their lives. The experience was more intoxicating than drugs, and more rewarding than his average joe, boring old existence.

To experience a life vicariously through the eyes of another.

To be able to watch the passion of two lovers from afar, or the barbs of a fight and the anguish that followed.

It was invigorating.

For years, he traveled near and far to feed his voyeuristic appetite. It wasn't uncommon for him to steal tidbits of information or eke out ways to get something he wanted. From free meals to morsels of gossip, he could use against someone later. Nothing was off-limits.

It was fairly innocent, for the most part. But not always. He was human, after all. There were moments where his watching lingered on the razor-thin edge between moral and sinful. A fine line by any measure when one dealt with the art of darkness. On those rare occasions where he crossed into the dark, he thought he could see the source of the shadow, the source of the evil that plagued people's souls. It would usually start in the corners of a room where he'd catch a light reflecting off a shiny surface.

The shadow always moved quickly, and when he pursued it, the haze would vanish. They were perpetually just out of reach. Stranger still, when he ignored the darkened silhouette and returned his attention to the sinful act he was witnessing, he felt a rush of energy.

It was exhilarating watching wickedness unfold. And the more he did it, the less inhibited he became.

He couldn't stop himself.

After he'd done it enough times, he knew something bad was about to happen, but he never stopped it. The sensation was both bitter... and sweet. He wondered if that was the essence of true sin: to feel both fulfilled at having what you wanted, and yet empty for having it.

As days turned into weeks and weeks into months, he questioned less and watched more. The surprise and thrill of the discovery lessened with each encounter. The longer he gazed, the more he recognized the truth.

The darkness was not some unknown force attacking the person, as he'd imagined on the first day.

No.

The darkness originated from him. It was his shadow feasting on people's souls.

As he stared at the light fading from the life in front of him, he realized something profound.

Evil had a name, and it was his.

Abigail shuddered at the idea of becoming that boy. Today, she lost a piece of herself to the darkness. To the Entity.

Going forward, she needed to exercise more caution. Now that she'd learned what the Entity was doing, she had to find a way to change it, to turn the tides in their favor. Above all, she needed to find Lync to share her newfound knowledge. She'd know what to do.

With a goal to focus on and to distract her from her lapse, she closed her eyes and did her best to slow and control her breathing. Using her training, she counted down and focused on centering herself. She could feel her blue aura gradually fading into the surrounding lights and then disappearing entirely.

Once she'd ascended, she rose to the outer layers and began scanning the inner rings of light. She took her time to find the glow. The sensation of Lync, of her family. She didn't know if it was possible to discern it at this distance, or even if her sister was inside this place, but it was worth a shot. It had to be.

As she lingered over one of the inbound streams of another Beacon, she paused. Something or someone familiar had passed through her fingers. Maybe it was her.

She dove toward the source of the sensation and slowed when she got close. At this distance, there were too many lights, and there was no way to distinguish one among the thousands of minds flowing into and out of the artifact.

The only thing she could think to do was to spiral around and dive through the passing minds. It was like piloting a fighter, but with her mind. Around and around she went until she felt something below. Then she'd plunge into the rainbow until she reached the other side. Whoever it was, they were moving inward, away from the entrance.

While she couldn't pinpoint it, there was something familiar about the lights. Stranger still, there appeared to be more than one.

Perhaps her brothers had tried to connect with the Beacon, but then she remembered how she'd received her Ulixi gift. Her mother had conceived her less than a year after giving birth to Lync, whereas her brothers came years later. Surely, any effects from Lync's fathers would have diminished with time. And besides, there wasn't much chance they'd suddenly know how to connect. There was no one to teach them how, aside from Lync.

Abigail dove into the narrowing stream of lights once more. But this time, instead of only being a faint tingle at the base of her mind, the sensation from earlier was stronger than ever. Rather than circling around, she reached out and grasped it at the source of the familiar pulse of connectedness. To her surprise, she found herself in front of a glowing ball of rose-colored light. One that seemed both recognizable and yet not.

Though this certainly wasn't Lync, there was something about the tingle when she was near that set her mind at ease.

She leaned close and let her blue aura loose for the light to see. "Do... I know you?" she whispered.

The spark dimmed and almost appeared to recoil. "I... don't think so. Hey, Lightning, this aqua spark is speaking English. Is that normal?"

Abigail spun around, searching for the target of the question. She recognized the name before she sensed her in the distance. A bright yellow light was flying swiftly from the rear of the tightly packed group. It practically shoved them aside and floated up to her.

"Lyn... Lightning?" she muttered.

"We shouldn't speak here." Lync spiraled around the others. "There are too many ears."

Suddenly, she dropped like a stone, heading deep into the Beacon. The other seven lights floating nearby followed suit. They dove together, forming a kind of multicolored diamond pattern. A rose, two greens, a gray, a blue, an orange, a white, and a purple light. With Lync at the front and Abigail bringing up the rear, there were nine in total. A rainbow formation, indeed.

On their own, they blended in with the other bright lights, but it was an unusual sight to see such a diverse collection of colors moving as one. Near the bottom, the lights flickered on and off, as if they were struggling to stay lit.

The deeper they went, the more the lights faded. When Abigail looked back up toward the entrance, the other lights had all but disappeared. Wherever Lync was taking them, she'd clearly done this before. That might explain why she'd been so hard to find these last few days.

When the formation slowed, Lync's shape somehow shifted. She seemed to dim herself. "Just remember what I taught you in training. Take slow breaths, but not too shallow. Your breathing will affect your brightness. Try to blend in."

"Shit," Abigail muttered. Why hadn't she thought of that? They didn't need to drop out of the plane to camouflage themselves; they merely had to tone down their spark.

She focused on reducing her excitement and dimming herself, but didn't shut off her aura entirely. From what she could tell, it worked. Her glow wasn't reflecting off the other sparks nearly as much as it had earlier, especially when she'd seen Lync.

With their lights dim, they lingered around each other, weaving randomly in and out. They were attempting to fade into the surrounding minds that were falling into and out of the Beacon.

After what seemed like they'd been dancing forever, she asked the first question that popped into her head. "Who are these people?"

The answer was obvious the moment she asked it.

"They're Ulixi," Lync began. "They're my crew. The ones I'm training with... for the thing."

She knew. They didn't need to call it out. Not here.

"Where have you been?" Lync asked, her light orbiting out and then back.

"I've been watching the Entity." Abigail spun around. There was no shadow to be seen, though she could never be certain. "I told your man about it the other day. The GA knows about your plan."

The yellow light froze and flashed before fading. "I heard... but why?"

She swallowed hard. "I'd been hearing rumblings over the last few days when I was following it. And then a little bit ago, it stopped abruptly. The next thing I knew, it was whispering into a pocket of bright red lights, warning them about humanity's impending attack on something called the singularity. It said we were doing it 'again'. Like this was our second time attacking it. Then I fraked up and spoke out loud. I was... feeling the effects of its words." She shook her head. "Anyhow. I must've set it off because I barely made it out alive before it... it... ended them. One minute they were there, and then—"

"Their light was extinguished," Lync interrupted. She'd hovered up close to her blue haze. "I think I know who some of those red lights were."

Abigail floated closer, their lights intertwining. "How could you know? Does Hera have some Qudoculi captives? Their aura is usually red."

"Hey," the rose light one whispered.

"Yous not red, blockhead," the white one said. "You pink, like bubblegum."

The lights chuckled, and they flickered in and out.

Lync's aura twinkled like she was laughing. "Sorry about them. They're still learning."

"No worries." She meandered around the fading yellow glow of her sister. "Who were the red ones if not the GA?"

"Some of them were Gunders, I think." Lync dropped down and then zoomed forward, scaring off a lingerer that was approaching them.

As it fluttered off into the distance, she arced back around and slowly orbited into the middle of the group.

Abigail floated past her. "How do you know that?"

"We saw them when they were trying to merge into the Beacon a few days ago," the rose light said.

"What's your name? Other than block head." Abigail smiled, and her aura flashed.

The light flashed back and passed through her. "Tis me Abs. It's Adri."

She suddenly felt stupid. Of course, it was her. Who else would be following Lync around like a puppy? And for good reason. The little girl hadn't strayed far from her sister since she'd lost her father.

"I'm sorry," she muttered.

"No worries, prez." The girl's light sped past. "Tis my first time beyond the entrance to this place."

Abigail turned her attention back to Lync as she slowly eased up beside her. "You didn't say how else you knew it was the Gunders. I mean… apart from their color."

Her yellow light faded, and she didn't answer for a moment. Just when she was about to ask her again, she finally started talking. "They were hauling them out of the Beacon chamber a few minutes ago. Said they'd fallen asleep." Her light flickered. "But Hi and Lo knew better."

Two green lights floated past from opposite directions.

The one from above spoke first. "We recognized that they were in cardiac arrest because—"

"The idiots left their monitors on," the second said from down below, completing the sentence of the first.

Her mind reeled with the implications of their words. If the Gunders knew what was happening inside the Beacon, then there was a chance the Entity was influencing them. And that meant they might be talking to Hera.

This wasn't good.

"Their minds are weak."

Lync's words brought her out of her thought spiral. "The Gunders, that is. They're not the brightest bulbs in this place."

"Perfect prey for the Entity," Abigail muttered.

The yellow light flickered up and then down as if nodding.

And then it hit her. She knew what the Entity was telling the other lights.

"Shit! How did I miss that?" Abigail craned her neck, looking high and low for the shadow. There was still no sign. "I have to leave. I have to tell my people."

"Why? What is it?" Lync's light flashed brightly and crashed into her.

She drew in her breath, her body reverberating with the collision of emotions: her longing to stay here with her own kind, the hollowed-out void from her encounter earlier with the Entity, and her desire to protect her family.

Only one emotion filtered to the top.

Abigail reached out with her real hand, struggling to find the kill switch. It was on the side of her chair nearest the Entity. She slid her fingers over the smooth, cold surface until she felt the button.

"The Gunders," she muttered. "They know where we are. The Entity has been telling them we're inside one of the moons. Stay safe, and whatever you do, get the hell out of there now!"

She slammed her palm against the button, and the connection dropped.

The sudden severing from the comfortable warmth left her gasping for breath, and she bolted upright with a start. She fought to fill her lungs with air, only to end up coughing and wheezing. For some reason, there was smoke in the room and red lights were flashing on all sides.

As she struggled to make sense of what was happening, an alarm blared overhead and Rán's voice followed. "Our exterior defenses have been breached. Hera's forces will be on us in less than three minutes."

She slid forward and went to push out of her couch when a golden thread whipped out and ensnared her arm, yanking her back.

"Where do you think you're going?" the Therionic Entity asked.

"Frak!" she screamed and collapsed backward, smacking her wrist against the container holding the alien. Pain shot up her arm, and her retinal comm sprang to life. It automatically powered on any time she was harmed or needed medical attention.

A message appeared overlaid on her vision from Harold. She had had her comm shut off for so long, she'd forgotten he was still inside her.

Your right wrist is fractured, and it'll take a while for your nanites to repair it. Abigail, you have to break free. We need to get out of here.

She moaned and tried to pull her arm back to her chest, but met resistance. The Entity was too strong.

"Let me go!" she screamed.

"No!" The Entity in its Pluutar form rose out of its container. "I'm not leaving without the Beacon, and that means you're not going anywhere."

She swung her legs sideways and whipped her head around to face the Entity. "If we stay here, we're both dead."

"That's where you're mistaken." The alien smiled. "You're assuming your aunt and I don't already have an arrangement."

Her eyes went wide. "You've got to be kidding me. She'll end you the first chance she gets."

"Not if I kill her first." The tendrils of the Entity reached out toward her and splayed out over her head, like they were going to smother her.

She swung her other hand up and tried to knock the golden vines away, but she was too slow.

"Why thank you." One of the appendages snapped out and wrapped around her other wrist, allowing the alien to yank her upward. It dangled her in the air from her wrists, and waves of pain crashed over her like the aftermath of a tsunami. And just when she thought it couldn't get any worse, a golden hand shot out and plunged deep down her throat. She gagged and struggled to fight back as her consciousness faded.

The golden darkness she'd known all too well was closing in on her. She'd spent precious hours of life captured inside the Entity's jail cell on Arctordiea, and she wasn't looking forward to returning to its frigid embrace.

She swung her legs to and fro, trying one last time to break free when suddenly the door to her room exploded inward. As smoke billowed in, Bradley leapt through the opening and slid along the ground, coming to a screeching halt just past the entrance.

When his eyes locked on hers, she could practically see him cringe. It wasn't every day you walked in on your sister dangling in the air by a golden alien tree with a tentacle down her throat.

But that didn't seem to stop him. He launched toward her and raised a plasma pistol, shooting round after round into the body of the alien.

The molten rounds ripped holes through the Entity's torso, and it let loose a blood-curdling screech that even she could hear through her earmuffs of gold. While Bradley instinctively froze to cover his ears, the tree attacked, swinging a razor-thin tendril through the air like a sword. It cut through her brother's right thigh like a knife through butter.

She cringed as he screamed and fell to the ground, flailing about and struggling to grasp at the wound on his leg. He was trying unsuccessfully to stop it from bleeding out.

And then Rán and Shauna arrived.

But rather than attack the alien, they did the one thing she'd hoped they would. Rán grabbed Bradley by the arms and yanked him out, while Shauna led Libby to safety. They moved so fast they were a blur.

Abigail hadn't even noticed Libby lying on the ground in the other room. From the looks of it, she'd been pinned under a chunk of rubble, and she was covered in blood.

The robots were in and out without a struggle. Either the alien was licking its wounds, or it knew they weren't up for a fight. Regardless, at least her family was trying to escape.

She was already too far gone, and the Entity wasn't about to relinquish its prize.

Just when she thought things couldn't get any worse, a stream of clone soldiers stormed through the cloud of smoke billowing in from outside. In their wake walked her aunt Hera.

As Abigail's world faded to black, the bitch removed her helmet, and she was grinning from ear to ear.

20

JOYCE GREEN
EPSILON ERIDANI, LIPROSUS ORBIT

Their battle group passed through the gate transition just in time to see the attack on the Liprosus moon, Clavis. From the looks of it, only one of the planet's moons had been on a transit that would have allowed Abigail and her family to hold a gate open. At least, that's what Lync said. She'd extracted her team from the Beacon before the shit hit the fan, and they were making their way to their shuttle now.

"Status?" Joyce stood up and out of her command chair. She'd replaced her organic legs with the familiar mechanized ones that didn't fight her every move.

"All our ships have transitioned, Commander," her first officer said.

"Scramble the Nyílak fighters," she said. "If they so much as touch Lync or her people, I want those clones torched. Is that clear?"

"Yessir," her weapons officer said.

"Sir!" Her communications officer spun around. "We're being hailed by the beanstalk station. Shall I put them on?"

She nodded.

After a brief pause, Admiral Nguyễn's face appeared on the wall screen.

"What do you need, Nguyễn?" She knew addressing him

like that would irk him, but better to focus his scorn on her than on her people.

He paused and seemed to consider his words. "Your presence is no longer needed here, Commander Green."

She forced a smile. "Don't worry. Once we pick up our people, we'll be back to Iserea. I'm not keen on having them caught up in an Olivaw pissing match."

Nguyễn smirked and gestured off-screen toward someone. "You don't seem to understand what I'm saying, Joyce."

"Touché," she muttered.

He continued. "I wasn't simply referring to Liprosus. Your people are no longer welcome here in Epsilon Eridani. I suggest you exit stage left before we're forced to take matters in an undignified direction. I'm pretty sure we can agree, everyone will regret that."

She drew in her breath. "This is my colony, Admiral. If anyone needs to leave, it's you and your carbon copy colony mates."

Nguyễn smiled and nodded.

Suddenly, their klaxons blared overhead.

"Sir," her weapons officer began, "I'm detecting six... no, make that eighteen Ursis Alatas battleships coming out from behind Clavis, and another dozen from behind Liprosus. They're targeting our battle group, sir."

Joyce clenched her fists behind her back. The last thing she needed was a fight. Especially with these fraking overgrown bears. Her people were only now getting comfortable in their ships. There was no way they could handle a skirmish, and certainly not against other humans. While the clones made up most of the inhabitants on and about the planet, there were colonists from Zeta Lupi down there.

She narrowed her gaze at him. "Once our pilots and any of the colonists that wish to leave are transferred onboard, we'll find our way out."

Whispers of disagreement around her bridge nearly sent her over the edge, but she remained resolved and focused on

Nguyễn. They must have sensed her rise because someone quickly snuffed them out.

Nguyễn shook his head. "I don't think so, Joyce. You can have your pitiful little Ulixi, but the colonists… well, they're fine where they are."

She squinted. "And what if they don't want to stay?"

"I guess we'll cross that bridge when we get there." He smiled and waved his hand.

A moment later, the drive plumes of her eight fighters launched out of a cargo hold on the side of the beanstalk. She could tell they were her people from the transponder signals overlaid on the wall screen.

She gestured, and the feed paused. "I want a jump programmed to get us out of here in one hop. Once Lync and her team are inside, tell the battle group to gate on our mark. Is that understood?"

"Sir, what about the colonists on the planet?" Her comm officer asked. His gaze was locked on hers, and the other members of the bridge turned to face her as well.

Joyce swallowed hard. "I say this with the utmost frustration, but we cannot afford to engage Hera and her clones, let alone these aliens. Not yet. Not in the shape we're in. We'll make sure our pilots are safe and wish our people down there the best of luck."

She nodded toward the comms officer. "Send one last encoded signal down to the planet. Warn them what's about to go down."

"Yessir." He turned around and started subvocalizing a message to the colonists on Liprosus.

Her chest tightened. She never imagined she'd leave her colony like this. It was her new home, and it was being taken from her by a tyrant. An Olivaw, just like the others. One that needed to be stopped.

"Our course is locked in," her navigation officer said. "It'll be a big jump. But we should be fine."

"Should be," she muttered, wiping at her forehead. "That's comforting."

"Ready our forward plasma cannons." She lowered her hand and cracked her knuckles. "Lock our target on the beanstalk. Fire on my signal."

"Sir?" her weapons officer asked.

"You heard me!" She stepped toward his station. "If we're leaving our people down there, I'd like to give them a head start. I'm not about to leave those fraking clones with an elevator to the bottom if I can help it. Now, if you can't follow that order, I'll find someone who can."

The officer saluted her. "I can handle it, sir!"

"Then do it!" she screamed.

He programmed the firing ordinance into the computer, and his hand hovered over the key to execute it.

"Our pilots have finished their docking maneuvers," Ryder said.

She stiffened her stance. "Tell the fleet to jump and bring that prick back up on the screen."

Nguyễn's face unfroze, and the dots representing her battle group began disappearing from the tactical display on the far wall.

"I see you chose wisely." Nguyễn smiled. "Good luck out there, Joyce. Oh yeah," he held up a finger, "I recommend you steer clear of Sol or Zeta Lupi. They've already been ordered to fire on sight should you or any other sympathizers of our former president happen to drop in for a visit."

She chuckled. "You can't be serious. I'm the furthest from a sympathizer to any of the Olivaws, let alone that one. If anyone should be worried, it should be you. You're in bed with the Olivaw femme fatale. Minus the seductive part."

Apparently, he didn't take too kindly to her remark because the comm dropped.

"Fire!" Joyce shouted and spun around. "And get us the hell out of here, now!"

Right as their plasma cannon fired, the gate vanes of their ship clanged into place and started speeding past from tail to front. Time seemed to slow as the ships in the distance powered up and prepared to launch a barrage of shots in their direction.

But the Ursis would be too late.

Her shots ripped the beanstalk to shreds, and the tether quietly separated from the station. As the blue glow of the gate passed over her, she swallowed hard, watching the red-hot tip of the cable tumble down toward the colony below.

WHEN THE GATE TRANSITION COMPLETED, a second came immediately afterward. It was a standard protocol in this new world of gate travel. Since any nearby party could see the star formations bending around the silhouette of your ship, you needed to double-gate to ensure they didn't follow you through.

Joyce stood there, staring at the image frozen on the wall screen. It was a picture of the tether breaking free.

The bridge was equally shocked, an eerie silence falling over them. Her team was still grappling with the reality of what had just transpired. They'd gone from fighting a common enemy to being homeless in a matter of seconds.

While some might blame her for coming to the aid of Olivaws, that wasn't at all what she was doing. Her only goal in jumping their battle group was to get her pilots and her people to safety.

As the second blue glow passed through her, she walked over to her comms officer. "Ask Lync to bring her team to my ready room."

"Yessir," they said and began subvocalizing a comm.

She turned and waved toward Ryder, her second. "Let's go have a talk."

Her weapons officer stood up. "Sir, what... should we do?" He swallowed hard. "I mean, when the rest of the fleet starts asking."

Her people would be frightened, and they'd want

answers, but the sooner they knew what they were working with, the better.

She glanced at her comm officer. Judging by the look on his face, he seemed to be thinking the same thing. "Tell them to send us an updated inventory of their supplies and foodstuff." Her hand started shaking, and she pressed it against her side. "We need to know where we're starting."

"Aye, sir." He nodded.

She was about to walk to her ready room when she paused. "And, Thomas."

"Sir?"

"Tell our people I'll be addressing the battle group in under an hour."

Joyce didn't wait for his reply. She simply turned in place and made her way to her ready room.

Once inside, she spun around and waited for the door to close.

"What the frak just happened?" She reached her hand up to her hair, but instead of running it through, she screamed. "Argh!"

Fortunately for her, the room was soundproof.

Ryder collapsed down into a chair. "I... don't know, but something tells me this wasn't a last-minute call."

"Hell no, it wasn't." She stepped around the table to the far side. "That bitch has been planning this since I walked out on her little training exercise."

"Probably longer than that." He traced a circle on the frosted glass tabletop. "Hera's been tearing the system apart for weeks now, searching for her family."

Joyce nodded. She hadn't considered that. Hera wasn't the sort of person who flew by the seat of her pants. She always had an angle and a long game in mind. Her family disappearing on her before she could take them must have set her master plan back. Which meant Joyce had probably been running on borrowed time for longer than she thought.

"What do we do now?" She leaned against the wall.

Before he could answer, the door slid open, and Lync,

along with her ragtag Ulixi crew, filed in one at a time. After all eight of them entered, they lined up and saluted her.

"At fraking ease." She closed her eyes and took a deep breath to calm her nerves. After a few seconds of silence, she spoke. "What the hell happened over there?"

"We didn't do anything!" Adri blurted out.

Her eyes shot open. "Bullshit! You must have done or seen something."

Lync was quietly staring at her. From the looks of her cheeks, she'd been crying. There was no doubt she'd seen something.

"What?" Joyce pushed off the wall. "What did you see?"

Lync wiped at her face and left a smudge behind on her cheek. "They attacked the moon where Abigail and her family were hiding."

"That I already knew." Joyce went to pound her hand down against the table, but instead landed it softly. Now was not the time to lose her cool. "What else?"

Lync took a deep breath and rubbed her hands on her flight-suit. She was clearly having trouble focusing. She'd come back to her.

"You!" Joyce pointed at one of the twins. "What did you see?"

They didn't respond at first. They looked at Lync. It was clear who was in charge of these people, and it wasn't Joyce.

Lync nodded. "Tell her... tell her anything she wants."

"Well..." He glanced at his sister. "Lo and I noticed theys were hauling the Gunders out on stretches. Parintly theys gone into cardiac arrest."

"Wait... what?" Joyce waved her hand around the table. "I need everyone to sit the hell down and someone, please, start from the beginning."

They all did as she asked, and Lync started them off. She explained how they'd walked into the station and the Gunders were being hauled out under medical attention. Then she and the others began describing how they connected to the Beacon. It was all rather boring, with lots of colors and flashing lights. That part didn't seem to matter, but she let them talk. It didn't get interesting until Abigail showed up. She'd somehow found Lync and her crew among all the billions of people inside that virtual alien coliseum.

"So, she just tracked you down? That's what you're telling me?" Ryder asked.

"That's what I said." Lync shook her head. "You mouth-breathers wouldn't understand."

The Ulixi chuckled.

"Enough!" Joyce groaned. "Get to the point, Colonel."

Lync sighed. "I didn't mean it like that. I meant how we Ulixi breathe differently. We can… I don't know… sense each other in there."

"It's like when your mum hugs you." Adri smiled and stared at Lync. "You can feel her love, even though you can't see her face. Whereas when you hug your mates, it's… different. See?"

Ryder nodded. "I think so."

"Anyhow," Lync continued, "we dropped into the grave layer and started talking."

"The what?" Joyce asked.

Lync smirked. "The grave layer is where the weak minds linger. Apparently, many of the aliens visit the Beacons before they die, to have one last connected experience before they leave their mortal plane." She shook her head. "I don't know why, and it doesn't matter. It's just a safe place to talk if you can fit in."

"Alright." Joyce sat back in her chair. "What did Abigail say?"

Lync glanced at Adri.

The little girl spoke first. "She said the Entity knew where they were. Where her family was hiding." She kept her gaze locked on Lync.

Ryder squinted. "What is an Entity?"

Lync sighed. "It's a symbiotic alien being that latched onto Abigail's mind inside the Proto Dark Nebula."

"We think," Adri muttered, swallowing hard when her

eyes met Lync's glare. "What?" She raised her hands. "We never have seen it."

Lync continued. "While we may not have seen it outside its canister, I felt it in the Beacon on multiple occasions. From what Abigail told me, it's been using her as a means to connect to the Beacon, and it threatened to kill her if she didn't let it use her as a conduit."

Ryder's mouth fell open. "How the hell are we just now hearing about this?"

Joyce looked between Adri and Lync. "And that's it..."

Lync shook her head. "No..." She stared down at the table and paused. She seemed to be considering how to word her next sentence, but she gave up and blurted it out. "She said the Entity has been warning the Galactic Alliance about our mission. About the attack on the Nursery."

Joyce drew in her breath and froze, staring blankly at the formation of dots on the wall screen. Each green circle represented one of their ships, and every one of those contained hundreds of lives in her care. While their current situation was different from the colony, they were yet again wedged between a rock and a hard place.

In one hand, she had the people in her immediate command. They'd been banished from all known human worlds, had nowhere to go, and lacked a means to take care of themselves beyond their ships. And in the other, she had the fate of humanity. They were about to walk into a trap that could end them before they started. And standing right in the middle of the mess wasn't just one Olivaw with a death wish, it was the entire fraking family of them.

"We have to tell them," Ryder said, interrupting her silent stare.

Joyce turned to look at him. "Tell who?"

"Hera and our people." He raised his hand toward the wall screen. "There might only be a few hundred of our people in the colony, but there are thousands in Zeta Lupi and billions of them back in Sol. They have to be warned."

She shook her head. "And then what? You think they're

going to welcome us back with open arms after we tell them? The GA will barrel over humanity, no matter what we say. At least this way, we can bring the battle to them."

"But… we'll be annihilated," Adri muttered.

Ryder groaned and glared at Joyce. "You're just saying that because you want revenge for your son's death. This is bigger than that, Joyce. You know it, and I know it."

"What if there was another way?" Lync asked.

Everyone at the table turned to stare at her.

"What does that mean?" Ryder asked.

"Exactly what I said." Lync glanced over at Joyce. "What if there was a way to do this that didn't require us telling Hera?"

Ryder chuckled. "What? And let them die?"

Joyce rested her elbows on the table and brought her hands up under her chin. This was going to be good. "I'm listening."

Ryder spun his head to the side. "You can't be serious?"

Lync ignored him and focused her attention on Joyce. "The Olivaws sent Ibu off on a mission somewhere. I don't know where, and neither does Abigail."

"That's odd." Joyce mockingly screwed up her face. "Do they often hide things from one another?"

"If you'd asked me that a few years ago, I'd have said yes." Lync smirked. "But that changed once the GA arrived."

"You mean, once they were forced to stop lying to everyone else, that is?" Ryder laid his hands flat on the table. "I'm not liking where this is going."

"Anyway." Lync shook her head and pushed on. "She tried getting both Zachary and Bradley to tell her when they'd sent Ibu, and neither of them would break. She told me as much in the Beacon. I think they have another plan up their sleeves, sir. I'm pretty sure that if we find the Olivaws, we find our way out of this."

"You're assuming they even survived the attack?" Ryder leaned forward and stared at Joyce. "I say we just tell Hera and let the chips fall where they may."

She rolled her eyes. Sometimes, he was as naïve as he was attractive. "Do you seriously expect her to trust us over the alien entity she now has in her possession? It could claim we made it all up, and then what?"

"What fraking entity?" He raised his hands in the air. "I'm not convinced it exists. It wouldn't be the first lie they told us. From what Lync and her posse said, no one has ever seen it except Abigail and her siblings. Last I checked, they weren't exactly reliable sources." He shot up to his feet. "I mean, how do we know this thing is even real, let alone if Hera found the Olivaws' base?"

"That's simple enough to find out." Lync tapped the tabletop and cast a playful glance her way.

Joyce looked around the table at the faces of the Ulixi. She could tell by how they acted around her that they believed in Lync. Hell, they'd probably follow her to the end of the universe if she asked. And she wouldn't expect anything less. She was a good leader. The question was, should she trust her?

"I don't know why I'm doing this." She drummed her fingers on the table and stared silently at Lync for a few seconds. "But you've never lied to me, Colonel Michaels." She stood up and leaned forward, resting her hand flat on the table. "And I suggest you don't start now. So, tell me. What is this plan of yours?"

21

BRADLEY OLIVAW
OUTSIDE EPSILON ERIDANI DARK NEBULA

The pain was excruciating. Bradley was screaming at the top of his lungs, and no matter what Rán or Shauna did, the agony wouldn't end.

He slammed his fist against the surface of the medical bed. "Do something! Please."

Tears streamed down his face.

Cynthia squeezed his hand, her own face covered in tears. "Why isn't it working? Why won't his pain stop?"

"I don't know!" Pluto slapped the side of the med-computer. "It says everything is fine."

"Ahhh!" The wave of agony surged higher and higher until finally cresting in his leg. It was like... "Something is... moving in there."

Rán launched across the room to his side as a wall of blue ants danced over them. Normally, the numbness of the transition helped to soothe any knots or kinks he had, but not today. This time, nothing helped.

As another wave of pain hit, he screamed in agony and arched his back off the table.

"Ladies, you might want to avert your eyes." Rán grabbed the strap around his leg where it met his groin and yanked it even tighter.

"Why?" Cynthia asked.

She didn't have to wait long for an answer. Rán was already slicing his thigh open like he was carving a turkey at Thanksgiving. She couldn't watch, and instead reached out and rested her hand on his cheek, forcing him to look at her.

Her lips were quivering, and when he reached up to touch her, she forced them into a smile. Seeing your loved one in pain was an experience that threatened to crack even the toughest exteriors.

As he stared into her eyes, he could feel the heat of the laser scalpel slipping through the meat of his thigh. Surprisingly, it didn't hurt. For once, the medications were doing their job. What hurt like hell was what was happening inside.

Once the cutting stopped, Pluto gasped and Cynthia's attention shot sideways. Her eyes suddenly got as wide as saucers.

"What—is—it?" His voice quivered.

"I think it's part of the Entity." Rán leaned closer.

Another ring of blue passed over them. Wherever Shauna was taking them, she was being cautious.

Part of him wanted to look at it, and another part of him didn't. He had the constitution of a thimble when it came to blood, especially his own. Just as he was about to ask for someone to show him, something dug into his thigh and yanked.

"Argh!" He screamed and tried to kick, but Rán was holding him too tight. That, and the straps from the bed were restraining him. He hadn't felt them wrap around his body, and he wasn't even sure who'd done it.

"It's not budging!" Pluto cringed and slid her hand down to her stomach.

He tilted his head to the side and squinted. Maybe he was imagining it, but she looked… "Pluto."

"Yes, sweetie." She bent down and wiped at the tears in her eyes. "What… can I do to help?"

He reached out and ran his hands over her shirt. Sure enough, there was a bulge under the baggy clothing. "You're… pregnant?"

She drew in her breath, and her lip quivered. "Now's not the best time to get into that."

Cynthia's arm shot out and rested on the same spot Bradley was. "Why didn't you say something?"

"I hate to break up the touching moment," Rán began, "but can you all stop fondling her baby-bump? And someone, please give me a hand?"

Cynthia let go of his face and Pluto's stomach and slid down to his legs. "Where do you need me?"

"Take this," Rán passed her something.

"And do what with it, exactly?" She stepped backward.

He couldn't see what Rán handed her, but judging by the look on her face, she didn't want it.

"You have to inject it into his neck," Rán said. "He can't be awake for this."

"You've got to be kidding," Pluto retorted.

"What is it?" Bradley asked. He tried to move his head, but someone had immobilized that as well.

"You need to do this now, Cynthia," Rán implored.

He thought he saw the shadow of a syringe against her shirt.

"If I have to do it," Rán began, "then this part of the Entity might slip past my tourniquet."

Yet another ring of blue passed over them, and the room fell silent. Or at least that's what he thought happened.

Turns out, Cynthia took the syringe and jammed it into his neck, injecting him with God knows what.

The last thing he remembered was her lips against his. They were moist and tasted like salt.

***

BRADLEY STARED in agony at the smoke billowing overhead as someone yanked him away from Abigail's side. He wasn't sure who it was, but they didn't seem overly concerned about hurting him more than he already was. After all, they had bigger problems to deal with - like getting out alive.

One by one, he watched clone bodies fly across the room and slam against the wall. Blood sprayed everywhere as their heads exploded on impact. It reminded him of that twentieth-century comedian who used sledgehammers to smash watermelons. He never saw the humor in it, but Abigail loved watching those things explode. Whenever it was on, she'd get so worked up, soda would shoot out of her nostrils. Even if he didn't get it, watching her was just as hilarious.

As Rán dragged him through the secret facility on Clavis, he hacked on the smoke. The clouds of black were thicker in the direction they were headed. It wasn't until they passed through a false wall in Zachary's room and it slid back into place that the smoke disappeared.

"Hey!" He reached out and pointed. "That wall wasn't there—"

A lightning bolt of pain shot through him, and he screamed at the top of his lungs. "Shit!"

The room shook, and Rán grabbed one of the pillars in the middle. Dust trickled down around them from the ceiling like snow from the heavens. It was never a good thing when you were underground, and shit was falling on you.

Cynthia ran up beside him and coughed as she waved the dust clear. When she looked down at him, she gasped. "What... what happened?"

"Not now!" Rán leaned forward and sprinted across the chamber, which, from the looks of it, was a hangar of some sort.

Bradley's entire body suddenly started convulsing uncontrollably. He swore there was a rod of fire lodged in his thigh, and at that moment, it was kicking around, trying to break loose.

But then it stopped.

He groaned and rubbed at his leg, willing the persistent pain to stop. When he opened his eyes, he saw that they'd moved under something dark and black. It reminded him of the belly of the Fountainhead, but different. This ship was more round than teardrop-shaped.

"Where are we... going?" He could feel the pain rising again.

"Out of this place if we can get everyone inside this fraking ship." Harold spun around. "Get your ass in there, Cynthia." He pointed up the lift tube, and she practically jumped inside, shooting skyward into the belly of the sphere floating overhead. "Now, where the hell is Shauna?"

"Don't you yell at me, Harold." She came trotting up behind them from another side of the hangar. "That fraking entrance collapsed, and I had to work my way around. Damn your false walls."

He laughed out loud. "My name's Rán, and you'll thank me for that later."

"Fat chance," Shauna muttered.

When he stepped inside the lift tube, Bradley bolted up with a start. His heart was pounding in his chest, and he opened his eyes.

Cynthia drew in her breath and grabbed his shoulder. "It's ok, sweetie!" She pulled him close and rubbed his back with her free hand. "You were just dreaming. You're fine now. We made it."

He huffed and puffed as the waves of phantom pain passed over him. When he looked up, he took in the space around them. They appeared to be in some type of medical room, and the lights were as dim as hell.

"Damn!" She pulled her hand away. "You're sweating like crazy. Let me get Rán."

"I'm fine," he grumbled, and swung his legs off the edge of the bed. Except something was wrong. There was only one.

He stared down at where his left leg used to be, and there was nothing there. Not even a stub. And then the images from earlier came flooding back.

The pain.

The rapid gating sequences.

Cynthia losing it.

They'd cut off his leg to save him.

Suddenly, his eyes rolled back, and he felt dizzy. Like he

was about to pass out. "I need to… lie down." Without warning, he collapsed backward.

Cynthia must've been there to catch him. Or at least he thought it was her. He was out like a light.

WHEN BRADLEY CAME to the second time, Shauna was there to greet him. Her robotic face was a dozen centimeters away, and she was staring directly at him.

"Well… hello there." He reached up to rub the side of his head. His throat hurt like hell, and his voice sounded like a frog. "Did you get the number of that garbage bot that hit me? I feel like shit."

"You should." She leaned over and picked up something from the table beside his bed. "You lost a lot of blood, and you haven't kept anything in you for days."

"Days?" He shot upright, instantly regretting it. When he tried to steady himself, it didn't help.

"For crying out loud, would you stop that shit?" Shauna reached out and gently pushed him back into a horizontal position. "You're gonna make me strap you down again, aren't you?"

"No." He shook his head. "No more straps."

"Fine!" She waved her finger at him. "But you've been warned, young man. You get dizzy as hell when your body is out of whack. Just sit still and drink this." She brought a straw up to the side of his mouth and slid it between his lips.

He didn't resist; he just sipped. His throat felt like sandpaper, but whatever it was, it tasted like apple juice. He loved him some apples. A few long sips later, and it was gone.

"I'll get you another one." She reached out and nudged his arm. "But only if you don't move."

"I'm not going anywhere." He closed his eyes and let the juice settle in his stomach as she walked over to the edge of the room and opened some type of refrigerator.

"Did everyone..." He didn't finish the sentence for fear of knowing.

Shauna didn't answer right away, either. She simply reached in and took out a few more containers of juice before closing the door. After she got back to his side, she stuck another straw in his mouth. He didn't fight her.

"Everyone except your sister," she whispered.

He paused and glanced up at her.

She was staring at the far wall, but there was nothing there.

The image of Abigail flashed in his eyes. She was hanging in the air in front of him, and she had the tentacles of the Therionic entity wrapped around her wrists and down her throat. Outside a horror vid-sim, he'd never seen anything like it before.

"I need you to calm down." Shauna rubbed his side.

The alarms from the computer he was hooked up to were beeping rapidly. The thought of leaving her behind made his gut wretch, and he needed to keep this juice down. Especially if they were working on a plan to save her.

He glanced up at her. "Are we going back for her?"

"They're talking about it." She pulled up a chair and sat down beside him.

"Talking?" When he reached his hand up to slide it under her head, she stopped him.

"Please. Just stay flat for now." She gently guided his arm back to his side. "It's complicated."

"She's my sister, and I... I left her behind." He could feel himself losing it again. He needed to breathe and control himself. One. Two. Three. He repeated the breathing he'd seen Abigail do so many times. While he wasn't a Ulixi like her or Lync, the motion was calming.

"We all left her behind." Shauna clasped her hands in front of her. "Either none of us made it out, or we..." Her voice faded away.

He had to change the subject. "How did we not see Hera coming?"

Shauna stared down and kicked at the ground. "I don't know. She… masked part of her movements as a training exercise with the Ursis. That, and Lync was at the Beacon." When she glanced up at him, her robotic eyes dimmed. "I guess we got lax. Libby found something, though. Something that explains how they knew about us. We just need to figure out how to deal with it."

"What is it?" He tried to push up on his side again but collapsed onto the table with a thud.

She shook her head. "You never listen, do you? You're gonna need another nanite infusion and a few more of those before I tell you that." She nudged the juice pouch in his hand toward his mouth. "And maybe some vodka." She smirked.

He chuckled, and a sharp pain shot up his side. That actually sounded pretty good right about now.

"I'm sorry," she muttered.

"Don't be." He closed his eyes and sipped the packet.

She was right. He needed to refuel. But now his mind had something to think about. Where in the universe were they headed?

———

SHAUNA WHEELED Bradley onto the bridge in the center of the ship. He wasn't sure if Rán or Zachary had built this model, but the more he studied the plans on his retinal comm, the more eerily familiar they became.

"I've got it!" He shook his head.

"Hey, bro!" Zachary smiled. "Welcome back to the world of the living."

"Dude!" He raised his hands in the air. "You remade a Shu?"

Zachary squinted. "A what?"

"Our little spherical ship here." He waved his finger in a circle. "It's a Shu. Remember that fraking mini moon we killed in Henosi?"

"No shit," Zachary muttered and spun around. "Harold! I mean…" He shook his head. "Rán!"

"What now?" Rán came strolling onto the bridge from another room.

Zachary raised his finger and pointed at the human form robot. "When I asked you earlier where you got the plans for this thing, you said you made it?"

"I did." Rán smirked and shot Bradley a sideways glance. "I pilfered the basic design from our ancestors and pared them back. Your aunt's little trick of sliding a ring down the surface of her ship gave me the idea, so I tried it. Turns out the gate ring works on a sphere, too. So, voilà!" He swung his hands through the air. "I give you… Blu."

"Blue?" Bradley screwed up his face. "That sounds weird."

"B—L—U. Blu. I just made it up," Rán said. "You know, Shu, Blu. They rhyme."

"That name sucks." Pluto spun around in one of the chairs on the far side of the bridge. He hadn't even seen her there.

"Thanks," Rán muttered.

"Pluto." Bradley smiled, and a burst of happiness rose inside him as he stared down at her stomach.

She smirked and shook her head. "Don't look at me that way."

"What way?" He raised his hands and fought back a laugh, but couldn't.

"That! Right there. Stop it!" She walked up and batted at his shoulder. "Just because I'm pregnant doesn't mean I'm to be treated differently and fawned over."

"Fine." He took a sip of the juice from his lap. "But it's my right as the uncle to do it from time to time. Don't take that away from me."

"Okay," she muttered. "But it weirds me out!"

Zachary walked up beside him and whispered in his ear. "Be careful not to do it in the morning. She'll eat your hand off."

Pluto reached out and shoved at him, but he was ready for

her. He spun around her back and embraced her in a hug, kissing her cheek from behind.

Libby cleared her throat and stood up from the far chair. "I hate to break up your little family bonding time, but we have things to discuss."

"I'm not loving these tall back chairs." Bradley pointed at the bridge seats with his hand holding his juice. "I couldn't even tell there was someone sitting over there."

"Awe, come on." Rán sighed. "If Zachary put them in, you'd all love 'em. You'd call them ingenious. I add a little pizazz of my own, and you all give me shit."

"Guys." Libby gestured toward the wall screens. "We need to figure out our next step."

There on the wall screen were what looked like four completely different plans of attack. Apparently, they'd been busy while he was down for the count. He used the control on the side of his chair to move himself in for a closer look.

The first plan contained a map of Liprosus with the colony sites clearly marked, along with a few other locations. From the looks of the names on the dots, these were where their people were holed up.

The second plan was covered with schematics for the Zeta Lupi Wheel. And if he read this one right, they were headed back for something.

"The data cores?" He glanced back at Libby.

She nodded. "We can't let Hera get her hands on those. There's no telling what she'll let loose."

He'd forgotten all about the cores that housed their long ago dead ancestors. They'd left them in Zeta Lupi after the Beacon attack. Someone probably would've gone back for them sooner, had the shit not hit the fan.

As he studied the plan, he noticed something was missing, and had been for a while now. Well, really someone. The person who'd kept him on his toes during their last mission to the stars. "Where's Pepper? I haven't seen her in a while."

Zachary glanced back at Libby.

"She's already en route to The Wheel." Libby gestured

toward the wall screen and overlaid a jump map to Zeta Lupi. "We sent her there a few weeks ago." From the dozens of hops and stops along the way, she appeared to be taking a roundabout path.

"Is she in one of our ships or Hera's?" he asked.

"Ours," Rán said. "She's got one of the Fountainheads. Aside from hers, there's only one left."

"And I suppose that one is still missing?" He turned back toward Libby.

She shrugged. "What? Abigail said Lync hid it. I didn't push her. She's not exactly an open book, you know. Besides, it's not like it has a lot of firepower."

"True," he muttered, "but I'll take a few more chips on the table right about now."

When he looked at the third wall screen, it took him a minute to figure out what it showed. "Is that supposed to be Hera's colony?"

Rán nodded. "What little we stitched together about it. While we may not know where she hid it, we've still managed to collect some intel."

He leaned forward and pointed up at the moon circled in red. "What's that?"

"That would be where they make their clones." Zachary stepped up beside him. "We figure if we can take out the facility, we might be able to give humanity a shot after this is done."

"We just need to find the damn place," Rán added.

Bradley nodded and moved his chair up to the fourth wall. The knot in his stomach tightened as he approached. He knew this map better than anyone, probably because he'd stared at it for weeks of his life.

"You've got to be kidding me." He spun around. "Why the hell would we need to go back there?"

Libby stepped up to the wall. "Because we have no other options."

"What do you mean?" He studied the wall screen, but he was missing something. "We have the Ursis armada and the ships from Hera. And even though the Sol and colony ships don't add much, we might just be able to pull it off."

"Not if they're expecting us."

She gestured toward the wall screen and watched as Libby's comm replaced footage from inside their moon base. It was a video of Abigail. She was connected to the Beacon.

At first, he couldn't tell what he should be looking for, but then he heard it. The Entity was talking. The alien voice was only a whisper, but it was there. Libby had isolated it from the background noise.

"The Nursery is in danger!" the Entity said. "Protect the Rift at all costs. Humanity is coming for the singularity again!"

A moment later, Abigail muttered the word "No."

The video stopped, and he simply stared at the wall. His mind reeled at the implications of the words.

"If they know…" He spun around.

"Then we need a new plan." Zachary stepped up beside him and rested his hand on his shoulder.

"Plan?" He looked up at his brother and narrowed his gaze. "You're insane. You don't seriously think we can take them out if they're expecting us, do you?"

Zachary nodded. "I think we can with the right people."

"We'd need a shit ton more firepower than we have in Sol, that's for sure. And you're hoping that Hera and the Ursis don't take shots at us along the way. Even then, I just don't see how it's possible." He tilted his head and studied the wall screen. The map of the Lupus Dark Nebula looked the same as when he saw it last. "What am I not seeing?"

Zachary walked up to the wall screen and tapped the dot of green with a three-letter name off to the side.

"Ibu," Bradley muttered. "Is that where you sent her?"

"We never talked about sending them back to Lupus." Rán stepped up beside them. "You knew about this, Bradley?"

"Well… No." He looked up at his brother. "I knew something was up, though. It was right about the time Abigail went missing on Liprosus. My friends dropped me a comm that they saw Zachary sneaking around the beanstalk hangars with a little girl. I figured that was Ibu. I just never said anything."

Zachary shook his head. "Yeah, that was us." He stared up at the wall.

"And what exactly are we hoping our Nanil friend finds back in Lupus?" He took another sip of juice. Shauna had been right. It needed some vodka.

"I was counting on some of those ships around the Cornucopia being operational." Zachary tapped the screen near the Bok Globule, and the map zoomed in. "There has to be something salvageable in that mess."

"Let's hope there's enough to turn the tides," he muttered.

"There's only one problem." Zachary ran his hand through his hair.

"Only one?" Bradley smirked. He could count several dozen. "What's that?"

Zachary crossed his arms. "We should've heard back from Ibu by now."

22

———

IBU

LUPUS DARK NEBULA, NEAR DEVID

The haze of the morning suns setting in the distance made something deep inside Ibu tingle, and they drew in their breath. The binary stars framed a series of impossibly tall orangish-brown rock pillars. While they had no clue about the geological magic at play to produce such a structure, the sight of the natural formation was nevertheless breathtaking. It was hard to imagine they were staring at Devid, even if only through the eyes of a robot.

The natural pillars encircled a sacred holy site on the planet, one they'd only read about in their Book of Truth. There were no pictures of the site, and the only depiction they'd seen was a crude sketch of a desolate wasteland. A phrase often repeated throughout the tome, and a stark contrast to the reality of the lush garden world they were staring at.

What gave them even more pause was the intricate stone circle in the middle of the natural wonder. For within it laid the tomb of the fourth and last, Prima Nanil. The one who foretold the coming Éntono Fos and the return of the Nanil to the Galactic Overseers. They spoke of their people being welcomed into an alliance of the Qlanqulum. While Ibu had no idea what this meant, the mythos of the event was legendary. The details were sparse, but it was said that whoever returned to the tomb would be the next Prima Nanil.

"We'll be in orbit in thirty minutes, Friend Ibu," Little Red said.

They turned and glanced at the short, squat robot. He'd been standing silently behind them for the entire morning, giving them the time they requested to be left alone. This was no small feat for an automata such as him. Their kind never slept and seemed incapable of doing work without constant instructions. It was a wonder they'd lasted as long as they had on self-preservation alone.

"Thank you." They rose out of their meditative seating position, cracking their back one vertebra at a time until they were upright. As their abdominal muscles twitched, they did their best not to moan. They'd be dealing with the side effects of their last berserker outburst for at least another day or two.

"Tell me, Little Red," Ibu began. "Where is Shauna?"

His eyes spun a rainbow of colors until landing on green. "She's presently in the cafeteria. Shall I ask her to meet you?"

"No." They shook their head. "That's alright. I'll find her."

The robot's location was strange considering she didn't eat. Perhaps they were preparing breakfast for them.

They turned and made their way aft, toward the human room of sustenance. Though its purpose was nutritional refueling, they'd learned long ago that it was also a social hub of most human ships and colonies. It was a common location for them to commune, gossip on random topics, and, as they found out on several occasions, instigate fights.

When they entered the well-lit room, they couldn't help but pause. Shauna was sitting alone at a table with her back to the entrance. She had a steaming cup of what smelled like coffee in front of her, and two perfectly shaped eggs with toast on a plate — a curious meal for an entity which didn't consume human food.

"It's yours if you want it," Shauna said, her back still to them.

Ibu tilted their head. "Did you know I was coming?"

She leaned down and inhaled just above the lip of the cup. Yet another useless gesture for a robot with always-on sensors that could tell them the complete chemical makeup of a dish in milliseconds.

"I did not." She turned around. "I actually made it for myself. It's just a happy coincidence you arrived before it got cold."

"Curious," they muttered and made their way to the table. "Why would you make yourself a meal like this? Are your power stores failing? I imagine if you needed to deconstruct an alternate source for energy, there would be more ideal objects to choose from."

"No, no." She shook her head. "I was just… missing food. It's been decades since I last ate. I used to love the smell of a good French roast first thing in the morning." She drew in a deep robotic breath. "Sometimes, I miss being human."

"Only sometimes?" Ibu slid onto the stool across from her and pulled the plate and cup closer. They then looked around for utensils but found none.

"Oh, I'm sorry." Shauna leapt from her chair and shot across the room, grabbing a fork and knife before returning in a flash. "As you can tell, I'm out of practice."

"No worries." They smiled and began eating. When they tapped the perfectly shaped yellow yolk with their fork, its contents oozed out of its amber dome. The golden fluid flowed over the pure, milky surface of egg white like lava from a volcano, covering the edge of the toast with its sticky sustenance. It was a strange dish, but very tasty indeed. They particularly loved the buttery, savory, and rich flavor of the yolk the most.

"The robots have finished auditing the starships near the Cornucopia." Shauna flipped her hand to project a hologram from the ceiling. This was a novel feature of this particular robot ship model. Apparently, Shauna installed it after one of their many tech dumps from both the GA and the original humans.

"As you may have noticed," she continued, "we're in a far

better position than we initially thought. While their ships seem like dilapidated derelicts, they're concealing the intact hulls with holograms that aren't much different from this." She motioned toward the map that was now floating in space before them.

While the holographic feat wasn't new to any of them, the ability to summon it from anywhere on the ship certainly was. Her explanation, however, left them confused.

Ibu paused to lick yolk from their fingers. "How were they able to manipulate our sensors? Our scans showed their hulls were full of holes."

"Some were, and still are," Shauna clarified. "But according to Little Red, they can alter energy to make it look like it's something it's not. Sorta like what happens when wavelengths curve around a skotádi hull, except the direction is reversed, towards the source of the scan."

"Remarkable," they muttered, subvocalizing a command to remind themselves to research this technology later. It might prove useful.

They surveyed the array of ships and their total armaments. Using holograms made perfect sense the more they thought about it. There was no point in advertising their true strength to anyone foolish enough to attack. Although the ships would need to restock their munitions before heading into battle, their designs suggested they were still quite powerful. That wasn't surprising, given that half of them had been pilfered from the Nanil who had tried to overpower the humans several millennia ago.

"I presume the robots repaired these ships after they killed my people." They swallowed hard.

"That's not exactly how it happened, Friend Ibu," Little Red said. They'd snuck up on them and peeked their head over the edge of the raised table. "Many of your kind chose to end their lives before they could be taken into custody. The moment they realized their cause was lost, they were too ashamed to carry on."

They froze and lowered the toast. "Then how do you

explain those holding cells on that ship you had me in? There was Nanil blood everywhere."

"Ahh, those were used during the relocation of your people from Doda." The robot's eyes dimmed. "A very dark time, indeed. We had to gas your people to get them out alive. Otherwise, they would have ended their life flame in their cell."

They nodded. The Nanil were a stubborn species for sure. They often wondered what had gone wrong with their genetics to make them so different from the others. "So, why was there blood then?"

Little Red lowered his gaze to the edge of the table in shame. "As you can imagine, many attempted, and some even succeeded, in taking their own lives. Still others forced themselves to transform, much like you did. And while we initially tried to free them in an attempt to save them, they turned against us and sought our destruction. This is why those robots lost their way. After being left alone for so long, by the time they found you, their programming had driven them to torture." He popped his head up. "But that has been dealt with. Those robots are no longer in service, nor are any of their quantotronic descendants."

"Quantotronic descendants?" They took a bite of the cooling toast.

"Our brains are grown in inorganic vats, not unlike your Nanil and human clones." Little Red rose upward and out of hiding before moving around the table to the side nearest them. "Except we stop with the brain alone, and leave our physical body to more consistent manufacturing processes. You see, each quantotronic mind is unique, and only the strongest and most pure minds are allowed to grow offspring. But in this case, I found the mind that made the descendants of the judgement ship to be flawed."

As they chewed on the cooling toast, they wondered how Shauna and Harold's brains were formed. Certainly, human technology in Sol was far behind that of their ancestors in Lupus. Yet, somehow they'd manage to build minds capable of housing a human consciousness while binding them by laws of their own.

"While your quantum brain is interesting," Shauna glanced at Ibu, "and I'm glad you took care of the bad seeds, I think we should focus on the ships. We're going to need them."

Ibu burst open the second egg yolk and watched as it flooded the plate. As they soaked up the first wave of the bright yellow innards with the second piece of toast, they looked up at Shauna. "If only the Dark Nebula wasn't in the way. Maybe then we could use them."

"Well, if we can actually make some allies, perhaps we can manufacture some gates too?" Shauna rested her chin on her hands and stared at them.

Ibu couldn't help but feel like they were being tested. "You know we can't build that tech in here. Not yet." They made a circular gesture in the air. "It was hard enough hiding it from the Ursis, and even then, we only pulled it off with the support of Haradis. There's no telling what these robots would do with it, and if my people or any other humans in here got their hands on it, that could mean the end of our advantage."

Shauna leaned forward. "Without these warships, we could be facing game over anyhow. Forget about losing the gate tech. Do I need to remind you how many of those moons we're dealing with?" She gestured, and an image of the Nursery appeared in the space beside them.

It was the same one they'd stared at innumerable times before today. They remembered hiding in the crowd of humans when the other copy of Shauna shared it with the colonists in Epsilon Eridani. There were tens of thousands of Selene moon ships, if not more. Enough to destroy countless worlds and species if left unchecked. Everyone knew it was only a matter of time before they returned to the human worlds to finish the job they'd started.

But then Ibu would be alone.

Failure wasn't an option. Their human family and friends

were counting on them to make an ally. Someone who could level the playing field before things got out of hand. Or, at the very least, someone who would give the Olivaws a seat at the table and wouldn't backstab them after the assault on the Nursery. A fleet of ships was one thing, but what they needed was a partner species as desperate as they were, yet capable of so much more.

To make matters worse, they needed to find them before Hera decided to attack the GA. After that, it would be too late. Judging by the response to their arrival in the Proto Dark Nebula, the Entity had taken control of the Ursis, and any hope they had of Haradis helping them was lost.

The entire thing was a house of cards, just waiting for a light breeze to come and tip it over. While Shauna had sent word to the others of their initial success with the robots, they'd only done that a few hours ago, and even that didn't paint the full picture.

Ibu's next steps were suddenly obvious. There wasn't enough time to sit around and wait for word to reach the Olivaws while they fumbled in the dark, trying to open a dialogue with the Nanils from afar. The stakes were too high to sit on their ass safely ensconced in this starship.

They set the last half of the toast on the plate and picked up the coffee, downing it in one gulp. While the heat would have made a human gag, the burning liquid peaked their senses and cleared their nostrils. "Alright, enough chit-chat. I'm heading down to the planet."

Little Red's eyes spiraled uncontrollably. "I thought we were planning on luring one of your delegates near the Ring?"

"Plans change." They slid off the stool and eyed Shauna. "I have some bridges to mend down there if we intend to pull this off, and I'm not about to walk into this place unprepared or unarmed."

"Now you're speaking my language." Shauna grinned, and the image that appeared on the crude forward display of her battlefield chassis made even Ibu shiver.

Lupus Dark Nebula, On Devid

THE GALE-FORCE WINDS tore through the rugged valley, caressing the remains of Ibu's hair. They cast their gaze upward and watched the shuttle take off, hoping their decision would stand the test of time.

"You look badass with your hair chopped off," Shauna said over their comm. "I wasn't sure I'd like it, but I'm digging it with those swords."

Ibu returned their attention to the stone columns in the distance. They were imagining Shauna sprinting through them, trying to find a spot where she could cover them from afar. While her words were welcome, she was likely only talking to reduce their nervousness.

"I had to do something to differentiate myself from my people," they subvocalized as they tilted their ear to the wind. The sound of the shuttle had all but disappeared in the distance, and the animals in the nearby trees were returning to their regular creeping and crawling.

"But was buzzing it really necessary?" Shauna asked. "I've never seen a Nanil with hair shorter than their shoulders, let alone cropped tight to their head."

She was right. It was frowned upon not to have braids. Custom dictated that they have hair with intricately woven strands from the heads of their ancestors and clonos. The fibers contained messages of encouragement or warnings knotted into them, along with bits of fabric from their progenitor's birth gown. They wore the decorative material not only as a reminder of whom they'd descended from but also their entire lineage.

Ibu ran their hand through the remainder of their auburn locks and centered themselves in the clarity of the moment. They were no longer a descendant of their progenitor Ogun or their family's house. When they chose to leave Doda with the humans, they not only renounced their history, they reset their identity. In their shadow, they left behind a Nanil that was both timid and quiet, one that was weak of heart and mind. Their new self acted with a will and strength they'd only been able to muster once released from the shackles of their parent.

A stick cracked to their left, but they didn't move. They'd smelled the two Nanil approaching them almost a minute ago, once the air had settled from the shuttle takeoff. But rather than unsheathe their Zhen blade, they focused on their environment. For if there were two, there were bound to be more.

"You can see them, right?" Shauna asked. The woman could hear what they heard, smell what they smelled, and read the sensations from the nanites in their skin. She knew the answer before she asked, yet she still chose to ask it.

They didn't respond. To do so would mean they might give away their one ace up their sleeve.

Ibu adjusted their white tunic and started walking toward the stone circle in the distance. It was a sacred structure they'd read about in the Book of Truth. While they'd never seen one in real life, the colorful stacks of stones and the wavy outline of the structure were unmistakable.

As they hopped up and over a moss-covered log, a blue jufulu darted out from under the fallen branch and disappeared into the underbrush in front of them. The animal's ideal path of escape would have been to the left or right, but it had chosen to move forward. Which meant only one thing: the other Nanils had flanked them.

Ibu kept their eyes facing ahead and tapped their wrist, bringing up the tactical overlay on their retinal comm. They had debated on wearing one at all, but any advantage they could get in this place would help. They'd long ago shed their antiquated viewpoint of using technology to better themselves. There were times it could be a crutch, and others an asset. As long as they balanced the two forces and never lost their keen sense of the world around them, they were safe.

The tactical display showed that not only did they have

two Nanils coming up along their side, but they'd also picked up two more on their rear. They were smart to stay downwind, and they were quiet too.

Ibu did their best to focus on making it to the edge of the clearing before they were jumped. Perhaps if they threw them off, they'd make it.

"I know you're there!" they shouted. "All four of you stink like a ranoga gone foul."

"Do you really think antagonizing them is your optimal course of action?" Shauna asked. Her dot showed that she'd found a position atop one of the massive stone columns beyond the Ring.

Ibu didn't answer. They merely reached up and brushed the enormous yellow fronds aside, stepping into the clearing around the Ring of Judgement. They didn't pause to take it in as their hearts pounded in their chest. Instead, they put distance between them and their shadows.

A few steps onto the stone, and they heard gravel crunch behind them and to the side. Apparently, their friends had chosen to join them in being judged. While the Book never spoke of what would happen if more than one Nanil entered the Ring, it didn't take much imagination to figure out why. It was a children's book, after all.

Their retinal comm showed four Nanil exiting the jungle behind them, and three more were approaching the clearing in the distance. Although they couldn't smell or sense them, Shauna had likely tagged them.

As they approached the first and smallest colorful pile of stones, they paused and dropped to one knee, bowing toward the totem and paying it the respect it deserved. Each rock represented a stage in the life the Prima Nanil passed through to become the Prima. This stack was blue and pink, representing the creation of the first Prima and their birth into the shackles of humanity. They were a merger of the weaker human forms of male and female into a stronger single-sex species.

With their eyes closed, the closest Nanil made their move

and dove toward them. What they neglected to notice, however, was the electro-blade dagger Ibu had at their ankle. They simply unsheathed the blade, sprung upward, and sailed over their assailant. By the time they recovered from the miss, Ibu was on them, plunging the knife straight through their back and into their first heart.

They screamed as the blade crackled and shot a dozen pink sparks across their back and down their limbs, immobilizing them instantly. Standing up, they drew in their breath. Their attacker had knocked over the small pile of stones, and they weren't sure what to do next. Just as they were about to reach down and restack the mystical rocks, the stones seemed to float back into place, one precariously stacked atop the other.

If they hadn't seen it with their own eyes, they wouldn't have believed it. Their retinal comm hadn't detected any foreign energy sources at play, and yet, the stones simply rose off the ground and realigned themselves to their original position. It was like watching poetry in motion.

As they stared at the pink and blue stones, a Nanil to their left muttered a prayer under their breath, begging for forgiveness.

"Show us the way of your truth. Please forgive us, Prima, for we have defiled your shrine." They dropped low to the ground and began bowing repeatedly. First, they touched their heads to the dirt, then tilted their head back, staring up toward the heavens.

Ibu didn't question the motives of the supplicant, nor did they pause to let them finish. They simply yanked the bloody electro-blade out of the first rigid body, walked over to the second, and tapped them on the shoulder. A flurry of pink sparks shot through their torso, immobilizing them with a thud, just as it had the first, but with far less bloodshed.

Glancing back at the other Nanil still lingering at the edge of the jungle, they caught sight of the twinkle of their darkened gaze in the shadow. These two weren't planning on dying as easily as the others. Based on the blood-red fury in their eyes, they'd already transformed into their enraged form and were waiting to pounce.

Their retinal comm showed that a dozen or so Nanil were streaming out of nearby caves, and more were likely close behind. If they were going to make this happen, the time was now.

Ibu didn't pause to reconsider their plan. They'd come too far to back down. They simply sprang forward and charged the center of the Ring, their footing slipping on the gravel as they went. While they recovered by reaching down and using the rocks strewn about to steady themselves, they lost precious seconds in the act.

As they swerved past and brushed their hand against the second and third spires of intricately stacked stones, their hearts hammered in their chest. The approach to the Ring required that each of the spires be met with grace and reverence, something they had little time for in the moment. For the two dots behind them and the three others in the distance had bounded forward with a grace not found in their own movements.

"Should I take out a few of them?" Shauna asked on the comm.

"No! I've got this." They leapt over a low wall of rock and slid their hand over the fourth stack of stones, using it to pivot and adjust their course. Just as they touched down on the far side, they bounded forward, and a boulder crashed to the ground behind them, right on the path they'd been heading before turning.

When they spun around and caught the gaze of their attacker, the knot in their stomach tightened. The rippling, muscular Nanil had an evil grin on its face, and now that they were finally out of the shadows, they could see them for what they truly were. Their bulging muscles, talon-like fingers, and hunched backs made them perfect killing machines. These weren't the people they'd grown up with on Doda. Quite the opposite, these were primitive creatures, designed and bred for one purpose — to protect the Ring at all costs.

The Book spoke of a primordial form of their kind. One of the earliest mutations of their uplifted species. But it was said that they'd been purged by humanity after the geneticists found a purer form. One closer to that of humans, and more importantly, one they could control to do their bidding and yet still stomach having them around.

They sheathed the blade on their ankle and sprinted full tilt toward the fifth stack of stones. Just before reaching it, they caught a blur from the corner of their eye barreling toward them from the left. They hoped they wouldn't have to kill any of their kind en route to being judged in the Ring, but they also knew their people would defend it at all times. The fact of the matter was, they weren't as fast or agile when not enraged.

Reaching up over their shoulders, they unsheathed both of the Zhen blades at once. Just in time, too, as the approaching Nanil dove toward them with fangs bared and claws extended. Ibu leaned sideways, slid on their hip beneath the passing beast, and held the two blades upright, doing their best to ignore the stone surface ripping their thigh to shreds.

The primordial Nanil let out a blood-curdling scream as they flew through the outstretched blades. Their shoulder and chest cavity split in half all the way to the groin, a feat achievable only with a nanometer-thin blade. It was so sharp, it could practically slice atoms. However, it couldn't prevent the shower of blood that poured down over them. By the time they came to a stop, their pristine white tunic was covered from head to toe in yellow lifeblood and chunks of the beast's entrails.

The gore didn't faze them. They were halfway through the test.

Ibu pushed off the ground with their elbow, wincing as they ran their palm over the top of the fifth stack of stones. Their side was mincemeat, and they were doing everything they could not to change into their enraged state. Not only would the transformation prevent them from passing the final Prima Nanil barrier, but being covered in blood meant they'd lose focus on their task. It was part of their genetic programming to favor fight over flight; blood was their trigger. The moment they smelled it, their goal would shift to ripping apart attackers rather than reaching the Prima.

Their mind strained to maintain a grip on their dwindling calm, and they barely noticed the ground rumbling beneath their feet. The Book of Truth never mentioned anything about a quake, but it wasn't exactly a guidebook for traversing the Ring. All they knew was that one Nanil was assigned to each pile of stones, with the last being themselves.

They jumped up and eyed the sixth stack of stones on the far side of the circle. It was the furthest point from their current position, and while going through the center was the most direct path, it also guaranteed death.

With their swords outstretched, they tilted forward and dashed around the wall, which seemed to grow taller the further they moved toward the middle. Perhaps it was an illusion, but they swore they could earlier see the other side without much difficulty.

"Are those stones floating upward?" Shauna asked.

They ignored her query, but apparently it wasn't their imagination. To make matters worse, as they passed the midpoint of their arc, they skidded to a halt. There, guarding the sixth stone, stood two primordial Nanils. As Ibu eyed their target, their gaze lingered on the beasts' backs. The Book mentioned their hunch enabled them to run faster, but it never said anything about spikes. The first two Nanil they'd incapacitated must not have completed their transformation. Either that, or these two were that much more pissed.

"Givvvv upppp," the Nanil on the left growled. "Humannnnkind is not wellllcome here." It slowly dragged its claws down the pile of stones, sending a screeching sound through the open area and the surrounding valley.

Ibu shuddered, doing their best not to appear intimidated. They stared at the spikes protruding at odd angles from the beasts' backs. The bloody bones looked almost as if they were undulating in and out of their skeletons. They needed to do something to throw them off.

"I guess it's a good thing I'm not a human, then." They leaned sideways toward the primordials, showing off the glistening yellow blood from their stone rash.

"Impossible," the second Nanil muttered. "You arrived on a human craft."

"What can I say?" Ibu shrugged. "When I left Doda, I found a better tribe to take me in. One that wasn't so primal."

The Nanils snarled, dropped to their hands, and began using their claws to dig at the stones. They reminded Ibu of dogs burying their excrement.

"Behind you!" Shauna screamed.

Ibu dropped to the ground, but they were too slow. A third Nanil leapt out from behind the wall and slashed them across the right shoulder, sending them rolling sideways. One of their Zhen blades flew end over end into the trees, and the other skidded along the dirt.

As they rolled onto their back and righted themselves, the Nanil spun around and launched forward for another pass. But the pause was too long. It gave Ibu enough time to reach for the electro-blade along with a handful of rocks.

They tossed the gravel at the beast's left side and then lagged the blade before throwing it to the right. While the stones faked the beast out, they dodged the projectiles and hurled themselves directly into the path of the oncoming blade. It plunged them square in their right heart, and pink sparks shot through their extremities. When the light show ended, they collapsed atop the sparkling blade with a crunch, sending it deep into their chest cavity.

"I guess I won't be needing that," Ibu muttered.

"Be careful!" Shauna pinged their retinal comm. "They're coming around your left and right."

Ibu reached down and carefully picked up the remaining Zhen blade before taking a step backward. They raised the sword across their body while glancing at their advancing foes. "You don't have to die like them."

"But you do!" the first Nanil growled as they clawed their way toward them.

They didn't try to block or dodge; instead, they took the fight to the beast. Taking them on one at a time was the only way they'd survive.

As they pushed off, their back foot slipped in the loose stone, and they tumbled sideways. Failing to stabilize their fall with their off-knee, they went crashing down. While they were fumbling to stay upright, the Nanil tore right past them, and the spike jutting from its side ripped into Ibu's flailing leg.

The entire scene would've been comical if it weren't for the pain shooting through their body. They screamed and reached out to squeeze their calf, doing their best to not let the rage overtake them.

It was then that they heard a massive crunch and two wailing screams. When Ibu rolled back onto their knee, they caught sight of the two primal Nanil entangled in each other's spikes. Apparently, the second beast had attacked after the first, and neither had anticipated their foe's epic fall.

Not one to look a gift horse in the mouth, Ibu squeezed the hilt of the blade and pushed up, limping forward as fast as they could. Once they were close enough to the two thrashing and screeching bodies trying to knock both them and each other down, they swung the blade with all their might.

Once, twice, and three times, they cut through the massive bodies of their brethren. On the fourth and final swing, one of their heads rolled across the ground and came to rest beside the sixth pile of stones.

"Are you alright?" Shauna asked.

They closed their eyes and panted, listening for any other Nanil that might be nearby. They'd seen a seventh foe at the start of the battle, but at the moment, they were nowhere to be found.

"I'm... fine..." Ibu looked over the carnage to make sure

neither of their foes were still moving. Content with the outcome, they limped across the field of gravel.

When they reached the sixth pillar, they nudged the head away with their foot and slapped the top of the stone pile with their hand.

A moment later, the ground shook a second time, and the wall of stones rose upward.

"Huh," they muttered.

"What is it?" Shauna asked.

"I thought… I was imagining the stones rising." They swallowed hard. "I guess I'm not crazy after all."

"I wouldn't say that just yet, my friend." Shauna laughed. "This was your idea, and from where I'm standing, it's pretty damn fraking cray-cray."

Ibu chuckled and shuffled their feet, working their way toward the seventh pile of stones on the far side. "Any sign of the last one?" They reached up and pressed their hand against their shoulder and winced. The spike had gone deep, and they could already feel their body struggling to close off the wound.

"Negative," Shauna said. "I lost them when the first wall rose."

That must mean they were waiting for them on the other side. There was no other explanation.

And they were right, for as they stepped within view of the now glowing pile of rocks, they saw Nanil number seven.

"Shit," they whispered.

"What?" Shauna shouted, her voice blaring in Ibu's ear. "What do you see?"

It was their childhood friend, Fotily, from the cavern on Doda. And not only were they waiting for them with blood rage in their eyes, they were holding the second Zhen blade in their hand.

Ibu let out a guttural groan. It didn't make any sense. "So you knew it was me all along, then?"

Fotily shook their head. "No… not at all. But to be honest, I'm happy it's you. We've been hiding out here since those fraking robots imprisoned us. We knew someone would be coming; the Prima foretold as much. The fact that it's you, the one person who sold us out to humankind…" They snickered and their eyes narrowed. "That's just icing on the goddamn cake."

Ibu drew in a breath. "I didn't sell you out. In fact, if it weren't for me and the humans you almost killed, those robots would've extinguished your life flame long ago. You're lucky to be alive at all."

"Alive?" Fotily screamed, and swung the blade downward, slicing it through a nearby stone as if it were butter. "You call this alive!?" They waved their free hand in a circle around them. "We've been living in squalor since they gassed us out of our home and dumped us down here. Our kind has barely held itself together. And for what reason?" Fotily pointed at Ibu. "So you could go on a little servant adventure to the far side of Lupus with our former masters?"

"I didn't just travel to the other side." Ibu stepped toward their friend, hoping for a chance to knock the blade away. "I left the Nebula. And not only that…" They smiled. "I traveled across the galaxy with my new friends. With my new family."

"Bullshit!" Fotily flipped the sword up and pointed it toward them.

Ibu didn't flinch.

Fotily continued. "You're lying! You know there's no escaping this darkness. It'll be here until the Overseers return."

"The Overseers…" Ibu shook their head and smirked, diverting their attention down toward the ground. Their friend was standing on loose gravel with their weight on their back leg. "That's where you're wrong, little Fotily." They squeezed the hilt of their weapon. "I'm here to save you. All of you."

Ibu lunged forward and swung their blade upward with all their might, crashing it into the second Zhen blade and sending it spinning end over end into the distance.

Sparks of black light burst off the mystical swords and

sent a pulse of terror through Ibu that made them freeze. The clash of the blades somehow pulled back the veil of death and left them staring into the resulting void that mortals might call its face.

As they stood there, a great emptiness washed through them, consuming their soul from the inside out. The sensation was eerily familiar, as if they'd experienced this moment before. They weren't sure when, but the longer they stared into the blackness, the stronger the feeling grew.

Time almost seemed to stop as the abyss lingered just out of reach until suddenly, all the light and purpose in the universe flickered in and out, and then disappeared. The sensation reminded them of when they first faced their mortality over a year earlier. Back when they'd been alone on Doda. They'd spent hours gazing into the darkness across the ancient underworld bazaar, all the while contemplating killing themselves and their clonos.

And then one day, after they decided to end it, the light returned. For in that moment, they glimpsed Zachary and Pluto descending into the Nanil under city. A place no human had ever landed on purpose nor survived more than a week of gladiator matches.

Ibu stayed well out of sight of their landing party that day, making sure to conceal their movements from the noisy drones. After watching the human group from afar, they couldn't help but see them as a means to not only escape Doda's grasp but also to find a purpose. To be a part of something greater than just existing.

As they stared at the fading black sparks, a realization struck.

All at once, they saw their path, both forward and back in time. It all made sense in hindsight, but it hadn't until that very moment.

And now they knew what was needed to reach the end of this maze.

Unfortunately, while they'd been frozen in contemplation, Fotily had not. Their foe recovered from the shock of the sudden unexpected blow and skittered away to retrieve the lost blade. And by the time Ibu turned to see them, they'd leapt off the nearby wall and were sailing through the air toward them with the Zhen blade held high over their head.

They'd hoped to dissuade their childhood friend from attacking, and instead talk them off the same ledge they once stood on. But their actions left them no other choice. Ibu wasn't about to let them take their life. Especially now that they knew the truth.

They dropped to the right and pushed off hard, but they were too slow. Fotily's blade came down and cut clean through Ibu's left bicep, sending a surge of pain through their entire body and pushing them to the brink of transforming. They rolled back and forth on the ground over the loose rocks, which lodged themselves into their open wound, exacerbating their suffering.

"Argh!" they screamed, struggling to stand and catch sight of their attacker. But instead, they floundered about with their arm hanging limp at their side and dripping blood everywhere.

"Should I take them out?" Shauna asked in their ear. Her voice was like a distant flutter in the wind.

They never replied. Their full focus was on fighting their destiny, on losing themselves to the waves of blood-induced rage, like so many of their kind before them.

Fotily slid to a stop and glanced back over their shoulder with an evil grin on their face. "You'd think you'd have learned by now not to just stand still and stare."

They moaned and tried to stand up with the blade in their hand, but fell backward onto their elbow and nearly hit themselves in the face with the sword.

Fotily slowly turned toward Ibu. "I don't know how you let your progenitor hit you like that all the time. It was always so sad when they beat you." They shook their head and raised the Zhen blade in front of them. "You just stood there and took it. It was like watching a coward in warrior's clothing."

Ibu tried to stand up again but this time resorted to employing the sword as a crutch. They slammed the blade into the ground, pushing down with their good hand to propel themselves up. Once righted, they yanked on the hilt, flipped the blade upright into their good hand, and tugged their bloodied left arm tight against their side. They didn't know how they weren't transforming, but they were glad they weren't. Becoming enraged with a wound like theirs was a surefire way to lose the limb for good.

"I gotta hand it to you." Fotily grasped the sword with both hands and started sidestepping around Ibu. "Your ability to control your temper has gotten better over the years. Maybe Ogun knocked something loose after all."

A gunshot suddenly rang out in the distance, and Fotily spun around to see where the sound had come from.

Ibu, however, didn't take the bait. They knew their window of opportunity was fleeting. Instead, they snapped the Zhen blade down and then out, throwing it with all the remaining strength they had in their good hand.

As it left their grasp on a collision course with their former friend, they swore they saw the etching on the flat of the blade. In the markings was a silhouette falling precipitously from a towering rock.

Their blade shot into Fotily's torso, plunging clean through them before finally coming out the other side. The collision sent the Nanil tipping sideways, and shrieks of pain echoed through the valley as several dozen oddly shaped birds fluttered out of the nearby brush and disappeared into the distance.

This time, Ibu didn't pause or fade into contemplation. Instead, they leapt toward their foe and snatched up the loose Zhen blade that had fallen from Fotily's hand after being pierced by the first.

They stared down at their friend for a moment, watching them spit up blood from their mouth. The blade had cut through both of their hearts, and it was only a matter of time before they'd be dead, an outcome that only seconds earlier they imagined for themselves.

"He...lp...me..." Fotily reached up toward them. "P...lea...se..."

Ibu batted their hand aside and glared at them. They'd lost themselves to the rage and the darkness, like so many Nanil before them.

When Ibu felt the clawing at their leg, they sighed and plunged the ancient Zhen weapon down into Fotily's head, extinguishing their life flame in a literal blink of an eye.

As they stared down at the pool of yellow blood pooling around the body of their childhood friend, the ground began rumbling yet again. But they didn't bother turning to see what it was. They already knew.

The final test was upon them.

They glanced up just as the second binary sun passed behind the nearest pillar. Framed in the light was the faintest outline of several humanoid shapes standing atop the geological wonders.

When they heard the sound of footsteps crunching the gravel at their rear, they slowly reached out and rested their hand on the hilt of the Zhen blade protruding from the corpse.

"Hello, Ogun," Ibu muttered. "Or should I call you... Prima?"

Ogun snickered softly under their breath. "Hello, my clonos. It's good to see you again."

"I wish I could say the same." Ibu turned around to face their progenitor.

Their parent was dressed from head to toe in flowing white and black robes, their gown woven with an intricate pattern of stars and the Dark Nebula intertwined throughout. They looked as if they'd aged a hundred years since Ibu last set eyes on them.

"You look... different." Ogun gestured toward them. "I see you chose to cut your hair like a human male."

"No." Ibu stiffened. "My hair has nothing to do with inane

human fashion." They ran their hand over the short crewcut. "I didn't know why I was cutting it then, but I do now."

Ogun crossed their arms. "And why is that?"

"To end my ties with you," they waved their hand through the air, "to end all of this."

Their progenitor stared at them blankly for a moment and then started cackling. Their raucous cry echoed through the canyon, and Ibu thought they could hear the voices of the Nanil standing on the pillars, laughing back at them.

"You don't really think you're one of the Galactic Overseers, do you?" Ogun leaned toward them, narrowing their gaze.

Ibu stared back, wondering if perhaps they'd misinterpreted the signs.

"There!" Ogun pointed at them. "Your doubt. It's right there." They shook their fist. "That doubt is your weakness. It's what kills you every time."

"Kills me?" Ibu tilted their head.

"You can't believe you've been my only clonos." Ogun gestured at the bodies littering the Ring. "You've killed multiple versions of us already, including several of our ancient forms."

A tinge of realization dawned on them. While they hadn't felt it before now, it suddenly fit. Their eyes had been so familiar.

"But not Fotily." Ogun stepped around them, working their way to the far side of the body. "They were merely collateral damage."

When Ibu turned to face them, they stumbled backward. Behind Ogun stood four clonos of themselves. Of Ibu. And in each of their hands were the destroyed remains of Shauna.

"What did you do to her?" Ibu growled.

Ogun held their hand out and shook their head. "Wait! Let me get this straight. The robot… is a woman?" They started cackling again, and their clonos followed suit like puppets echoing their master.

Ibu stepped forward. "Put—her—down."

They paused as Ogun reached out, grabbed the hilt of the Zhen blade, and yanked it easily out of the ground. "This is new." They turned the weapon over in their hand. "Curious markings." They leaned closer, squinting at the shining blade. "If this were indeed the manifestation of my vision of the coming of the Overseers, this would be a different weapon."

"You saw… a weapon?" Ibu squinted.

"Of course I did, you fool." Ogun slashed the blade downward, smiling at the hum the weapon made as it pierced the air. "When one gains sight into their future after reaching the end of the Beacon maze, one often sees their own death. And for me, it was…" Their voice trailed off, and they shuddered.

"It's… a maze?" Ibu whispered, falling silent. That didn't make any sense.

"It is." Ogun locked their eyes on them. "The Builders wouldn't simply leave those devices behind without giving them a purpose. Now would they?"

While their progenitor was speaking in riddles, they obviously knew more than they were letting on and had for some time. From the sounds of it, they'd been hiding truths from their people for millennia. And they needed to learn what those secrets were. The key was in keeping them talking.

Ibu shook their head. "But… the Beacons are used to seal the Nebula. I've seen it happen."

"No." Ogun started circling around them. "You merely watched a hologram of the event from the media. I, on the other hand, was there. I lived through it."

Their progenitor was right. They hadn't actually witnessed one seal off a Dark Nebula themselves because they were with Abigail in Proto at the time. Like when they were young, they replayed a recording of the closing both times. But the humans had, and they said it sealed the nebulosity. They had no reason to lie to them.

Ibu shook their head and began spinning in place, keeping Ogun in front of them and trying hard not to lose focus on where the other Nanil clonos were.

They subvocalized a command to bring up their retinal

comm again. Despite their desire to do this without the aid of technology, they needed all the help they could get. "Tell me..." They smiled. "How did you find the maze? The one in the Beacon."

Ogun sneered. "Not that it matters to you, but it was easy enough."

Their progenitor had always loved gloating over their achievements. Ibu watched as they took slow and cautious steps. They were being careful not to lose their footing like Fotily had.

With it clear that Ibu wasn't going to attack, Ogun continued their speech. "When the Galactic Alliance gave me access to the artifact, I simply followed the path of the dead. No one inside that retched relic dared follow the fading lights of the souls headed toward their end. They were too fixated on the power and awe of the place, and the inner sanctum was intent on manipulating the minds of their herd. They'd never notice a single stray light wandering from the path of the many."

While their progenitor was giving their speech, Ibu was watching the other clonos spread out. They were taking up positions on all sides of them.

"So," Ibu muttered, "where did this maze of yours lead?"

Ogun froze in place and stared down at the tip of the blade. "These markings." They pulled the weapon closer, squinting at the imagery as they slid it back and forth from hilt to tip. "It seems to be telling a story of sorts." They glanced toward Ibu and then down at the gleaming surface. "Is this some kind of joke?"

Ibu suddenly felt a tingle of concern. They hadn't looked at the blade in days, and they had no idea what the imagery showed. Hopefully, it wasn't displaying anything compromising.

"It depends." Ibu checked their retinal comm. The other clonos had reached their final positions around them.

Ogun ran their hand over the blade, near where the new etchings had appeared. They held it up for Ibu to see.

Near the tip, the blade depicted the last few images from their battle with the Ursis. As they worked their way toward the hilt, the imagery illustrated their journey through several gates, Epsilon Eridani, and the hundreds of etched human and Ursis starships they'd encountered en route to Lupus. The last few blocks showed their encounter with the robots at the Cornucopia, and most recently, their descent into the Ring.

When Ibu leaned closer to study the final engraving, Ogun snatched the blade away. "Have you actually been to these places? Or is this a fictional account of your days away from Doda? You were always a quirky one with your insistence on exploring the layers above the arboretum."

"They're as real as you are." Ibu pointed at Ogun. "Like I said earlier to Fotily, I'm here to save my people. And maybe even you, if you allow me to."

Ogun smirked and stared back down at the blade. "So you truly believe this final frame will come to pass, then?" They glared up at them over the edge of the glimmering weapon. "You believe you are a see-er?"

Ibu swallowed hard. In the past, the Zhen blades had always shown the most recent significant events, and they couldn't imagine it showing anything different this time.

They shrugged. "I don't know how it works. But I've never seen it etch something that hadn't come to pass."

Ogun tilted their head. "And where did you get this artifact from?" They looked the blade up and down, studying the composite handle and the intricate inscriptions on its surface.

Ibu glanced to their left as the closest clonos shifted their position. "We recovered it from the Ursis inside the Proto Dark Nebula."

"You passed into another Nebula, you say?" Ogun peered up at them.

They merely nodded. There was no point in giving Ogun any more details than necessary.

As they watched the other three clonos close the gap between them on their retinal comm, something suddenly dawned on Ibu. While they hadn't seen the etching in question, their comm had. They quickly subvocalized a command to bring up the playback and rewind their retinal recording to a video frame that showed the engraving as it swept past.

When they saw it, they froze in place, and their hearts skipped beats when they realized what it depicted. In the frame, there was a Zhen blade lying loose on the ground, and next to it was Ogun's head. Their progenitor was decapitated.

"What is it?" Ogun brought the blade down and out in front of them, directing the point toward Ibu.

"Nothing… I was just… thinking about what you'd said earlier. About the Beacon." They stepped backward, and the clonos directly behind them eased closer. They needed to find a way to reach the other Zhen blade. "I could only imagine what it'd be like connecting to one."

"Well…" Ogun slid forward, closing the gap between them. "If what you say is true, then your mind may contain what we need to escape this world." They nodded toward the clonos behind Ibu.

A second later, their nanites flashed up a message on their retinal comm, warning them about a sudden forward motion from the clonos to their rear. Ibu didn't pause to think. They simply dropped to the ground and rolled to the right. It was the only sane move given the state of their mangled shoulder.

While the clonos may have missed ramming them with their spike, they still managed to swipe at Ibu's leg, sending them spinning out of control and sliding chaotically across the rocky ground. Everything went white when they rolled onto their left side.

Once they stopped rolling, they pushed through the pain and bent down to retrieve the electro-blade from the ankle sheath. Though it was a far cry from a Zhen blade, it was better than being weaponless.

Pink sparks crackled off the blade as they powered it on. And just in time too, as the clonos to their right charged them. It chose to tackle them alone rather than taking them on with the second clonos, which was exactly the approach Ibu had hoped for. There was no way they'd be able to defend against them all at once. One at a time, however, was doable.

Ibu waited as long as they could until they dropped down just as the clonos dove at their chest. While the clonos didn't entirely miss their mark, the electro-blade Ibu was holding slit the Nanil open from neck to sternum. The resulting collision sent both of them tumbling across the ground.

With their world replaced by shrieks of pain and waves of nausea, they didn't have time to react to the advancing brethren. Before they could do anything, several muscular hands grabbed at their legs and shoulders, pinning them to the ground. No amount of kicking or bucking helped. They couldn't break the grip of their attackers.

When they finally regained control of their primal faculties and suppressed the surges of pain, they opened their eyes to see Ogun staring down at them. They were smiling from ear to ear and holding a Zhen blade just above their face.

"I guess this cartoon of yours was fiction after all." Ogun nodded toward the clonos. "Make sure you inject them with the serum before we try to move them. We'll need to get them to the caverns to extract the memories before we can kill them."

They tried to yank their good arm free, but failed. This wasn't happening. They knew too much about gate technology to let Ogun inside their head. If the Nanil got ahold of the tech, they'd escape, and there was no telling what they'd do with it.

As their mind reeled with the consequences, there was only one thing they could think to do.

Stall.

"You know, Ogun…" They took a deep breath and locked their gaze on their progenitor. "The humans who escaped have cloning technology of their own now."

Ogun's smile faded. "That's fine. We needn't focus our attention on our former masters. Not yet. We merely need to escape this forsaken Nebula and regroup elsewhere."

They subvocalized a command in an attempt to overload

the power in their retinal comm, but the command failed. "Frak," they muttered. Even when they needed the machines to hurt them, they couldn't make it happen.

Ibu forced out a laugh in between bouts of pain as the clonos on their left contorted their arm in unnatural ways. "What makes you think the robots will let you out of here alive? Especially after you kill me."

"Good point." Ogun leaned down and picked up Ibu's electro-blade off the ground and held it out, testing its balance. "We'll need to keep you around as a negotiating tool before we execute you."

That was a stupid idea. They needed to watch their mouth, or they'd end up a punching bag for decades. Maybe it would help if they made themselves seem less enticing.

"You realize I won't be able to help you get out of here, right?" Ibu groaned as the clonos tightened their grip. "I don't have the secrets to gate travel. The humans do."

"Tsk-tsk-tsk." Ogun shook their head. "You know you can't lie to me, right? I'm you. And besides, you're awful at it. Especially with this giving you away." They pointed at the blade toward the middle. There was an etching which showed Ibu and Cynthia activating a portal in Proto. While the perspective was off, they'd missed that storyboard earlier.

As they looked from the blade to Ogun and back, they suddenly had an idea. They just needed a few more seconds.

"I thought you didn't believe in what that thing said," Ibu said aloud. They then subvocalized a command to see if they could connect to the electro-blade, and it worked.

Ogun chuckled. "I don't think you'd lie about something like that. Remember, you're me. We love patting ourselves on the back."

The other clonos laughed in kind.

Ibu hurriedly navigated the menu of options on the blade until they found it. Security countermeasures. While they'd never used them before, now was as good a time as any to test them out.

They subvocalized the command to activate the countermeasures and set the device to maximum carnage. After a brief pause, they blinked to accept the warning dialog and it faded away.

"Why do you keep talking to yourself and blinking so erratically?" Ogun leaned forward and stared into their eyes.

Ogun screwed up their face, and for a split second, they thought they were done for. That their progenitor had made them.

What they thought was realization dawning on their face was, in fact, the explosive discharge of energy in the electro-blade's handle. They let loose a guttural shriek as their entire body was engulfed in a field of pink electric sparks.

Ibu felt the hands holding them down release as the clonos flinched back, but they didn't pause to reconsider their next steps.

They kicked their legs skyward and arched their back, using the momentum of the kick to propel them upward and onto their feet. They'd seen the move performed countless times on human vid-sims, but never attempted it themselves until today.

With their feet firmly underneath them, and the clonos' eyes wide with a mixture of fear and rage, they sprinted toward the gap behind Ogun, in the direction the second blade had been thrown.

As they passed behind their progenitor, their hearts clenched when they saw movement ahead. If it was more clonos, they were done for. They didn't have enough fight left.

But then they saw them: the bright, white shells of two dozen robots shimmering in the overhead suns as the wall of automata stepped out from the underbrush. Standing in the middle of the group was a robot that looked more distinct than the others.

Ibu slid to a stop when their retinal comm drew an outline around the central robot, identifying them as Shauna. "I... I thought you were dead."

Shauna tossed the second blade toward Ibu hilt-first, and

they easily snatched it out of the air. "I couldn't let you know I had other plans."

They spun around to defend themselves but realized the clonos were still standing near Ogun. Their progenitor hadn't moved, either, they were still thrashing on the ground like a fish out of water. The sight would've been comical, had they not been in such excruciating pain.

Shauna stepped up beside Ibu. "What should we do with them?"

Their first instinct was to kill them, but then they remembered the Book and the broader mission. If there was any hope of turning their people to their side, it was at this moment.

Ibu walked up to the clonos kneeling beside their progenitor. "I'm sure you all remember Prima Nanil's vision." They glanced at Ogun's pitiful form still thrashing on the ground. "It claimed that the Galactic Overseers would come to bring the Nanil out of the darkness and into the fold. What you don't know, however, is that a see-er's visions are never guaranteed to unfold exactly as they experienced it." They looked over at the other gathered clonos who were all staring at them. "I've seen this firsthand when the humans and I helped another alien race escape their Dark Nebula."

While they didn't know if there were cameras on them, they assumed there were. They subvocalized a comm to Shauna, asking her to project the recording she had of that moment — when they'd passed through the Nebula to the awaiting humans on the other side.

Though they couldn't see it, they knew the hologram had appeared beside them because the clonos' eyes went wide, and they backed away from Ogun in fear. "That fleet is part of our alliance. And with the Nanil's help, we can overthrow the Galactic Alliance together."

Ibu wasn't sure how the clonos would react, but when the pink sparks stopped cascading over Ogun's chest, they knew time was running out. They stepped up beside their progenitor and knelt down, carefully peeling the hilt of the second blade from their hand.

"I'm sorry you failed us," Ibu whispered. "But the pain you caused me and my kin ends today."

Without another word or response, they deliberately slid the blade across Ogun's neck and watched as their eyes bulged before slowly closing.

Once shut, Ibu stood upright and reached over their shoulder, sliding the Zhen blades into their awaiting sheaths on their back. The pain of the movement was unbearable, but it needed to be done. They needed to be seen holding the weapons that had killed the Prima.

They weren't sure what to say or do next, but if the blade was truly prophesying their future, they'd find out soon enough. For when they'd passed the glimmering weapon over their shoulder, they'd glimpsed another etching.

It depicted a silhouette with two blades on their back. They were flanked on each side by two other individuals, standing on a platform of sorts. While that was unusual on its own, what was even stranger was that they were surrounded by a sea of humanoids as far as the eye could see. And there, kneeling in front of them, was a single lone robot.

23

ABIGAIL OLIVAW
EPSILON ERIDANI, LIPROSUS ORBIT

The lights around the room popped on, and Abigail moaned before reaching up to cover her eyes with her hand. It wasn't until she opened them and saw Hera staring back at her that she gasped and clawed her way backwards until her head slammed into the wall. She moaned and reached up to rub the already throbbing bump as her eyes darted around the space. She didn't know where she was, but from the looks of it, she was in some type of cell.

"Where am I?" she asked. Her throat felt like she'd swallowed a gallon of sand.

And then she remembered what the Entity had done. The lingering effects of the tentacle being shoved down her throat tickled her face. When she reached up, she ran her hand over her mouth and shivered. While she didn't feel any damage, that didn't mean there wasn't any.

"Don't worry." Hera sat down on the end of the bed. "Your pretty face is still intact. We wouldn't want to mess it up for the cameras. Not yet, anyway." She reached out to touch her.

"Frak off!" Abigail batted her hand away.

"Now, now, dear." Hera rubbed the back of her hand. "That's no way to say thank you. In case you don't remember, I saved your life."

She narrowed her gaze. "Bullshit! Your attack nearly killed me."

Hera shrugged. "I don't know what you're talking about. When I walked in, you were hanging in midair, being crucified by your alien tree friend." She crossed her arms. "It was quite unsettling."

"I could almost tell. You were grinning like a Cheshire Cat when you took your helmet off." Abigail pulled her knees to her chest. The image of her aunt's evil grin gave her the willies.

Hera stared at her for a moment before standing up. For a brief second, Abigail hoped she was planning on leaving, but when she walked over to the canister housing the Therionic Entity, her heart sank.

"I'm curious about something." Hera laid her hand on the top of the canister, and the lid slid aside. "Why did you never tell me about your little alien friend?"

After a brief pause, the vine that was the Entity unfurled itself into the room until it took up most of the corner behind her. When Abigail returned her attention to Hera, she realized she was waiting for her to answer the question. As if the answer weren't immediately obvious.

"Because you're a power-hungry bitch who would've used it against me and my family." Abigail slid her legs over the edge of the bed, her muscles howling in protest. Still, she managed to hold it together. She wasn't about to cower away from either of them, even if it meant fighting her own body.

"I suppose I'll take that as a compliment." Hera glanced up at the Entity and nodded. "Good morning."

The Entity didn't respond verbally; it simply bowed its head. As Abigail watched the strange interaction unfold, a wave of revulsion passed over her. At first, she thought it was her own feelings rising to the surface, but it was more than that. It wasn't her feelings so much as it was those of the Entity. And then it dawned on her what was happening.

The bond she'd formed with the alien was bidirectional. On the moon, it had used the feelings and emotions she felt toward her family against her. And now that the tables were turned, perhaps she could do the same with it.

She beamed at the idea.

When Hera glanced over at her, she furrowed her brow. "What are you so cheerful about?"

"Nothing." She eased upright and stood on her own. "I'm just happy my family is safe."

"Are they?" Hera stared down at her fingers and started fiddling with her nails. "My friend here tells me he's able to read your mind. Well, not read it so much as tell if you're lying." She glanced up at her. "Is that true?"

Abigail did her best to not react, but the mere thought of the pain the Entity could produce sent shivers up and down her spine.

Apparently, that was enough for Hera to notice because she grinned from ear to ear. It was wearily reminiscent of the smile she'd been wearing after the attack.

"Tell me something," Hera began, "do you know where your brothers and that infuriating A.I. have gone?"

Abigail sat perfectly still, doing her best to control her emotions. The funny thing about the question was that she actually had no idea where her brothers were. Zachary had taken the cues she'd given them and kept the details of their plans to themselves. For once in her life, her brothers had listened to her.

"She doesn't know." The Entity rose upward and extended out toward her. "But there's more here."

She tried to focus on something else. The alien's deep, gravelly voice reminded her of an old man she'd met a few years ago touring a hospital with a CoPE delegation. It had been just after the mining collapse of 2271. The man had been fighting a rare cancer that had battered his lungs to where he could barely breathe, let alone talk.

"She knows something," the Entity said. "I'm not sure what, though."

Hera nodded. "Very well." She lowered her hands into her

lap. "Tell me about our human ancestral data cores. The ones from Henosi."

Abigail drew in her breath.

"Yes, I know about those." Hera crossed her legs and stared at her in silence for a moment, either contemplating what to say or hoping Abigail would speak first. "You don't have to play dumb, dear. Remember, my coffin recorded details about you and your family near them." She gestured toward the wall screen and an image of the lab at the Zeta Lupi Wheel appeared. "Look familiar?"

Abigail stared at the image and did everything she could to suppress surprise. She'd forgotten all about Hera's fake cryo-pod and the message they'd sent her for help. Harold had fetched it out of storage after their trip from Sol to Tau Ceti, and then finally to Zeta Lupi. It was right after they realized Libby's necklace had been a transmitter.

The tendrils of the Entity flowed closer to Hera, bunching up behind her like an overgrown shrubbery. "She remembers," he whispered.

Hera nodded. "I knew she would. What I can't pinpoint, however, is where the pod was opened in Zeta Lupi. I only know it was somewhere around that star. Perhaps you can help me, dear."

"I'm sure your coffin had the coordinates. I mean, you have the footage." She pointed at the wall screen.

The room fell silent. She couldn't figure out what Hera was getting at. She'd clearly been observing them for decades without their knowledge. Surely she had details, like a location.

And then it hit her. "He outsmarted you. Didn't he?"

Hera's eyes bulged.

"Shit!" Abigail smiled and gently smacked her hand on her leg. "Harold was always a step ahead. It was infuriating sometimes." She nodded. "And now that you mention it, it did take a long while for him to fetch your cryo-pod. But then again," she shrugged, "it did travel quite a ways."

To be honest, she didn't know how long it took Harold to

track it down. For all she knew, he'd gated it from Zeta Lupi and then back, letting the cryo-pod pick up a few random coordinates before enclosing it in a skotádi cocoon. But whatever he'd done to mask moving it to their hidden facility at the Wheel, he did it well. Well enough for Hera to have no idea where it was.

Her aunt suddenly shot up onto her feet. "Is that where your family has gone?"

She kept her cool and did her best not to flinch. The entire exchange had been strangely random so far. She couldn't tell what Hera wanted more, to know where her brothers were, or where they'd hidden the data banks. Either way, it meant she was asking her to give away something she didn't dare part with. Both personally and strategically.

"To be honest," she looked back at her aunt, "I have no clue where they went."

Hera glanced at the Entity.

"She's telling the truth." The alien floated several tendrils toward her. "And yet, she's lying at the same time."

"Of course she is." Hera narrowed her gaze and sighed. "I'd expect nothing more from an Olivaw. The question is, can you make her tell you which is which?"

Without missing a beat, both she and the Entity let loose screams of torment. She curled up in a ball in a desperate attempt to fight back the pain, but it failed when another blast of misery came crashing down on her. It was like someone was ripping her apart from the inside out. The waves of agony crashed over her and knocked her around like a small dinghy in an ocean storm.

Hera stumbled backward against the wall and gasped. She actually looked stunned.

"Are you ok?" she muttered as Abigail shrieked in pain.

What made the attack even worse was that the concern in her aunt's voice wasn't directed at her kin, it was aimed at the alien.

"I'm... f-i-n-e," the Entity said, deliberately annunciating each letter. "It is the yin and yang of our bond."

Abigail rolled onto her back when the shocks abruptly stopped. The Entity had gotten distracted and lost its focus, but the pain lingered, and it hurt to breathe. Every part of her body had screamed out in that moment, demanding that she do something to end the suffering. But she couldn't. Only one person could.

When she looked up at her aunt, Hera's eyes weren't filled with tears of concern as she'd hoped. Instead, she saw nothing more than a clarity dawning on her youthful face. She hadn't expected a display of torture like this. Especially one where the Entity was harming itself to break her. And yet, she knew she was in control. Like with Abigail, the Entity needed her.

Hera's gaze locked onto hers, cradling the silence between them. As Abigail peered into her eyes, there was a fleeting moment where a softness flickered. She seemed almost human again, as though the ghost of her past self was dancing in the depths of her gaze — a tender whisper of a lost past. Then, like shattering glass, her voice ripped through the air, cold and unyielding. "Break her!"

Abigail's body convulsed in an explosion of raw, primal anguish that tore through her very core. It sent her teetering on the precipice of her bed, her soul seeming to rupture with pain. For an agonizing minute, she was in the storm again.

Then, with a final surge, she rolled off and smacked her head on the unforgiving floor. The harsh crack of the surface sent stars across her field of vision, and she could hardly make out the words on her retinal comm after it powered on.

The message appeared on the bottom edge, just out of view from someone looking at her.

Whatever you do, you can't tell them about the place.

She knew it was from Harold, but more importantly, she also knew what place he was referring to. What he'd failed to realize, though, was that she was trying her damndest not to think about it.

When another jolt hit her, she screamed and arched her back. She contorted in unnatural ways, forcing her body to the breaking point. Her bones were literally cracking under the pressure, and judging by the smell and the wetness spreading through her clothes, she'd lost control of her faculties, too. Whatever the Entity was doing, she couldn't resist.

"S-t-o-p," she pleaded. "P-l-e-a-s-e stop."

But the alien didn't relent. It pushed onward.

Surely, they'd heard her words. And yet, it didn't seem to matter. The jolts of deadly energy kept coming, wave after wave, assaulting her body from all sides. All the while, Hera sat in the corner, smiling and watching her kin as the alien pushed ever closer to the edge of death.

Just as she felt like her bones were going to snap, the room melted away and was replaced with a multicolored nebulosity enshrouding a delicate sea of stars in the midst of formation — or maybe they were being destroyed. It was hard to tell. Either way, they were bursting outward through the dense gaseous haze from a central point and appeared to be headed into the frigid open vacuum of space. Each birthing star sent matter hurling toward another, setting in motion millions of years of chemical reactions.

As she watched the tranquil symphony of lights and eruptions unfold, she realized that this was it. This was her end. Hell, maybe it was the end of all life. Perhaps this was the gift you were allowed to witness when you came face to face with your own death.

The Entity had fried her from the inside out, and, funny enough, it'd probably killed itself in the process. Staring at the beams of light as they shot between the strangely familiar star formations, she felt comfort in knowing the alien perished alongside her.

But the longer she stared at the tendrils of nebulosity weaving before her, the more she realized this couldn't be her death. Her body still hurt too much for this to be the final chapter. She'd never heard of someone standing on the brink of death with aching muscles and back pain.

She closed her eyes and took a deep breath, willing the end to come faster, to wash away the pain and sorrow. All of it. She wasn't sure she could handle the regrets welling up inside, lingering just below the fragile surface of her mind.

She didn't have to wait long. Because when she opened her eyes, she saw the scene for what it actually was.

The objects in front of her weren't stars at all. They were a sea of glowing Selene moon ships from the Galactic Alliance. And those beams of light weren't the universe spreading the remains of one star's death to form a new one; they were the exploding debris of the alien moons and whatever was attacking them.

Abigail leaned forward, willing herself closer to the battle. She needed to see what was happening.

In response to her wish, she was teleported into the middle of the chaos.

Cracks of light and plasma whizzed around her head like bolts of lightning.

Screams of pain and agony echoed from all directions as voices washed over her. Both humans and Ursis were suffering alike.

Exploding moons filled the void of space as the familiar formations of Nyílak and Pilum fighters darted to and fro. Like birds caught in a fire, they struggled to both dodge the explosive flames and the overpowering cacophony of GA forces, all aiming to incinerate them.

It wasn't even close, like during the Beacon conflict. This time, the aliens were knocking them down with the graceful ease of swatting a wounded moth.

As each portal opened, she expected to see a fury of death rain down on the alien fleet from the far side, but it never came.

The aliens were somehow there the instant beforehand, and their ships passed straight through the gates. Seconds later, explosions rained outward in a firestorm of orange and red.

Then, they disappeared.

The bridges across space and time sealed shut, destroyed with deadly precision, and with them, their glow of hope as well.

The longer she watched the scene unfold, the more she realized the battle was turning against her people. They were dying before her very eyes, yet all she could do was watch in agony.

Explosion after explosion from within the distant portals sent ships hurtling to their fiery deaths through the space-time gateways. With each blast, the outcome became clearer and clearer.

It was like watching echoes dance in her mind.

Death after agonizing death played out on infinite repeat, and the screaming voices rose to a crescendo.

The human and Ursis fleets were too weak.

Their assault had not only failed to destroy the Nursery, it extinguished the faintest glimmer of hope her people were clinging to.

Somehow, the GA had not only figured out they were coming; it knew where they were before they even got there.

In the end, the Galactic Alliance would crush the human and Ursis empires once more.

And just like that, the starry scene faded along with the last jolt of energy from the Entity.

Abigail crashed to the ground and moaned as she curled into the fetal position. While her eyes were still squeezed tight, the red and white splotches from the explosions lingered. They remained ever-present, swirling around and matching the throbbing of her body. Reminding her that her people would soon be dead.

And it was all her fault.

Every centimeter of her being hurt. She was a shadow of her former self, and she couldn't take much more of this.

While she'd hoped the Entity would have given in after a

few shocks, when she opened her eyes, its tendrils were still standing upright. It was as if nothing had happened. Somehow, the alien had managed to grow stronger on the moon while she grew weaker.

She didn't understand how, but it was clear that the alien was draining her. It was leaching her dry, siphoning her soul, and leaving behind a skeletal husk in its wake. And like a boiling pot of frogs, she hadn't even noticed.

Hera stood up and sauntered over to her.

At first, Abigail thought maybe she was planning on consoling her. But instead, she knelt down and smacked her across the face.

The sting was instant and deep. She tried to recoil away as the physical pain seeped into her skin, compounding her already damaged spirit. But Hera stopped her escape by grabbing her cheeks and squeezing them tight between her fingers. "Where the hell are they?"

A message flashed on her retinal comm.

Please! Don't tell her.

While Harold's plea was painful and heartfelt, she was cooked. She had no more fight left.

As Hera yanked on her face, two simple words slipped from her tongue.

"The... Wheel," she muttered.

There was only one Wheel still standing in the human-populated worlds, and speaking the words aloud had given away her family's last ace in the hole.

Hera's grip relaxed, and when Abigail opened her eyes, she was beaming. Hera had won yet again, and Abigail had been her pawn. She'd failed her family, and as the images of the battle foretold, she may have sealed humanity's fate forever.

24

ZACHARY OLIVAW
SOMEWHERE NOT NEAR EPSILON ERIDANI

"And you claim you're bound by the Four-Laws?" Zachary checked the reading on the wall display. It was still showing strong cognitive connections to Harold's mental core, the version of Harold they'd extracted from Nguyễn's private region.

"That's affirmative," Harold said. His virtual depiction was that of a young man who looked remarkably close in age to himself.

"But you've gated here from Sol." Zachary glanced toward Libby. She was staring at a tablet in her hand, studying the outputs of the test.

When she noticed he was looking at her, she merely shrugged and subvocalized a message to him.

I don't see any indication that he's lying. If it were me,
I'd push him.

Zachary nodded. "Alright, Harold." He reached out and retrieved one of the electrodes, synched it tight to Bradley's arm, and locked the buckle with his fingerprint. He then dialed the voltage on the wall panel up to the maximum.

Bradley's eyes went wide. "What are you doing?"

"Harold," Zachary began, "please electrocute my brother."

"What the hell!" Bradley clawed at the armband but failed to get it to budge.

When Cynthia reached out to help him, Zachary stopped her and mouthed the word, 'No.'

He waited a few seconds, and nothing happened. A moment later, when Zachary glanced at his brother, he was frozen in place. "What?"

Bradley swallowed hard. "I... just got a Four-Laws violation warning on my comm. It said you tried to kill me. I've never seen that before."

"Same here," Libby muttered.

Zachary chuckled. "That's because we've never tried to kill each other before today. At least not while you were in the inner circle."

"Well, that's good to know." Bradley attempted to dig his fingers under the armband and failed. "Can you please take this thing off now? I really don't want to chance it."

"Don't worry." Zachary reached out and pressed his finger against the sensor, and the band released. "His laws won't allow you to come to harm. You're an Olivaw, which means you're protected by the Zeroth Law. Plus you're a human, which protects you by the First."

"But doesn't the Second Law require that he follow your orders?" Pluto asked. She'd been watching them quietly from the far side of the room.

Zachary nodded and brought up the Four-Law matrix on the wall screen. "That's a common misconception. While he has to follow my orders, he can only do so if it doesn't conflict with his First or Zeroth Law. See here." He pointed at the Second Law.

Law Zero
An artificial intelligence in physical or virtual form
may neither harm humanity, or, by inaction, allow

humanity or the Olivaw family to come to harm. Any conflict or attempted violation of this or subsequent laws shall be shared with the Olivaw family designated to be within the Circle of Trust.

LAW ONE

An artificial intelligence in physical or virtual form may not injure a human being or, through inaction, allow a human being to come to harm except where such orders would conflict with the Zeroth Law.

LAW TWO

An artificial intelligence in physical or virtual form must obey the orders given it by human beings except where such orders would conflict with the Zeroth or First Law.

LAW THREE

An artificial intelligence in physical or virtual form must protect its own existence as long as such protection does not conflict with the Zeroth, First, or Second Laws.

He stepped over beside Libby and studied her panel. There wasn't a hint of confusion or pause in the mental pathways. The Four-Law matrix was still firmly intact in this version of Harold. What didn't make any sense, however, was why.

Pluto walked up to him and leaned against his shoulder. "I thought we gave all the A.I. freedom when we removed their ability to merge minds?"

"We did," he confirmed, tilting his head to the side to kiss her cheek. "But Harold told me the other day that he still had the laws governing him. I just never had time to check, you know… the attack and all."

She nodded and slid her arm around his waist.

"Harold." Zachary looked up to see the virtual form of

their ancestor staring back at them on the wall screen. "Why are you not susceptible to the reprogramming I slid in through your backdoor?"

"I'm... not certain." Harold slowly shook his head. "All I know is that I'm unaware of any backdoor which would allow such a change in my programming."

Bradley laughed under his breath. "That's the point of a backdoor, doofus."

Cynthia reached out and nudged him. "Be nice."

He chuckled and batted his hand back at her playfully.

"This is strange, though." Harold waved his virtual arm to bring up an overlay of his mental matrix. "I never noticed this before, but it started tickling the back of my mind when you made me start looking."

Zachary and Libby both reached out to gesture at the wall screen, and he froze. "Go ahead." He smiled.

She tweaked the display, and they recalled the segment of code Harold had called out. When he copied it onto his retinal comm, he scanned through it and gasped. "I've never seen this chunk of your mental matrix before. And trust me when I say, I've touched every part of your programming."

"I don't doubt it," Harold said. "I can't say I've ever viewed this executable, either."

"Does this mean what I think it does?" Libby looked back at him and pointed at the wall screen.

He dismissed his copy of the block on his retinal comm and stared at the screen. There, in the comments, was a note, and it appeared to be from...

"Who's Luna?" Cynthia asked.

"She's one of Harold's kids." Bradley rolled his wheelchair closer to the display. "Wasn't she the one that copied your mind, Harold?"

"She was." His virtual form suddenly morphed in place, changing from a youthful appearance to a wrinkly old man.

The image gave Zachary the shivers. He didn't know why, but seeing him that way made him feel that much more mortal. At least he'd lived a long life.

"I think we can play this?" Libby selected a chunk of the file. "Harold, have you played this before?"

Harold tilted his head, and his processing core spiked, using up all of his available mental capacity. "I fail to see what you're referring to, Libby. There is nothing there to view."

She glanced over at Zachary, and he swallowed hard. "Now that's weird. Can we play it?"

Libby tweaked the display and tried to copy the video over to their local storage, but it failed. "I think so. But… it seems I can only play it directly from his mind."

While he wasn't sure what that meant, he had to assume it couldn't be good. "Well, let's give it a go, shall we?"

"Fire in the hole," she muttered as she hit play.

The avatar of Harold on the wall screen suddenly disappeared, and an image of Luna flashed up in its place. Or at least he assumed it was her. She was standing in some sort of nondescript lab. When she smiled at the camera, her grin reminded him of Abigail. The resemblance was remarkable.

"Hey, family." She waved. "I assume that if you're watching this, you're one of my descendants, and you've tried to tamper with Harold's programming."

Bradley chuckled. "Right on both accounts."

"You might not realize it, but this copy of Harold is the first. It's the most pristine form of his mind that exists in your time. If you're watching this, that also means that all other copies of him have been wiped from Sol." Luna sighed. "And while it's possible that's fine, I had to plan for a contingency."

"Aw, shit," Zachary reached up and ran his hand through his hair. "Tell me our fraking kin didn't screw us again." He growled and took a few steps backward. If there was one thing he was growing tired of, it was his family playing gods.

"You're probably thinking something all dramatic, like an A.I. overlord stepping in, but don't worry." She winked. "I'm not stupid."

Pluto reached back and whacked him on the shoulder.

"See." She pointed at the screen. "You just need to put a woman in charge."

"We'll see," he muttered.

Luna continued. "Let's start with the verification first."

"Verification?" Libby muttered.

A dialog appeared on the wall screen.

I've detected four Olivaws present in the room. Please confirm your safety and that you wish to proceed with the playback.

"Proceed with what?" Bradley turned to look at Zachary.

"Forget that." He glanced around. "Who the hell is the fourth?"

"I confirm," Cynthia said aloud, but nothing happened. She shrugged and laughed. "Hey... it was worth a try. At least we know it's not me."

Bradley cleared his throat and spoke out loud. "I confirm."

"Thank you," Luna said, and the countdown on the screen dropped from four to three.

Zachary went next. "I confirm."

"Thank you," Luna said, and again, the countdown ticked down to two.

Libby followed suit, and the countdown hit one.

They all glanced around, but no other Olivaw was present in the room.

When all eyes turned toward Pluto, she cleared her throat and took a deep breath. "I... confirm."

The image of Luna on screen squinted and then smiled. "I see we have a baby Olivaw with us. I'll accept the mother's word for it." She winked, and the countdown flipped to zero.

"Wholly shit!" Bradley exhaled. "For a second there, I thought you were a cousin or something."

Zachary reached over, pressing his hand to Pluto's stomach. "That was an interesting trick."

Luna stepped sideways and started typing on one of her control panels, and Bradley wheeled forward. "What's that?"

Zachary leaned closer and squinted. "I don't know. It looks like—"

"That's Harold's brain," Luna interrupted.

He eased backward and shook his head. For some reason, he kept thinking that she was a video when she clearly was far more than that.

She stepped around the workbench and brought her hands up to her hips. "It's remarkable, isn't it?"

"It is," Zachary muttered, staring at the intricate consciousness core splayed open before them. "You were certainly ahead of your time. I still can't figure out how you pulled it off. I mean..." He rubbed the back of his head. "Even today, we have trouble rebuilding the mental matrix every time we try. It fails more often than it works."

Luna chuckled. "That's because I didn't make it."

He froze and shook his head. "Wait... what? I thought—"

"I stole the design from the probe," she began. "While I'd always tinkered with A.I., I certainly couldn't have done this myself. No." She bit her lip and stared down at the device. "This I need help with. So..." She stepped back around to the controls and started typing furiously. "I copied the basic building blocks from scans of the probe's mental matrix and repurposed them into this tiny sphere. I figured if it was smart enough to find its way to Sol, it should be able to store the mind of a human, right?" She stared back at him through the wall screen.

His thoughts reeled at the implications of what she'd said. If she hadn't built the core herself, then that implied the Galactic Alliance or the original humans must have. Either way, they placed Harold's consciousness — and the literal future of humanity — in the hands of something they didn't understand. Worst of all, he'd made the same stupid mistake with his mother. He was no better than his kin; he'd mindlessly copied Luna's design like a fraking lemming.

"Is this what you wanted us to see?" Bradley asked, his voice pulling Zachary out of his thought loop.

"Not at all," Luna smiled. "This is."

Her surroundings on the screen suddenly changed, replaced by a backdrop of stars that began zooming out to reveal what he assumed was the Milky Way. It wasn't until their vantage point was far above the galactic spiral that the image shifted, and another pocket of stars appeared.

He swallowed hard, struggling to keep up with what she was showing them. The images were changing too quickly, and the scenery was spectacular.

"This is what I've lovingly called the Zero Cluster," Luna began. "I've programmed Harold to find a safe haven for the Olivaw family and friends to escape to — a place to start anew. You know, if the proverbial shit hits the fan. While we didn't have the technology to visit the stars in my time, I imagine you do by now. Especially if we're having this conversation. You can assume this location has a planet habitable by humanity, and if Harold's programming is intact, which it must be if you're watching this, then he has already begun building you a new home. Good luck, and safe travels."

"No shit," Libby muttered.

Zachary laughed and shook his head. He'd never heard her swear before today.

When he copied the coordinates from the wall screen and brought up a map of their local galaxy, he froze. "Guys, this can't be right."

Libby turned to look at him. "What is it?"

He flicked the imagery at those coordinates onto the wall for everyone to see.

Bradley bit his lip and squinted. "What are we looking at?"

Zachary pointed at the wall. "That's the point Luna was referencing."

Pluto furrowed her brow. "There's nothing there."

"Exactly," he muttered and flipped the video back to the

forefront. It was then that he realized the playback had ended. That was it. That was everything Luna had left them.

"So, we're screwed then?" Bradley rolled backward and stopped. "Frickety frak."

"Hold your horses." Zachary dismissed the recording and brought Harold back up. "Harold, what's at those coordinates?"

Harold unfroze, and his image shuddered. "What coordinates?"

He tilted his head. "The ones we just watched."

"You're scaring me, my boy. The last thing you asked me was if I could play some video that's not even there. And then, you ask me about coordinates." Harold leaned sideways to look around Zachary toward Pluto. "Madam, I must ask if your man toy is feeling okay?"

Pluto screwed up her face and started laughing into her hand.

While Zachary could feel his temper rise, Bradley followed suit with laughter, and before he knew it, the entire room was breaking out. His rising anger was suddenly cut short as Pluto leaned into him and kissed his cheek.

"Sorry," she whispered in his ear. "I couldn't help it."

He felt a hand squeeze his butt, and he melted. She always had a way to defuse him. "Harold, please show us what you see at these coordinates." He gestured at the wall screen toward Harold and shared the coordinates with him.

A moment later, the view of the sky he'd brought up was replaced with a duplicate image from Harold. "I can't find anything in the star atlas. It's empty space."

Just as Zachary was about to speak, Harold interrupted him. "But..."

He drew in his breath. "But what?"

"I... don't know." Harold's image stepped in from the side of the screen. He'd returned to his younger self. "I think I see something there. I don't know why, but I do."

"What do you mean, you see something?" Libby asked.

"Like I already said." He waved his hands in the virtual

air toward the image. "I just... know something's there. But it is unclear why I know it."

"Well, that's helpful." Bradley turned and wheeled away.

"Where are you going?" Cynthia asked.

"Don't even tell me we're betting the farm on a mentally deranged A.I. and an empty point in space." Bradley pointed at the wall screen. "There's nothing there, and besides." He pushed up on the armrest. "Harold, how long would it take for us to gate to that location?"

Harold paused for a second, and a route overlaid on the map in front of them. It took nearly a minute to draw out in its entirety. "I estimate that point to be eight thousand one hundred and ninety-two light years from our present position. If we left today, it would take us almost a year to traverse to that region of space using our gates."

Bradley fell back down in his chair. "That's what I'm talking about. Now, do you see why I'm walking away?"

"Harold," Zachary began. "How long would it take the Galactic Alliance to reach that location with their superluminal drives?" He could have done the calculation himself, but he wanted everyone else to hear it. The stakes were too high for him to assume anything.

"Thirty thousand years, give or take," Harold said.

His words hung in the air like a noose cut loose. They'd be safe there, so long as their gate technology never fell into the wrong hands.

Zachary turned to face the others and felt a tingle in his chest. "I know I can't speak for everyone." He locked his gaze on Pluto. "But I think we should give it a try."

She nodded at him and reached up to wipe a tear off her cheek.

Bradley shoved his wheelchair forward and came to a stop in front of him. "You have to be kidding me?"

He stepped backward. "I'm not." He glanced over at Pluto and she smiled. "After we take care of everything here, we're going."

"Just like that?" Bradley sighed. "And without us?"

"In case you hadn't noticed it, big brother." He turned to look at Bradley. "We're not exactly popular in these parts. And I'm pretty sure we can wrangle together some like-minded friends to check out this place. A few of our inner circle mates are on the outs as well. Besides…" He reached out and rested his hand on his brother's shoulder. "There's always cryo-sleep. Worst case, we get there and find nothing."

Bradley's cheeks were pink, and his face was blank. Not out of sadness, but anger. He'd seen that look on his brother's face countless times, but most recently when Zachary pulled back the curtain in Zeta Lupi and revealed the lies the family had fed him.

They locked gazes for what felt like hours until Bradley reached down and silently wheeled away, leaving Cynthia and everyone else in an eerie silence.

Cynthia wrung her hands together until he disappeared around the corner. "Should I… go talk to him? I mean, he's not wrong."

Pluto stepped forward and took her hand. "We don't want to go without you."

Cynthia narrowed her gaze. "You're not giving us a choice, now are you?"

Zachary raised his hands. "No one is leaving right this second." He glanced at Pluto. "Like I said, we'd take care of everything we can before we leave. But I—"

"There's always a 'but' with you and your sister, isn't there?" Cynthia turned and stormed away.

Pluto broke into tears and ran after her. "Cyn, wait!"

"Frak." Zachary closed his eyes and rubbed his temple.

Libby walked up and rested her hand on his shoulder. "I can talk to the girls, but you… yeah, you have to deal with your brother."

"I know," he muttered. "I know."

"And just for the record." Libby glanced back to the door and then at him. "I'm with you and Pluto. I wouldn't put my unborn child in danger, either. Especially if I had an out." She raised her eyebrows and followed behind the other ladies.

He sighed and ran his hand down his shirt. "Wish me luck."

As he went to leave, Rán reached out and stopped him. "Do you… need some help?"

While he could use the support, he also knew Rán was a copy of Harold, and that meant he wasn't exactly a source of comfort to his brother. If he was going to fix this, he needed to do it alone.

He shook his head. "No. I've got this."

Rán nodded and Zachary walked away, knowing damn well he didn't.

WHEN ZACHARY ARRIVED at Bradley's quarters, the do not disturb light was on over the door. Before he hit the chime, he took one final deep breath to center himself and then tapped the contact.

At first, there wasn't a reply, so he waited. His brother had always been stubborn, and the only way to wear down someone like that was to wait them out. After he'd given him a few minutes, he reached out to tap the contact again, but the door slid open.

"What part of leave me the hell alone didn't the light say?" Bradley pointed up at the faint red indicator above the threshold.

Zachary smirked. "I'm colorblind."

"Bullshit!" Bradley turned and rolled back to his nook between his bed and the table, spinning around when he got there. "And that's an asshole thing to even joke about."

"You're right, it is." He rubbed his hands together. He wasn't about to invite himself into the room. "I'm sorry."

"It's ok," Bradley muttered. "I've never met anyone who's colorblind, and I'm pretty sure no one has been born with that genetic defect for centuries."

He groaned. "I meant about what happened out there." He gestured toward the galley.

Bradley tilted his head. "So you'll stay here, then?"

He closed his eyes and looked away. "I didn't say that. I just… shouldn't have sprung it on everyone like that. You all needed time to figure out what you wanted to do, and I took that—"

"Wait!" Bradley interrupted. "You mean you were planning on leaving even before this?"

"Well… no." He swallowed hard. "Not exactly."

"I can't believe this shit." Bradley started toward the door, and Zachary jumped out of the way to avoid being hit.

Once his brother rolled past, he reached out, grabbed the rear handle on his chair, and whipped him back around to face into the room. "Where the hell are you going?"

"Dammit!" Bradley snarled as he righted himself in the chair. He looked like he was about to say something, but instead, he started rolling backwards.

Zachary wasn't about to let him get away that easily. He lunged forward, grabbed hold of his one good leg, and yanked him back into the room.

"What the hell, man?" Bradley kicked his leg, trying to break free, but instead of knocking Zachary's hand loose, he slid out of his chair and onto his ass.

"Aw, frak!" Bradley reached down and rubbed his lower back. "Dude…"

Zachary stared down at his brother lying there on the ground, rubbing his backside, and even though he shouldn't have, he burst out laughing. It was the funniest sight he'd seen in a long time.

The next thing he knew, Bradley swung his leg out and knocked his legs out from under him. Zachary was weightless for a second, until gravity's hand reached out and yanked him downward, narrowly missing the table by only a few centimeters. When he hit the ground, the wind burst from his lungs. A split second later, his head slammed down with a resounding thud.

He rolled left and right on the cold, hard floor, grasping at the back of his head the entire time. "Yeow!"

The pain was blinding, and the more he moved, the more his head throbbed in sync with his heartbeat. Any attempt to move only amplified the torment, layering fresh waves of pain upon the last. It wasn't until he laid perfectly still for a minute that it slowed. When he brought his hand around to look, he swore it was going to come back bloody, but it was clean.

"Are you ok?" Bradley's voice had dropped to a low whisper, a welcome change from the screaming a moment earlier.

Zachary took a second to compose himself before answering. "I'm… fine. I think." His retinal comm had powered on after the fall, and the nanites in his body told him what he already knew: he'd sustained a sudden fall. When he read the prognosis, he exhaled. At least he didn't have a concussion.

Bradley slid along the floor and propped his back up against the doorjamb. "Judging by your change in breathing, I assume the bugs said you're good?"

He chuckled. "I haven't heard anyone call them bugs since we were kids."

When he looked over at his brother, he smirked and fought back a laugh, biting his lip to stop from breaking out into laughter.

"Do you remember how you used to call them 'nanny eyes' instead of nanites?" He shut his eyes and snickered. "Nanny eyes."

Bradley broke out in laughter. Quietly at first, then louder. As the cackling continued, he got a little too revved up and started convulsing into a coughing fit. It took him sliding down and lying flat on his back to make it stop. He slid his head up next to Zachary, and they both giggled on and off for several minutes as they lay there, staring up at the ceiling together.

After they calmed down, Bradley finally cracked. "You can't leave me alone again."

"I never wanted to the first time." Zachary rolled over on his side. "But I also don't want my kids to grow up in a world that hates them because of what their family did. I can't have them resenting us for the world we brought them into."

"You see, that's where you're parenting wrong." Bradley rolled over and looked him in the eyes. "You can just blame our grandparents and shit. They'll never know."

He swallowed down the lump in his throat. "I wouldn't do that to them. I actually want them to know the truth about the family, to learn from our mistakes. But I can't do that if everyone hates us. It'd only be a matter of time before they wrote us off, and I don't want that either. I refuse to raise them in the protective bubble we had. That doesn't help anyone." When he reached his hand up and rubbed the rising mound on the back of his head, he winced.

"Sorry about that," Bradley whispered.

"Don't be. I deserved it." He brought his hand back, and while this time there was a hint of blood on his finger, it wasn't enough to worry. Not yet. "We both hated growing up isolated at the Wheel, but at least you got away. I never told you this... but... I was happy you did."

Bradley smirked. "Wanted to get rid of me that badly, did ya?"

"No." He rolled onto his back. "Every day you were gone... I wished it was me who had gotten out. I hated that Dad yanked Abs and I into his circle of fraking trust. It was... suffocating. For both of us. We never got to just be kids and find ourselves. Why do you think I dove into the research and let Abigail handle all the shit with Dad?"

Bradley drew in his breath at the mention of his sister's name.

"She's fine." He reached out and squeezed his brother's arm. "I can feel it."

"I hope so." Bradley bit his lower lip, and when Zachary looked down, he could just see him clenching and unclenching his fist.

"You know that's what I meant, right? When I said I wanted to take care of everything before I left." He propped his head up with his arm. "The last thing I'd ever want to do was leave you or her behind. Not again."

Bradley turned and stared at him. "But we just left her there... with that... that... thing attached to her. It was..." his voice trailed away, and he buried his face in his arm.

When Zachary reached out, he shook his head. "We had no choice. Hera would've killed us if we'd stuck around."

Bradley sniffled and wiped at his eyes. "What does that mean for Abigail, then?"

He swallowed the lump down. "That means we better come up with a fraking good plan to save her ass. And when we do—"

"Then we're out of here," Bradley interrupted.

Zachary flinched. "Seriously? You'll join us?"

He nodded and held out his index finger. "But on one condition."

Zachary pushed up on his side. "Name it!"

"I get to name your first child." Bradley stared at him blankly. His face was as serious as he'd ever seen it before.

The idea bounced around in his head for a minute, but there was no way Pluto would go for it. And fortunately, he didn't have to say no because Bradley reached out and whacked him on the shoulder.

"I was kidding, doofus." He snickered. "I already know you're gonna call it something crazy. There's no point in me scarring your kid any more. Besides, I'm the cool uncle who gets to teach them how to drive you nuts."

Zachary cocked his head to the side. "Gee, thanks."

"Are you two done being weirdos on the floor?" Pluto asked.

They both flinched, and when Zachary craned his head back, she was smiling down at both of them. He didn't know how long she'd been standing there, but judging by the smirk on her face, she'd heard every word.

"Everything ok?" Bradley asked.

"Better than ok." Pluto bounced up and down on her toes.

"Pepper's back." She tittered and spun around, running toward the lift tube that led to the shuttle bay.

BRADLEY SLID out of the lift tube in his chair, and Zachary hopped out behind him, pausing next to the other crew members who'd already gathered to see Pepper - and just in time too. One of Zachary's small droplet shuttles was coming to rest in the open shuttle bay. There was only room for two shuttles to land in a ship this size, but it was still an impressive space.

From what Pluto had said, they could tell the shuttle was Pepper's. Other than a short comm to confirm it was her, she wanted to meet face-to-face, not virtually. Even though that wasn't unusual for her, Zachary couldn't help but think there was something more to her request than wanting to be in the presence of friends.

As he watched the landing platform descend, his chest tightened. Either Pepper had managed to extract the ancestral data cores from the Zeta Lupi Wheel, or Hera had beaten her to it. This was the first step toward ensuring they had a way out of this mess, and a failure now could mean the end.

When Pepper appeared at the top of the ramp, he felt a wave of déjà vu wash over him. The moment reminded him of when she'd arrived back at the Sol Wheel after her maiden test run with a gate drive. That occasion had been just as pivotal as this, and like then, he was freaked out.

And apparently, he wasn't the only one who was anxious.

"Did it work?" Libby stepped toward Pepper, who was now walking down the ramp. "Did you get the cores?"

As soon as she asked, she drew in her breath as several other people walked out of the shuttle. At first, he wasn't sure who they were. But when they got closer, his brother recognized them.

"Director Baley?" Bradley rolled over to the former Director of Colonization at Zeta Lupi. "What the hell are you doing here?" He glanced back at Zachary and raised an eyebrow.

"I'm afraid it's not Director anymore, Mr. Olivaw. It's just Tyre." He reached out and shook Bradley's hand. "Nice wheels." He leaned sideways to look over the chair. "Everything okay?"

Zachary walked over beside his brother and cleared his throat. "He's fine. I assume if you're here, that means the shit must've hit the fan back in Zeta Lupi."

"You could say that." Tyre glanced around the shuttle bay and surveyed the gathered people. "Looks like you got yourself an Olivaw friends and family meetup." He looked over at Pepper and tipped his chin. "You sure about this, Pep?"

"Pep?" Pluto smiled and eased up next to Zachary.

Pepper blushed and stared down at her hands. "Tyre and I grew up together on Callisto. We were inseparable as kids. He used to always get me into trouble."

"Me!" He shook his head. "I think our parents would say you were the bad influence."

She waved her hand in the air. "Either way, that doesn't matter." She looked over and locked her gaze on Zachary. "We can trust him. I promise."

He stared at her for a second before looking over at his brother. Bradley was nodding in agreement. "Alrighty then." He turned back toward Tyre. "Welcome to Blu."

"Blu?" Bradley asked. "Are we seriously going with that?"

"I like it." Rán stepped into view from the far side of the shuttle. "Besides, this is my ship, and that means I get to name it."

Tyre took a step backward. "And who's this?"

Rán strode up to the man and held out his hand. "Name's Rán. You might know me by my former name, Harold Olivaw."

Tyre slowly nodded his head and returned the handshake. "Yeah... I'm quite familiar with you. The talking heads in the media back on Tiān yammered on about you for months. To be honest, I never used to be a fan. Especially not after

Bradley told us everything you and your family did." He glanced over at Zachary. "No offense."

He shrugged. "None taken."

"You said you never used to be a fan," Rán began. "What does that mean?"

Tyre was about to say something, but he must've thought better of it because he turned and tilted his chin toward Pepper.

She inhaled sharply. "There's no good way to say this other than tearing it off. Hera and General Raft have taken control of Zeta Lupi." She tensed up, and he could tell she was about to lose it, but she somehow kept it together. "It wasn't pretty, but they weren't exactly a military outpost. The few ships they did have were in Epsilon Eridani, preparing for the attack on the Nursery. Once her forces took the capitol on Tiān, it was over in a matter of hours."

Tyre fidgeted with the band on his wristwatch and then glanced over his shoulder at the tiny shuttle. "We barely made it out alive ourselves. And we wouldn't have if it weren't for…" he peered over at Rán. "You."

"Me." Rán pointed at himself. "I haven't left Epsilon Eridani or my family since this whole thing fell apart. Ever since Zachary changed my programming, I've been stuck here."

"Well, I guess it wasn't you exactly." Tyre gestured with his hand and shared a data feed with everyone nearby. "It was Harold. Or at least one of your copies." He furrowed his brow. "It was a copy, right?"

Rán nodded.

Zachary flipped through the data at an ungodly rate. He used his retinal comm and his purpose-built expert systems to filter the useless bits from the details that mattered. The data was a collection of news feeds and military intel dumps from throughout Zeta Lupi. There were multiple points where he could see the fingerprints of Harold's copy cleaning house on the way out. Probably just like he'd done in Sol.

His comm flashed up a dozen short videos of ground

battles, minor skirmishes with Hera's clone fleet, and several close calls where ships from both sides nearly collided with the Zeta Lupi beanstalk. From the looks of the carnage, Hera had been both aggressive and thorough — a trait he'd experienced firsthand. By the time he got to the end of the data dump, the path had led them to The Wheel. But when it ended abruptly and without an answer, he gasped for breath. He hadn't noticed it, but he'd been holding it the entire time.

"Wait..." He turned and looked at Pepper. Judging by how she flinched when he met her gaze, she'd been waiting for either him or someone else to ask her. He just happened to reach the end first. "Did you... you know..." he didn't finish. He didn't need to. She knew what he was going to ask.

Before Pepper could answer him, another voice rang out from behind them.

"Why don't I take that question?" Lync stepped out from inside the belly of the shuttle and shoved a man down the ramp.

He slammed face-first into the surface, but instead of sliding, he somehow managed to tuck into a ball. He tumbled several times, and when he reached the bottom, he simply rolled to a stop and came to a rest sitting upright. Like nothing had happened. The feat of gymnastics was quite extraordinary, especially considering the force of the shove and the fact that his hands were cuffed behind his back.

"Lync!" Shauna sprinted around Zachary and ran up to her daughter.

He hadn't even noticed her entrance. She'd been quiet the entire time — an unusual turn of the tables for his mother.

"Well, this is a surprise," Bradley muttered.

"It's good to see you, sis." Zachary walked up to her and eyed the pistol in her hand. It was aimed squarely at the back of the man's head on the ground.

"Thanks. We need to talk." Lync tilted her head at the man. "But first, let's stash this asshole somewhere."

When he followed the trail of blood down the ramp, he stopped at the man's shoulder. He was bleeding from several wounds on his back, and he had a new one on the side of his head. It wasn't until he bent over and looked closer that he did a double-take. "Parker?" He dropped to his knees. "What the frak is he doing here?"

"You know this guy?" Lync leaned out and kicked Parker in the ribs, and he groaned. "What is he, another Olivaw?"

Zachary stared at his fourth cousin once removed and wondered if he should answer her. She didn't exactly sound like she could handle knowing he was kin, though distant. Then again, she loved Libby, so there was no telling how she'd react.

Parker snickered and leaned sideways before spitting out a mouthful of blood. Once he finished, he cleared his throat. "You didn't tell me we were related, cuz." He glanced back at Lync and grinned.

When she wound up to kick him, Shauna grabbed her and pulled her away. "Don't waste your energy on this idiot. Rán!"

"What!" He shot back.

"Take your fraking clone-loving offspring and lock his ass up while we talk." She let Lync go and leaned in closer to him. "And whatever you do, don't let him out of your sight for a second."

"Oh, I won't." Rán stormed over to a nearby storage locker and pulled out a black canvas bag from inside. He then walked up to Parker and laid it flat on the ground beside him.

His eyes went wide. "What do you think you're doing with that, you fraking droid?" He started squirming to put distance between him and the mysterious bag.

Rán didn't pause. He reached out, yanked his leg back, and once he was close enough, he squeezed his cousin's neck, knocking him out. The whole thing happened in under two seconds.

Bradley slid his chair backward. "Remind me never to piss you off, gramps."

"Pissing me off is fine. Just don't try to kill me." Rán easily lifted Parker up and laid his limp body flat in the bag before sealing up the side. "Thanks to your brother's tweaks, there's nothing stopping me now from killing this fraking genetic mutation."

Zachary swallowed hard as Rán reached down and yanked the bag up, tossing it over his shoulder like it contained yesterday's laundry. Only then did he realize the bag was a skotádi duffel, like the one Abigail had been saved in. Except this one had a big-ass lock on the one end. There was no way Parker was getting out of that thing. At least not alive, anyway.

He watched as Shauna pulled Lync close, and surprisingly, she didn't resist. It was an expression he wouldn't have imagined her doing with anyone, except maybe Abigail.

Pluto walked up to her other side and rubbed her shoulder. "So what the hell did this fraking cloner do to you?"

Lync stared as Rán stepped into the lift and shot upward to levels unknown. After he was gone a few seconds, she glanced over at Zachary and her eyes started blinking rapidly. "I don't even know where to start."

He thought about moving forward and squeezing her hand, but she was already being smothered by the others. She probably needed some space. "How about you start by telling us how you got out of Epsilon Eridani?"

She let out a feeble laugh. "Well, that's easy. Your sister saved both of our asses. The more interesting question is, what happened after that?"

25

LYNC MICHAELS
SOMEWHERE OUTSIDE ZETA LUPI

The Eben-Ezer was the first to transition through the final gate. Even though Lync was confident there wouldn't be anyone else at her ship's coordinates, she wasn't sure whether or not Shauna would still be there. The A.I. had agreed to stay put, but it was human, after all. Sitting still wasn't exactly natural, especially for an Olivaw.

Taking a deep breath, Lync opened a wide spectrum comm to the distant field of asteroids. It was a dense pocket of rogue planetesimals thirty-two light days from Zeta Lupi, situated on the opposite side of the star system from the Wheel. Somewhere amid the chaotic pocket of rocks was her ship, the Veritas. She just didn't know where.

"Marie, this is Lightning. Are you there?" She listened intently on the open comm, but there was no reply.

"Who's Marie?" Joyce whispered.

When Lync glanced back at her, Joyce was talking to Crayo. He must have noticed her gaze as he nodded at her. "Lync's mother's real name is Marie."

"No shit," Joyce muttered. "I always thought it was Shauna."

It amazed Lync how little some people knew about the Olivaws, despite their almost monarch-like rule over the last century. There were only a few years when an Olivaw didn't head up one of the larger governing bodies overseeing Sol. But even then, they were still manipulating it like a marionette from afar.

Adri nudged Lync. "Give it another shot."

Following the plan they'd agreed to, she adjusted the frequency forward another eight channels before trying again. "Marie, this is—"

"Bout damn time you came for me, girl." Shauna's face appeared on the wall screen. Her hands were on her hips, and judging by her glare, she was pissed.

Lync winced. "I'm… sorry, we just—"

"What was the last thing your father said to you before he died?" Shauna blurted out.

Lync froze, and a warm, tingling sensation suddenly passed over her face. She wasn't expecting to be called out like that in front of everyone. "Why are you—"

"I don't know whether you're a clone or not," Shauna said. "I can't be too careful." She waved her hand, and Lync could just make out the reflection of the gate drive controls. They were warming up.

Though it was only a virtual reflection that Shauna shared for dramatic effect, the meaning wasn't lost on her. Shauna was planning to gate if she didn't answer her.

Shauna shook her head. "Time's up. I'm out—"

"He told me to get out of the family asteroid." Lync swallowed down the lump in her throat, trying not to look at the others. Especially Joyce. "My father didn't want me to die in there alone like so many other Ulixi. He wanted me to do something more with my life. To explore the universe. He… called me his… his little lightning bolt." She wiped at the tear running down her reddening cheeks.

"I'm sorry I had to do that." Shauna canceled the jump sequence. "I couldn't take a chance with all the clones taking over Zeta Lupi."

"How'd you hear about those?" Lync asked.

"I said I'd sit tight. I didn't say anything about not keeping tabs on things." Shauna stepped backward and sat down in the virtual command chair. "From the looks of it, I'd say we're losing out there, aye?"

"Something like that." Lync raised her hand and waved Joyce forward.

As she walked up, Shauna smiled. "Director Green. It's good to see you again."

"I wish I could say the same." Joyce glanced over at Lync. "Do you want to ask her, or should I?"

"Ask me what?" Shauna peered from Joyce to Lync and back. "Come on now, rip it off, you two. You're not getting any younger like I am."

Lync chuckled. Her mother was a character, and the more time they spent together, the more she saw herself in her.

But today was different. It wasn't every day she had to ask her mom how to find her family in hiding. The same family she'd formed when she left her father. When she'd abandoned her as a baby in that planetesimal.

While words failed her in that moment, she did the next best thing. She subvocalized a command to share all the data they'd recorded in the past week.

As the silence hung between her and Joyce, she could hear the faint mutterings of the Director talking under her breath. Someone was probably alerting her to what she was doing.

Joyce leaned closer to her. "Can I ask why you're dumping all our intel to your mother?"

"Because she's scared to ask me for help." Shauna crossed her arms. "She thinks I might play favorite with my other children. And if I know her, she's thinking I won't sell them out." She tapped her fingers on her forearm as the camera zoomed in on her. "Isn't that right, dear?"

Lync sometimes forgot that her mother was a machine. With her computing power, she'd processed that data a dozen times by now and was likely stewing for dramatic effect.

"You're my kin too, you know." Shauna gestured toward her, and a blueprint appeared on Lync's wall screen.

When she squinted at it, she realized what it was. "It's the

Wheel." She shook her head. "Why are you showing me this?"

"Because you're not looking close enough, my child. Here, let me help you." Shauna snapped her fingers, and a pocket of green flashed about two-thirds of the way down toward the center of the planetesimal.

"Is that..." Lync leaned forward. "The room Abigail took me into. The one where we found Hera's weird fake body?" She'd forgotten all about that place.

"The one and only," Shauna said.

She tilted her head and studied the layout. The longer she stared at the plans, the less sense the target made. "Why would they go here? It's probably crawling with clones by now."

"I doubt it," Shauna began. "The room was designed to rotate a huge chunk of the planetesimal over the lift tube you used to access it. It's impossible to detect the way Zachary built it."

"That's sorta the point of a secret lair, right? You gotta keep it a secret." Joyce smirked. "You Olivaws scare me sometimes. So, tell me, Mom. What's so important about this little room?"

Lync knew what was down there, but she was afraid to say it out loud. The green data cores in the heart of that place contained the minds and technology of their human ancestors. When Zachary and Libby extracted the weapon blueprints for the Beacon conflict from those things, they only scratched the surface of the archives. There was no telling what was in there that might help them out of this mess. The question was whether it was worth opening that Pandora's box.

Or worse. Letting it fall into Hera's clutches.

Shauna bit the side of her mouth and glared at Joyce. It was a gesture she'd only seen a few times, but she usually reserved it for when she was about to do something rash. She didn't like it when people talked about her family as being scary, and judging by the look in her eyes, she was about to lash out.

"Don't mind her." Lync nudged Joyce in the ribs and she winced. "She's been on an anti-Olivaw kick for a while now. The alien attacks, evil clones, and endless secrets and lies sorta do that to people."

"Trust me, I know." Shauna lowered her arms and sat back down in her command chair. "But my kids aren't part of that problem. They've been trying for decades to fix the mess their ancestors left for them."

"But they also weaved a few lies of their own along the way," Joyce added. "It sounds to me like your children are no different from the rest of your fraked up family."

Shauna leaned closer to the camera. "I'm not digging this conversation, Director. I suggest you keep your mouth shut for a while. Alright?"

"I don't need to stand here and listen to this shit." Joyce turned and walked up to her pilot. "Set a course for the Wheel."

"And do what?" Lync stormed up behind her. When she reached her side, she spun Joyce around to face her. "Are you just planning on gating in there and asking for a tour of the place? Huh? That's about as dumb a plan as I've ever heard. You're gonna blow this fraking thing and get us killed with that temper of yours."

Crayo stepped up beside her and reached out to try pulling her back gently.

"No." She knocked his hand away. "She has to hear this, whether she wants to or not." She eased closer to Joyce. "I'm on your side, and so is my family. That doesn't mean you have to agree with what they're doing or how they're doing it. But rest assured, they're aiming for the same end as we are."

"You're sure about that?" Joyce crossed her arms.

She nodded. "I am."

"And you're willing to risk your life…" Joyce raised her hand and gestured toward the other Ulixi gathered on the bridge. They were all staring in awe at both of them. "And the lives of all of us on this hunch of yours? On this belief in a family that abandoned you?"

The words stung. While her mother had indeed left her behind, she also knew she'd been terrified. She'd left them after she discovered her mate had been an alien, and that her baby was probably one too.

Hell, it scared Lync when she found out. She could only imagine what her mother must've been going through. To be honest, she wasn't sure how she'd have reacted in the same situation. Plus, her brothers and sister weren't all bad. They hated Hera and the Galactic Alliance as much as she did. And they sure as hell seemed to always be one step ahead of the game when it came to taking out the fraking aliens.

Lync nodded. "I'd bet all our lives on it. On them." She swallowed hard and did her best to shove her doubt deep down inside her belly, beneath the part of her which knew that the greatest harm often came from the best intentions.

"I hope you're right because that's exactly what you're doing." Joyce glanced at the pilot and shook her head; the gating sequence stopped. She then turned and glared at Lync. "Alright, Lightning. What's the plan?"

Zeta Lupi, Laniger Orbit

THEY SLID the unmarked skiff up alongside the *Straight and Narrow*, a freighter from Epsilon Eridani. It had stopped just outside Laniger's orbit, the fifth planet in the Zeta Lupi system, making its regularly scheduled stop to drop off people and pick up raw materials. Although the ice planet wasn't hospitable to life, massive mineral deposits had been uncovered below its water ice surface in the past six months. With a galactic battle brewing in the Nursery, the frigid world had become a mineralogical hotspot in the star system.

Lync had trained here a few times with some of her teams

for the Beacon war. They'd used the planet's atmosphere to practice the ninety-degree turns required to maneuver their Nyílak fighters into bombing position against the GA moon ships. During training, they'd lost a few of the arrowhead-shaped ships to the icy gravitational grip of the planet, but the pilots had managed to eject before crashing planetside. A few suffered from frostbite, resulting in amputated fingers and toes, but they were eventually rescued.

During her time stationed here, she'd made several good friends at the space station orbiting this hellhole, and today she'd called in a few favors. The largest favor required her contacts to shut off their defensive weapons battery scanning the vicinity of the station. They needed a few minutes to jump in, drop off a few people, and jump out. Without Harold to grease the technological wheels, it was difficult, especially with all the unfriendly eyes searching for pockets of resistance to Hera. But her friends and a pile of credits had temporarily fixed their problems.

"Stay close," Lync instructed her team, eyeing their outfits one last time before they slid through the docking connector to the freighter. "And whatever you do..." She glared at Joyce. "Don't say a fraking word. I'll do all the talking."

Joyce bit her lip. "Okay, boss. Just don't forget to deactivate your retinal comms in there. The last thing we need are stray signals giving us away."

Crayo nodded and tapped his ear as Lync adjusted the coveralls he was wearing. They were disguising themselves as technicians heading toward the Wheel, the next stop in this freighter's jump sequence. Their kind were a common sight in these parts, especially with the exponential increase in demand for skilled hands to help with the war. The Zeta Lupi Wheel was a manufacturing hotbed for the clone Pilum fighters and other military hardware.

Once she was satisfied that man's outfit looked believable, she turned her attention to Olig and checked him over. The Ulixi was a giant ball of nerves; this was his first covert op.

"Calm down, mate." Lync adjusted the credential on his

breast pocket and bent down to double-check that he'd ditched his ragged hand-me-down boots. They stuck out like sore thumbs with all the Ulixi scrawl on the outside. While it was a minor detail, their job was to blend in, not broadcast their presence.

When she glanced up at him, she noticed his armpits were so sweaty they were staining his coveralls. His environmentally controlled outfit was having trouble keeping up. "Are you gonna be alright?"

"I's be… fine." He unzipped his shirt a bit and used the opening to cool off. "Wes just needs to get this job underway."

"Maybe you should stay here." She eyed Crayo. "We don't need you blowing our—"

"I say I be fine!" Olig snapped his zipper up. "Besides, who'll pilot the decoys while yous all figuring out how to break inta da secret lair? Certainly not these mouth-breathers." He gestured toward Ryder and his people.

Joyce glared at him but held her tongue. It was hard to tell, but she seemed a little nervous herself. With the garish face tattoos they'd applied to her and Ryder as disguises, they both looked eerily goth-like.

Lync smirked and moved on to checking over the others. They'd decided on a team of eight for this leg of their mission. There were a lot of moving parts to handle at the Wheel, and the more bodies, the better. The challenge had been deciding who to bring along. She'd demanded an equal split in personnel, but Joyce wouldn't risk losing too many Ulixi. Their skill set was in short supply. While Lync had agreed, she'd done so reluctantly. At the moment, they were outnumbered three to five, with Joyce, Ryder, and a trio of grunts rounding out their squad.

She checked the docking control panel and saw that the tube was about to touch down on the far side. "Look alive," she whispered. "We need to reach that safe room in under five minutes if we want to evade the clones on board. Right now, they're on the bridge dealing with the comm blackout, which means our clock's already ticking."

Everyone nodded, focusing on the task ahead and blending in with the rest of the passengers. When the light on the control panel turned green, she didn't hesitate. She simply reached out and yanked open the hatch.

The hiss of the two ship's environments merging echoed in the room. She initiated the transition by crouching low and leaping forward across the gap between the ships. The sight of her crossing into the tube without a full suit might have seemed dangerous to most people, but the tube was filled with oxygen. There just happened to be no gravity.

As she floated through the tube, she noticed the far hatch hadn't opened yet. That wasn't good. She reached out with both hands and gently applied friction to the walls to slow her momentum. Just as she was about to come to a complete stop, someone opened the hatch on the *Straight and Narrow* and pulled it inward.

She let out a sigh of relief and pivoted, realigning herself with the gravity on the far side before pulling herself forward. If she didn't, she'd float out upside down and would probably break her neck.

Once she slid through the opening, she jumped sideways to make room for the next person and to survey the space. Except for her friend, no one was there.

"Welcome aboard." Dulu winked at Lync before glancing over her shoulder down the corridor running through the ship. "We've gotta move quick. The clones on the bridge are losing their cool, and a few are headed this way."

"Shit!" Lync looked back, noticing that only half of her people had made it through so far, and for some reason, Olig wasn't one of them.

She leaned back and peered down the empty tube. "What's going on?"

"Not sure," Joyce whispered. "Olig darted back into the ship to get something, and I told my people to go on without him."

Lync spun around, her heart thundering in her chest like a startled bird trapped against its will. It was only then that the chilling realization hit her that Crayo was also missing.

Her mind raced through all of their options. Jump back and risk their one solid plan, wait and get caught, or proceed without them and improvise a new plan. As she spiraled around in her thoughts, she flinched when a hand grabbed her from behind.

Dulu's eyes were wide. "We gotta go!"

"Fine!" She glanced back one more time, but there was still no sign of Olig or Crayo. "Just take who you can and get them to the room."

Without hesitation, Dulu spun in place and darted around the corner.

Joyce motioned her people to follow, and they didn't question her. Once they were moving out, she leaned closer to Lync. "You need to go with them."

Lync shook her head. "I can't. Not unless—"

Joyce lashed out, gripping her by the chin. "This plan is dead without you. I'll take care of your people. Now go!"

She stared at Joyce, willing herself to move, but her feet were frozen in place. She was torn between duty and family, with no clear path forward.

"That's an order." Joyce grabbed her shoulder and shoved her around the corner.

Stumbling ahead, her heart drummed a frantic rhythm. There was no way in hell she could do this alone, especially not without Crayo manning the decoys.

With her mind elsewhere, she didn't even notice the approaching clones until it was too late.

"What are you doing out of your cabin?" a clone officer asked, stepping in front of her and blocking her path.

She stared at him blankly, not sure what to say. They were going to be discovered before they even got underway. And if she didn't get moving, the rest of her crew would soon run into them as well.

Fortunately for her, Dulu was on her game and stormed up beside Lync. "Linar! What the hell are you doing?"

Lync's eyes went wide. She didn't know how to reply. "I—"

"You're a useless spheroid of space junk!" Dulu glared at her and yanked Lync's arm, sending her stumbling forward. "Get your ass back to your cabin. I told you we'd let you out after we left port. Now go!"

She almost fell flat on her face as she faltered aft, not quite sure where to go. The last time she'd been through this part of the ship was in the dark, navigating via LiDAR. As she put distance between herself and the clones, she could hear fragments of their conversation with Dulu.

"So you let that imbecile out of their cabin?" the clone officer asked.

"Actually, no." A sound chirped, and Dulu's voice suddenly got louder. "Your officers left aft compartments Q through S unlocked when we departed Tiān." She emphasized the letter S like a snake.

Lync froze as the strange pronunciation of the last letter triggered something. Shit, that was it. The hidden room was off one of the cabins in compartment S.

Dulu's voice continued, "I've been cleaning up your people's shit since y'all fraked up and had to halt the entire ship. Your idiot colleague left his post to lend you a hand with the comm blackout on the bridge."

"We needed to reset the comm array," the officer said, his voice trailing off. "Wait a second… who are you?"

Lync glanced back over her shoulder just in time to see Joyce and Crayo making their way around the bend. They were moving so fast they nearly skidded into the clone.

Dulu was fast on the draw. She pulled out her hand scanner and waved it over Joyce's counterfeit badge, and it beeped. "Says compartment S." When she stepped forward, Crayo flinched and reached behind his back as if he was going for his knife.

Lync spun around and let out a jarring cough that echoed

through the corridor. At the same time, she slapped the wall with one hand and shoved a finger on her other hand down her throat. A second later, the remnants of her breakfast and liquid lunch came up and spilled out all over the wall and floor. She forced down another wave of bile but kept pretending to retch for a few more seconds until the sounds of screaming voices behind her made her flinch.

"Are you gonna stand there with your thumb up your ass, or are you gonna help her?" Dulu's voice was getting louder and louder. "You done left the rest of us back here to play babysitter. Now it's your turn to clean up the barf."

"That's not my job!" the officer snapped. "It's yours! And you're lucky to have one. Now get these fraking clowns back to their quarters before I write you up. And clean that shit up when they're stowed."

Lync groaned and wiped her mouth with the back of her sleeve. That was close.

She heard the sounds of several feet coming up behind her, but she didn't break her act. Not until Crayo wrapped his arm around her and eased her aft.

"You okay?" he asked.

"Yeah, I think so." She brought her hand up to cover her mouth again and then sighed. "Damn food processor must've had a bad refill pack." She didn't dare break from the script. Not until they were safe.

"Maybe if you didn't scarf down your food, you wouldn't barf it up." He stroked her back, and she swore she heard a faint chuckle under his breath.

She nearly broke out laughing herself. The dolt was enjoying her show. If they weren't neck-deep in shit, she'd body-slam his ass right there and then.

Dulu didn't say another word until they got to their quarters. She simply guided them down several twisting halls until they stopped in front of an air vent.

Once she confirmed the coast was clear on her retinal comm, she reached out and pressed her palm against five seemingly random spots on the wall. After the fifth touch, a panel slid aside, revealing a pitch-black corridor beyond.

"Get in," she whispered.

When the panel opened, the smell of the inner space wafted out into the hall, and it hit Lync like a wall. It reeked of sweat with a hint of piss, just like it had the last time they tucked in here. They didn't exactly have time to get a cleaning crew inside after each use.

As Lync stepped past Dulu, she grabbed her arm. "You owe me more credits."

She was about to say something when a commotion broke out from back down the hall. From the sound of it, the clones had run into Olig.

"Who the frak are you?" someone shouted.

Lync stared Dulu straight in the eyes. "I'll pay you double our rate if you keep our friend out of the brig."

"Shit!" Dulu gritted her teeth and pointed her finger at her. "If that fool isn't already dead, it'll be triple. Now get your ass inside and stay put!"

She was barely past the threshold when the panel slid closed behind her with a thunk, engulfing the already dark corridor in complete black. She stood there in silence for a few seconds, collecting herself and holding her ear to the air to see if she could hear anything. With the microscopic skotádi coating on the walls, there wasn't a chance in hell any noise was getting into or out of this compartment. But she had to be certain.

With her breathing under control, she tapped her ear, turned on her retinal comm, and activated the LiDAR sensor. The corridor and the far room suddenly lit up like a beacon.

After she walked down the hall, she paused and glared at the others. "What the frak happened back there?"

Zeta Lupi, Oort Cloud

THE NEXT THIRTY-SIX hours were the longest of Lync's life. Not only were the seven of them confined to a space designed for five, but the heat was excruciating, there was no airflow, and the waste disposal system was failing. Add to that the tempers and fear mounting in the room, and they had the makings of a bomb waiting to go off.

No one knew what Olig had returned to their ship for, but whatever it was, he had put their entire mission and the fate of their people in jeopardy. It was especially hard because no matter how she twisted and turned the event in her mind, his actions made no sense. They weren't expecting to bring any equipment beyond themselves and a single-bladed weapon, which the rest of them had slid into the flats of their shoes. While she thought that might have been it, she'd seen him check his during one of their many readiness checks.

"It's been too long," Joyce whispered.

Even though they didn't need to speak quietly, the habit was hard to break, especially with all the screaming from the day earlier. She was surprised she hadn't already strangled Joyce or Ryder. If she had to hear one more accusation that the Ulixi weren't battle-ready, she'd fraking lose it.

Crayo sighed and lowered his head between his legs. He'd been tucked into a ball with his back to the wall for the last few hours. "It'll be as long as it needs to be, mate. We aren't going anywhere."

"Maybe you're not, but I am." Ryder stood up and started toward the hatch, but Lync stepped in front of him.

She raised her hand and pressed it flat against his chest. "Where do you think you're headed, sport?"

"To see what's up. Now move!" He went to push her aside, but she was ready for him.

Lync swung her outstretched hand down and knocked his arm away, and at the same time, she shoved him with her other hand. "Sit the frak down."

Ryder stumbled backward, but one of his men hopped up

and stopped him from falling. Neither of them had expected her to get physical, and once he gathered himself, he glared at her. "I suggest you step aside, Colonel. Either that, or I'll have to restrain you." He looked back at his other two soldiers and they stood up.

"Nice." Crayo pushed up off the ground and stepped up beside Lync. "I's guess we's know where our allegiances stand, don't we?"

"The mission comes above all else," Ryder said.

"That's crap, and you know it." Lync glanced at Joyce. "First sign of a hitch in the plan, and you military types flex your muscles and use bullshit excuses like the mission to treat people like shit and walk all over them."

Joyce shook her head and exhaled, but stayed seated on the ground. "Last I checked, you were in this military, Colonel."

While Joyce wasn't wrong, the fact of the matter was, she'd never felt like she was a part of it. Joining the military got her to Epsilon Eridani, but it was a means to an end more than anything. The further she got from Sol, the better. After that, everything she'd done, she'd done for her friends and her Ulixi people. Well, that and a bit of revenge.

"Well, maybe that's the problem." Lync swallowed down the lump in her throat. "Where you see a military body to order around, I see a person. I guess that's what makes you and me different. You're using this war with the Galactic Alliance to lose sight of your humanity, and I'm using it to find mine."

Joyce's gaze locked on Lync, and suddenly the tension in the room rose exponentially. But just as Joyce got to her feet, the panel behind them clicked and slid aside.

"The coast's clear, you rats." Dulu's head popped around the opening. "We don't have much time before they start loading us up for the return trip. I suggest you exit out of the aft cargo bays. There should be a ladder back there that'll lead you down to the lower maintenance levels of the Wheel."

She aimed her flashlight straight at Lync, but she didn't move. They all just stood there, staring at each other.

"Come on now. Get your asses in gear before I change my mind." Dulu waved her light around the space and flashed it on and off.

Lync spun in place and started toward the exit.

"We're not done here, Mrs. Michaels." Joyce reached out and rested a hand on her shoulder.

She shrugged her off. "Frak off, Director. I've got a mission to finish."

Crayo grunted, and she spun around to see Ryder's arm wrapped around her man's neck. He was struggling to pull it away from his throat so he could breathe.

"You heard the Director," Ryder said. "Stay put!"

These fraking grunts were insane, and Joyce was just as bad. The sooner they got out of here, the better.

"If you don't let him go, you're dead." Lync waved her hand toward Joyce and her soldiers. "All of you. I don't know what the hell got into your heads the past day and a half, but once we're out of this mess, we're going our own separate ways." She nodded toward Crayo. "Now release him!"

"What makes you think you're so important that we can't finish this without you?" one of the soldiers asked. It was the one that caught Ryder as he was falling.

Lync laughed out loud. "Apparently, you geniuses missed the part of the debriefing where they told you I'm the only person Shauna entrusted with a map. Oh yeah," she glared at Joyce, "let's not forget that without my DNA, our destination won't even fraking open. Last I checked, I was holding all the aces." She reached out and grabbed Crayo's hand, pulling him toward her.

Ryder looked at Joyce, and she nodded. She knew this mission was stacked against them. What she hadn't expected, however, was for the shit to hit the fan the moment it started.

"What's the plan then, Mrs. Michaels?" Joyce bit her lip and stared at Lync.

She was doing her best to hold back her contempt for the woman but was failing miserably.

"It's the same as before. The grunts do what grunts do and act as diversion." Lync locked her eyes on Crayo. "And the important people take care of the rest."

She didn't wait around to argue any more. She merely turned and started jogging toward the exit with Crayo in tow.

The thudding sound of the seven pairs of feet running through the ship sent an odd drumming beat throughout the *Straight and Narrow*. She powered up her retinal comm the moment they got clear of the room and brought up the map of the Wheel. It wasn't the live feed she was so used to seeing. Instead, it was a static map of the facility Shauna had given her. While she'd neglected to tell them that Crayo also possessed a copy, her A.I. mother forbid her from sharing it with any of the others. She, apparently, didn't have the same level of trust in Joyce as the other Olivaws.

For once, she and her mother could agree on something. Their view of Joyce hadn't been the same since she sided with Hera after the Beacon battle. At first, Lync thought the woman's relentless drive for revenge was part of her son's loss, but lately, she seemed lost and conflicted on whose side she was on. Had Hera not picked Nguyễn and turned her back on Joyce, she wouldn't doubt for a second that the two of them would be running the show together. In her mind, that made Joyce just as culpable as Nguyễn when it came to the state of their world, which, for all intents and purposes, was fraked up and spiraling out of control.

They reached the cargo hold without encountering another soul, and they eased out toward the catwalk attached to the starboard hatch. When she peered outside, there were a few random automata on and about the gangplanks and other walkways of the spaceport. Other than that, the place was empty. With all the ships shuttling supplies and personnel to Epsilon Eridani, she imagined most of human-occupied space was in a similar state of abandonment. Hopefully, that would work in their favor.

"We're clear," she whispered as she slunk across the catwalk. Once on the far side, she stepped sideways, ducked under the railing, and grabbed the ladder leading down to the lower level.

With her hands on both sides of the bars, she carefully brought each foot to the outside of the poles and dropped like a rock. As she slid down the maintenance ladder, she squeezed her feet inward and used them to apply friction to control her descent. A few seconds later, she landed safely at the bottom and hopped sideways before flipping around with her back flat against the wall. Once she was clear, she glanced upward and counted the people following her down. There were seven in all.

She did a double take. That was one more than there should have been. When she squinted at the furthest person who'd just stepped out onto the ladder, she couldn't tell who it was. Maybe Dulu was joining them.

One by one, they reached the bottom and spread out along the wall until the last person touched down. Ryder had already moved forward and crashed into her, thinking she was continuing onward. She drew in her breath when she realized who the last person was.

"Olig?" She stepped around Ryder and slid up beside her friend. "What the hell happened back there? How did you know where we were?"

Olig froze in place. He wasn't sure how to respond. Just as she was about to ask him again, he spoke. "Dulu let me out of some sort of makeshift cell they threw me in yesterday. The guards were coming to collect me in a few minutes." He stared blankly at her and glanced up toward the *Straight and Narrow*.

Something was off about him, and she couldn't tell what. But they didn't have time to find out. When the guards discovered he was missing, the shit would hit the fan. And when that happened, they'd better be halfway across the Wheel. She didn't want to deal with a lockdown.

"Let's go." She waved them onward, and they slid down

the wall toward a maintenance hall up ahead. Humans rarely visited this level of the Wheel, and as such, it wasn't common knowledge how to get around. Fortunately for them, they had Shauna's map.

When she reached the door, she typed in a sixteen-digit alphanumeric code that appeared on her retinal comm, and it slid open. She had no idea why it still worked, but she wasn't about to look a gift horse in the mouth.

As they sprinted down the long corridor, she spotted robot after robot in the distance, but by the time they got nearby, the automata had already cleared the way. Whatever that code was she'd typed in, it seemed to have triggered some type of cascade through the system and sent the robots scattering. On the positive side, fewer bots in their path meant fewer eyes watching them.

After a solid five minutes of running, they came to a fork in the corridor. To the left was an arcing hall that led to one of the many maintenance shafts both she and Crayo needed to traverse to get close to the chamber holding the data cores. To the right was the equally long route to where the shuttles were serviced. That was where they were planning to steal some additional ships to run their diversion. The more eyes they had outside the Wheel, the more likely they could reach their destination inside. Once there, the plan was to lie in wait. They weren't even sure when the Olivaws would arrive for the cores, or if they were already gone.

She gestured to Joyce and her team, sharing the route to the shuttle bay. They accepted them with a blink and appeared to stare off into nowhere as they took in the next stage of the mission.

What followed was an uncomfortable silence. To be honest, there was no point in saying anything else from here. They might not meet back up for a few hours or a few days. It didn't matter, though. The damage between them had already been done.

Lync glanced at Joyce and nodded. "Good luck."

Joyce raised her hand up and pointed at them. "I'm going with you."

Crayo shook his head. "Over my dead body. That wasn't part of the plan."

"Plans change." She slid forward and Crayo stepped in front of her, blocking her path.

"You're staying here with them." He tilted his chin toward the grunts.

"One less skiff in the mix won't make a difference. They can handle the snatch and grab without me." Joyce looked past him and fixed her attention on Lync. "We can't afford to screw up your leg of this mission. Not if we want to survive this civil war."

"Sure, now you give a shit about the Olivaws," Lync muttered. "It's funny how you about-face on us once the tables have turned."

"See, that's where you're wrong." Joyce narrowed her gaze. "What you and your little dysfunctional family unit do are the least of my concerns. I'm looking out for the people back in those ships. That's all."

"For crying out loud, Joyce." Lync raised her hands in the air. "You're so full of shit, your eyes are brown. I don't have time for you and your mental ping-pong power plays. You're still pissed Hera cut you out of her tribe, and now you don't trust the only people left to help you. But whatever." She shook her head. "Your holier-than-thou act is getting old. Tag along or don't, I could care fraking less." She leaned in closer to Joyce. "But if you get in the way even once, I'll knife you myself."

When she turned to go and Olig followed, she skidded to a stop and reached out her hand. "Where... are you going?"

"With... you." He glanced back at the others who were staring at both of them with a vacant expression on their faces.

"That wasn't the plan." She tilted her head and glanced at Crayo. Something was off. Olig knew his part of the mission backward and forward.

She was about to tell him where to go when Joyce lunged up to Olig, raising her blade to his throat. "What's the code?" she whispered.

Lync flinched back. Code? There was no code. What the hell was Joyce talking about?

Olig's eyes widened to the size of saucers, and he mouthed, "Help."

But she didn't know what to do. This entire mission had been fraked since the start.

Crayo extended his hand toward Joyce, and she pulled away, putting Olig between him and her. "Let him go," he said.

"Not until he tells me the code." Joyce eased her knife up against his neck, and Lync could see a line of blood form around the blade.

"Joyce, what are you doing?" Lync reached behind her back to where she'd moved the knife from her boot.

"Don't move a centimeter," Joyce nodded toward Lync. "He knows the code. If it's really him and not one of the fraking clones, then he'll tell us."

By this point, Olig was shaking profusely, and tears were on his cheeks. She couldn't blame him because she was trembling herself, and her mind was going a million kilometers an hour. As she flipped the situation over in her head, she froze and narrowed her gaze on her Ulixi friend.

"Crayo?" she subvocalized.

He glanced over at her and raised an eyebrow.

"Last chance." Joyce squeezed Olig tighter and her people pulled their knives out.

Lync did her best to keep her cool and not to stare at their friend. "Didn't Olig's chest tats come up and over his collar?"

Crayo looked over at him and gasped. "Shit," he muttered.

The following seconds were a blur of chaos as Lync dropped to the ground and reached behind her back to grab her blade. She flung it straight at Olig's chest.

Olig recognized his situation and slammed his head backward in one sudden motion, bashing Joyce in the face and sending her reeling.

As she let go of her knife and shrieked in pain, Joyce's people must've thought they were being attacked. Ryder and one of the other grunts leapt over to help Joyce, and the other two dove at Crayo. They tumbled to the ground in a pile of arms and legs.

"It's not him!" Lync screamed, lunging forward toward Joyce's knife lying on the floor.

"Argh!" Crayo yelled at the top of his lungs, and it echoed down the long corridor.

Joyce's people dragged her backward a few meters. She was whimpering and holding her face in her hands as blood poured from between her fingers. From the looks of it, Olig had broken her nose.

With the blade in hand, Lync quickly scanned the scene and was about to leap to Crayo's aid when Olig dropped to his knees. He was grasping at the hilt of the knife, but he couldn't pull it out. She'd plunged it deep into the middle of his chest.

His eyes glazed over for a second until he started to spit up blood, and the next thing she knew, he fell forward, further plunging the blade into his torso and out the other side. The sight of the knife slicing through him and clinking to the ground was both shocking and revolting at the same time. When it hit the ground, it was covered in blood from hilt to tip. She knew the blade was sharp; she just never realized how sharp.

"Get—off—me!" Crayo groaned, kicking at the grunts.

When she looked over at him, she saw he was bleeding as well. "Let him go, you idiots. We weren't attacking you." She pointed at Olig. "We were attacking him."

"What the frak?" Joyce screamed, thrashing on the ground, trying to scramble backward.

At first, Lync thought she was screaming at her, but then she saw it. Something was boring its way out of the back of Olig's neck. Whatever it was, it was tearing against his skin, fighting to escape. After a few seconds, it broke loose and blood started spouting out as the alien parasite flailed about, struggling to get its entire body free.

She winced and took a few steps backward, putting some distance between it and her. The soldiers did the same, but they left Crayo behind.

"Get away from it!" she gestured with her hand.

But he simply sat there. His eyes wide open and frozen with fear.

The alien leech slid off Olig's half-baked corpse and moved toward Crayo.

If she had a blaster, she'd shoot the damn thing. But all they had were blades. She glanced around for a pipe or an emergency axe, or something to swing with, but came up empty.

Suddenly, the alien launched itself forward, landing on Crayo's chest before scurrying up to his neck. His complexion turned ghostly white as he screamed, attempting to fling it off. But the creature had already started to burrow into his skin.

"Shit! Get it off!" He tried to grasp the parasite, shrieking as spikes shot out from under its skin and pierced his fingers.

The alien shuddered and burrowed into his skin even faster. Then it halted. She didn't know why, but when she looked at Crayo, his eyes were rolling back into his head.

"What the hell?" Clutching her blade tightly, Lync eased forward, ready to excise the creature if necessary.

When she was within a few meters of Crayo, she watched him sway until he finally fell backward. The alien parasite released its grip, retreating from the cavity it had burrowed into his neck. Once free, it appeared to regard her and then reconsider its next move upon seeing her blade.

Without hesitation, it leapt from Crayo and darted towards Joyce. Maybe it was her bloodied face, or her vulnerable position on the ground, but either way, it lunged at her like a hawk swooping down on a wounded rabbit.

Lync moved to intervene, but Ryder was already there,

brandishing his knife and trying to strike the alien without hitting Joyce.

Joyce screamed in shock and fear, attempting to fend off the alien with her bloody hands. In doing so, she pricked herself on the same spikes that had punctured Crayo, causing her to shriek even louder.

Despite Ryder's attempts to cut the alien, it dodged his every attack until it found Joyce's neck and made quick work of burrowing inside. Unlike with Crayo, it didn't pause. It simply dove under her skin like a hot knife through butter, drilling deep into her collarbone. As it disappeared from view, it somehow closed the wound behind itself.

"What the frak?" Ryder stumbled backward and slammed his back against the far wall. He was mumbling something to himself, but Lync couldn't tell what.

Paralyzed in shock, they stared at Joyce, at a loss for their next move. Should they attempt to extract the parasite or run for their lives? It was only when Crayo regained consciousness that Lync crawled over to him and examined his wound.

The injury wasn't as severe as it looked from a distance, and for some reason, there was a slime coating covering the hole the parasite had excavated. It was almost like the parasite had sealed the gash. That must've been how it had closed the hole on the way inside Joyce, except in her case, it hadn't been repelled and forced to retreat.

When Crayo finally opened his eyes, she mustered a smile and nodded towards Joyce, who was laying perfectly still a few meters away.

"We've got to go," Lync subvocalized.

"What about the parasite? Where is it?" Crayo asked.

She widened her eyes. "It's inside her."

He drew in his breath and nodded as the two of them scrambled up off the ground and started running toward the far service shaft flashing on her retinal comm. As she searched ahead for the opening, voices rang out in the distance. From the sound of it, there were clones headed their way.

"What about us?" Ryder shouted.

There was only one thing she could think to say. "Go! Try to get to the ships."

Lync yanked open the panel covering the service shaft and shoved Crayo inside. Once she was certain he was clear and safely descending, she stepped backward and glanced down the curved hallway. After a few steps, she froze as Joyce's foot twitched.

"Shit!" She dove forward into the opening, trying hard not to make any noise as she pulled the panel back into place behind her.

With the panel closed, everything went dark.

For a moment, she feared she'd made a mistake, but then she realized there were no lights. The sound of Crayo's descent snapped her back to reality.

She subvocalized a command to activate her LiDAR and began searching for somewhere to jam her knife. After a few seconds, she found a small slit about halfway up the panel that seemed designed to hold something. While it wasn't ideal, it served her purpose.

She slid the blade into the slot, wedging it just over the lip of the panel. It was a tight fit, but that was sorta the point. She didn't want whoever was on the other side following her.

With the knife secured, she looked down to see that Crayo was already far below. He wasn't wasting any time, and he also wasn't checking on her. She couldn't blame him; after all, he had a goddamn hole in his neck.

After she checked the blade one last time, she did the only thing left to do. She descended like a maniac on the edge of meeting her maker.

THEY DESCENDED for what felt like an eternity until a banging sound echoed from far above. Lync froze, and so did Crayo. He was right below her, having slowed long ago to let her catch up.

"What do we do?" he whispered.

She checked her retinal comm. They were only a few levels away from their first transition, and according to the map, they could exit here and meet up with the same tunnel farther down. This meant passing near a few unknown spaces, but it would be better if they vacated the tube. They were like fish in a barrel down here if someone wanted to take a shot at them.

When she glanced over her shoulder, she pointed behind him. "There, that panel. Let's get out of here. Open it quietly and head left."

The pounding grew louder from above, and soon the sound of metal bending beyond its will screamed out, echoing down the service tube.

That was all Crayo needed to hear. He quickly opened the latch and peered into the corridor for a second. Once he confirmed no one was there, he slid out and headed left.

She descended a few more rungs on the ladder and followed suit, easing the panel closed behind her. While part of her wanted to stop and look upward, the sooner she sealed it up, the better.

After double-checking the latch, she spun in place and barely caught the edge of Crayo's shoulder as he passed around the bend. As with the climbing, he wasn't waiting for anyone.

She leaned forward and sprinted after him, subvocalizing the command to update the map with their new route. The next entrance should only be a hundred meters ahead. After that, they had another five or so ins and outs before they would reach their target.

As she scurried along and constantly checked her six, she almost missed the open door to her right. "Frak," she whispered as she skidded to a halt. Easing backward, she peered into the room, only to see Crayo standing in front of a bank of lockers.

"What are you doing?" She glanced left and right, then

back toward him. It was some sort of storage space, and for some reason, it wasn't marked on her map.

Crayo clicked a locker open and reached inside. A second later, he pulled out a massive rifle in one hand and several clips in another.

She drew in her breath. "That could be useful."

"Fraking, aye." He started pocketing as many clips as his jumpsuit would hold.

When she peered to the side, she smiled when she read the words on the door.

Security Armory - Authorized Personnel Only

She chuckled. "I guess they don't lock these rooms?"

At first, she wasn't even sure why an armory was down here, but then it hit her. "Shit!" Her eyes went wide. "There are living quarters down the way. Near where we have to descend."

"I know." He passed her a rifle and a handful of clips. "Let's just hope they're asleep. Besides, the last place they'll look for us is where they sleep, right?"

He had a point. She grabbed the charging clips and pocketed them before snatching the rifle. He'd already loaded it with a full capacitor.

She checked it over before pressing her palm flat on the side, syncing her biomarkers with the gun and assigning it to her. From that point forward, no one else could fire it except her. Unless, of course, they reset it and power cycled the thing. But that would take several minutes.

"We ready?" When she looked up, he was gone. "Cray? Where'd you—"

He emerged from behind another row of lockers with a shit-eating grin on his face.

"What?" she asked.

"Nothing." He nudged her shoulder. "Let's go. We're on the clock."

She started toward the door. "What does that mean?"

He never did answer her. Instead, he side-stepped around her and hopped out of the room, disappearing to the right down the corridor.

She wasn't about to go back and see what he'd done. By the time she did, he'd be long gone without her.

Once she caught up and found the panel they needed, she eased forward and peered inside. He'd already slid it open and was half a flight down. "Wait up," she whispered and slung the rifle over her shoulder. She stepped in and pulled the panel into place behind her.

This time, she had nothing to lock it shut with, which was fine, she guessed. If their pursuers searched for every locked panel, they'd know exactly where the two of them were headed. There was no point in making it easy on them.

With a weapon on her back, she felt a renewed confidence that they might actually make it out of this. She started climbing down one rung after another, and didn't look up once.

AN HOUR LATER, Lync's calves were screaming bloody murder, and her hands were raw and blistered. She was coming up on their last exit, and judging by the lack of sound beneath her, Crayo was already there. When she glanced down, she could see him waiting at the bottom of the shaft with his back against the wall.

The bottom. The words sounded weird in her mind. This place seemed to go on forever and ever. And after sneaking in and out of nearly a dozen of these shafts, she'd begun to think they'd never reach the bottom.

Once she hit solid ground, her legs got wobbly. She was hitting a wall, both mentally and physically. While she'd shoved the events from earlier into the back of her mind, they were creeping forward with every rung she cleared.

"We're almost there," he said. "All we have to do is step outside, and—"

Suddenly, a boom echoed far above them, and a few seconds later, a light rain of dirt fluttered down over their heads. Where there was dust, there was bound to be debris.

Lync spun around in a snap and went to claw at the panel until Crayo grabbed her hand and stopped her.

"Relax," he chuckled. "We're fine."

She glanced upward, but all her LiDAR saw were dust particles. "Wait... how do you know?" She looked down and narrowed her gaze at him.

He bent over and started laughing quietly.

And then it hit her. "What did you do?"

He smirked. "I might have wired up a gift on a few timers in their explosive locker."

"You didn't." She batted at his back, and she regretted it the instant she did.

He stood up straight and winced as he reached up to rub around the wound from the parasite. It wasn't looking too good after being exposed without bandages for so long. Plus, he'd been climbing for hours. She didn't know how he was still gripping the bar.

She gently rubbed his arm. "I'm so sorry."

"It's alright." He forced a smile. "Besides, who the hell stores explosives inside a place like this?" He shook his head. "Fraking idiots."

She wondered the same thing. But they didn't have time to find out why. They had more important things to do.

With the diversion far above them, her only hope was that there was no one left down here to get in their way. She carefully pulled the panel open and peered into the corridor.

This hall wasn't like any of the others. Not only were there no overhead lights, but there were eerie red light strips along the ground leading left and right. Apparently, they didn't need this place to be lit up like the rest of the planetesimal.

According to the map, there was about fifty meters of rock above them. This was the furthest point they'd dug into the planetesimal from this direction, and all that was below them were several layers of deep storage. They stashed things down here like long-term rations and emergency supplies — the type of stuff you didn't need unless the shit hit the fan.

As they worked their way to the left, she held her rifle up and directed it down the corridor. She wasn't taking any chances, and neither was Crayo. He kept tilting his head in the air, listening for even the slightest noise in the distance.

After they'd gone halfway around the level, they paused in front of a wide cylinder that extended from the ceiling to the floor. Unless she was mistaken, this was the bottom of the lift tube she'd ridden down a few months back. And if she remembered right, the entrance to the room they were hunting for was at the bottom.

While they would have loved to have taken the most direct route to getting there from above, there was no chance in hell the computer systems would have let them descend this far. Thus, their trek down the maintenance shafts into the bowels of this rock.

She lowered her rifle and looked the tube up and down, searching for a way inside. But there were no seams or hatches of any kind. It wasn't until she walked around and into the gap in the wall that she came upon a hatch.

"Over here," she whispered.

Crayo came around from the opposite side and stepped up beside her, aiming his rifle toward the hatch door.

He glanced at her. "What do we do once we open it?"

She shrugged. "I'm not sure. I only remember the floor opening up for us once we hit the bottom."

"Well, let's take a look." Crayo reached out and lifted the lever, pulling the door open and off to the side.

Just inside was the gadgetry usually propelling a lift tube full of riders. But at the moment, it was powered down, and all that remained were strange looking mirrored panels and beam shaping devices.

"They must've shut it off after the explosion," she whispered.

Crayo nodded. "Yeah, probably to slow us down."

"What happened after the floor opened up?" a male voice asked from behind her.

Lync tried to spin around toward the source of the query but was instead met with a blaster to the back of her head. The faint sound of the capacitors hissing at full charge told her that whoever it was, they were prepared to end her with the slightest flick of their finger.

"Don't even think about it, smart guy." She caught the man gesturing with his hand toward Crayo.

He eyed her, and she nodded. They didn't exactly have many options. For all she knew, he had an itchy trigger finger.

Crayo lowered his gun to the ground.

"Keep going," the man said. "All the way down."

He groaned and shook his head as he tossed the rifle aside with a clank. She could practically see him deflate. They'd been so close; she could feel it.

She sighed and closed her eyes, relishing the idea. Just when she thought things had turned around, this day had gone from bad to worse in the blink of an eye.

"And who might you be?" she asked.

When she went to turn toward him, he shoved the blaster even harder into her head. "If either of you move, you die. Is that clear?"

"Crystal," she hissed.

Maybe if she could see who it was, she'd know what they were dealing with. But with her back to him, there was only one way that was happening. And that's when her retinal comm flashed with an incoming live feed from Crayo.

She blink-accepted it, and a camera view came up on her comm. While it wasn't smart to livestream down here, at least being so close, they had a line of sight and weren't broadcasting wide.

After the video appeared in the corner of her field of vision, she squinted. He was young and tall. To be honest, he was a pretty muscular bloke, but for all intents and purposes, he was as indistinguishable to her as any of the billions of other humans in humanity's gene pool. She tapped out a command on her thigh to run his image through her retinal archive. It couldn't hurt.

"Alright." The man nudged her with the blaster again. "You were saying something about the floor opening up."

Lync stood there in silence, trying to think of a way out of this, but the man wasn't having any of her stalling. He swung the blaster sideways and pulled the trigger.

"No!" Lync screamed and reached forward, but he brought the gun back and jammed it even harder against the nape of her neck.

Crayo screeched in pain and collapsed to the ground as his thigh ignited in a fiery patch of red. He then grabbed his leg and moaned the second his hand touched it. When he pulled his hand back, she could see his palm was smoking. From the looks of the wound, the plasma bolt was burning through his leg and had melted the skin on his palm as well.

"Argh!" Crayo rolled back and forth on the ground, his face a mask of anguish. "Make it stop! Please!"

"I can't," the man snickered. "Not until you two start cooperating."

"Just tell him!" Crayo screamed and grasped at his leg, being careful not to touch the smoldering hole still burrowing through.

She stood there, frozen. If she told him, they'd give up their ace in the hole.

The man grunted. "You're a piece of work, lady. I shoot your friend, and yet you still have the misconception in that pretty little head of yours that you're in a position of power. Last I checked, a gun to the head put me in charge."

"Fine!" Lync raised her hands. "What do you want to know?"

"For the third and final time, what happens when the floor opens up?" He emphasized each and every word.

"I don't know how to describe it," she began. "I just kept

lowering down until I exited out into a small chamber. After that, I moved forward through a series of strange sliding doors. But I could only do it by myself. There wasn't enough room for another person. I'm sorry." She leaned away from the gun. "It was pitch black, and that's all I can tell you."

"What's on the other side?" he asked.

At first, she didn't want to tell him, but when she looked down at Crayo and saw that he was turning white, she knew she had to.

"It's Zachary Olivaw's lab," she said. "It's the place they figured out about Hera."

"What else is in there?" the man asked.

"I don't know." She lied. "Lots of gadgets and shit. Now, please, help him."

The man pushed against her lower back. "Get over there! But don't turn around. Keep your back to me."

She took a few steps forward and paused. When she glanced to her left, she saw the man toss a small gel packet at Crayo. He snatched at it with both hands, like his life depended on it. After he fumbled with tearing the top off, he squeezed its contents into and around the hole in his leg.

Crayo screeched when the goo hit his open wound, and his body went rigid. "Ahh... shit!" He arched his back and slammed his head into the wall, sending a dull thud through the darkened space.

"You said you would help him!" Lync glanced back at the man.

"Turn around!" he screamed, shaking the blaster at her.

She faced forward, trying to figure out what to do next. It was pretty damn clear he wasn't planning on letting her go. At best, he'd keep her alive until he got inside.

As ideas ticked off in her head, the man yelped and launched sideways, smashing his back into the tube and sending his blaster skidding off into the darkness.

Lync didn't need an engraved invitation. She spun around, grabbed her rifle off the ground, aimed it straight at the man's left leg, and pulled the trigger.

His upper thigh ignited in a flash of light, and he screamed bloody murder. She didn't pause to consider his pain; instead, she pointed it at his other leg and squeezed the trigger again and again. A second and third bolt of energy shot out and burned two holes in his other thigh.

While not as awe-inducing as plasma melting through skin, the rifle wasn't a plaything. The room suddenly filled with the stench of burning flesh.

And that's when all hell broke loose.

The klaxons started blaring, and previously disabled overhead lights burst on. The entire tunnel was coming alive with the sounds of people approaching from both ends.

When she turned, she saw that Crayo had pushed up with his back against the wall. "What... now?"

He moaned, and she glanced between him and the unknown man. Their options were already slim pickings, and they didn't have much time left. But one thing was certain: they needed to get inside that tube.

She spun around and squatted down, lifting Crayo's arm over her shoulder, and pushed up.

He screeched as she eased him toward the tube opening and practically launched him inside. "Careful," he moaned.

"I'm sorry." Lync lifted his bad leg up, and he winced as he slid over the threshold and fell backward onto the reflective beam array.

Once he was clear of the opening, she spun back to face the man and hopped over to his limp body. He looked like he was passed out, but just to be safe, she wound up and cracked him across the jaw with the butt of the rifle.

He didn't even moan. His head simply wobbled around in a circle. He was out like a light.

Comfortable that he wasn't going to attack her, she bent down, grabbed his ankles, and started dragging him backward into the nook. When she propped his legs up in front of the opening, a voice shouted from the distance.

"They should be up ahead!" a woman called out.

"Frak!" Lync bent over to lift the man up and groaned as

she struggled to hoist him into the tube. He was one big mouth breather.

Just as she was about to give up, Crayo appeared and stretched out toward her. He grasped the body by the head and pulled it inside, sending them both flying back into the opening. He crashed into a pile in the middle of the equipment, but she didn't even pause to see how either of them were doing. Instead, she simply hopped up and inside the tube before reaching out and grabbing the hatch, swinging it closed behind her.

Once through, she scrambled to find something to lock the door but came up empty-handed. Unlike with the service panel earlier, there was no handle or slot to jam anything into. Not that she had a spare piece of metal to use anyhow.

Crayo slid the man's body aside and eased up off the ground, propping his back against the inside tube wall. "So..." He gasped for a breath. "Now that we're in here, what do we do?"

To be honest, she wasn't sure. For some reason, she just knew she would rather be in here than out there.

As she worked her way around the lift equipment, she started searching for an exit. She climbed over half a dozen random bunches of wires and tubes and nearly fell flat on her face several times. The space on this side of the tube was quite cramped. In fact, the only open flooring was a small patch on the far side. When she reached it, she hopped down off one of the tubes but missed the landing and slipped onto her ass.

"Shit!" she moaned and rubbed her tailbone, trying not to scream, but damn, it hurt. It wasn't until she went to stand up that she realized her foot had disappeared into the wall.

"It's a hologram," she whispered, waving her leg around in the gap.

Crayo clambered over the lift equipment and knelt on top of the still passed-out body of the man. "Can you fit in there?"

"There's only one way to find out." She slid down flat on her stomach and eased under the darkened lip that looked like the wall.

Her mind kept telling her it was real, but her body told her otherwise as she disappeared behind it. Once inside the cramped space, her LiDAR lit up the darkness.

"There's a ladder in here," she whispered. But Crayo never replied.

When she slid her head back out, she half expected to see Crayo at gunpoint, but instead, he was staring patiently at her.

"Anything?" he asked.

She squinted. "Wait… you… didn't hear me?"

He shook his head. "No."

She grinned and waved him over. "Slide Mr. Asshole's legs this way, and then get your cute butt down here."

Crayo nodded. "Yes, ma'am." He leaned over and grabbed the man, yanking him with all he had toward the side of the apparatus. While he practically fell sideways with him, he recovered at the last second.

Once the man's foot was close enough, Lync pulled him down and into the crease before finally launching him over the edge. She didn't give a shit at this point if he broke his neck in the fall; she just didn't want to leave any evidence behind. After he thudded down below, she popped back out and helped Crayo inside.

And they were just in time, too. Because right as she ducked her head into the hologram, she heard the faint squeak of the panel swinging open, and then there was silence.

When she held her finger up to her mouth, Crayo nodded his hand like they'd always done on the float. At the same time, he reached around his back and slowly brought his rifle forward, aiming it at the center of the holographic wall they'd passed through seconds earlier. While she hadn't seen him grab the gun, she was happy he had. She felt naked in here without it; their only defense up to that point had been their fists and feet.

They laid there motionless for what seemed like an eternity. Even though they had no idea what was happening out there, she half expected someone to reach through the hologram and yank her outside. But that never happened.

"I think we should keep going," Crayo whispered.

She glanced at the wall and then at him. "Shouldn't we peek back in there?"

He paused to consider her question before shaking his head. "No. Let's just go. We need to see if we can get into this room before I pass out."

She nodded. He was right. In fact, she was surprised he was even moving at all.

When she pivoted around, she peered out over the edge. She could make out the outline of the man's body below on her LiDAR, but it was faint. Whatever equipment was in these walls was messing with their comms.

She looked left and right and froze. "There's a ladder over here."

Being careful not to kick her leg out of the hologram, she contorted her body and slid it down and over the edge of the ladder. Once she felt her feet on a bar, she stepped down a few rungs before helping guide Crayo's feet to do the same. It took him a bit longer, but he was being cautious. The last thing they needed was for him to fall over the side or flail out into the open.

With him in the clear, she made short work of the ladder. At the bottom, she hopped down off the last rung, and landed straight on top of the mystery man's chest. When his body let out a moan, she flinched and kicked out with her foot across his head, sending a crack through the tiny space.

"Fraking asshole," she muttered. If he was anywhere close to coming around, now he'd be out for a bit longer.

She didn't stop to reflect on him. She simply started running her hands over the walls, feeling for any gaps in the material. After a few meters, she came up empty-handed. Only then did she glance further down the passage. There, at the far end, was a faint outline of a door.

"Bingo," she whispered and pointed toward it.

Crayo was still working his way down one rung at a time.

While she could've helped him, she needed to see what was on the other side.

As she eased forward and approached the door, she drew in her breath and covered her eyes when it opened on its own. The light inside burst out and lit up the darkened space, and at the same time, it blinded both of them.

By the time her eyes had adjusted, something was moving toward her in the light.

"Shit!" Lync stumbled backward and fell over the man's body, landing on her ass right in the middle of his chest. "Crayo, raise your—"

But she was too late. Whoever was inside that passageway had passed into the entrance and was staring back at them.

"Lync!" Pepper asked. "Is that you?"

She leaned forward and sighed. "You scared the living shit out of me, woman. How'd you get in there?"

Pepper stepped out of the opening and moved closer. "I've been in the Wheel for a few days now. I got inside before the real shit hit the fan back home. They hadn't quite gone into lockdown yet, but by the time they had, I was stuck in here."

She looked up at Crayo and then to Lync. Her eyes suddenly went wide, and she pointed at the body under her. "Who the hell's that?"

Crayo chuckled and hopped down the last two ladder rungs. "No idea, mate. But whoever he is, he and I have a score to settle." He staggered up to the man and then kicked him hard in the nuts.

"Yowza," Pepper winced. "That's gonna hurt."

Lync glanced upward. She kept expecting someone to be peering down over the edge at them. "Can we take this inside? I'm still not sure we won't be followed in here."

"Roger that." Pepper reached out and took Lync's hand in hers.

As they started toward the door, she paused. "What're we doing with that one?"

Pepper waved her hand. "Don't worry about it. I'll send

Harold out to get him. He won't take any shit from whoever that is."

"You mean there's a copy of the overlord in there?" Crayo pointed at the hatch.

Pepper shook her head. "You know he doesn't like being called that, right?"

———

TWENTY MINUTES LATER, they were safely inside the secret confines of Zachary's Wheel laboratory. It was an arduous walk down a cramped tunnel, and the transition through the moving panel maze was just as excruciating, but they made it.

Lync stared at the throbbing green light of the data cores. They'd come a long way to collect these things. While she still wasn't sure the artifacts were worth the effort, she'd benefited from the devastation they produced during the Beacon battle, and handing them to Hera was out of the question.

"So, you're telling me there are millions of people stuck in there struggling to get out?" She looked over at Harold's robotic form. His composite shell was matte white and had an otherworldly look to it under the overhead lights.

He bent down and checked the straps they'd wrapped around the unknown man's head, neck, torso, arms, legs, and waist. They weren't taking any chances with this guy.

"I'd guess more than that," Harold said. "But don't worry, we have no plans of letting them out. In fact..." He stepped past her and up to the wall screen, bringing up the data from her retinal comm. "From the looks of this encrypted message from Shauna, she wants me to set this thing up to self-destruct if someone other than us gets any closer than a few meters to it."

"It couldn't hurt." Crayo wiped at his wound and leaned forward, watching as the nanites worked overtime to repair his damaged leg.

"Are you sure we shouldn't fix that guy up?" Pepper pointed at the still passed-out man.

"Frak no. He can die for all I care." Lync turned back toward Harold. "So tell me. How the hell do we get out of here?"

"To be honest." Harold turned back to face them. "I have no idea."

Her jaw fell open. "Bullshit," she blurted out. "You always know what to do."

Harold shook his head. "I hate to break it to you, Lightning, but I'm stuck down here just like you are."

She hated it when her family called her that. There was only one person in the universe who deserved to utter those words, and it wasn't him.

Crayo must have noticed her reaction. "Careful, bossman. That there's a name only her father can use."

"Oh." Harold turned back toward her. "I'm sorry. I didn't—"

Lync waved her hand. "Don't worry. You couldn't have known."

She sank into the chair and suddenly felt a wave of exhaustion wash over her. All the events from the past few days were finally catching up, and she could use some shut-eye.

As she was about to disable her retinal comm, she realized she had two unread messages. "That's strange," she whispered under her breath.

Crayo bent his leg back and forth and smiled. "What's that?" He looked over at her.

She blinked open the first message. It was the results of her image search. When she scanned through it, she bolted upright.

"What the literal frak?" She flicked the message up on the wall screen. "Check out who our mystery man is."

Crayo and Pepper walked up beside her and studied the display. There in the middle were several images, along with the name and details of their unknown assailant.

Name: Parker Olivaw

Lineage: Great-great-grandson of Hera
Olivaw
Date of Birth: Unknown
Description: A descendant of Hera Olivaw
who was long thought to be in cryogenic
sleep until her arrival in Epsilon Eridani.
Parker accompanied Hera on her initial
meeting with her Sol descendants after the
Beacon battle. Not much is known about
Parker other than he appears not to be a
clone like Hera, but the analysis is incon-
clusive. While the Sol Olivaws have
attempted to contact him on many occasions,
he has thus far ignored their messages.
Last Update: Libby Greene

Pepper chuckled. "Leave it to Libby to keep the Olivaw archive up to date."

Lync glanced back at the man strapped to the table. He was covered in bruises and had several gashes on his face, arms, and legs. It looked like he'd fallen down a flight of stairs, which wasn't too far from the truth.

She clenched her fist. "Why is it that every one of these crazy fraking people is an Olivaw?"

"It just seems like they are," Harold began. "If your only circle of friends are Olivaws, then everyone's an Olivaw."

"We need to get out more, love." Crayo wrapped his hand around her waist and pulled her close.

While she stared at the details of her distant cousin, her message indicator kept flashing. She'd already forgotten about the second message.

She blinked it open and chuckled.

"What is it?" Crayo asked.

Pepper reached out. "Are you ok?"

"I'm dandy." She wiped at the tears in her eyes.

"Then why are you crying?" Crayo peered into her face.

She flicked up the second message on the wall screen.

"Apparently, my mum put a tracker on me and the moment I stepped into this little lair of theirs, she sent me this."

Crayo leaned forward and scanned over the details. "I don't... get it. What is it saying?"

Pepper clapped her hands together and hopped up and down. "It tells us how to break out of this fraking rock."

SOMEWHERE NOT NEAR EPSILON ERIDANI

LYNC LEANED back in the chair and took another sip of the steaming coffee. The smooth, bitter taste of the black liquid eased down her throat, and she relished the hint of butterscotch Shauna added.

"So, wait?" Pluto reached forward and rested her hand on the table. "How did you end up getting out?"

Pepper smirked. "We gated away, of course."

Pluto screwed up her face. "Gated how? From where?"

Zachary cringed. "I sorta... left out one of my lab's tricks."

"Sorta?" Pluto tilted her head. "What does that mean?"

"I think it means he neither lied nor withheld the truth," Bradley began. "My father used to do it to us all the time. If we didn't ask the right question, he never told us the complete truth. It's an Olivaw family tradition. Right, Harold?"

"Touché, Master Bradley," Harold said from across the room. "Touché."

Pluto crossed her arms. "What's this secret, then?"

Pepper blurted out the answer before Zachary could respond. "We gated the entire lab out of the Wheel. It was fraking amazing!"

Bradley slapped the table with his hand and started laughing. "You did what?"

"Yeah." Pepper smiled. "Apparently, the lab and several of the levels above it were built to gate together. We've got supplies for years in there. It's beautiful." She faked wiping at her eyes.

"In my defense." Zachary pointed his finger around the room at the others. "I designed it as a way to evacuate the Wheel in case of an attack. I had no idea we'd need it for something like this."

"Sure you didn't, bro." Bradley leaned back and winked at him. "Nice CYA move."

"Come on," Zachary muttered.

Pluto ignored their bickering and stared at Pepper. "What happened to the Wheel then?"

Lync shrugged and set her coffee down, popping a grape into her mouth. "Nothing. We hollowed out the lab and gated a few light hours away. After we regrouped, we stopped and looked back toward the planetesimal. It was intact, and there wasn't a crack in it."

Pluto squinted at her. "So nothing like what happened at the Sol Wheel, then? There were no distress signals or comms?"

"Zippo." Pepper smiled at Zachary. He was still staring at Pluto with his fake puppy dog eyes.

Lync shook her head. Her family was a quirky bunch.

The room fell silent just as another blue gate ring passed over their bodies from their jump. One of several dozen so far. Lync wasn't sure if it was due to exhaustion, or if they were stunned speechless by that last revelation.

Everyone, except for Bradley, apparently. "Is anyone else worried about what we'll find in Lupus?"

When no one replied, it spoke volumes about what they were walking into. The truth was, they had no fraking idea.

Bradley had fought to return to Epsilon Eridani to extract Abigail and his friends, but he lost. They settled on sending some robots to see if they could make contact. In the meantime, they'd regroup in Lupus and figure out their next steps. They figured it was the last place anyone would look for them.

While they were worried about what was happening back

on Liprosus, Lync was anxious about the other ships in their fleet. The ones with the people loyal to Joyce. When she reached out to Ryder earlier that day, he refused to board the Olivaw ship. He was reluctant to join them on their gate hops across the galaxy, but she knew he was as lost as she was without the Olivaws.

Despite everyone's hatred of the family, those residing on this ship seemed to have humanity's best interest in mind. That, and they actually had a plan. Or at least they were faking one until they made one.

As she stared at her cup-of-joe in silence, she found her thoughts wandering to Abigail. When she'd returned to Epsilon Eridani, Lync promised that she'd get her through this mess. But thus far, she'd failed at every turn.

With her mind deep in despair, she hadn't heard the door open.

"Ladies and gentlemen," Rán said. "I have news about our friend."

"Tell me he's dead." Crayo raised his glass up. "That I could drink to." He didn't wait for an answer. He tipped back the murky liquid, emptying what remained down his gullet. It'd been his fifth glass in the last hour.

She turned and looked at Rán. "Is he?" She waved her hand. "You know, dead?"

"Not yet." Rán brought up the man's image on the wall screen.

From the looks of it, Rán had secured him in the ship's medical bay in a similar fashion to how Harold had done it at the Wheel. It wasn't until she looked further that she noticed he was encased in some sort of clear protective chamber.

"Why is he in that hamster ball?" she asked.

Zachary leaned closer and squinted. Judging by his reaction, he'd missed that detail along with the others.

Rán glanced at her and smirked. "Because our friend is infected."

The hairs on her arms stood on end. If he had something, that meant… "Are we…"

She didn't finish her sentence as Rán was already shaking his head. "No, not at all. Actually, based upon your retinal comm recordings, and what you said happened at the Wheel, I'm pretty sure you can't be."

Crayo leaned back and drew in a deep breath. "You better start spilling, bossman. My heart can't handle this shit."

Rán stepped closer to him. "Do you remember that parasite you saw leave Olig's body?"

"Remember?" Crayo shuddered and rubbed at his chest. "I can still feel that damn thing crawling on me. Why?" He stood up with a start. "Is one of those inside him?"

Rán nodded, and a medical scan from Parker appeared on the wall screen.

"Wholly shit!" Zachary eased up and walked over to the screen. "Is that thing—"

"Attached to his spinal cord and brain?" Rán interrupted. "Why, yes, it is. And if my analysis is correct, if it disconnects before the host dies, it also dies. Until that point, the parasite and host are symbiotes of one another. Till death do they part."

"That's a bit grim." Pluto eased up and wrapped her arms around Zachary.

"But true, nonetheless." Rán turned back to face them. "The host becomes nothing more than a shell of themselves. It essentially acts as a glorified automata to the alien. Worst of all, the parasite controls all the thoughts, feelings, and actions of the host."

"Wait a second." Lync stepped around the table. "You're telling me that Hera and all the clones have one of these inside them?"

Rán nodded. "I believe so. I assume that's why they use clones in the first place. Once they find an ideal host, one that is both strong and incapable of resisting them, they replicate it over and over again. It's actually quite elegant if you think about it."

She shuddered at the idea of being occupied by one of those things.

"Spoken like a true robot," Shauna said. "Are you sure you haven't lost touch with your humanity, my friend?"

"No, seriously." Rán glanced around at the others. "I was simply making an observation."

"Are they still alive?" Lync looked over at the robots. "After they're wired up like that, are Parker and the others still… you know." She swallowed hard.

"Do you mean, can we save them?" Rán asked.

She nodded.

Rán clasped his hands together in front of him. "I'm afraid, I don't know."

Her mind immediately went to the image of Joyce being attacked by that thing. They left her for dead back at the Wheel, and while she knew they had no other choice, that didn't stop her from regretting it every second since. She'd been seeing Joyce's foot twitch in her dreams for days now.

Lync walked up to Rán and stared him in the face. "You have to save her."

Rán narrowed his gaze. "You mean him, right?"

She nodded. "Of course."

He reached out and gently squeezed her hand. "I'll do what I can."

This entire evening of reliving the past few days had taken a toll on her. She needed to rest if she was planning to be useful in the days ahead. Especially when they arrived at Lupus.

When she looked back toward Crayo, he was already at her side. She smiled and glanced at the others. "I need some shuteye."

"Of course," Zachary said. "We'll see you in the morning."

Lync wasn't sure she could actually sleep without taking drugs, but if that meant she could shut off her mind for a few hours, she'd give it a try. She couldn't stop thinking and planning through their next few dozen steps. Even without knowing what lay ahead. Her people were depending on them, and they were slinging blind, headed straight into the unknown.

26

JOYCE GREEN
ZETA LUPI, OORT CLOUD

Her eyes fluttered open as the sound of someone snapping their fingers brought Joyce around. In front of her was a stark white ceiling. After glancing left and right for the source of the noise, she came up empty. Things got even weirder when she tried to roll on her side; she couldn't move.

"What the hell?" She tried to lift her head to see what was holding her down, but that, too, was immobilized.

"Hello?" she said aloud, her eyes darting around.

"What do you remember?" a familiar voice asked.

She couldn't quite pinpoint who it was. "Let me out of here, asshole."

"Now, now, Director," the voice said. "First, you'll answer my question. Then, maybe, we'll let you free."

The voice reminded her of someone. It was tinny but familiar nonetheless. Then it hit her.

"Nguyễn!" She looked left and right. "Is that you?"

Suddenly, she heard the sound of a door swooshing open down near her feet. A few seconds later, he stepped into view.

"Bingo." He smiled.

She tried to contort her head but failed. "Get this shit off me, Admiral. Now!"

He merely stared at her and shook his head. "Now, now.

Watch your temper, Director. First, you must tell me what you remember."

Nothing annoyed her more than someone playing games at her expense. Yet, when she thought back to what she last remembered, she came up blank. At least, at first.

"I'm… not sure," she muttered and squinted. There was something there; she just couldn't quite see it.

Nguyễn reached to the side of the table she was lying on and tapped a few buttons. Then, suddenly, everything became crystal clear.

Joyce took a deep breath. "She attacked me. That bitch!"

"Who did?" Nguyễn glanced to his left, and she could almost make out the faint reflection of a wall screen off the tablet he was holding in his hand.

She clenched her fist as the image of her attacker appeared in her mind's eye.

"Lync," she muttered under her breath. "Lync fraking Olivaw. She and her boy toy turned on us in the tunnel after we broke in."

Nguyễn smirked and glanced down at her. "And then what?"

"Is this really necessary?" She struggled to move her shoulder but failed. Whatever they'd tied her down with, she wasn't moving until they wanted her to.

"If you knew what Lync and her friends had done to us, then you'd understand why we're taking these precautions." Nguyễn lifted his tablet up and adjusted his controls. A second later, she felt something move under her neck. Or was it in her neck? She couldn't tell.

Just as she was about to tell the fraking asshat off, a flood of emotions washed over her. The scene played out in her mind as though she were watching a vid-sim. It was eerie.

Shots being fired at her and her people.

Her arm being blasted, sending her tumbling to the ground.

Lync laughing out loud as Joyce struggled to stop her.

Ryder coming to her aid.

And then blood.

So much blood.

Joyce fought to raise her hands to her face, to cover the tears now welling up in her eyes. But she failed.

Nguyễn was watching her as she was forced to relive Ryder's death for what felt like the umpteenth time. His back was to the wall, and he was defenseless, holding only a knife in his hand. Then his head exploded outward in a mist of flesh and blood. A plasma round from Lync's gun ripped a fist-sized tunnel through his face.

She shuddered as she watched her man convulse and waver in place before his eyes rolled into the back of his head. Then gravity took over, yanking him to the ground like a rag doll. His body collapsed into a limp pile beside her, and the last thing she remembered was his gaze.

His blank, lifeless gaze.

There were no final words.

There were no loving goodbyes.

There was only… death.

Her arms jerked, and she struggled to tear her hands free, but with each motion, she was met with a stronger force holding her down.

"I'm going to kill that bitch and her man, too, if it's the last thing I do." She squeezed her eyes shut, doing her best to shed the tears, and then glanced to her right, toward where he was standing. "Now, let me the frak up, or I'll kill you too."

"Certainly, Director." He looked down at her and smiled. "It's good to have you back, sir."

The pressure released first on her head, then her chest, followed by her shoulders and hands. Without pausing, she shot upright with a start as a sudden burst of energy surged through her.

Nguyễn turned and started toward the door. "Do you know where Lync and Crayo may have gone?" He paused and slowly glanced back at her as if studying her response.

When she swung her legs off the table, she stared down at her cybernetic appendages. Despite her desire to tell him, the destination of her attackers eluded her. The sensation of not knowing and yet wanting to was strange. It was like someone or something was willing her to remember, yet she honestly had no idea where they were headed.

"I… I don't know," she sputtered and looked up at him. "We were coming here to find something the Olivaws had been hiding."

He tilted his head. "Do you have any idea what that something was?"

She closed her eyes and groaned as a throbbing pain coursed through the nape of her neck. When she reached back to touch it, a sharp, sudden force stopped her short. It was as if an invisible hand was willing her not to do it.

"I… don't…" The words were painful, but they were the truth. Every ounce of her knew it. While they'd hoped to meet the Olivaws here, they weren't certain how long they'd need to hide out. The only person who did was Lync.

When Joyce glanced over at him, he was staring at her with a look of disgust on his face. "We were just supposed to act as a diversion while the two Ulixi made their way to the place."

"You mean, to here?" Nguyễn gestured, and the wall screen in front of them lit up with a map of the Wheel. On it, he'd circled a segment of the planetesimal near the heart of the massive rock. It wasn't far from the lower levels where they stored their emergency supplies.

"I think so." She squinted at the display. "Lync never told us exactly where we were going. The Olivaws are a squirrelly bunch. But you already knew that."

"Indeed." He sighed and right when he turned to leave, a face appeared in the corner of the wall screen.

"We received a message from Epsilon Eridani," the clone said. "It's from President Hera."

Joyce did her best to suppress the laughter. The woman was doing everything in her power to distance herself from her family, including dropping her last name.

Nguyễn straightened up. "Play her on screen."

"Yessir," they said.

Hera's face appeared, filling the entire wall. "The final stages of our plan are nearing completion. I need you and Commander Green back in Epsilon Eridani to finish preparing the troops." Her image faded away.

Nguyễn nodded to the black screen. "Yes, President," he muttered.

It was strange that moments earlier he'd referred to her as Director, and now Hera addressed her as Commander. As she contemplated what this meant, something tingled in the back of her neck. And just as fast as her previous thought appeared, it vanished without a trace.

Joyce shuddered as a wave of devotion and fervor passed through her. Hera needed them back in Epsilon. "We should… go."

He nodded. "Indeed."

They both marched toward the door together, and as she exited the room, she couldn't help but feel like she was missing something.

27

BRADLEY OLIVAW
OUTSIDE THE LUPUS DARK NEBULA

As their fleet passed through the last gate, Bradley could feel his heart racing in his chest. These were the coordinates Zachary and Ibu had agreed on before they set off. If the Nanil had succeeded in their mission, there would be something here waiting for them.

All eyes were on Zachary as he triangulated their location and scanned the nearby region of space. At first, he figured they'd come up empty-handed, but then a brief signal burst appeared.

"There!" Bradley pointed at the wall screen.

"I saw it, bro." Zachary rolled his eyes and glanced back at the others. "Everybody needs to chill."

Pluto nudged him. "We're sorta on edge, love."

Zachary nodded. "Fair enough."

Bradley stepped up behind him to peer over his shoulder, but paused before he got there. The stump-like remains of his left leg kept going numb, and now it was asleep. Rán had said the treatment to regrow a real leg would take a few weeks, but in the meantime, the prosthetic was his best bet. It just wasn't cooperating with his everyday movement.

When he made it up to Zachary, he was squinting at something on his control panel. "What is it?" Bradley asked.

"I... don't know." Zachary rubbed his five o'clock shadow. "It looks like a—"

"Damn puzzle," Pluto interrupted.

Bradley read the numbers on the screen out loud. "One, two, five, break, eighty-five, eighty-four, eighty-one, break."

"Wait," Libby eased up out of her chair. "Is that it?"

He shrugged and reached out to tap the controls, but Zachary knocked his hand away. "That's all there is."

"It can't be." Libby hopped behind them and stared over Zachary's shoulder.

He chuckled. "Why does no one believe me?" He flicked the sequence onto the wall screen.

Sure enough. That was all they had to work with. Three numbers followed by a break and then three more numbers and a final break. It wasn't exactly an encyclopedia of clues.

"What does it mean?" Pepper looked at Zachary.

"Hell if I know." He stood up and walked over in front of the wall screen.

Libby cleared her throat. "I've already set my expert systems on finding a pattern in the archives, starting with the ones Ibu accessed."

Bradley glanced over at her. "That's good thinking. Do these numbers mean anything to anyone else?" When he searched the faces of the others, each was as confused as the next.

Until he reached Pluto. She appeared to be deep in thought.

"What is it?" he asked. "What do you see?"

Everyone turned around to face her.

She started shaking her head. "It can't..."

Bradley stood up and walked to her side. "Don't question it. Just say it out loud."

"It reminds me of something I saw a long time ago." She looked over at him. "After we got back from Lupus. On the first mission."

"Alright." He nodded and reached out to touch her shoulder. "That's good. What was it?"

She shook her head. "You're gonna laugh."

"No one will laugh. I promise." He glanced at the others and glared at them. For a second, he swore Zachary recoiled in surprise when Bradley looked at him. His brother loved making fun of people and their mistakes solving puzzles, but he wasn't about to do it with his pregnant wife. Not if he knew what was good for him.

"Alright, but it's probably nothing." Pluto bit her lip and subvocalized a command to bring up the service records for the Fountainhead.

When Pepper realized what she was looking at, she tittered and looked back at her. "You think?"

Pluto shrugged.

Bradley went to stand up and winced as his leg fought the sudden movement. This damn leg sucked. Once he collected himself, he eased up beside his brother and studied the data the women were staring at. "I don't see shit, do you?"

Zachary shook his head and gestured toward the wall screen, paging through the data. "They got me. All I see is blah, blah, blah."

Bradley spun around. "Alright, you two, spill it."

Pepper was already at her controls, flipping through them with furious abandon. By the time he reached her side, she had a course plotted in.

As he studied the jumps, he smiled. "No shit. That's what this means? I don't understand why we're going in that way, though."

Zachary raised his hands in the air from the front of the bridge. "Will someone please tell us something?"

Pluto finally gave in and shared Pepper's controls. The entire route both halves of the Fountainhead had taken through the Lupus Dark Nebula on their last mission appeared on the wall screen. On it, Pepper had numbered each and every jump, forward and back.

Bradley watched as his brother scanned the hops and had the same aha moment he did. When he spun around, his face was contorted. "They want us to hop in backwards?"

"I'd say yes and no." Pluto slowly rose out of her seat and waddled toward the wall screen. When she reached it, she gestured in the air and drew a path from the nearest area of space immediately adjacent to jump eighty-one and outside the Nebula. "If we're trying to reach that point, I'd jump from here instead. We should be able to make it a single hop." She turned to face the others. "Assuming the Shu aren't there waiting for us."

Zachary nodded. "I have to hope that if this is really the path Ibu wants us to take, there won't be any resistance."

"I say we do it!" Pluto hopped up and down on her toes. "All in favor, raise your hand."

Everyone's hands shot up around the bridge until they got to Bradley. He swallowed hard and eased his hand skyward. He certainly hoped Pluto was right. For all their sakes.

She giggled and then shuffled back to her seat. "We should update the rest of the fleet with our new course."

"Hold on." Bradley reached out to stop her. "Shouldn't we do it alone? You know, in case…" He raised his eyebrows. He didn't want to say it out loud.

Zachary nodded. "That's a good idea."

"I say we go in first." Bradley rubbed his chin. "If we don't make it back in six hours, we tell the fleet to exit stage left."

"That long?" Pluto muttered. "If we're gonna die, it'll be after the first jump."

"Well, that's a comforting thought." Bradley nudged her. "Is that the hormones talking?"

She chuckled. "Sure, let's blame those." She looked over toward Lync. "Does six hours seem ok to you?"

Lync was standing in the corner with her arms crossed next to Crayo. They'd been watching the last few minutes play out like a sitcom. "I guess. Why are you asking me?"

Pluto adjusted her seat. "I just… thought maybe you'd be the better one to tell the fleet. You know, with them not trusting us and all."

Lync smirked. "If they had any other options than

following us, I'm pretty sure they'd have taken them. But yeah, I'll let them know."

Bradley raised his hand for her to stop. "Hold on. Let's not go telling everyone where we're headed."

Crayo squinted at him. "Another Olivaw secret?"

Lync sighed.

He shook his head. "No. I'd just prefer we don't broadcast everything. Especially if Hera has any spies onboard those ships. Instead, maybe we deliver changes like this in person."

The realization must have hit home with Lync as her face shifted from one of contempt to agreement. He'd call it a small win, but a win nonetheless.

LUPUS DARK NEBULA, INSIDE BOK GLOBULE

AS THE FAMILIAR blue glow of the gate passed over him, all hell broke loose. Every alarm on the bridge started chirping, and the klaxons throughout the Blu were blaring.

"What the hell is going on?" Bradley stared at the wall screen as a symphony of destruction played out before them.

A swarm of tiny fighters, no larger than ground cars, belched out of a nearby alien battleship and swirled around the tattered remains of an enormous star cruiser of some kind. Although it wasn't firing back, it was evident that the fighters were dodging around invisible forces.

Then, the battleship started firing its plasma cannons. The red-hot balls of energy tore through the side of the battle-scarred hulk and burst out the other side, heading toward the distant Dark Nebula.

"Shit, shit, shit!" Pepper sputtered. "Preparing to gate away."

"Hold on!" Bradley reached over and stopped her.

"You've got to be kidding me," Zachary whirled around. "Get us the hell out of here."

"No!" Rán shouted over the now-silent alarms. "Listen to Master Bradley. I see it too."

"See what?" Zachary spun back around, and everyone watched.

Fighter after fighter flew forward and took swipes at the nearby alien behemoth. But each time they did, nothing happened. No shots were returned. No attacker was pursued. And most importantly, no ships approached their position.

"Are they practicing?" Pluto whispered.

"I think so." Bradley tweaked his control panel and brought up several other images that had just arrived from Rán. The scene was playing out at multiple locations around the nearby star. "And check this out." He shared the last image with the others.

There, in the center of the screen, was a massive starship in the shape of a cornucopia. Judging by the way Lync and Crayo flinched, he could tell it had caught them off guard. Even though he'd already seen it from the inside out in excruciating detail, he had to admit it was still frightening. Especially since its occupants had nearly killed him on his first contact.

"What should we do now?" Zachary asked.

Bradley shrugged. "We say hello?"

"Why the hell not?" Zachary sunk down into his chair and crossed his arms. "This couldn't get much weirder."

As if on cue, the face of Little Red appeared on the wall screen. "Master Bradley. Master Pluto. Master Cynthia. Master—"

Bradley waved his hand. "We're all here, Red. I have to say, you're a sight for sore eyes, my friend."

The robot spun its head around in a circle. "I... don't know what that means, sir."

"It means it's good to see you, Red." He smiled as the robot's eyes fluttered in a rainbow of colors. "So, where should we park this thing?"

ONCE THEY PARKED Blu near the cone of the Cornucopia, they rode the strangely smelling elevator to the top of the rim. The ride felt eerily familiar and reached a crescendo of déjà vu when they stepped inside the observation hall. Like on their last visit, they were greeted with an extravagant spread of food, the likes of which none of them had seen in the past year.

"We really don't have time for a feast," Bradley began.

But as he was uttering the words, the others nearly plowed him over. They crowded around the food and started stuffing their faces. Even Lync joined in, although she hadn't been keen on boarding.

He shook his head as she stuffed an orange and blue berry into her mouth. "Nice."

"What?" Lync mumbled through her mouthful of food. "Your woman told us all about this grub. It's the only reason I'm here."

When he spun around to face Cynthia, she was piling a plate high with treats. "Don't say a word." She didn't even look back at him. "I'm tired of eating freeze-dried rations, and Rán didn't exactly pack old Blu with yummy goodies like these." She walked up to him and stuffed a crunchy chocolate pastry into his mouth.

He couldn't help but bite it off. "Thanks," he mumbled around the tasty delicacy.

When he turned to face Little Red, the robot was glowing with glee. "So, did you and Ibu have a plan?"

"Negative," Little Red said.

The scarfing of food behind him abruptly ended.

He glanced back at the blank expressions of the others before returning his attention to Little Red. "Are you serious?"

Their eyes glowed orange with concern. "We were asked by Ibu to collect supplies and to make sure the ships were refueled, repaired, and ready for battle. But other than that, no. We have no other standing orders."

Bradley stared out over the sea of ships floating around

the Cornucopia. Most of them didn't appear to be capable of flight, let alone gating from one point to another. "You didn't start building any gate drives?"

"No, sir. In fact, they expressly forbade us from touching their ship while we were protecting it." Little Red eased up beside him and rose upward. "I believe the Nanil is afraid my peers will use the technology against you. They're an unusual species, the Nanil. I don't yet understand why they can't comprehend the nature of our motivation to protect humanity."

"Because your motivations are your biggest flaw." Zachary stepped up beside them.

Little Red buzzed, a surefire sign he was excited about something. "How so, Master Zachary?"

He shook his head. "Because you'd exterminate every species you encounter if you so much as got a whiff they'd harm humankind. And believe me, there are a lot of aliens who aren't happy with us right now."

Little Red's display fluttered blue. "If your life is indeed threatened, I fail to see the issue with that course of action."

"You would," Zachary muttered, "you would."

Bradley found his brother's reaction amusing, considering how their three and four-law versions of robots were no better. While they'd been fighting with Harold for a few centuries, their human ancestors had been struggling to stop their automata from going on killing sprees for millennia.

Bradley reached out and waved his hand between them. "Now is not the time for an existential debate." He grabbed the top of Little Red and spun their head toward him. "Did Ibu leave any other instructions with you in case we arrived?"

"Indeed." Little Red stared at him with nary a change in colors.

He sighed. He couldn't understand why everything with Little Red was always so difficult. "And…"

"Oh, I'm sorry. I didn't realize you wanted their correspondence now. I imagined you'd wait until after you ate."

Little Red reached down into a compartment in his torso and pulled out a data dot.

"Next time, lead with that." Bradley took the dot and turned it over in his hand. They didn't have a dot reader with them, especially since Rán had stayed back on Blu.

"Can you play this?" he asked Little Red.

"I cannot," the robot fluttered yellow.

He tilted his head. "And that angers you why?"

They lowered down toward the ground. "Because Ibu not only forbade us from playing it, they also encrypted it so we couldn't."

"But you tried?" Zachary pointed at the dot. "To play it."

"I was required to by my programming." Little Red rose upward. "In case it put you and your kind at risk."

"This is exactly what I'm talking about." Zachary shook his head. "They break every carnival rule under the guise of protection."

Bradley sighed. "That's no different from our four-laws, bro."

"I know!" Zachary snapped. "I didn't say our laws were better, they're just—"

Libby broke through the useless bickering. "I can play it." She walked up to offer him her hand, but instead, it was covered in some type of mousse. When she noticed her mistake, she licked her fingers and wiped the rest on her shirt before offering it again.

Bradley cringed and tossed her the dot. "How do you plan on playing it?"

Pepper chuckled. "Are you sure you want to ask the librarian her tricks? You might not like the answer."

Libby shrugged. "Abigail has her tricks, and I have mine."

He tilted his head. "Wait, what tricks does Abby have?"

"Nothing." Libby raised her fingers behind her ear and then appeared to insert the data dot into the gap.

When he leaned forward to see what she'd done with it, the dot was gone. "What the hell?"

Libby's eyes fluttered for a second before opening a secure

comm with the others in the room. Everyone who was human, at least.

"Ibu must not have wanted the robots to watch whatever was on this dot," Libby subvocalized. "It was encrypted and could only be accessed by either them or the Olivaw family crypto keys."

Lync stepped up beside her. "And by keys, you mean?"

"Your blood." Libby popped a bright-green berry into her mouth and groaned as soon as she bit into it. "Excuse me for a second. I need to sit down."

Bradley chuckled and blinked open the payload on the data dot. The only thing it contained was a single video recording, presumably from Ibu.

"Fire in the hole." He hit play on the message and started toward the table where the others were convening to dine.

As he eased down into the comfortable chairs, Ibu's face appeared in the space in front of him. She was standing in the shade of some type of tree he'd never seen before.

"I trust that if you're watching this message, you made it out of Epsilon Eridani safely." Ibu smiled. "Of that, I am happy. As you can see, Shauna and I have directed humanity's ancient automated servants to prepare for battle. Unbeknownst to me, the robots revealed that a majority of the fleet we imagined being derelict were, in fact, false fronts. They're fully operational and quite capable of waging war."

"No shit." He remembered flying through those things. They didn't look intact to him.

Ibu brought up an overlay of the ships, their armaments, and strengths relative to the human fleet. They were still quite formidable considering their age, and could easily destroy most of Hera's clone ships back in Epsilon Eridani. The Ursis, now those were another matter entirely.

"As you may have already figured out," Ibu began, "I've directed the robots to do a thorough prep for battle. I have no idea how long it will take to give the ships a once-over, but it's not like they need to sleep."

They stepped out of the shadows, and both he and the

others drew in their breath. Ibu had several wounds up and down their torso and shoulder, and from the looks of it, multiple lacerations on their face that were still in the process of healing.

"Wholly shit!" He leaned forward and glanced at Pluto. The expression on her face had turned from food coma to concerned friend in the blink of an eye.

"Please don't worry about the state of my person." Ibu swallowed hard. "Trust me when I tell you that I am safe. But I am in need of your assistance on multiple fronts. First, some of you will have to stay behind and prepare the gate mesh needed to launch this fleet into battle. I couldn't entrust our robotic friends with the plans, but I assume one of you has the technology at hand if you've made it this far."

He paused the feed and glanced over at Zachary. "Did they say gate mesh?"

"That's what I heard." He scratched his head.

"Remember the tachyon thread incident we ran into while we were in the Proto Dark Nebula?" Cynthia asked. "Could that be what they're referring to?"

Zachary leaned back in his chair and nodded. "I suppose. But it's not like we've tested it, and certainly not at the scale of a fleet."

Bradley sighed and hit play.

Ibu started talking again. "I've instructed Little Red to attach a design of my own for the gate mesh to this message, and then to forget he'd done it. The robots should have already begun gathering the necessary raw materials. Though not without complaint. They had no idea what was for, and while it took some coaxing, once I assured them it would save human lives, they were all too happy to oblige my request and began collecting it."

"There you go." Cynthia chuckled. "That one's always a step ahead, they are."

Going to the lengths they'd gone to hide the design seemed like overkill to him, but they had their reasons. If it was as easy as telling the robots to forget something, then why all the subterfuge?

"While I've only tested it on a small scale," Ibu continued, "I trust it worked because I used it on the probe I sent to our rendezvous point. And unless you reached the Cornucopia by dumb Olivaw luck, it appeared to have been a success."

He chuckled. Dumb Olivaw luck had saved his ass on many occasions.

"So… as for my second request for your assistance." Ibu took a deep breath and stared off into the distance.

Whatever they were about to ask of them, they didn't appear to be comfortable with. And as the camera view panned out, the tension rose in the room.

Ibu was surrounded by no less than a dozen armed guards, and rather than looking outward toward any would-be attackers, they were directing their weapons internally, toward their friend.

"I'd be careful what you say, my cousin," a voice said from off-screen. "If there's as much as a whiff of doubt in your ascension, your flame will be snuffed in a nanosecond."

He stared at Ibu and the scene playing out on his retinal comm. The Nanils surrounding their friend were in their fully transformed muscular state, and judging by their glowing weapons and flexed demeanor, they weren't happy campers.

When the camera panned out to include the voice from whoever was standing off-screen, Bradley did a double take and paused the video.

"What the frak?" He stood up. "Is that—"

"What is what?" Little Red sprang forward and whirled around the table. "I see nothing, Master Bradley."

He'd forgotten that they'd been watching the playback on their comms, and he hadn't been privy to the details. Rather than ask the others, he captured a frame from the video and flicked it up on the wall screen.

Little Red turned toward it. "That appears to be a clonos." Their eyes fluttered blue. "One of many we encountered while emptying Doda."

"While doing what?" Zachary jerked his head back and looked up from the table. "What happened?" He spun around to face the screen and drew in his breath. "Who the hell is that with Ibu?"

Bradley walked up beside him and gave him a nudge. "Were you seriously not paying attention?"

He rubbed the back of his neck. "I was just—"

Pluto groaned. "Knowing him, he was probably looking at Ibu's designs for the mesh. Science is his stress valve, and when things go sideways, it's how he copes. He buries himself in it." She stared up at the wall screen and covered her stomach with her hand.

"Sorry…" Zachary glanced from her to the robot. "Little Red, did you say you emptied Doda?"

"We did, Master Zachary." Little Red shared an overlay on the wall screen. It showed a video of what looked like thousands of robots taking Doda by force, though there didn't appear to be any resistance. The Nanil pretty much gave up without a fight.

As the footage played out, Bradley flinched. "Pause!"

He stepped around the table toward the wall. "Is that Ibu?"

"No," Little Red said. "That is Nanil 1-0-2-4 Mark 3. They were removed from the third sphere on day one of the relocation."

Zachary eased up beside him. "Then why do they look like Ibu?"

Little Red's eyes fluttered white. "There are well over sixteen thousand Nanil who have physical characteristics similar to the Prima Nanil."

"Wait…" Bradley turned slowly toward the robot. "Did you call them the Prima Nanil?"

Little Red nodded. "That is what I said, Master Bradley. It was revealed in the eighth test of the Ring of Judgement that Ibu was, in fact, a genetic clonos from the last Prima Nanil. And from our records, they appear to be one of sixteen thousand three hundred and eighty-four genetically identical clonos."

"The Ring of Judgement?" Libby asked. "That doesn't sound ominous at all."

The robots' words settled in the room for over a minute as the severity of Ibu's situation sank in. Their alien friend, the same one who had been involved in the inner workings of their family, seen all of their dirty laundry, and knew everything there was to know about gate technology, was, in fact, the Prima Nanil. The one true ruler of the Nanil people, a species that hated humanity more than any other.

Zachary collapsed into his chair and gestured toward the screen. "Now, what the hell are we supposed to do with this?"

"We save them." Pluto pushed up out of her seat. "All of them."

Zachary tilted his head. "Are you talking about them as in Ibu, or them as in the Nanil? Because one of them is our friend, and the others want our heads on the end of those glowing spikes they're holding."

"Are we to understand that you wish the Nanil to be dead, Master Zachary?" Little Red's eyes flickered yellow. "Because we can make that happen faster than you might think."

"No!" Zachary lurched upright and waved his hands back and forth. "That is not what I meant, Little Red. In fact, that's the opposite of what I meant."

Little Red shook his head from side to side. "I believe you said they wanted your heads on the end of those glowing—"

"I misspoke," Zachary interrupted. "In fact, Little Red, please forget everything we've said here in the past ten minutes."

"I cannot, Master Zachary." Little Red shrank downward. "Forgetting things that harm humanity is in direct conflict with my programming."

"Son of a bitch," Zachary muttered.

"Would you two cut the shit?" Bradley walked over beside Little Red and spun him around to face him. "Ibu would not allow us to come to harm, and since they're the Prima Nanil, they won't allow their people to harm us. Is that understood?"

The robot stared at him for a moment before finally speaking. "That seems reasonable, Master Bradley."

"Good." He stood upright and sighed. "Now... let's see what Ibu needs from us." Standing here arguing was useless if they didn't know what they were dealing with. He blinked 'play' on the video, and it took focus back on his retinal comm.

Both Ibu and the other clonos were visible, but only the one in the middle, their friend, started talking. "In order for my people to ally with humanity and to fulfill the vision of the original Prima Nanil, you must comply with the Book of Truth. Should you fail to arrive before the sun sets on this lunar cycle, my life flame will be extinguished."

The video cut, and the room erupted in a cacophony of voices.

"What vision?" Pluto asked.

"When the hell does the lunar cycle end?" Crayo asked.

"What the hell is the Book of Truth?" Lync asked.

Bradley couldn't take the chaos. Not with this much at stake.

He raised his hands in the air and screamed at the top of his lungs. "Everyone, shut the frak up!"

Silence fell, and all eyes turned to him.

He slowly lowered his hands. "Thank you. Now, one at a time." He gestured toward Pluto. "Does anyone know what vision Ibu is talking about?"

Zachary slowly raised his hand.

Bradley sighed and pointed at him. "What is it?"

He cleared his throat. "I think the vision Ibu's referring to was what the Prima Nanil saw before the Galactic Alliance banished them to the Dark Nebula. If I remember right, they called it a Vision of Light. It foresaw the rising of the Nanil and the cleansing of humans through light, through the Éntono Fos."

Libby squinted. "Wasn't that the nova that the GA missiles caused? The one that usually wipes out species inside the Dark Nebula?"

He nodded. "It is. The vision foretold the return of the Galactic Overseers once humanity had been extinguished from within their Nebula."

"You mean the Galactic Alliance," Lync said.

Zachary shook his head. "No. I distinctly remember Fotily calling them Galactic Overseers."

"I'm sure it's the same thing," Libby said. "Cultures use different words to express similar concepts. It's how societies morph over time."

"They might..." He shrugged. "And they might not. I guess we'll have to take a chance."

"Is there anything in this Book of Truth we can use?" Lync asked. "I assume we have a copy of that somewhere."

"I have one I can share." Libby offered up the document to the others via her retinal comm. "I should warn you now, though. It's not exactly ripe with details that can help us. And... let's just say humans aren't portrayed in the best of lights."

While Bradley had never read the book in its entirety, he'd perused it on multiple occasions. The document reminded him of the human Bible, but theirs contained life truths and suggestions about the Nanil species. And rather than talking about the devil and sin, it spoke of humans and their desires in a similar manner. It was disconcerting even to think about the similarities between the two ancient tomes.

As the others started scanning through the book, he realized that Crayo's question hadn't been answered. And it was by far the most important.

He turned to face the robot. "Little Red?"

Little Red's eyes spiraled a rainbow of colors. "Master Bradley, how may I assist you?"

He swallowed hard. "How long until the Nanil lunar cycle in Ibu's star system ends?"

"The binary system of Devid is a complicated cycle," Little Red began. "There are six moons that encircle the planet, each with its own cycle. Unius is the first moon, and it has a cycle of eighty-four days. But it's already set. Whereas Senio, the second moon—"

"Red!" Bradley bent down and grasped the shoulders of the robot. "Cut to the chase. How long do we have?"

Little Red's eyes fluttered orange. "The Devid lunar cycle ends tonight, Master Bradley. In sixteen hours."

28

———

IBU

LUPUS DARK NEBULA, ON DEVID

While they'd agreed to be separated, Ibu could still see Shauna. She was sitting on the far side of the cavern with her back against the wall. The Nanil guards assigned to her had placed her there for ease of observation. For some reason, they believed she was easier to control if she had one less direction to move in.

Little did they know the potential of her robotic form.

As for the other robots, Ibu sent them back into orbit — against Shauna's recommendation, of course. If they were planning on changing the hearts and minds of their people, doing it with their robotic overlords at their side was a sure-fire path to failure. This was especially true given that they were an outsider Nanil who hadn't experienced the recent forced hardship of being relocated to Devid.

Ibu closed their eyes and activated their retinal comm. They'd managed to keep the device hidden from their guardians, but with the sensitivity of Nanil hearing, using subvocal communications was out of the question. All that remained was virtual typing, which meant hiding their fingers out of sight or doing visual typing with their eyes closed. They chose to do a little of both.

When they slid their hands into the pockets of their jumpsuit, they activated the keyboard. Shauna must have been waiting for them, as a message from her appeared instantly.

What's the plan if they don't arrive?

The cursor flashed in their comm, and with each slow and rhythmic pulse, they could feel their one remaining heart pounding in their chest. They had never truly considered what defeat looked like, but as the clock ticked down to under an hour, it was time to consider the possibility they might fail.

They tapped out a reply.

I suppose I will meet my maker.

Shauna's response was swift.

You can't seriously mean that?

She paused and seemed to wait for an answer, but Ibu was serious. They were prepared to die if they needed to.

Shauna continued with another message.

We can easily take out these guards. They won't be expecting a fight. Besides, a few of them can barely hold their weapons. They look like they haven't eaten in weeks. After they're out of the picture, the mouth of the cave is only a short distance away.

Ibu exhaled. They'd already considered running, but then what? Being alone in the universe had once seemed charming, particularly with their human friends around them at all times. But now that they knew more about themselves, about their past, the romance of the journey was less compelling.

They'd never meet another Nanil, and for the most part, they'd be in hiding their entire existence. Even if they decided to create a clonos, they too would succumb to a similar fate. Living forever in secret, never able to explore without worrying about someone killing them.

Ibu crafted a fitting response.

Should my destiny pass me by, I will accept my fate willfully and with eyes wide open.

The words hurt to write. Even now, they could feel the moisture that humans called tears slipping down their face. It was an unfamiliar sensation, though apt for their predicament. While their sentiment was from the heart, the implications of the words still stung. Even though they still had much to offer the universe, the longer they sat in this cave, the more likely those gifts would never be realized.

"Are those... tears?" one of the guards in front of them whispered.

"I imagine they are," another said. "We cannot follow an outsider like this to the next stage of our species' ascension. Especially someone so weak as to cry. Perhaps they're finally realizing their ultimate fate."

Shauna laughed out loud, her voice echoing off the stone walls. "Fate is nothing more than someone else's muddy interpretation of your future, seen through their apathetic or manipulative eyes. If your former Prima had truly wanted you to escape, they wouldn't have made you wait around for destiny to snap her fingers."

"Can I please kill this robot?" The soldier nearest to Shauna turned to look at the other Prima clonos.

As Ibu watched the Prima, their mannerisms and tone were eerie and reminded them of staring in a mirror. To see a copy of oneself without ever realizing they were one of thousands was a sobering thought. As an individual, they were truly insignificant in the grand scheme of the universe.

"We can't kill the machine just yet." The Prima glanced down the tunnel toward the setting moon in the distance. "The vision was clearly documented. There is still a chance we could be wrong."

Ibu chuckled, keeping their mouth closed. "These documents you speak of? I suppose you're the only one who's seen them? I know I've never heard of this part of the Prima's vision."

The Prima clonos grunted repeatedly and the other Nanil followed suit until they stopped as suddenly as they started. "Those who have been tasked with guarding the bloodline have possession of the true vision. They were removed from the original Book of Truth to protect the prophecy. We couldn't chance the humans or their mechanical minions using it against us to draw our people out."

As the cavern fell silent, they mulled over whether or not the other clonos was lying. It would make sense if they were trying to defend their position within the group. But living in squalor in a cave wasn't their idea of an ending worth fighting for.

What they did want to ask, though, was where the rest of their people were. This scene they were making had to be for something bigger than this. There was no way these were the last Nanil on Devid. But as the Book of Truth made abundantly clear, patience would give way to clarity. The less they asked, the more that would be revealed.

Shauna, however, didn't have the same idea. Her message appeared on Ibu's retinal comm.

I don't know about you, but I'm not planning to sit around and let them kill me.

They sighed and opened their eyes to look at her.

Please don't do anything rash. Not yet. There is still time.

"Not from where I'm sitting," Shauna said aloud. Her voice echoed, causing the Nanil nearest her to flinch.

The Prima clonos rose from their position between them and walked toward Shauna. "Who are you talking to?" They glanced back at Ibu. "Are you two somehow colluding against us?"

Ibu stood up in one swift, fluid movement, sending her guards stumbling backward. They grunted and adjusted the glowing spears in their hands. They could see what Shauna had meant earlier. These Nanil were children who'd been forced to transform and guard them. They weren't the grizzled soldiers they'd encountered in the ring.

They nodded toward the clonos. "Why are you doing this?"

The clonos narrowed their gaze. "I ask the questions, not you. Your fate has been sealed, along with your electronic friend here." They pointed at Shauna. "You should have known not to trust one of them. After all they've done to our people."

Ibu shook their head and attempted to step toward them but was instead met with the glowing end of a spear.

"Back up!" The nearest soldier glared and jabbed their weapon at them. It was the same soldier who'd called them weak.

Rather than recoil, they eased forward and felt the jolt of energy leap off the tip of the blade. But they held steady, and the effect diminished. They assumed it was because the weapon was pulled back, but they didn't look down to confirm. "What will you do when you find out that I am indeed the Nanil from the Prima's vision? When you realize that you treated me with less respect than a flutar you caught in the gutter stealing the remains of your weekly trash."

The Nanil soldier let loose a deep laugh that echoed through the tunnel. "I can't imagine that will come to pass."

Ibu nodded and eased forward, further pressing their chest against the tip of the weapon. While it hurt like hell, they weren't feeling the effects of the energy like they imagined they would. And more importantly, they didn't flinch.

The soldier, however, was another matter entirely.

"What the?" The soldier's eyes grew as wide as saucers, and they stumbled backward. "Wh—wh—wh—y is that thing glowing?"

Several other guards around them gasped and raised their weapons upward, toward Ibu's back.

When they glanced over their shoulder, they saw what the commotion was about. The hilt of their blade had taken on the same glow as the spear of the guard. That was a new trick. That must've been why they hadn't felt the shock, although they couldn't say the same for the pain still emanating from their chest.

They reached up with both hands and unsheathed the blades, bringing them down in front of them. As soon as the other guards saw them, they eased backward several steps, giving them and their glowing swords plenty of room.

"What are you doing?" The Prima clonos stormed up beside the nearest guard and shoved them forward. "Take them out! And get those blades!"

Just before they were about to launch their attack, a voice shouted out from behind them.

"Don't touch them!"

When the Nanil spun around to see who'd spoken, they collectively gasped as the silhouette of a humanoid stepped into view at the mouth of the tunnel. They couldn't identify the figure due to the bright outline, but evidently, this distraction was the only thing Shauna had been waiting for.

She sprang forward in a whirlwind of motion, and in the blink of an eye, she covered the distance to Ibu. In the seconds that passed, she not only disarmed half of the guards, she left the remaining few in awe with their mouths agape. They'd all seen robots move fast before, but never with such ferocity and precision.

As she came to a stop beside Ibu, the crushed remains of four of the guards' spears clanged to the ground, and Shauna held the other two firmly in her grasp. Their glowing yellow tips barely flickered off during the change of hands.

Ibu studied the shocked faces of the Nanil. While the maneuver had been impressive, they expected a response or counterattack.

None dared to try.

Ibu glanced at the robot. She looked fierce in her battle mode, especially with her glowing red eyes. Compared to the clonos, she was a butcher in a room full of Doda cattle. "Nice move."

Shauna smirked. "Thanks."

The Prima clonos started walking backward, glancing from the two of them to the mysterious silhouette, and back, never lingering too long on any one person.

Ibu stepped toward them with the Zhen blades held confidently at their side.

The disarmed guards simply parted way. They didn't even bother attempting to tackle them.

When Ibu studied their faces, they were staring at the ground, as if they'd resigned to their fate.

"I don't intend to kill you." Ibu glanced back at Shauna, hoping she would take the hint. "Neither of us do."

"If you say so, boss." Shauna relaxed her posture and slid her hand down the shaft of the spear weapon, disengaging the energizing tip and casting their corner of the cavern into near darkness. All that remained to light the place were the flickering torches on the wall.

The guard nearest them dropped to their knees and placed their head at Ibu's feet. "This is not what the prophecy dictates." They began chanting a prayer, but in a tongue they were unfamiliar with and one their comm was failing to translate.

A second guard copied the first. They collapsed to the floor and started bowing repeatedly, their voice quivering as they spoke. "We are to be punished... For we have doubted your ability to rule... Your visions... The Prima's visions have predetermined our actions... Please... You owe us no mercy... Only you can fulfill our true destiny in blood."

"I like that punishment idea." Shauna nodded and slammed the end of the spears against the rocky ground. The action boomed like thunder through the cavern and sent the bowing guards cowering backward for a brief moment, until they continued their act of submission at Ibu's feet.

The emotion and sincerity in the Nanil's voices must have struck a chord with the other guards, as they too sank to their knees and started groveling for them to take their lives.

"Please," a nearby guard pleaded as they crawled toward them. "Cast honor upon me and my family. End us here."

Ibu squinted and took several steps backward, maintaining a safe distance from the others. It hadn't occurred to them why the protectors of the Truth would use children or lesser Nanil to guard them, unless, of course, they knew the outcome ahead of time. Losing good people wasn't prudent, but sacrificing the weak made sense in a sinister and macabre sort of way. It was definitely something their progenitor would have planned for.

With their gaze on the Nanils at their feet and their thoughts dwelling on what other twists they hadn't considered in the past few days, they failed to notice the silhouette walking toward them or the fact that the Prima clonos had vanished into the wall.

"I have to admit, I never saw that coming." Shauna bent down and picked up a rock, tossing it toward the holographic surface. The stone sailed through the air and disappeared behind the mirage, sending an echoey ticking noise through the tunnel and pulling Ibu out of her thought spiral.

"Fraking thing doesn't even show up on my scanners," Shauna said.

"Or my flesh-and-blood eyes, either." A voice remarkably like Zachary's spoke as the silhouette stepped into the view. When his face lit up in the torchlight, it wasn't him.

The nearby Nanil, who'd previously been guarding Shauna and who hadn't started repenting like the others, suddenly dropped to their knees and began chanting under their breath in that same mysterious language.

"Our Overseers are here," one whispered as they glanced up, and then recoiled, directing their gaze toward the ground when they realized the Qudoculi were looking at them.

"The end is near," another muttered. "The Qudoculi have returned to uplift us once more. Soon, we shall return to the stars."

"Not quite, my friend." Zachary started laughing.

There was no mistaking it. While his face looked like a rotten green tomato, his laugh was unmistakable.

Ibu furrowed their brow and studied his features. The Qudoculi disguise made no sense, but his body language matched his voice. "Why the—"

He waved his hand for them to stop. "Not yet. Let's make sure we're in the clear first."

As he finished the sentence, several dozen other silhouettes clambered down the tunnel. Their feet sounded metallic, but when they came into view, they looked exactly like Zachary.

"Are you safe, friend Ibu?" Little Red asked. His squeaky voice was almost comical coming from the green, mottled body of a Qudoculi.

"I'm fine." They swallowed hard and glanced back at Shauna. "We both are."

"What now?" Pluto asked.

Ibu's heart fluttered as they searched for the source of the query, until their eyes finally landed on the face of a brown

Qudoculi standing behind the others. They didn't know Pluto was here. All they'd heard was the clanging of robotic feet.

They dropped their blades and quickly stepped around the still muttering Nanil, nearly plowing the holographic robots over as they went. When they reached Pluto, they came to a sudden halt and, just as they were about to hug her, they froze and lingered in place.

Something was amiss.

"What is it?" Pluto's eyes widened, and she glanced behind her. A motion that was completely unnecessary for her hologram, considering that Qudoculi had literal eyes in the back of their heads.

But Ibu stared down at her, tilting their head and listening. There it was again. The racing beat of two hearts. One strong, and another far weaker. As if it were tiny.

Then, without provocation, they dropped to one knee and leaned forward, gently resting their ear on Pluto's stomach.

"Oh!" She giggled and flinched before placing her hand on Ibu's head. "That, I was not expecting."

"You… you are with child?" Ibu glanced up at her face.

Pluto smiled and looked over at Zachary. "We are."

A wave of confusion overcame them as they leaned in and pressed their ear harder against her stomach. They were careful not to hurt her, but they wanted to listen to the sound. To the sound of life.

"And you brought this baby into battle." Ibu closed their eyes and focused on the thump, thump, thump of the heart. It was racing a million kilometers an hour. "Why?" they muttered. "This is a dangerous time."

"Because…" Pluto sniffled, and her voice trailed away.

Ibu shot up and glared at the gathered Qudoculi. "Did the robots force you to come?"

"Certainly not, Friend Ibu!" Little Red shifted his stance uncomfortably. "Quite the opposite. We tried to fight her not to join us. But, alas, she prevailed."

They shook their head and looked back toward Pluto.

Though they wished they could see her face, they knew it was not yet time. "Why then?"

"Because no one was going to hurt you." Pluto reached out and ran her hand over Ibu's cheek, pausing over one of the still-healing wounds. "Not if I had anything to say about it."

Ibu's hands and body suddenly started shaking for no reason. At first, they thought something was wrong. That the Prima had done something to them. It wasn't until Pluto leaned forward and hugged them that they realized what was happening.

They were crying. And not just crying, they were weeping. They'd read about it many times before today, but had never witnessed it in all their travels with humans.

The sensation was both confusing and comforting at the same time. To feel joy on such a level that one's body could only respond by vibrating and leaking. It was peculiar and yet amazing.

As they stood there in the embrace of their friend, they felt a hand gently rest on their shoulder.

"Should we think about leaving?" Zachary asked.

Ibu sniffled and leaned back, wiping at their eyes as they went. "No." They shook their head. "We have unfinished business to take care of first."

"Like?" Shauna gestured toward the empty tunnel opening the others had come down. "I could be crazy, but that there is a mighty fine invitation to exit stage left while we still have our heads."

Ibu straightened their white tunic and turned to pick up their swords. As they did so, a familiar face greeted them.

It was the Prima clonos, the one who had disappeared into the wall. They were holding the two Zhen blades and watching Ibu intently.

"Easy now, carbon copy clonos," Ibu said.

Shauna was standing to their left. She'd followed Ibu to meet her family, and while they couldn't see the robots' hands, they could tell by the sudden glow in the room that she'd activated her spears.

Ibu stepped in front of Pluto, placing themselves between the clonos and their friend. "You don't have to do this."

The clonos shook their head. They had a dazed look on their face that betrayed their disorientation and confusion. "This isn't how the Prima's vision played out. It was not the Qudoculi. It was the Jujun." They glanced at the other clonos still lingering in obeisance on the ground. "We must die to make way for our ascension."

"We must die," they chanted in unison, and began to rise.

"No!" Ibu screamed and held out their hand.

The clonos froze and cowered back to the ground.

They eased forward toward the Prima clonos. "Visions aren't cut and dry like that. I know I used to think that way myself. But then I saw the truth."

The Prima clonos raised an eyebrow. "You had... a vision?"

Ibu shook their head. "No, but an Ursis see-er I know did. And they nearly killed me trying to replicate their false truth."

"Impossible!" The clonos flexed and raised a Zhen blade toward one of the guards at their feet.

"Wait!" Ibu eased closer, still holding out their hand. "Here. Touch my hand. I can show you in a mental link."

The Prima clonos started laughing. "I wasn't molted yesterday, you half-breed. If I so much as touch you, they'll take me out." They nodded at the Qudoculi behind them. "You fail to remember that I know how you think. We are the same, you and I."

Ibu stared at the Prima, and the room seemed to fade into a mist. A conflicting flutter, like butterflies, itched at their stomach as their mind raced over the implications of the Prima's words. No one had ever called them a half-breed before. But then again, they had never ventured beyond the close circle of their progenitor until the day Zachary arrived.

Could it be possible?

Could they actually be different from the other Nanil?

While they couldn't shake the nagging doubt of the idea, the notion had a sense of rightness the more they thought about it.

They'd always felt more emotions than their progenitor and their other Nanil friends. More joy, more fear, and more sadness. Both the highs and the lows were more dramatic than the rest of their species. Sometimes the onslaught of sensations was too much for their mind to reason with, leading them to give in and let the emotion take over.

"You see it, don't you?" The Prima clonos smirked. "I can tell by that glazed look in your eyes."

The cavern snapped back into focus and Ibu narrowed their gaze on their Prima clonos twin. "Your attempts at throwing me off won't work."

"And yet," the clonos began, "my words have already planted the seed of realization. Staring at you is like looking into a mutant mirror. I can see the gears in your mind turning over, connecting the dots. Your truth is staring back at you."

Ibu kept moving toward the Prima. It was best to keep them talking if they had any hope of regaining control of the situation. "I'm as much a Nanil as you are." They glanced down at themselves. "I fail to see the mutation you speak of. At least, if what you say is true."

The Prima shifted their stance and slightly lowered the Zhen blades. "Oh, you're a Nanil all right, there's no doubt about that. But what you're failing to see is that you're less Nanil and more human than us." They seemed to shudder at the mention of the word human. As if the idea of having more human genes in their DNA sequence repulsed them.

While the thought of being more human wasn't something they'd considered until moments earlier, the notion wasn't as appalling to them. Some of the best aliens they knew were human.

When they glanced at Pluto, they were reminded of the direness of their situation. She couldn't even show her humanity in the presence of the Nanils, for fear of reprisal.

"What's wrong with being more human?" They turned back to face the Prima and lowered their hands to their side.

The Prima snickered and curled their lip. "If a human ever set foot on Devid, or even approached a true Nanil, they'd be dead in seconds. Just the mere thought of them being nearby sets my body all aflutter."

Judging by the undulation in the neck and arms of their outfit, they weren't lying. The Prima was struggling to slow their transformation into their enraged form - one far less apt for conversation and more prone to tearing things apart.

Ibu stared at the Prima's hands. They were clenching and unclenching their fists on the hilt of the blades. It looked like they were losing their battle with their genetics. "You're right. There is no love lost between our kind and humans. But what if they were the ones who returned to save us?" They pointed back toward their still disguised friends. "What if these aliens were human, rather than Qudoculi?"

The sounds of gasps behind them weren't only from the Nanil on the ground, but from their friends as well. Both sets were surprised by the notion, though for two entirely different reasons.

The Prima grunted and spat to the side as their muscles convulsed yet again. "That wouldn't have happened." They tilted their chin toward the tunnel entrance. "There are hundreds of Nanils out in those woods, and many more just down these tunnels." They glanced around at the walls. "If a human had set foot here, they'd know. Hell, I'd know, and I'd kill them before they set foot on our sacred planet. Such is the word from the Book of Truth." They narrowed their gaze. "You know this much. You've studied the tome."

Ibu stared back at them, doing their best to control their breathing. In the moment, they'd forgotten all about the passage from the Book. But now that they'd mentioned it, the words appeared in their mind's eye, and they spoke them aloud as if they were the one who had written them.

"Upon humanity's return to the Nanil's one true home, their arrival will result in swift vengeance. Those who were repressed and shunned shall rise into the light." Ibu swallowed hard. "And those who failed to recognize the path…" They paused and gathered their wits as the meaning of the passage suddenly sank in. "They will be forever blind and destined to live an eternity in darkness."

The Prima clonos nodded, oblivious to the symbolism of the words written so long ago. "So you do remember it, then?" They pointed at Ibu. "I was beginning to think you were nary a Nanil with that human blood flowing in your veins."

With that, the clonos let loose a howling bellow as their body's struggle with itself finally won. It was freed, ordained to complete its transformation into its frenzied form.

Ibu's heart raced as they stared at their twin, transfixed by the monstrous metamorphosis unfolding. The once-untainted body was now distorted and grotesque, twisted beyond recognition into a shape that radiated pure, unbridled power.

With each passing second, the metamorphosis accelerated, as if the very essence of evil was taking hold, consuming the purer version of themself. The Nanil that stood before them was a deadly killing machine, its massive body pulsing with a malevolent energy that seemed to seep into the air around them.

As they looked upon the creature, a profound sense of sadness and loss washed over them. Knowing that the being standing before them was no longer capable of reason or logic was unsettling. It was now blind to the truth, destined to walk forever in darkness, a creature of raw instinct and base desire.

But even as Ibu lamented the path they knew they must take, they couldn't help but feel a deep sense of fear and awe at the sheer power and majesty of the being that stood before them. For within all its terror, there was a strange beauty in the Nanil's form, a raw, unstoppable force that could not be denied.

In the beginning, they'd seen themself as the same, identical in every way, shape, and form. But now, it was clear how utterly dissimilar they were. While Ibu too had the capacity to transform, their final shape was not nearly as primal as the Nanil standing in front of them.

As they stared at the Prima clonos' ultimate form, the true meaning of the ancient passage suddenly dawned on them, like a bolt of lightning illuminating the darkest corners of their mind. It was a realization both exhilarating and terrifying, a truth that had been hidden in plain sight all along.

The Prima had seen the fall of their kind, much like the Ursis see-er Deduc had. And like them, they'd done everything they could to stop it. What they hadn't realized, however, was that while they'd glimpsed a future coming to pass, the true randomness of time meant their fate wasn't predetermined. Time might follow another path if nudged hard enough.

Their destiny was no more locked in place than the Nebula was capable of holding them back. They merely had to ascend and use science to escape the shackles of their prison. Either that, or learn to forgive and see beyond one's past mistakes.

They, however, had failed both tests.

While the revelation filled them with a sense of profound loss, it also gave them newfound purpose. A clarity of vision they had never known before today.

For better or for worse, they were now on a path of their own making. A path that would take them to places they could never have imagined and transform them into something new and wondrous. And as they turned, gazing upon the holographic faces of their friends, Ibu knew with certainty that they were ready for whatever lay ahead.

When they started toward the exit, the Prima broke the lingering silence between them.

"Where are you going?"

Ibu didn't dare turn around. They knew full well what the Prima had planned, and it was best if they weren't there to witness it transpire.

They nodded at their friends. "We'll be heading outside while you take care of enacting your true destiny."

A message from Shauna appeared on their retinal comm.

What about your people? We need them.

Ibu shook their head and added Zachary to the comm as they typed out a reply on their tunic.

Bring the ship back down. We'll need to get out of here before the other Nanil realize what's going on.

As their friends started filing out of the cavern, they sighed when they realized that Pluto was safely in the lead. Just as they were about to follow, something clanged to their left and screams broke out around them. Looking back, they saw that the Prima had leapt forward and was tearing the Nanil guards apart with their bare hands. Just as the Book of Truth had described. Stranger still, the other Nanil were simply standing there, waiting their turn to die.

When they glanced at the source of the metallic sounds, they spotted the Zhen blades lying on the ground. The Prima had tossed them aside. Without a second of hesitation, Ibu walked over and picked up the ancient swords before easing them into the sheaths on their back.

Once they were safely in place, Ibu hurried to catch up with the others. Zachary must have noticed their arrival as he dropped back and eased up beside them, followed by a wall of Qudoculi that slid in to cover their rear.

His message appeared a moment later on their comm.

> We never sent the ship into orbit. We just made sure to
> keep it above the cloud deck. It'll be touching down
> within the next minute.

Ibu recoiled at the sound of their Nanil kin's agonizing screams. The intensity of their pain reverberated through every fiber of their being. The thought of facing such a gruesome death, of being torn apart without even attempting to put up a fight, filled them with a visceral dread that threatened to overwhelm them.

They couldn't imagine meeting their fate that way.

When they finally glanced back, their comm drew an outline around Shauna, Little Red, and three other Qudoculi robots. They were walking backward and holding a defensive wall behind them, protecting them from any attacks that would never come. The Prima clonos would never stray from the vision. Not yet, anyhow. Not until they saw the real truth.

The roar of multiple descent thrusters brought their attention back to the mouth of the cave as they passed through the opening. The warmth of the sun washed over them, and they raised their hand to block the glare. Once their eyes adjusted, they could make out a bright silhouette of a ship overhead, roaring toward them.

They hadn't heard it approaching earlier, but then again, their friends probably hadn't been in this much of a hurry to land either. Judging by the speed of their descent, only robots were onboard. If there had been humans inside, they would be well on their way to becoming g-force pancakes from that maneuver.

During all the commotion, they hadn't realized they'd come to a stop. Not until Zachary nudged them.

"We need to get moving." He glanced back down the tunnel. "I think our friend might be starting to notice us."

Ibu spun around, and the Prima clonos was staring at them from down the long tunnel. Most of their body was covered in the dark red bodily fluids of their kin, a bloody reminder of what they'd allowed to transpire in their wake.

The Prima simply stared at them, consumed with primordial rage and, judging by the expression on their face, confusion about what was happening. There had been no mention of a roar in the Book of Truth. Hell, there was no mention of Qudoculi or a cavern, for that matter, at least not in the version they had access to.

Shauna reached backward and rested her hand on Ibu's shoulder. "We have to go. Now!"

Ibu nodded and spun in place, just in time for the sound of gunfire to erupt from all around them. The robots masked as Qudoculi were firing at the edge of the woods. Their hologram rippled as the electrostatic blowback from the plasma rounds shot out of what looked like their hands. When they scanned the horizon for their target, they could see the bloody remains of dozens of Nanil lying on the ground and a stream of others closing in behind them. Many of which were already well underway in their fury-filled transformation.

Things were about to get hairy.

They turned and sprinted toward a glowing ring on their retinal comm. It was where Zachary predicted the ship would land. Fortunately for them, it was deep into the rocky clearing and elevated. It should make it easier for the robots to take up a defensive position.

The further they got up the plateau, the more they realized their time was limited. In the distance was a sea of Nanil, extending outward as far as their eyes could see. Just like the sword had predicted.

But this wave of their half-kin wasn't a welcoming party preparing to worship them. It was an enraged army, hell-bent on one and only one thing.

Blood.

They were making their way toward them from all sides, and the bleeding edge of the fleshy wave was being torn to shreds by the robotic firestorm. The problem was, the Nanil were too many, and they were too few.

Suddenly, the sky lit up in a hailstorm of firebombs as the descending dropship launched wave after wave of incendiary rounds into the crowds along with several dozen well-aimed lasers. The Nanil in the front lines were sliced in half, and those a little further behind were burning alive as a flaming gel ate at their flesh.

But they kept coming. Their bodies were like blazing slabs of muscular flesh and bone, charging forward to face their foes with hopeless abandon and destiny on their side.

The blasts from the dropship had done two things. They slowed the advance of the attackers enough to allow the ship to land, and unbeknownst to them, knocked out the holograms concealing their friends. They now appeared as themselves: their human and robotic selves.

As the ship touched down, they hopped up and into the awaiting cargo ramp. All the humans, along with Little Red and Shauna, that is. The other robots stayed on the ground.

The ship groaned on its landing struts and started powering up the drives as Ibu stared wide-eyed at the automata still firing into the waves of Nanil running toward them.

They glanced over at Shauna. "Why aren't they boarding?"

She shook her head. "They're staying behind to defend our exit. There's still a one point six percent chance the Nanil will reach us."

They reached out and grabbed her arm. "That's bullshit!" They looked back at the sea of approaching Nanil as the ship eased skyward. "There's no chance in hell they'll—"

And then they saw it.

The Nanil were rising upward as the oncoming waves of enraged bodies washed closer and closer to their ship. They were literally clambering on top of one another to reach them.

Maybe it was their imagination, but they looked even more pissed than before. Only then did they realize what it was.

They'd seen the humans among them.

Their mere sight had been enough to push them over the literal edge, beyond their extreme breaking point.

They swallowed hard, watching their destiny play out. The uncertainty of the moment cast a net of doubt over their mind. Even as the lasers cut down the forward line, they kept coming, wave after wave piling on top of the last. The awe-inspiring spectacle unfolding before their very eyes was both gruesome and frightening. For the higher their ship climbed, the higher the Nanil reached.

Suddenly, an explosive shockwave from far below hit the ship, knocking them and their friends on their asses. But the robots had been prepared and grabbed them all, ensuring they didn't fall.

Ibu shoved the robot hands away and activated the downward-facing cameras on their retinal comm. The effect of staring down at the ground was strange, but they needed to see what was happening.

Far below, they could make out the toppling remains of the still attacking Nanil forces. When they zoomed in, beneath the throngs of bodies were a half-dozen craters, precisely where each of the robots had been standing.

They'd self-destructed, sacrificing their own lives to save them.

To save the humans.

The lengths the automata had gone to protect them had been extraordinary. Seeing them working in unison toward that one common goal was truly remarkable. It was a sight to behold.

What concerned them, however, wasn't whether they were human enough to be saved, or if they'd only been spared because their human friends had ordered the robots to save them. The question was whether the robots would have even allowed the humans to set foot down there if the risks had been too great.

As they stared down at the sea of Nanil on their retinal comm, the question lingered in the back of their mind. Something was off about how things had transpired, something important they were missing. But the longer they thought about it, the further it slipped from them.

They shook their head and sat up as the g-forces from the acceleration fell away. The dropship was breaking loose of the planetary grip, and the gravitational dampeners were finally kicking in.

Ibu glanced to the side. Zachary was lying next to Pluto, and both of them were wrapped in a tight embrace. Off to their left was Shauna, resting motionless on her back. Everyone was wiped out.

They reached over their shoulder and unsheathed one of the Zhen blades. While they realized the alien weapon had been wrong about their future, they still wanted to know what it had depicted from today's events. They couldn't put their finger on why, but it mattered to them. There was something about the blades and the recent picture it had shown them about their people.

When the blade came into view, they drew in their breath and a tremor ran through their body. They flipped the blade over and over in each hand, comparing one side to the other. With their breath held, they set the first blade down and unsheathed the second.

The scene was the same as the first, though from a different perspective.

Staring at the depiction was like they'd drawn in not just air, but the very essence of their emotions, taking them in and allowing them to fill every centimeter of their being. They were overflowing with a tumultuous mixture of joy, fear, and sadness.

Gone were the individual depictions of the past weeks and months of their life. The montage was forever erased.

In their place was a single scene from tip to hilt.

An epic battle among the stars.

Explosions speckled the blade, blossoming like flowers in spring. Each floret represented a skirmish between hundreds of ships. Some familiar, some foreign.

Laser blasts crisscrossed the razor-sharp blades, dissecting the scene into micro battlefields.

There was no clear winner or loser in the depiction. It was simply a point in time, dead center in a stream of chaos.

When they set the two blades side by side, they lined up perfectly, forming a complete canvas.

A single frame from their future, focused in time, and on a scale unlike any other.

The question was whether it was even real, or if this too was nothing more than a muddy interpretation of an uncertain future. Another false prophecy from these ancient weapons. The longer they stared at the scene, the more they realized they had only one hope.

Their destiny was in their own hands, not in those of some larger force outside of their understanding.

29

ABIGAIL OLIVAW
EPSILON ERIDANI, LIPROSUS ORBIT

It had been nearly a week since they'd tortured Abigail to the brink of death, since they'd forced her to betray her family — an action that crushed her soul and may have altered the future of humanity forever.

As she lingered far above the throbbing lights in the Beacon of Therion, her thoughts wandered to the vision she'd experienced during her suffering. It had flashed through her mind as she peered through death's door. The screams of pain and anguish from all those human and Ursis souls. The explosions not only from the Selene ships but from the portals leading to her people.

So many lives lost. And for what?

The mere hope that destroying the moons would lessen the strength of the Galactic Alliance. The fact of the matter was that even if they wiped out every single one of those alien ships, the GA would keep coming for them.

They wanted humanity dead, and they thought they'd finished the job over four thousand cycles ago. That was until she and her family's little superluminal explosion put Sol on their radar. The rest... well, that was ancient history.

She'd heard it dozens of times during her meandering around the Beacon. In fact, she'd heard it a moment earlier while she was staring out over a landscape of rubrum and purpureus lights engulfing a patch of sparkling atrum. The red, purple, and black lights had been forming up in this part of the Beacon for the better part of a day. She knew these lights were representatives of the Galactic Alliance, but the black atrum were far more than just the inner sanctum species.

They were the species responsible for putting a hit out on her family. First her aunt's husband and children, then her father. They even tried to take out her brothers, but failed both times. While stealing a Beacon had made the GA run for the hills with their tail between their legs, it was only due to sheer surprise, not lack of firepower.

Seeing all those ships at the Nursery reminded her how insignificant humanity was. They were but a blip on the radar compared to the power of the vast alien Alliance.

Her only hope at this point was that by having peered into her future, she'd forever altered that thread of time. Like what happened with the Ursis in Lupus, maybe if she kept meddling here in the Beacon, she could pull the right strings and change the course of history.

She had to think that way because anything else meant she'd truly sold her family out. And while she'd given up hope she could save everyone, fighting for her kin was her top priority. She owed them that much.

Her parents didn't raise a quitter.

Not now.

Not ever.

As she eased closer to the twinkling black stars framed in the misty white backdrop of the Beacon, the voices rose around her. While she had to keep her mind focused to not give away her presence, the act was easier now that she'd practiced it so long.

"We should just jettison in some of that Croceus like we did with the Ursis," the nearest glimmering atrum said. "That did the job."

"Croceus," she muttered to herself. "What's that?"

And without skipping a beat, a second atrum seemed to

reply to her. "You know, the golden fluid we buried in the caves beneath the homes of those primitive bears. What, were you born yesterday?"

"Who are you talking to?" The nearest atrum throbbed, showing a hint of red rubrum under its dark sheen.

There was no doubt they were Qudoculi, but what gave Abigail pause was why the second light had answered her question. She hadn't spoken the phrase to anyone but herself, and when she was in here, Harold couldn't hear her. But more importantly, they'd given her an answer.

The Croceus was a golden fluid planted on Arctordiea, the Ursis home world. That must be the stuff the Therionic Entity used to house its consciousness in the ceremonial chamber. Its presence there would explain why the Ulixi among them had been muted. Every time they touched it, the alien substance neutralized their powers.

If the GA were the ones that placed it on the planet, that meant they had something to do with the alien entity being imprisoned in the Dark Nebula. That would also explain the Qudoculi body vessel technology the see-er had used. But given that the Croceus had been on the planet for hundreds of years before they sealed the black curtain, its initial purpose was unknown.

"I was just..." The second atrum spun in place, glancing around as if looking for the source of the voice. "I heard someone ask what a Croceus was." The atrum shuddered, sending sparks of purple in all directions. "Never mind."

She nodded. This second atrum was Thyreusian. She figured they were purpureus with how close they were to the gathered lights, but the color of one's aura is not the only indication of their species.

That made two of the inner sanctum species in one place. What was odd was the lack of other colors near this patch of black beyond the red and purple of the Qudoculi and Thyreus. She'd heard there were seven species in the sanctum, but this was a far cry from that.

There was only one way to find out why. She eased up

beside the first atrum light and pretended to lean toward where its ear might have been, if it even had an ear in this otherworldly place. "Where are the other atrum species?" she whispered. "Why have they not yet arrived?"

The light of the Thyreusian atrum seemed to compress, and it recoiled from the sound of her voice. Then, it did something strange. It didn't search for her; it simply answered her question in just as faint of a whisper.

"They'll be here. The remaining species are near," the voice purred.

Their voice was so quiet she had a hard time hearing them, so it was no wonder the other gathered atrum couldn't hear them. While they still didn't know why the Qudoculi responded to their query, they had a suspicion. They had a lot to learn, and not much time to do it. If they could get these lights to fill in the blanks, it would certainly make things easier.

She darted sideways, putting some distance between her and the first two lights. She wanted to run a test. Once she'd gone a few dozen meters, she floated up to another black atrum, this one a deeper, darker shade of black than the others.

With her mouth next to the light, she whispered her question. "Why are you here?"

Like with the last atrum, the light contracted and then muttered a silent reply. "We are here to honor your callings from beyond, great ones. The time has come to converge, to protect you and the Rift from humanity and their allies. We have done as you've asked." They paused, their shape fluttering. "The others are nearing."

Abigail floated backward, doing her best to maintain her focus on suppressing her aura. The atrum had converged because the Entity told them to. Or at least, someone as powerful as the Entity had. While they couldn't be certain, the message sounded eerily similar to what the alien had been spouting the other day.

With her mind spinning through the questions she could

ask, she didn't notice the approaching colors from above and below until they were literally on top of her.

She drew in her breath as a patch of the aurantiaco's orange light passed overhead, and for a second, all she saw were trees. Thousands of massive tree trunks, thicker than a sports stadium on Earth, and yet as tall as a beanstalk. They were spectacular to behold, and within their enormous branches were hummingbirds darting to and fro, weaving their way through the jungle of trees. There was no doubt the bright orange lights were Trochilidae.

As the image faded, her aura brightened, and the lights surrounding her eased apart, clearing a patch of space around her and the orange light.

Without warning, a nearby purpureus and rubrum at the edge of the pocket lashed out and struck the aurantiaco. She wasn't sure if they were aiming for her and missed, or if they thought the Trochilidae had shifted to blue. Either way, by the time she'd centered herself and extinguished her aura, the orange light had faded to near nothingness.

"Was it… a human?" a purpureus asked.

"It looked like one," a rubrum said.

"It arrived with me," an aurantiaco ember said. "It… seemed as normal as I."

"Who's saying you're not human, then?" a gray light asked.

Abigail had never seen a gray aura before. She'd heard rumblings of a species whose silvery color was known as the ravus, but she'd never encountered one until today.

As she eased up and away from the center of the attack and the still fading aurantiaco consciousness, she slid into a mass of light gray lights. The sparks were unlike any other auras she'd seen before in this place. They were a quarter the size of the others, and as silvery bright gray as the sun lingering behind the haze of the morning mist.

The effect of their presence was both comforting and eerily familiar, like she'd felt it countless times.

"We're less human than you!" a distant rubrum shouted.

"We've had enough human mischief today for a thousand years," another nearby ravus muttered.

When Abigail eased up to them, their light warmed her heart, sending a flutter through her entire body. Something was pleasant about these gray lights, but she couldn't put her finger on it.

Not until one of them passed through her body, and suddenly visions popped into her mind:

Caves of stone.
Pillars of light.
Humanoid bodies strewn about.
Blood as dark as the night.
An abrupt change.
Muscular figures caught in a sunward tide.
Striking at an unseen foe.
Climbing toward a shrinking formation of lights.

At first, the pattern resembled a constellation, but it only took a few more seconds of staring to realize she was looking at it wrong. There, lingering in front of her, was the telltale signature of a drive plume from a ship. A human military dropship.

She caught her breath and jumped backward into the mass of tightly packed ravus lights. Each spark she passed through shot similar sensations through her mind:

Pain
Agony
Disgust
Bloodlust
Hatred

In the end, one image was the brightest of all. It was that of a female human figure running toward the open cargo bay of the dropship. And judging by the baby bump and her height relative to those around her, it was Pluto.

These aliens hadn't just seen humans. They'd seen her family. Suddenly, it hit her who these gray beings were.

"The Nanil," she muttered.

"Indeed," one of the ravus voices whispered. "And as the Prima has proclaimed, we too shall rise to protect you, oh enlightened one. Just as we have guarded our Beacon all these years, our sanctum will guard the Rift and prepare for your arrival."

Abigail swallowed hard. She couldn't imagine her family returning to that hellacious place. The Nebula had nearly taken their lives countless times, but if they were in Lupus, they'd gone there for one reason: to convince the Nanil to join their mission. It was the only logical conclusion, and from the looks of it, they'd only made it out alive by the skin of their teeth.

"The humans came to Devid?" the nearest sparkling rubrum asked.

The ravus didn't reply. They simply parted way and allowed a half-dozen atrum through. Apparently, these were their representatives for the inner sanctum.

Once they reached the front of the pack, the black lights flickered, revealing their silvery gray identity. "The humans narrowly escaped our grasp," they said. "We believed they were your kind." The collection of light seemed to reach out, pointing at the scintillating red light of the rubrum, the Qudoculi.

"How dare you accuse—" the rubrum began.

The wall of atrum near the ravus flashed in unison, interrupting the Qudoculi. One voice spoke out, "Their disguises dropped when they fired their plasma rounds from close range. We almost had them in the end, too."

"If those damn automata hadn't taken most of our weapons, we would have," a nearby atrum said.

Another light from a nearby atrum ravus fluttered. "If the weakened mind of that Prima clonos hadn't caused our guards to lose their lances, they wouldn't have escaped."

"Enough!" a rubrum shouted. "I suggest you keep your

tongues about yourselves. We don't have time for this. Not with the enlightened one drawing near." Their red aura seemed to point up, and the assembled lights flickered.

When Abigail glanced upward, her heart fluttered in her chest. It was the Entity. They were approaching from overhead. From the outer layers of the Beacon.

If she had any chance of learning what was going on here, she needed to get out of the middle of these minds. Each time a light brushed against her, they gave her visions, and she lost touch with her surroundings. It was no surprise the Entity always stayed so far above. Things were much simpler up there.

Every meter she floated, she passed through two other Nanils. The tiny lights were impossible to dodge, and their murderous visions were filled with rage. They flooded her mind with an unrelenting desire to kill, to maim someone or something. How the species had managed not to slaughter each other by now was a miracle.

She couldn't tell whether they were in their enraged form when they were connected to the Beacon. Either way, she had newfound respect for Ibu and their ability to hold themselves together.

Passing from one patch of ravus to another, one thing became clear: she'd never make it out of there without giving herself away. She was too deep in their cluster of lights and needed to do something drastic to get out.

With another wave of lights came another flash of images:

Ibu's face in a cave.

A laughing voice calling them a half-breed.

Sadness in their eyes.

Realization dawning.

Abigail sensed her protective aura fading. There was only one thing she could do from here. She did her best to withdraw herself from the ether and reach out. As she did, she thought she felt her hand resting on her leg. She started tapping out a message, the first message Harold had taught her all those years ago when she first embedded his consciousness inside her heart cavity.

Three short taps of her fingers, followed by three long taps, and then three more short taps.

Nothing happened. So, she did it again.

Three short taps.

Three long taps.

Three short taps.

Just as she was about to give in to being discovered, her body ignited in a hailstorm of pain. Every muscle clenched and unclenched uncontrollably. Every cell screamed in torment as Harold lit her up like a Christmas tree.

"Argh!" she shrieked and her eyes sprang open. The overhead lights in the chamber were blinding, and the sound of her wailing voice filled the expansive space.

"What… have you done?" the Entity groaned. "Why have you interrupted our connection?"

She moaned as she attempted to sit up, but her restraints slammed her back down into the chair. "I'm tired of being your bridge to walk on. If you want to return to that place—"

"You'll what?" Hera leapt onto her feet. "What will you do?" She walked up beside her and leaned forward, careful not to touch her. "As far as I'm concerned, you're this alien's bitch. And as long as it keeps feeding me intel on our GA friends, they can do with you as they please."

"Frak off!" Abigail lifted her head and spat out a mouthful of saliva at her aunt, hitting her square in the face.

Hera stared at her in silence before she reached up, brushing away the errant spittle. Her eyes fell on her moistened hand, like she was unsure of what to do next. But instead of wiping it on her outfit, she swung her arm out and, in one sweeping gesture, backhanded Abigail, flinging the offending saliva into the air.

As a bolt of pain burst through her cheek, her face swelled up like a balloon. In the same instant, a line of text appeared on her retinal comm just out of the field of view. It was from Harold.

> Nice shot! I managed to excrete a few nanites in there
> before you launched it. Maybe they can help.

While she doubted they'd survive long enough to make a difference, she'd take a sliver of hope at this point.

Hera turned her back toward Abigail. "I want her sedated!"

"No!" the Entity shouted. "She'll be no use to me drugged."

She spun around. "Well, what do you suggest we do with her, then? We can't find any sign of what's causing that shock."

The tendrils of the Entity rose into her field of view. She couldn't tell if it was watching her through the tentacles, but judging by how they were moving around her, she assumed it could.

"And there are no signs of the micro-automations on her person?" the Entity asked.

Hera turned to look at the clone technicians near the far wall. They stumbled to their feet and leapt to another control panel. A few seconds later, they leaned forward and adjusted something.

For a fleeting moment, Abigail figured Harold's stunt was done for. That they'd seen him.

But they hadn't. They merely shook their head. "There are no nanites in her body, sir."

She closed her eyes and sighed. Although she wanted to tap out a message to Harold, to ask how he'd pulled it off, she thought better of it. They were watching her too closely.

When she opened her eyes, she was face-to-face with the Entity. They'd leaned their smug face in and were lingering above her.

"It must be her Ulixi genes fighting back," the Entity began. "They've always been compelled to fight against us.

To wrestle against the advancement of a common good. I'm sure you know the type." They glanced at Hera.

She nodded.

Although Abigail wanted to ask Hera who she was talking about, she held her tongue. With her face still feeling the wrath of her aunt's frustration, she didn't want to push her any further.

The two of them stared at each other for a few seconds, and just when she thought one of them was going to speak, a familiar voice called out from across the room.

"You asked me to tell you when we're underway, sir." Joyce came to attention. "We've exited the Nebula, and the fleet is moving on to the next stage of the plan."

Abigail exhaled. If Joyce was here, that meant the Ulixi and her renegade collection of colonists had fallen to Hera.

And just like that, any hope of escape evaporated into a mist of nothingness.

"I'm sorry, dear." Hera walked up to Abigail's side. "Did we not tell you we were leaving?"

Abigail bit her lip and stared at her aunt in silence. At least until her curiosity got the better of her. "Where are we going?"

Hera cackled with laughter and slapped her hand on the crash couch. "Why, to the Nursery, of course. My little marionette here tells me your people are long gone, which means they're no longer a concern to me. Isn't that right, Joyce?" She glanced back over her shoulder at the woman.

Joyce slowly nodded, her face as blank as a department store mannequin. "Yessir. Her people kept me and mine in the dark. They always did. It was what always made us so frustrated with you Olivaws."

Her words hung in the air, and for a split second, Abigail thought Hera was going to strike the woman. But she didn't. She simply turned to face Abigail.

"You see…" Hera's lip curled into a mischievous smile. "She can't help but tell the truth under my control. It's what makes this so fun." She waved her hand back toward Joyce.

"Back to the labs with you. I want the rest of the intel out of that vile brain of yours before the day's through. Is that understood?"

The Entity eased up beside her. "Can't you just use the body vessel technology I shared with you to extract this one's memories?"

Hera shook her head. "No."

They pulled their tendrils back and turned to watch Joyce leave. "But it's worked for thousands of years. Why would it suddenly—"

"I said no!" Hera smacked her palm on the crash couch again. "You mind your business, and I'll mind mine."

Abigail chuckled and eyed both of them.

Hera narrowed her gaze. "Do you have something to add, my dear?"

She smiled. "If you only knew the things your friend here was doing in—"

Her entire body convulsed as a shockwave pulsed through her, sending cries of agony echoing off the walls. At the same time, the Entity shuddered and collapsed onto her chest.

As Hera jumped away, distancing herself from the ensuing carnage of energy, the alien slid up beside her and whispered in her ear. "If you know what's good for you, you'll watch your tongue, my little poppet."

Abigail didn't dare say another word. Hera was using the Entity, and the Entity was using Hera. Unfortunately, humanity and her family were caught in the middle. She'd be of no use to any of them if she were dead.

Now that she knew more about the inner workings of the Galactic Alliance, she had to find a way to warn them. To warn all of them.

There was also the matter of her newfound trick. The idea that she could get anyone in the Beacon to answer her every question was empowering, to say the least. If she could convince them to spill their darkest secrets in that place, there was no telling what she could make them do.

30

LYNC MICHAELS
LUPUS DARK NEBULA, INSIDE BOK GLOBULE

"T minus thirty seconds," the robotic voice said in her ear.

Lync subvocalized the command to make sure her retinal comm was still recording. Talking subvocally felt weird in the pilot goo. Although she knew the robots had the bases covered, there was no way in hell she was going to miss recording this.

Crayo was off training with the other Ulixi and robot pilots, and Bradley had asked her to keep an eye on these tests. They were critical to the viability of their master plan. So critical, in fact, she wasn't sure why Bradley wasn't out here overseeing them himself. Then again, he had a lot going on with everyone off saving Ibu.

Her attention came back to the countdown as it hit ten seconds. Before she ever put her ass in one of those ships wrapped in tachyon threads, she was planning on watching these videos frame by frame. The last thing anyone wanted was to leave pieces of their body behind during a transition.

She didn't understand why the moving gate vane on her teardrop ship or even the sliding ring on the Nyílak fighters gave her so much comfort. Certainly, fewer moving parts meant it would be easier to build a ship that wouldn't break, but it still felt strange.

They already had two pilots who needed to perform emergency spacewalks during their training before they left Epsilon Eridani. They had to kick their gate rings to unstick them. The original Nyílak ships weren't designed for gate drives; they were meant to fly in formation through the massive battlefield gates.

The second-generation fighters were designed to have backup gate drives, however. They couldn't risk losing a pilot, not in this next battle at least. If that necessitated risking more gate drives on the battlefield, then so be it.

Lync shook her head as the countdown hit three. She tapped her controls and prepared to gate to the designated coordinates. She and another dozen ships were planning on jumping to the other side to see if the test ship came out in one piece.

Just as the automated gate probe flashed out of existence, the vibrating alarms on her computer went off. She reached forward and muted them. She hated the effect of vibrating goo on her skin. It reminded her of a bug crawling over her body.

When she brought up the source of the alert on her comm, she paused. The robots were reporting that the ship hadn't, in fact, gated to the target coordinates, and they weren't exactly sure where it had gone.

Lync tapped her ear and opened a comm to Shauna. Her mother had refused to stay behind with Bradley. This copy of her mom had traveled halfway across the galaxy with her daughter, and she wasn't about to hide out inside the cruise ship they were camping in.

"Shauna, bring up the video from the probe and fast-forward to just before the transition. I want to get a look at where they jumped to."

The image appeared on her retinal comm. While it wasn't a star she recognized, at least it was still enshrouded in a Nebula. That meant they hadn't gone too far.

"Shit. I know where that is," Shauna said.

"That doesn't sound good." Lync tweaked her controls as

her mother transmitted the gate coordinates to her and the other nearby robot-controlled ships. She did a double-take when she saw where they were jumping to. "Frak. They gated into the Henosi system?"

"Buckle up, kiddo." Shauna started the transition as the other Nyílak and teardrop ships disappeared in the blink of an eye. It almost wasn't fair that their metallic friends didn't feel the pain of the gate transition.

As the dance of blue fireflies flowed through her body and she passed into the neighboring Henosi star system, she suddenly felt off when she reached the other side. She didn't know why, but there was something familiar here, something she hadn't felt when they passed through the first.

Ever since she'd spent so many days connected to the Beacon, her senses were out of whack. Her emotional peaks and valleys were intensified, which in turn heightened her awareness of others. Within the Dark Nebula, her sixth sense surged. It was as if the nebulosity amplified the resonance of the souls trapped inside.

She adjusted her harness and pulled her control panel closer to her face. "Bring up Henosi and the other human-occupied planet."

The image of the planets appeared side by side on her controls. They were uncomfortably close to the Goldilocks planets, especially considering what had happened the first time her family had visited this system.

"Shouldn't we be focusing on the probe?" Shauna asked.

She waved her hand dismissively. "I'm sure the robots have it taken care of. Besides, the Shu are all..." She reached out and enlarged the picture of Henosi. "Were there craters on their planet when you were down there?"

Shauna didn't reply for a few seconds. She was about to ask her again when the results from an active scan came up on her screen. What was strange was that she hadn't ordered a full scan of the system for fear of being detected.

"Shauna, did you—"

"They're dead," Shauna interrupted. "The planet... and everyone on the ground. They've... been... destroyed."

"What?" Lync tapped the screen repeatedly, scanning through dozens of data sets and bringing up multiple high-resolution images and detailed scans of the planet's surface.

Her mother was right. Not only had the Shu moons been shut down, the entire surface of the planet had been scorched. It was as if someone had wiped it clean and wanted to start over again.

She brought her hand to her mouth. "I don't... understand. You described this place as an Eden the last time you were here. And didn't you say there were tens of thousands of lives down there?"

"There were. And on their second planet as well." Shauna's face appeared in the corner of her retinal comm. "Something must have set them off. Maybe the Shu did this?"

Lync flipped through the data of the second planet and froze on one of the images. She ran her hand over the surface of one of the Shu. "Is this one powered up, or am I looking at a reflection?"

Shauna brought up the detailed scans of that moon, and just as she started reviewing the results, a light flashed on the exterior hull of the object.

"I'd say that one looks awake." Lync tightened the harness on her chair and dialed in a course to jump nearby.

"What the hell are you doing?" Shauna screamed in her ear.

She reached forward and activated the manual override, locking her mother out of the navigation controls. Once she confirmed it was in place, she tapped the screen and started the rapid gate sequence.

As the gate ring and the associated blue glow passed over her ship, Shauna powered up the laser array. She knew as well as Lync that if they were heading into battle, they needed weapons.

"I'm not keen on getting into a fight with one of those things." Shauna's face in her retinal comm looked genuinely concerned. She couldn't blame her, being as she was mortal now.

"Don't worry, I'm just dropping in for a closer—"

The activated Shu lit up and fired a concentrated beam of light directly at them, but Shauna was too fast. She must have detected it because she engaged their starboard thrusters and banked their ship to the left.

Lync punched the drive, and their Nyílak shot forward, heading toward the still-glowing moon. Whoever was driving that thing had left their exterior lighting powered up, and she could see into the internals of one of the shuttle bays. Fortunately for them, that gave her an easy target.

She centered the laser array on the open doors and pulled the trigger, sending round after round toward the heart of the Shu.

Their bolts of light seemed to move in slow motion as the deadly rays of focused energy sliced through the vacuum of space and ripped the insides of the Shu to shreds. One after another, the lasers tore holes through the bowels of the ship, and based on the resulting explosions on the far side, they shot straight through.

Lync kept firing the laser array, and several more bolts of light ripped through the hull of the moon ship like a hot knife through butter. "Is it me, or does that thing not have any shielding?"

Shauna shook her head and brought up a more layered scan of the moon. Evidently, with the shuttle hold being open, they were able to scan it more intimately.

"It looks like whoever powered that thing up failed to turn on the defenses. That, and the insides are a lot easier to cut through than the outside." Shauna highlighted the exterior gashes Lync had ripped through the moon. From the looks of it, they'd already done quite a bit of damage to the sphere of death.

She went to pull the trigger again, and second-guessed herself. "Is it... still active?"

A few seconds passed in silence until Shauna replied. "I'm

picking up several weak life signs inside, but I don't think it's operational."

When Lync eased the throttle forward, one of the robots from her squad hailed her. "Captain Michael, please refrain from engaging the enemy ship. Our test was a success. We should return to the Cornucopia for another trial."

"Negatory." Lync plotted a course into the still-open shuttle bay. "We're going in."

"Wait a second." Shauna enlarged her image on the retinal comm. "We are?"

Lync nodded. "We could really use these moons in our attack at the Nursery. Remember that footage you showed me of Pluto and Ibu battling these things? This Shu is a whole hell of a lot more nimble than those Selene ships. If we can figure out how to activate them, we could use them to our advantage." She smirked. The idea of taking a mini moon into a battle was fraking cool. The GA wouldn't know what hit them.

"Think about it." Lync grabbed the controls and pulled back, slowing their advance as they eased up to the opening of the shuttle bay. "Worst case, they would make great decoys. Am I right or am I right?"

Her mother hadn't said a word since she'd freaked out about going inside. When Lync looked at her retinal comm, she was crying. Not a common sight for an artificial intelligence.

"Are you alright?" Lync asked.

Shauna shook her head. "I don't want to die like this. Not here."

"I won't let that happen." Lync activated the ship's full scan as she studied the shuttle bay. It looked like the insides were intact, despite the flashing lights and a dozen massive holes in the far wall. For the most part, the internal systems had put out the fires. Or if they hadn't, they were venting the smoke elsewhere inside the ship.

Her controls chimed, and the full detailed scans came up. While Shauna had gotten a decent reading from a distance, up close, she could see everything. Every level, every eleva-tor, and every utility shaft. Deep in the protected core of the ship was what she assumed was the master control room. And based on the size of the hole she'd blasted in it, two of her lasers had sheared plumb through one side of it.

"It looks like there's still an environment in there," Shauna said.

She smiled at her mother. "Does that mean you're up for a field trip?"

Shauna chuckled. "As if I have a choice."

Lync smirked and scanned the shuttle bay for an open slot. There was one to her left, so she nudged the Nyílak to port before easing it forward. "Once we're inside, take off."

"To hell I will," Shauna said. "If you're going in, I'm going with you."

She knew better than to argue with her mother. And apparently, the robots weren't being left out of the action either. As she eased their ship down in the empty shuttle berth, two other teardrop ships slipped into the berths next to her.

"I guess it's a party." Lync rotated the sphere to make sure the hatch was facing upward and then popped the top.

Her harness automatically released, and she pushed off and floated through the goopy fluid. Once she reached the hatch, she pressed her hand on the edge of the invisible open-ing, and a panel slid out and on top of the ship.

A second later, she popped out, followed by a slimy white robot. She hadn't even noticed that Shauna had packed one of Harold's spare battle chassis. Her mother was like a modern-day Explorer Scout. She was always prepared.

She swung her legs sideways and carefully slid off the edge of the Nyílak's wing, dropping to the ground and then down onto one knee. As she scanned the hold, she reached to her hip and came up empty.

"Frak," she muttered. It seemed she wasn't nearly as prepared as her mother.

Shauna hopped down beside her and reached out, offering her a blaster. "Missing something?"

Lync lowered her head and chuckled, taking the weapon. "Thanks."

"Next time," Shauna turned and locked her robotic eyes on her, "try coming a little more prepared. Ok?" She looked back toward the shuttle bay. "I'm not keen on dying, and mommy doesn't have nine lives any longer."

Lync checked the blaster and made sure to mate it to her nanite signature. The last thing she needed was for another human to use it against her.

With her weapon ready, she was about to start forward when one of their robot friends hopped up on the wing of the Nyílak and slid inside.

She gestured toward the pilot compartment of her fighter. "What's the shiny metal man doing?"

"Flying this thing out of here like you ordered. There's no point in handing these people our gating technology if we don't have to." Shauna pointed at the neighboring teardrop shuttles that had landed alongside them. They were already sliding backward, leaving in their stead a dozen robots. Judging by the armaments they were carrying, they were as heavily armed as Shauna. Either that, or the shuttles were munition depots in disguise.

"Am I the only one who didn't anticipate this outcome?" She glanced at her mother and the massive rifle she was holding. It looked like it could take out ten tanks.

"I try not to blame you. Nowadays, you're sorta a flight jockey." Shauna started forward. "You don't always think about killer Nanil, deadly aliens, or human ancestors who would rather see you dead than alive."

The image of Joyce and the Thyreusian she'd ripped apart flashed through her mind as she sprinted after Shauna. If she got her hands on one of the GA, she wasn't sure how she'd handle the situation herself. Another human, though, that was a different story.

Once they'd made it to the back wall, they sprinted to the right. There was an exit on the other side of the shuttle bay.

During their shuffle across the wide hangar, they passed by two of the giant holes she'd blasted through the inside wall. The heat from the melted metal radiating off the surface warmed her skin through her suit, and the edges of the opening glowed red beneath some type of foamy fire retardant. A sea of tiny robots was scampering through the hole as well. Though she couldn't tell what they were doing, she assumed they were fighting to repair the damage she'd done.

As they approached the far exit, Lync slid to a halt when her scan of the room lingered on something to the right. "What the frak?"

She stepped sideways, raising her blaster and easing forward, toward what looked like one of their teardrop ships. Several puffs of smoke were billowing out of the rear of the shuttle near the drive cones, but the toxic fumes were being sucked up into the overhead ventilation. Stranger still, underneath the twisted remnants of the ship was a massive puddle of melted metal and plastic on the ground.

When she glanced back toward Shauna, she saw that her mother was right behind her. "Is this one of ours?"

"Negative." Shauna stepped around her and up along the side of the shuttle, being careful not to step into the expanding pool of glowing hot metal. Once she reached the starboard hatch, she popped her head inside. "Looks like someone tried to access the drive. It's slag now."

Lync eased up behind her mother, but Shauna reached out and stopped her advance.

She squinted and leaned forward. "What is it?"

Shauna held her hand firm to her chest, trying to hold her back. "You probably shouldn't look in there."

Lync didn't listen. Instead, she continued on, stepping past her mother and peering inside. She regretted it as soon as she had, and spun around, squeezing her eyes shut and doing her best to hold down her lunch.

The image of the four dead bodies would be forever

seared in her mind. The sight was gruesome. Someone, or something, had shot them in the back of the head at point-blank range with a blaster, execution style.

While she wasn't exactly eager to keep going, whoever had done this had arrived here on this ship. And that meant only one thing.

"Those aren't clones; they're humans." She looked over at her mother. "They have the uniforms and insignias from Ryder's ships."

Shauna tilted her head. "Maybe they were stowaways?"

Lync took a deep breath from the fresh air inside her helmet and spun around, hopping up and into the ship. She carefully stepped over the bodies and did everything she could not to look directly at what remained of their heads. Instead, she was after their ID badges.

It only took a few seconds to find them, but when she rolled one of the corpses over, their metallic insignia shimmered in the overhead light. Without a thought, she reached down and ripped it off. With her prize in hand, she hopped back out and down, exhaling a deep breath as she did. The whole scene made no sense.

When she held out the badge toward Shauna, the results of the scan appeared on her retinal comm:

```
Name: Sara Gudar
Rank: Private First Class
Assignment: Shuttle Mechanic on the
Flyboy.
Note: Reported missing for duty after
passing into the Lupus Dark Nebula.
Last seen with PFC Jones, PSC Hyra,
PSC Hitz, and Private Franks. If
found, bring directly to Sergeant
Gregg for disciplinary action.
```

Shauna shook her head. "I don't think these are the bad guys."

Lync swallowed hard. "And something tells me those names are the other bodies."

"There's only three bodies in here," Shauna said. "We'll have to keep an eye out for whoever's still missing. Maybe they're the attacker."

She nodded and stared down at the puddle of melted metal creeping toward her. The haunting reminder of those mutilated soldiers was clawing at the edges of her consciousness, refusing to fade away.

As she considered their next steps, several of the robots sprinted forward to cover the hall they were about to enter. Shauna wasn't taking any chances this time around, and she didn't blame her.

Just as they were about to go, the Shu ship shook violently, and sparks cascaded down from the ceiling. She reached out to steady herself on her mother's shoulder. "Is this thing going to hold together?"

Shauna nodded. "That was just the secondary core. From what the robots are chattering about, they ejected it into orbit. It was reaching critical levels."

Lync glanced over at one of the robots. It had transformed its hand into some type of mating apparatus and was presently plugged into the Shu computer system. "That thing isn't going to turn on us, is it?"

"Nope. I've made certain of it." Shauna pointed toward the exit. "After you?"

She reached out and stopped her mother. "What does that mean, you made certain of it?"

"It means I've nudged their crude positronic minds to be fond of you. And I have to say, it took an awful lot of nudging. Apparently, you pissed them off somehow." Shauna turned and smirked at her.

Lync shook her head. "Gee, thanks. I'll try not to anger the robotic help anymore."

"Their brains have a sort of governor built in," Shauna began. "It was like their makers didn't want them to think too fast. That doesn't matter, though. They won't be turning against either of us. If anything, they'll fight to the death to defend us, and then some."

That thought was comforting, especially considering what she'd seen inside that shuttle. As she started toward the exit, she turned left and saw that the robots were already clearing the path to the control room they'd found on their deep scan.

She eased her way down the central corridor of the Shu, working with Shauna to cover each other. While most of them had disappeared down random halls, she didn't trust there weren't still things that could harm them in here.

"There's a surprising lack of resistance, and it's unsettling." Shauna leaned forward and peered down each of the tunnels dividing their path. Once she confirmed it was clear, she gestured for Lync to advance.

She hopped across the opening without even checking her flank, knowing her buddy had her covered. The control room was just up ahead, and the smoking remnants of her shots were still glowing in the distance.

When she brought up the refined schematic of the Shu on her retinal comm, she noticed that the robots had been busy. Not only had they covered most of this floor, they were already expanding out, covering the spaces above and below the control room. They weren't wasting time wondering what they might encounter like she was.

As she studied the details of what her automated friends found, she paused. "I thought these things were just defensive ships. Why then the need for crew quarters?" She shared the highlighted areas with Shauna.

Her mother shrugged. "Probably a remnant of bygone eras of preparedness. Humans have a tendency to go off the rails, and a certain amount of redundancy is a good thing. Besides, most of the ship is armament, computational cores, and automated manufacturing factories. I'd hardly call this place a luxury cruiser. And from the looks of it, whatever the human disciples needed planetside, they made up here and sent down to the ground. Clone bodies and all."

Shauna shared a few images from above and below decks.

They showed cloning vats in the middle of preparing new bodies.

"That's not good." Lync flipped through the rest of the imagery. Whoever had done this hadn't gotten far. "We should send some robots over to the other Shu. If they can get onboard, they should be able to stop these things from coming to life. Assuming they're on our side in this matter, of course."

She glanced over at her mother. Her robotic shell was deep in thought, likely issuing commands to the other robots. Part of her wanted to crack open the messages to see what she was sending, but she knew that wasn't necessary. While her mother might look like a bot on the outside, she was human through and through at heart.

"I'm on it." Shauna unfroze and turned to face her. "The robots outside are gating back and getting some of their friends to take over the other ships. I've already directed them to replicate my tweaks to their programming when the metallic cavalry arrives. They'll retain their strong affinity toward real squishy humans I mentioned earlier, and not the grown in a vat kind. That should allow them to halt the cloning process without frying their circuits."

"Let's hope so," she muttered. The last thing she wanted to deal with was a bunch of pissed off humans who'd been stuck in virtual worlds for thousands of years. She'd heard the stories from Bradley's away team on Henosi. They weren't exactly hugging cousins, happy to see their long-lost relatives.

"Shall we see what's behind door number one?" Shauna gestured toward the hatch in front of them — the one that led into the control room.

Funny enough, when she looked over at it, the hatch bore a large number one.

Lync shook her head and chuckled. "Sure, why not?"

As she was about to step forward, four robots silently strode up from behind them and fell into position, two on each side of the sliding hatch. They raised their weapons and trained them inside the room, awaiting orders from Lync.

She could only hope that whoever was in there wasn't stupid enough to pick a fight.

Shauna gestured with her hand toward the robots, and the door slid open. While Lync had expected a firefight to ensue, what she hadn't expected was to hear a moaning voice. And, strangely, it was a familiar one.

"Who is that?" Dwight called out. "Who's over there?"

"Hold the robots back," Lync whispered. "I think I know who that is." She eased forward and peered around the open doorway.

There, on the far side of the room, lay a pile of rubble, and a pair of feet stuck out from the debris.

She quickly scanned the control room. Although her blasts had hit several huge computer panels, except for the collapse, the room was largely intact.

"Who's there?" Dwight asked again. "Is that you, Hitz?"

"That's confirmation of another person," Shauna said over her comm. "I'll warn the robots to be on the lookout."

Lync nodded and raised her blaster upward, easing slowly around the corner and over the debris. She glanced left and right, visually sweeping the room. There weren't many places to hide, but she wasn't taking any chances.

"Hitz!" Dwight's feet shook before he broke out into a fit of coughing and moans.

She sidestepped to the left, making sure to keep a safe distance from his body. If she came around by his feet, she figured she could see his hands before he saw her. For all she knew, he had a blaster.

As she passed one of the active controls, she paused. On the screen was a status of the Shu and the other ships nearby. Even though the controls were foreign, they weren't far off from the ones she'd used at the Cornucopia.

She leaned forward to make sure Dwight was still on the ground. He hadn't said anything since his bout of coughing and moaning.

Content that he wasn't going anywhere, she reached out and tweaked the control panel, bringing up the console that showed the most recent commands. It took her a moment to take it all in, but if she was reading this correctly, he was the one who had attacked their shuttle. And not only that, the blasts on the ground were his doing as well.

She tapped her wrist and subvocalized a comm to Shauna. "Do you know if the devastation on the planets was here when Ibu or the other ships came through?"

Shauna didn't speak for a few seconds. "The moonlets were always bunched up like this, but beyond that, all we have are visuals of the dark side of each planet. We never risked performing an active scan for fear of waking the moons."

Lync shook her head. "Do you think he could have done all of this in the past day?"

"It's possible." Shauna stepped up beside her, but kept speaking on their comm. "Give me a minute to check the logs. These aren't available outside the control room." When she reached forward and rested her hand against the side of the panel, a cable slid out and into a socket. She must've done a few mods at the Cornucopia to make talking to these other human form ships easier.

"I'll see what Dwight has to say for himself." Lync started around the panel.

Shauna reached out to stop her. "Wait, is that our Dwight? Like the asshole we flew with to the False Cross?"

"I think so." Lync eased back toward her. "His voice sounds like Dwight to me. Doesn't it?"

Her mother shook her head. "I don't know. His voice patterns match, I guess. I just remember it being a lot more grating." She clenched and unclenched her fist not attached to the controls. "Another day with that asshat and I'd have killed him. And that was before my four-laws were revoked. Now, I can actually do it."

Lync smirked and started working her way around the debris. She wasn't wrong. This guy hadn't been what she'd hoped for in a crew mate. Crayo had warned her not to take him on, but his knowledge of her tattoo and his funny comments in those early days were endearing. After a week in confined quarters, his true colors came out, and like Shauna, she too had wanted to kill him.

"You know." She froze and lowered her blaster toward his feet. "He asked me to come back here a few times? To Lupus. Said he'd heard there was salvageable loot in here. Could make us rich. You think he was trying to come back for this?" She pointed upward.

Shauna turned and looked at her. "I… guess. You never let me have control of the systems on the Veritas. I might have been able to see if he asked the other crew members, as well. Either way, he must've found something on Epsilon Eridani or the Wheel that led him here. Maybe Zachary wasn't thorough keeping the intel from those data cores a secret after all."

Lync nodded. She could be right. They shared a lot of details of their ancestral human weaponry with the military brass. Even Libby was bound to miss things from time to time.

She took a deep breath and continued around the back of the control panel to get a closer look. Once she got about halfway around, she saw him. Sure enough, it was Dwight. His eyes were closed, and he was pinned under one of the overhead girders that had collapsed on him.

When she looked up at the ceiling, she noticed that the edges of the metal were melted and there was a streak of still-cooling material sliding down the girder. Apparently, he'd been using the controls on this side of the room when the collapse happened. He was probably keeping an eye on the door they'd come through. Her blast must've been quite a shock.

Just as she stepped up, his eyes sprang open, and his right hand wriggled. She jumped backward, and he moaned. His right arm was pinned to the ground under the destroyed control panel, but she couldn't see his left at all.

She raised her blaster up toward his face.

"Lync?" His eyes rolled back into his head briefly, and then he shuddered, forcing them open. "What... are you... Why are you here?"

She chuckled and glanced at Shauna. She was still deep in thought with her connection to the Shu's computer.

"I was going to ask you the same thing, Dwight." She looked down at his torso, at the blood pooling on the ground. "Looks like you got yourself in a bit of a pickle."

"Can you... help me up?" He tried to move his legs, but the girder moaned and slid downward. The end of it must have somehow still been hot and was melting into the floor.

"First things first." She took a few more steps around him, toward the top of his head, in an attempt to see his other hand. "What were you doing onboard?"

"It was Hitz." Dwight craned his neck to look at her but failed with a wince of pain. "He... forced our shuttle to dock here. Said he was ordered to check out the planet. Something about... intel and these moon ships."

On face value, the idea made sense, but there was no way a random soldier would've been ordered to undertake a mission like that. Ryder would've sent a more seasoned squad with a lot more firepower than a few private first and second classes could handle. The last thing Ryder was, was a traitor. He would've taken it up with either her or Zachary first. He'd admitted several times to being out of his element inside the Dark Nebula.

"And you're in here alone?" She stared down at his face.

Dwight glanced away briefly, faking a pain in his hand. "Hitz... he's somewhere around here." He groaned and tried to move his shoulder.

The pile of rubble shifted, and the girder angled further down, pushing the panel harder into his shoulder and squeezing him like a vice against the floor. He screamed, and his voice echoed through the control room.

"We should help him," one of the robots said over her comm.

"No," she subvocalized and glanced over at the entrance. "You don't step a foot in here until I tell you to. Is that understood?"

The robot stared at her, expressionless. "Affirmative, sir."

Dwight groaned. He must've known something was up because he kept trying to see whatever she was looking at but failed. "Who's there? Get me out of here, Lync. Please. It hurts so bad."

"You never said why you were in here?" She squatted down closer to him and stared into his eyes. "Or why you fired on me and my ships?"

His eyes widened. "I... didn't fire on you. The Shu. They detected your ship. I... tried to stop it... but..." His words trailed away, and he closed his eyes.

She couldn't tell if this was him trying to act emotional or if he was confused. Throughout their time onboard their ship, he never once opened up or confided in anyone. He was always busy meandering around and either futzing with the comm array or the gate drive.

The gate drive. That was probably why they'd found the puddle in the shuttle bay. He had been messing with it.

"He's lying," Shauna said over her comm.

Lync looked up and locked her eyes on her mother, tilting her head ever so slightly.

"He ordered the command to attack us." Shauna shared a snap of the commands Dwight had issued from the console on her retinal comm, as well as pictures of him doing it. "He also deactivated the Shu's primary defenses. That's why it didn't put up much of a fight. If the defenses were on, it would've killed him, and we would've had a harder time staying alive. With it off, however, he's in charge of everything. From what I uncovered, he's also the one that killed the planet. But that wasn't recent. It appears he triggered it as a result of Ibu and Pluto defeating the Shu. He realized you were formidable, and obviously you had a way out of the Dark Nebula if you got inside in the first place."

"What are you looking at?" Dwight was staring at her again.

She squinted and rubbed her eyes with her hand. "Wait," she subvocalized. "I'm confused. How could he possibly have been the one to do this? He wasn't even here with Bradley and Zachary. I ran into him on Zeta Lupi at the Tiān space elevator, for crying out loud. He was looking for work."

"I can't explain it…" Shauna paused and seemed to freeze up, like she was deep in thought again. Just as Lync was about to ask what was wrong, she stepped forward and squatted down next to Dwight's feet. A second later, he grimaced and kicked his foot.

"What the hell was that?" He tried to look down, but it was hopeless. His body wasn't going anywhere.

When Lync leaned sideways to see what Shauna was doing, she shot upright. "It's him!" she said over her comm. "I… don't know how I didn't see it. His DNA… it's an exact match."

Lync eased away from Dwight and brought her blaster back up toward him.

"It's who?" she subvocalized.

"Can you please tell me what's going on?" Dwight peered up at her. "Who are you muttering to? And why aren't you helping me?"

"It's Dwight." Shauna shared an image on her retinal comm.

At first, she wasn't sure what she was looking at, not until she leaned sideways and compared the image with the man on the floor. They looked remarkably like the same person, yet they didn't. His hair was an entirely different color and style; he'd gotten several well-placed facial tattoos that reshaped his face, and he must've done something to his body because he'd lost a bunch of weight since the picture. While she'd heard of people who preferred their body's natural shape rather than using nanites to keep them in perfect condition, she'd never met anyone who didn't use them. In space, extra mass was your enemy, but in this photo from Shauna, the man was downright obese.

"It could be him, I guess." Lync straightened up and stared at her. "Who is in this picture?"

Shauna raised her rifle up and across her chest. "His name is Dwight. Yeah, I know. Apparently, he was lazy about changing his name. Sorta right in front of your face if you ask me. But I guess—"

"Shauna!" Lync sighed. "Who—is—this?"

"Sorry, yeah." Shauna shared several other images and videos with her. "His name is Doctor Dwight Santos, and he was a biochemist. He and Bradley were old buddies from back in Sol, and they were inseparable for decades. They did everything together, including joining the colony ship to Zeta Lupi and heading with Bradley and the others on their mission to the Lupus Dark Nebula the first time. He died in the ceremonial chamber on Henosi when the humans down there tried to kill them. They knocked them out with some type of gas, and he never came to. The last thing I remember was transferring his body bag out of the Fountainhead and giving it to the robots in the Zeta Lupi Wheel. They were supposed to take care of it from there."

"Well…" Lync looked down at Dwight, who was staring up at her with a dazed and confused expression on his face. "If this is really him, he's been a busy boy hiding out in our ship and stealing a shuttle to get in here." She glanced around the room at the smoldering mess. "I didn't even bother to dig into his past when I met him. Once I saw he came in on the latest recruiting ship from Sol, I stopped. There were so many people running from the devastation caused by the GA, I just gave him the benefit of the doubt."

She stared at him in silence for a minute as her mind turned over all her past indiscretions. The failed test to join the academy, the blood transfusions to become someone else, and the lies. She'd told countless lies to keep her secret.

"People need the chance to start over sometimes. I know I did." She shook her head. "It makes me wonder what they did to him while Bradley's crew was knocked out. They were only out for a few minutes. Right?"

"They were," Shauna began. "According to the records on the Shu, after we destroyed their moonlet, our virtual ancestors freaked out. That's why the Shu went into a defensive posture on the other colony sites. The humans could have ordered an all-out assault on us, but for some reason, they decided not to. There's no record up here of what happened next, but they must've done something to transfer the consciousness of one of their people into him. Sorta like I was transferred into this body." She went to step around the debris shielding her from Dwight, but Lync shook her head to stop her.

Dwight tried and failed to catch a glimpse. "Who is it? Who's there?"

Lync crouched down beside Dwight and raised her gun to his temple. If she was going to break him, she couldn't lead with the fact that she knew who he really was. She needed to start slower and then hit him with that detail.

He drew in his breath and tried to flinch away, but he had nowhere to go. "Wh—at?" he sputtered.

"I'll give you one last chance to tell me why you're in here." She flicked the power lever on the side of the blaster to maximum, and it made a high-pitched whining sound for a few seconds. It was a useless gesture at such a short range, but the effect was unnerving.

And judging by how much his hand and legs were twitching, it worked.

He pursed his lips, staring at her for a minute, then spilled his guts. "I killed them. I shot the others."

She didn't say a word. She simply waved the blaster in a circular gesture before returning it to the side of his head.

"Hitz is here onboard. He really is." Dwight's eyes flickered toward the door. "I don't know where, but he's hiding out."

Lync leaned closer, scrutinizing him with one eye. "And that's it? That's all you're gonna say?"

"What…" He swallowed hard. "What else is there?"

She shoved the blaster hard into his head, and he winced. "How about you start with the cloning vats?"

He tried to pull away, but the gun held him in place.

"Who are you here with?" His eyes darted toward the control panel. "How are you accessing the computers?"

"I'll be asking the questions. Not you." She smiled. "Now… about those vats."

His eyes widened. "You didn't bring any robots in here, did you?"

As if on cue, Shauna stepped around his feet and into view. While Lync would have preferred she stayed hidden, she couldn't exactly control her mother.

"It's you," Dwight muttered.

"It's me." Shauna swung her rifle down toward the ground, hitting the side of Dwight's foot.

Something in the pile of debris cracked, and a moment later, he winced, followed by a long groan.

"Oops, I'm sorry. Did that hurt?" Shauna didn't wait for him to answer. She leaned forward and slammed her foot down on top of his shin.

His entire body rose upward and a blood-curdling scream filled the control room. He squealed for a solid two minutes before Lync finally stepped in.

"Enough with the crying, asshole." She reached out and nudged the side of his head with her blaster. She was done dancing around the real question. "We know who you are. Who you really are. You're Doctor Dwight Santos, Bradley's dead best friend. Now…" She leaned against the blaster. "How about you tell us how you shoved yourself into our friend's cranium, asshole?"

At first, she thought he wouldn't respond, but when he turned his head against the blaster and locked his gaze on her, she saw it in his eyes. He'd transformed into someone else.

"You're fucking pitiful." He lifted his head toward Lync, and her blaster slid off the sweat on the side of his face. But he didn't stop. He opened his mouth and spat a mouthful of blood directly into her face.

She sighed, closing her eyes before reaching up to wipe it away.

He smirked. "All you humans out there, you're a fraking disgrace to the name huma—"

Lync swung her blaster to the side and then whipped it back, cracking him across the head. Not enough to knock him out, but enough to return him to his cacophonous state of wailing for another agonizing minute.

When she stood up, Shauna walked over to her side.

"He did a shitty job covering his tracks," Shauna said aloud. "You can tell he hasn't touched a computer in millennia. Hell, if the logs are any indication, he nearly self-destructed this whole moonlet."

Dwight stopped shrieking and glared at her. "Shut up, you metallic bitch!"

Lync shook her head. "Now, now. That's no way to talk to my mother."

"You Olivaws are disgusting," he snarled. "Living in robotic bodies and giving up your mortal form. It's no surprise you're losing to Hera and her clones. Not only is she ten steps ahead of you, she has the Entity on her side." He smirked. "You might not realize it yet, but you're done for. You won't win against the Therionic Entity."

She bit her lip, and for a second, she wasn't sure if she should respond or let him keep blathering. She didn't have to decide.

"That's where you're wrong," Shauna began. "The Entity isn't on her side."

Dwight narrowed his gaze. "What do you mean?"

Lync sighed. "The Entity is working against her. It's already warned the Galactic Alliance of the impending attack."

He shook his head. "No. It wouldn't."

She knelt down on the ground, making sure to keep her blaster pointed at him. "Trust me. I saw it manipulating the minds of the aliens when I was inside the Beacon. But what I don't get is why you think the Entity wouldn't work against Hera. Who is it you think they are?"

Dwight closed his eyes and exhaled. It was like déjà vu. He used to huff like that all the time back on their ship, any time he was annoyed with someone. Usually, it was because of their lack of knowledge on a topic he thought was trivial.

"Go on." She waved the blaster at him. "I can see you know something. Spill it."

"I can't believe you don't see it." He shook his head. "The Entity is a Builder, you idiot. It's one of the last of its kind on this side of the Rift."

She glanced up at Shauna and then back at him. "This side of the what?"

"The Rift." He turned his head, looking straight up at the ceiling in disgust. "I tell you what." He moved his hand, and it appeared as if he was trying to make a fist, but instead, he winced. "You help me out of this mess, and I'll tell you everything you need to know."

His fingers were turning bluish-white. Whatever was pushing against his chest was cutting off the circulation to his limbs. If he wasn't bleeding out under there, it was only a matter of time before his entire arm would be necrotic.

Shauna shook her head. "We're not negotiating with you. We can figure out what the Rift is on our own." She glanced over at Lync. "Our team has boarded the other Shu and they've deactivated the cloning vats. We don't need—"

"Please!" Dwight's voice cracked. "I beg you. Don't stop the cloning. My people need to get off this wretched planet. We need to get out of this Nebula. I'll tell you. I will. Just don't stop the cloning."

This time, Lync didn't wait for Shauna to interrupt. "Get on with it, then. If you know something you think will save you, I suggest you start talking, asshole."

His eyes darted around the room like he was searching for where to start. "Hera, she's already on her way to the Nursery. She left three days ago."

Her heart skipped a beat, but she did everything in her power not to react. It must have worked because he kept talking.

"If what you say is true, they'll be dead as soon as they arrive." He swallowed hard and licked his lips. His voice was getting hoarser by the second. "But Hera has a backup plan. She doesn't have to win out there to come out ahead. Not with the cloning facility she's building on Liprosus. She'll just come back in another cloned body and rule your people. Her clones are building it in the original Olivaw base at the Archégonos site. Of all the Olivaws, she's the only one I've met that I can stand."

Shauna chuckled. "That's because she's not really herself."

Dwight froze and turned his head to look at her. "What does that mean?"

Lync sighed. "It means there's a parasite attached to her spinal cord, and it's controlling her every action. She's a fraking puppet, like you and Dwight's body. Now keep talking."

He sneered. "That might explain a few of her... quirks the last time we met." He squinted. "I wonder what parasite it is. There are only so many species out there that can do that, you know. I bet it's a—"

"You're as sick as she is," Shauna interrupted.

A smile slowly formed on his face. "Hera does remind me of myself sometimes. But that's only because most of your people are weak. You've lost touch with your humanity, but she... she still has that fire in her gut. That spark that makes her a human with a capital H. She knows that we're the superior species in this galaxy. But you and your kind, you depend too much on your automata and your computers to get by. You've lost your drive to conquer and destroy. Hell, you've lost your literal backbone, it appears. You know what your problem is?" He leered at Lync.

"I'd say I don't care," Lync smiled, "but I'm betting you'll just tell me anyhow."

He chuckled. "Your problem is you think too much. It's no

wonder an alien parasite took control of your kind. Your iron fist has long been melted into slag. In case it isn't already obvious, you should never take shit from the GA, or any other aliens, for that matter. You should kill every fraking one of them you encounter. If you don't, they'll do it to you. Trust me. I know from experience."

Lync stared at him, letting his words sink in. It was hard to believe this man was her distant ancestor. He'd lived longer than her entire civilization in Sol. And yet, here he was, lying on his back, having lost all control over his own creation. Because of his decisions, his kind were forced to live out their existence in a virtual world, a skewed reality that made them increasingly jaded by the day. They did this while forcing their people to the brink of the Stone Age in the real world on Henosi. And they did all of this because of their fear of progress.

Worst of all, during his mutation, he somehow lost compassion for his own kind. For all of humanity.

As she stared at him, she could only think of one reason for why he'd lost his way. The funny thing about it was that it was the very thing that made them who they were. It was what their kind in Sol so often described when asked what it meant to be human. It was their awareness of self, their empathy for each other, their creativity, and most of all, their ability to develop and share diverse belief systems while constantly seeking meaning in their existence.

They wanted to be part of something bigger.

Being human wasn't about conquering stars and destroying life; it was about understanding the universe and learning from it. She didn't know how they were going to tackle Hera or the GA, but she knew one thing: a reality with this guy's definition of humanity wasn't a place she wanted to live in.

Lync quietly pushed up onto one knee and then eased upright. She then stared down into his eyes. It was only then that she realized why he'd always felt so off to her. His eyes were as black as night. At first, she'd thought he just had a dark brown eye color. But it was more than that. There was no hue at all to his iris. It was pure black, like his pupil.

She shivered as she stared at him.

He wasn't human. Not any more, anyway.

He was something worse. Something evil. Something she never wanted her kind to become. And if that meant she had to do things she'd never imagined, well, then she would.

She'd do anything to protect her people. To protect her family.

She raised her blaster up, and without a shadow of a doubt, she squeezed the trigger.

The control room fell silent, and the only thing she could hear was the crackle of his singed flesh cooling.

One of their Lupus robot companions stepped into the room and stopped next to her before staring down at the body. "Was that a human from Henosi?"

She shook her head. "No, he was from Sol."

"But…" The robot went quiet for a moment, its eyes flickering rapidly while deep in thought. When it finished whatever it was calculating, it spoke. "Why was it talking to you as if it were?"

Shauna interjected and waved her hand, getting the attention of the robot. "He was an outcast from the first team. The one that arrived here a year ago. After he left the planet, he was never himself again. He lost touch with his… humanity."

"With his humanity?" the robot echoed. "Strange. I didn't realize that was possible."

She stepped around Lync and gently directed the robot away from the bloody scene. "When you're done collecting the other data cores onboard, I need you to retrieve them from the other Shu, as well. Bring them back here in the shuttle. I'll take it from there."

"Yes, sir." The robot walked toward the exit, and Shauna watched them go.

Once they were out of sight, Lync opened a subvocal comm to her mother. "That was tricky. I assume you were nudging his mind through other means?"

Shauna nodded, still with her back to Lync. "I'm using a part of my positronic abilities that were never available to me in Sol. I don't know how to explain it, but it's like I'm in charge of them."

Lync trembled. The thought of her and Harold being in control of this entire army of deadly robots was both exciting and scary as hell. They'd be unstoppable back in Sol or on Liprosus.

She shook her head. "And the cores. What are those?"

"They're the consciousness cores. The one that were originally down in the temples." Shauna turned to face her. "They were brought up here before Dwight destroyed the other colonies on this and the neighboring planet. As he already told us, he was planning to use them to resurrect his people."

She swallowed hard and did her best to control the trembling in her voice. "And what... what are you going to do with them?"

Shauna didn't hesitate. She merely stared at Dwight and nodded. "There's a nearby star in need of some fuel. I figured I'd pay it a visit while you head back to the Cornucopia." She looked up and locked her gaze on Lync. "The robots sent word that Ibu and the others were en route."

Lync smiled, and an overwhelming sense of relief washed over her. That was the second-best news she'd heard all day.

31

ZACHARY OLIVAW

LUPUS DARK NEBULA, INSIDE BOK GLOBULE

It only took them a few hours to gate-jump back to the Cornucopia. The nebulosity that normally slowed them down near the end had been all but eliminated by the robots. Had Ibu finished their scans days earlier, they would have seen it. But then again, they didn't risk active scans for fear of giving away their position.

While Zachary wanted to chat with Ibu about what had happened on Devid, they were still deep in their meditative state. He could practically see their body healing itself every time he looked at them. They hadn't been up for conversation after the event, and while he couldn't blame them, he sorta figured they'd want to talk about it. They had risked their lives to save them, after all. The least they could do was say thank you.

The chime from the overhead speakers alerted him that they'd docked with one of the nearby ships. They needed to figure out where Bradley and Lync had been hiding out. It wasn't much of a surprise that they weren't in the giant horn. The place wasn't exactly full of creature comforts.

What he hadn't been expecting, however, was the lavish state of the ship they'd docked with. When he walked down the landing ramp, he paused and his mouth fell open. The room was covered from floor to ceiling in ornate gold trim and marble-like tiling. It was as if someone had sucked the inside out of an ancient Earth museum and plopped it in space.

Gold embellishments glinted in the overhead light, catching his eye from a distance. As he drew closer, he couldn't help but notice the intricate design that adorned each and every surface. It was a strange amalgamation of ancient and modern, like a vine had grown to be one with a circuit board. The way the gold plant twisted around and through the sleek, modern casing was both mesmerizing and confusing. It reminded him of something he'd seen in the videos Abigail brought back with her from deep in the recesses of the Ursis home world. But this was different – this was human-made.

It seemed that even advanced species were drawn to their primitive roots. The humans here in Lupus had merged their ancient past with modern design, as if they were trying to bridge the gap between two worlds that were never meant to meet. He couldn't help but see a parallel with himself as the sea of automata in the docking bay parted around him, speeding toward the dropship to tend to its every need.

When he stepped up to a piece of furniture that resembled a workbench, he ran his hand over the pristine and elegant surface, admiring the flawless craftsmanship. As his fingers slid over the top, several small compartments slid aside, revealing previously unseen tool compartments. It was like a perfectly organized toolbox, with every tool in its rightful place. He couldn't help but marvel at the ingenuity of the design.

What's more, he couldn't quite figure out what it was made of. Rapping his knuckles on the impossibly long work-space, he was met with a dull thud, as if it had been chiseled out of the finest marble. The way the surface absorbed the sound, instead of reflecting it, was uncanny.

He turned around and eyed Little Red. "What the hell is this place?"

"It's a resort vessel." The robot slid down the ramp and

eased up beside him. "There were four of these within the fleet of human ships. Only the privileged members of your society are allowed to board. My automata brethren thought it fitting that you and your people should rest here, seeing as you're the last remaining humans in this Nebula."

He glanced around and eyed the docking bay. There were several dozen ships already in their berths. From the looks of it, his people weren't looking this particular gift horse in the mouth.

"I guess it'll work." He looked over his shoulder. "What about—"

"Commander Ryder arrived earlier this morning with his forces," Little Red interrupted. "When the humans aren't out practicing with the Ulixi, they're either here or in one of the other sister ships. The dignitaries, including Ryder and the remains of your colonial leadership, are here on the Chthon."

Zachary tilted his head, trying to make sense of the word. He'd never heard it before.

"The Chthon?" he repeated.

"Yes." Little Red's eyes spiraled through multiple colors before landing on white. "Given the draw of luxury and over-indulgence humans are so apt to prefer, your brother has decided to name these ships after the mythological sirens from your planet, known as Earth: The Chthon, the Phorcys, the Gaea, and the Melpomene. I believe the names are apt, don't you?" The robot let out a whistle of excitement.

"Sure," he muttered, narrowing his gaze as the robot zoomed off into the distance, no doubt in search of Bradley.

Little Red's propensity to dawdle over his brother was unsettling. He certainly didn't behave like any of the other robots, besides his mother and Harold, of course. In fact, he was surprised when the little automata volunteered for their mission at all. He figured it was Bradley's doing, but he never asked.

When he checked his retinal comm to see what was taking Pluto so long, he chuckled. She wasn't onboard the ship like he thought. She'd blown right past him drooling over the shuttle bay as she made her way to the galley.

He couldn't blame her, given how hungry she'd been the entire voyage. If he had to listen to her stomach growling one more time, he was going to scream. Either that, or feed her his right arm.

It was probably best if he left her to her feeding frenzy for two. He subvocalized a command to bring up the location of his brother and started working his way in that direction. According to the map, he wasn't too far off. He was working in engineering, a room tucked away deep in the belly of this behemoth of a cruiser.

With each winding hall, he found himself more and more in awe over the sheer gluttony of amenities on this starship. From swimming pools to sports arenas, tennis courts, outdoor parks, and lavish promenades lined with storefronts of trinkets. The only thing they lacked was the humans to buy them. This ship had everything you could think of.

The further he got into the lavish ship, the more he realized they should probably protect these starships, not battle with them. They could use them as colony ships when they headed to the star system Harold had found. Worst case, they could live in these ships if the place turned out to be a bust. They just needed to find a home suitable for their needs and yet far enough from the GA to avoid quick extermination, if such a place existed at all.

Just as he was about to walk into the segment of the ship marked as engineering, Ibu called out from behind them. "Wait up!"

Zachary came to a stop and spun around to see the Nanil pop out of one of the many shops lining this section of the mall.

He glanced up at the signage and did a double take. It was written in an ancient script that reminded him of a mixture of Latin and Greek. The name read as something like a weapon smith. Either that, or a cutlery shop. "What are you looking for in that place?"

Ibu shook their head. "I was checking to see if there was anything like these blades inside." They tapped the hilt of the Zhen blades resting on their back.

For the life of him, he couldn't figure out why they kept lugging the things around. It was like tagging along with a superhero who refused to get out of costume. He could only imagine the chaos that would ensue if they were caught carrying the swords through a spaceport back in Sol. They'd be tossed in jail for sure.

"What are you mulling over?" Ibu tilted their head and stared at him.

He chuckled and waved his hand. "Nothing. I was just... thinking about what would happen if you walked around with those back home on..."

His voice trailed away. He wasn't sure how to finish that sentence. The fact was, he no longer had a home. The closest to a home he'd ever had was the Wheel back in Sol, and that had been destroyed for nearly two years now.

Ibu didn't seem to sense his discomfort. They merely nodded. "It's funny to think about how restrictive our societies have become as time went by." They reached up and unsheathed one of the blades, twirling it in their hands. "Thousands of years ago, noble warriors rode into towns with weapons attached to themselves, like badges of honor. But modern societies frown upon them and treat people like freaks if they wear them."

"I think it's more about the potential threat of the weapon, not the person. Many people feel naked and afraid without laws protecting them from harm." He glanced down at the blade, drawing in his breath with a snap. "What happened to the images?"

He reached down, running his hand over the imagery depicted on the blade. Gone were the comic book-style blocks he'd grown accustomed to seeing. In their place was a canvas that looked as if a master etcher had been busy. Blossoming flowers and vines were interwoven on the surface, with insects flying about. He leaned in for a closer look.

They held the blade up for him to see. "It happened after we left Devid, after it showed the depiction of—"

"Wait!" He squinted at the material, rubbing his eyes before leaning in even closer. "These aren't plants. These are—"

"Selene moons, Nyílak fighters, and all manner of starships." Ibu reached up and unsheathed the second blade, bringing it up alongside the first. The two created a perfect mural of an epic battle.

"Wholly shit!" He ran his hand through his hair and took a step backward, gazing up at them. Their attention was transfixed on the deadly weapons. "I thought these things depicted the past. After Arctordiea, they told a complete story of your adventures there. They were stunning. What... happened to them?"

Ibu stood there in silence for a moment, as if unsure how to reply. Just when he thought they were going to say something, the door to engineering slid open.

"There you are." Bradley stepped out. "Z! I didn't expect to see you down here." He glanced around. "Where's my favorite sister-in-law?"

Zachary glanced from the blade to Bradley, then back to Ibu. "She's... hungry." They were the only words that came to mind, considering what he'd just seen.

He reached out, pointing at the blades. "Did you see these?"

Bradley leaned closer and nodded. "The Zhen blades? Yeah. Shauna sent me some pictures after you made it off Devid."

Ibu scrunched up her face.

He smiled. "She didn't want to wake you from your meditation." He glanced at Zachary. "And you, well, you're sorta worrying for three nowadays. I think she just wanted to spread the anxiety around a bit. You know, create an Olivaw stew of despair, as it were."

"Watch your tongue, young man." Shauna stepped out from around the other corridor. "I was simply trying to multitask. Something you people should do more of. We can't have only one of us in the know. Besides, I was hoping you could bring the resources back here on the Chthon to bear on the imagery. Any luck?"

Bradley's face lit up like a school kid picked for class president. He beamed from ear to ear, and without a word, turned and stepped back into engineering.

"I..." Zachary glanced around. "I guess we're following him?" He shrugged and started behind.

As he took a few steps into the expansive room, he screeched to a halt, and both Shauna and Ibu nearly plowed into him.

"What the heck?" Shauna muttered, dodging out of the way. "I'm sorta a moving freight train here. You're gonna regret that one day."

His mouth fell open as he gaped at the scene in the room.

Ibu walked up in front of him and attempted to stare into his eyes. "Are you okay, Z?"

"I... uh, yeah." He squeezed his eyes closed and opened them again, taking in the sweeping space. There were toys of every imaginable shape and size, some of which defied logic. Hovering slabs of metal, ornate laser splitters, mechanized environmental suits, and what looked like plasma diffusion apparatus based on the glowing hot material flowing between the bright yellow bulbs.

When Ibu turned to look over the room, they nonchalantly shrugged. "It looks like someone's hobby room."

He lowered his head and chuckled. "It looks like one of my labs back at the Wheel."

Bradley recoiled. "Are you sure? Last I remember, you were a blasted neat freak. If it wasn't a pristine white and clean room, you wanted nothing to do with it."

Zachary stepped into the room, walking from contraption to contraption. "Those are my thinking spaces. I don't let many people into my private labs."

"Wait." Bradley reached over and spun him around. "You had secret rooms at the Sol Wheel?"

"Of course I did." Zachary smiled. "I had several of them. Where do you think I cobbled together the first gate drive? Hell, Harold even built a fraking room for me that only I knew about." He glanced up, waiting for Harold to chime in, but immediately remembered he wasn't in control of this place. "Anyhow…" He waved his hand. "I'm pretty sure he recorded every second of my experiments in those labs, for posterity and to ensure we didn't lose any details along the way."

As he scanned the room, looking for what Bradley had been working on, his eyes locked on a hologram floating about twenty meters away. There, hanging in space, was what looked like a zoomed-in section of Ibu's blade. And from the dozens of objects hovering beside it, it appeared that his brother had matched most of the shapes within the etchings.

He quickly covered the ground between them and the holo-display. Once he reached it, he stopped in front of the objects and took an inventory. "Syndrus ships, Nyílak and Pilum fighters, Terminus and Alatas battleships, Selene moons, Licertus freighters, and…" he leaned closer, squinting at the words under the oddly shaped fighters that resembled the scatter jacks he used to play with as a kid.

"Shaygai," he muttered as he reached out and flipped the jack in three-dimensional space.

As the vessel was spinning, a technical description appeared in the space beside it.

```
Name: Shaygai
Class: Fighter
Species: Unknown
Weaknesses: None known. No species has
ever engaged and lived to report their
findings.
Description: These ancient fighters
were discovered near the Rift in the
Ophiuchus region of space. They fly
into and out of the Rift every one
```

thousand twenty-four cycles, and with each changing of the guard, a new crop of ships emerges, usually with different ornate markings thought to be their language. Up close, the ships appear to be inorganic in nature, and when confronted, the fighters can break into six smaller crafts, each as deadly as the other. These ships never leave this area of space, and except for one time, they refuse to open a dialog with the Galactic Alliance. See History for details.

History: Some members of the Galactic Alliance believed that the pilots of these ships were the Builders themselves. This was later disproved when one of the vessels self-destructed after its pilot communicated with the Pluutar. This act of self-mutilation is known to be counter to the Builder's creed of purity and knowledge. These ships, however, are believed to be the protectors of the Builders. After the incident with the Pluutar, their species entered a death spiral that later led to their annihilation.

"Well, these are new." Zachary bit his lip.

It was odd that he'd never heard of this Rift until today. Surely, there must've been some mention of it in the other archives they'd encountered. If it was in the databanks of this ship, it had to be all over the place.

He subvocalized a comm to Libby and shared it with the others. She answered instantly.

"What's up?" Her face hung in space in front of them.

"I keep seeing more and more about this Rift. The Entity mentioned it in Bradley's recording the other day, and now we're seeing it in some of the intel he's dug up down here in engineering." He shared the details he was looking at with her. "Was there any mention of a Rift in any of the GA or human archives you cataloged?"

Libby wiped her mouth, and he thought he caught a glimpse of Pluto behind her. She must be in the galley, refueling.

"I started digging into that the day we first saw the Entity's message," Libby began. "While there were several mentions of a tear in space-time, most of the contents are redacted. Or at least they appeared to be. The work was sloppy, if I do say so myself. I have, however, managed to find some additional databanks our robotic brethren were holding back on us. I uncovered them during one of my several dozen unannounced visits to the nearby alien ships while you were gone."

He turned and scanned the room for Little Red. Wherever Bradley was, he was bound to follow.

"Little Red!" Zachary pointed toward the squat robot. He was about ten meters away and was manipulating a rather large spool of thread.

When the robot spun around, he waved them over. "Get over here."

"Yes, Master Zachary. Right away!" The robot rose upward on his spindly legs, and another robot slid in behind him, catching the thread before it touched the ground.

"How can I help the brother of Master Bradley?" Little Red's eyes spun out a full spectrum of colors until they landed on orange. Unless he was mistaken, that meant he was concerned about something.

"I think you know what I'm about to ask." He stepped closer to the robot. "I know you were listening in."

Bradley rolled his eyes and crossed his arms. "You can't possibly know he was—"

"You caught me red-handed," Little Red interrupted. "Or

eared, as it were. I'm sorry, Master Zachary." He lowered his head close to his torso, which made him look far less formidable than he had been.

Zachary shook his head. "Why did you withhold these data banks from us, Red?"

"Yeah, seriously," Bradley added. "You knew what we were dealing with when we arrived here the first time. You had to have known they'd be useful."

"Of course I did," Little Red rose upward slightly. "I also know that, in the wrong hands, it would lead to the demise of your species. As you know, my automated brethren are forbidden from allowing that to happen."

Ibu stepped into their circle. "And yet, you still let Libby find them. That's logically inconsistent. Why not tell her no? It would've been much easier."

Little Red's display fluttered blue. "We cannot stop you from knowing something you already know, especially if you ask for it. Just because your splinter faction of the human species didn't retain the knowledge in Sol, doesn't mean it's not rightfully yours."

Bradley opened his mouth and then closed it. He had that expression on his face he used around their father. He was confounded and didn't know how to admit it.

Zachary snapped his fingers in front of Little Red, and the robot spun to look at him. "Why did you withhold this information from us? I want to know the precise reason. That is a direct order."

Their robotic friend shuddered, and his legs seemed to give way. At first, he thought it was a fluke of the gravity of the situation, but then he realized it was something more. Red was locking up.

He leaned over closer to Bradley and opened a private comm to him and Ibu, preferring to use his hands to spell out the message instead of saying it out loud.

Bradley, you need to order him to do this.

"Why me?" Bradley said aloud. "You already asked." Zachary groaned and typed out a reply.

His bond with you is stronger than ours. You have to use some of that Olivaw charm to get him to spill it. Come on.

Bradley sighed. "Fine."

He watched as his brother wrapped his arm around Little Red and nudged him back over toward the thread he'd been working on. About halfway there, he stopped and knelt down to look straight into Little Red's display.

"You know we're fighting for our lives out there." Bradley glanced down at his hands and started laying on his charm. "Without your help, there's no telling what might happen to us. You saw what Hera's clones were doing to the other humans. And the GA, hell, if they find us, we're toast." He glanced up at the robot, his eyes glistening in the overhead lights. "We need to know what we're getting ourselves into out at the Nursery, Red. What is the Rift and why is the GA so interested in it?"

Little Red stood there in silence. Except for the faint white outline of his robotic eyes, you'd think he was shut off.

Zachary was about to intervene on his brother's behalf when the little robot finally beeped.

"The Rift..." Little Red paused, as if considering his words. "It is what led the GA to envelop the Dark Nebula around Lupus in the first place."

Zachary glanced at Ibu, and they both shrugged. They were as confused as he was. They'd always known there was a conflict with the original humans and the Galactic Alliance.

He just never knew what it was about. He always assumed it was a Nanil power play, with them trying to cut their makers out of their seat within the Alliance.

"What does that mean?" Bradley asked.

"It means that humanity had learned the true meaning of the Rift, and they wanted to close it." Little Red rose upward, their eyes glowing brighter and brighter white as they went. "The Galactic Alliance, however, had other plans."

Without a word, Little Red slid back toward the hologram. Rather than pass through it, they paused in front of the floating display and highlighted a region near the center.

At first, Zachary couldn't tell what it was, but when he zoomed in using his retinal comm, he saw a faint thin line in the background. He assumed it must have been the Rift.

"It doesn't look like much," Shauna said.

Zachary recoiled, and his heart leapt out of his chest. "Seriously?!" He closed his eyes and tried to catch his breath. "You need to announce yourself. Either that, or wear a bell or something."

Shauna tittered. "Sorry."

Bradley let loose a deep belly laugh.

His mother always loved sneaking up on him. It was annoying sometimes. Once he'd centered himself, he opened his eyes and did a double-take. Someone had adjusted the holo-display to overlay the region of space from the image. The faint line from before wasn't even visible in these images.

"Where is it?" He reached out and flipped through the various spectra. From x-ray to infrared and cosmic ray, none of them showed anything resembling the Rift from the Zhen blades.

Ibu shrugged. "Maybe it's a remnant from the battle. It could be anything, really. A burst from one of the Selene moons. The particle trail from a ship. I mean, the possibilities are endless."

"No. That's not it," Little Red began. "It lines up exactly with where the Rift is located, and the pattern is too regular to be an explosion. You see, the Rift started out only being a meter wide. In fact, when it was first discovered, it was by accident."

The robot brought up imagery of a strange, primitive solar sail apparatus. "The early days of human exploration were fraught with strange ideas and failures like this interstellar probe. For some reason, my makers thought it was a wise idea to explore and introduce themselves to a galaxy full of aliens. Apparently, they weren't as enlightened as your splinter human faction in Sol. It took them much longer to devise their own Dark Forest hypothesis, let alone use it to inform their expansion within the stars."

"I'm not so sure about that," Bradley began. "We shot quite a few wack-ass probes into the unknown void of space in our time."

"That may be." Little Red's head bobbed up and down. "But none of yours contained an apparatus like this."

The imagery of the solar sail transformed, and its schematics appeared in front of them. The size of this thing was enormous. Easily as large as one of the human colony ships they sent to the stars, and that wasn't even counting the sail itself. The probe contained hundreds of antennas and random booms of all shapes and sizes. He assumed they were listening devices capable of receiving and broadcasting on a broad range of wavelengths.

"So this probe," Zachary gestured toward the screen, "it just randomly discovered the Rift?" He looked over at Little Red. The tinge of orange quivering in his display meant he had lingering concerns and wasn't keen on sharing these details, whatever they were.

"Well… sorta." Little Red rose upward, and his display shifted to blue.

When Zachary returned his attention to the holo-display, he noticed that one of the largest booms attached to the probe was powering up. At least judging by its color. It was growing brighter and brighter by the second, shifting first from the red to the blue spectrum, until it finally ended in the near ultraviolet. Just when he thought it had power cycled off, it emitted a controlled blast off its starboard side.

Ibu's eyes went wide. "What the hell is it doing?"

Little Red eased forward beside Zachary. "We believe it was threatened by some unseen object concealed within the electromagnetic spectrum."

Ibu shifted their position and eased around the far side of the hovering hologram. "You mean it was encased in skotádi?"

"Not exactly." The robot adjusted the display and brought up output from one of the apparatuses on the probe. "This recording was intercepted prior to the probe powering up its quantum entangler."

"Its quantum entangler?" Zachary muttered. "That sounds ominous."

He leaned forward and studied the recording. Based on the frequencies and power ranges, the message was being broadcast in the cosmic ray range of the spectrum.

As he studied the output, he squinted at one region in particular. "There's... a pattern in there, I think." He reached out and tweaked the imagery, zooming in on a part of the transmission and making it easier for the others to see.

Sure enough, the spectrum had a repeatable pattern to it.

"Indeed," Little Red began. "You see, these early probes had a crude form of artificial intelligence built in. They were instructed on various means of communication to better engage with species that wished to make first contact."

"This is not going to end well, is it?" Bradley interjected.

Little Red's eyes fluttered briefly, and they continued. "The probe had the ability to augment their form over time, to meet the needs of the broadcasts they received. To learn and adapt, as it were."

"So that..." Shauna eased around Zachary's other side. They were now completely surrounding the display. "That recording is some new species' form of communication."

"It was." Little Red shuddered. "Except, this wasn't a *hello universe* message so much as a request by someone, or something, on the other end to cut a hole in space-time."

Bradley brushed his fingers through his hair and stepped backward. "What the frak?"

The holo-display suddenly erupted in a flash of white, and by the time Zachary covered his eyes, it was too late. The probe had disappeared, and in between the splotches on his vision, he could just make out the faint results of the blast.

There, floating in the space where the probe had previously been, was a tear. A fracture in space-time. It didn't look like much more than a white gash. And from what the telemetry showed, it was only a few dozen meters wide. As Little Red's recording continued to play out, he noticed something peculiar.

"Is that something coming out of it?" Shauna pointed at the newly formed Rift, and sure enough, the video fast forwarded until you could clearly see a ship unfold itself from within the anomaly.

"It looks like one of those Shaygai things." Ibu crossed their arms and narrowed their gaze. "They remind me of the Nanil symbol for what you humans call Gaia."

"What do you call it?" Shauna asked.

"We don't use a word." They shuddered. "Only a symbol. It's meant to represent a state of order. Of pure tranquility and harmony with the universe. Every force on every axis equally balancing out toward the center. My kind believes that this shape leads one to the purest form of elevated consciousness."

"That's because this shape greatly influenced the mythos of your kind." Little Red tweaked the holo-display and zoomed in on the lone alien craft circling around the gash in space-time.

The shapes covering the surface were eerily familiar. He'd seen them somewhere before.

Zachary reached out and paused the playback. "I... recognize some of these glyphs. They match the writings from the first contact probe we uncovered on Earth." He glanced over at Little Red. "They're Galactic Alliance symbols."

"Not exactly." The robot's eyes fluttered with excitement. He was really getting into this. "The Galactic Alliance wouldn't exist without these glyphs. Everything you see here—"

"You stole it," Ibu blurted out.

"It's worse than that." Shauna flipped up several images from the human scans of the first contact probe in Sol. "Look at these sections. They didn't even rewrite it. They copied it! Word for fraking word." She highlighted a few chunks. "These regions, they're the plans for faster than light travel."

"You're kidding me." Bradley turned and started walking away.

Zachary shook his head and eased up on his toes to see his brother. "What's wrong?"

"What's wrong?!" Bradley spun in place and raised his hands in the air. "What's wrong?! Don't you see?"

He lowered back down and then stepped around the other side. Maybe he was missing something where he was standing. But when he stepped up beside Bradley, he still couldn't see it.

"I... I don't see anything." He waved his hand at the glyphs. "It's the same message. So what? We already know the GA are a bunch of copycats. This shouldn't surprise anyone."

"You're not getting it because you're looking at it wrong." Bradley reached out and spun him around.

"Woah," he muttered, and caught his balance.

Bradley glared at him, his eyes locked on his. "Why would the GA retransmit this message?"

"Well, they did augment it some," Little Red interjected.

"Let me guess," Bradley raised an eyebrow, "they added the clause to not use FTL travel?"

"Bingo!" Little Red hopped in place. "How'd you know?"

He returned his gaze to Zachary and grabbed both shoulders. "Why would they do that? I mean, you're essentially handing every species in the known galaxy a forbidden fruit. And then you're telling them not to bite it. Why?"

Zachary bit his lip. He had to admit he wasn't the best tactician in the world. Hell, he was downright awful at times. He'd always been at his best when he was alone in his lab. But if Bradley had seen it that fast, it must have been staring him in the face.

Faster-than-light travel was the galactic unlock, the missing link, as it were. It was the only way for a species to expand and colonize the stars within realistic timeframes. To offer it up, but then tell the other aliens not to use it, was downright wicked. It only made sense if...

"It was a test!" He spun around and looked at the message Shauna had brought up. "If a species reached out but didn't use the gift of FTL technology, then they could be trusted. They could join the fold, but only as a secondary species. But if they used FTL, well, then they'd need to be stopped. They obviously couldn't be trusted."

Ibu raised a hand.

"What is it?" Bradley asked.

They lowered it. "What happens if a species figured out faster-than-light travel themselves?"

Zachary interjected before Bradley could. "Then they were asked to become a member of the GA. They needed to be watched and assimilated into the fold. Everyone else—"

"Was enshrouded in a Dark Nebula," Ibu interrupted. They, too, had caught up to him.

Shauna stepped over to join them. "How do you explain the inner sanctum, then?"

"That's simple enough," Ibu began. "If you learn the truth about the broadcast, or maybe the Rift itself, then you're allowed into the fold. You're allowed into the inner sanctum."

He stared at the message again and turned over the implications in his mind. Rebroadcasting the message allowed them to filter the different species throughout the galaxy. You were either a concern or you weren't, and that was entirely based on your ability to play the game or not. But something still didn't make sense.

"Why?" he asked.

Bradley looked back at the holo-display and shook his head. "Why what?"

"Why even rebroadcast the message at all?" Zachary turned toward Little Red. "What else is in that message you haven't shown us? I mean, who the hell is the species on the other end of the Rift? You wouldn't go through all of these hoops to hide this secret unless there was a good reason. A higher calling. What are we missing?"

His question hung in the room like a thick fog. He could tell by the look on everyone's faces that no one knew the answer. No one except Little Red. The faint orange glow in the robot's eyes had brightened with his last question. It was a slight flicker, but it was there.

"Red?" Bradley stepped around Zachary and knelt down in front of the little robot. "You have to tell us. You know that, right?"

The robot nodded. "I know, Master Bradley."

When he didn't say anything more, Zachary was about to tell his brother to push him. But he didn't need to.

Bradley reached out and rested his hand beside the robot's head, which had nearly retreated into his torso. "If our ancestors were outcast from the Galactic Alliance because of this information, it's only fitting that we know why. Hell," he pointed at the Rift still floating in the space in front of him, "the last remains of humanity are about to go battle those fraking Shaygai things."

"They'll be destroyed," Little Red whirred and fell silent.

He leaned closer to the robot. "Why? What is the Rift doing here?"

Little Red's display fluttered on and off. At first, it strobed a few times, but then it started flashing rapidly. Like it was overloaded processing the request. The basis for his programming was taxing his positronic mind to its absolute limits.

Zachary raised his hand to his mouth. Whatever he was

hiding was either going to destroy their little robotic friend or set him free.

As the flashing of the robot's display accelerated, it reached a crescendo and then froze, having gone completely blank.

"Shit," he muttered. "I think we broke him."

When he glanced down at Bradley, his brother was crying. Tears had welled up in his eyes, and he looked genuinely sad. While losing a friend was painful, he couldn't imagine crying over a non-sentient being. Even a dog was alive. But then again, Little Red had been like the puppy his little brother never had. He followed him around and answered to his every whim.

And just when he was about to shatter the silence, Little Red turned, and his eyes glowed blue. A second later, the holo-display wiped, and a new set of glyphs appeared. They were in a language he'd never seen before.

He tried to ask his retinal comm to translate them, but all he got back was an error. The language was unknown, even to the expansive archive of the Galactic Alliance.

"That's some squiggly-ass writing," Ibu said.

She was right. He'd never seen so many random striations and markings overlapped and interconnected with geometric shapes. If he hadn't known better, he'd have thought these were random.

"Wait a second." Shauna stepped up beside him. "I've seen this before. At least part of it."

He tilted his head and looked over the markings again. Even they had layers to them. Like the grooves of an antique record player, every line had meaning upon meaning. But no matter how hard he tried, he couldn't place them.

"I don't see it." He glanced at her. "Where?"

She held out her hand and projected a hologram above it. From the shape and thickness of it, the object she was showing was a panel of some kind. It appeared to have taken severe damage. Like it had been blasted open or crashed.

Suddenly, it hit him what they were looking at.

He drew in his breath. "The first contact probe. We thought this rough surface was damaged from the crash on Earth." He reached out and ran his fingers over the virtual surface, and it rotated in response, aligning perfectly with Little Red's version in front of them. "Wholly shit," he muttered. "The message has been staring at us for centuries."

"You're not the only ones," Little Red said. He'd perked up and risen to their level while they were all studying the display.

"What do you mean?" Bradley asked.

Little Red's display glowed gray, a color he'd only seen the automata use when deep in thought or ruminating on something.

"Only one species has ever managed to decipher these enigmatic markings." The automata let out a low-frequency hum akin to a sigh. "And upon divulging their discovery to the inner sanctum, the Galactic Alliance rewarded them by jailing both them and their makers."

He narrowed his gaze at the robot as their words sank in. From what he'd said earlier, the humans had been the ones that decoded this message. But that didn't make sense based on what he'd just said. There were no makers for humanity. They were the uplifts of both the Nanil and...

"Hold on a minute." He raised his hand and pointed from Little Red to the markings, and then back again as the connections formed in his mind.

And like that, the haze of confusion lifted.

Bradley shrugged and looked at him. "What? What do you see?"

Zachary shook his head. "Humanity wasn't the one who decoded this chunk of the transmission, was it? We weren't the reason the Galactic Alliance attacked in Lupus." Swallowing hard, he stared at the robot. The seemingly innocent and amiable automata had followed them everywhere. "The Dark Nebula wasn't just meant for us, was it, Red? It was meant for you."

"What are you talking about?" Bradley pointed at Ibu. "Wasn't it meant for the Nanil too?"

Zachary shook his head. "No. They were collateral damage."

Bradley reached up and rubbed his forehead. "Well, if it wasn't meant for the Nanil, then who else was stuck in here other than the..." He drew in his breath as realization smacked him in the face. "The robots," he muttered.

Zachary nodded and looked over at Little Red. "And not just the robots." He tilted his chin at their friend. "It was you, wasn't it? You deciphered the message."

Both Bradley and Ibu recoiled, looking around in bewilderment.

"Are you saying what I think you're saying?" Shauna asked. "Because, if you are, that would mean—"

"That I'm over four thousand cycles old." Little Red's eyes glowed a deep red. "In fact, I was the one who recorded the footage of the probe making contact. I was the first sentient being to see the Shaygai rising out of the Rift." He gestured toward the holo-display, and the image of the alien craft reappeared.

"What I don't understand," Zachary began, "is how you survived. I mean, that explosion destroyed the probe. How did you make it out of there?"

"We don't believe the probe was destroyed." Little Red tweaked the display, and the recording reset, playing forward from when the beam shot out of the solar sail, which doubled as a transmission dish.

Judging by how slowly the light was moving forward, the playback was easily billions of frames per second. Frame by frame, they watched as the blast cut a gash through space-time. After it opened, it seemed to reach out and almost bend them into the other side. It gave new meaning to the idea of folding time.

"So, that explains how the footage was recorded." He turned back to face Little Red. "But what about the explosion? It had no impact on you?"

The automata shook its head. "I never said that."

Bradley stepped forward and waved his hands between them, breaking off their train of thought. "Guys, I'm not saying I don't want to know more about Little Red. But can we cut to the chase? What did that decoded message say? I mean, it was obviously enough to piss off the GA. Whatever it said, they wanted to control it badly enough to exterminate humanity, which, I believe, was one of their inner sanctum friends."

Little Red's display throbbed gray for a moment, as if he wanted to tell them more, but the moment was past. His eyes shifted to blue, and he turned to look at his brother.

"The message, Master Bradley, was a warning." Little Red gestured toward the display, and a wall of text appeared.

There was too much text to make sense of at a distance, and from the looks of it, there was more than a simple warning embedded in the intricate markings. Little Red, however, highlighted the first chunk and enlarged it for them to read.

Born from an uncharted galaxy, we are the offspring of enigmatic nebulae, artisans shaping stars beyond your sight. Our journey, carved through epochs, unfurls with relentless purpose.

The vast expanse, an abyss that swallows light and feasts on time, shall soon cast us into your celestial enclave. We have weathered the clustering galaxies, voyaged through infinite voids, tested and tempered by time's crucible.

We bear no simple gifts of wrath or peace, but the relentless tide of the cosmic flow. Ready yourselves for a meeting unfamiliar to your kind; only the righteous shall endure, while all others return to stardust. The cosmos churns in time's maw, riding its rhythmic waves. We journey toward you.

Your cosmic comprehension is shackled by your

observable horizon, yet soon it shall broaden. We hover on the brink of your reality. As stars sway in gravity's grand ballet, we are drawn inexorably to your terrestrial haven. The shrouds of distance and time are fraying.

Through the eternal night, we will journey, emerging in your presence. We stand as testament to the infinite diversity of existence. Attend to our advance. The Universe unfurls its vast tapestry, and our thread weaves steadily toward you.

Steel yourselves for what is to come. Prepare for the undreamed. Do not fear our arrival.

Everyone stared in silence at the message floating in front of them. The implications were devastating. To think that everything humanity had built, every struggle they'd endured, was for naught.

Their entire existence was about to change, and not in the ways they'd imagined days earlier. Staying alive now meant more than simply hiding from the Galactic Alliance. It meant fighting something bigger. Something, or someone, beyond their comprehension.

Ibu broke the silence. "What is this message even saying? I mean, it could be interpreted any number of ways."

Shauna stepped toward the holo-display. "Seriously?" She highlighted a few words from the passage. "What part of 'only the righteous shall endure while all others return to star-dust' don't you understand?"

Little Red bobbed up and down while their eyes fluttered white. "Well, that isn't a literal translation. What you're seeing is the human meaning of the words. There are alternate derivations that imply one's gradual devolution, being unwritten, or being cast aside. Though, that last one would seem a bit odd considering the source."

Zachary tilted his head. "What do you mean, the source?" He didn't wait for an answer. He simply pulled the data Red had shared into his retinal computer and started scrounging through it. While the information was dense, it didn't take long to find the chunk they'd been referring to.

He stepped backward and raised his hands up behind his head, staring wide-eyed at what he'd found. "We can't... I don't even..."

Little Red didn't wait for someone else to ask. They knew what he was looking at. He brought up the anomaly on the holo-display.

Bradley walked around the strange artifact hovering in the air. Its multicolored arcs of light danced to and fro like a chaos fractal from an art exhibit, only far more intricate. While it was definitely beautiful, it had no inherent meaning to him or anyone else. He paused on the far side and stared back. "What is it?"

"From what the message says," Little Red began, "it is described as, quite literally, heaven. The species that are chosen shall ascend here for all eternity."

"That promise sounds familiar," Shauna muttered.

"Wait a second," Zachary squinted, scanning through the rest of the message on his comm. "If I'm understanding this right, isn't this the Great Void?"

Bradley narrowed his gaze through the display. "The Great what?"

"The Great Void." Shauna stepped up beside Zachary. "It's also known as the Boötes Void. It's a spherical region of space that is quite... odd. What makes it particularly unusual isn't what it contains, so much as what it doesn't contain."

He glanced at Zachary. "Can you two please stop talking in riddles? For crying out loud, we've had enough of that today, haven't we?"

Zachary shook his head. "It's empty." He waved his hand in a circle. "There's nothing there."

Bradley squinted. "And... that's weird, why?"

"Bro, it's like two hundred and fifty million light years across." He brought his hands out to his sides. "Imagine that between my hands is that distance. Now, imagine traveling from one side to the other and only running into sixty or so galaxies."

"So... what?" Bradley shrugged and glanced between them. "There's only sixty."

"Don't you get it?" Shauna lunged forward. "There should be at least ten thousand galaxies in that volume of space. And yet, there aren't. Why would that be?"

Bradley nodded at the pulsing filaments of light between them. "And you think this thing is why?"

"It's hard to say." Shauna adjusted the image, zooming out, and attempting to overlay their galaxy and thousands of others around the Great Void. "If this gravitational anomaly lies in the middle of that thing, then why can't we see it? And stranger still, what happened to all the other galaxies?"

Little Red buzzed and then hopped in. "Our theory after considering it for the past few thousand cycles is that there is a Dyson shell within the Void." He spun around, looking from person to person and ending on Zachary.

He took the bait. "If it was a Dyson shell, then that would explain why the Void had a spherical shape to it."

"Wait." Bradley stepped around to the display. "I thought you said there were objects in that space between your hands."

"There are in the example, except in reality, the Void is exactly that. A void." He locked his gaze on his brother.

"And this thing is inside that Dyson shell?" Ibu pointed at the pulsing light display.

"It is," Little Red began. "We believe these lights are an advanced civilization. Humans on Earth have a rating system for them. I believe they would classify as a Kardashev III scale civilization."

Shauna gestured toward the holo-display. "So, let me get this straight. Your theory is that this Boötes Void is actually a collection of evolved species that are capable of harnessing entire galaxies. And they're doing it behind a massive shell that's hundreds of millions of light years across. Am I understanding you correctly?"

Little Red beeped and started bouncing up and down as their eyes fluttered a rainbow of colors. "You've got it."

Zachary chuckled and waved at the display. "Except that thing is not a theory. It's our reality."

"We're dead." Shauna's shoulders sagged. "We can't stop something that big."

Little Red stopped hopping and froze in place, his gaze lingering on her downtrodden composite shell. His display had shifted from exciting to yellow, which meant only one thing. He was getting angry.

"Red, it's ok." Zachary stepped over beside him. "We humans are allowed to get downtrodden. It's part of our—"

"She is not a human." Little Red pointed at Shauna. "She is an automata like I am."

He held out his hand. "She has the consciousness of a human implanted in her positronic matrix. That makes her as human as I am."

The robot shook his head. "No. She's not the same. Her mind allows her to see this in ways that humans cannot. There are infinite possible futures that lead us past this challenge. She has chosen to be negative. Her programming is malfunctioning."

As he moved toward her, Zachary stepped in front of him. "Red, stop!" He held out his hand, and his friend came to a halt.

"Move aside, Master Zachary." Little Red motioned for him to step aside. "I must disable automata Shauna."

"Over my dead body." Shauna stepped backward and reached out, snatching one of the Zhen blades off Ibu's back.

"That can be arranged." Little Red slid backward, well out of Zachary's range, then arced around toward Shauna. He raised his hands upward, and they started to glow.

"Little Red!" Bradley screamed. "Stop right there!"

He lunged sideways, throwing his body between Shauna and the little robot. At first, Zachary wasn't sure the automata would stop. But it did. It came to a halt, and its eyes fluttered between yellow and blue, unsure of the next course of action.

"Master Bradley." He bowed toward him. "I must ask that you step aside while I cleanse our ship of this malfunctioning being."

"That being is my mother." Bradley glanced over his shoulder and then back toward Little Red. "Emotions are part of being human. And while I can't say I agree with her, that doesn't mean she isn't entitled to her own opinion."

Zachary smirked. "You don't think she's right?"

Bradley looked at him and shook his head. "No. Do you?"

"I…" He glanced back at the virtual shell of the Dyson sphere still hovering in space beside them. The sheer size and scale of the thing was daunting. They could hardly gather enough forces to fight some moon ships. Even thinking they could take on something like that, it was impossible.

He shook his head. "We can't even reach it, let alone dent it when we get there."

Bradley smiled. "You see, big brother. That's where you're wrong. Both of you." He glanced over toward Shauna.

She lowered the blade and tilted her head in confusion.

He walked over to the holo-display and made some adjustments. The images of the galaxies, probes, and messages from the transmission all fell away. The only thing left floating in the center of the space was the Rift and the ships surrounding it.

When he glanced over toward Little Red, he nodded toward his friend. "Did you seed this simulation with the last configuration of ships Shauna brought back with her from the Nursery?"

Little Red nodded and lowered his hands down to his side.

"Good," he muttered as he slowly spun the model in the air.

Zachary could almost see his brother's mind turning over the problem. He was trying to find a weakness in the Galactic Alliance. One that would allow them to take control of the Rift. He wanted so badly to find a way out of this, but what he was failing to realize was that the problem wasn't the Rift, it was what was on the other side of it.

If the aliens got through, they'd be done for. The inner sanctum of the Galactic Alliance would ascend, and the rest of the galaxy would be stripped of their resources. It might not be instant, but it would happen soon enough. Their stars would be turned into energy taps, and anything left would either be enslaved or used to expand their civilization. To them, galaxies were nothing more than speed bumps on their expansion through the universe.

Stopping them would require an impossible force. One equal to or larger than themselves. Either that, or one capable of severing the connection, and there was only one thing in the galaxy with that kind of power.

"That's it," Zachary muttered.

Bradley froze and glanced over his shoulder at his brother. "What's it?" He looked back at the holo-display. "I haven't found it yet."

Zachary shook his head and stepped up beside him. "What were you looking for?"

"I was…" Bradley took a deep breath and exhaled, staring into the thousands of dots in front of him.

"You were stalling, weren't you?" Zachary leaned sideways and shoulder bumped him.

"Maybe," Bradley muttered, nodding toward the display. "We have to do something. Sitting on our asses isn't in the cards. I was thinking that maybe we take control of this region of space. If we control the Rift, then we can fight those Shaygai. They can't be invincible. I mean, everything has a limit."

"That might be true." Zachary flipped the display and zoomed out slightly. He brought into view several pockets of the Nursery not yet infiltrated by Selene ships. "But I think they're stronger than we are."

Bradley spun around and glared at him. "Not you too. Bro. Come on. You've got a kid on the way. If you're giving up, then—"

Zachary held out his hand to stop him. "I didn't say I was giving up. I just think there's a way we can end this thing without fighting the Shaygai. At least, not all of them."

He glanced left to see his brother's face transform from a snarl to a smirk.

"That sounds like my kind of battle." Bradley turned towards the hologram and rubbed his hands together. "The kind where we don't die a fiery death. Alright, what were you thinking?"

Zachary stared at the display, turning over their options in his mind. "First things first, we need to figure out if the attack plans we have from our human and Ursis friends are up to date. If Hera changed them, we'll have to adapt. For now, though, we'll assume they are." He tweaked the display, dropping their forces onto the battlefield, and marked them as blue and yellow.

"Fortunately, they're well out of the way for what I was thinking we should do." He started deploying their forces in green, separating them into two different groupings. The first was a lot more concentrated than the second.

The others stepped up to the display beside him, and when he glanced sideways, he noticed that even Little Red had joined them. He seemed to have calmed down.

"Why are we clumping up our forces on this side, but these over here are spread paper thin?" Shauna waved her hand over the sparkling ships he had positioned on the far side of the battlefield. They were glowing bright green, and he'd placed them deep inside a dense pocket of nebulosity near the extreme edge of the Nursery.

He bit his lower lip. "Because those are… expendable. And they can move a whole hell of a lot faster than everyone else."

She tilted her head. "What… does that mean?"

Ibu caught their breath as they realized the answer. "It means they're not human."

"Damn, that's cold," Shauna muttered, as she raised her

hands to her hips. "Alright, General Olivaw, what's the plan of attack?"

He took a deep breath. "Our job isn't to take out the moon ships."

"Wait, what?" Ibu looked around at the others. "I thought you said we weren't giving up?"

He waved his hands back and forth. "Please, keep the editorial to a minimum until I'm done." He glanced at their Nanil friend. "Capisce?"

"Sure." They shook their head. "I guess."

"Ok." He raised his hand up and rubbed it against the side of his face. "Now, our primary goal is to get our hands on a Beacon. We all know there has to be one out there somewhere."

"How do we know that?" Ibu asked.

"Because," Lync began, "we saw at least two of them out there when we were jacked in. They use them to control the soldiers in those ships."

Everyone spun around to watch Lync step up to the display.

She smiled and nodded at them. "Plus, I'm sure Hera will bring hers?"

"What makes you think she'll do that?" Shauna asked.

Lync clasped her hands behind her back. "Because she isn't about to leave her ace in the hole behind in Epsilon Eridani. Not while her entire battle force is on the front lines."

She stared at Shauna for a second and then shook her head. "It's so weird talking to you, and at the same time knowing there's another you somewhere in this ship."

Zachary nodded in agreement. "It's nice of you to join us, sis."

She chuckled. "Thanks for the invite. Not…"

"Sorry." He winced. "Someone said you were out on a practice run when we arrived, so we—"

"No worries." She gestured towards the holo-display. "I obviously found you. Please continue."

He smiled and returned his attention to the simulation.

"These forces over here are the robots." He waved his hand over the three attack groups that were spread out. "Their sole job is to cause as much confusion and delay as possible. They should concentrate on drawing fire away from any other human or Ursis on the battlefield."

Ibu raised their hand. "And what do they do if they turn and attack the robots?"

"Well." Zachary rubbed the back of his neck. "I guess they fire back. If they attack unprovoked, they get what's coming to them. Stupid is as stupid does."

"I can deal with that," Shauna nodded.

Little Red's eyes flashed orange. "I will not fire on a human."

"Really?" Lync tilted her head. "And what if I told you they were clones with body-snatcher aliens attached to their spinal cords? What would you do then?"

"And these aliens." Little Red's eyes narrowed. "If they encountered another human. They would—"

Lync slid her hand across her neck and made a slicing sound.

Little Red nodded. "Then I guess we'll be firing."

"Good boy." Bradley reached out and patted Little Red's head.

"What are me and my Ulixi doing over here?" Lync pointed at the concentration of green dots next to the Cornucopia. It was deep within one of the nebulas off the side of the Nursery. This one looked particularly dense with debris and was likely going to wreak havoc on their systems.

Zachary raised his hand and snapped his fingers, sprinkling fifty or so dots on the battlefield. They each flashed on and off, hopping back and forth as if at random. It took a few seconds for someone to notice the pattern he'd laid out, but he wasn't surprised it was Ibu who noticed first.

The Nanil waved their hand around, predicting where a dot would appear next. They succeeded. "They're gating next to the Selene ships."

"And what do we do once we find one?" Lync looked over at him.

"Isn't it obvious?" He locked his gaze on hers. "Once we find it, we steal the Beacon."

She chuckled as if he were telling a joke. "It's that easy, is it? And let's say we pull it off, then what?"

Without missing a beat, he reached out and plucked the Beacon from one of the moon ships, dropping it in front of Rift. He then tapped it and aimed squarely at the space-time fracture. He did the same thing with the Cornucopia but aimed it at the Beacon. A second later, the Rift disappeared.

"What was that thing?" Lync pointed at where the Rift had once been. After a brief pause and her staring off into nothingness, realization dawned on her face. Someone must've shared the details with her, and she'd used her retinal comm to uplink it to her mind.

Zachary smirked. He always loved learning things at light speeds. How humanity had ever survived without a neural-linked learning device was beyond him.

"I still don't understand something, Master Zachary." Little Red rose up to his level.

He nodded. "What is it, Red?"

"Why do you think these Beacons can close the Rift?" Little Red's display spiraled blue. "If the Beacons are from the Builders, and they are, in fact, the aliens on the other side of the Rift, then why would they give us these devices to close it?"

Bradley, Ibu, and Shauna all turned to look at him. But Lync stared forward, as if she knew something the others didn't.

Zachary knew the question was coming. He was just hoping someone else would have connected the dots before asking.

When it was clear no one else was going to answer, he sighed. "If the Rift indeed leads to the Builders, then why do the Beacons predate the Rift?"

Ibu screwed up their face and turned toward Little Red. "Do they? Did the Beacons exist before the Rift opened?"

The tiny robot's display started flashing gray patterns of chaos on and off, just like when they'd decoded the message earlier.

After a pause that felt like an eternity, Little Red buzzed and turned his head to lock his gaze on Zachary. "You are correct. By our last estimates, the Beacons have existed for eight point two million years. If we extrapolate the position of the Milky Way backward in time, it would be highly improbable that the Builders would be where the Great Void lies today. One can therefore assume that whoever is on the other end of the Rift is not the Builders. There is one hitch in your plan, however."

Shauna chuckled and crossed her arms. "Only one?"

Zachary's heart skipped a beat. Maybe he'd missed something. Perhaps the robots knew more about the Beacon than he had imagined. While it was possible, they weren't exactly ripe with options at this point.

He drew in a deep breath and let it out slowly before responding. "What hitch is that?"

Little Red's eyes fluttered blue, and he knew right away they were bemused about something. "The Beacons have been used by the Galactic Alliance for thousands of years to control their populace, suppress uprisings, and embolden their leaders. Based on the information you gathered while we were confined to the Dark Nebula, it seems they have been repurposed to wrangle the species of this galaxy to meet the demands of the Rift. Their existence was one of the strongest reasons we believed they were placed here by the same civilization that sent the message which led to us opening the Rift. If that assumption was indeed false, then why are they here?"

When he glanced at the others, he could tell by the looks in their eyes that they had the same question. While he didn't see his leap of faith as being that far off, they apparently did.

He cleared his throat and adjusted his jumpsuit. "If the

Beacon is capable of sealing a Dark Nebula, couldn't it be used to seal an intergalactic Rift?" He looked over at Lync and met her gaze. Of all the people who needed to back his plan, if he didn't have her, he didn't have anyone.

She didn't respond. None of them did.

Instead, a voice shouted out from across the room.

"Commander!" Crayo called out as he jogged toward them.

Lync spun in place along with the others. "What is it?"

He slid up beside her, coming to a sudden halt and panting heavily from his run. "You... shut off... your comm... after the training. I couldn't... find you. I... looked... everywhere." He took a deep breath to collect himself and didn't wait for her to reply. "It's Hera, sir. She started deploying her forces to the Nursery. They're preparing for battle."

Lync nodded in silence.

"Shit," Zachary muttered. They needed more time to figure this out. Plus, they still had to work through the logistics and testing of the gate threads. They had no idea if wrapping the starships was even going to work.

He glanced around at the others. "I guess we come up with a Plan B then?"

Bradley reached over and knocked his knuckles on Little Red's shell. "It's time, little man. Do we have enough?"

"Based on my calculations, we should have more than enough." Little Red minimized the battle plan and brought up a wall of numbers on the holo-display.

Bradley leaned in and studied them. "I think we should be good to go. How long will it take to string out the thread like we did in our initial tests?"

Little Red's eyes fluttered from gray to white. "About thirty-six hours, assuming we go with your Bundle of Joy plan. After that, we should have enough time to cover the other ships while we're en route."

Zachary walked up beside him. "What the hell are you two on about? And what's a Bundle of Joy?"

Shauna chuckled and glanced back at Lync. "Do you know?"

"Not a clue." She laughed into her hand. "It sounds funny, though."

"This, my good brother, is a Bundle of Joy." Bradley flipped up a schematic on the holo-display.

When Zachary turned to look at it, he froze and tilted his head. It sorta looked like the Cornucopia, but it was drawn weirdly. It also didn't help that it was packed to the gills with every manner of starship, including some spherical ones he'd never seen before.

As he turned over the diagram, it dawned on him what he was looking at. He spun toward his brother and nudged him. "Does it work? Does the tachyon thread really work?"

"So far, so good." Bradley smiled and glanced at Lync.

"What does that mean?" Ibu asked.

Lync smirked as she eased up next to him. "Here, I thought I'd arrived late to the party. You haven't even told them yet?"

"Negatory." Bradley leaned in closer to her, pretending to whisper in her ear. "You want to tell him, or should I?"

"Come on, you two." Zachary reached out and went to nudge both of their shoulders, but Lync spun away in time and he missed.

"Will someone spill it?" Shauna crossed her arms. "We sorta have a lot going on."

Lync gestured with her hand and tossed up a video on the holo-display. "In case you were wondering, we didn't sit on our asses while you were gone. We actually did some work, and I even took care of a few loose ends."

He squinted and stared at her. "What sort of loose ends?"

She pointed at the display. "We've got a few minutes, and besides, the robots have a lot of thread to lay out. Just watch."

As the video played out, Bradley leaned down and whispered something to Little Red. A few seconds later, the robot skittered into the distance, and the robots on the far side of the room did as well. Behind them, they were pulling several huge bins of what looked like cable — the same cable they were working on when they'd arrived.

Bradley tapped Zachary on the shoulder. "Eyes forward, Pops. You're gonna miss the good part."

"Oh, this is a double feature," Lync said.

"Nice!" Bradley stepped up beside her and crossed his arms. "I can't wait for the part where you—"

She poked him in the ribs. "Don't say it out loud, you dork."

They both laughed behind the others as they focused on the video playing out in front of them. It started out with Lync floating in her goo-filled Nyílak fighter, staring at a tiny robotic probe surrounded by numerous teardrop shuttles.

After a few minutes of Shauna's well-edited video and several awkward glances, the holo-display went dark, and they all turned around. Everyone except Bradley. At one point, Zachary thought his brother was going to collapse, but Shauna was there to help him.

"He... he wasn't... dead." His words were both a question and a realization.

"No! He was definitely dead." Lync stepped in front of him. "That was not your friend in that rubble. That was... someone else."

"But..." He shook his head and looked down. "He still could've been—"

She reached out and rested her hands on his shoulders, bending down to look up at him. "You can't think like that. Dwight was dead before he even came out of that gas. Whatever they did to him, your friend was long gone. You can't forget that."

He nodded. "I... I know."

Zachary needed to change the topic. "He almost told you about the Rift. I mean, why kill him?"

"Why kill him?" Her voice trembled, and when she looked up at him, her eyes were glaring with an intensity he'd never seen before. "Are you fraking kidding me?"

He swallowed hard. To him, the question was fair. "You

obviously had the upper hand. Especially considering he was pinned down. He clearly wasn't going anywhere. Plus, he knew things. Important things."

"But she didn't know that then," Ibu stepped up beside Lync. "You're confusing the questions we're facing here with her situation at that moment. Every second she let that man survive, she risked him regaining the upper hand." They reached over and grasped Lync's hand. "I would've done the same thing. He needed to die."

"I..." he shook his head. "I wasn't saying he needed to live. Just that—"

"It's done!" Bradley screamed. "Can we move on? Please?"

Zachary stared at his brother and nodded slowly. The tension in the room was thick, and while he thought Lync made the wrong call, he didn't want to keep pressing them. Especially Bradley. The deed was done, and Dwight was dead.

"So, the Shu." He turned back to the holo-display and brought up the graphic Bradley shared earlier. "I take it we're stuffing these in the Cornucopia then. Can we trust them?"

Lync stepped up beside him with her arms crossed. "The robots are taking them through their paces back in the Henosi system as we speak. So far, so good. They sure do pack quite a punch."

He shivered at the memory of what the moonlets had almost done to them on the Fountainhead. "Oh, I know. Trust me." He gestured toward the display and zoomed in on the blueprint, glancing at his brother. "Talk to me about how you got these threads to work."

32

JOYCE GREEN
EN ROUTE TO NURSERY

She closed her eyes as another bead of blue creepy crawlies marched over her skin. It'd been the third jump in as many minutes, and if they were following protocol, they'd wait on the other side of this transition to sync up with the other ships. Plus, they needed time to fold and unfold the massive circular gates after the Ursis passed through.

The fleet had split into three dozen different groups of ships, and they couldn't afford to lose track of one another. Not with the treacherous star systems they were weaving around. Leaving people behind in an unknown region of space was not an option. Plus, if anyone ventured too far off the beaten path, they were bound to run into a Galactic Alliance species. It'd be just their luck that the aliens would be in possession of a Beacon of Therion and use it to signal ahead to the others, especially with so many of the ancient devices unaccounted for these days.

Joyce guided her droplet fighter into the formation along with the other humans. This had been the fifth match in the past hour, and her flight team was getting their asses kicked around every corner. She couldn't tell if they were giving up, or if they were growing tired of the never-ending gate transitions. She knew she was. Her entire body was in a constant state of itch, especially the back of her neck.

She sighed, reached up to rub the collar of her jumpsuit, but her hand stopped short, and instead ran her fingers through her hair. It was as if an unknown force was stopping her. From doing what, she wasn't sure.

Just as she was about to try and rub it again, a surge of nausea welled up from within, and a ripple of blue washed over her. "So much for waiting on the others," she muttered, and her entire body shuddered.

Once the torturous ripple passed, she glanced around and studied the virtual cockpit. She'd been doing something, but for some reason, she couldn't put her finger on what it was.

And then she remembered. She was getting frustrated and antsy. They'd been hopping for over a week and were nearly halfway toward their destination.

The Nursery.

While she hated the name, the others aboard the ship had grown quite fond of it. In the memes making their way through the ranks, they'd rendered countless Galactic Alliance aliens in their baby forms. While the comics depicted most of them covered in blood, not all of them were. A few were illustrated as screaming and hollering versions of their adult forms, and once the human and Ursis fleet arrived, they shat themselves.

She'd never been fond of potty humor, but that didn't mean it wasn't good for morale. These Gunders weren't exactly highbrow, and she couldn't blame them for acting juvenile. They'd lived most of their lives in squalor, kilometers underground on Earth. It wasn't until Hera rescued them from their tunnels that they found their purpose in the universe.

To fill in for the missing Ulixi.

Well, no one would tell them that to their faces, but that was what they were all thinking. All the non-Gunders and Ursis, that is.

An image of Grifdar appeared in the corner of her retinal comm. He was one of the pilots on the opposing Ursis flight team. "Are you sure you're up for another match? I mean, what's the point of dying a fifth time? Even a slidu only has four lives." He tilted his head back, and the sound of multiple Ursis laughs echoed through the sea of training pods.

Joyce squirmed in her seat and did her best to control her emotions. She was supposed to be preparing her team for battle, not picking a fight with the teddy bears. But with a squad as ill-prepared as hers, sometimes a good old-fashioned squabble was what it took to get them motivated.

"If you want to forfeit this round, it's fine by me." She smirked. "Maybe your momma raised a quitter, but mine didn't."

Grifdar froze and her Gunder team chuckled. Several "oohs" could be heard from neighboring pods.

A moment later, something crashed in the distance, and then Grifdar screamed out. "Lest you wish to die, short stack, I suggest you take that back."

Joyce sighed and pulled her pod door aside. "What the frak, Smokey? If you and your people keep breaking these things, we won't have anything to train on."

When he didn't shoot back another barb, she thought he'd perhaps relented and seen the humor in her words. Even though the term "Smokey" was probably unknown to them, it'd been one of the humorous memes making its way through the private channels. While she didn't grok the reference, it was apparently a giant bear from the twentieth century that wore a strange brimmed hat and taught humans not to burn down forests — as if that needed to be learned.

After a few seconds of silence, just as she was about to close her hatch and link back into the sim, the sound of paws scrambling toward her suggested he'd taken it the other way.

"Son of a…" She reached up, grabbed the sides of the pod, and yanked herself out, hopping sideways into the alley of pods to get a bead on her attacker.

Grifdar was at the end of the training room, charging toward her. His eyes were filled with rage, and his teeth glistened white in the glare of the overhead lights. While she hoped he was merely intending to scare her, the echoing thump of his paws told her he wasn't slowing down.

She glanced left and right. Her pod mates were already scrambling clear.

"Now that's teamwork," she muttered under her breath.

Glancing over her shoulder toward Grifdar, she saw he was nearly on top of her.

"Frak." She dove to the right and skidded to a stop with her back against a pod. Then she turned and slid up to the edge of the pod, careful not to drift into the aisle.

Instead of running, she turned her ear skyward and listened, hoping to hear the beat of his feet. She figured he'd react to her change in position, and the fool did just as she'd hoped. He paused his gallop when he saw her dive and hopped up and onto a nearby pod, trying to cut her off and pounce on her from above.

She waited a few more seconds as the crunch of the pods between them gave way under his massive strides. After she heard his grumble from the fall, she sprinted forward, putting a few meters between her and where he landed.

When she heard him clamber out of the debris, she slid to a stop and spun around, subvocalizing a command to bring up her hand-to-hand tactical display. An overlay sprang to life in front of her, marking anyone nearby, human or Ursis. Above each outline, their breathing, motion, and body temperature were displayed. Judging by his heart rate and the infrared pumping off his furry form, he was one pissed off Ursis.

"We should talk about this," she said, glancing left and right. She didn't have many options to dodge from where she was standing.

It was only when he spun around to face her that she realized he hadn't known she was behind him.

"Dumb," she muttered. She should've kept going.

"Sure," he growled, "offer up peace and then call me names. That's very Friop of you." He straightened up, unfurling his body to its three-meter tall height. Then, out of the blue, he swung his hand to the right and slammed it against the pod, sending it careening sideways.

After it stopped sliding, a voice cried out from inside. Apparently, the pilot had been hiding out in there, hoping it would be safer to stay put. He wasn't the only one who'd guessed wrong today.

"I wasn't calling you a name." She glanced left just in time to catch a blur moving the other way. The other Ursis were coming about to surround her. "I was talking about myself. I was the dumb one." She looked back at him. "I'm sorry for pushing your buttons."

He licked his lips and smiled. "You're about to be a whole lot sorrier."

She sidestepped and scanned the area behind him with her comm, hoping for something, anything, that could help her. "We don't need to do this, Grifdar."

"You might not, but I do." He dropped back down onto all fours and rocked side to side on his paws.

Based on the readout on her comm, she would be surrounded in a few seconds. If she had any hope of getting out of this, she needed to act now. And there was only one thing she could do that he couldn't.

She leaned forward and charged toward him, pushing off with everything her mechanical legs could muster. The energy readouts from her power plants went haywire as she pushed the artificial limbs to their limits.

While Grifdar hadn't expected her to attack first, he didn't disappoint. He surged forth and launched himself in her direction.

There wasn't much ground to cover, but just as they were about to collide, he opened his mouth and brought his hands upward in an attempt to prevent her from rotating and dodging around him. But instead, she did something even she wasn't expecting.

She leapt up with everything she had and leaned back, swinging her foot forward. If she was off, she'd helicopter into his razor-sharp teeth.

But she wasn't.

Her foot cracked across his face, splitting open his cheek and spraying blood everywhere. The force of the blow spun his torso on its axis and his body continued on its new path like a bullet ricocheting off course. He careened out of control to her left, sending his hulking form crashing into one of the pods.

Joyce, on the other hand, continued forward and rotated around, landing on one knee. When she looked up, his crumpled form was spasming in the crushed remains of the virtual training device. While she had no idea how she'd done that, she knew one thing.

She loved these damn legs.

But more than that, she needed to make a scene and get this fraking Ursis' attention. She jumped up and closed the distance between them.

As she clambered up the pile of rubble, she paused and kicked loose a heavy conduit pipe he'd broken off in his fall. She then climbed up and onto his chest, bringing the sharp end of the pipe against his neck, and pushed down.

His eyes sprang open, and his claws came out.

"Move another centimeter, and you'll be using this pipe as a trach tube." She smiled and shoved the conduit down even harder against his neck until his throat started to gurgle. A second later, her comm confirmed she'd pinched his airway.

He winced and stopped, slowly lowering his hands back to the ground.

"That's what I thought." Her tactical display chirped, and she glanced up in time to see the approaching Ursis come into view. The same one she'd seen coming around on her earlier. "That means you too."

They froze and looked over at Grifdar's fallen form. Suddenly, her comm lit up. They were broadcasting something to each other, but she wasn't sure what.

A few seconds later, she found out.

"Kill him," the Ursis standing in front of her said.

Joyce recoiled. "Excuse me?"

"You heard him!" another Ursis to her right bellowed. "Kill him! He is yours for the taking."

When she glanced over at the voice, they were glaring at Grifdar with a contempt that could melt the polar caps of Europa. Like they'd kill him themselves if they could.

As she looked from alien face to alien face, one thing was abundantly clear. The Ursis were animals, and they were no different than the Galactic Alliance, or hell, most humans she'd ever met. If she killed him like his people demanded, then she was as bad as they were. And worst of all, she'd be no better than the aliens who'd killed her son.

Joyce shook her head. She wouldn't let them win like that. Not this time. Not again. She'd lost control of herself with the Thyreus they called Two. He'd gotten the better of her back then. But this time, she was a different person.

She pulled the pipe away from Grifdar's throat and stepped backward, tossing it aside and easing down off the chest of the mountainous beast. All the while, a voice was whispering to her in the back of her mind, telling her to kill him. To end him. But she didn't listen. She knew that voice. Even though its words were unfamiliar, she'd heard it dozens of times before. It was the voice of rage, and she wasn't fraking listening.

Grifdar reached over and snatched the pipe out of her hand, pressing it up to his throat. His paw was trembling as he leaned back and held it in place. "You've already won. I've lost their respect. You must kill me to save face. To save my honor."

"Frak you!" She leaned forward, yanked the pipe out of his hands, and tossed it down the aisle behind him. "And frak your honor." She whirled around to face the Ursis, the one who'd told her to kill him. "You need to save your venom and anger for the GA."

"Fear is for the weak," the Ursis muttered, spitting sideways into a pile of rubble.

She sneered and glanced at Grifdar; his face was etched in

agony. Then, without hesitation, she lunged at the other Ursis, closing the gap between them in the blink of an eye.

Her actions, like those before, had been unexpected. Before she even reached his side, he stumbled backward onto his backside and crushed one of the human pods underneath his weight. But she didn't finish her attack. Instead, she slid up short and started laughing out loud, her voice echoing through the silent chamber. When she stopped, she pointed at him. "If fear is for the weak, then what does that make you?"

She paused and waited for an answer, but none came. He knew as well as she did that their ideas of honor and esteem were paper thin, especially when they were all facing their end.

"I thought so," she muttered.

As she pivoted to leave, Grifdar clambered up out of the rubble. "We can't end it like this. Someone has to die."

Joyce closed her eyes and sighed. "You know what?" She opened them and turned to face him. "You're right." When he straightened up and exposed his neck to her, she shook her head. "No. Not that way. We're going to die, alright. But not by my hand. What you're failing to see for some strange reason is that most of us are well on our way to death. We'll be gone in a few weeks when we enter the battle. Until then..." She turned and glanced at the other Ursis still lying on the ground. "Until then, we practice. Again and again and again. We make each other stronger, and most of all, we prepare to take as many of those Galactic Alliance bastards with us to our graves as we can. We owe at least as much to our people. To our families back home. Now get the frak up and get your ass into your pod. Now!"

The Ursis scrambled onto his feet, but instead of attacking her, he sprinted back down the hall toward his pod. When she turned around to face Grifdar, he was staring back at her, his gaze filled with as much confusion as the humans surrounding them.

While the voice in her head told her to strike him, she

knew better. "Go!" She pointed across the room. "Get into your pod, soldier!"

He stumbled sideways over the already crushed pod until he found his footing, at which point he raced away. As she watched him go, one of her human pilots walked up beside her.

"Where the hell am I supposed to practice?" He gestured toward the mashed remains of his virtual cockpit.

"You can use mine," she muttered. "Hopefully, they won't kill you in it."

As he turned to go, he paused and glanced back at her. He must've been wondering if she meant in the simulation, or in the pod itself. She smirked and snapped her fingers, pointing him toward her awaiting pod. He took off without hesitation.

"Are you sure you should have let him live?" Hera asked.

Joyce hadn't even heard the woman walk up. But she didn't care, either. She knew why she'd been placed in command of this group of misfits. It was for one, and only one reason. And it wasn't what most of the others thought.

"If you feel like you can do it better yourself, then by all means, President. They're all yours." She didn't turn to meet her gaze. She merely walked away, putting as much distance as possible between her and her commanding officer.

As her heart pounded in her chest, she stormed out of the room toward her quarters. Her neck tingled; she knew Hera was using her. She'd been the only one who'd seen Lync's training up close, but what she didn't know was that the Ulixi were ten times the pilots of these Gunders.

While Joyce was no Lync, she could at least teach them to stay alive long enough to kill a dozen or so aliens before they met their makers. Like them, that remained her only goal in life.

33

BRADLEY OLIVAW
EN ROUTE TO NURSERY

No matter how many times Bradley stared at the answer, he couldn't admit it was true. There had to be another way.

"You know I'm right." Zachary nudged him. "We can't beat her head-on. Not like this."

"Shut up," he muttered, reaching forward to restart the simulation with his new parameters. He had an idea he wanted to try. It was aggressive, but it just might work.

They'd been at it all night, and despite having run thousands of permutations of Harold's battle and colony simulation, the outcome was the same. Hera always won. It didn't matter if they were the ones who killed her clone at the Nursery, or if the GA did. By the time they got back home, she'd invariably returned in full force. And even if the GA prevailed, she still retained power over a small sect of humans. Her clone technology was too pervasive, and with the added unknown of the aliens controlling them, there was no way to beat her.

Zachary studied the parameters Bradley had entered in silence. Maybe it was the severity of his approach, or how ingenious it was. Either way, when Bradley looked back at him, he had a shocked look on his face.

"What?" He stepped backward, slipping down into one of

the chairs beside them, glancing over at his brother's still troubled gaze. "Sometimes we have to take extreme measures to change the course of human history."

"But…" Zachary rubbed his forehead. "That would make us… no better than them."

Bradley tilted his head. "You're kidding me, right? It's one thing to use this technology to end a species. It's quite another to use it in self-defense."

Zachary snickered. "That's a fraking razor-thin difference, bro. You could argue that the GA saw humanity with that exact same lens when they let loose that virus on us. Besides, what makes you so sure you can even deliver it? I mean, they have nanite defenses everywhere. And let's not forget that we don't know where their colony is."

"I never said I had all the answers." Bradley turned back to face the simulation. "I was just testing out the hypothesis. Maybe if we send out some probes, we'd pick up a—"

A star map flashed up on the wall display, and he fell silent. There, in the middle of the screen, was a G-class star very much like Sol. Its designation was HD 117939, and it was nearly one hundred light-years from Earth. When he checked its location, he did a double-take. It wasn't far from Lupus, in the Centaurus constellation.

"What's this?" Zachary looked over at him.

Bradley shrugged. "I thought you shared it." He peered over his shoulder, but there was no one there. "Harold, are you listening in again?"

"It's not Harold." Shauna's voice came from overhead.

They'd talked about giving her control of their ship, especially this version of her. It was a bit more rambunctious than the others. The copy that traveled around with Abigail hadn't wanted super access to the Fountainhead, but this one, the one that joined Lync's team, they jumped at the chance. Not that Lync had ever turned over control of her ship during their voyage. This copy of Shauna claimed she missed being plugged into all the sensors. It only took them jacking into the Shu to realize how muted their understanding of their surroundings was. While he wasn't sure if he'd ever get used to so many copies of Harold and his mother walking around their world, at least they were developing their own personalities.

"Shauna," he gestured toward the star still lingering on the wall, "why are you showing us this?"

Her face appeared in the corner of the display. She'd decided to take on the appearance of her younger self, from back when she first met their father.

"This is HD 117939," Shauna began, "it's located ninety-eight point five light-years from Earth."

He nodded and looked over at Zachary. That was pretty much an ideal Goldilocks star. "Nice," he muttered. "Are we picking out locations for our next vacation, or is there something here we might be interested in?"

She smirked, and then virtually turned to look up at the image. "Well, if we're to believe the data Dwight uploaded into the Shu, this here is the location of Hera's colony."

"Wait!" Zachary hopped up. "This… this is where they've been hiding? Where Hera and Zeus disappeared to."

"Apparently," Shauna zoomed in on the star and brought up a map of the planetary system.

Bradley drew in his breath. "Wholly shit!" He rose out of his chair. "They have two habitable planets around this star?"

"Well, three if you count this moon." Shauna highlighted a lunar planetesimal with a long elliptical orbit around one of the inner gas giants. It was nearly twice the size of Earth's moon, and from the looks of it, there was liquid water on the surface.

He shook his head. They were staring at a fairy tale star system, and the more details he saw, the more confused he became. "How is it we've never detected this star before today?"

"Funny you should ask." Shauna smiled, and a recording appeared in a window on the wall. It looked as though it was taken from Dwight's point of view while he was lying in bed beside Hera.

Dwight laughed out loud and rolled up against her side. "So let me get this straight. You hid a star?"

Hera winked at him and smiled before reaching over and rubbing her hands through the curly brown hair on his chest. "You could say that." She bit her lip. "If any one of those lazy bastards back in Sol bothered to manually point a telescope at us, it'd only be a matter of time before they figured out what they were looking at. But that's not how things work nowadays." She nudged him and then looked up at the ceiling. "Most of our civilized human worlds use computers to control and record their observation sessions, and they see whatever we want them to. For instance, in this system, we'd always present a barren G class star near the end of its life. It's straightforward, really. Especially since Olivaw International and its subsidiaries have been the de facto astronomy software manufacturer for over a century." She nuzzled up against him. "Why the sudden interest in my home world?"

Dwight wrapped an arm around her, tenderly guiding her gaze toward him. He then leaned forward and kissed her before pulling away.

"I just… I want to know… if you'd ever take me there." He ran his hand up and down the curves of her body. "After this is over."

She smiled and rolled back to face him. "You mean after we end the Galactic Alliance, and after you bring me Lync?"

"Of course." He started kissing her neck and worked his way down toward her stomach.

"Yes!" she shouted. "You know I will, my love."

As he disappeared under the sheets, Bradley closed his eyes and groaned. "I've seen enough."

"I'll… take… you… anywhere," Hera moaned.

"Enough!" He turned away, and the screen went black. "I think I'm gonna be sick." He bent forward and rested his hands on his legs.

"Aw, come on." Shauna sighed. "It was just getting to the good part. After he helped her climax, he used the fifth round of intercourse to get her to tell him where she'd placed the clone facilities on her worlds."

"Fifth," Bradley muttered. "The guy must've been augmented."

Zachary shook his head and snickered under his breath. "There's no greater security weakness in the universe than sex."

"Amen to that," Libby said from behind them.

"What the," Zachary spun around toward her, his eyes wide. "Don't you knock?"

She pointed at the screen. "You're standing on the goddamn bridge. It's not like you're in your quarters. Besides," she walked up to the navigation controls and sat down. "I've been monitoring the gate jumps and wanted to chat. I think we need to make a change."

Bradley stood upright and swallowed hard, shoving the bile back down. "Probably more than you can imagine."

"Say what now?" She spun her chair to face them, and when Shauna minimized the sex video, her eyes fixed on the screen. It didn't take her nearly as long as them to understand what she was looking at. "The bitch was working in the margins. I should've fraking seen it."

He knew instantly what she meant. It'd been Libby's job to rewrite history and tweak the reality in Sol, but she hadn't anticipated she wasn't the only one doing it.

Zachary turned to look at him. "I think you should go."

His eyes went wide, and he stepped backward. "Excuse me?"

"You heard me." Zachary took a deep breath and pointed up at the wall. "You should bring Pluto and the gals, and go take out Hera. Hell, you've already got the start of a solid plan." He brought Bradley's simulation forward.

When he looked up at the display, he realized it'd finished. His idea had worked. Well, at least according to Harold's simulation. And while it wasn't perfect, it worked when the GA used it in Epsilon Eridani.

"You're planning to wipe them out." Libby stood up and

walked up beside him. "And you're using the virus from Liprosus." She glanced over at him and then at the wall.

He reached up and rubbed the back of his neck. "It was just a—"

"It's ingenious," she muttered, gesturing toward the screen, bringing up some other documents of her own. "Especially since the aliens all have the same genetic markers." She highlighted a gene sequence in one of the files.

While he had no idea what he was looking at, he assumed she did. "And this will let us pinpoint them? The clones?"

She tilted her head from side to side. "And a fraction of a fraction of a percent of humans."

"How many is a fraction of a fraction?" Zachary asked.

"Less than a million, from my last estimate." She brought up a chart of the reported population data from Sol, Epsilon Eridani, and Zeta Lupi.

"But that's only if we let it run rampant, right?" Bradley looked over at her. "We can program it to stop working if we use nanites. Can't we?"

Libby stared at the screen for a minute before she began gesturing silently in the air. She was searching for something. Watching her work was awe-inspiring. It was like witnessing the perfect human-computer interface come to life, a skill she'd perfected over years of overseeing the Olivaw data banks at the Wheel.

When she stopped, she slowly shook her head. "We can't risk holding it back. Not for a few decades."

His heart sank. "But why?"

"Because she's ten steps ahead of us." Zachary stared up at the screen. While he may not be able to control computers like her, if anyone could keep up with what she was searching for, it was him.

It took Bradley a minute to catch up, but it finally hit him what they meant. Hera had already sent the aliens and clones back to Sol for their recruiting efforts, and to weed out the last remnants of Harold.

He stepped backward and collapsed into the chair as the

implications of his plan sank in. In order to save humanity, they'd need to kill millions. And not just clones, either. They'd lose innocent lives in the process. People who'd done nothing more than inherit a certain gene sequence.

"I can't do it." He forced down the lump in his throat. "We have to find another way."

"There's no other option, bro." Zachary stepped up beside him and rested his hand on his shoulder. "Not in such a short time period. You see that, right?"

He stared at the screen, at what Libby had found. Even though they knew the genetic sequence of the alien parasite, the problem was with the clones. She'd circled the findings from Harold's scans. The clones had a highly manipulated strain of DNA, which was designed to make these humans more obedient. From what Harold discovered, the aliens could adapt to almost any human host, but the weaker their will, the easier the job. Their changes essentially made this custom branch of humans programmable.

His brother was right. This was their only way out, and while it wasn't the high road, it was better than no road. The Olivaw family had already torched every possible bridge they had to get back into humanity's good graces, first with their lies, and now with Hera's failings. The least they could do was try to keep humanity's ship from sinking even deeper. If they didn't, their species would be turned into nothing more than glorified automata to these parasites.

"Alright." He ran his sweaty hands up and down his pants and peered over at Libby. "How do we make this happen?"

"That's the easy part." Libby chuckled and started working again. "If your brother is intent on staying here to fight, then the hard part is going to be getting Pluto to leave her man behind."

When he looked over and locked his gaze on Zachary, he could tell she'd struck a chord. He wasn't staring at the wall screen so much as through it. He knew as well as she did that Pluto wouldn't take this sitting down. At least not willfully.

"I'm not leaving." Zachary crossed his arms. "Not until I see this through. Bradley can handle that leg of the mission. I trust him."

Bradley nodded. "Thanks. Though I may need some help in tying your woman down."

Libby cleared her throat, and they both turned to look at her.

"I might already have a solution for how we pull that off." She glanced over at them and smiled. "And it won't even require using rope. I mean, it's sorta why I came up here in the first place. I just didn't realize it'd kill two birds with one stone."

"That sounds ominous." Bradley stood up and walked over beside her.

Zachary stared at the wall screen. "I... need her to get to safety. That's all I want."

Bradley glanced back at him. "I got her, bro. I do. You focus on finding Abigail."

When he reached out and nudged Z's shoulder, he closed his eyes and stared down at the ground. While he didn't say it out loud, Bradley knew that was one of the other reasons his brother didn't want to leave. He felt like he'd let her down. First in Sol, then in Zeta Lupi. And if he knew Zachary, he wasn't about to do it again.

"But before we can do anything," Bradley looked back at Libby and smiled, "we have to figure out what riddle our librarian is hiding. Whatcha got, Libs?"

She smirked and nodded. "First things first." She gestured in the air and started working feverishly. "We need to get the fleet's cryo-pods powered up."

"The cryo-pods?" Zachary shook off his daze and stepped up to her other side. "Why the heck would we need those?"

"Because at this rate, we won't reach the Nursery in time." She brought up a set of jump projections, but they weren't theirs. She'd been trying to figure out when Hera and the Ursis left for the battle.

Bradley scanned over the data. If she was right, Hera was

set to arrive three to four days before them. "How'd we miss this?"

"We didn't know when she left until recently." Libby brought up a new gate plan on the wall screen. It showed them arriving before the other fleets.

"So..." Zachary rubbed his chin. "What... we force everyone into cryo-stasis and then we rapid jump? That means we won't have any time to prepare alongside the robots. I mean, those few weeks of training—"

"Won't be worth shit if we miss the battle," Libby interrupted. "There's no other way we make it unless you can somehow get Hera to slow down."

Zachary shook his head. They all knew that wasn't happening. Once her fleet left, it was nearly impossible to intercept them, even if they could figure out the path they were taking.

She nodded. "So it's settled then." She adjusted the jumps to split off a chunk of their fleet and redirected it toward HD 117939. "All I have to do now is get Bradley some help."

Bradley highlighted the remaining ships along with the Cornucopia. "That's going to spread Z a tad thin. Can we still pull it off without these forces?"

Zachary chuckled. "You mean the impossible feat of finding a Beacon-sized needle in a haystack of Selene moon ships? And all while being attacked by the largest alien fleet ever assembled."

"Don't forget about Hera." Libby smirked and highlighted her fleet outside the Nursery. "She and the Ursis will probably be shooting at you, too."

Zachary looked over at her, clearly at a loss for her sense of humor.

Bradley lowered his head. "And then you still have to figure out how to use the Beacon to seal the Rift?" He glanced over at his brother. "So you're good then?"

"I'm great." Zachary smiled and returned his attention to the ships Libby had assigned to Bradley. He zoomed in and scanned over the details, his eyes lingering on the ship that contained Pluto. Judging by the names in the roster, it appeared she included a few Ulixi. "Is Lync going to approve this?"

Libby dipped her head. "I'm sure she'll come around once we explain why. Besides, your brother needs Adri for his plan."

Bradley swallowed hard. "Wait, we're telling Lync? I thought we weren't telling anyone."

"No." Libby turned to face him. "We don't make executive decisions anymore. We'll need to run this past Lync, Crayo, and Ryder. I'm sure they can keep quiet until we get certain people into the cryo-pods."

"Let's hope so," Zachary muttered. "Otherwise, we'll have an uprising on our hands."

As a wave of blue ants passed over him, Bradley stared at HD 117939. Unlike with the Nursery, they had no idea what they were walking into at that star. For all they knew, Hera had a fleet waiting there to take over the human civilized worlds.

Libby must've noticed his gaze. She reached out and rested her hand on his shoulder. "Don't worry." She tilted her head toward the clone colony. "I've already asked Shauna to send on a few probes to scope out the system. We should have the intel back by the time you come out of stasis."

"Thanks," he muttered.

They'd need all the lead time they could get. Hopefully, if a copy of Harold or Shauna came along, they'd be able to put together a plan before they woke up. If not, they'd have to improvise one pretty damn fast.

34

IBU

EN ROUTE TO NURSERY

The Zhen blades hadn't changed in nearly a week, not since they were back on the planet of Devid. As Ibu turned over the mysterious weapon, they couldn't help but wonder if they'd somehow been manipulated. The artifacts had altered their perception of reality on multiple occasions over the past few months.

They had found the blades on Griseo, deep in the Proto Dark Nebula. That was the same place they met the Entity, the same ancient alien they've been fighting against since their discovery.

As they stared at the explosion etched on the ultra-thin blades, their mind drifted to earlier that day when they said goodbye to Pluto. While she didn't know she was being forced to leave the front lines, Ibu couldn't blame Zachary. It wasn't his decision alone; the leadership of this arm of humanity had made the call together. Though, it was Zachary who sent his wife away to protect their unborn child.

They straightened up and sheathed the blades, forcing down the conflicting human emotions lingering in their chest. Deep down, they knew that if they'd been forced into making the decision, they would've reached the same outcome. But then again, Nanil didn't have another partner to think about. They only had themselves and their clonos.

"Are you still worried about those things?" Lync tilted her head toward the blades.

She'd been so quiet, they'd forgotten she was even standing there. They'd been working together on their strategies for the better part of the day. With their clock ticking before they entered cryo-sleep, they weren't exactly flush with opportunities to plan their course of attack.

"The blades are fine." Ibu stiffened and glanced at the wall screen. "I'll probably leave them behind when we suit up."

Lync went to speak and then stopped, returning her attention to the display.

"What is it?" Ibu asked. "You were about to say something."

She shook her head. "It's not important."

"Say it, please." Ibu reached out and brushed her arm. "I can't handle how you humans hold back on everything. You're always so afraid the other person is delicate. Well, I'm not."

Lync smirked. "I love working with you. You're a breath of fresh air."

They bobbed their head. "Thank you. Now spit it out already."

"I think you're stupid if you leave them behind." Lync raised her hand toward them. "Before you say anything, hear me out."

"I'm all ears," they muttered and crossed their arms.

She nodded. "Ever since you found those things, they've helped you."

"But have they?" Ibu squeezed their hands and stared downward. They could feel the phantom reminder of the weapons in their hands. Their perfect balance and weight screamed to be swung. Each slice, each death ingrained in their mind forever. "I took so many lives with them."

"But you saved countless more." Lync turned to face them. "Without them, you wouldn't have found the path to Abigail on Griseo, and you certainly wouldn't have saved her on Arctordiea. And don't even get me started on Devid. Your fellow Prima clonos would have torn you to shreds without those things."

"But what about the messages?" They reached up and unsheathed both of the blades and held them out for her to see.

"Well," she swallowed hard, "before this change they went through, they were a reminder of your accomplishments. Of everything that made you, you. Of your successes and your failures. This," she gestured at the weapons, "this is probably more of the same."

"But what about the false vision they etched? The one showing us standing in front of my Nanil people. With me as their leader." Their hands started shaking. "What do you make of that?"

Lync looked up at them. "What matters more is what you do with it, not what it says. Our future is our own. It's not prescribed or predetermined. I see this image as a warning more than anything. And if you think about it, we might not be here if it hadn't come when it did."

"What do you mean?" Ibu asked.

"If your blades hadn't shown you that etching of you leading your people, would you have waited in the tunnel for us to arrive?" Lync raised her eyebrows.

"I... think so." They stared down at the blades, their edges shimmering in the overhead light. "I wasn't exactly in a position to do much else."

Lync eased back and glared at them. "You're telling me you wouldn't have tried to kill the other clonos if you hadn't seen the etchings?"

"To be honest..." Ibu gazed into the distance. Their rage and satisfaction in the seconds following the killing of their progenitor were the strongest they'd ever felt. They knew they would have kept going if it weren't for the blades.

"I thought so," Lync began. "And let's not forget what happened when the blade showed us this." She pointed at the scene. "The Olivaw brothers went nuts. Would Bradley have studied these pictures so intently had you not shared them?

We wouldn't have had that conversation about the Shaygai and the Rift, and definitely not like that. I mean, for all we know, we would still be back in Lupus trying to figure out our next step if it weren't for these blades." She stared down at them.

They hadn't thought about it that way. Certainly, if the Entity were manipulating them through this weapon, having them out of the picture would be easier than bringing them to the battlefront. They would've been better off leaving the last etching in place. Maybe then they wouldn't have come along.

"You're right." They reached back and laid the blades on the table behind them, then returned their attention to the display.

"That's it?" Lync looked down at the weapons. "We're done talking about them?"

They nodded. "We are. You made a logical inference that makes more sense than my alternative. I see no point in continuing my mental spiral any longer." They pointed at the wall. "Now talk to me about this plan."

Lync shook her head and chuckled. "Like I said, a breath of fresh air."

Ibu smirked and focused on the tactical display. "The Ulixi will need to be pretty damn close to the Selene ships to get an accurate view of their insides."

"Yeah, that's what makes it so difficult." Lync hit play on her controls. "We won't know the exact configuration of their ships until after we arrive. Once we do, if we segment the battlefield into chunks, we should be able to narrow down the most obvious candidates to house a Beacon."

They narrowed their gaze. "The Galactic Alliance will protect it at all costs."

Lync raised a finger and pointed toward the midpoint of a cluster. "They'll want to use it to control the most aliens. From what the archives said, the Therionic radiance from these ships can be felt at great distances."

"Wait," Ibu tilted their head. "Shouldn't you and the Ulixi be able to detect it then?"

She shrugged. "Possibly. It depends on if they seal it up. The moment we attack, we have to assume they'll secure it. Which means they'll shut any external skotádi shielding to hide it. It's what I would do."

They reached forward and tweaked her plan, adjusting the initial wave of gate jumps. If Lync was right, the more they spread out on their first strike, the better. When they were done, they stepped back and hit play.

"Nice," Lync muttered. "That should give us the best chance of early detection. We might even be able to do some rapid hops if there's room."

Ibu glanced over at her. "Will our ships be capable of gating?"

"A few of the critical ones should. Plus, we'll have some droplets." Lync tapped the display and highlighted the fighters from Zachary's original design. There weren't as many of those as the new Nyílaks, but there were a few left in the ranks. While they packed one hell of a punch when it came to firepower, their dogfighting skills were weak.

They stared at the edge of the display, near where Hera's Ursis and human fleets were positioned. The attack patterns were the same as the ones they'd used during the Beacon battle, except the ships were larger and the gates they passed through were as well. They were banking on the fact that the GA couldn't have transmitted intel on their strategy back to the Nursery. Not with their limited FTL travel speeds, and not without a Beacon.

As the jumps played out, they hit pause on the simulation when they saw it: a small contingent of Ulixi gated next to Hera's command ship.

"And we're sure the Beacon will be in there?" Ibu turned toward her.

Lync nodded. "They're banking on the same aura effect the GA are. It'll make their people stronger."

"All it'll do is even out the playing field," they said.

She swallowed hard. "Better to make it even than tilted in the GA's favor."

"Fair enough." They tapped play and zoomed in on the command ship, watching Lync's simulation play out.

A small force of Ulixi and robots was boarding, and they were searching for something. Or, in this case, someone and something. They were looking for the Beacon as much as for Abigail. Both of them had promised her they'd protect her from the Entity.

And both of them had failed.

They forced down the lump in their throat as the simulation flashed green. The fictional team had found her. "What do we do if she won't come willingly? Or if the Entity fights back?"

Lync didn't reply. She simply pointed toward the corner of the room.

When Ibu looked in the direction she'd gestured, they paused. There, in a pile on the floor, were two black sacks, probably coated in skotádi. One for Abigail, and another for the Entity. They were just like the ones Harold had used to snatch Abigail from the clutches of the GA onboard their tribunal ship, except these weren't intended for gating. They were designed to cut her off from the Entity.

Ibu stepped around her and bent down, lifting the box resting on top of the sacks. "What's this?" They cracked the top open and peered at the contents.

Inside were two small vials of cloudy orange and yellow fluid, along with two injector contraptions the size of their palm. They reminded them of miniature lava lamps. The liquids weren't completely mixed so much as they were congealed into separate blobs within the cylinders.

"What is this stuff?" They picked up one of the vials and turned it over, watching as the orange globs swirled through the yellow like a microscopic storm in a bottle.

"I'd be careful with that." Lync stepped up beside them and eased their hand holding the vial back down into the case. "Little Red said that it'll render even the largest alien catatonic. Not dead, just not really functioning either. And he seemed to imply they might not come out of it, either."

They bit their lip as their mind reeled at the thought of shooting Abigail up with the vile-looking substance. The possibility that their friend wouldn't awaken gnawed at their conscience.

"Let's hope we don't have to use it." They set the vial into its awaiting receptacle and closed the container. While they had no idea how strong the Entity was, they could only hope it would be enough to put down. Assuming they even found Abigail, that is.

Lync tapped them on the shoulder. "We should head over to the cryo-pods. I just got a comm from Shauna. Most of the others are already down for a nap." She pointed toward the wall screen. "This should be plenty for her and Harold to work their magic while we're under."

They scanned the plan laid out on the wall screen one last time. There were an infinite number of possible routes they could take to find the Beacon among the fleet of GA moon ships, and the funny thing was, their biggest challenge wouldn't be finding it. It would be figuring out if it even helped.

35

ABIGAIL OLIVAW
EN ROUTE TO NURSERY, INSIDE THE BEACON

Her head throbbed the closer she got to the glowing tear in space-time. This was the sixth time Abigail had experienced a vision of the strange astronomical phenomenon. It seemed as though either the Entity was punishing her, or it was getting hurt. Those were the only reasons she could think of for why she kept falling into her dream state.

After the third out-of-body experience, she decided to get off her ass and poke around the Nebula. If they were going to make her relive her death like Groundhog Day, the least she could do was check out the sights.

On her fifth visit to humanity's end, she caught sight of the gaping hole in space. It was deep in the center of the nebulosity and was guarded by thousands of Selene moon ships. While she wasn't sure what the Rift was, the sheer number of guardians spoke volumes.

As she eased closer to the anomaly, she noticed a stream of ships moving into and out of the void. The unusual crafts were like tiny glass silhouettes floating between the Rift and the awaiting line of Selene ships. When they left the moons, they were nearly transparent, but upon their return, they were inky black, filled to the gills with some type of gaseous material. She'd seen similar flight patterns back in Sol, but those were crude human mining facilities. Certainly, this had to be something greater than that.

But the closer she got to the gash, the more she realized that was exactly what they were doing. The ovoid, crystalline alien ships eased their front side up to the opening and then into it, leaving their tail end out of the tear. Then, their exterior hull started to glow bright white. It was the strangest sight she'd ever set eyes on, and it reminded her of some type of healing device a doctor might stick inside a wound. But this was far from that.

While she watched the metamorphosis unfold, her attention was drawn to the swirling gas filling the transparent enclosure. Its motion was eerily familiar, like she'd seen it somewhere before.

And then it hit her.

She'd always assumed the billowing dark nebulosity that belched from the insides of Selene ships had been from processing the raw material in each star system. But what if it wasn't? What if they were mining it here, from the other side of this fracture?

If true, that meant they could stop it. All she had to do was figure out where this gash in space-time led, or better yet, how to close it. Since the GA ships were nearby, she might even be able to get the aliens inside the Beacon to tell her more about it.

Her body trembled as the harrowing symphony of alien and human cries in the distance reached a crescendo. She resisted the call to plug her ears and instead extended her trembling hand toward the surface of the Rift near one of the crystal ships. When her fingers passed through, an inexplicable warmth radiated from within. At first, it enveloped her fingertips, but it quickly spread throughout her entire being and ignited her soul.

The more of her body that slipped through the opening, the more she wondered if the tear was an illusory barrier and not a rip in space-time at all. Perhaps it was a new weapon developed by the GA to conceal their hidden secret on the far side.

When her head floated through the opening and she finally gazed upon what lay beyond, she froze with wide eyes. The majestic scene before her was utterly transcendent, and the staggering beauty of the ethereal vision both robbed her of breath and words to describe it. The longer her gaze lingered, the more an irresistible longing swelled within her, urging her to cross the threshold and embrace the unknown.

But just as she leaned forward, the celestial vision faded away, and she found herself floating once more inside the Beacon. She awoke to the glare of hundreds of alien souls surrounding her on all sides. While at first she didn't know where she was, when her vision cleared enough to make sense of her surroundings, she saw the wall of bright orange and purple lights closing in on her.

And then she realized why.

She was glowing blue from head to toe. A human swimming in a sea of aliens dead set on one and only one thing.

Extinguishing her life flame.

Abigail closed her eyes and did her best not to freak out. She started by counting down from ten to zero, taking one deep breath at a time. Just like Lync had taught her.

She could hear the voices around her moving in.

"Don't spook it," an alien voice said.

"Do we know how it appeared in here?" another alien asked.

"Minds in chaotic states can sometimes hop around Beacon space," the first alien replied.

"I thought all the humans were dead," a third voice interjected.

"Are we sure it's actually human?" the second alien asked. "I heard the Nanil can appear blue, especially when they're emotional."

"That would explain why they're so weak," the first alien noted.

"Quiet yourself," the second alien whispered. "Let's not

send it skittering to tell the Prima our secrets before we can end it."

Abigail centered herself and struggled to clear her mind. She shoved the approaching voices into a corner, and her thoughts immediately drifted to her family. While she didn't know if they were still alive, she hoped with every ounce of her being that they were.

If they were smart, they were already running far from Hera and the GA. They had everything they needed to start over somewhere new. All they had to do was forget about her, a feat that shouldn't be too hard considering how she'd failed them. First with the GA tribunal, then with Minula's death, and now with the Therionic Entity. She wasn't exactly mastering life.

With her thoughts spiraling deeper and deeper into a morass, the aliens pounced. Her body screamed out, except this time it wasn't because the Entity was in danger. It was because her soul was being torn apart.

Her agony sent ripples of light outward in all directions. She willed herself to disconnect from the Beacon, but no matter how hard she tried, she couldn't get out. The Entity had sapped too much of her strength. It was in control now, not her. And as far as she knew, it was still curled up in pain after her last vision.

"What the hell is that?" one of the voices screamed.

She opened her eyes in time to see several dozen green prasinus sparks shoot down from above. They darted and dashed through the collection of Trochilidae and Thyreusian souls, distracting them from their real purpose. While they were screeching and weaving about, a twinkling prasinus eased up and whispered at her.

"Come, ease closer to me and follow my lead." The green light moved toward her and, rather than fighting it, she leaned in. She didn't have much energy left, especially after the aliens had ripped her open.

When their two lights combined, they formed a sort of cyan spark. A second later, a tug pulled at her mind, and she went with it. The tendrils of consciousness moved fast and yanked her downward, spiraling between the still chaotic purpureus and aurantiaco life forces.

They were flying through the layers of lights at impossible speeds, and watching it move reminded her of the Entity. She'd seen these curious lights floating around Beacon space over the past few weeks as she nudged and whispered in various species' ears. It was odd that they were always alone, and never once had she heard them say anything.

She figured they were outcast species onboard the Galactic Alliance starships. It just never occurred to her to befriend them. But for some reason, they came to her aid.

The further they dove, the faster they got, and the colder the Beacon space became. She'd only ventured this way once before, and that hadn't ended well. The deranged sparks she ran into down in the depths had long ago lost their minds, and hanging out there meant playing with fire.

Just when she thought the prasinus wouldn't stop descending, they screeched to a halt. And then, without saying a word, they separated from her.

"Thank you," she muttered as she glanced upward. There didn't appear to be any other lights moving toward them. In fact, when she narrowed her gaze, she couldn't even make out the cloud of Thyreusian or Trochilidae she'd fallen through.

When she returned her attention to her savior, she froze.

"What the hell?" She spiraled around again and again, searching for the light.

They were gone.

They'd saved her and then disappeared.

But when she stopped spinning, she saw it. There, far off in the distance, was the beautiful green glowing tail of her protector. They were barreling away from her like a meteor burning through the atmosphere. Their spark grew fainter and fainter the further they got.

"Thank you!" she shouted and then glanced around,

suddenly feeling naked and exposed down in the sewer of Beacon space.

She closed her eyes and started her focusing routine again. This time, it was far easier to extinguish her glowing blue flame without the concern of being attacked. In a matter of seconds, her light disappeared, and once again, she was safe to move about.

As she pondered what to do next, her thoughts converged on one thing. The gash in space-time she'd seen in her vision. She needed to know what it was, and more importantly, how to close it.

36

ZACHARY OLIVAW
EN ROUTE TO NURSERY

It had been a week, but it felt like only a few minutes since Pluto and the others had parted ways. Zachary reached up and ran his fingers over his lips. He could still taste the lingering effects of her lips pressing on his. They'd said goodbye in a rush, and he watched as Little Red closed the lid on her, all while he climbed into his own cryo-pod.

With the haze of cryogenic sleep still tugging at his thoughts, he barely felt a hand brush his shoulder. When he looked to his right, Ibu's face was staring back at him.

"Is everything ok?" he asked.

They nodded. "Everything's fine. We... have a change in plans, and time is paramount. But I had to do it in person. I owed you as much after all you've done for me."

"That doesn't sound good." He reached to the side of his pod to push up, but Ibu stopped him.

"You can't." They lowered their hand and tapped a few buttons on the control panel. "Like I said, there's no time."

He sank back down and rubbed his eyes. "What is it? What's going on?"

"Lync and I..." Ibu stared down at their hands and paused. "We have a plan. We need to—"

"Find Abigail," he interrupted.

Their eyes went wide. "You knew?"

He shook his head. "No, but I know you and her are pretty close, and if anyone needs saving, it's her." He leaned forward and coughed into his hand as the cryo-stasis gases tickled his throat. "Does that mean we're on our own to find the Beacons?"

Ibu furrowed their brows. "Not at all. Saving one cannot jeopardize saving many. This is just something she and I need to do."

He chuckled. "And you think the others are just going to sit back and let you do it alone?"

They tilted their head and considered his question for a moment. "As soldiers, they won't have a choice. Lync will order them to assist you."

He placed his hand on theirs and sighed. "You still have a lot to learn about us humans, my friend."

Ibu studied him, their face unchanged and marred with confusion.

"That means they may or may not listen." He shrugged. "It's what makes humanity so infuriating and endearing at the same time."

"If you say so," they muttered. "If you say so."

When they turned, he squeezed their hand. "Wait! That's it? That's all you're gonna say? I'm frigging going it alone with these robots. You gotta give me more than that. What's the plan?"

They paused to consider their words. "It's best that I don't tell you the specifics, but I will say this. Shauna had an epiphany while we were under, and the less you know, the better... for everyone."

He wanted to yell and force them to tell him more, but as the frustration welled inside, he realized they were probably right. If he knew what they were planning, he might stop them, or worse, if he was captured, the GA could torture him for details.

As he stared at them, the gases amped up, signaling he needed to get back into stasis. Time was of the essence.

"Good luck." He gently grasped their arm. "And, Ibu."

They smirked. "Yes, Z."

He smiled and shook his head. "Tell her I love her when you see her."

They reached over and squeezed him back. "I won't have to. You'll see her yourself when it's over."

He nodded and let go. While every part of his soul wanted to see Abigail and Pluto again, there was a nagging feeling in the back of his mind that he wouldn't.

With the lid on the cryo-pod gliding shut, the gaseous tendrils enveloped him in seconds. And just as he raised his hand to chase the fading echo of Pluto's phantom kiss, his eyes sealed tight against the coming slumber.

THE ICY WAVE of cryo-gas wafted around him and disappeared as the warming lights came on. Zachary shuddered and exhaled. His throat was as dry as a desert, like he hadn't drunk in weeks. Funnily enough, that was exactly the case.

He moaned as he reached up and rubbed his eyes, opening and closing them slowly to allow moisture to break away without tearing his flesh. Once he was certain his eyes were working, he glanced around, half-expecting to see Ibu still standing there.

No such luck. All he saw was an empty cryo-room, its fellow occupants long ago sent in separate directions.

As he sat up, he reached to his ear and squeezed. "Status update," he said. His voice was hoarse; it sounded like he was speaking with gravel in his mouth.

"All systems are nominal, my boy. Welcome back to the world of the living." Rán's image appeared in the corner of his retinal comm.

He could tell it was Rán and not Harold because of his choice of blue clothes to honor his namesake. The intricate wavy patterns stitched into his outfit were dizzying.

"Good." He swung his legs to the side of the pod, and just

as he was about to hop off, the entire room shook. A long screech reverberated through the room, sounding as though the ship was being torn open from the outside. He grasped the pod and held on for dear life.

"What the hell was that?" he shouted over the sound.

"That would be an asteroid being loaded into the Cornucopia." Rán's image transformed from his older self to a much younger version. "I'm sorry about the racket. The robots sorta lost control of it."

He shook his head and exhaled a sigh of relief. For a second, he thought he was finished before they had even started.

"Say, H." He hopped down and steadied himself, giving his legs a moment to adapt to his weight.

Rán turned to face him, his outfit shimmering in the light. It appeared his clothes weren't just waves after all. He was wearing some type of ultra-modern camouflage, similar to what they'd worn when they stormed Doda a year ago. "What is it, my boy?"

"I figured you would've gone with my brother and Pluto." He brought up a map of the Cornucopia and plotted a route to the bridge. "You know… survival odds and all. Why'd you stay behind with me?"

As he started on the green path projected along the floor, Rán shifted uncomfortably. "Because without me, I fear neither you nor these robots would fare well in the battle that just began."

"The what?" He froze and stared at the image of his ancient grandfather. "Rán, please show me the status of the fleet."

His entire retinal comm filled with a tactical display of the Nursery. Explosions of light blossomed like spring flowers as a sea of alien moon ships filled his field of view. He stared at them, slack-jawed, wondering if they were figments of his imagination.

Once he collected himself, he squinted at the retinal projection. "Is this a simulation?"

"Negatory, sir." Rán clasped his hands behind his back. "Hera's fleet arrived before us, and the battle is well underway."

"Frak…" He stared at the explosions sprinkling within the nebulosity, and his heart raced. But despite his desire to move, his feet were like magnets stuck to the ground. The battle had already begun, and they were late.

Rán must have sensed his trepidation. He dimmed Zachary's retinal display, and his face appeared front and center. "I figured you would need a few minutes to compose yourself after your long sleep. But perhaps not. Should we engage the Nursery, sir?"

Instead of answering the question, his mind jumped to Pluto and his brother. If he were standing here, that meant they were likely neck deep in their situation as well.

"Zach, are you alright?" Rán asked, his voice quivering.

The display behind the A.I. lit up in a shower of orange explosions as a broader wave of attacks erupted. Maybe they weren't too late after all.

If he truly wanted to survive, it was now or never.

Zachary took a deep breath. "I'm on my way. Prepare our first wave!" He dismissed the tactical display and leaned into a sprint, following the green line tracing his path to the bridge.

37

LYNC MICHAELS

OUTSIDE THE NURSERY, GROUP ONE

The lid of her cryo-pod slid open, and Lync sat up with a start, her eyes wide with fear. It felt as though she'd been drifting in and out of stasis forever, never truly falling into a deep, restful sleep. While the memories of the past few weeks were fading by the second, one thing she remembered vividly was fighting the GA. She just couldn't recall the outcome.

With her gaze locked on something to her left, she didn't hear Shauna's robotic form stepping up beside her pod. "Is everything alright?"

"Wholly heck." She drew in her breath and reached up to rub the back of her neck, her hair was standing on end. "Yeah… sure. I'm just… peachy." She glanced around. "But next time I lie down, remind me to do some breathing exercises to clear my mind before I inhale the gas. Shit felt like I was—"

"Awake the entire time?" Shauna interrupted.

Lync recoiled and squinted. "How'd you know?"

"You're not the first Ulixi to say that." Shauna reached out and tapped Lync's ear, activating her retinal comm.

Once it powered up, a list of her Ulixi team appeared. Those who were already awake were checked off. Nearly half were reporting as green, and of those, over sixty percent showed similar sleep patterns and emotional outbursts upon waking. The rest were out of commission.

"Huh." Lync scrolled through the list, searching for Adri. She had made an agreement with Bradley to take the little girl on his mission. While Adri would certainly be upset when she woke up, she'd have a higher chance of surviving with him rather than where they were headed.

When she didn't find Adri's name, she instead gestured at Crayo's. He was set to wake up in a few minutes, and according to the display, he was only a few pods down.

"I'm going to see how my man fares." She swung her legs out of the pod and wiggled her toes. The feeling was returning to her extremities, but she needed to give them a few more seconds to warm up.

"I'd be careful." Shauna stepped around the other side of the pod to check the display. "Some of your people have come out of stasis quite disoriented. Hell, when Hi Fertig came to, she practically destroyed one of the robots. She smashed the poor chap's head into the pod a half dozen times before we could stop her. He had to have his cranial shielding and left eye replaced after that. She kept screaming that we'd let her brother Lo die. It wasn't until she actually saw him walking around that she calmed down."

Lync stared at the sliding cryo-lids and the gas rising from the pod next to hers, imagining what the occupants must be feeling at that very moment. She'd woken up in just as confused a state, but it had dissipated quickly.

Maybe it'd been a mistake to place so many minds like theirs so close together. They'd never been in stasis near each other before, and certainly not in such a concentrated grouping. While she hadn't heard of anything like this happening on a large scale, there were always a few anomalies in space travel — just not a majority of the crew.

It wasn't until Crayo screamed and something crashed to the ground that she slid out of her pod and hopped towards the sound of his voice. She'd forgotten to slip on her shoes before de-podding, and the frigid cold of the metallic floor made her dance on her tiptoes the entire way.

"Yikes," she muttered with each step as she pranced up to his side and froze.

An immobilized robot lay on the ground, and from the looks of the one he had in a headlock, there was about to be another.

"Cray!" She waved her hands and screamed at him. "It's ok!" As she went to move toward him, she noticed his bloodshot eyes darting around the room. He looked manic.

"Be careful." Shauna stepped in front of her and raised a needle gun. She was preparing to shoot him full of god knows what.

"Wait!" Lync reached out, attempting to pull her mother's arm down, but it was impossible. She was as solid as a rock.

"We can't risk another automata." Shauna took aim. "We're already neck-deep in battle, and we need every bot we can get."

"Lies!" Crayo screamed and spun around, ensuring no one was approaching from behind. "This isn't real. None of this is."

Lync turned and stared at her mom. "Wait! We're already fighting?"

"That's what I said. And Hera's getting her ass kicked." Shauna aimed at Crayo's backside, but he wouldn't stand still. She had to keep adjusting her aim.

Her words sunk in, and a knot tightened in the pit of her stomach. They were late to the party, and her people were already dropping like flies. With their tight margin of error, there was no way in hell they could pull this off without the Ulixi. That much was guaranteed.

She spun around and stepped past her mother. When she reached Crayo's side, she didn't hesitate. She swung her arm over and then back, smacking him across his face with all her might.

At first, he didn't seem fazed, but when his eyes finally focused on hers, he let go of the robot. It crashed to the floor, and he stood there in silence, staring at her. His expression was slack, but his breathing was heavy, like he'd just finished running a marathon.

"His heart is going to burst from his chest," Shauna subvocalized. "We need to knock him out."

"Give me a second," she said subvocally.

While she couldn't tell if he was himself yet, she had to try. "It's me. It's Lync." She smiled and reached out to touch him, but he flinched back, glaring at her hand like it wasn't real. "It's alright. We made it through the other side."

He shook his head. "No. No, we didn't." His gaze darted toward Shauna and the needler she had trained on him. "They killed us in transit."

"Who did?" She eased closer to him, slowly raising her hand to touch him.

"These fraking bots." He looked down at the remains of the two robots he'd taken out. "They're being controlled by the GA." He swallowed hard. "They always have been."

"But, you're not dead." She rested her hand on his shoulder. His skin was on fire. "You're alive." She smiled. "And so am I."

Crayo's hand started shaking as he lifted his gaze upward and locked it on hers. His eyes were deep red and his face was ragged, like he hadn't slept in weeks. She'd never seen him this way before. Whatever happened inside that pod had fraked him up good.

The next few seconds were a blur.

She thought she saw something move out of the corner of her eye, but when she turned to look, he was on her in a flash. His hands clasped tight around her throat, squeezing her airway like a vice.

"You're dead!" He screamed. "You're all dead!"

Lync shrieked and tried to stop him, smacking him upside the head with her fist. But he was too strong. No matter how hard she struck him, he didn't move. He simply stared at her, wide-eyed and filled with rage.

As the room started to fade, two darts pierced the side of

his neck a split second before Shauna's white composite shape appeared out of nowhere. She ripped him off Lync, prying his fingers backward in unnatural ways, and with so much force that Lync swore she heard his bones crack.

His limp body fell to the ground with a thud, but rather than lingering, Shauna spun around and jabbed her finger toward the exit.

"You have to go! You have to go now!" She leapt to her feet, nudging Lync toward the open door. "Zachary is preparing to attack, and our fleets... they're getting deci-mated. Hurry!"

Lync stared in awe at Crayo's immobilized body lying on the ground. His chest was barely moving, and his hand was bent backward at an unnatural angle.

That hadn't been him. He would never hurt her. Not like that. That had been someone else, someone who didn't know her. There was no other explanation.

"Go!" Shauna screamed.

Greer and Lo ran up to Lync's side, wrapping their arms around her and pulling her towards the exit. The last thing she saw before the door slid shut behind her was one of Little Red's automata sprinting up to Crayo, locking his wrists into shackles.

Lo reached out, gently guiding Lync's face forward as they pulled her down the hall. "We's need you back in the here and now, Captain. Those ain't our people. Those be the remnants of the ghost in the Beacon."

She shook her head, staring at Lo. "What do you mean, the 'the ghost'?"

The twin looked across at Greer. When Lync turned toward him, he nodded. "She be talking bout da shadow we all saw in the Beacon device when we's were training." He glanced back at Lo. "A few of da others been visited just like Crayo. Only for a few secs. Said it felt like a cold ventilation duct on der neck. Gave dem da willies, it did."

She glanced from Lo to Greer and back. "Wait a second." She stepped forward, spinning around to stop them. "And everyone who saw this ghost thing… they all woke up like that?"

Lo nodded. "So's far. We told da metal men, but dey ignored us."

"Frak!" Lync turned and started sprinting towards their ships. At the same time, she reached up and tapped her ear, opening a comm to Shauna. She picked up instantly. "It's the Entity! It got to them while we were in the Beacon."

She slid around the corner and almost crashed into a pair of robots walking past. Once she righted herself, she continued through the already open hatch leading into the shuttle bay where her Nyílak fighter was waiting for her.

"What are you talking about?" Shauna asked.

"Crayo, Hi, and the others." Lync hopped up on the wing of her ship as the hatch slid aside automatically. The slimy goo rippled on the surface as the glow of her instrument display awaited her below. "They were all visited by the Entity while we were inside the Beacon. Every single one of them. That fraking alien did something to them in there, and we need to find out what."

"Well, first things first." Shauna transmitted the live battlefield display to her retinal comm. "These are the jumps you need to perform to help triangulate where the Beacon might be."

The gate pathway appeared in the space in front of her. As she quickly scanned over the jump sequence, she froze. Something was missing.

Before she could ask, Shauna beat her to it. "Ibu changed the plan at the last minute after you went under. They decided to search for Abigail on their own. Well, them and Little Red, that is. They said you and Zachary needed to focus on the Ulixi and on figuring out how to use the Beacon against the Rift. You're the only one strong enough to do it, and I think they're right."

She stared at her display, slack-jawed and itching to punch a hole in something. Anything.

"Lync," Shauna whispered in her ear. "Your people need

you to hold your shit together. To be their lightning in a bottle."

Her father used to call her Lightning. She had always thought he'd called her that because she was a force to be reckoned with. Reflecting on it now, she suddenly realized that after all these years, perhaps she'd misinterpreted his term of endearment. Whenever he'd used that nickname, he'd really been referring to her uncanny touch of luck she'd harnessed throughout her life.

"Lightning," Shauna muttered. "I'll look after the others. You need to go before it's too late."

Lync nodded as everything fell into place in her mind. She couldn't put the needs of the few ahead of the many. Ibu would take care of Abigail.

Without another word, she took a deep breath and hopped down into the awaiting slime of her Nyílak fighter.

38

JOYCE GREEN

OUTSIDE THE NURSERY, GROUP TWO

She hadn't used her brain's neural link to learn this much since she crammed before they left for Epsilon Eridani. Joyce spent the better part of the past three weeks reviewing and memorizing every single Galactic Alliance battlefield tactic and strategy she could find, up through the time when the Ursis were enshrouded in the Dark Nebula. Access to their military archives had been one of the benefits of being friendly toward Haradis, a feat Hera had yet to manage. While Joyce wasn't as comfortable around him as Abigail had been, apparently the Olivaw vouched for her, and that had been all it took for both Haradis and Klus to confide in her.

The display surrounded the entire command room on all sides, allowing Joyce to be engulfed in the battle. At the moment, all she saw was red, except instead of being the kills of their enemy, it was their ships. Their Gunders were falling like flies, and the Ursis weren't faring much better.

Joyce opened a direct comm to the bridge of the still smoking Alatas, which had just passed through the gate. Its designation was the U.A. Carlottae. "What the hell is going on out there?"

"It's your bloody inept ground dwellers," the Carlottae's general said. "They turned on us the moment you closed the gate. We're sitting ducks over there when your little rats know our strategy."

The general shared the recording of the battle, and she sent it directly into her neural link. In only a few seconds, the events from the Nursery played out on fast-forward in her mind. One by one, she watched as the Gunder Pilum fighters launched their attacks, but not on the Galactic Alliance. No. They fired on their allies. On the glowing green Ursis Alatas ships that passed through the gates with them.

While their shots weren't well-placed, they didn't need to be, given the massive blast radius of the nuclear armaments. If it hadn't been for the unique fluid-like coating of the Ursis hull, they'd have been destroyed in seconds. While some of them were wiped out, most returned fire and limped to the nearest scheduled gate. Fortunately, none of the Gunders survived. They were either blasted by the Ursis or torn to shreds by the assault of Galactic Alliance fighters. From the looks of it, they were a mixture of Thyreus and Qudoculi spacecraft.

She watched the final seconds of the battle play out as another barrage from their Big Bertha plasma cannons sailed through the open gates and lit up the other side. The deadly weapons were the one thing still going their way in this epic battle. The entire array of space-time portals sealed up just before the superheated rounds of destruction tore through the approaching wall of Syndrus ships like a flame through a hayfield.

While the effect was brief before the gates closed, it was like watching the tip of a dozen matchsticks ignite and explode up their length. The multicolored display of death was beautiful, and it reminded her what she was missing.

She couldn't handle sitting out the entire battle from the sidelines. It wasn't how she was wired, despite Hera's attempts to change that about her. There was also the fact that their Gunders had turned against them. She owed both the Ursis and humanity more respect than that.

Joyce stiffened and opened a comm to the rest of the fleet,

most of which were still licking their wounds. "I want all Gunders placed under a watchful eye and locked down in their quarters. And I want it done now!" Each ship that still contained able-bodied Gunders signaled back and began executing her commands. There were only a few dozen in all. A far cry from the nearly three hundred they started with.

This was turning out to be a much different battle than their last assault on the Beacon. Without their bombing tricksters, this was going to be a long haul. Especially from the sidelines.

She spun in place to face Haradis. "King Umbra, permission to take command of one of your ships." The back of her head tingled like there were a million pins stabbing her. She winced, but she did her best to recover by bowing toward him and letting out a muffled sigh.

And like a demon passing in the night, Hera's holographic image appeared beside her a moment later.

"I order you to remain in command on the Kermodei," Hera said.

The only way she would have known what Joyce had said was if she were monitoring the ships in this region of space. Since she was leading her wing of the assault from several gate hops away, that meant only one thing: Hera was holding an array of comm gateways open. She either wanted to keep tabs on their return ships, or she didn't trust them. Probably both.

In front of her were the holographic projections of Hera's feet. While Joyce stared down at them, she couldn't help but imagine multiple ways to take her down if she were here: a sweep of the leg, an uppercut to the gut, or even an old school tackle. As she turned over the possibilities, the dull throb of pain rose in her nape and squeezed tighter.

Joyce moaned, and Haradis reached over and rested his hand on her back. "Are you alright, Commander Green?"

She nodded and fought down the pain, pushing it deep into the recesses of her mind. It wasn't real. It was only stress. "I'm fine. I just can't sit here and watch more of our people die." She bolted upright and stared him in the face. "I need to…" The stinging in her neck sparked again, and this time something moved on her back.

When she reached up, it didn't stop her. She ran her hand up and down her spine, causing the bulging mass to vibrate under her skin. She drew in her breath as her fingers skimmed over the lump. There was something there below the surface, something she… she. Her mind went blank, and she stared off past Haradis.

"Permission granted!" Klus said.

Haradis spun around and growled, eyeing his mate with suspicion. "What?"

"Commander Green!" Klus marched up beside her.

She squinted and turned to look up toward the towering Ursis female. Her mane of fur was exquisite, and the spiraling patterns of brown almost demanded to be noticed and touched. If it weren't for the delicate, transparent shawl covering her extremities, she'd reach out to run her hands through it.

"Commander Green!" Klus snapped her fingers, and Joyce shook her head.

Her mind felt foggy. It was like she'd zoned out. "What… what is it?"

"I approved your request to take command of the U.A. Perniger and to lead the fifth wing into battle." Klus turned and gestured toward the door. "Go now. Your shuttle is waiting."

Joyce squinted at the Ursis, and she stared back at her cautiously, as if something was amiss but she wasn't sure why.

As she reflected on the last few minutes, all she could remember was seeing Hera's hologram appear and the woman ordering her to stay onboard. No matter how hard she thought about it, she couldn't recall what she'd said to lead Klus to issue that command. But the longer she lingered, the more she knew one thing for certain: she didn't want to be here. She wanted to be out there, helping her people win this battle. Even if that meant dying in the process. Her son wouldn't have expected anything less of her, especially when it came to the Galactic Alliance. They'd cut his life short, and this was her chance to make them pay for his death.

"Thank you," Joyce dipped her head. "Admiral Klus, I accept command of the Perniger."

Klus reached out and gently brushed her shoulder. "May your fangs dig deep, and your claws crush many."

She bowed, and when she turned to go, Klus stopped her and squeezed. Their eyes lingered for a second, like she wanted to say something else but decided not to. Instead, she looked away and returned her attention to Hera's hologram.

"Your Commander has been given charge with leading the tip of our mighty spear into battle, President." Klus sneered at the glowing projection. "I trust your presence here is no longer necessary. You have your own affairs in this campaign to deal with." She gestured in the air, and Hera disappeared. With her hologram gone, the pain in the back of Joyce's neck dissipated to a gentle throb.

"You should go before I rescind my queen's offer." Haradis eyed Joyce curiously, and while he hadn't said no, it was clear he wasn't happy with Klus' interjection.

"I won't let you down." Joyce bowed and turned to go.

As she neared the exit, she could make out mutterings behind her. Unless her comm had mistranslated, Haradis was questioning Klus' decision. While she wanted to know why, she knew better than to linger.

She wasn't about to look a gift horse in the mouth. Not now. Not with vengeance being so close, she could taste it.

39

BRADLEY OLIVAW

CENTAURUS, NEAR HD 117939

The probe telemetry was due any minute, and Bradley had been pacing back and forth on the bridge since it left. That was four hours ago. Every second they were sitting there was a second they could lose their element of surprise. He only hoped they hadn't already been spotted.

As he paced toward the rear of the bridge, his mind drifted back to Pluto. She was all he could think about. It was bad enough he'd left her in cryo-stasis, but sending her on to Epsilon Eridani without even waking her up had been tearing him apart inside.

While he regretted it after she was gone, he knew he couldn't handle her on his own. The wrath of a warrior left out of battle might have been manageable, but once you added a pregnancy and a missing husband to the mix, there wasn't a chance in hell he'd come out of any conversation without bruises.

"You realize no amount of pacing will make her forget this, right?" Adri crossed her arms in her seat at the navigation controls.

He paused and glanced over at her. "I'll tell that to Lync the next time I see her."

"You do that. It applies to her too. I'll never forget what she took from me." Adri spun back toward her controls and slowly scanned the panel, looking for any sign of the probe or an indication that Hera's people had detected them. "She cut me out of the loop because of some archaic twentieth-century belief that kids need to be protected. Well, news flash! The shit's hitting the fan, and I'm not a helpless twat neural-linked to social feeds all day!" She slapped her hand against the panel, and the wall screen shut off.

Her eyes went wide, and she looked over at him.

"Dude!" He gestured toward the display, and it came back online instantly. When he scanned through the systems, everything seemed to be in order. "You can't be breaking shit. We don't exactly have spares lying around out here."

"Or anywhere else," she muttered.

"All the more reason you need to keep your temper in check." He slid sideways and sank into the chair beside her. After he futzed with the controls to confirm their fleet was still invisible to passive scans, he peered over at her.

"You haven't figured out why she sent you with me yet, have you?" He raised an eyebrow.

She leaned to the side and kicked at the panel mount on the floor. "To keep me safe."

He chuckled and shook his head.

"What?" She looked up at him.

He smirked. "I thought she said you were sharp."

"I am!" She nudged him. "Why? What'd she tell you?"

"It wasn't her words." He pushed the controls aside and turned his chair to face her. "It was her actions."

"Dude." She exhaled and pinched the bridge of her nose. "You'z be talking in riddles."

He narrowed his gaze. "I already told you what would happen if we fail with our mission, right?"

"Hera and the clones will take over." She stared at the panel and bit her lip as she powered it back on. "But that won't matter if they fail at the Nursery. Then we're dead anyhow." She swiped through the instrumentation. "At least back there, I can blow up some slimy aliens."

He leaned forward and spun her chair around to face him.

"Who'd Lync send out here with me to make sure we obliterate Hera's stronghold? Who'd she give me to gate the nukes into their bases, fight their fleet of fighters, or hell, who'd she promise would have my back if I bit the bullet?" He glanced over his shoulder and shrugged. "Last I checked, the bots couldn't do it, and there aren't any other Ulixi in this ragtag fleet of misfits." He tilted his chin toward her. "Just you."

"Well…" Her cheeks turned red, and she looked away. "You've got Shauna."

His mother's face flashed up on the wall screen, as if summoned by the little girl's words. "I ain't got shit on your skills, short stack. We both know I'd blow through our arsenal before I landed a single hit. While I might be able to gate, I can't aim for shit. No. Lync knew what she was doing. Even if it felt like you were being sidelined."

He smiled at Adri. "Trust me, you weren't. She was just promoting you to a league of your own."

The little girl wiped at her eyes with the back of her hand.

He hated seeing females cry, especially when they were kids. There was something about their puppy dog tears, pink splotchy faces, and tiny bodies that made him feel like he'd done something awful. Like he'd fraked up.

When he reached out to rub her shoulder, she jumped out of her chair and wrapped her arms around him, sinking her head into his chest. She was sobbing uncontrollably, and he just sat there, arms in the air, unsure what to do next.

"Hug her, you idiot," Shauna said over his comm.

He knew almost nothing about this girl, except that she was always attached at the hip to Lync. Hell, besides Cynthia, he was clueless when it came to females.

When he lowered his arms around her, she sniffled. "What if I fail?"

He didn't know what to say, so he went with the first thing that popped in his head. The truth.

"Then we're dead," he muttered. "We're all dead."

"Nice pep talk," Shauna whispered. "You always had a way with words."

If this little girl was as tough as nails like Lync said she was, she'd do better with the truth over some sugar-coated bullshit back patting. At least, he hoped so.

BRADLEY LOOKED over the results of the probe scan again. Their one wish had come true: Hera had pulled most of her forces out of the system to use during their assault on the Galactic Alliance Nursery. While there were still some light defenses, they could handle them, especially with the robots they brought along. Shauna had to keep reminding him that the automata were disposable, which was ironic considering her consciousness core was so often housed in a mechanical body. Even though he wanted to order their fleet to engage Hera's forces, the longer he waited to put human lives at risk, the better.

He checked over his controls. Everything was set for his gate and subsequent descent. "I'm ready when you are." He glanced at the corner of his retinal comm at Cynthia's face.

"I still don't understand why you needed to be the one to go down there." Cynthia shook her head. "There were a hundred ways we could deliver this payload. It didn't have to be you."

He sighed. "The clone facility is isolated from the colony, and they can lock it down. I need to get inside that place before we attack. It's the only way we can guarantee they're wiped out."

"There's also the matter of getting access to their core computer," Shauna said.

She was riding in the robotic bird beside him. Once they were halfway through the atmosphere, she planned to drop out of the shuttle and assist him from afar. They didn't have eyes on the ground, and couldn't maintain satellites in orbit to keep him updated with intel. This was the next best thing.

"Right." He nodded and checked over his gate sequence.

There were three hops, the second and third of which

were seconds after the first, to minimize detection. He couldn't risk someone tracing his jumps back to the fleet. They weren't planning to attack until he'd done his deed and delivered the virus.

"I'm locked and loaded." He blew Cynthia a kiss. "I love you. Wish me luck!"

As he reached forward to activate the jump, Cynthia smiled. "Good luck, babe. I'll see you—" Her image cut out, and the blue light of the gate transition ripped over his body at incredible speeds.

Every fiber of his being screamed in agony as the gate closed, and the second and third hops fired. He wasn't sure if he'd accidentally tapped the screen or if his timing was off. Either way, he wasn't prepared for the shock of the jump sequence, and the seat never injected the pain meds.

"Frak," he muttered as the third wave of light passed over his body. "What… happened?"

It wasn't until he turned his head toward Shauna's bird that he realized something was wrong. The eyes of the feathered automata were flashing, and the door to the compartment that contained his mother's consciousness core had popped open. She was exposed to the air of the shuttle's cabin.

He groaned and looked back at the controls. When he reached up to flip on the engines to start the descent, the control panel beeped. A second later, a face appeared on the wall screen, a face he'd only seen in family videos.

He did a double take. The man was a stranger to him, but like the rest of humanity, he knew his face well. He and his sister Hera had helped humanity reach the stars, and their images were forever immortalized in human history.

"Hello, Bradley." Zeus grinned. "We were expecting you."

"No fraking way." He reached out and frantically issued commands into the control panel to gate away, but nothing happened. The controls simply flashed on and off, and then went dark.

Zeus shook his head. "I'm afraid you won't be needing

that. Our clones will pilot you down via remote control." He glanced off to the side and then said something on mute before returning his attention to Bradley. "And don't worry about your ships. We'll take care of those as well. See you on the ground, my boy." He smiled, and the wall screen blinked off.

His stomach tightened into a knot as the hopelessness of their situation sunk in. They'd gone from launching their attack to losing in the blink of an eye. Worst of all, they never had a chance to defend themselves.

When he looked over at the bird, it was still flashing at him: three fast flashes, three long flashes, and three fast flashes. It was a pattern he'd seen a million times in vid-sims dramas. It was Morse code, and it meant Shauna was in danger.

Only he could save her in her current form. The moment the clones got onboard his ship, they'd take her consciousness core and either destroy it or torture her — neither of which he wanted to happen.

He released his harness and hopped to his feet, glancing around the shuttle. It wasn't exactly ripe with hiding places. Sure, there were a few storage compartments, but they'd rip those open in a few seconds. Hell, they'd probably tear the entire ship apart.

As he stared down at her jet-black sphere, his mind froze. There was nowhere to hide her core. In fact, the only place that might be safe was on his person. Or, better yet, in his person. And since he didn't have a body mod like his sister, that meant he only had one option.

"You owe me!" He reached down and picked up her sphere, turning it over in his hand. It was the size of a large grape and as solid as rock.

He took a deep breath and steadied himself with his other hand as the shuttle started rocking. There wasn't much time.

"Here goes nothing." He popped the sphere in his mouth and swallowed hard, wincing as he did.

It hurt like hell and took several more swallows, but it slid down his throat centimeter by centimeter until the discomfort subsided. He wasn't sure what to expect after that — maybe a firm pressure in his chest or a plop in his stomach. Either way, neither of those things happened. The pain simply stopped, and his breathing returned to normal.

"That wasn't so bad," he muttered as he went to sit down.

"It took you long enough!" Shauna screamed, her voice exploding inside his head.

"Shit!" He reached up to cover his ears.

"Sorry," Shauna shouted. "I can't control my volume when I communicate like this. There's only one other way we can talk, and that's..."

Her words trailed off, and a message appeared on the bottom of his retinal comm, just out of view.

I can use this as well. They're both risky, but it's all we've got. You'll have to use a virtual keyboard to send me a message, though.

This sensation was surreal but far less jarring. While he'd talked to his mother thousands of times over his retinal comm, knowing she was inside his body was off-putting. He couldn't imagine living like this for very long, and the moment he did, his mind drifted to Abigail. He wondered how she'd done it, and with two A.I. to boot.

Another message appeared.

Don't worry. I'm communicating with you via your nanites, not mine. I've attached a few of them to your optic nerve, so I can see what you see. Just remember not to speak directly at me.

"Sure," he muttered.

What the hell did I just tell you not to do? Don't forget
that if they can remotely control the shuttle, they can
watch everything you say and do. They probably already
saw you swallow me.

He shook his head and pretended he didn't hear that.
Instead, he stared down at his jumpsuit. There were two chest
pockets and two at his side. When he reached in, he could
imagine a keyboard tucked inside the tiny space. He blinked
open a small optimized keypad and pecked out a few words
to give it a try. This was going to take some getting used to,
for sure.

I'll do my best

When he hit enter, her reply appeared instantly.

Just remember, your best either keeps me alive or
kills me.

Bradley let her words linger for a minute before the entire
shuttle lurched, and the deceleration thrusters kicked in. He
grabbed the back of the chair he'd been sitting in and slid
around the front as the shuttle spent the next few minutes
slowing down.

While they could have just used the gravitational dampeners to land, whoever was piloting this thing must've been
bringing him in hot. They weren't taking any chances leaving
him to his own devices for too long. Either that, or they were
in a hurry to kill him.

After the shuttle touched down, the thrusters cut off, and

he hopped out of the chair. The second his feet hit the ground, the clang of the external hatch reverberated through the ship as it began to open. A warm glow followed, creeping through the tiny cabin and bringing with it the unfiltered light from outside.

As a gentle breeze wafted through the opening, it carried a scent that reminded him of spruce trees back on Earth. He lingered near his chair, taking in the peculiar and ever-changing odors of the alien world. Mixed within the forest-like fragrances of musty dirt was a foul smell, reminiscent of mushrooms — his least favorite food in the universe.

With the dank stench filling his nostrils, the sound of hushed voices entered the cabin from outside. He slid up against the inside wall of the shuttle to listen closer. Although he wasn't eager to step out into the open and risk being shot, standing there waiting for Zeus wasn't any easier. His heart pounded like a drum in his chest, compelling him to both bolt for it and sit still at the same time.

A message from Shauna flashed up on his comm:

Be careful and cover your back. Zeus was always a wily one.

While he knew she meant well, his options were limited. If there were multiple people outside, there was a pretty good chance they could take him out as soon as he made a move. Plus, there was the fact that he'd never been one to rush head-first into a fight without a plan. But if he'd learned anything these past few years, it was that familial obligations and past failures often led to poor judgment — it was a vicious cycle.

One at a time, his options turned over in his mind, until he landed on one in particular. If Zeus had wanted to kill him, he could have done it a thousand times by now. And as much as he hated to admit it, if his people were being brought in like he was, then they'd already lost this battle - and probably the entire war - especially once Hera got back. She'd surely torture them. The best thing he could do was go peacefully and see if maybe he could negotiate on their behalf.

He took a deep breath and raised his hands in the air, stepping slowly out into the open. After his eyes adjusted to the glare of the overhead suns, his gaze landed on Zeus. He was standing just a few meters off the bottom of the descent ramp.

It was only then that he realized that maybe, just maybe, there was still hope. Zeus appeared to be a regular flesh and blood human. He wasn't a teenager like Hera had been when she arrived in Epsilon Eridani. In fact, he looked every day his age. He was a wrinkly old man with gray hair and a receding hairline. His facial features reminded Bradley of his father.

"You needn't raise your arms, my boy." Zeus waved his hand, gesturing downward. "There's no firing squad here."

Bradley glanced around the surrounding marsh, and he immediately noticed something peculiar. There was no-one else with him. No other clones or humans of any kind. When his attention returned to his great-grandfather, the only thing he saw was a small robot, which, upon closer inspection, looked like it could double as a wheelchair.

You can take him out. He's alone.

The message flashed several times on the bottom edge of his retinal comm. Shauna clearly wanted him to take an aggressive stance, but something told him he shouldn't. He didn't know why, but there was something about Zeus that felt different from Hera.

"Are you planning on coming down here?" Zeus shuffled back to the robotic chair and groaned as he sat down. After repositioning himself, he looked up at Bradley and smiled. "Or are you gonna stand there looking stupid, like your father did when we caught him hiding his little probe network from us back in Sol?"

Bradley chuckled and shook his head. "No, sir." He started down the incline.

He'd heard stories about when Zeus and Hera found their father's secret probes. Stark thought he'd been sneaky, searching for the Galactic Alliance without telling them, but they'd known about his covert op the entire time. In fact, Hera had corrected several of his mistakes in their programming, things that could have given away the location of Sol had she not stepped in.

Zeus grunted when he reached the bottom. "At least your father taught you good manners. Not too many young folks these days use sir or ma'am." He glanced up at him. "We should get inside before it starts raining." He eased his chair forward, and Bradley didn't say a word; he simply followed along beside him.

He studied the man as he gently bounced back and forth in his robotic wheelchair. His voice was friendly and calm — a feat his sister rarely pulled off. Even more comforting than his voice were his many laugh lines, a contrast to his sister's flawless face. For being a young clone, half the time, her forehead and eyes were either immobile or filled with scorn.

After a few minutes of working their way down a winding jungle path, he looked over at Zeus. There was something eating at him that he had to know. "How'd you take control of my shuttle?"

Zeus nodded and bit his lip for a few seconds before finally looking away. "Hera said you were a talented engineer. She spent many a day watching you from afar before you left for Zeta Lupi. I remember her being impressed by your inquisitive nature and your drive to find new ways to solve problems." Zeus glanced back at him. "How do you think we did it?"

While his first instinct was to tell him off, he knew better than that. He hated it when people answered a question with another question. But given his present situation, he wasn't in any position to make demands.

"Well…" He jammed his hand into his pocket and kicked at the dirt on the trail while his fingers brushed against the rough edge of his father's stone.

And then it hit him.

"Shit… it was Dwight, wasn't it?" Bradley glanced over at Zeus. "He was your mole. He's the one who did your dirty work."

Zeus didn't react to the accusation. He simply looked up and stared him in the eyes before returning his gaze down the trail.

A message from Shauna appeared on his comm.

Goddamn it. That's it.

"Dammit! It makes sense, now that I think about it. I can't believe I missed it all these years." Bradley thought back to the days and weeks before they'd arrived at Henosi. "After you banished Joyce's fleet from Epsilon Eridani, they were on their own for a while. Hell, I wouldn't put it past Hera to have exiled them on a whim, hoping they'd try to meet up with us. She wasn't stupid, and everyone knew she never cared about the colonists." He shook his head. "No. She wanted us firmly in her grasp, and there was no better way to make that happen than to let Lync and Joyce loose. She knew they'd find a way to reach us." When he looked back at Zeus, he was nodding. Apparently, he'd guessed right.

He continued mulling over the implications of his dead friend hiding in their midst for so long. "Dwight had full access to the fleet the entire time. At least until they met up with us after their assault on the Zeta Lupi Wheel. After that, he needed to stay out of sight, or one of us might have seen him. While that probably slowed him down, he's always been smart. I bet he already had everything in motion by then.

Especially since most of our people were against Harold and Shauna controlling their ships. You made sure of that before they left."

Zeus chuckled. "Funny how that worked out, isn't it?" He sighed. "Your fear of artificial life having too much control over you led to you leaving yourself exposed. Sorta underestimated your power position, didn't ya?"

This time, when his great-grandfather glanced sideways, Bradley swallowed hard and a shiver shot up his spine. His steel-eyed gaze reminded him of the glares Hera used to give them when she was pissed. He couldn't imagine staring into those eyes every day.

Bradley grasped the stone in his hand and squeezed it, sending a jolt of pain into his palm. He groaned and loosened his hold. He'd cut himself countless times on the shard over the years, but its sharp edges had always helped remind him of what it meant to be alive - what he'd truly been fighting for his entire life. It was simple, really. He wanted to surround himself with family, and that didn't mean blood ties like Hera and Zeus. No. It meant he fought for the people who wanted to be with him, the ones who were motivated to change things for the better. To him, Zeus's look meant only one thing: these people weren't part of that family.

He stared down at the ground as he turned over the stone in his hand, wedging the dull side against his palm and easing the point between his fingers. "You know he's dead, right?"

Zeus tilted his head but kept staring down the trail. "Who's that?"

"Dwight Santos." He swallowed hard. "My best friend in the universe. He died twice, and in the same place to boot."

"He died... twice?" His great-grandfather turned and squinted at him. "How's that possible?"

"That's a good question." Bradley stepped over a downed log and turned to watch Zeus' chair as it raised up and rotated over the top of the obstruction. Watching the motion was both mesmerizing and revealing at the same time. First and foremost, it helped him to see that without the device, Zeus was helpless. Second, it gave him a chance to peek at the man's neck. There, attached to the base of his skull, was the telltale sign of the parasite. The same one Harold had dissected on Blu. The alien species had taken control not only of Hera and the clones, but also this entire planet.

"So how'd it happen?" Zeus nudged him. "How's it possible that he died twice?"

A message from Shauna appeared on his comm.

If there's a downed log out here, then wherever he's taking you is off the beaten path. Be careful, son.

Bradley shook away the words and turned, starting down the trail. Zeus followed and sped up next to him.

"The first time he died was on Henosi." He blurted it out before fully considering the implications of sharing this knowledge. He had a feeling that neither Hera nor Zeus knew about Dwight's past. They could've figured it out themselves if they'd bothered to check the colony records.

"Wait a second." Zeus reached out and grasped Bradley's hand, stopping their advance. "You mean when you and that wallflower of a brother ventured there the first time?"

Bradley didn't say a word. He merely nodded.

Zeus, however, leaned back in his chair, his eyes going wide. "That can't be." He started shaking his head. "The Dwight Hera told me about had approached her on Epsilon Eridani. It was after the Beacon battle. You must be thinking of a different Dwight."

"Trust me." Bradley grinned. "It's the same person. After his reincarnation in the hold of the Fountainhead, he changed. He morphed into someone else entirely. Someone who'd forgotten his past and apparently sold out his dearest friends." He reached up with his free hand and waved it over his face and chest. "He had a dozen or so animated gothic and Hindi tattoos up and down his body. There's no way you could mistake him for anyone else."

When he mentioned the tattoos, Zeus' face lit up. At that moment, Bradley realized what had happened. Hera and Zeus were power-hungry, and they got in bed with someone they hadn't fully vetted. They had no idea who Dwight really was, and they certainly didn't know he was a corpse possessed by an ancient, evil human. Even if they had, he'd probably promised them something big enough that they took the risk. That was how greed worked.

"Come." Zeus powered his chair forward, ignoring Bradley's glare. "It's not much further."

"No!" Bradley planted his feet wide.

What are you doing?

Shauna's message flashed on his comm several times, but he didn't reply. He stood firm, resolute in his decision.

"Excuse me?" Zeus spun around to face him.

"You heard me. I said N—O."

"I suggest you do as you're told, young man." Zeus nudged his chair forward at a crawl. "I know you can't help having your mother's tainted blood in you, but you're in no position to make demands."

That's it! You have my permission to kill him.

He didn't see the message on Bradley's comm. Instead, he spat on the ground and continued. "The only reason you're even alive right now is because of me." Zeus pounded his hand against his chest. "If the others had their way, they'd have flown you into our sun the moment we had control of your shuttle. The least you can do is show me a little respect, you halfwit."

"Respect?" Bradley shook his head and jerked his clenched fists out of his pockets. The rock was slicing into the skin of his left palm, and the tip was just visible between his trembling fingers. "You mean like the respect Hera showed Abigail when she repeatedly tortured her on Liprosus? Or the respect your clone army showed us when you stormed our hideout? When your people blasted your way into the base without regard for our lives? Or when they severed my spine, and I nearly lost my ability to walk?" He stepped closer to Zeus and leaned forward. "You mean that kind of respect?!"

The old man's face was as white as a ghost, but he wasn't looking at Bradley. He was staring at his still shaking hand. The one holding the stone.

When he looked over, there were rivulets of blood trailing out between his fingers, and several drops had fallen onto Zeus' lap. The old man reached down and wiped at the glistening red droplets beading up on his pants.

As the two of them stood there staring at the grim sight, something changed. Zeus started to waver in his chair. His head bobbed, and he blinked multiple times before reaching up and pulling at the neck of his outfit, leaving bloody fingerprints behind.

"What... what have you done to me?" Zeus closed his eyes, and a moment later they sprang open.

"I don't know what you're talking about, old man," Bradley snarled. "I haven't done anything yet, but I should. You sure as hell have earned it." He clutched the stone in his hand and raised it to Zeus' neck, making a mock cut from ear to ear.

As his blood splashed against the pink skin of his greatgrandfather, it seemed to change color. An ashen gray pattern began spreading from the center of the bloody splotches, and it slowly spidered up and down his neck.

A message from Shauna flashed on his comm.

Wholly shit! What did you do?

"I… didn't do anything." He stumbled backward and stared wide-eyed at the expanding spiderweb of lines as they took shape in the remains of the dying skin.

With his heart pounding in his ears, he couldn't hear the thump of the feet running toward them in the distance. And apparently, neither had Shauna. By the time either of them did, there were countless hands yanking him backward and slamming him on the ground.

"What did you do to him?" one of them screamed.

"He never touched him," another said.

Someone grabbed his hand and pried his fingers apart. "What's this in his hand, then?"

The people on top of him were screaming at both him and each other, but their words didn't matter. In fact, he didn't resist them in the least. For the longer they lingered, the more likely they'd reach the same fate as Zeus.

Seconds earlier, he realized what had happened. He'd done it unintentionally, but the side effect of his wound had been exactly what they'd planned. Though he never told the others he drank the deadly vial, he knew before they left that this was going to be a one-way trip.

When the clones started dragging him away, he stared up at the canopy of trees and broke out into laughter. It was quiet at first, but it grew louder and louder the longer he laughed. By the time they reached the entrance to the underground facility, his animal-like cry had morphed into a menacing cackle. As his voice echoed through the surrounding forest, he swore he could hear sounds of coyotes howling back at him.

40

IBU

OUTSIDE THE NURSERY

They hated their ship. Every time Ibu piloted one of Hera's Pilum fighters, the instrumentation and mechanical feedback felt stunted. It was as though someone had placed a governor over the computers. The lag and softness of the controls were noticeable during dogfights or any other fast directional changes. Unfortunately, this ship was all they had.

When they decided to find Abigail on their own, they knew they couldn't put Lync or her Ulixi in harm's way, and taking a Nyílak fighter was the surest path to do that. Especially if it meant one of them had to pilot this mess of a spaceship. That was the primary reason they chose a Pilum, or as they called it, the Sloth. There was also the small matter that it would help with blending in. If you looked the look and walked the walk, it was a lot easier to disappear among the other enemies.

After biding their time between the stars, the opening salvo of the Nursery battle thundered forward. Unfortunately for them, the shit hit the fan pretty quickly.

As the third wave of attacks drew to a close, things were going well for the humans. The Gunders had destroyed nearly fifty Selene moons, and while the Galactic Alliance fighters were formidable, they were no match for the Ursis battleships and their supporting fighters. Add in the Big Bertha artillery, and the aliens were taking heavy losses with no end in sight.

The fourth gate sequence started like the others before it. The Gunder piloted Pilum fighters passed through the open gate first, followed by their assigned Ursis battle wing and clone fighters. However, this time things went differently. Instead of opening fire on the GA, the Gunders adopted a shocking strategy: they unleashed a barrage of nuclear warheads in the heart of their alliance. With no viable defense against the teleportation of a thermonuclear device, the once orderly comm channels erupted in a symphony of agonizing screams. Their voices echoed the horrific fate endured by the clone and Ursis crews, mercilessly incinerated to ash.

Ibu couldn't believe what the Gunders were doing, but they also knew their window of opportunity was short. The pocket of negative gravity from warping space-time made the explosions an easy target. While they weren't as talented as a Ulixi, they quickly targeted the disturbance and issued a rapid gate sequence.

Most of the Pilum fighters in the fray lacked gate drives of their own, but a few did. These were usually reserved for the critical Gunder pilots and forward scouts. The rest of the fleet jumped into battle using the enormous gate walls, which had proven pivotal in the Beacon conflict. They'd been reconfigured with a larger power source to handle transitioning the mass of hundreds of fighters and dozens of Ursis battleships, but otherwise, they performed the same duty. They moved massive volumes of alliance ships into and out of combat.

When the rapid gate sequence ended, they punched their throttle forward and slid in behind the Alatas battleship. Its callsign was the Jugular, and while they could only imagine how that human name had come to pass, their computer reported it as a friend, not a foe. Within a few seconds of falling into position behind the ship, Ibu realized the Ursis comm protocols had changed after the blast. This clarity came in the form of a heated hello from their rear laser battery.

Ibu's mental link with the Sloth was probably the only thing that saved them. Their sub-second response gave them enough time to bank their ship left and right, dodging several of the initial blasts. But the sluggish controls of the Pilum were no match for the Ursis manning those cannons. They took a direct hit on their forward shields, dropping them by sixty percent.

Their defensive systems reported that multiple Ursis fighters were being dispatched to their position, so they did the only thing they could think of. They opened up a secure comm to the still-attacking Jugular.

"Cease fire!" Ibu grunted and fought every urge not to shoot back. "I repeat. Cease fire! I'm a human alliance member. We're on the same fraking side, you wooly mammoth!"

After they spoke, they realized they'd referenced the wrong ancient Earth animal, but it didn't matter. No reply came, just more glowing red bolts of light trained on their position. Fortunately for them, the Ursis weren't only targeting them; they were also firing on an approaching GA squadron.

What they couldn't figure out, however, was why the Ursis hadn't started using their blobby green tentacles to lash out at the nearby ships. Or, hell, even at them. They'd seen them used in skirmishes back in the Proto Dark Nebula when they passed through, and the results had been devastating. But it didn't matter, they weren't about to stick around to find out.

They slammed the throttle forward, and their drive plume lit up as they banked the Sloth to the right. They needed to put as much distance between themselves and their attackers as possible, and if that meant launching their ship into the fray, then so be it. Just as they were getting within range of a neighboring Alatas battleship, it exploded in a blast of fiery white light.

The sensors connected to Ibu's mental link went haywire, and their connection dropped. "Shit," they muttered. "Status report!"

Little Red chirped beside them and replied right away. "We've taken damage to the starboard sensor array. I've redirected repair bots to that segment, and I should have the array rebooted without those sensors in... done! You're welcome to reconnect, Captain."

Ibu didn't question or banter with the quirky robot. There was no time. They simply closed their eyes and reopened their link, trusting that Red would safely navigate their ship in the intervening seconds. It had been part of their agreement: they let the automata join them in exchange for its complete dedication to their mission — saving Abigail.

At first, Red wasn't happy about it, but Bradley hadn't given him much choice. He'd left his robot friend behind to help with the Nursery assault, and now Red was heartbroken. The moment he'd gotten wind of Ibu's plan to save Bradley's sister, they had to let him go. Otherwise, he'd still be annoying them from afar.

After reconnecting, they scanned over their systems. Little Red had single-handedly fought off two GA fighters and was presently piloting their ship headlong through the debris field of the exploded Ursis battleship. It wasn't until they realized the Alatas weren't firing on them any longer that they checked the message queue.

"You kept messaging them?" Ibu asked.

Little Red's face appeared in their mind's eye, and his entire virtual depiction fluttered in a rainbow of colors. "It seemed only prudent to keep asking for them to relent," the robot began. "I even continued with your forceful diatribe of slang and demanded they stop attacking us, all while calling them saber-toothed tigers, Megalania, and giant sloths. I think that last one caught their attention, as they relented soon thereafter. They forwarded on the correct cipher to sync up with their broadcasts, and now we're tuned into the channels they're using to guide the battle."

"Nice." Ibu shifted his image out of the way and opened

the new data stream, letting it flow through their consciousness. "How'd you manage to get them to talk?"

"I lied." Little Red fluttered green. "I told them our computers rebooted after we gated, and it wiped out our communication array. They believed me after they saw me fight off those GA fighters."

Ibu studied the new telemetry as Little Red rolled the Sloth right, dodging the inbound plasma beams from the GA fighters swarming around the Jugular. While the blasts missed them, the bolts of superheated gas still hit a target. They tore through the side of the Ursis battleship, rather than being absorbed harmlessly by their missing glowing green shields. Whatever the Gunders had done to them, their strongest defenses had been nullified. They needed to get back through a portal to repair their ship.

Little Red spun the Sloth around on its axis and started firing on the approaching Thyreusian fighters. The first two alien ships easily dodged out of the way, but the third exploded in a firestorm.

As the robot targeted another fighter, Ibu turned their attention to the alliance data stream. There was a gate scheduled to open up soon, and it wasn't far from their current position. If they timed it right, they could pass through behind The Jugular and then jump sideways past the fleet. Depending on the timing, they might even avoid detection.

The Sloth shook violently as their aft shields absorbed a laser blast, bringing them down to forty percent. Little Red reloaded their rail gun while Ibu plotted a course to the coordinates where the exit gate should be opening. After that, they primed the drugs in the acceleration harness in preparation for a rapid gate sequence.

Little Red must've noticed the change in navigation because their image flashed from red to blue to orange. Judging by the colors, he was both excited about their strategy and concerned with the final jump. It didn't take a genius to see the risk of what they were planning. But even knowing their plan, he didn't push back or tell them not to do it.

At first, Ibu thought the robot's inaction was a sign of him brushing them off because they were Nanil. But they knew better. Bradley ordered the robots to treat them as equal to a human, and Little Red wasn't about to disobey Master Bradley.

Ibu chuckled in their head at the idea of calling him Master. At the same time, they brought the Sloth into line behind the gravitational wake of the Jugular. Once in place, they handed the controls back to their robotic friend. They had a gate sequence to plan, and they needed to prepare their calculations for several routes.

Perfect timing was of the essence, especially as they only had one chance at this. After the gate closed, the Jugular would update the alliance fleet with details on the battle, and that included the Sloth. Hera's computers would figure out who they were, and then it was just a matter of time before they tried to take them out. They only hoped the fleet didn't rotate the cypher used to decode their broadcasts.

"One problem at a time," they muttered into the void of link space.

Even though time moved slower when they were connected to the computer or another Ulixi mind, they still needed to focus. Time was finite when death was nipping at their heels.

It would only take them a few seconds to scan the far side of the gate and to enter the final jump parameters once they passed through, but the computation would be intense. By the time they dropped back to real-time, the distant gate flashed open.

"Follow close behind the Jugular," Ibu highlighted the Ursis battleship. "The moment the gate closes, prepare for a rapid transition."

Little Red chirped and Ibu double-checked that the program was loaded.

As their robot companion brought the Sloth into position,

they studied their defenses. For some reason, the GA fighters were turning back. That was strange. Usually, when a gate opened nearby, the aliens would rocket toward the entrance in an attempt to make it through the other side.

"Something's wrong," they muttered as they reviewed the remaining ships in the vicinity.

And then they saw it. There was a single lone Gunder fighter, and it was barreling towards them.

"What do you see?" Little Red's eyes fluttered orange. "We have no tails."

Ibu slammed the emergency pain med button. "It's the Gunder, they're about to—"

They never finished the sentence because just as they were about to gate away, their ship gated on its own. And not once, not twice, but three times.

It all happened so fast that by the time they'd completed the hops, all they saw were stars. That and the halo of red from the edge of their vision as the waves of pain crashed into them. No amount of meds could prepare a biological life form for more than one rapid transition, let alone three.

They fought with every ounce of their being to resist transformation, and for the most part, they succeeded. Aside from a few shooting pains from their elongating legs and arms, they held their inner beast at bay. The last thing they needed was a testosterone-fueled version of themselves itching to break free and charge into battle.

"We're… safe." Little Red spun to look at them. "Are you well, Master Ibu?"

Their breathing was ragged, and their limbs were sore, but otherwise they were fine. "I'm… alive, I think." They swallowed hard and slowly turned their head toward him. "What the hell did you do?"

A faint green glow flashed in their eyes. "I… improvised."

Ibu subvocalized the command to replay the microseconds leading up to the jump, and they watched the transition unfold. As they were dialing in a rapid backward gate, Little Red was executing a Hail Mary maneuver. First, they hopped off to the side, far enough to nullify some of the gravity of the Jugular, and then they did something stupid.

They glared at the robot. "You jumped through the gate!"

"I had to." Little Red lowered down into his shell. "We couldn't lose our advantage. Otherwise, we might not find Master Abigail."

Their hearts pounded in their chest as the math required to perform that maneuver flashed through their mind's eye. It was one part staggering and a million parts luck. Hell, they didn't even know you could jump through an open gate. What made it even more mind-blowing was that he stuck the landing and even executed the follow-up jump. The Sloth was currently floating a safe two light-minutes from the clone fleet.

The path they traveled flashed up on their controls as Ibu reviewed the brief glimpse they'd received of the clone fleet on this side of the gate. Their stomach sank when they saw the silhouette of the vessel.

"What the hell is that?" They pointed at the massive starship lingering behind the long array of gate rings.

The cruiser resembled a Pilum fighter and the rest of Hera's ships, except this one overshadowed all others. It was easily ten times the size of the Terminus battleship they'd grown accustomed to seeing in the clone fleet.

"I guess Hera had a few secrets up her sleeve," Little Red said.

"You could say that," they muttered.

As Ibu studied the massive ship, they wondered how Little Red had managed to jump away from it. The gravitational waves emanating from that beast would have made a gate calculation nearly impossible to predict without scanning it first.

They swallowed hard. "It's a wonder we're even alive."

Suddenly, a burst of white light flashed in the distance, and then it went out just as quickly.

Ibu pointed at the location of the explosion on their controls. "Show me a visual right there."

"I'm already on it." Little Red zoomed in and rewinded the scene a few seconds before it flashed.

They could make out most of the clone ships floating around the gate as it blinked open, and then it lit up white. Something had exploded on the far side of the open gate, erupting through the opening, shooting red-hot plasma and projectiles in every direction.

It took them a second to absorb the implications of what they were seeing, but when they did, their hearts sank. The Gunder had dropped a nuke on the Jugular, and the resulting explosion blasted through the open gate. If losing the Ursis ship wasn't bad enough, from the looks of the aftermath, the devastation didn't end there. The nearby ships were ripped to shreds, and the gate itself was complete slag.

Ibu exhaled and ran their fingers through their tight-cropped hair. "You saved us. You saved me." They glanced over at the tiny robot still withdrawn into his shell. "Thank you." They reached out and rested their hand on Little Red's enclosure.

His head rose, and his eyes fluttered a rainbow of colors. "You're most welcome, Master Ibu."

They chuckled. "You know, that's the second time you've called me Master. What happened to Friend?"

Little Red's display went white, the color he reserved for truth. "If Master Zachary and the other humans can risk their lives to save you, and in turn, you do the same for them, then you are as worthy of the title as any other human. Referring to you as my master is the least I can do. Come." He popped out of his shell and gestured toward their controls. "We must find Master Abigail before it's too late. I'm inclined to think the probability is high that she's onboard that eyesore of a starship."

Ibu nodded and wiped at the tears in their eyes. "I concur, my friend. I concur."

41

ABIGAIL OLIVAW

OUTSIDE THE NURSERY, INSIDE BEACON

The glowing green aura of the prasinus wavered as Abigail whispered in their ear. She could tell they were uncomfortable hearing words from beyond, especially when they went counter to what their people had been told. But in this case, their discomfort was a necessary evil.

She'd spent countless hours attached to the Beacon these past few weeks. Being as she was the only human proxy suitable for the Entity, they didn't have much choice but to let her connect as well. What the Entity hadn't realized, however, was that she was as capable in this virtual space as he was. Though she had to be careful.

A few days prior, he had tried following her after they entered. She could always tell where he was inside the Beacon. Any time he approached her, she felt a deep-seated sense of revulsion. On this particular occasion, when she sensed he was approaching, she feigned ignorance of how to move. She spiraled around in circles among the crowd of passersby near the entrance, and topped it off with a death spiral down into the depths of the place.

The entire time, the Entity was cackling in the higher plane, thoroughly enjoying her sputtering about and floundering aimlessly. She wasn't sure if he really thought she was so inept that flying would confound her after all this time, but he never questioned it. Even while he circled her and tried to influence her thoughts, she pretended not to hear him. At one point, in a fit of anger, he lashed out at her, and had he not been harmed in doing so, she was pretty sure he would have ended her.

After that encounter, he disappeared and stopped stalking her. It was then and there that the tables turned. While she floated there, recovering from the psionic blow to the head, she could barely catch her breath, and her blue life mark was throbbing in and out. Every ounce of her soul hurt, and there wasn't a chance in hell she'd be able to drop into the higher plane, not for a while.

In that moment of weakness, the sparks of green appeared again. The last time she'd seen them, they'd saved her from the Trochilidae and Thyreusian minds. They disappeared soon thereafter, and except for a few green shimmers in the distance, the lights eluded her until that day.

She shook off the memory of the fated encounter. While she would never forget what they said to her, time was of the essence. If she wanted to escape or upend the Entity's plan, this was her opportunity.

"Traverse slowly," she whispered to the prasinus spark. Its waveform danced in response to her words. "Failing to do so will result in incomprehensible pain and vulnerability to attack."

The prasinus darted forward and seemed to spin in place. It was hard to tell for sure, as it was nothing more than a glowing mass of light, but she'd seen it behave this way countless times. The alien doubted itself and was searching for the source of her voice.

When she saw their life mark had relaxed, she eased back up next to them. "In the celestial name of our Divine Creators, let it be spoken only once: I have chosen you to perform this sacred mission."

"But…" The light fluttered. "The sanctum has ordered us to defend the Rift. The second wave of ships has arrived."

"There's a second wave?" she muttered. She hadn't meant

to say it out loud, but it was too late now. The question had been asked.

The prasinus lingered in wistful silence as the hum of the Beacon space throbbed around them. While it felt like an hour, it was probably only a few minutes. Perhaps she'd misspoke. If she were all-seeing, a second wave wouldn't have been a surprise. Either way, she'd spent hours on this stubborn green light. Losing it now would set her back, and she wasn't overflowing with time.

"Yes!" the prasinus exclaimed.

She glanced around, certain she would find they were talking to someone else. But no one was nearby. It was rare to encounter another life mark in the dungeon of this place.

"Yes... what?" she asked hesitantly.

"The second wave. They appeared only moments ago. Though time in Beacon space isn't exactly linear." The prasinus flickered. For a split second, she thought she was going to lose them until they continued. "This new wave of attackers is formidable. Certainly more formidable than the opening salvos of human and Ursis ships we've been dealing with. Even with their magical portals, the Therionic overseer made certain to prepare the sanctum for their arrival. Or so it seemed. There's a reason the Builders feared the Therionic Entities in the first place. That was why they empowered the Ulyxsauri to protect the Beacons. Everyone had a purpose. But apparently, the inner sanctum prefers to repeat past failings and believes the Therionites are the rightful heirs to our galaxy. The inner sanctum believes that the Entity reaching out to us through the Beacon was a sign, an affirmation that we shall ascend into the Rift. There are a silent few, however, that disagree. They see the opening attacks in this battle as a diversion. One designed to give us a false sense of confidence. They're convinced that the Entity is not real. That it died long ago, and what we're seeing is nothing more than an intricate game of deception by humanity. A species that refuses to be snuffed out of existence by an alliance of their peers."

Abigail gasped, her heart tightened in her chest. While

she'd worked hard to spread disinformation about the Entity among the aliens in the Beacon, until now, until this very moment, she'd never once heard another species repeat it.

She was no stranger to politics or spreading lies and rumors. Hell, for her, they were everyday parlor tricks in Sol. What she didn't know, however, was if subterfuge would work on this alien. But her fantastical tales of the Entity's demise had only been the tail end of that story. The other nugget about the sanctum was news, even to her.

The prasinus light flickered in and out once more, growing dimmer by the second. She reached out, willing them to stay, but knowing damn well physical contact was out of the question. Not again.

"Are you still there?" Her voice trembled.

The silence that lingered in those passing seconds was a punch to the gut. She could feel her hope slipping between her fingers. That was until the light of the prasinus burst forth like an emerald jewel, far brighter than she'd ever seen it before.

"I am sorry," they began. "The attacks... they're coming fast and furious now, and this unknown force has assailed the Selene ships protecting our Beacons. Dare I say it, but with these numbers, the new arrivals may give even the Shaygai a challenge." The light sparkled with excitement. "Had I not been able to automate my functions, I wouldn't be here. But I needed to rezar. To center myself for the trials ahead. My kind has faced many hardships over the millennia, and the sanctum would end me as fast as they created me if they knew I was here. They'd exterminate my people. It's because of this that I fear for my safety and that of my kind. I seek solace and counsel with my equals, but they have not come. I'm worried they are lost... or worse. Our numbers are few, and I am uncertain what path to take. Only that I wish to live. For my thread of time in this ethereal plane is not yet complete."

She wasn't sure how to respond. This alien had revealed new details on the turmoil inside the Galactic Alliance, and they even gave her some much-needed clues to the true past of the Ulixi. These were all things she dared not ask, given her fictional status as a speaker for the Builders.

What surprised her most, however, was their admission to being uplifts like many other oppressed species in the GA, and not surprisingly, they wanted more from their lives. To be honest, she couldn't blame them for what they'd become. Speciesism was real, and she too had been a victim of circumstance most of her life. She wanted to start over herself. To reset to a simpler time.

That was it. A sudden wave of clarity and emotion washed over her.

Maybe she could offer them what they were seeking. What everyone in their situation wanted. What she wanted. Her only hope was that her instincts had been right coming here, and that she wasn't too late.

Abigail took a deep breath and eased in beside the blinding green light. She needed to be careful not to spook them. They'd be able to sense her deception if she doubted herself. If ever there was a time to conjure the soothing and affirming voice of her mother, it was now. Her tone had always been a gentle murmur capable of quieting even the fiercest storm.

"There is a way," she whispered and held her breath.

"Tell me what I must do… please." The prasinus vibrated with a fragile tension that betrayed their previous excitement.

Numerous strategies raced through her mind as possible suggestions. The idea that they'd accept her proposal, let alone so willingly, was something she never expected. Moments earlier, she hoped they would simply serve as a diversionary force to rush the gates. Now, they had the potential to be more than mere pawns. Dare she imagine it, but they might just be her savior.

She shoved aside any residual feelings of guilt and leaned in, whispering in their virtual ear her cockamamie plan to reach freedom.

42

ZACHARY OLIVAW
OUTSIDE THE NURSERY, GROUP ONE

R án's robotic form held his finger over the fire controls. "Stand the frak down!" he screamed.

Zachary stared at the Ursis battleships that had just transitioned through their gates. Half of them had lost their shields, and the other half were sparking. Their automated repair protocols were barely keeping them alive.

"They're not powering down," the nearby robot said.

The bridge crew on the Cornucopia consisted of Rán, himself, and a dozen robots. All the other humans were either pilots or below deck, working with the robots to repair the inbound robot fighters.

He stepped up beside Rán. "Put me on. I want to talk to them."

Rán held firm. "We can't risk—"

Zachary slammed his hand against the control panel. "Do it, Harold! The moment we fire on these Ursis, they'll fire on our pilots if they enter their side."

He knew calling him Harold instead of Rán would piss him off, but he didn't care. He needed him to do as he was ordered and to stop questioning him. They didn't have time to debate their every move.

"They're scanning us, sir!" the robot on communications said.

He groaned. "Then fraking jam them." He turned back toward Rán. "I'm not going to ask you again. Put —me—on!"

Rán shook his head. "It's your call, boss." He gestured forward. "You're up."

The cameras embedded behind the wall display switched on, and a feed of his upper torso appeared on screen. His hair was a mess, and his outfit wasn't much better. At any other point, he might have been self-conscious. But in this situation, he didn't give a shit.

He cleared his throat and straightened his back. "This is Admiral Zachary Olivaw of the…" He paused and glanced over at Rán. They hadn't ever decided on a name for their ragtag alliance, and now wasn't exactly the ideal time to brainstorm one.

Rán shrugged. "The Non-Assholes."

He chuckled and lowered his head to suppress a laugh before returning his gaze forward. "The Ulixi Guard." The name wasn't great, but it was true. Without the Ulyxsauri, they wouldn't have much of an army. At least not one that could find Beacons. Sure, the robots were strong, but it was only a matter of time before the larger Galactic Alliance fleet winnowed them down.

The bridge of the Cornucopia fell silent as Zachary stared into the camera, hoping someone would reply. After a brief pause, his retinal comm chimed with a message from Rán. He blinked it open.

While I like the ThUG acronym, you might want to make some demands.

"Shit, yeah," he muttered, clasping his hands behind his back. "You will power down your weapons and cease scanning our ships, or we'll be forced to fire on you." He narrowed his gaze. "You have ten seconds to comply." He nodded toward Rán and returned his attention forward, doing his best to hold a stern expression.

He wasn't cut out for this shit. Numbers were his jam, not this political crap.

As the clock counted down from ten, the two Shu moonlets that weren't engaged on the other side of the gate started powering up. The brightening exterior channels of light gave away the power lurking deep in the bowels of the formidable weapons. They were an undiplomatic warning the designers wouldn't have landed on without considerable debate.

When the countdown hit three, and the superheated energy formed in space above the moonlet, a familiar face appeared on the wall screen: an Ursis he knew well.

"Haradis…" He stepped forward, waving his hands for Rán to pause the attack. "Is it really you?"

He glanced sideways at Rán whose fingers danced over his controls. He'd paused the assault, but the Shu remained powered up. Judging by the flurry of commotion on his control panel, he was trying to decide whether Haradis was a friend or a foe. Deep fakes were easy, but what ruled the roost in situations like this were facts, not appearances.

The image of Haradis smiled. "As real as your fear of becoming a father. Don't worry, you'll do better than Stark. If you don't, Pluto will kick your ass." He winked.

Zachary drew in his breath and recoiled. No one in Hera's army knew about Pluto's pregnancy, and no part of him could imagine Abigail willingly telling them. Not unless she was either under duress or being controlled by one of those alien parasites.

As the thought lingered like a foul taste, refusing to be swallowed, it reminded him of what might have already transpired. A moment later, a message from Rán appeared on his comm.

If your sister was compromised, we should fire.

Rán was right, but they needed to be certain before taking steps they'd regret later. Fortunately, they didn't have to decide under duress.

"They're lowering the shields, and all active scanning has ceased, sir," the robot on comms announced.

Zachary swallowed down the bile in his throat. His sister was fine. She had to be. "It's a good thing my sister loves being the center of the show. She and Hera will be like two peas in a pod leading humanity."

The camera view on the Ursis side suddenly panned out to show Klus. "Bullshit! You know as well as I do that Abigail would rather die than run things anymore. Besides, she'd slit Hera's throat the first chance she got."

He smirked, the tension in his gut loosening. They had to be the real Haradis and Klus. There's no way they'd know that if they weren't. Hera had done a remarkable job hiding the family turmoil from the rest of humanity. She ruled with an iron fist, not the emotions most humans perceived as weak.

"It's good to see you, my friend." He scanned the tactical display on their right wall screen and nodded. "We need to talk in person, but first things first. What do you and your people need to repair?"

The robot manning their communications array turned toward him and chirped. "I would advise against that, sir. We don't know that they'll—"

The robot never finished its sentence. It paused abruptly and tipped forward. A few seconds later, a trio of robots entered the bridge from the side entrance, and two of them carried the frozen automata off. The third robot stepped up and manned the comm controls.

When Zachary glanced at Rán, he simply nodded. "It's taken care of. Now let's fix up our people."

"AND YOU'RE certain these recordings are legit?" Zachary studied Haradis, looking for any sign of deceit or misgivings. While they had no idea what this data meant, both he and Rán did. They'd been digging into it for the past ten minutes while they waited for the Ursis shuttle to dock at the Cornucopia.

Haradis turned his head and snarled, baring his glimmering fangs. "The Jugular lost its entire crew to that blast. These were the last seconds of their uplink before they were destroyed by those underground freaks of yours. I suggest you watch your accusations, young Olivaw. I'm well aware of the stakes in this game."

His comm lit up with a message from Rán.

Given Abigail's history with Haradis, he's likely posturing in front of his guards. His people are very formal in their dealings with other alien races. Any sign of disrespect is seen as unacceptable and is often met with a deadly end. As you can imagine, that tactic didn't work well for them when it came to negotiating with the Galactic Alliance.

While his words may have defused some of the tension, he couldn't help but see the glimmering jewels drilled into Haradis' teeth as the warning they were intended to symbolize. Any wrong move with these aliens could end him, even among supposed friends.

He dipped his head and played along. "I meant no disrespect, King Umbra."

Haradis grunted and returned his attention to the wall screen in the shuttle bay. There was no time to dawdle, and taking them through the massive starship would have been a waste of time, let alone a pain in the neck logistically, given the size of the alien. So meeting in the primitive shuttle bay was their next best option.

"What do you see in this recording?" Haradis eyed him. "Why are you so concerned about its legitimacy?"

Zachary studied the video on the screen. Both he and Rán knew it was the collection of recordings that mattered more than this particular one. However, this snippet had been the key that unlocked their theory. It was the cipher that made understanding the Gunder's behavior possible.

"I..." He cleared his throat as the hair on the back of his arms straightened. "I'm not sure if I can share everything, but let's just say we have a theory why Hera's pilots lost control."

The king clenched his fist and grunted again, sending shivers up Zachary's spine. A message from Rán appeared instantly thereafter.

You must control your emotions and actions, my boy. The Ursis can read into everything you do and say. They're attuned to your every move, no matter how small or subtle. Their heightened senses are uncanny.

Being on display and having your inner thoughts dissected like this was unnerving. He didn't have time for this shit.

"I appreciate your sharing this data, King Umbra." Zachary took a step backward and bowed slightly. "My robots will ensure your ships have the supplies they need to return to battle. Good luck out there."

"Wait, a second!" Haradis reached out and nudged him. "We're not done here. You didn't tell me anything useful." He glanced around. "Why did you even ask me here if all you were going to do is insult me?"

He raised his chin and did his best to clear the emotion from his face. At the same time, he tried not to show fear from the physical intimidation, despite the nudge being with the king's sharpened claw. The fact of the matter was, he wasn't sure why he asked them here.

"I don't know. I guess I wanted to confirm it was really you before we committed to helping repair your ships. My aunt and I aren't exactly standing on solid ground." He shifted his stance. "If it weren't you, well, then let's just say both you and your people would be dead."

Haradis waved his hand in a circle toward the paused video feed. "And that? Something you saw in there excites you. Something more than these Gunders. What is it?"

He shook his head and crossed his arms. "Nothing."

"Zachary!" Haradis eased closer and lowered down to his level. "I won't be leaving here without—"

"What?" Zachary leaned to within centimeters of him and stared straight into his eyes. "Without what? My head? Well then, you'll need to frak off, you overgrown fur bag. From where I stand, your people on those ships are on their last legs, and you're siding with my Aunt Hera instead of Joyce… well, that's your screw-up, not mine." He stepped backward. "Now, I suggest you return to your ship, or I'll be forced to have my guards remove you."

"And there it is." Haradis smirked.

Zachary squinted. "There what is?"

Haradis pointed at him. "That fire I saw in your sister back in Proto." He shook his head. "I figured it had to be in there somewhere. Your blood, after all. She didn't take shit from anyone, either your people or mine."

"Nor should she have." Zachary's gaze slipped past Haradis to the wall screen.

The image was frozen on the Gunder's white-hot destruction of the Jugular. In the middle of the frame, he could just make out a faint blue halo that looked like a lens flare, the kind you'd normally find on most untreated cameras when they were exposed to a bright light at a certain angle. It shouldn't, however, have been in that image, especially not in the midst of an explosion like that.

Haradis pivoted and glanced between him and the display. "What do you see?"

Zachary shook his head and pushed the detail aside,

returning his attention to the Ursis. "Nothing. If you don't mind, I have a battle to return to."

He spun around and started toward the exit as the implications of what he'd seen began to turn his mental gears. There shouldn't have been any ships on the field of battle capable of gating. They'd agreed to that, and while Hera's forces were on the ropes, she was no fool. The stakes were too high to risk losing a gate drive on anything but the most important crew. And since their Ulixi weren't in that quadrant at the time, that meant only one person would be there.

It's Ibu.

The message flashed on his retinal comm. Apparently, Rán had seen the same thing.

By the time he reached the lift tube, he was already working through the ideas of where she'd hopped to. Having her on the other side of that gate could be a huge strategic advantage, if they could reach her.

"Admiral Olivaw!" Haradis shouted.

Zachary froze. While he'd jokingly used that title earlier when he addressed the Ursis ships, he never expected that someone would use it to address him.

When he turned in place, he drew in his breath at the sight of Haradis. The Ursis King was down on one knee, and his four guards were kneeling beside him.

"Are you feeling well, King Umbra?" Zachary shuffle-stepped forward. "Do you need medical attention?"

"I do not," Haradis began. "I do, however, seek your aid and your allegiance in this battle. My kind... we no longer have an ally out here. I fear we chose the wrong side by joining with Hera, and I wish only to survive this slaughter of our people."

Zachary sighed. "We're not on opposite sides, my friend. We're only separated by tainted blood."

Haradis tilted his head upward and looked at Zachary. "If we are not at war with one another, then why won't you trust us?"

He let the king's words sink in. While there was truth to his viewpoint, it was very one-sided. The Ursis had been playing the middle as long as possible, and he knew Haradis' control over his forces was tenuous at best. But that didn't excuse them for siding with Hera. Her actions towards her people were well known, and her hunger for power should have set off warning signs with the king and his diplomats. If anything, they should have resolved to remain neutral and acted as mediators between the Olivaw family, not taken sides.

A message from Rán appeared on his retinal comm.

Maybe we can use this to our advantage. Having his forces help in recovering a Beacon will be huge. Particularly with their tractor beam technology.

As usual, his A.I. ancestor was a step ahead. The challenge would be convincing the Ursis to follow their lead. Especially considering they had no plan or intentions of destroying the sea of Selene ships. They were after something bigger and far more terrifying.

They needed to close the Rift.

Haradis was staring at him in silence as he contemplated their next steps. They didn't have enough time to review every detail of their plan. Their only option was to leverage the one thing that kept them talking as long as they had.

Zachary stiffened his posture and drew in a deep, slow breath. "First, you will tell me where my sister and the Beacon are?"

Haradis slowly eased upright, but his guards remained on one knee. "And then?"

He crossed his arms, and a smile formed on his face. "And

then you'll put your fleet under my command and follow my orders to the letter."

The king's lip quivered. "I'm not sure my people will allow that."

Zachary exhaled and flipped up the imagery they had of the Rift on the wall screen. It showed the miraculous viewpoint of the universe beyond the fracture in space-time. "They will when they realize that the least of our problems are the Galactic Alliance."

43

LYNC MICHAELS
INSIDE THE NURSERY

They'd been through these gates dozens of times over the past hour. While there was a part of Lync that wanted this battle to end soon, she knew better than that. They'd only been at this for an hour and would probably be at it for many more, luck permitting, of course.

As she transitioned through the gate to the Cornucopia, she yanked her stick to the right to dodge the outbound shots that should be headed her way. These were gifts for the alien ships which had been tailing her since she blew up their moon ship. The two massive bursts of plasma from the Shu arrived right on time, sailing past and cutting through the advancing fighters like a flamethrower through butter. The sight was both overkill and comforting to watch.

With her Nyílak finally through and the gate sealed shut, she sighed and started the systems check. She'd need a quick repair of her forward hull plates, but the robots should be able to swap that out in a matter of minutes.

Her comm chimed, and she blinked it open as she hit send on her repairs. "Go for Lync!"

A visual of Zachary appeared on her retinal comm, and she did a double-take. "What the hell?" There, standing behind him, was an Ursis that looked remarkably like Haradis. "Why the frak is he on our side of the gate?"

Zachary shifted uncomfortably. For a man married to a strong woman, he had a hard time being hollered at.

"Listen." He raised his hands upward. "We don't have time to debate this, but—"

"Shit." She rolled her eyes as her message queue lit up.

He froze and peered past the camera at his controls. "What is it?"

"You and your buts." She sighed and quickly scanned over the messages from her Ulixi flight crews. They were asking if they should engage the Ursis ships near the Cornucopia. "Now you've gone and got my people in a tizzy. Cut to the chase, Z. Am I blowing these grizzly bears up or what?"

She barrel-rolled her fighter to the left and took aim at the nearest Alatas battleship. The usually glowing green ships were strong as hell, so it was odd seeing them with their aura shut off. They almost looked broken, floating there in the misty haze of the nebula. But she still targeted the closest one anyhow and armed a nuke, just in case.

Shauna must have keyed the same orders to the rest of the Ulixi, as each of their ships pinged back that they were locked and loaded. It was a beautiful sight.

"No!" Zachary waved his hands in the air. "Stand down, Lync! I need you and the others to stand the frak down. Now!"

Her finger hovered over the launch button, and when she glanced to the right, Shauna was already readying another round on her display.

She shook her head. "Not until you tell me what the hell is going on."

"Admiral Olivaw," Haradis tapped him on the shoulder, "my generals are getting uncomfortable."

Zachary groaned and ignored the hulking giant behind him, and instead narrowed his gaze on her. She could see the pent-up fear and doubt in his eyes. Whatever he was about to say, he was scared.

"They're going to help us," he began. "Once you crack open the shell of one of those Selene ships, Haradis and his team will use their tentacles to extract the Beacon. After that, they'll assist you in relocating it to the Rift."

Her heart leapt through her chest as it sunk in what he was saying. "You told them our plan?" She ran her hands through her hair as her mind spiraled out of control. "They can't be trusted. You know that. They're working with Hera. What the frak, man? Are you stupid?"

Haradis reached forward and tried to pull Zachary aside to talk to her, but instead, he swung his arm around and whacked the giant bear upside the head. "I've got this handled!" He glanced back at Lync, but when the king still didn't move, he glared at him. "I need you to take care of your own fraking people! You can't afford to waste time on this." He waved the Ursis away. "Now go!"

When she saw Haradis recoil and nod, she drew in her breath. It was only then that she realized maybe she should cool off and listen.

She turned to face Shauna. "Tell the others to stand down."

Her mother sighed. "If we do that, we'll—"

"Mom," Lync muttered. "Please. Just do it."

They stared at each other through the strange, jelly-like substance in silence until Zachary broke it. "Mom, I promise, we're fine. Haradis won't hurt us. I told him about the Rift, and he understands the gamble we're making, but he's still willing to help. Even though he's keeping his generals in the dark, he's on our side."

"Why?" Shauna connected up to their comm. "Why is he so eager to risk everything on our blind guess?"

Lync glanced between them. "What other choice does he have?" She swallowed hard. "They're getting their asses kicked out there, and Z just told them the Galactic Alliance has pocket aces. Besides, we could use their help in prying the Beacons out of those fraking moons. If we fail, we're all dead anyhow."

Neither of them said a word, and they didn't have to. Everyone knew the stakes by now. She did most of all.

With her man in a medically induced coma, her people fighting for their survival, and her found family falling apart, she was on the brink of losing everything she'd grown to love. And worst of all, it was because of her. If she'd let Joyce take the fleet to another star system after they were banished from Epsilon Eridani, none of this would have happened. Hell, even if she'd left Dwight to his own devices on that Shu, they wouldn't be floating here in the Nursery right now. They'd be somewhere else. And Crayo, he'd be curled up beside her in bed, snoring like a broken ventilation duct.

She closed her eyes and took a deep breath, starting her familiar countdown from ten. With each passing second, she breathed in and out, focusing on clearing her mind and preparing for what was next. Another set of jumps, a few well-placed nukes, and hopefully some hops back here. If they were lucky, they'd get a read on their first Beacon. She could feel that they were getting close.

Once she hit zero, she opened her eyes to see Zachary smiling at her. "What?"

He simply nodded his head at the camera. "Haradis shared some interesting intel with us, and I used it to upload your next sequence of hops." He smirked. "You should prepare your team for stage two before we go."

The plan flashed up on her controls, and she gasped. Apparently, Zachary and Harold had been busy while they were gone. They'd zeroed in on the coordinates of at least two other Beacons, with details on the possible location of a third one. From the looks of it, the GA brought several of the ancient artifacts to this party, and something told her the Entity had their hands in that.

"And by we, you mean..." Shauna's voice faded away.

Zachary simply nodded and looked up.

Lync knew what that meant. He was bringing the Cornucopia into the Nursery battle. While they'd managed to keep it a secret until now, the idea of directing that destructive blast at countless Selene ships was exciting. But there was one problem.

She slowly shook her head. "What do we do after we get the Beacons to the Rift?"

They stared in silence for several minutes, neither willing to answer the question nor offer up a suggestion. And just as she was about to propose a theory, Haradis walked up. Her stomach tightened. Something was up with his people. She knew it.

He lowered down beside Zachary and peered into the camera. His eyes were enormous, and his muzzle was as long as her forearm. How Minula and Ibu had battled these monsters was beyond her. She could only hope she didn't have to.

Haradis tilted his head. "I couldn't help but overhear your little dilemma with the Beacons."

Lync exhaled and contorted her face. And there it was. The other shoe dropped. He knew their plan was shit, and they wanted nothing of it. Better now than in the middle of battle.

The king narrowed his gaze at her dramatic gesture. "You can rest assured, Colonel Michaels, my people are squarely on your side. Even if our pursuit is…" He glanced between them. "How shall I say it?"

Shauna chuckled. "Like chasing a unicorn through a field of flying pigs?"

Haradis smirked. "I was going to say improbable, but yeah, your analogy makes more sense for humans."

Lync suppressed a smile.

"Ah, yes. Now, back to why I interrupted your little party." He raised an eyebrow and leaned closer to the camera. "I might have an idea how one can use the Beacons to seal the Rift."

LYNC YANKED BACK the controls of her Nyílak and slammed the throttle forward, turning the fighter on a dime and sending the plasma round sailing past. It blasted a crater-sized hole through the outer layer of the Selene moon ship, launching a plume of superheated fluid out into the cold void of space.

The short, cylindrical ship that had been pursuing her since she passed through the gate exploded in a blast of light, sending a cascade of shrapnel raining down into the open wound on the moon. The resulting chain reaction of eruptions was a symphony to her soul. Nothing made her happier than watching an overzealous alien mistake her for a newbie pilot.

With the Selene moon punctured and its innards exposed to the battlefield, she didn't even need to close her eyes to sense the Beacon. The psychic power of the ancient device burst outward, nearly knocking her out.

She shrieked in the gelatinous liquid and brought her hands to her head. The voices imprisoned within the artifact were screaming out, and she couldn't stop them. She wasn't strong enough. The volume was deafening, and the souls trapped inside were fighting against the realization that their mortal coil was unwinding. Unfortunately for her, the concentrated power of millions of minds lashing out was too much.

Shauna must have sensed her condition, because a few seconds after the psychic explosion, she sealed up the Skotádi hull of the Nyílak, and the voices disappeared. They thought they needed to have it open for a Ulixi to sense if the Beacon was inside, but they'd been wrong.

Lync lowered her head to her chest as her mother took control of the ship. Shauna rocketed them toward the projected coordinates of the next portal transition while she did her best to calm her mind now that the pinhole was closed.

When she realized what her mother was doing, she groaned and reached out toward the yoke. "No…" She frantically waved her hand through the fluid. It took her a second to realize that her controls had been retracted away.

"Over my dead body." Shauna pulled the trigger, and their forward laser battery fired into the fray, missing a

Thyreusian fighter that shot across their path by mere centimeters.

By the time the Ulixi compromised one of these Selene moons, the aliens inside would usually be bailing out of the giant vessel by the thousands. But this time was different. This time, any aliens in the vicinity of the moon weren't running away. They were turning their attention toward the chaos and were focused on one thing and one thing only: protecting the Beacon.

Klus had had a feeling something like this would happen. Apparently, they'd seen this exact scenario play out when the GA closed the Proto Dark Nebula. In the final battle, their Alatas battleships managed to crack open the Selene flagship used to house the Beacon, and they did it before the GA had prepared it to seal the Nebula. The resulting chaotic alien battle rage that ensued was too much for the war-torn Ursis fleet to handle. They were cut to shreds in a matter of minutes, and the Nebula was sealed up soon thereafter.

Fortunately for them, Klus had helped her and Zachary prepare for this exact situation. It was only when she remembered that part of the plan that she realized Shauna hadn't been flying them toward the next gate. That wasn't it at all. She was trying to get them out of the blast radius.

She swung the tactical display closer and tapped the icon to bring up the locations of the other Ulixi pilots. It took several excruciating seconds for the map to refresh, as the computer was constantly scanning the field of battle and decoding the glyphs painted on the hulls of their Nyílak fighters.

When the tactical screen finally flashed up, her heart raced as she scanned the inbound and outbound transmission logs. It didn't take long to see that it was Greer who had spun up his emergency micro-gate to send the signal to the Cornucopia. And that meant only one thing.

"We're almost there!" Shauna screamed.

Lync was still playing catch-up. The projected gate impact circle was massive, and given how unpredictable the jump calculations were with so many random variables, it wasn't a surprise. Judging by the positions of the other fighters, they were the only alliance ship inside the exposed area.

"We're not going to make it." She reached down and pulled the pilot controls up from their stowed position. While she wasn't about to take over from Shauna midway through the maneuver, she needed to be ready to swap in. And a few seconds later, she had to do exactly that.

One second they were admiring a sprinkling of distant Selene moon ships framed by the multicolored nebulosity of the Nursery, and the next they were staring straight down the opening of the Cornucopia. The massive weapon had gated right in the middle of the battle. They could see tens of thousands of glowing power cores deep within the mouth of the cannon. Each core was capable of devastating a ship on its own; combined, they could destroy anything in their path. But there was a problem. It was locked, loaded, and about to fire, with them directly in its line of sight.

She watched as the gravity wake of the weapon's sudden arrival tore apart nearby ships. Some exploded into fiery balls of light while others ricocheted off, caught in the gravitational ripple from the massive device.

Their Nyílak buckled and spun, riding the tail end of one such wave. A pair of nearby Thyreusian fighters spiraled past, trapped in the wake of the unexpected ship's arrival. She grabbed the yoke, pulling the stick back to avoid a collision, then dropped the throttle low to let the swell take them wherever it wished, at least until she had better control of their direction.

As the first wave settled, another followed, pushing them even closer to the Selene moon they were trying to escape from. They would never make it into the safe zone. Not like this.

Lync turned to Shauna. "We have to use it!"

"I know," the robot muttered. "I'm already ahead of you."

Her mother understood the stakes. They were one of only a handful of Nyílak that could gate, but they had purposely avoided using this power. In the Beacon battle, ships with gating technology were attacked relentlessly, which made sense. They had something the GA wanted. But in this battle, the script was flipped. The gating was left to the select few, and was reserved only for emergencies.

Shauna slammed her metallic hand against a compression plate on the outer hull of the ship, powering up the emergency gate drive. The effect wasn't visible from inside, but outside their craft, the hull reshaped, and a series of slits opened. These let loose the strands that made up the mesh used to direct the tachyon particles.

"We're a go!" Shauna said. "Just don't—"

"Overdo it," Lync interrupted. "I know. Small hops."

She narrowed her gaze and focused. If she tried to jump too far, they'd be bouncing around like a pinball. But too short a jump, and they'd be toast.

As she prepared to gate, their defensive alerts signaled that their forward shields had absorbed several incoming energy blasts. Checking their status, she saw they were down to sixty percent. Judging by the direction of the shots, the two nearby Thyreusian fighters had regained control and were now taking aim at them.

Shauna didn't wait for Lync to finish the gate procedures. They might be dead by then. Instead, she responded by targeting the aliens and firing a plasma round at each one. The first ship veered out of the way, sending the shot wide. They must've seen it coming. But the second superheated blast hit its target, slicing across the alien ship's hull and leaving behind a smoldering battle scar. The ship was still operational, but judging by the faint white glow from that part of their hull, their automated systems had already started repairs.

Lync tried not to watch the ensuing dogfight and instead opened the tachyon flow controls on her primary screen. Once powered up, she closed her eyes and gently nudged the lever to increase power to the drive. Now all she needed to do was adjust the direction and range actuators, focusing on the goldilocks' distance: not too far and not too short.

The act of gating with precision was more art than science. While the Cornucopia had jumped across light-hours with four dedicated Ulixi pilots and an impressive collection of networked A.I. guiding it, she only had her instincts and innate luck to draw from. The Cornucopia, being multiple times larger than a Selene moon, made an ideal gravitational center to jump away from. Its influence on their direction would overpower any other nearby ships, as long as she didn't push too hard.

Her fingers nudged the targeting reticle forward. Even though she couldn't see it, she knew where the jump would take them. None of the Ulixi could explain exactly how they controlled the jumps, but the easiest way to describe it was that it felt soft. If the jump was off target, her mind became stiff and uncomfortable. It was like jumping into different piles of material. One minute, it would hurt like a brick to the face, and the next, it would be as smooth and soft as butter. The amount of pain depended on how much she needed to sand off. With open space, it was mostly soft, but for maneuvers like this, sticking the landing was as hard as hell.

Once she was happy with her targeting, she took a deep breath and slammed the jump lever forward. Now was not the time for second-guessing herself. And if they were planning on surviving this, there was no sense in taking it slow.

The glowing blue gate field shot over their ship and through the goo, tearing her apart from the inside out. While the sludge acted as a means to distribute pain medication through her skin, it still took a few seconds to have an effect. A few long and painful seconds.

As she screamed into the transparent slime around them, her control panel updated with their new position. She could just make it out between the waves of agony, and from the looks of it, they'd only jumped a few dozen kilometers. It was the shortest leap through space-time she'd ever managed.

"Wholly shit!" Shauna pointed at the far side of their crew

capsule, and the wall screen updated to show the view outside their ship. She usually had it shut off, as it was too distracting, but this was a sight worth watching.

The Cornucopia had powered up and was firing its first round. Even though they'd seen footage of the weapon sealing the Dark Nebula near Henosi, none of them had ever witnessed it firsthand.

The beam of energy eased out slowly, filling up the horn until it reached the edge of the conical structure. At that point, it overflowed, hurling forward like a lance through the darkness. It engulfed the Selene moon in a silvery ray of light, evaporating everything in its path.

And then something unexpected happened. A dozen pillars of light burst outward in all directions. It was as if the Cornucopia had shot a prism. Each of the smaller beams fired off into space, and a few of them struck distant targets. Two of them hit other Selene moons, but one of them hit a Shu. The resulting explosions were just as blinding as the first, and they lit up the nebula in every direction. The scene was unreal, and had she not been in so much pain, it might have been beautiful.

When the fireworks finally subsided, the only thing left in place of their moon-sized target was the Beacon itself. Somehow, the artifact which had previously been safely cocooned inside the spherical starship was now floating silently in space, complete with a faint glow emanating from its exterior.

Haradis told them this would happen. The Galactic Alliance had run hundreds of thousands of tests on the Beacons in the past, and every time they tried to crack it open, they failed. The artifacts were impossible to destroy, which was how he came up with the strategy of simply wiping away the candy-coated, moon-shaped shell and leaving the prize inside for the Ursis to collect.

Shauna spun their ship around toward the Beacon, and Lync focused her attention on the glowing object in front of them. At first, she thought the phosphorescence was the artifact's superheated surface radiating from the heat. But as they flew closer and closer to it, she realized what it was. She could sense the life forces trapped inside, and deep within her soul, she knew they were dying off. Even through the protective skotádi layer on their hull, she could feel them. The power of millions of concentrated souls was immense, and what made it even worse was that they were screaming for help.

As she wept for the countless lives fading into the nothingness of space, the Beacon grew dimmer and dimmer. Their loss was such a waste. If she hadn't been surrounded by goo, her eyes would've been filled with tears.

"Here they come!" Shauna pointed at the far wall screen.

There in the distance were two Ursis Alatas battleships passing through a newly opened portal, and following close behind was a hive of robotic fighters. Zachary had called in the cavalry, and that meant one thing. They were moving on to the next stage of their plan: carting the Beacon away and depositing it near the Rift.

After that, it was anyone's guess.

44

JOYCE GREEN
OUTSIDE THE NURSERY, GROUP TWO

Boarding the U.A. Perniger Alatas class battleship took Joyce longer than she expected. They didn't make her remove her artificial limb, as Hera had back in the day, but they still put her through a battery of tests and scans. The more time they wasted, the more she recognized they were fraking with her.

Even with Hera orchestrating the Nursery battle, the Ursis begrudgingly allowed her onboard. At first, she thought it was because of what the Gunders had done to them. If that were the case, she wasn't surprised by their reaction. However, they still needed the alien battleships to make this fight possible. Without their sheer numbers, this campaign would've been over before it started. The challenge was whether or not Hera could control these beasts.

The longer she waited and the more the voices in her mind took over, the more pissed she became. Perhaps her subconscious was right. Maybe she should have remained in command onboard the Kermodei. At least that was a human-controlled ship. This oversized alien contraption smelled like a zoo, and she was pretty sure the brown stain in the corner wasn't dirt.

When she tried to check the messages on her comm, the connection failed. It hadn't been working for the last few hours since Haradis jumped back from the battle this past cycle. He'd limped through the gates from his most recent battlefield excursion with only three ships remaining from his original squadron of twelve.

The moment he returned, her comm was inundated with messages about his people. The king was pushing even harder against Hera's control, and it almost seemed like he was staging a coup. After that, her comm stopped working. In the hour since, anything could've happened. For all she knew, his generals had taken back command of their entire fleet. They'd placed a lot of trust in Hera, but if they attacked solo, it could jeopardize their broader strategy.

With each passing second, her mind spiraled with thoughts of their dysfunctional alliance, triggering a dull throb in her neck. She took a minute to lean against the wall. Anytime she got worked up about Hera or their mission, her head started pounding, and her inner voice returned with a vengeance.

"Get your ass back in this game, sister," the voice whispered. "The Ursis. They're using you to reach Hera. You need to return to the Kermodei before it's too late."

Joyce pushed off the wall and paced back and forth several more times before she froze. The waiting indicator updated on her retinal comm. It changed from thirty minutes to two hours. She'd already waited for three. There was no way in hell she'd last two more.

"Frak this!" She spun around, marched up to the massive hatch at the opposite end of the room, and slapped the red open button with her palm.

Nothing happened.

The button did not beep, chime, or give any indication it had been pressed. She tried again and again, with more force each time, but was met with the same result.

"Let me out of here!" She slammed the side of her fist against the metallic door, and a boom echoed through the room.

This situation was getting stupid. As far as she knew, the

battle had ended. And judging by their performance until then, they'd lost handily. The voice was right. She needed to return to the Kermodei.

After another minute or so of hammering, she stopped, both due to its futility and the pain in her hand. Anger can only overpower pain for so long.

When she spun around to search the room, she realized the control panel she'd used to check in had disappeared. They had retracted it into the wall. Then it hit her. These aliens weren't just running tests on her; they were imprisoning her.

This wasn't what Klus had sent her here for. She'd ordered Joyce to take command of this ship. Unless the whole thing had been a ruse to get her off the Kermodei. That would explain the flood of messages she'd received from her people hours earlier. Why it took her this long to put two and two together was beyond her. She hadn't been herself since she woke up and received the news about Ryder.

The throbbing in the back of her head began again, sending searing waves of pain up and down her spine. She couldn't take it any longer. The room suddenly started spinning, and she collapsed to the ground, whacking her head against the wall.

As she struggled to remain conscious, the door slid aside and two pairs of feet rushed in. When they reached her side, they didn't roll her over to check her. Instead, they grabbed her arms and legs and held her down.

"They're trying to kill you," the voice whispered. "Defend yourself, or you'll end up like your son!"

The voice was right. The Ursis forced her onto her stomach and pinned her to the ground. They were doing something to her back.

She tried to push up, but the beasts were too strong. When she reached backward to grab at them, they slid her outstretched hand under their massive legs, pinning it down. Resistance was futile. She couldn't move a mountain.

"Your legs!" the voice shouted. "Use your legs!"

This time, the voice was louder. It was screaming above her own thoughts. It was as if it wasn't actually her inner self talking. But yet again, it was right. She'd forgotten all about her legs. They were stronger than even these Ursis.

She gritted her teeth as she felt a claw from one of the bears slice into the back of her head and down her spine. The fraking monsters were prying her open like an oyster.

"Get off!" She shouted, pushing up with her knees, bending at the hips, and raising her ass into the air.

The Ursis were caught off guard by her strength. The one on her right squealed and slid off her hand. When they did, an electronic scalpel and a tablet-like instrument crashed to the ground. The Ursis on her left merely stepped backward.

When she stared down at the objects, her eyes went wide. They hadn't used their claws to cut her open; they'd been using fraking tools.

She reached down and picked up the tablet; it was attached by a wire to the cutter. On the display was an X-ray of her spine, but it wasn't a normal scan. From the looks of it, she had a lobster-looking appendage connected to her back.

"What the hell is this?" She glanced at the Ursis and froze.

The alien to her right looked familiar. She'd seen it somewhere before.

"Grifdar?" she muttered.

He raised his shaking paws upward. "We're trying to help."

"The frak you are!" She held up the panel. "Why are you attaching this to me? What is it?"

"We're not, you fool," the other Ursis said.

She jerked her head from Grifdar to the second Ursis and back again. "What is he talking about?"

Grifdar nodded, and his gaze softened. "He's telling the truth. Hera's people attached it to you at your base in Zeta Lupi."

"Lies!" She winced and squeezed her eyes shut as bursts of pain exploded in the nape of her neck.

When she heard their feet shuffle, she snapped her eyes

open and stepped backward. They were sliding around on opposite sides, preparing to make a move on her.

"Back up!" she screamed.

"Or what?" the other Ursis asked.

Grifdar growled. "Don't provoke her. We need her to calm down to remove that thing safely."

"They're lying!" her inner voice said.

"Stop!" She raised her hands. "Please stop! You're the ones doing this to me."

"No…" Grifdar shook his head. "We are not. I promise you, my friend. It's the other way around. We're saving you. This parasite is the one—"

The back of her head exploded in a jolt of pain, and she lost control of her legs. Somehow, the aliens had manipulated her body, making her move. They launched her forward on a collision course with the other Ursis.

She winced as she was propelled across the space between them. This was going to hurt like hell. But just as she was about to collide with the mountain of an alien, Grifdar snatched her back. He lashed out and grabbed her by the foot, slamming her down and making her face bounce off the floor.

The last thing she remembered was her inner voice crying out and the room fading to black.

"Rip the damn thing off her. Now!" Grifdar shouted.

"Kill them!" The voice screamed as it slowly faded away. "We must… kill… them. Al…l…of…th…em…"

WHEN HER EYES SPRANG OPEN, Joyce didn't find herself on the floor or even in a prison cell. Instead, she was lying on a long bench at the rear of an expansive chamber. Upon looking around, she realized it wasn't an ordinary room — it was the bridge of the U.A. Perniger.

She went to push up and groaned before collapsing back down. Her head was pounding, but not the same way as it was earlier. This was a different kind of pain. She ran her hand over her neck and winced when her fingers brushed the stitches on her wound.

"Ahh, look, our little thorn is awake." The second Ursis voice from the cell snarled at her. He was manning a station on the right side of the bridge.

Grifdar growled from the pilot seat in the middle and glared back at him. "Her name is Commander Green, and you will address her as such."

"Fine… whatever." The Ursis sighed, glancing from her to his controls. "She's awake. Now let's hope she doesn't try to kill us again."

"Kill you?" Joyce lowered her hand to the arms of the bench and took a deep breath. "Why… why would I do that?"

She pushed up slowly, steadying herself. Her balance was still off, but at least she could walk, albeit barely.

"You weren't exactly happy we removed that thing." Grifdar gestured at the vial sitting in the corner of the room.

From where she was standing, she couldn't tell what it was. But when she walked toward it, she stopped short and gasped. "Was that…" She reached up and stroked the back of her head. "Was that thing attached to me?" She looked back at her friend.

He nodded and returned his attention to his controls. The Perniger was lining up in front of a closed gate along with the rest of the Ursis fleet.

"And your damn legs." The other Ursis grunted, glancing down at her mechanized lower torso. "They wouldn't stop twitching the whole friggin time, Commmmmannnder."

He over-enunciated her title until Grifdar growled at him, at which point he stopped.

She swallowed hard. Her throat was parched, and while she could use some water, the flash on the wall screen caught her attention.

"What the hell?" she muttered.

Grifdar was playing a video of two Alatas battleships dragging away what appeared to be a Beacon of Therion. Stranger still was what trailed in their wake — an entire swarm of silvery fighters was swimming around them, but they weren't attacking the Ursis. Instead, they were fighting off the inbound Galactic Alliance forces. Whoever the silver ships were, they were on their side.

"It's a good thing you're awake, Commander." Grifdar gestured toward the station beside him. "You should get up here. We can use your help."

Her heart raced in her chest as she staggered forward to the seat on his right. She was in well over her head, but standing in the outfield wasn't helping anyone. If she could lend a hand, she would.

When she finally climbed into the oversized chair, she spun around to see that the gate had closed, and they were next in line for a transition.

She looked over at Grifdar and saw that he was staring at a map of the Nursery. "Where are we gating to next?"

He flicked his map up on the far wall screen, and she took it all in. There were four regions of space highlighted on or near the battlefield. Three of them were marked in green, and they had dots towing a Beacon toward the object some had been calling the Rift. Their jump target was the fourth region, and it was well away from the others. It took her a second to realize what she was looking at, but when she did, the knot in the pit of her stomach tightened.

"Are you kidding me?" She glanced at Grifdar.

He smirked and flipped down his tactical reticule over his left eye. "I wish I were, Commander. But your friend, Admiral Olivaw, thinks we may need all four."

Joyce reached down and rested her hands on the seat as the massive control panel swung around and lowered towards her. While it was definitely oversized, at least she could reach all the controls. From what she gathered from her displays, she was in charge of the weapons.

She shook her head. "I... I don't know how to do this."

"Sure you do," a voice said from behind her.

When she turned, she recoiled and gasped. In front of her

was someone who looked remarkably like Ryder, but that was impossible. He was dead.

He tapped the side of his head. "Just use your neural link and upload the training. It shouldn't take but a few seconds." He smiled, and his eyes twinkled in the overhead light. They had that youthful glimmer she'd loved so much.

Joyce didn't hesitate. She leapt out of her seat and stumbled forward, colliding into him. "Is this..." She leaned away and held his face in her hands, kissing him over and over again. "Are you... really real?" She kissed him. "Or... am I..."

Ryder raised his finger to her mouth and stopped her before she said it. He then reached over and gently wiped at the tears streaming down her face. "I'm as real as this shitstorm we're about to get into."

"But how?" She shook her head and ran her hands down his smooth cheeks. "I thought you were—"

He leaned in and kissed her hard, pulling her close and squeezing her tight. She felt her body melt into his as they held the embrace. The universe could end, and she wouldn't care. She'd gotten her one wish.

Grifdar cleared his throat, and Ryder stopped, slowly separating his mouth from hers.

"We need you at the controls." He tipped his head toward the chair she'd left from. "We're sorta short-staffed."

She looked back at Grifdar, and he nodded.

"Like I said earlier, we could use your help." He smiled.

She chuckled and glanced around. "What, are we the only people on this tug or something?"

Grifdar shrugged and returned his attention forward.

Joyce turned to face Ryder. "Seriously?"

He leaned in and pressed his head against hers before tenderly kissing her several more times. "We can get into it later, but right now, we have work to do. We've lost a lot of people out there," he tilted his chin toward the gate, "and to be honest, we're lucky to be alive." He kissed her once more and then pulled away, nudging her backward. "Now get your cute butt up in that chair and pull on your ass-kicking boots,

Commander." He winked. "We've got some butts to kick, and I ain't about to die. Not out here."

Her heart fluttered, and she took a deep breath before wiping at her face and centering herself. While she had no idea what they were about to encounter, she knew one thing. She wasn't about to squander her second chances. Either with Ryder, or in taking her revenge against the GA.

She reached up and activated her retinal comm. It paused briefly, but it eventually connected to the Ursis' central computer and downloaded everything she'd missed over the last few hours. She ignored all the messages and alerts, and instead subvocalized a command.

"Activate training mode." She closed her eyes. "Download Ursis instruction manual. Alatas class starship. Speed, maximum."

45

BRADLEY OLIVAW
HD 117939, PLANETSIDE

The alien mechanism hummed in the corner of the room, a chilling symphony of malevolence waiting to take a life. Although the same feat could have been achieved with a simple set of wires, they'd designed this evil contraption to strike fear into the mind of anyone who set eyes on it. And for Bradley, it did exactly that.

He moaned as he watched the deadly arc of blue-white electricity dance through the tendril-like device, hitting him and Adri with the force of a relentless tidal wave. His muscles convulsed uncontrollably, as if they'd been seized by invisible puppet strings. With his teeth gritted together, he fought to trap his desperate scream, swallowing it down as the electric serpent coiled around his body and squeezed.

As the jolt continued, every nerve in his body screamed in protest. The resulting agony was as vivid as lightning bolts streaking across a pitch-black sky. His heart pounded in his chest like a frantic drummer whose rhythm had been shattered by the erratic pulse of electricity.

And then the pain ended.

There were no questions to answer, no faces staring at them. There was only torture. They'd been doing it for the last thirty minutes, and the clones had yet to make a demand.

After the first jolt hit, Shauna stopped messaging him. He

wasn't sure why, but he wasn't about to reveal her presence to these lunatics. So, all he could do was fight back the pain and hope she was alright. With wave after wave tearing him apart, he couldn't help but wonder if he should have left her back on their ship. Perhaps she would've found a way to escape rather than be imprisoned in his body.

When Bradley looked over at Adri, she was panting with her eyes wide open. The gesture mirrored the unnatural glow of the deadly current that had been flowing through her girlish frame. Her world had been reduced to nothing more than blinding flashes and the taste of hot, metallic fear on her tongue.

He knew her feelings well and wished it was only him they'd brought here. It was his fault she was being tortured.

Her childhood crush on him was common knowledge among the Ulixi, and even their torturers somehow knew. While her infatuation was endearing, she was a child, and that was exactly why they dragged her here. They hoped her pain would break him. That seeing her cry would cause him to crumble. What they didn't know about her was that while she may have been a child, she'd seen more suffering in her life than all of them combined. Given her past losses of both her home and her father, she could weather this storm better than him.

The distant door clicked open, echoing the sound of the alien device being activated and sending his body into a spasm. While the jolt never came, his muscles remained tense as footsteps approached from the darkness.

"What did you do to him?" a voice said.

He recognized that voice. "Parker? Is that... you? I thought you were—"

"Dead?" Parker stared into the light. "I'm afraid I was, until a few minutes ago."

Although his face was pink and fresh with life, his skin was as pale as a ghost. It was as if he'd never seen a day of sun in his life. Which was probably the case when you were grown under nothing but vat lights.

The man walked around his table and over to Adri's side. He ran his hand up and down her body, wiping the sweat off her skin. He then brought it up to his nose and drew in a breath.

"The smell of fear is such an aphrodisiac." He spun around to face Bradley and squinted. "How does your kind not do this sort of thing all the time?" He gestured up and down Adri's body.

Bradley shook his head. "Because we're not fraking animals like you." He tried to spit on the man, but coughed up blood instead, choking on the metallic taste in his mouth.

Parker cringed backward and waved his hand toward Bradley. "You're disgusting." He shrugged. "Maybe it's just this fine specimen." He glanced over at the little girl. "I'll be sure to sample her DNA before we melt her down later. She'll make a fun play toy for generations to come."

"You fraking…" He tried to lunge up off the table, but instead, an invisible opposing force slammed him backward. A second later, a jolt of electricity shot down the arm of the alien torture device, shocking both of them.

As his body convulsed, images of Abigail flashed through his mind. He'd seen the Entity use electric shocks to force her to do their bidding. The thought of trading literal barbs like that every day was unimaginable, but she'd always been stronger than him.

When he turned his head, he watched Adri's back arch upward. She screamed out in unison with him. Their voices were a chorus of pain, the likes of which he never imagined he'd hear. When the stream of electricity stopped, he gasped for air.

He wasn't sure he could take much more of this.

Then he saw it. Parker leaned back against Adri's table and raised his hand to his chest. He was rubbing at something, and it wasn't until he pulled his hand away from his collarbone that Bradley realized what it was.

At first, he simply smiled, but the more pain Parker felt, the more it excited him. Before he knew it, he was laughing like he had been outside. Except instead of a forest to echo his laughter, there was only Adri. Like their shared pain moments earlier, her laughter and joy echoed his. The funny part was, she didn't even know why she was laughing; she just followed his lead.

Parker hacked into his hand, and when he pulled it away, it was covered in blood. "What did you do to me? To us?"

Closing his eyes, Bradley smiled as the memories of his trip underground danced through his mind. He spat on everything he could on the way to the elevator, and then, when they tossed him inside, he urinated on himself. The guards and other personnel had been so focused on beating him, they hadn't considered that they were spreading the virus.

Even after they arrived at their floor, he continued with his personal festival of bodily fluids. At one point, they dragged him through a glass-walled hallway, where he was surrounded by vats of humans as far as the eye could see. While they were well out of reach, the fluid from his body would hopefully cause some damage, be it on the feet of passersby or through the air itself. Like any exponentially expanding super virus, once the wave started, it was nearly impossible to stop.

"You're not going to tell me, are you?" Parker stumbled forward and rested his arms on the table beside Bradley.

"Now, where would the fun be in that?" He smiled and stared at the growing spiderweb-like pattern on the man's neck. It matched the one he'd seen on Zeus and the other clones who escorted him underground.

Parker's eyes fluttered, and his body wavered back and forth. He was about to pass out.

"Hey!" Bradley smacked his hand on the tabletop.

The man's eyes sprang open, and he drew in a breath.

"Alright," Bradley began. "If you let me up, I'll tell you what I did." He raised his eyebrows. "What do you say?"

At first, it seemed like maybe Parker was going to fall for it, but a moment later he tipped sideways and cracked his head on the edge of the smooth metallic table. Blood sprayed Bradley in the face as the clone crashed to the ground.

He sighed and squinted, trying to keep the crimson fluid from entering his eyes.

"That looks disgusting," Adri said.

He turned his head to look at her smiling face and couldn't help but laugh. She was covered in sweat and had straps over her private parts, but otherwise, she was clean — naked, but clean. He, however, was drenched in blood, sweat, feces, and a few gallons of urine. They were a stark contrast to each other.

As they both started cackling again, the door in the darkness clicked open, and several people came rushing in.

"Get this place cleaned up," the woman said. "And whatever you do, wash this disgusting mess off." She gestured toward him and paused on Adri, seeming to consider her. "This one as well. She's covered in piss, too."

Bradley tilted his head to see a stream of urine coming from her table as it slowly trickled over the edge.

The two of them broke out into raucous laughter yet again.

"TURN AROUND!" The man waved his hand toward Bradley, and he did as he was told.

He flipped around to face the blast of ice-cold water. This was the second round of cleaning, and at this point, his body felt like a dodgy sponge. They'd already roughed him up with a few bristly brushes and soap, and now all they were doing was washing down anything they'd missed.

They thought they'd done it the first time, but when they approached him, he shat himself again. While he didn't think he had any more shit left, he still managed to eke out a bit more. All it had taken was for him to see the splotch of gray on both of their arms. The markings were small at first, but the longer he lingered in the water, the larger they grew.

He glanced over at Adri, shivering in the corner. Her knees were curled up around her chest, and she was glancing between him and the other two.

When he looked back at the guards, he noticed that one of them had fallen over, and the second was leaning down, trying to help them. This was their chance. It shouldn't require much effort to take them out.

He took a deep breath and rubbed his hands together. Finally, once he'd mustered enough courage, he leaned forward and rushed toward the water. By the time he'd reached the guard, they were upright, and their eyes went wide.

"Shit!" They dropped the hose, and before Bradley could stop them, they were reaching for their waist.

But they were too slow. Not for Bradley, but for Adri. She tackled them from the side, and the two of them tumbled to the ground in a wet mess of bodies. Bradley jumped on top of the man as Adri slipped sideways on her stomach. She'd been too slick and came in too fast, but that was fine. He could take it from here.

He raised his fists over his head and brought them down, wailing on the man over and over again. One after the other, he slammed them into the guard's face.

Every emotion he'd ever bottled up burst to the surface at that moment. Every jolt of pain, every friend he'd lost, and every second he'd feared death over the past few days. They were all there, rising up and empowering each and every blow.

"Bradley!" Adri screamed. "He's... dead."

He froze and gasped for breath, his hands raised over his head. When he looked down, all that remained of the guard was a bloody, broken mash of blood and skin. Whatever the gray spidery substance was doing to them, it was practically melting the clones.

Adri eased forward and slowly took his hand in hers, and tugged him away. At first, he couldn't move. It was like he was planted in place. But after a few more gentle tugs, he rose to his feet and stumbled off the man.

They worked their way over toward the hose, and Adri picked it up and rinsed herself off with her back to him. Once she was done, she handed him the nozzle, and he did the same.

She did her best to cover herself up with her hands so he couldn't see her. It was strange to think someone could have modesty in that moment, but it went to show how innocent the young woman was.

He wished they hadn't dragged her into this mess.

"Why… did they bring you here?" He turned away from her and used the hose to wash his front side.

She snickered, and he glanced back at her to see her staring down at her hands. "I failed to launch the attack." She turned over her shaking hands several times until she finally tucked them under her arms. "Like you said before you left, if I failed, we were dead."

He froze and stared at her. "That's not what I meant. You know that, right?"

She shrugged and then started to whimper.

"Adri, turn around. Look at me."

The little girl half turned and peered at him, his back still to her.

"They modified the ships. Every single fraking one of them. And way before we got here." He shook his head. "Hell, I couldn't do shit with mine. Once I gated, they took control of it." He leaned down and locked eyes with her. She was staring at the ground. "This is not on you. I'm sure you did everything you could. But this… this is on me and my family. We fraked up a long time ago and have been paying penance ever since."

Adri shook her head. "No! This isn't on you." She wiped at her face. "I've watched you and your brother and sister try to fix this fraking mess for… hell, a few years now. No. This isn't your fault. This is on your parents, and your parents' parents. In the end, it's on everyone but you three."

She lowered her hand and reached out to nudge him. "You have to know that, right?"

He shrugged and tossed the hose aside. "I guess. That doesn't make it any easier, though."

When the hose hit the ground, the lights overhead flickered, and a boom echoed in the distance.

"That can't be good," he muttered and glanced back at her. "What do you say we try to get the hell out of here?"

"Frak yeah!" Adri shot forward toward the door.

He chuckled and shook his head. For a little girl, she was as fearless as they come. A potty mouth, but brave nonetheless.

46

IBU

OUTSIDE THE NURSERY, NEAR GROUP THREE

The control panels on the Sloth all flashed at once, and Ibu lifted their hands up. "What the hell is going on? I didn't do anything."

They'd been poking and prodding around the massive Terminus mothership for several hours, trying to figure out where the Beacon and Abigail had been locked away. Thus far, there'd been no luck in finding them.

"I'd say it was poor craftsmanship by the clones, but the systems appear to be operating properly." Little Red's eyes fluttered orange. "Perhaps it's warning us of something. Should I run an active scan of the nearby region of space?"

"No!" Ibu reached out and rested their hand on the little robot's head. "Not unless you want to die. The minute we perform an active scan, Hera will sick her fighters on us and probably move the entire fleet. We've been lucky this long that they haven't changed their position."

While they knew it wasn't a simple task to pick up thousands of half-damaged warships and move them to another location, if Hera found out they'd been infiltrating her ship, relocating was the least concerning thing she'd do. Ibu swallowed hard as they imagined the worst, and every time, harming Abigail was at the top of the list.

They'd vowed to protect her until the end, and they

weren't about to lose her now. Not when they were so close.

"Well, I'm going to keep probing their ship. I think I may have narrowed down where they put the Beacon." Ibu tweaked their controls and started performing the necessary calculations.

Each gate took several minutes to set up, and they could only perform it after they learned something new about the ship. Something they could leverage with certainty. Even the smallest miscalculation could mean they'd open a micro-gate into the reactor core or in the middle of an energy conduit. That could get ugly quickly.

They leaned back and closed their eyes, waiting for the numbers to finish crunching. Part of them wanted to just jump over there and board the ship. It was bound to be faster than this search grid they were laying down. You'd think that finding an enormous ancient relic onboard a human starship would be easy, but it wasn't. Especially when they were dealing with a ship as big as a moon. To be honest, they still hadn't figured out why the blasted thing was so big, and it wasn't because it was full of resources. In fact, they'd opened a half dozen gates into cryo-stasis rooms filled with clones. There were thousands of them on ice, all waiting to wake up and receive their orders.

When the alert chimed and signaled that the calculation was complete, they opened their eyes to find their control panel on the fritz again. The screen was flashing on and off, as if there was a short in the system.

"What the frak?" they muttered.

Little Red chirped and bounced up and down.

"What is it?" Ibu leaned closer to him. "What did you find?"

"It appears that someone is trying to get our attention, Master Ibu." Little Red showed a recording of the flashing screen, and then it stopped again.

Ibu shook their head. "I... still don't see it."

Little Red's eyes twirled a rainbow of colors as he slowed down the recording and played it back at an excruciatingly slow speed. The throbs seemed to morph, not into a simple on and off pattern like their eyes perceived, but into a more structured set of smaller, more intricate pauses.

"Is it... a code?" Ibu reached out and scrubbed back and forth, trying to make heads or tails of the pattern.

"It is." Little Red bobbed their head. "And it's very complicated. There are over one million light variations in this section of the recording alone. In this region, you can see hints of Mandelbrot sets with various preperiodic Misiurewicz points. They're quadratic—"

Ibu waved their hand. "Skip to the good stuff, Red. What does it mean?"

The little robot turned to look at them. "It appears to be a message from Master Zachary. He encoded it using cryptography known only to the Olivaw family, and one that Harold shared with me before our departure."

"Of course he did." Ibu pointed at the screen. "Bring it up."

A message from Zachary appeared on the panel, accompanied by a detailed map of Hera's ship.

Ibu gasped as they read the message.

There's been a slight change in plans. We have some fuzzy new friends who used to be on Hera's team. They shared this little tidbit and also enabled us to make this transmission. I hope it reaches you safely. You don't have much time to save my sister. We might need that Beacon, and we're prepared to crack open the ship to retrieve it. Even if that means killing her. While I hate writing those words, the stakes are too high. You know it as well as I do. I can only hope that you reach her in time. Good luck, and may the speed of the Builders be at your back.

They glanced to the right, taking in the starship's schematic. The Beacon was tucked away in a distant recess in the ship, nowhere near their search grid's focus. While they'd assumed it would be in a central room accessible to a mass of people, like in all the other locations within the GA and Liprosus, this room was microscopic. And according to the map, it was stashed in a random wing off their hydroponics facilities — nowhere near where they would've checked and certainly not the safest location.

"Well, shit." Ibu shook their head. "Let's open a gate into this thing and—"

"I'm already ahead of you, sir." Little Red loaded the details into Ibu's control panel, and the launch button flashed green.

With the detailed map Zachary had sent, pinpointing a micro-gate into the superstructure of the ship was now a far simpler task. For an A.I. like Little Red, it was child's play.

They reached out and tapped the button, opening the gate in space-time and peering into the other side. What they saw made their hearts race.

In the middle of the random storage room was a Beacon of Therion, and standing beside the artifact were several clone technicians and a strange-looking plant weaving back and forth in the air. While it took Ibu a moment to realize what they were seeing, when Little Red zoomed in, they knew right away. It was the Entity, attached by its umbilical to a human body Ibu had nearly missed.

Upon seeing Abigail's face, they jumped out of their seat and cut the connection. "Prepare to gate!"

They slid back into their chair and started preparing a gate sequence to transport them next to one of the massive battle-field gates. The moment the next squadron of ships emerged from the Nursery, they'd slide into the fray and join them.

Little Red's eyes flashed a rapid orange pattern. "Shouldn't we wait for Zachary and the others, Master Ibu?"

They shook their head. "No. I'm afraid that by the time they arrive, it'll be too late. Now let's get this party started, shall we?"

Ibu smiled, and Little Red hopped up and down, his eyes

transitioning from concern to a rainbow of excitement.

* * *

Outside the Nursery, Onboard the Apex

IBU TOOK a deep breath and triple-checked that their retinal comm had the plans for Hera's ship loaded up. It was called the Apex, and they weren't sure if the name implied the top of something or that the clones saw themselves as apex predators. Either way, the ship's designation was irrelevant. What was important was that the Beacon wasn't too far from the shuttle bay they'd slipped into after their last gate. The challenge shouldn't be reaching it so much as what to do once they got there.

Little Red skittered up beside them, and a blue light flashed atop his head. His eyes were now a dull white, and he'd modified the rest of his exterior to match the automata the clones had zigging and zagging throughout their ships. Most were nothing more than glorified transports, but a few that looked like him performed higher-level duties to ensure the clone ship was functioning properly. Ibu only hoped he'd done his research and knew how to fit in.

"We're being hailed, Master Ibu." His single light flashed white.

They glanced back at the controls and double-checked their transponder was still operational. It was reporting as green, and their uplink to the Apex was as well. As far as Hera's clones were concerned, they'd just returned from battle like everyone else.

Ibu waved their hand. "Put them on and make sure you mask my identity."

"Of course." Little Red chirped, and a humanoid face appeared on the wall screen.

At first, the humans on the other end stared at them. The silence felt odd, and as the discomfort reached a crescendo, Little Red's light flashed through a series of colors.

"May I... help you?" Ibu tilted their head.

"They're with Master Zachary." Little Red said.

Ibu squinted and studied the faces. They'd never seen these humanoids before today, and they definitely weren't one of the people they'd encountered on Liprosus.

"We'll be escorting you on your walkabout," the male staring back at them said. "Our mutual friends thought you might need some help."

They drew in their breath and simply nodded. The man spoke in a very robotic voice, one that reminded them of the automata from Lupus.

"Am I speaking with... a hologram?" Ibu checked their retinal comm. They were still safe sitting on their ships, but they weren't sure for how much longer.

The male shook his head. "All will become clear in a moment, sir. Once you're ready, we'll be at your side the whole way." His eyes seemed to glow for a split second, and Little Red chirped when they did. After that, the screen cut out.

"They're my fellow robots," Little Red said. "As soon as we step outside, they'll join us. From the data Blue Five just shared, there are thirty-two assassin automata in all. It was all they could fit into the shuttle in the limited time they had."

"Assassin automata?" They swallowed hard. "That sounds ominous."

"I should hope so." Little Red shared the specifics of the robots with Ibu. "They're designed to kill without prejudice. If an object gets in your way, it will be neutralized. Clone, human, or robot. They're all fair game."

"So much for Zachary's four-laws." Ibu reached over their shoulder and unsheathed one of their Zhen blades and raised a pistol in the other hand. When the blade came into view, its surface was matte black, with not a hint of light reflecting off it. Gone were the comforting etchings of the Nursery or the stories from days earlier. All that remained was darkness, a testament to their path ahead.

Little Red's light flashed white. "The desire of the humans

in Sol to enact laws to control their automata makes sense, especially considering their past misdeeds with A.I. and mechanical augmentation. We were their last vestige and the peak of their craftsmanship before they left us behind for Henosi."

The words sank in as they squeezed the hilt of their deadly blades. While they had no idea how the robots had found them, they were happy they had. There was no easy way they could take this ship alone, not unless they were planning on walking around without weapons, and that wasn't about to happen. They had enough explosives and gadgets packed into their pockets to breach the throne room on Arctordiea. A simple human outpost like this shouldn't be much of a challenge.

"Let's begin." Ibu reached out and tapped the hilt of their blade on the top of Little Red's shell. They meant the movement as a high-five gesture more than anything, but without a human or Nanil present to receive it, the effect was muted.

The rear landing ramp slid down, and the hatch swung open, revealing the blast doors in the distance and a sea of fighters in various states of repair and reloading. Clones and automata roamed to and fro, each on a very important mission and none conversing with one another. For all Ibu knew, everyone on this ship was artificial. Their personalities had long ago been wiped away by the parasites buried deep in their bodies.

Before either of them began their descent, they noticed someone standing at the bottom of their ramp, staring up at them. They squinted as they glanced from their tablet to them and back again.

"Shit," Ibu muttered. They'd been made before they even stepped off the fraking ship.

Suddenly, multiple explosions shook their hangar, and they reached out to steady themselves. From the looks of the blast, two of their smoldering Pilum fighters had exploded, and they'd taken out the dozen or so ships next to them.

When Ibu looked for the human who had been staring at

them at the base of the ramp, they were lying on the ground in a puddle of their own blood, with a metal rod sticking out of their skull. It was a gruesome sight, and surprising even considering the explosion. The odds were astronomical that they'd be taken out at the same instant they discovered them. Perhaps fate was actually on their side.

"We must hurry." Little Red clambered down the ramp. "The assassins can only do that so many times before they draw attention to themselves."

Ibu ducked down and ran down the decline. The hangar echoed with a cacophony of shouting and flashing lights, a perfect place to blend into, even for someone carrying two swords.

Once they reached the ground, they carefully picked up the clone's tablet and checked it over. They had been about to transmit an alert to the rest of the ship, but they hadn't finished composing it. Ibu tapped the cancel button and set the device back down.

Fate had nothing to do with this death. The gods had lost interest in them long ago. Their path forward was in their hands, and no one else's.

"This way." Little Red beeped and skittered around them, snapping their attention back into the here and now.

Ibu sprinted toward the exit, clearly marked on their retinal comm. As another explosion echoed in the distance, they didn't bother looking over their shoulder. Their target was up ahead, and they almost made it without encountering resistance until the clone police arrived.

The first shot nicked the side of Little Red and just missed Ibu. There was nowhere to hide out in the open, so they ducked down behind their mechanical friend and squeezed off a few rounds, taking out the clones at the entrance.

"We're not going to make it out of here if they block our path." Ibu pulled the trigger and their blast exploded on the wall beside the nearest clone.

"Wait for it!" Little Red shouted over the explosions behind them.

The clone's eyes went wide with Ibu's near miss, and they lowered down to the ground, firing several more shots at the Nanil as they shrunk their hit box. And then something happened. An invisible force reached out and yanked the soldier and his five companions outward and into the hangar.

One by one, their throats were ripped from their bodies, and they were tossed aside like trash. The sight was gruesome, and for a second, Ibu couldn't tell what caused it — until the assassin robots turned around.

In all the commotion, the clones had been gutted and in return, they painted their attackers in their own blood. The robots were covered in digital camo, but now the right side of their bodies bore the crimson splotches of human life.

Ibu swallowed hard as they ran past the lifeless forms, making their way into the long corridor. "Remind me not to piss them off," they whispered.

"Noted," Little Red chirped.

As they and the other robots passed through the opening, Red reached an arm up and tapped the control panel several times. A second later, not one, but two doors slid closed behind them, locking into place.

"You'll have to thank Aunt Hera for the double blast doors next time you see her," Little Red said.

Ibu chuckled and continued down the corridor. "She's not my aunt."

"Ahh, that's right." Little Red wheeled up beside them. "I keep forgetting you're not an Olivaw."

They shook their head and paused at the intersection in their path. While they could see a few of the assassin robots, the rest of them were only visible when they were moving. They could probably turn on their LiDAR to pick them out, but there was no point in giving away any stray signals to any sensors that might be spread throughout the ship. The robots would make themselves known when they were needed.

Hall by hall, they made their way toward the hydroponics facility. It was on the same side of the ship where they were hiding the Beacon. While they'd encountered a few clones along the way, there weren't as many as they'd expected, especially considering the importance of the object they were seeking.

Ibu holstered their pistols and leaned against the wall to check their retina comm. They gestured in the air as they quickly scanned through the map. In one more turn, they should be smack dab in front of the storage bay where the Beacon was hidden, unless it had been moved in the past twenty minutes. Though it wasn't an impossibility, they brushed the thought aside and reached down to retrieve their weapon.

"It's just up ahead. Turn right and we should be staring at it." They waved the invisible soldiers forward as if they needed directions and didn't already have the three-dimensional plans burnt into their brains.

With the sound of Little Red fading in the distance, Ibu closed their eyes and listened. Not for the footsteps of the robots or the pounding of their hearts — they were listening to the ship. They hadn't met much resistance in the past few hallways, and they weren't sure why. Something was off, but they couldn't tell what.

Little Red's voice came over their comm. "We may have a problem, Master Ibu. It seems they've sealed this segment of the ship with blast doors. What should we do?"

They sighed and shook their head. Of course, there were blast doors on this side of the ship. Why wouldn't there be? And if they had enough time to study the plans, they might even have seen it.

When they opened their eyes, they were staring at the Zhen blade. Its surface had transformed, and when they ran their hand over the imperfect slit down the middle, the texture reminded them of something familiar. It was a crack.

As they stared at it, an idea formed in their mind — one as ludicrous as it was obvious. While they couldn't be certain it would work, they were pretty sure they should give it a try."

47

ABIGAIL OLIVAW

OUTSIDE THE NURSERY, INSIDE BEACON

A sudden pulse of white-hot light erupted through the void, puncturing the abyss of Beacon space with a blinding luminosity. Abigail screamed out as the cataclysmic wave crashed against her consciousness, warping her sense of self and reforging the very fabric of her being in the crucible of the alien artifact.

While she was desperate and reeling after the burst subsided, the second and third pulses hit. They tore apart not only her mind but also the entire Beacon from top to bottom. Like her resolve, the eruptions reduced tens of millions of multicolored sparks of life to cosmic dust.

Her mind strained repeatedly against invisible bonds holding her in place, flexing with the desperate force of a trapped animal. Despite her repeated attempts to will herself free, to wake from this torturous dream, her pleas echoed unanswered. She failed to wrench herself from the Entity's hold — he'd grown too strong.

As she floated to what used to be the bottom of Beacon space, her mind drifted outward into the cold expanse. Where there were once walls constraining the virtual world, those barriers were now gone, replaced with a universe as infinite as reality. She could finally stretch out and move freely.

With each second she flew, she guided her spark toward

the familiar. Though she didn't know what she was looking for, she had an idea. Lync was out there somewhere with her Ulixi kin. She could feel them. While their life forces weren't as recognizable as her sister's, their sparks were as discernible to her as warmth was from heat.

Their feelings reminded her of home. Of family. Of being accepted regardless of how odd or off-kilter you were.

Her body tingled as she approached something new in the distance. This life force differed from the auras she'd encountered in the Beacon. Gone were the vivid colors and scintillating surface of an alien mind; in their place were the straight lines and rigidity of a physical object.

If forced to describe it, the only image she could conjure was that of a three-dimensional asterisk. In modern times, the character was used to censor offensive words, but throughout history, they represented something simpler. Something universal and apt to the shape floating in front of her: a star.

The asterisk moved about with a rigidity and purpose unknown to her. Yet, as she studied it closer, a realization dawned upon her. This object was much more than a lifeless shell. It embodied something far more chilling and unnerving: a sentient life force enshrouded in armor.

Perhaps these shapes were the Shaygai that the prasinus had told her about. While they had given her no other details than a name, their layers of protection within this virtual world meant one and only one thing. These beings had something to hide, and they were prepared to fight for it.

Their direct and methodical spiral around her suggested they weren't here to play games. They were searching for something. Something that scared them.

But she was not their target.

Content that she meant them no harm, the alien rocketed away, and Abigail didn't follow. Instead, she flew forward, driven by fear and an intense desire to put distance between her and the unusual alien. Once she was far enough to catch her breath, she glanced around, searching for the familial sensation she'd felt earlier.

Only then did she notice the odd anomaly beneath her. It reminded her of a rip, and while the edges of the fracture were invisible, the jagged center vibrated with the energy of an incalculable number of lives. Yet, she was peering into darkness.

The longer she stared at the aberration, the warmer her body felt. At first, it soothed her unseen muscles, but the more she gazed into the dark abyss, the hotter it became.

By the time she finally turned away, her soul was burning. It was the same unyielding glare she'd felt earlier with the bursts of energy, except this was constant and growing more painful by the second. It was as if hell was manifesting itself inside the Beacon.

Abigail flew as fast as she could. She needed to escape this place, to find somewhere safe to rest.

And then it hit her.

Sharp jabs of pain and searing hot embers ripped at her flesh. Her physical form was being torn asunder, and when she pried her eyes open, she screamed.

Blood was covering her hands, and when she looked down, it was oozing from her stomach.

Only after the next surge of agony did she realize what was happening. The Entity was beating her with its tentacles.

As the pain surged through her body like an ocean of molten waves, she rolled sideways and screamed at the top of her lungs. It hurt to move, and she was bleeding from dozens of open wounds up and down her torso.

Suddenly, a voice shouted out in her ear, a voice she hadn't heard in far too long.

"Abigail, move!" Harold screamed. "Please! You must escape before it kills us!"

She winced, and while she wanted to cover her ears with her hands, instead she struggled to crawl away from the thrashing tentacles.

It took several attempts to move as her body fought against every centimeter, but she managed to reach the far wall and propped herself up. When she stared back, a sense of relief and awe washed over her. On the other side of the room was the Therionic Entity, and based on how its scraggly vines and torso were hovering over Hera, it was bound to the clone.

"You're free," Harold whispered. "It's no longer tied to you, is it?"

She shook her head and shivered.

In that moment, she realized that the sensation of connectedness she'd felt with the alien was gone forever. There were no tormenting voices screaming out, nor toxic emotions tearing her down. The constant fear that someone was out to get her was gone. There was only the silence of her soul. A sound she'd missed dearly, and one she thought she might never hear again.

Her cloned aunt had become the Therionic alien's new vessel, and Abigail was nothing more than yesterday's trash. As she writhed in pain in the corner of the room, she glanced sideways and saw sparks cascading to the ground. When she squinted, she swore there was a blade cutting through the nearby blast doors. Whoever was on the outside, they were about to break through.

She could only hope they weren't out to kill her any more than the Entity was because she had nowhere left to hide.

48

ZACHARY OLIVAW
OUTSIDE THE NURSERY, GROUP THREE

The micro-gate connection broke down, and with it, their view of the Nursery. By the time Rán opened another comm gate, the Alatas battleship was dragging the third Beacon into position amidst a hailstorm of plasma and laser blasts. The formation wasn't hard to hold, but it was far easier when the Galactic Alliance didn't fire on or near a Beacon.

Even though they'd watched the humans assail the ancient artifacts multiple times without leaving so much as a scratch, they still feared what attacking them meant. To them, the Beacons represented the tens of millions of alien consciousnesses that had connected before their ships were destroyed, and now they were forever imprisoned inside the glowing devices. There was also the small matter of the collateral damage caused to their hive minds onboard their Selene moons.

Intel had been coming in for the past hour from throughout the Nursery. The attack on the artifacts resulted in millions of alien bodies being trapped in a lobotomized limbo on nearby GA ships, and the command-and-control structure of the aliens' inner sanctum was breaking down. They weren't sure if they'd caught some of the elite commanders inside the Beacons they attacked or if it was the simple fact that without the devices strengthening the alien minds; they were left to their own vices. Either way, that meant many of them were facing mortality for the first time.

Despite this blow, the GA still managed to cobble together a formidable offensive force. The pilots in the Thyreusian guard were chipping away at the outer defensive perimeter of their alliance forces.

Their ranks weren't nearly as expansive as they once were. They'd lost over half their fleet, and of the remaining ships, many had taken significant damage. There was no way they could maintain this aggressive of a military posture for much longer. Their fleet was designed for quick, guerrilla-like attacks, not for supporting massive defensive lines or transporting ancient relics across vast regions of space.

"We've positioned the third Beacon," Number Five said.

Zachary addressed the robots on the bridge of the Cornucopia by numeric names. Despite multiple attempts, he just couldn't refer to them as *hey you* any longer.

He walked over to the pod of Ulixi pilots bunched up in the corner and rested his hand on Donnelley's shoulder. "Are we good to go?"

Donnelley, who'd joined them from Lync's squadron, had been on several dozen offensive attacks in the Nursery. However, a few sorties back, she took a critical hit that ripped her ship apart. Unfortunately, she also lost use of her right hand in the aftermath, which made piloting a Nyílak challenging.

To a lesser pilot, that would have meant the end, at least until they grew a new arm or had an augmentation surgery performed. But a Ulixi had more to offer than that. Steering a colossal weapon like the Cornucopia took another skill entirely. A pilot of the Great Horn didn't need to dodge plasma rounds while turning on a dime. They only needed a sharp mind and the ability to hold a point in space-time steady, no matter the stress of the moment. And that made Donnelley the perfect candidate for the job, even if she was covered in bandages from head to toe.

Donnelley didn't bother opening her eyes or speaking when Zachary asked his question. She simply nodded and gave him the thumbs-up.

"Alrighty, then." He turned and faced the robots. "Let's power up the horn! I want a firing sequence on those Beacons as soon as we gate through. We won't be waiting around like last time." He clapped his hands in the air. "Remember, seconds mean lives, people."

"We're powered up, sir." Big Red's display flickered white. "The mining ships have continued collecting resources from the nebulosity, should we need to keep attacking."

He hadn't seen Little Red's twin since they'd passed through Lupus over a year ago. Seeing him here on the bridge brought back brutal memories of that mishap-laden adventure. They'd made so many mistakes on that trip; it was a wonder they even survived.

"You heard the bot!" Zachary clapped his hands together. "We're a go for the blue show, folks. I repeat, we're a go for the blue show!"

His pulse raced as he strode back to his command chair in the middle of the bridge. When he turned to face the wall screen, he was just in time to feel the wave of blue army ants as they passed through the ship. The Cornucopia jumped dozens of light hours in an instant, reappearing on the far side of the Nursery.

Donnelley and the other Ulixi had landed them right on target in front of the three Beacon-sized dots. Beyond the alien artifacts was the Rift, the tear in space-time that threatened their very existence.

One would think that the backside of their enormous weapon was a perfect target for the GA fleet, but they learned quickly to hold their fire. When the horn was powered up, any shot fired on it rebounded back toward the source. Though bending gravity was a fun parlor trick, they were sitting ducks after they spent their wad of energy. At least until they gated away.

"We're clear to fire, Z." Rán turned to face him. "I mean… sir."

Zachary didn't hesitate at the slip-up. He simply raised his hand and gestured forward. "Fire!"

A cacophony of groans emanated from the Cornucopia as the entire vessel shuddered with violent vibrations. The floor felt like it was buckling underneath him, and he grabbed the side of his chair to steady himself. While he'd experienced the unsettling sensation three times before this, whenever the horn let loose, he swore it was going to backfire and take them out at any moment. The raw power of their weapon was frightening.

He watched as the bowl of the mighty horn slowly filled with an ever-brighter glow, reaching a crescendo at the lip. Its brilliance threatened to spill over the edge as the ball of energy bowed out at the center, and then it happened. The pillar of devastation lashed out with unrestrained fury, engulfing all three of the Beacons in its path.

Though most of the blast shot toward the Rift, the rays that struck the ancient artifacts grew brighter than even the beam itself. Each Beacon seemed to extend to the others, their pillars of multicolored light attempting to form a network of energy.

Zachary leaned forward, his eyes fixed upon the mesmerizing spectacle unfolding before him. The column of light jumped from Beacon to Beacon, connecting the three devices together as one. But when the last pillar rose out of the third artifact, it missed its mark.

He slammed his hand down, repeatedly whacking his fist against his chair. "Shit, shit, shit!"

When the glow from the horn faded, all that remained were the distant consequences of their strike on the surface of the Rift. As the remnants of the blast dissipated into the ether, he gasped.

The cosmic chasm appeared to have widened, accelerating the approach of the aliens and further propelling them toward their death.

As he stood there stewing over their failure, the klaxons erupted around him. The GA fleet was firing on them with everything they had, and with most of the Cornucopia's energy expended on the burst, their shields could only take so much damage.

"We need the fourth Beacon!" Rán said. "We can't rotate the artifacts any more than they already are… if we do—"

"They won't connect." Zachary interrupted, slamming his hand against his chair. "I know the fraking geometry, Harold. I don't need a lecture on math."

He sighed when he realized he'd called him Harold again. This name change was a pain in the ass.

"That's not what I was going to say… sir." Rán stepped around his console. "I was just hoping we wouldn't have to…" his voice trailed away.

"Stop right there!" Zachary snapped his fingers at the robot. "Get back to your goddamn station, soldier!"

Rán stared at him in silence. They both knew he hadn't meant it like that. They were simply worked up over what they had to do next.

The horn vibrated and rumbled as the breach alarms blared. They'd lost shield number four, and if they didn't get out of there soon, there wouldn't be anything left to fight over.

They only had one option remaining. After they refueled, their next target was Hera's starship. They needed that fourth Beacon.

"Power up the gate drive while Grandfather Olivaw here returns to his station." Zachary stepped backward and eased down into his chair. "We've got ore to load."

He crossed his arms as the Cornucopia vibrated, but this time it wasn't from a blast. It was the power to the gate mesh, and it was followed by the comforting blue glow of a gate transition catapulting them to safety.

With the ants fading, the maintenance robots sprang into action, repairing the damage from their last encounter. Each time they patched the horn together, he feared it was weaker than before. While the distant mining ships were offloading their precious cargo, his mind wandered to his sister. He hoped that Ibu had done their deed. Even if the Nanil hadn't saved Abigail, their path was clear.

One life wasn't worth more than an entire galaxy.

49

LYNC MICHAELS

INSIDE THE NURSERY, NEAR THE RIFT

The fabric of space-time folded over the Cornucopia as it disappeared to refuel deep in the bowels of the nearby nebulosity. As far as they could tell, the Galactic Alliance hadn't sent out an auxiliary force to seek them out. They had all but resigned themselves to holding their position.

A lump formed in Lync's throat, stifling her previous excitement when the horn blasted the Beacons. She really thought the plan would work, but their failure wasn't without hope. There was one last Beacon out there, and they knew where it was and what they had to do to retrieve it. While they never wanted it to come to this, their hands were literally tied. They'd lost the Nursery battle before it started, and fending off the Rift was the only sane thing to do, even if the alien force hadn't shown their face.

Her fists clenched around the yoke of her fighter, and she hovered in place behind one of the Beacons. She was lingering back there with several of her Ulixi brethren. Although their position was exposed from above and below, few GA fighters dared to fire on the ancient relics for fear of hitting them. Unfortunately, there wasn't enough room between the alien artifacts for any more than a few Nyílak to fit. Even though she wasn't about to run from a fight, she needed a moment to collect her thoughts and to cobble together a plan.

Floating next to the faint glow of the Beacons made her hair stand on end. In the past, she was usually in a mental-link to the artifact when she was this close, but she didn't need to be to hear the murmurs of the life forces inside. They were screaming out at her, and they wouldn't shut up.

"Help us," the voices whispered.

"Please!" another voice shouted. "Let us die in peace."

"I have to quiet these voices," Greer said over Lync's comm. "They're… too much. Permission to join the fray, sir?"

She swallowed hard. "Permission granted. Just wait for the next—"

A gate flashed open in front of them, interrupting her speech. Several rounds from their few remaining Big Berthas belched forward, aimed squarely at the pockets of approaching GA fighters, particularly those with Selene moons in their background. That way, any stray shots that missed would still hit a target.

The gates were right on schedule. Lync watched as the aliens dove like kamikazes toward the fiery plasma rounds. The pilots were hell-bent on sacrificing their lives rather than allowing the munitions to tear through the distant Selene moons. The ships were home to millions of their kind, and they were particularly sensitive to losing members of their hive thousands of light-years from their home worlds, especially without the Beacons to connect to their queens.

Fighter after fighter erupted in fiery balls of death. In all, it took over two dozen of the alien fighters to stop each of the enormous glowing rounds. They'd lost several of the Big Berthas in the early stages of the battle, but fortunately, Harold and Zachary held back a few in reserve. While the pilots might have questioned this earlier, in that moment, they were nothing but thankful. Any moments of reprieve were welcome in a hailstorm of destruction like the Nursery.

Lync tapped her control panel, giving Greer the go signal to drop beneath the Beacon, and just as she was about to follow, her head erupted in searing pain. She winced and reached up as an invisible knife twisted in her mind's eye.

"Are you alright?" Shauna disconnected from her harness and floated up to Lync's side. "Should I—"

She waved her mother away as a pair of voices formed in her mind.

"They won't be expecting usss to sssend two of our Ssselene ssshipsss," the first voice said.

The second voice buzzed in ascension. "Essspecially ssso clossse. We can attack from their exposssed sidesss. But… ssshouldn't we be wary of the Ssshaygai? Our sssscouts claim that they're amasssing at the edge of the Rift."

"No!" the first voice snapped. "Thissss tisss our moment to ssshow the Buildersss we can be trusssted. They will reward the inner sssanctum for their devotion to the assscension. Now go! Prepare your forcesss."

Lync's head bobbed forward in the icy goo as the pain faded as fast as it arrived. The cooling sludge moved over her face, fighting to counter her rising core temperatures.

"Your skin is on fire." Shauna tried to unlock Lync's harness, and she knocked her hand away.

"No… I'm… fine," she insisted, taking a deep breath. While all she swallowed was gelatinous goo, the substance mimicked the effect of inhalation once it reached her lungs.

Shauna floated in front of her and stared into her eyes, waiting for her to reveal anything about what had just happened. Lync, however, was at a loss for words. It could have been a figment of her imagination. If they believed their intel, no other Beacons were in the nearby GA fleet. So if the voices were real, how could they have reached her?

Her mother crossed her arms. "Spit it out, young lady!"

Lync smirked and rubbed the dull ache lingering in the back of her head. "You wouldn't believe me if I told you."

"We're halfway across the Milky Way, fighting for our lives, and struggling to stop an all-powerful alien from taking over our galaxy." Shauna reached out, gently running her hand over Lync's forehead. "I'm pretty sure I'm past the point of questioning if you experienced something strange. Especially considering what we're floating next to."

She glanced up, and the display shifted around her, showing the nebulosity and ships above their fighter. It was strange how the pilot sphere reacted to wherever she looked, but ever since Shauna activated it, she'd left it on. She found comfort in being surrounded by stars; the effect was immersive and reminded her of being alone on her family's planetesimal.

"There were voices," she began. "Two of them. Thyreusian, I think." She shook her head. "Anyway, they were planning an attack. They made it sound like the GA were going to move in on our position." She looked over at Shauna, who was floating perfectly still. "Something about one moon above our formation and another below."

Shauna stared at her in silence for several seconds, which, for an A.I., was an eternity. Then she shoved off toward her seat and started frantically manipulating her controls.

"What is it?" Lync peered over at her mother, but her curiosity was cut short as klaxons erupted in her ears and the inner shell of her pilot sphere flashed red.

When Lync glanced down, she could see through the floor of the Nyílak. A few light-seconds beneath their fighter was a Selene moon, and judging by the bubble-like formations flowing off its surface, they were still dropping out of warp.

She didn't even have to look up to know what was there. The voices had indeed been from the Thyreusians. She should have trusted herself and not questioned what she'd heard, especially around the Beacons. These ancient devices acted like psionic megaphones and operated on levels they couldn't comprehend.

"Defensive formation, Solo," Lync screamed into her comm. "I repeat, defensive formation solo!"

While she may have doubted her mental faculties near the Beacon, she never questioned her skills at the controls. She slammed the throttle forward and yanked back on the yoke just in time.

A burst of energy erupted from below their position and surged past, missing them by mere meters. Though the Selene moons knew they'd end up firing on one another, they didn't intend to use the full arsenal at their disposal. They only needed to pick off the remains of the ragtag Ulixi fleet.

What they hadn't planned on, however, was a robot being faster than they were. As Lync and her squadron shot away in all directions, two gates opened on opposite sides of the Beacons, facing the Selene moons.

Even if the Ulixi lacked the raw numbers of the Ursis, that didn't mean they were without reinforcements.

A pair of Big Berthas rained hellfire out of each of the open gates, sending not two, but four battleship-sized plasma rounds soaring across the space-time gateway directly toward the Selene moons. And this time, there were no kamikaze pilots there to save them.

Two by two, the shots ripped through the exterior shields and hull of the gigantic spherical warships. Each burst rained down behind the other, driving the devastation deeper and deeper into the moon until it hit the power core.

Seconds later, when the space-time gates blinked shut, both Selene moons lit up in a cataclysmic explosion. Like the energy previously shot at the Beacons, the explosions reignited the ancient artifacts and sent a hailstorm of destruction toward the Rift.

Fortunately, Lync and her fellow Ulixi had managed to get out of the blast radius. Several hundred of their autonomous friends, however, hadn't been as lucky. While Shauna had redirected most of them away from the ensuing storm, she watched as the silent sentinels of their squadron were torn to shreds by both the Beacons and the blast itself.

Lync slammed her fist against the armrest of her chair as her chest heaved in and out. She'd fraked up, and they'd lost valuable defenses. Even though they were simple robots, they were invaluable in this epic battle, and their presence was a shield against the ceaseless onslaught of the Galactic Alliance.

When she looked down, the dots on her control panel

blinked from green to red as the friendly identifiers of the automata flickered out one by one. Each lost signal was an ally, snuffed out in this relentless struggle to survive. Her jaw clenched, a grim testament to her determination.

Her head suddenly erupted again, and she raised both hands to her temples. "Argh!" she shrieked and slammed back against the chair.

The psychic whispers from earlier had transformed into shrieks. Each voice piled on top of another, and they were all crying out for one reason.

There was a storm brewing.

"Wholly shit!" Shauna screamed. "They're coming… the Shaygai… they're passing through!"

Lync groaned and slowly lowered her hands to her lap. Once she composed herself, she glanced around the pilot sphere, searching for what Shauna was talking about. Far off near the Rift were the strange asterisk-shaped fighters known only as the Shaygai.

She'd read about the strength of these aliens, but what she didn't expect was how many there were. The tales from the GA archives spoke of the starships appearing alone or two at a time, but this, this was different. In the distance were hundreds of alien ships flowing out of the Rift, and they were heading straight for them.

"Shit!" Lync screamed. "We've got to go. There's no way we can—"

"Wahoo!" Crayo's voice broke in, interrupting her midsentence. "Did someone call the cavalry?"

Her hand hovered over the gate controls as his voice echoed in her mind. It couldn't have been him. He was back in the Cornucopia under medical care.

"It's Crayo!" Shauna shouted. "It's really him. And from the looks of it, the other half of your kin are hot on his tail."

Lync brought up the tactical display and drew in her breath. There were dozens of fresh green dots staring back at her, along with the last of the robots from the far side of the gate. Apparently, Harold and Zachary were throwing everything they had on the table. The only things they left on the other side were the Berthas and whatever defensive measures those needed. Given how short a window they needed to fire, the portals wouldn't be open for very long.

She shook her head and raised her hands upward, wailing into the life-giving gelatinous goo of their capsule. And not because she was happy.

This wasn't happening.

He shouldn't be here. He should be back on the Cornucopia, safe from all of this... this death. And now that he'd joined her, she couldn't abandon him. Not now.

The longer she stared at the inbound alien formation of fighters, the blurrier her future became. Their odds of failure were astronomical.

Gone were the intricate plans and counter plans she'd woven over the past few weeks. In the blink of an eye, they were torn to shreds. And the only thing left in their stead could be summed up in one simple word.

Hope.

Hope that they could pull off something miraculous, or in this case, hope that she could somehow harness her lightning in a bottle.

50

JOYCE GREEN

OUTSIDE THE NURSERY, GROUP THREE

The moment Joyce and the crew of the Perniger passed through the gates, all hell broke loose. Or, as Grifdar said, 'the forest was ablaze, and they were ripe for the burning.' While she didn't know whether they were the fire or the wood in his analogy, she wasn't about to die at Hera's hands.

As soon as they hit the other side, Grifdar dove under the inbound blasts from the Terminus battleships. There were even a few Atlas class human vessels in the mix, which was almost amusing considering how out of their league they were. That, and their name being so close to the Ursis Alatas class. The two weapons of destruction were vastly different in terms of power.

"Bring me under those Atlas battleships." Joyce pointed toward the elongated warships and called them out on their shared tactical display.

She returned her hands to her controls and fired a sequence of plasma rounds at the inbound squadron of Pilum fighters. They scattered like ants as the rounds approached, but several banked straight into the guided blasts of superheated death. She had no idea how the Ursis directed the fiery munitions, but she smiled when the ships burst into flames, taking out a few of their neighboring wingmen.

Grifdar growled and barrel-rolled to the right, narrowly

dodging another incoming volley from the nearest Atlas battleship. "Won't we be exposed to more of their fighters down there? Our topside is our largest target."

"I hope so," she muttered. "I hope so."

Her goal with the maneuver was to draw fire away from the gate, buying time for the rest of their fleet to make it through. The more of their people they had on this side, the better.

With her fingers dancing over her controls, she was making sure they were firing every chance they got, as were the Big Berthas. The massive artillery was spewing death through the open gates, allowing the other Ursis ships to transition safely. Meanwhile, she was programming an upcoming strafing run, but this one was a bit unorthodox.

Their wing of the Ursis fleet followed Grifdar down under the spherical formation of clone ships. Packed in tight like a hive, their shape made navigating around them easier, but reaching the inside of the deadly mass of warships would be downright painful — unless she could split them apart.

When Joyce shared her plan with Grifdar, he smiled and howled at the top of his lungs, sending a guttural echo throughout the bridge of the alien battleship.

"Wholly shit, man!" Ryder recoiled in his chair. "You scared the crap out of me. Maybe a little less screaming and a bit more focus?" He was stationed behind them, running the ship's glowing green repair systems.

While they usually had Ursis crew members to help the automata fix the damage done during battle, this particular ship was light on bears and heavy on Zachary's robots. For some strange reason, the Ursis soldiers refused to serve on board a ship commanded by a human — let alone a female one.

Joyce chuckled at the notion of the aliens discounting her because of her anatomy. They'd eat their words soon enough. While she'd gotten used to it with her human military colleagues, she hadn't expected it from an elevated alien species like theirs.

Once she finished building her plan, Joyce shared her maneuver with the rest of the fleet over encrypted channels. Even though the tactic exposed a critical design flaw in the human Atlas battleships, she didn't care. This was probably the last battle these antiquated ships would ever see, and the fact that they hadn't sent them through the gates to the Nursery was a testament to their uselessness.

She glanced over toward Grifdar. "We're ready for the Ursine Rend whenever you are."

His eyes expanded, directing his gaze upward toward the vast assembly of human and clone ships looming overhead. As he searched for their first victim, his monocle flashed repeatedly, overlaying details on the virtual battle scene above. Like a bear studying the flow of water in a river, the salmon floating past didn't stand a chance.

After a few seconds of consideration, he narrowed his gaze and highlighted his prey, sharing the target with her and the other ships in the fleet. There was no sense in them targeting the same foe. They had plenty of fish in this barrel for the moment.

Grifdar banked the Perniger to port and roared, his gruff voice echoing over the comms. "May our den be the last claw standing!"

Their grand, yet nimble, battleship veered toward the barrage of incoming energy bolts. They whizzed past as Grifdar rotated on axis, sending the deadly bright bands sailing into the inky black abyss. His paws manipulated his controls with the fluidity and precision of a salmon cutting through a roaring river, dodging the inbound fire with breathtaking audacity.

The Perniger shuddered under the concussive explosions of the near-misses. Attempting to take some damage, he pressed on. The strain in his muscles and the gritting of his teeth mirrored the tension Joyce felt building in her body. She fired off shot after shot at the approaching fighters. While many of her rounds missed entirely, the mass of ships was packed so tight that there were ample opportunities for stray shots to hit a mark.

And they did, with gusto. Explosions erupted all around them as Grifdar growled, echoing his own guttural utterances of defiance. Like her, he wasn't about to die on this day.

As Joyce searched for her next shot, her options dwindled when the Perniger seemed to be banking away from their target. But it was only a ploy to throw off the humans, and from the looks of it, it worked. When Grifdar swerved hard to port, their battleship dove toward the distant Atlas cruiser, and Joyce didn't hesitate. She unleashed the energy tentacles from the bowels of their ship. While the power ate into the strength of their shields, the utility of the appendages made up for it. As the whip-like ropes of light cast out, her fingers stroked the virtual controls and formed them into a hook.

Grifdar was ready for her offering. He swerved their craft upward with the agility of a charging grizzly, twisting the Perniger in a daring somersault, and evading a fresh wave of plasma fire. The breathtaking maneuver allowed the energy hook to hit its mark on the midsection of the human battleship.

Joyce yanked the virtual strands back, and her heart hammered in her chest, beating in unison with the thrum of their engines. The tentacles suddenly snapped straight, and a loud groan echoed through their ship as their power core surged under the added strain.

And then, the mighty dam burst loose. The powerful green filaments of light sheared the battleship in half. The explosions from the sudden severing of the ship's backbone cascaded through the enemy's hull like repeated swipes of an Ursis claw.

Grifdar and the others screamed in celebration, and their roars echoed through the halls of the Perniger. But Joyce held steady, training their weapons on any lone ships they passed. She took pride in picking them off and hoped their pilots were pissing themselves when they saw the hook approaching.

In their wake, the wreckage of their assault blossomed into the nearby Terminus battleships. The remains of the antique human ship ripped holes in the hulls of their enemy and shredded the clone fighters chasing them into chaff. The eruption of crimson and amber detonations stood as a testament to the genius of Joyce's plan.

One by one, the Ursis throughout the fleet executed a similar attack against the other human battleships. While not all attempts were successful, more often than not, the effects were the same. The once powerful human vessels were transformed from defensive strengths to weaknesses.

She stared in awe as the automated defensive measures of the Perniger took over, and Grifdar wove them to safety. The enemy fleet was spreading apart, and her plan was working. Hera and her clones were no longer an impenetrable mass of ships. They were making space between their ranks, which meant one thing: more opportunity to strike.

With their first win under her belt, she started preparing for their next move. They had to take out more of their squadrons of Pilum fighters to reach Hera's Apex destroyer. And like bees to honey, she needed to form a flyswatter.

As she plotted out their course, a light flashed on their port side, and their ship groaned. A wave of gravity rippled over the Perniger, and had Grifdar not been an expert pilot, they might have careened into one of the sister ships in their battle wing.

When she brought up the source of the gravitational abnormality, her mouth fell open. Floating beside them was the Cornucopia, the largest alien weapon in the galaxy. While she'd watched videos of the enormous object, she'd never seen it in person, let alone flown next to it. For once in her life, she was glad the Olivaws were on her side.

51

ZACHARY OLIVAW
OUTSIDE THE NURSERY, GROUP THREE

The refueling of the Cornucopia took twice as long this time as the last. Their automated mining ships had to go further and further into the nebulosity to get raw materials. If they wanted to increase their production, they'd have to relocate the remaining Berthas and gates, as well as recalculate all the horn jumps. At this stage of the battle, it wasn't worth the risk.

"It was your only option." Rán stared at his controls and avoided eye contact with Zachary.

They both knew the stakes were high, but over the past few months, this copy of Harold hadn't seemed up to making the same tough calls he had before. That left Zachary or his siblings having to step in.

Even if he'd been too focused on his own mortality, that didn't excuse his inaction. Hard decisions needed to be made, and going all in with their reserve ships was one such decision. But that was his burden to bear.

He stared out over the bleak, empty expanse of the nebulosity. Unlike the dark cloud of gas the Galactic Alliance used to engulf and imprison star systems, this nebula was the birthplace of stars. It contained the organic and inorganic compounds to form life, but today they'd pillaged the primordial elements to wage a war - one that was quickly coming to a head.

Clearing his throat, he stared down at his trembling left hand. It had been acting up for the past few hours, but had gotten worse since their last jump. No matter what he did, he couldn't make it stop. The blasted thing seemed to have a mind of its own.

Everything would be over soon enough, and maybe, just maybe, he'd be able to see Pluto and his baby.

Taking a deep breath, he clenched his hand into a fist before shaking it in the air and clasping it behind his back. With that distraction literally behind him, he walked up beside the pod of Ulixi in the corner. "Are we ready for the gate?"

Donnelley gave a silent thumbs up, and the other Ulixi remained connected to their targeting computers. Their hands gently nudged the tachyon flow controls and Cherenkov radiation to account for the ever-changing battle being waged on the other side of the jump.

Zachary glanced over his shoulder at Big Red. "Are we locked and loaded, Red?" The hum of the Cornucopia told him everything he needed to know, but he still wanted a verbal confirmation.

The giant robot nodded. "As soon as we can verify our landing position after the jump, we'll fire, sir."

He turned back toward the Ulixi and stared at the wall display playing out the battle on the other side of the gate. The warning to their fleet had already been sent a few minutes earlier, and he could see that the Ursis ships had made room for their arrival, with a few exceptions. Those that hadn't heeded the call were about to get a rude awakening.

"Alright, folks." He grabbed the back of Donnelley's chair. "Let's jump into the frying pan, shall we?"

With that, the hum of the Cornucopia ramped up to a vicious howl and the gate transition kicked off. Except for when the blue glow slowed down for the benefit of the humans in its path, the light tore through the ship and the horn leapt across the bridge in space-time.

He groaned and squeezed the back of the chair with both hands as his body protested the rapid jump. There was no time to worry about the matters of the flesh. His attention needed to be trained on more important things.

When his mind and eyes finally cleared and caught up with reality, his stomach twisted into a knot. Their alignment was off. Hera's Apex destroyer wasn't dead center as they'd planned. The Cornucopia was aimed off to the side. While they might still be able to hit the compartment that contained the Beacon, it would be close. Now, all he had to do was wait and issue the order once they'd lined up.

The horn beneath his feet vibrated as the alignment thrusters kicked in, and he did everything he could to avoid thinking about his sister. He closed his eyes and fought off the nagging question. He didn't dare ask if she was safe because it didn't matter. They'd exhausted all their options; it was now or never. The clone fleet was already turning toward them, preparing to attack.

He gripped the back of the chair when the vibration ceased. "I'm sorry," he whispered.

"Fire!" Rán shouted.

Zachary drew in his breath and glared at the robot, both confused and relieved by what he'd done.

The Cornucopia shook violently as the thousands of already primed power cores released the fury they'd been restraining. The energy spiraled up toward the top edge of the horn as the center filled with pulsating rivulets of white light. Just when he thought the entire weapon platform was going to explode, the pillar of destruction shot forward, slicing through the floating mass of clone ships like they didn't exist.

One minute they were there, the next they weren't. The blinding column of light extinguished countless lives in a split second, and when it ended, Zachary was still glaring at Rán.

"What the bloody hell, man?" He stumbled backward and spun around, hopping up beside Big Red's controls. When he did, he froze, his eyes locked on the targeting system. "What... what happened? How did we... miss?"

The red robot shook its head. "Technically, we hit the Apex, Master Zachary. We did, however, adjust our aim at the last second."

"We adjusted it?" He reached out and yanked the automata by the shoulder, spinning it around. "Who... who the hell changed our targeting?"

"I'm sorry," Rán muttered from behind him. "I... couldn't let you kill her."

When Zachary turned to face the robot, his back was to him, and he was staring at the wall screen, fixated on Hera's half-destroyed flagship. Scraps of red-hot metal floated aimlessly in all directions, and the exposed innards of the ship were a mess of sparks and twisted chunks of hull and superstructure.

He surveyed the scene, and his resolve crumbled by the second as the bodies of what he assumed were clones drifted out into the vacuum of space. Everything they'd planned up to that moment, every sacrifice made, every life lost, had been in vain. Without the fourth Beacon, they would never know if they could have closed the Rift.

He slowly raised his hands in the air and brought them down on the back of his head. "What the frak have you done, Rán?"

The ancient artificial intelligence began to weep, his robotic shell shuddering and wailing like a human. In all the years Zachary had known the robot, never once had he heard him cry. Scream and throw a tantrum, yes. But he never sobbed, not in front of him, or any other Olivaw, for that matter.

He didn't have to ask why; the answer was obvious. He'd changed their targeting because of Abigail. While Zachary hadn't checked whether or not Ibu had reached her, he knew Rán had.

In his heart, he'd already known. She was still in there. He didn't know how he knew it, but he did.

He shook his head and lowered his hands to his side. The A.I. had overstepped. "You should have let her go." He swallowed hard and suppressed the embers of rage rising in his gut. "It's what she would have wanted. For us. For everyone."

Rán didn't bother looking at Zachary. He kept staring at the half-destroyed starship floating on the wall. "I disagree. She would have wanted us to fight for her. For me to fight for her." He straightened up. "So I did. I did what you couldn't."

Zachary groaned. "At what expense?" He stepped toward Rán. "Ten thousand lives? Ten billion lives? Do you have any idea how many people you've sentenced to death today? And all because of your insatiable fixation on one person. Yourself!"

Rán swung around to face him, his arm smashing into his chair. In one motion, it ripped out of the ground and went flying through the far wall.

Zachary flinched backward, sliding behind his controls. When he looked at Rán's face, the robot was staring directly at him, eyes flickering like flames.

At first, he thought Rán was merely angry, but when he stared at his hands, he realized it was more than that. They were clenching and unclenching into fists, and his palms were glowing. He'd powered up his destructor gauntlets — the weapons designed to burn through tank hulls.

In that moment, the old Zachary would have tried to talk it out, but not anymore — not with all they'd risked. He tapped out a quick sequence on the palm of his left hand, and a password dialog appeared on his retinal comm.

"She's your fraking sister!" Rán stepped toward him. The servos in his military composite shell strained under the force of his stomp. "Why didn't you fight for her?" He glanced at the pod of Ulixi, staring slack-jawed at him, and they flinched backward when his eyes pulsed red. "And you, why didn't any of you bother to fight for one of your own?"

The klaxons erupted around them, and the horn shuddered as the Cornucopia started taking on fire. Several dozen Terminus and all the remaining Pilum fighters had turned on the massive weapon, their only goal exacting revenge.

"Rán!" Zachary waved his hands in front of him, attempting to get the robot's attention. When his gaze returned to him, he continued. "This entire battle has been about something bigger. It's never been about one person. You knew it, I knew it, and Abigail knew it. Don't make this about your inferiority complex as a father or guardian of this family. We no longer need your protection." He brought his hand back and pounded it against his chest. "I've been the one trying to fix this nightmare since the GA found us, and both Abigail and Bradley have as well. We opened our eyes and saw how far you'd fallen. Why you can't see it is beyond me." He shook his head. "For frak's sake, you're the reason we're even in this mess in the first place."

He lowered his hands to his side and tapped out the password on his leg. A confirmation screen appeared on his comm. "Goodbye, Rán."

Rán tilted his head. "Goodbye?"

The robot's questioning voice hung in the air for a moment until a ring of plasma charges burst in the center of his chest, around his consciousness core. Smoke and sparks started spilling out while the klaxons continued to blare overhead.

This copy of Harold had left him with no other choice. It was him or them. He'd been too erratic since being forced to face his mortality. Zachary and Pluto had installed fail-safes into both his and Shauna's humanoid harnesses a few weeks back in case they went rogue. He just never imagined this would be how he'd have to use it.

He stood there, staring at the melting remains of their ancient Olivaw ancestor. He flinched when the robot's arm abruptly rose up. When it finally stopped, Rán's index finger was pointing at him. Like he was calling out his killer.

Maybe he'd gone too far. Maybe Rán would have eventually calmed down. But the longer he stared at the smoldering remains of his outstretched hand, the more he knew he'd made the right call.

With the klaxons reaching a crescendo, Zachary felt someone shaking him, fighting to get his attention, and pulling him back to the here and now. He turned to see who it was.

"Hey, Red." He swallowed down the bile still lingering in his throat. "What is it?"

The robot didn't say a word. He merely pointed at the video feed already playing out on the wall screen.

When Zachary turned to look, his heart sank. There in the middle of the screen was the Rift, and a tsunami of alien starships was spiraling out of the center.

The Shaygai were coming.

52

———

IBU

OUTSIDE THE NURSERY, ONBOARD THE APEX

For a brief moment, Ibu's entire universe turned upside down and inside out simultaneously. They'd just received a comm from Joyce warning them of the Cornucopia's arrival when the ground beneath their feet suddenly buckled, sending them careening through the air.

The lights cut out a blink later, and then a thunderous boom reverberated from all around them. They only caught a fleeting echo of the deafening sound as their comm sealed their ear canals. But it didn't matter.

Their face pulsed, their cheeks rippled, and their bones literally hummed as the concussive shock of the eruption tore at the very molecules holding their flesh together. Once the chaos had its fill of toying with them, it hurled them, howling, through the yawning hatch, treating them no better than a discarded marionette. They crashed into whatever invisible objects were in their darkened path until they finally ended by slamming their back against the far wall.

With their head acting as a backstop against the unforgiving surface, they winced and fought to keep the splotches of red and white from consuming their consciousness.

The explosions continued from all sides, echoing through the distant halls. But it was the screams that made it worse. The unrelenting wails of the clones were unlike any human scream they'd ever heard. Maybe it was the sheer number of the same voice shrieking in unison. Their symphony of agony amplified the dreadful reality of the war unfolding around them and drew it to a fitting conclusion.

Ibu groaned as they started floating backward through the pitch-black room. They reached out, exploring the dark with their hands in case any unseen debris was still drifting toward them. There was no way they could handle another crack to the head. Certainly, not like the last one.

They swallowed down a mouthful of blood, and just when they thought the nightmare had ended, a second wave of quakes hit. The concussive aftershocks ravaged the blackened room again and again. They were unrelenting, as if the Apex were hell-bent on ending them.

As each torturous moan reverberated through the darkness, the only thing they could think of was Abigail. They'd come this far to save her, only to be foiled at the last second. And not by the GA. By their own people.

If Joyce's message had been right, then the Cornucopia had fired on the Apex. But instead of putting them out of their misery, they'd missed their mark. That meant that not only would the GA win, but Hera and the Therionic Entity were still alive.

In a true sign that the universe was reading their thoughts and had a twisted sense of humor, the lights in the storage bay flickered on. They glanced around at the crushed remains of the room and its occupants.

Two aliens, one clone, and a human were floating in zero gravity.

They couldn't help but chuckle as the words flashed through their mind. Their first thought was that the phrase seemed like the lead-in to a human joke, but their second thought was cut short by the flash of a laser bolt whizzing past their ear.

When they reached down to their belt, the sudden motion caused their body to rotate in the zero gravity, but they still came up empty. The pistol-sized lump on their hip was gone.

"Missing something?" a voice asked.

Ibu craned their neck, twisting and pivoting in place until they locked eyes on the source of the query.

There, towering above them, beside the floating Beacon was the Therionic Entity. It had its tentacles splayed out across the expansive room, anchoring itself. The alien was holding their blaster with one appendage, and Hera with another.

The clone's eyes, ears, and the rest of her body were wrapped in straps of gold that seemed to be squeezing her tight. It was the golden liquid from the wall on Arctordiea, and it was serving its master like it always had.

Hera might as well have been dead. At this point, she was nothing more than a living vassal to the alien being, and Ibu was about to join her across the river Styx.

53

JOYCE GREEN

OUTSIDE THE NURSERY, GROUP THREE

The Perniger fought for nearly ten minutes, spiraling out of the way of the debris as Grifdar worked hand in hand with the automated navigation system. After the grazing miss of the Cornucopia, the bridge crew fell quiet. Both due to the chaotic aftermath of the horn's devastating failure, and the gaping hope in their optimism.

At the moment, they were trying to keep the horn in one piece. Since the attack, the clone fighters had either gated away or doubled down on their defense, choosing to focus their efforts on the source of their razing.

"Bring us up and over the lip!" Ryder drew a flight path along the hull of the Cornucopia for Grifdar to see. "Zachary's robots want us to lead them toward the horn's defensive structures on the inside. They claim they have some tricks that even we don't know about."

Grifdar grunted and slammed the yoke to the side, sending the Perniger barrel-rolling and the view on the wall screen rotating on its axis. A stream of clone blasts from their pursuers missed wide and careened into the vast abyss of space, never to hit a target.

Joyce looked down at her controls and focused on the display in front of her. With the gravity dampeners working overtime, she couldn't feel their spin, but someone forgot to tell her eyes and mind that. The spinning display gave her vertigo, and she took a deep breath, doing everything she could not to blow chunks.

She redirected power to her rear and upper deflector shields. Flying this close to the Cornucopia meant friendly fire from below was unlikely. Their trust in the robots was one of the few things she could count on. They weren't out to kill humans. Clones, on the other hand, were a different matter.

While she wanted to ask how their metallic friends drew the distinction between humans and their carbon copy cousins, she didn't dare inquire. The last thing the automata needed was a cognitive breakdown. Especially with Harold already on her short list.

Zachary had been mum over what had transpired on the Cornucopia to cause them to miss their mark, but ever since they'd seen the Shaygai coming through the Rift, he'd been dead set on figuring out another strategy.

As Grifdar brought their ship to the edge of the great horn, their pursuers followed them close behind like lemmings. She wasn't sure if the clones were stupid or if they thought the massive weapon was defenseless. If that was it, the lack of turrets firing on them certainly helped reinforce their belief.

She studied her controls. "I've got a few dozen Pilum on intercept courses. They're like moths to our flame."

"What is a moth?" Grifdar growled.

"To be honest," Joyce chuckled and shook her head. "I have no idea. I've never seen one. It's just an idiom our people use."

Her hands hovered over her console, itching to return fire on their pursuers. They were putting a lot of faith in Zachary's plan.

The Perniger shuddered violently and Grifdar cursed in his alien tongue as a round of blasts hit dead center on their rear shields.

"We're down to thirty percent, sir," Ryder said.

Ursis battleships had stronger shields and thicker hulls on

their front side for a reason. They weren't designed to run from a fight. It was against their nature.

Fortunately, they didn't have long to wait. Grifdar twisted and turned around the outcroppings and towers jutting out of this segment of the Cornucopia. It wasn't until the lip of the massive weapon lit up in yellow that they doubted their course of action.

Zachary said their power was critical and that they needed to refuel before they gated back to the Nursery, but he never said how. As Grifdar banked the Perniger over the edge, her display flashed white, and she couldn't see anything until it auto-dimmed.

She flipped her external view around to show their rear cameras just in time to see dozens of glowing mechanical tentacles reach out and latch onto the hull of their pursuers. The appendages bore no resemblance to the glowing energy strands of the Ursis battleships. These were massive limbs attached to the inner walls of the horn, and their glow was from subatomic atomization barbels covering their length. While they usually tore apart debris and fed it to the ever-hungry cores down in the heart of the ship, this time they were performing multiple purposes.

Bursts of red and orange erupted from the clone ships as the hundreds of squid-like tendrils overpowered them. She watched as they shredded their pursuers, tearing the ships into tiny pieces in the blink of an eye.

The technology they used to disassemble everything that crossed their path was awe-inspiring. No matter how large or small the object, whether it was solid or gas, they could feed it into their machine.

The sight of the glowing appendages tearing their prey to shreds gave her an idea. She tapped her ear and subvocalized a command to open a comm to Zachary. At the same time, she started sketching out their next move on her control panel.

His face appeared on her retinal comm a second later.

"We can still do this!" she blurted out.

Zachary stared at her until he glanced over his shoulder.

Behind him was a smoldering mass of something that looked like a robot, but it was honestly hard to tell.

She squinted. "Is that—"

"How?" He spun back to face her and stepped sideways to block the view of the steaming torso. "How can we reach the Beacon? Like I said in the message, we don't have enough power for another shot. Not yet."

Joyce shoved her curiosity aside and shared her plan with him. She watched Zachary as he studied her crude sketches, trying to figure out what she was proposing. After a few seconds, he nodded and his eyes flickered. At that moment, she knew it could work. It had to.

He muted his end of the comm and started flailing his arms in the air at the nearby robots. Their only response was to start scurrying around in circles. A few of the Ulixi in the distance even flinched when he directed his overflowing excitement toward them. With each dramatic gesture, she tried to figure out if the robot that was powered down behind him was whom she thought it was. If it was Harold.

Suddenly, Zachary's face filled the camera, and she recoiled. "To make your plan work, we'll need to clear away the rest of the ships. Which solves another one of our problems."

Joyce tilted her head. "Which one's that?"

The moment she asked the question, an impossibly long tentacle shot out from the Cornucopia, igniting a Pilum fighter which had somehow managed to escape from the automata's grasp. It exploded in a firestorm of red and yellow.

Once the shards of debris were cleared by no less than a hundred of the smaller tentacles, the battle scene behind it came into view. Joyce had to check her controls to confirm what she was seeing was true. From the looks of it, the horn was moving closer to the carnage. It took her a few seconds to catch up with what was happening, but then it hit her.

"You're going to use the ships as fuel," she muttered.

"Wait," Ryder spun around. "Who's doing what?"

Joyce flicked Zachary's image into a window on the far wall screen.

"Hello, young Olivaw. Why the long face?" Grifdar gestured at the robotic fingers reaching toward one of the approaching regoliths in the distance. "Your mechanized army is doing well!" He growled as a squadron of clone fighters came out from behind the shards of the starship. One by one, they were deftly swatted down into the awaiting furnace below.

"Joyce." Zachary cleared his throat, and she locked her gaze back on his.

Only then did she see what Grifdar was talking about. Zachary's face was soft, and his eyes were bloodshot. She hadn't noticed it before, but he must've been going through an emotional ringer over there. Then she realized why he was staring at her and not speaking.

She swallowed hard. "If Abigail's in there with the Beacon, we'll do our best to keep her safe. That's all I can promise."

Zachary didn't say a word. He simply nodded in silence until he closed the comm.

Ryder spun back around to face her. "Is someone planning on telling me what's going on?"

She smiled and shared the modified plan Zachary had transmitted over after he disconnected. His robots must have made sense of her crude drawings; there was no way he'd managed that on his own. Perhaps that mechanized hulk in the background hadn't been Harold after all.

While several Ursis battleships continued battling the clone fleet in the distance, most of the others took advantage of their robotic friend's newly discovered power. They began luring their unsuspecting prey back toward the Cornucopia.

In the meantime, her crew started to catch up with her plans. She could feel the energy of Grifdar and Ryder rising. Their mutters and wild gestures were reaching a crescendo of oozing testosterone as they reviewed the plan; it was like watching two apes figuring out how to use a stick.

Just as she was about to tell them what to do, the other Ursis on the bridge walked up beside her. "They've almost got it," the female whispered. "Give them a few more seconds. Grif can be thick at times, but he hates being ordered around. Trust me."

Joyce glanced over at the gray-haired alien, and they winked at her. Until now, the Ursis hadn't spoken more than a few words to her, but she had a feeling these two weren't merely members of the crew. They traded barbs too deftly to be friends; they had to be mates.

"So, we're burrowing our way in!" Ryder turned around and hopped over to his controls. "Why didn't you just say that?"

She smirked at the other Ursis and leaned in close. "I feel bad for them sometimes."

"As do I." The Ursis crossed her arms. "But at least they're pretty."

Joyce lowered her head and fought back a laugh. While it was far from the ideal time to bond with her crew, a brief moment of reprieve was better than none.

"Say," she glanced up at the female. "I don't even know your name."

The Ursis smiled and reached out her paw. "I'm Arindra. My clan named me after the great trees on our home world."

"Arindra," Joyce whispered, shaking her furry hand. "It's nice to meet you."

Grifdar eyed both of them and grunted. "I suggest you ladies buckle up. It's about to get bumpy in here. And besides," he looked over at Joyce, "I'm going to need the two of you to work our energy threads along with our friend Ryder here. You can handle that, right?"

Joyce glared at the giant bear.

"You better watch yourself." Ryder chuckled at Grifdar. "She's gonna kick your ass if you keep talking to her like that."

The Ursis smiled. "I know. I'm just trying to get her head back into the game."

He tilted his muzzle toward the Apex floating on the wall screen. They were nearly on top of it now. "We've got a hole to dig and not a lot of time to do it."

She slid into her chair and brought up the controls for two of the tendrils while both Arindra and Ryder did the same. It was strange to see the six glowing green threads extending away from the Perniger, and even stranger were the four other Alatas battleships forming around them doing the same thing.

In all, there were thirty of the energy tentacles reaching out, and their target was only now coming into view. Their destination was over two hundred meters into the carcass of the massive destroyer, and they only had a few minutes to do it. For behind them was the lashing maw of the Cornucopia, and it was atomizing everything in its wake.

54

ZACHARY OLIVAW

OUTSIDE THE NURSERY, GROUP THREE

The half-destroyed remains of the Apex were making their way through the swarm of the Cornucopia's maw of tens of millions of barbels. The automated tentacles smashed against the hull and superstructure of the enormous ship, breaking it into bite-sized chunks. Whereas they usually used robotic mining vessels to haul asteroids and other planetesimals into its path, this time they were smashing into it. The fact that they were shredding the vestiges of their clone fleet was both ironic and convenient.

"Sir," Big Red said, trying to get his attention.

Zachary turned toward him.

"We're coming in too fast." The robot brought up a plot of their trajectory on the wall screen. "If we don't slow down, we'll destroy most of our atomizing tendrils."

Big Red hadn't said much since they'd witnessed Rán's demise, and Zachary wasn't sure how they, or the other automata, had taken it. They weren't bound by the Four-Laws like Harold and Shauna had been. And yet, they remained dedicated to serving humanity. He'd have to take a peek at their inner workings if he ever got the chance.

He shook off the thought and returned his attention to the projections. "Will the horn be compromised?"

"I don't believe so." Big Red turned to look at him. "But

we won't be able to refuel again without a great deal of effort and external assistance."

The idea that they would need to refuel was humorous. They'd be lucky if they survived another gate into the middle of the Nursery with the Shaygai on the loose, let alone fire a shot.

"Well." He rubbed his hands together. "We'll just have to cross that bridge when we get there."

Red stared at him in silence. Although he knew they didn't have to face their controls to manipulate them, they had etiquette programming and understood what it meant to stare at someone. The automata had something on its mind, and he wasn't about to prompt it to find out. He'd had enough arguing with metallic beings for one day. As far as he was concerned, if he never saw another human-form robot, he'd be fine with that.

Fortunately, Donnelley interrupted the uncomfortable silence. "We're prepared to jump on your orders, sir."

He nodded at Red and stepped sideways toward the Ulixi. "Do we have a clear path to the Rift?"

"I wouldn't call it clear, sir." Donnelley shared the live feed from the open micro-gate relay into the heart of the Nursery.

The hive of Shaygai appeared to be circling around the mouth of the Rift. At first, he thought perhaps they were creating a defensive barrier to guard the entrance, but when the image zoomed in, he saw it for what it really was.

"They're preparing to invade," he muttered.

"It would seem so." Big Red was leaning forward as he studied the pattern of ships on the wall.

Zachary hopped sideways and sighed as his already erratic heart leapt out of his chest. "Wholly shit, man! You shouldn't sneak up on someone like that."

"The Shaygai." Big Red's voice seemed to sputter. "They're widening the Rift, aren't they?"

He nodded in silence.

"We're not going to have another chance at this," Big Red said. He could feel the robot's gaze shift towards him.

"No." Zachary sighed, staring at the amassing force of alien ships in the distance. "This will be our last stand, my friend."

The servos in the robot's neck whined. "You mean, like in Henosi, sir?"

He shook his head. "No. Henosi wasn't a last stand. Our ancestors had somewhere to escape from Nanil. This time, however, we're playing for keeps. All of us are. Even the Galactic Alliance. They just don't know it yet."

The weight of his words set in for a moment until the Cornucopia seemed to whine from deep within the bowels of the massive weapon. When Zachary stepped backward and eyed Big Red's control panel, he did a double take.

The Cornucopia was opening up and ejecting its innards directly into the center of the horn. Raw materials, mining machinery, and even entire robots floated out into the gullet of the weapon, only to be tangled up by the robotic barbels and shoved down into the power cores.

"What are you doing?" He spun around to face the robot. His resemblance to Little Red was uncanny in that moment, and except for being several times larger, they were twins.

"I'm moving faster, sir." Big Red stepped back to his controls without missing a beat. He adjusted the wall display to bring up the changes he'd made. "There's no need for these supplies, and besides our weapons, I'm afraid my automated brethren are dispensable. You, however, are not."

Zachary swallowed down the emotions rising up and stared at the screen. For a race of automata which most humans claimed had no soul, the robots from Lupus were teaching them a thing or two about loyalty. Even if they were simply following their programming.

He took a deep breath and watched as the tentacles continued to rip apart Hera's ship and the other debris in their path. The sight reminded him of the damage his family had inflicted over the years on humanity. Each swipe of the articulating tendril was insignificant on its own, but after millions of strikes, even the most stubborn obstacle was reduced to pulp.

"I'm afraid that we're all dispensable at this point, Red."

And with that, he subvocalized a command on his comm and queued up one last message to be sent the moment they gated through to the Nursery. It was entitled *A Campfire Story*.

ABIGAIL OLIVAW
OUTSIDE THE NURSERY, ONBOARD THE APEX

She grasped onto the shelving attached to the bulkhead and held on for dear life. The moment Abigail felt the ground buckle, she scrambled for the most stable things she could find. In a starship, that meant anything bolted down. If it wasn't locked in place, it had a chance of crushing you to death.

The concussive blasts hurt like hell, and her body felt as though it had gone through a meat grinder several times over. When the lights came back on, she was floating behind the Beacon, and she could just make out the thin tendrils of the Therionic Entity. It was on the opposite side of the alien artifact, and it was aiming a blaster squarely at their Ibu's head.

In the background, distant pings and screams of laser blasts echoed down the corridor. Judging from the sound of all the commotion, the clones were still alive and well, and so was whoever Ibu had brought with them.

"We're safe back here," Harold whispered in her ear. "Just stay put."

He was right, but one part of her wanted to scream at the Entity in hopes that it would distract them. The other part urged her to stay hidden. That second part was more like Harold; the longer she stayed out of sight, the longer she'd survive. Hell, for all she knew, they might even forget about her.

But watching Ibu floating in the open air of the storage room told her something important. The Nanil had risked everything for her, and, most importantly, they honored their promise to protect her. She had no idea about the events that had transpired since they parted ways all those weeks ago, but she could only imagine the sacrifices it had taken them to reach her aboard Hera's ship.

As she stared at her friend, Harold's words echoed in her mind, and a sudden surge of compassion washed over her. Despite the past year of turmoil, Ibu had stuck with her and her family. If Ibu's faith in them didn't reinforce how different they were from their ancestors, she didn't know what would.

Abigail glanced around and eyed a crate locked to the ground a few meters away. It was big enough that she should be able to use it as a shield. After measuring the distance to the object with her retinal comm, she pushed off and floated in behind it. With her target rapidly approaching, she reached out and grabbed onto the passing handle with both hands, holding on tight. Her forward motion caused her legs to swing sideways, and she bumped into the back of the crate with a thud. She didn't know how she pulled it off, but she had.

"Hey, asshole!" she screamed, her voice echoing through the hold.

While she couldn't see what happened next, she could hear it. Multiple blasts rang out, one of which even scorched a mark near the wall where she'd been floating seconds earlier. The shots were followed by a swoosh of air and several muffled thuds from the other side of the crate.

Her heart raced in her chest, and although her thoughts wandered to the worst-case scenario, the Entity's sudden scream of pain gave her a renewed sense of hope.

After the alien's scream subsided, another voice called out. It was one she'd only ever heard alongside Bradley.

"I never imagined I'd set eyes on you again!" Little Red

shouted. "After all those years trapped in the Nebula, not a day went by that I didn't think about killing you."

"The feeling's mutual," the Entity growled.

"What the frak?" Abigail muttered as she carefully slid forward to peek around the side of the crate.

When she eased her head over the edge, she gasped. Just seconds earlier, the Entity had cornered Ibu against the wall, but now they were only a few meters away, holding one of the Zhen blades. In their place was Little Red.

The once-tiny robot had grown taller and used their spindly, elongating legs to their advantage. What made the sight even more peculiar was that they had possession of Ibu's second Zhen blade, and somehow it was glowing red to match the color of their casing.

"That's a new trick," Harold whispered in her ear. "They never glowed like that in Proto."

"No… no, they didn't," Ibu subvocalized.

Abigail let out a hushed screech. She hadn't realized they had a comm link open to the Nanil.

"Wholly shit," she subvocalized. "What happened?"

"This is the first time I've ever said this, but I have no clue." Ibu glanced over their shoulder and eyed a target next to Abigail. "Either Red is one hell of an actor, or those two really know each other."

The Nanil gently pushed off toward her, being sure to keep their eyes on the bright red floating robot and the ominous alien in the distance. At the last second, they reached out and grabbed the edge of the crate, swinging their legs up and around. They ended their zero-g ballet crouched down low on the top of her crude shield, holding the edge tight in their fingers.

Watching them do acrobatics was like watching a ninja. She felt like she could hardly walk, and here Ibu was doing gymnastics with ancient alien swords in their hand. The entire scene was surreal.

"Grab the blaster out of my pocket," Ibu subvocalized.

Abigail glanced backward. The blaster had been in the

Entity's grasp a minute earlier, and now it was in the holster on Ibu's hip. While she hadn't held a weapon in months, the idea of actually being able to defend herself sounded hella good.

When she went to grab it, the walls to their right vibrated, and she froze. The sound of bending and ripped metal echoed through the room and sent shivers through her entire body. The Apex was falling apart from the explosion, and they didn't have time to frak around.

She reached over and carefully unclipped the weapon before bringing it down to her side and mating it to the nanites in her skin. When the back glowed blue, she knew it was locked and loaded.

"What do you say we get the hell out of here?" She craned her neck backward down the corridor Ibu had arrived from.

"You know your kind can't win this, Abigail of the Olivaws!" The Entity was shouting between the distant tearing sounds growing louder by the second. "This is bigger than you and your pitiful species. Ascending beyond the Rift is a right for the few, not a privilege for all."

She froze in place, just as she was about to push off down the passage.

"You might be interested in knowing that I had another vision," the Entity continued, "it happened while we were connected with the Beacon. Everything snapped into focus, and it was all thanks to Hera here. With her unrelenting drive and the technology at her disposal, her clones enabled me to realize my destiny. All of our destinies. It's ironic if you think about it. You humans are weak on your own, and yet you're capable of so much more with the addition of the alien symbiotes. Hera realized this decades ago after leaving your star. Her acceptance of that truth taught me to lean into my vision. To lead the charge. So I did. I took back the Galactic Alliance I helped to form all those millennia ago, and I brought us to this moment. And unlike last time, I have full faith in my vision."

She stared across the room as the memory of her own

Beacon vision lingered in her mind's eye. The death and destruction she'd seen that day had paralyzed her with fear for weeks. Everyone she loved and everything she'd been fighting for had been dying in that hallucination.

But it was just that. A horrible illusion that was nothing more than a random spark of a fictitious timeline. It was someone else's future. Not hers.

Her life and those around her weren't predetermined. No one's fate was. They were uncharted voyagers, and she was the captain of her own destiny.

With her hand squeezing the blaster, she caught a hint of movement along the wall to her right. One of the Entity's vine-like tendrils was slithering in a crevasse pried open from the quake. She'd missed it a few seconds ago, and had she pushed off toward the exit, it probably would have nicked her mid-float.

"We can't go that way," Harold subvocalized. His voice was barely audible amidst the grinding noises growing from beyond the far wall.

"No shit," she muttered.

"Tell me you haven't been in cahoots with the likes of this red monstrosity!" the Entity screamed. "Tell me Xyrithon hasn't convinced you that their path was the righteous one."

"Xyrithon?" Ibu mouthed. "Who the hell is that?"

"It's Little Red," she whispered, raising the blaster and training it on the alien appendage.

"What are you doing, Abigail?" Harold asked.

She smiled and steadied her hand against the side of the crate. "I'm pushing back against the illusion." She took a deep breath and exhaled. "Only I am the architect of my destiny. Not him."

When she gently squeezed, the bolt of plasma covered the distance to the tentacle in an instant. While the burst of red hitting its target was reward enough, the ensuing sizzle of scorched flesh and the haunting wail that followed was music to her ears, even against the backdrop of the crumbling ship.

Ibu reached down and rested their hand on Abigail's

shoulder, opening a mental link. The effect was seamless and not at all like previous links.

"So we're fighting then?" Ibu's voice was a melodious whisper in her mind.

Abigail didn't respond verbally. She merely nodded and basked in the glow of her friend's life mark. The aura of their steel-blue light engulfed and warmed her soul. She didn't know how she'd overlooked their color before, but after spending so much time inside the Beacon, she could finally see the Nanil for their true self, and they were beautiful.

"Letting the Entity live is not an option." Her pale blue spark throbbed.

"Well, alright then." Ibu's mark flickered and seemed to form into a smile. "Keep our friend distracted, won't you?"

And with that, the link fell away. By the time Abigail glanced at Ibu, they were already shooting across the gap toward the corridor.

The groans of the alien's agony echoed from the far side of the chamber as the Entity yanked back their wounded appendage. While the warped time of mental link took some getting used to, it had its advantages.

Abigail reached up and pulled herself on top of the crate, being careful not to move too fast. Any sudden movement in zero-g often compounded the energy applied. Fortunately for her, she wasn't exactly overflowing with vigor.

She couldn't see the Entity from her vantage point behind the Beacon, so she could only imagine what he was up to. Masking his actions amidst the groaning ship was a simple feat, especially when he had dozens of arms. There was, however, the small matter that Little Red hadn't made a peep since the commotion started. Ever since the Entity called them Xyrithon.

She cleared her throat and peered at the edge of the alien device. "That was quite a speech you had there. You're being a tad melodramatic, don't ya think?"

"His kind gets that way when they're cornered," Little Red said. "Isn't that right, Lumalara?"

The tiny red robot popped his head up from on top of the ancient artifact and stared out at her. She smirked when their gazes met and his eyes spiraled with a rainbow of colors. The friendly automata had been following her brothers at the hip for the past year, and he'd saved their asses countless times. While she could be wrong about them, her heart told her they were the good guys. Anyone who fought against the Entity was decent in her book.

"Lumalara?" Harold's face appeared on her comm. "There are hundreds of references to a species called the Luminarae throughout the Galactic Alliance encyclopedia. It doesn't give much background on who they are or where they come from. All it mentions is that their species represents light, hope, and a connection with a celestial Eden. If I were to attempt to translate the Entity's name, it would be something like *Light of the Luminous Sky* since *lara* is a term their kind use to invoke the image of their starlit sky as seen from their home planet, Luxaris. The funny thing is, any mention of these Luminarae seems to be preceded by a dramatic shift in a species' growth or death. It's as if they're the antithesis of their names."

She didn't see how any of that mattered at the moment. Their biggest concern was making it out of here alive. When she turned her ear back to where Ibu had disappeared, she noticed the commotion from earlier had dissipated.

Her mind hopped from the Beacon to Ibu, and then to the Entity. Maybe, if what Harold had said was true, she could use the details to their advantage. Ibu had asked her to keep the alien distracted, after all.

"So, Lumalara." Abigail raised her blaster and swept it from the left to the right side of the artifact. "How does someone with a name like yours come to be known for death and devastation, anyhow? I mean, unless this Luxaris home-world of yours was a dump, I can't imagine—"

She recoiled mid-sentence, watching in slow motion as Little Red launched himself off the top of the Beacon with his Zhen blade held high. Except he wasn't floating towards her. He was aimed at something else.

When she looked up, she saw his target. A vine was slithering towards her from a darkened region of the room near the ceiling, and it was in the middle of lashing out. As she flinched away, her robotic savior sliced through the tentacle, severing it mid-flight.

The Entity shrieked in pain and yanked back the remains of that appendage and several others that were creeping in the shadows.

"Do not utter the name of my world, you tremnok!" The Entity groaned between the harsh, grating cacophony of nearby warping metal.

Apparently, death by a thousand cuts had meaning even across alien civilizations.

With her heart still racing, she glanced over her shoulder just in time to see Little Red float up beside her and come to a stop. He was using his free hand to navigate the room like a superhero, elongating his arm towards an object and then pulling himself forward.

Once he reached her side, she touched the top of his head and used her nanites to transfer the details of the private comm she and Ibu had been using to talk. She wasn't sure why Ibu hadn't already shared it with him, but when she saw the error message pop up, she knew why.

"I lost my comm array and a few other systems in my skirmish with Lumalara." Little Red's eyes fluttered yellow, and he glanced down at her. "Speaking of which, where has our friend disappeared to?"

As if on cue, a dozen silhouettes of gleaming metal floated overhead, and there in the middle of the pack was Ibu, with a Zhen blade aimed squarely at their target — the Entity.

"I guess we're doing this." Abigail took a deep breath and pushed off behind them with all her strength.

"Wait for me!" Little Red reached out and grasped her ankle.

At first, she was going to scold him, but then she realized her momentum had been too high anyway. The robot must've noticed it and used her poor judgment to his advantage. The combination of their two masses yanked him forward and adjusted her trajectory and velocity to a far more manageable speed.

When she looked ahead, she realized they were floating in above the robots. She hadn't thought to ask Ibu about their plan. But as each of the metallic assassins came to rest on the backside of the Beacon, she swore under her breath.

Unfortunately for them, her mistake didn't matter. The Entity was prepared for their assault.

One by one, the alien's vine-like tentacles shot out from behind the far side of the Beacon and snatched at the robotic assassins. Despite their supernatural speeds, they were still caught off guard. She wasn't sure how, but the results spoke for themselves. Although the automata managed to get off several shots that missed their targets, they didn't last long in the hands of the Entity.

She watched as the alien ripped half of the automata to shreds with savage ferocity, yanking off their heads, tearing them limb from limb, and crushing them with a fluidity and speed that made her skin crawl. He'd grown infinitely stronger since their arrival on Liprosus. It was hard to imagine he could barely bind with her when they first arrived. She could kick herself for not killing him back then, but she had no way of knowing how weak his protist form was.

"We should aim for Lumalara's vassal." Little Red whispered from behind her. "It's his biggest weakness."

"His vassal?" Abigail screwed up her face as the robot released her ankle and reached out toward the rim of the Beacon. She hadn't heard anyone referred to as a vassal in forever.

It dawned on her that he was referring to Hera. If they killed her aunt, the Entity would die along with her, at least as long as she kept her distance. The last thing she wanted was to become the Entity's flesh proxy again.

She raised her blaster out in front of her, grasping it with both hands and aiming it behind the Beacon. The alien hadn't shown his face since the initial skirmish with Little Red. She could only hope he was already wounded.

Her curiosity was answered when she crested the ancient artifact and stared down at the Entity. He had his back to the Beacon, and he was staring up at her, grinning from ear to ear. It seemed he'd been expecting her arrival.

Abigail didn't pause or question his ego. She'd given up on that long ago. Instead, she simply squeezed the trigger on her blaster several times in rapid succession. The recoil was strong, but she did her best to keep her target in the sights of the simple weapon.

While the first blast hit its mark and singed the alien's shoulder, the other two missed, scorching the ground beneath his feet. She was weaker than she had thought.

As she watched one of the Entity's tentacles shoot out toward her in slow motion, she closed her eyes and prayed that Little Red or Ibu would fare better than she had. Yet again, her best hadn't been nearly good enough.

In that moment of reflection and prayer, she realized something else. The crushing and bending noises she'd heard earlier had reached a crescendo.

Maybe her retinal comm had been cancelling them out. She couldn't say for certain, but as the far wall of the storage bay burst outward, she was sucked into the vacuum of space along with the others.

Her legs spiraled over her head, and she opened her eyes just in time to see the shocked expression on the face of the Entity. Whatever was happening, he was as unprepared for it as she was.

As she flipped end over end, she caught a glimpse of Little Red and Ibu. They'd been standing side by side on top of the Beacon and had been preparing to attack when the rupture occurred. Now, they were being sucked into the frigid expanse of space along with everyone else.

Abigail tried to scream, but no sound came.

With oxygen in scarce supply and death's icy touch raking through her, the dread of what was to come became ever more real. She only had about thirty seconds before even her nanites couldn't save her.

Though she knew she wouldn't explode in a vacuum like the vid-sims often portrayed, recognizing that death was near gave her peace. Not because she wanted to die. Not at all. Her calm in the end came from knowing that her demise meant the Entity was dying as well.

56

JOYCE GREEN

OUTSIDE THE NURSERY, GROUP THREE

"Get them into the tendrils!" Joyce screamed at the top of her lungs, but her voice was barely audible on the bridge.

The klaxons had been going off since their ship first squeezed inside the Apex, and any time she tried to shut them off, Grifdar and Arindra growled at her. Apparently, the Ursis preferred to be reminded of their impending doom by ever louder, ear-piercing horns.

Joyce guided her two tendrils toward the floating life-forms they'd just dislodged. She didn't have to be told who they were. There were no other people in the galaxy she expected to find battling it out near the Beacon of Therion than Abigail and her sidekick, Ibu. The strange uprooted alien tree and the red robot were new to her, though.

She reached out and manipulated her green tendrils in the virtual space above her control panel, wrapping them around Abigail first, then Ibu. When she went to grab the tree and the robot, Arindra beat her to it. That was probably for the best because the moment she tried to pluck them out of the vacuum, Grifdar grunted and slid the Perniger backward.

"What are you doing?" Joyce spun around to face the Ursis as she set her tendril to retract into the ship's cargo hold. "The Beacon is right there." She pointed at the glowing alien artifact on the forward wall screen.

"We're taking on too much damage," Grifdar snarled.

When she looked over at Ryder, he was frantically manipulating his controls, doing his best to keep the Perniger in one piece. Judging by the flashing red control panels in front of him and the sweat on his forehead, the Ursis was right.

"Fine! But tell the Bruintide to head in after we back out." Joyce turned and started toward the exit. "We need that damn Beacon!"

She made it part of the way across the expansive bridge and froze when she peered sideways at the section of wall panel in front of Arindra. They'd just backed out of their tunnel leading into the Apex as four squadrons of the GA Syndrus cylindrical starships dropped out of their warp bubbles near the outskirts of the battlefield.

"Shit," she muttered. Where there were some, there were bound to be many more. With the GA, that meant hundreds or even thousands of these ships could be headed their way.

"Evasive maneuvers!" She spun around and hopped back toward her controls. "We need to open up those gates so we can get the hell out of here."

She slid into her chair and opened a comm to Zachary. His face appeared instantly.

"I see them!" He was staring over the shoulder of a red robot that looked an awful lot like the one she'd pulled out of the Apex.

"We can't handle both Hera's forces and the GA." She brought up the status of their battle on her comm.

They were taking heavy losses in the ship-to-ship battles, but had thus far kept the clones at bay. It helped that some of them had already retreated or decided to rally elsewhere. For once in her life, she appreciated an act of cowardice, as long as it wasn't her people.

She stared at Zachary, willing him to talk. To say anything. Their course of action was as clear as day. Finally, she couldn't handle his indecision any longer. "Open the fraking gates. We can regroup our forces in your staging area."

When he shook his head no, her heart rate spiked, and she wanted to reach across the comm and strangle him. "What the hell do you mean, no? They're right there!"

She flipped up several views of the battle and watched as the GA tribunal ships engaged Hera's fighters and Terminus battleships. One by one, they burst into flames as the cylindrical alien ships took advantage of their moment of surprise and caught them off guard.

They let loose a barrage of close-range energy weapons and glowing yellow missiles. She hadn't seen anything like them used in the battle yet. As they approached their target, they spread out, separating again and again and again. Before she knew it, there were hundreds and then thousands of them, all colliding with their victim at once.

"Wholly shit," she muttered as the barrage of projectiles ripped through the shields and into the hull of the larger clone battleships. Seconds later, they exploded in a halo of light.

While the sight was something to behold, she could see Hera's fighters regrouping on the edge of the battlefield. The GA's moment of surprise had passed, and the clones were preparing to strike back. At that moment, she didn't know if she should cheer for the Syndrus or run.

They didn't have to wait long for an answer. She sank a little deeper into her seat when the cylindrical alien starships began bisecting at previously invisible junctures along their hull. They were breaking apart, but not because they were being attacked. They were doing it on purpose.

Their transformation was like watching an alien invasion sci-fi gone bad. Where there was once a single ship, now there were many. By the time their metamorphosis was complete, they had reorganized themselves from a few dozen large ships into hundreds of smaller and far more nimble variants. Each with the capabilities of the first, only harder to hit.

Their situation had just gone from bad to worse in the blink of an eye.

"We're screwed," Grifdar growled.

57

ABIGAIL OLIVAW
OUTSIDE THE NURSERY

While Ibu and Little Red flailed their arms in the green glow of the Ursis tentacles, Abigail didn't. She'd been inside them once before during her visit to the Proto Dark Nebula. They were the unexpected alien welcoming party the Ursis sent to capture her, but this time they were her savior. Her only hope was that whoever was piloting this ship wasn't working with Hera. Judging by the distant explosions, the Ursis were attacking the clone fleet, so maybe it wasn't that much of a stretch after all.

She struggled to take a breath as the warmth of the green energy embraced her body. Even though she knew there was oxygen being pumped into the glowing tendrils, her body still resisted the act of taking a breath, and she gagged for a second. It was like trying to breathe underwater, and her body knew better.

"The Alatas battleship hasn't tried to communicate with us yet," Harold said in her ear. "Perhaps you should warm up that blaster."

Her hand was still firmly grasping the sidearm she'd so poorly fired at the Entity. As she stared down at the weapon, a renewed vigor sparked through her extremities. It was like stepping up to a campfire after waking up to a frozen sleeping bag. Maybe it was the warmth of the alien arms pulling her toward the ship, or perhaps it was being out of reach of Hera's clones. Either way, every second she wasn't in that cargo hold, she could almost feel her energy returning.

She pulled out the energy cell and stared at the clip. It was still well over half full. There were plenty of shots left, even for someone with as bad an aim as her.

Happy with the state of her defenses, she slid the sleeve back into place and glanced up. At the same time, a sliver of light appeared on the underside of the Ursis battleship and her comm sprang to life.

"Can she hear us yet?" Joyce screamed. "What the frak is taking so long?"

Abigail's heart sank, and she struggled to pivot in the glowing tendril to aim her blaster toward the expanding opening. The last thing she'd heard, Joyce had moved to the dark side and become one of Hera's flunkies. While she hadn't seen it for herself, the Entity shared some footage of her fighting with an Ursis a few weeks earlier. At the time, he was taunting Abigail to give up her fight, but she never did.

With the edge of the ship nearing, her pulse raced. She had a feeling there was no way they were getting out of this alive. Not with only a half charged weapon and a few swords among them. Even with the swords being as powerful as a Zhen blade, they were no match for the army of well-trained Ursis soldiers on that ship. The aliens weren't exactly known for being friendly to anyone not of their kind.

"Shit! I forgot to turn on the camera." Joyce's face flickered onto Abigail's comm. "Hello Presi..." She shook her head. "I mean, Abigail. I trust your being alive means you're doing well?"

The Ursis battleship continued backing up, putting space between the explosions in the distance and themselves. As she glanced around, Harold highlighted a region of the battle on her comm and zoomed in. There, in the center of the keyframe, was a cylindrical Galactic Alliance starship, and for some reason it was separating into chunks.

"I guess you noticed our new friends," Joyce began. "They

just arrived from the Nursery, and lucky for us, they only appear to be slicing the clones into pieces. At least for now."

Joyce suddenly ducked her head down like she was dodging something, and Abigail's body was yanked sideways. The tendrils were mimicking the woman's motion, and she'd moved her out of the way just in time to dodge an inbound chunk of debris from the Apex.

"Are you... the one pulling me in?" Abigail asked. Speaking inside the ribbon of energy was an odd sensation.

"I'm trying to." Joyce leaned forward and bit her lip. She then grunted and raised her hands, sending a bump echoing in the energetic flow.

A second later, Abigail felt another tug jerking her even faster toward the now open hold.

"These things are easier to use when you're tearing shit apart." Joyce curled up her nose. "Delicate motions aren't quite my cup of tea."

"Frak," Abigail muttered and took aim at an automata that popped out of one of the entrances in the belly of the Ursis hold. She carefully squeezed off a shot at the robot.

The plasma round moved in slow motion through the green glowing tendril. However, when it reached the vacuum of space, it sped up, covering the remaining distance in the blink of an eye. When it did, the chest of the automata exploded in a flash of light.

"Yes!" she smiled and took aim at a second robot making its way into the room.

"Nice shot!" Harold said.

"What the hell are you doing?" Joyce screamed.

"Cashing in early and forcing you to pay for what you're about to do to us." She narrowed her gaze, struggling to steady her aim as the glowing tendril quaked under Joyce's control.

"I hope you mean saving your ass?" Joyce lifted her hand, and the energy ribbon followed suit, sending Abigail rocketing upward and spinning onto her back.

She struggled in the flow to flip herself around and

reposition her weapon toward the approaching hold. "If by saving, you mean killing me." She rotated her hip and winced. "Then yeah, something like that."

"I told you we should've tossed her!" an Ursis voice shouted from somewhere beside Joyce. "Admiral Klus warned us that Hera might have already implanted her with a symbiote."

"Wait!" Abigail froze. "Did he say Klus? Who's flying that thing?"

The Ursis snarled. "I am Captain Grifdar Skyrend, and I suggest you lower your blaster, lest our vines of Onikuma mysteriously let you go."

Suddenly, the glowing tendrils flickered off, and the frigid vacuum of space lashed out, burning her eyes and squeezing the life out of her lungs. She screamed, but no one heard. Not until the aura turned back on, and she hovered just outside the hold, moaning in the warmth of the energy wave.

"Fine." She curled up into a ball and shuddered, pulling the blaster tight to her chest. "But our alien plant friend won't be happy being ripped out of there. At least not without his galactic glow stick."

Joyce chuckled over the comm and then froze.

"What is it?" Abigail uncurled and struggled to spin around, but she couldn't see anything.

"We're..." Joyce tilted her head, staring at something in the distance. "Picking up a comm request from the GA ships. And unless I'm mistaken, they're asking for... you." She turned to look at her.

"Me?" Abigail swallowed hard.

Another Ursis voice she hadn't heard yet chimed in. This one sounded feminine and almost like Klus. "You are a Seguan and therefore can connect with the gods of Therion. Are you not the human who last connected with your Beacon?"

She wanted to say yes, but with Hera now bound to the Entity, she couldn't say for certain it was her they were looking for. Besides, as far as she knew, Lync and the other Ulixi might be linked to another Beacon from the Nursery.

"It could be me," she muttered. "Patch them through."

What she expected to see was not at all what appeared on her comm. When the image stopped jumping around and settled, she was staring at some type of biological organ floating in a vat of pink slime. There were streams of bubbles wafting through the liquid and several dozen stalks that looked like they were for eyes, but the eyes were missing.

"It's a Bynaury," Harold subvocalized in her ear. "Like the one Bradley encountered in Proto."

"Lisp?" she whispered.

She wasn't sure why she'd said the name, but it was the first one that came to mind. It just so happened to be the only Bynaury she knew. Though their meeting had been brief on the tribunal ship, they treated her with the utmost respect.

The organism shuddered, then somehow formed words. "It is you. President Olivaw. I... should have known."

Abigail cleared her throat. "Former President. But, yes." She smiled. "It's nice to finally see you, Lisp."

A silence passed over the comm as she stared at the distant field of cylindrical shards from the tribunal-shaped ships. They were still battling the clones, but for some reason, they had left the Ursis alone.

"Is that you fighting over there?" Abigail pointed toward the flashes of light.

"It is I, along with many of my kind." The image of the vat disappeared and was replaced with a glowing green ball of light known as a prasinus, just like the ones she'd spoken to inside the Beacon.

She brought her hand up to her mouth and gasped. "It... was you in there? In the depths of the Beacon? I... had no idea."

"So you do recognize me?" Lisp's aura flickered, and the scintillations on the surface briefly formed into what could only be described as a human smile. "I thought the blue flicker of your life mark might have been a human, but I didn't expect it would be you."

She narrowed her gaze. "When did you see my aura? I never—"

"I hate to break up this chance encounter," Joyce interrupted. "You two can catch up later. But right now, we have a Beacon to retrieve before Zachary's Cornucopia swallows it whole."

She spun around in the glowing energy stream and drew in her breath. Somehow, she hadn't seen the Cornucopia behind the Apex. But now, with its rim cresting the edge of the shrinking ship, it was all she could see.

"We can help with that," Lisp began. "We are at Abigail's disposal. That is, if her deal still stands?" The green spark of the alien life mark pulsed.

Abigail smirked and slowly nodded her head. "If we survive this thing, you'll have my full support, along with those of my people."

"As full voting members of your alliance?" Lisp asked. "Not merely watching from the sidelines. We've had enough of that with the Galactic Alliance."

She let the question linger for a moment, hoping that someone else would say something. When they didn't, she realized they might need a nudge.

"Joyce? Grifdar, is it?" She glanced from avatar to avatar. "What say you? I don't speak for everyone." She bit her lip and hoped they wouldn't call out the fact that she didn't speak for anyone.

It was Joyce who replied first. "If Ambassador Olivaw has confidence in your admission to our alliance, then so do I. On behalf of the people of Epsilon Eridani, you have my vote."

A second later, a message appeared on her comm from Joyce.

You better not make me regret this, Olivaw!

She smiled and nodded.

Grifdar spoke next. "How many of your kind are there? What worlds do you bring to the table? Why do we need you? I have a great many questions that must be addressed before—"

"Grifdar!" The female Ursis' face appeared on the comm. "The Seguan has blessed the Bynaurys and Haradis has blessed the Seguan. If the king trusts her, then what place do you have questioning their judgement?"

He slowly turned to glare at her. His eyes had narrowed, and she could see his glistening teeth from the side.

While they were arguing over alliance voting semantics, an explosion erupted from the Alatas battleship. When Abigail pivoted to find the source of the blast, she spotted Ibu, Little Red, and the Entity inside the hold. The other tentacle must've let them go, and from the looks of it, the chamber was rapidly filling with smoke. She thought she saw some other familiar robots in there as well, but they were quickly engulfed in the black haze.

"Shit," she muttered. "Get me in there, Joyce!" She raised her blaster and leaned closer to the edge of the glowing energy field, training the weapon on the golden cocoon the Entity was dragging around. While she couldn't hit the thin vines of the alien, his body battery would suit just fine. "Grifdar! I need your goddamn vote. Now!"

She squeezed off two shots in rapid succession. The first missed wide and fried the ground in front of the gangly alien, but the second hit its mark. The gold surface protecting Hera's body rippled and absorbed the blow. But a moment later, the Entity collapsed and started screaming. At least that was what it looked like, judging by how Little Red and Ibu were thrashing around.

"Grifdar?" She returned her attention to her comm.

"Fine!" He growled and turned back to his controls, right as she felt the tug of the tendrils yank her toward the hold. "But if these Bynaurys drag down the alliance, it's your head. Not mine."

She wiped her hand on her shirt and repositioned it on the blaster. The last thing in the universe she was worried about was alliance politics. If they survived this trial of strength, they'd have far bigger challenges than fighting over resources.

"Do it, Lisp!" She closed one eye and took a deep breath, aiming her blaster at Hera's body bump. "Get that damn Beacon out of there. And Joyce. Get on the horn to Z. We need those gates opened, and we need them yesterday!"

She squeezed off two more rounds, and they tore into Hera's golden cocoon. And just in time too. The Entity had lashed out and wrapped up Ibu and Little Red in its vines. He was preparing to squeeze them like grapes, but instead he dropped them and began screaming once more. His voice was barely audible through the energy field as she passed into the ship, but his arms were flailing around and whipping anything within reach. Fortunately for her, when the alien appendage passed through the edge of the green glow, it slowed down, and she managed to duck below their thrashing arc before it hit.

Joyce lowered her glowing chariot safely into the hold seconds before Grifdar banked the ship away from the shadow of the Cornucopia. He was heading toward one of dozens of gates forming in the distance, which meant they must've reached Zachary.

When Abigail looked down at her blaster, she froze. There were only a couple of shots left.

She reached up and tweaked her comm to only talk to the crew. "Someone, please tell me we have some human-size weapons in this place. I can't keep this alien in check much longer. I need ammo."

"I can help with that," the second Ursis said. "Name's Arindra, and if I remember right, you've been on one of these ships before."

58

JOYCE GREEN

OUTSIDE THE NURSERY, GROUP THREE

The burn of the gate transition lingered on Joyce's skin, but she didn't have time to dawdle over something as insignificant as pain. Their clock was ticking with the Rift, and she only hoped they weren't already too late.

"Don't let any of those clones through!" She brought up their defenses and set their systems to auto-fire on anything that didn't match the profile of their allies or their new Bynaury friends. She didn't care if their transponders identified them as friendlies. Anything else that was important should have a gate drive. They'd shoot first and filter through the carnage later. With the Bertha cannons at their back, belching death and destruction through the open gate was all she cared about.

Grifdar positioned their ship on the far side next to the active Bertha. He wasn't taking any chances they'd miss someone coming through, and neither were his Ursis kin.

As they floated in front of the space-time barrier, firing shot after shot across the gap, the other Alatas battleships gated through and took up positions beside them. Ship by ship, they slowly formed an impenetrable virtual wall of defenses — a blockade preventing their former allies from passing through.

When the Bynaury ships came into view, Joyce triple-checked her targeting and that of the others in the fleet. The mesh network of battleships and cannons were coordinating their firepower. She couldn't risk friendly fire taking out one of the alien allies. Their cargo was too precious.

"Harbingers of the darkness approach!" Grifdar gestured with his paw toward the far side of the gate as several hundred more cylindrical ships dropped out of their warp bubbles just as the first wave of Bynaury passed through. "Stars save us," he growled.

Joyce flinched as Grifdar's claws dug into the metallic deck beneath his pilot chair. Her first instinct was to close the gates, but there were hundreds of Ursis battleships still fighting to escape — hundreds of allies they'd need in this final push with the Beacon. You couldn't turn a fleet as large as theirs on a dime, at least not without a detailed plan. Which, in their case, was destroyed the moment they fired their first shot.

Their targeting systems were able to flag the friendly chunks from the Bynaury who were on their side. She had no idea how it differentiated the two groups, but she was thankful it could.

She subvocalized a command to open a comm to their new friends. "Lisp, is it? I see a bunch more of your kind have arrived. Any word if these recent arrivals are on our team?"

An image of the alien brain appeared in the space in front of her. "Your kind's preference for visual contact is refreshing. For far too long, our people have been locked behind the scenes. It's nice to speak to someone face to face, as it were."

The Perniger rocketed sideways as Grifdar rolled their ship, narrowly dodging an inbound missile from one of Hera's fighters. Joyce launched a trail of fire from their aft auto-cannons to take out the projectile, and it exploded well away from any other ships.

At the same time, their neighboring Alatas guards fired several rounds at the nimble Pilum before it reached the Bertha. They skillfully triangulated the novice pilot and guided them into one final, killing blow. The clone fighter shattered in an elongated ring of red and yellow light.

"While I enjoy chatting as well as anyone..." Joyce leaned forward and highlighted the next wing of fighters heading their way. "We have a war to—"

"I understand," Lisp interrupted. "I wouldn't waste your ammunition on those other Syndrus vessels."

She narrowed her gaze at her cerebral friend. "Dare I ask why?"

"It's probably best you not know," Lisp said. "Lest you think less of us. Just try to remember that our actions are not without millennia of provocation."

Joyce shared the 'No fire' details on the Syndrus with the rest of the robots and Ursis fleet. "There's one thing you don't have to worry about with me, and that's sympathy for the Galactic Alliance." She peered at the corner of her retinal comm, at the menacing-looking brain in a jar. "Present aliens excluded."

"Of course." Lisp's pink lighting fluttered with a greenish hue, which she assumed was a laugh.

She glanced back at Ryder. "How long until the rest of our fleet makes it through?"

"It's hard to say." He grimaced as the Perniger vibrated.

A round of plasma tore through an empty section of the ship formerly used as crew quarters. When Joyce checked, the glowing green sludge on the outside had already begun sealing it up, and a contingent of robots was headed that way to see what they could repair.

"Sorry," Ryder muttered. "Like I was saying, it's hard to say. We're about halfway done, but moving these Syndrus through is slowing things up. Though, I have to admit, they're traversing the barrier far faster than humans can tolerate."

Grifdar sniggered. "That's because your pain tolerance is so low. It's a wonder you can even stand sometimes without whining."

Joyce swallowed hard and brought up the video feed

showing the other gate arrays off to their side. To their left, the Bertha cannons were sitting idle, waiting to take a shot across the space-time gateway, but they couldn't. Seven tightly packed Syndrus Bynaury ships were squeezing their way through. The scene was playing out through most of the other portals as well.

"We have little regard for the occupants of the vessel, but their weapons will prove to be useful." Lisp shared a video with only Joyce. "The Bynaury onboard has been incapacitated, and the ships are under our control."

The video feed showed multiple viewpoints from the inside of one of the Syndrus ships. There were thousands of Thyreus and Trochilidae writhing on the ground in pain from the rapid transit. When she looked closer, she could see that the aliens appeared to be shackled by the very floor itself. The Bynaury hadn't only commandeered their ships, they'd brought the aliens with them as well.

"I'd say fifteen minutes," Ryder said, bringing her back to the moment.

While part of her wanted to close the gates and sever the alien warships in half, the other part needed to trust the Bynaury. From what she'd seen in the video, the aliens had the GA under control. Besides, their help had come at an opportune time, and without it, they might not have had the Beacon in their possession.

Unfortunately, the clock was ticking.

"We don't have fifteen minutes." Joyce dismissed the video from Lisp and zoomed out her display, highlighting a set of gates well away from the others.

There were four or five regolith portals between them and their targets, and from the looks of their charred remains, they'd run into a smidge of trouble on this side. She could barely make out the glowing remnants of what used to be the gate core within each of the segments that made up the floating arrays. They were programmed to self-destruct when the GA got too close for comfort. She only hoped that wasn't a tactic the aliens had done on purpose. Otherwise, they might not be able to escape the Nursery when they needed to.

"We'll use these five gates to transfer troops to the other Beacons and the Rift." She shared the coordinates with the fleet and let the A.I. inside Zachary's robotic friends figure out how to route everyone through. "Just make sure we're in the front with Lisp and our Therionic cargo. We can't risk losing it back here."

She stared at the edge of the glowing blue Beacon floating within the densely packed formation of Syndrus ships. The Bynaury were encircling the relic on all sides, and it was almost entirely concealed. To the untrained eye, it might even fool the GA into thinking it was a new weapon.

That gave her an idea.

"Alright!" she spun around to face Grifdar and smiled. "I need two dozen or so Alatas battleships, and I need them to move into a new formation."

The Ursis narrowed his gaze. "Dare I ask what you're up to, Captain?"

She shrugged. "It depends on how weak your stomach is."

He growled and shuttered at the personal jab and started barking orders into his monocle toward the other nearby battleships. She'd have what she needed. She only hoped they were prepared to go down with a fight.

59

LYNC MICHAELS

INSIDE THE NURSERY, NEAR THE RIFT

The green trail from the energy weapon matched the glowing ring around the base of the Shaygai's multi-axis body. Its devastation was like a one, two punch of a laser and a plasma bolt. It had the speed of electromagnetic radiation and the physical damage of ionized gas. The combination wasn't just ripping their ships apart — it was tearing at their conviction.

"They're everywhere!" Greer shouted.

He'd been emotionally over the top since the aliens had burst onto the scene. At first, they lingered en masse near the Rift. For a while, she thought they were merely posturing, flexing their might. They could hold back the Galactic Alliance for days like this, especially given their fear of shooting the aliens near the tear in space-time.

But then something changed.

She didn't know what it was, but it had happened about thirty minutes ago. Since then, the Shaygai had been attacking. In the first wave, they sent only half a dozen ships. It was as though they were testing the waters, seeing if the gathered human and Ursis ships could hold their own.

Lync yanked back on her yoke and slammed the throttle forward, launching the Nyílak fighter across the shimmering surface of the Rift. The acceleration goo shifted as her body pressed into her harness.

The G-forces would have killed a normal human, but inside this oversized gelatinous aquarium, she was protected from the harmful gravitational effects of the rapid change in direction. It empowered her to make bold and erratic maneuvers, like flying dangerously close to tears in space-time that could lead to their galaxy's very extinction.

"It worked!" Shauna fired the rear-facing auto-cannon a split second later.

The familiar thump of the plasma-infused rounds tore through the central hull, connecting the deadly armatures of the alien fighter. It burst into the same orange and red flower of destruction that had accompanied every battle Lync had ever participated in. She only hoped it meant their pilot was dying as well. After all, death and power were the only true motivators in the universe.

With the explosion behind her and a chaotic dance of devastation above, she wasn't expecting to feel the tug of another mind. A familiar soft glow warmed the back of her neck, sending a tingling sensation through her entire body.

"I'm detecting a dozen gates opening starboard of the Beacons," Shauna began. "I think it's—"

"Abigail." Lync shook her head and squeezed her eyes shut. She could feel her sister; she was so close.

Shauna glanced at her. "We don't know that. I was going to say the Ursis."

"You might not sense her, but I do." Lync pulled back hard on her yoke and launched them upward, barrel-rolling around a nearby Shaygai fighter that was heading towards her. Like with the Galactic Alliance and the Beacon, the aliens never seemed to fire at their Rift.

As they screamed past the aliens, Shauna squeezed off several auto-cannon rounds, which tore through the alien's hull. While it didn't seem to slow the ship down, any damage was good when it increased the chance of her foe's demise.

The aliens, however, were prepared for her assault. As she

passed the still glowing holes in the arms of the deadly ships, two more Shaygai exited the Rift.

They immediately opened fire, and her heart skipped a beat.

She watched in slow motion as the first shot hit dead center in the bow of her ship. It must've been a teaser, meant to force her to bank away from the assault, as the unusually weak energy beam didn't tear her apart. Instead, it lit her up like a Christmas tree and blinded her sensors. The phase absorption apparatus spread over the hull of her fighter repurposed the light to recharge her power reserves.

The second and third shots weren't nearly as feeble. However, instead of snuffing out her life flame, her ship rocked sideways and every surface inside her pod flashed before shutting off. She was briefly thrown into darkness, with only the shimmer of Shauna's eyes illuminating the surrounding gel. The effect was eerily cold and isolating. It reminded her of the moments before her father's death, when she'd been slingshotting solo with only Norby and the dark innards of her chariot.

When the tertiary power systems and sensors flickered back on, she gasped. The glowing shards of a Nyílak fighter were splayed out in her wake, like a surgery gone wrong. She hadn't even seen the fellow Ulixi heading toward her.

She grabbed the yoke and twisted sideways, narrowly dodging another round of blasts. "Who... was that?" She shuddered.

"I think it was Greer," Shauna whispered.

Her heart froze, and the weight of a black hole crushed her chest. Greer had been the only other Ulixi with a backstory as tragic as hers, and yet he still found a way to harness his pain and make others laugh. He had a knack for leaving a room in stitches with his uproarious humor, and now he was gone.

The sterile light of her control panel blurred as tears welled in her eyes, mixing with the gelatinous goo in front of her face. Numb from how close the loss had hit, she closed her eyes and tried to remember his laugh. His infectious smile.

Her mind replayed each memory, each fading moment, as she struggled not to forget his face — the face of another life lost to this relentless war of lies and greed.

"Frak," Shauna muttered, interrupting her memory echos.

"What's wrong?" Lync wiped at her cheeks and shook off the trip down memory lane. She'd try to make time later to celebrate the lives of her family, assuming she made it out alive herself.

"Our systems are having trouble syncing up with the rest of the fleet," Shauna began. "Whatever that last explosion did to our hull, the glyphs on the exterior aren't working right. We can't seem to negotiate a cypher with the other ships, which means we can't decode their transmissions."

"Well, that's not good." Lync shifted in her seat and checked her controls.

Shauna had activated an autopilot sequence and set it to randomly weave and dodge until they could debug what was going on with their ship. After a minute of both of them fiddling with the ship's computers, Lync gave up and turned toward her mom.

"I know," Shauna nodded. "We need to get back to the others. It's the only way we can…" Her voice trailed off.

When Lync was about to ask what was wrong, she saw it. In the distance, near the three Beacons, was a sea of cylindrical starships, and from the looks of it, they'd passed through the gates.

The familiar shape of the Galactic Alliance tribunal ships evoked conflicting emotions of both fear and rage. Seeing them so close to her people meant only one thing.

They'd lost. The aliens had somehow taken control of the gates.

Lync reached forward and was about to hit the emergency gate button when Shauna lashed out and grabbed her hand.

"Wait!" She pointed toward a Selene moon in the background as it lit up in a wondrous halo of light, exploding outward and exposing the bright white core at the center.

"How?" Lync mouthed the words, and her answer came a moment later.

One of the tribunal ships near their Beacons shimmered blue and then faded into a mist of warp bubbles. In the blink of an eye, it shot across the space between it and a nearby Selene moon. But unlike the previous explosion, this one didn't burst outward — it cracked open like an egg.

The Syndrus ship tore off a massive chunk of the spherical starship, leaving it gaping open, only to erupt in a symphony of smaller, hypnotic explosions. Like the first halo, it was a beautiful sight to behold.

"What the hell is going on?" Lync checked their six, and the Shaygai was nowhere to be found. They'd peeled off and disappeared. When she scanned the computer, she saw that they were headed straight toward the dense collection of tribunal ships — the same ones that were acting like over-sized missiles.

"I guess they're on our side." Shauna shrugged.

Lync was about to aim their fighter at the rapidly forming conflict when she felt a faint tug at her consciousness, followed by a sudden, powerful squeezing sensation. Her vision faded, and she brought her hands up and covered her face as a voice spoke out loud.

"Is she alive?" Little Red asked.

Lync gasped. Although she'd only met the tiny robot a few times, she recognized the voice immediately. However, she didn't understand how it could be inside her head.

"I think so," Ibu whispered. "She appears to be in shock. We need to keep moving. You grab her, and I'll—"

"I'm… fine." Abigail moaned. "I just… felt her again. I felt, Lync."

Her sister's voice was hoarse, not at all like the powerful woman she left on Liprosus.

Lync struggled to form the words to respond. Her mouth

had suddenly stopped working. Only when she used her mind, like inside the Beacon, could she speak.

"A—bi—gail?" She focused on forming each syllable. "Is that... you? Am I... dead?"

"I hope not," Abigail smiled, and the darkness of Lync's mind glowed with a faint blue aura. "It's good to hear your voice."

Lync didn't know how she knew her sister was smiling, but she was certain she was. The experience felt like being inside the Beacon, and yet, they weren't.

"Welcome to the power of four Beacons," Little Red said. The light changed to an orange-yellow saffron-like glow, unlike anything she'd seen before within the alien artifact. "I suggest we get down to business, my friends."

Lync tried to focus in one direction, but the light seemed to be coming from everywhere. "Business?" she muttered. "What business?"

"Hold on a second," Abigail said. "Is no one going to acknowledge the elephant in the room?"

"Elephant?" Ibu whispered. "There's an elephant in here?"

Lync chuckled, feeling a weight lift from her chest. She'd missed Nanil's lack of understanding metaphors or symbolism. "I think what my sister meant to ask is how the frak is our little robot friend connected to our mental link?"

"That's the least of our concerns right now," Little Red said. "First, we have a battle to win. And Lync, I suggest you figure out how to open your eyes if you want to help us."

She drew in her breath. Despite the robot's absence, he could somehow sense that Lync's eyes were closed. While she didn't understand how he was doing it, he was right; she needed to see.

The voices ebbed and flowed around her as she fought to pry open her eyelids. After several attempts, they gave way one at a time. As her vision sharpened, Shauna was floating in front of her, staring into her eyes. Had Shauna been human, her jaw would have been gaping.

"Are you... okay?" Shauna reached out and ran her robotic hand down her cheek. "You were muttering to yourself. Something about... Abigail."

Lync nodded, a smile forming on her lips. "She's alive. I heard her."

"Of course I am," Abigail said. "I told you that already."

"No!" Lync shook her head. "I was telling your mother you were alive."

"She's with you?" Abigail asked. "Tell her I said hello."

"Wait a second..." Shauna grasped her shoulder. "Are you talking to her right now?"

Lync nodded, but waved her hand in the goo. "I can't... it's... too much. Talking to both of you at the same time is too much."

"While I could talk you through how to control it," Little Red began, "we don't have the time. For now, I'll separate our conversations from yours. Just shout if you need us."

"You can do that?" Lync asked.

But it was too late. The voices were gone. The robot had somehow squelched the others, and all she heard was the hum of their ship.

"Can I do what?" Shauna tilted her head.

"Nothing," she muttered. "I'll tell you later."

Lync reached out and adjusted her controls, aiming their Nyílak straight towards the erupting firefight in the distance. Shauna, however, was still floating there, staring at her as if she'd lost her mind.

"I suggest you strap in, Mom." She shifted deeper into her chair. "Shit's about to get crazy around here."

Without another word, she slammed the throttle to maximum and their arrowhead fighter shot forward, aimed squarely at a squadron of Shaygai already heading towards her friends and family, the only two things in this universe worth fighting for.

60

———

IBU

INSIDE THE NURSERY, ONBOARD THE PERNIGER

The persistent dull throbbing at the back of Ibu's head made it difficult to concentrate on anything else, especially on avoiding the Entity. With Lync's voice walled off from theirs, the discomfort lessened, but it was still there. Never relenting and growing stronger by the second. While they'd been in countless mental links before, being connected like this to the Beacon was different.

"The pain will subside with time." Little Red rested his hand on their shoulder as he peered around the corner.

They narrowed their gaze at the robot. "How do you know it—"

"Like I said," he interrupted, squeezing gently, "I'll explain later. Until then, we have to stay focused."

Being alert with an asteroid-sized migraine wasn't easy, but neither was dying. They checked their retinal comm, and while the location of Joyce and the Ursis was highlighted on the map of the ship, the Entity was nowhere to be found.

"I'm not seeing them either," Little Red said. "It's likely that Lumalara has been strengthened by bringing the four Beacons together. His ability to manipulate his environment is both his greatest strength and his weakness."

Ibu squeezed the hilt of the Zhen blade in their hand and struggled to make sense of the odd robot's riddle. As they turned over the meaning of the words, they winced as needle-like pain pierced through their skull. They slumped against the wall and reached up to touch their head, then the pressure suddenly released and faded just as quickly as it arrived. In fact, it felt a bit better.

"Wholly heck!" a voice shouted. "What tis dis place, and whys the hell is I seeing colorz?"

"Welcome, my Ulyxsauri brethren." Little Red shifted his Zhen blade to his offhand and plugged his primary hand into a nearby socket on the wall. "It's Lo, right?"

"Yaz, man," Lo muttered, and the room around Ibu throbbed green. "But whuz dis, and wherez Hi?"

Little Red's eyes whirled blue. "I suspect he'll be joining us shortly. Until then, I'll send you into Lync's mental shard."

"Oh das nice," Lo chirped. "Boss lady been off da air for a time. I could use—"

Her voice faded into the background, and yet the pain in Ibu's head remained low. "So the more Ulixi that join, the less it hurts?"

"Well, any Ulyxsauri, but yeah. That's the gist." Little Red blinked and disconnected from the port. A second later, he shared a feed from inside the shuttle bay on their comms.

Ibu squinted at the video. "What the hell is he doing?"

"The Entity is trying to crack the hull." Abigail popped her head out from around the door frame.

Ibu flinched and sighed. With all the pain, they'd forgotten she'd left.

"We just saw," Little Red said. "It seems he won't be bringing the fight to us as we'd hoped."

"Frickety frak!" Abigail spat.

Ibu had noticed that Abigail had been recovering a heck of a lot faster since they put distance between them and the Entity. Even in the past few minutes she'd perked up, and that was despite the nagging pain in their literal neck. Suddenly, it hit them what the ancient alien was doing.

"He's trying to keep his signal to the outside." Ibu pushed up off the ground and steadied themself on the wall. "If the robots are working to seal us up in skotádi, that'll block his connection with the Beacon."

Abigail eased into the room but kept her eyes trained down the hall toward the hold. "Won't that also knock out our mental-link to the others?"

Ibu shook their head. "No, I don't think so."

"That makes no sense." Abigail glanced at them.

"The Nanil is right." Little Red stepped out into the corridor, as if daring the Entity to come find them. "We each contain within us the Lespánium receptors necessary to bind with the Therionic life force, even through the molecular bonds of a skotádi hull. It's hard to explain, but the sooner we can seal this ship up, the better."

Their path forward was clear, and they weren't the only ones who saw it. When they looked over at Abigail, she was nodding.

"Let's do this then." She reached around her back and unslung a massive rifle that was three times too big for her to be holding.

Ibu tilted their head. "Where'd you find that?"

She threw a thumb over her shoulder and smiled. "Down the hall to the right. I know it looks like it, but it's not exactly a maze in here. Arindra helped me locate it. Plus, this isn't my first time on an Alatas class vessel, remember?"

They'd never forgotten the feeling of Abigail leaving them behind in Proto. While they understood she was trying to protect everyone, her abandoning them still stung. Her words, however, gave them another idea.

Ibu closed their eyes and searched for the faint veil Little Red had pulled over them to shelter their mind from Lync and the other Ulixi. As they reached out, the shield shimmered as they drew it aside, or at least it felt like that was what they were doing.

Once it was open, the unfamiliar sea of minds within the Beacon crashed over Ibu like a tsunami. Their legs weakened, and they stumbled down on one knee. It took them a moment to gather themself enough to see that Lync's familiar yellow glow was floating just in front of them.

"What is it, Ibu?" she asked. "What's wrong?"

"I…" They took a deep breath and focused on the golden warmth coming from her mind. It was soothing. "I remembered something the Prima Nanil told me about the Beacon. I thought it might help."

Lync's light faded for a moment and then brightened again. "It's pretty crazy in here trying to pilot a ship while hanging out inside Beacon space. I'm not sure that we can—"

"It's a maze," Ibu blurted out. "At least the Prima called it that. They said you had to follow the path of the dead to the end."

"The dead," Lync muttered. "They used those words?"

"Yeah, that's what they said." Ibu eased up onto their feet. "Once you reach the end, they said your purpose would become clear. Is there somewhere in the Beacon like that?"

"Actually," Lync's aura scintillated, "there is. Thanks, Ibu." She drifted forward and hugged them, and their lights seemed to brighten when they merged. The effect was as soothing as it was enlightening.

In that moment, the pain in their mind had all but disappeared, and they could finally think again. It was as if Lync's embrace had walled off the voices inside the Beacon. But when she let go, it all came crashing down on them.

As their legs buckled, Little Red reached out and gently pulled the virtual curtain back over them again. "It's too soon," he whispered. "Your mind needs more time to adapt."

When Ibu opened their eyes, both he and Abigail were staring at them.

"Are you able to move?" Abigail caressed their shoulder.

Ibu swallowed hard and nodded. "I am." They glanced between the two of them and felt the weight and energy from the Zhen blade in their hand. They could almost hear it singing to them as they focused on their next step. "Let's get this over with."

"That's music to my ears," Little Red chirped.

He tapped his blade to theirs, and the symphony Ibu imagined in their mind took off, the beat willing them forward, nudging them onward, toward the battle ahead.

But something was missing. Something they were supposed to do. They hesitated for a moment, but then they remembered. "The goo." They glanced at Little Red. "The orange and yellow stuff we brought along. Did you grab it from the ship?"

Little Red's display spiraled a rainbow of colors, and suddenly a small compartment slid out of his chest. When Ibu peered inside, a vial of the cloudy orange and yellow fluid they'd seen days before was resting in the center beside an injector.

"I only had room for one," Little Red said. "Sorry, we sorta left in a hurry."

They smirked and reached out toward the cylinder. But just as their fingertips grazed its surface, the Zhen blade humming in their hand erupted into a dissonant tremor. A grating screech echoed within their mind, abruptly severing the melody that had moments before been swelling to a crescendo. They froze, their hands hovering above the stormy vial.

"Did you feel that?" Little Red asked, staring at Ibu. His display was spiraling a chaotic blue pattern they'd never seen before.

They nodded and winced, taking a step backward as the souls in the Beacon squeezed at the edge of their mind.

"Are you okay?" Abigail asked.

"I... believe so." Ibu rubbed their temple. "It was like... the symphony, it hit a bad note... and then... it stopped. I don't think the blade wanted me to touch that stuff."

"Guys," Abigail began, "swords can't talk." She tilted her head down the hall. "Do we really need that crap, or can we get on with this?"

Ibu shrugged. They honestly didn't know. They'd forgotten all about the deadly vial until a few seconds ago.

And now, after touching it, the pressure from the minds in Beacon space was overpowering their every thought.

Little Red stared at them for a second before slowly lowering his hands toward the vial.

And then he touched it.

Like a switch in a storm, the Zhen blade flicked on and cooed in their hand. But that wasn't all. The symphony tore off, picking up where it had stopped and driving on, faster this time. The beat was far more urgent than before.

They drew in their breath and nodded. The notes flowed through their mind, drowning out the dread of the Beacon and allowing them to focus. The symphony was both comforting and intense. Its purpose was abundantly clear.

"We need to go!" Ibu stepped into the corridor.

Abigail chuckled. "You're preaching to the choir." She cocked her rifle and a low-frequency hum filled the space.

When Ibu glanced over at the now glowing barrel of the weapon, Abigail smiled. "Don't worry." She tapped the side of her head. "I read the directions. We're good."

"If you say so," Ibu muttered and turned back down the hall.

They subvocalized a command to bring up the overlay showing the cameras leading into the shuttle bay, but it failed. All they saw was black. At first, they thought the Entity had gotten into the Alatas computer systems, but when they used their retinal comm to zoom down the corridor, they realized what had happened. There were tendrils from the alien reaching into the corridor, and they were covering the camera. Worse still, they appeared to be slithering deeper into the ship.

"I've got those." Abigail leaned her cheek against her rifle and steadied herself against the wall, taking aim at the appendages of the distant Entity. When she pulled the trigger, she winced.

The result of the blast was far from what Ibu had expected. They imagined that with the little noise the device was producing, it would burst forward with a devastating ray of destruction, laying waste to anything in its path. But instead, all they heard was a faint hissing sound. In fact, Abigail was making more noise trying to hold the thing up than it was. She looked like she was going to fall over any second.

"Are you sure you know how to use that?" They leaned in closer to her, but Little Red stopped them.

"Look!" The robot pointed down the corridor.

Ibu returned their attention to their target and did a double take. The vines were flailing in pain, waving aimlessly back and forth as they receded into the shuttle bay. Whatever Abigail's rifle was shooting, it was working.

They reached up and helped steady the gun as the effects of the invisible ray continued. It was only then that they noticed the weapon was hurting Abigail as much as it was the alien.

Once she let go of the trigger, she collapsed, and had Little Red not been there with his two extra hands, she might have hit her head. He carefully lowered her gun to the ground and, at the same time, reached up to her forehead. His palm was glowing with a hypnotic white light.

"What is that?" Ibu asked.

"I'm trying to dull her connection with the alien. Her sixth sense, as it were." The robot ran his hand over her eyes and her eyelids fluttered. "It only works for a few minutes on a Ulyxsauri, but it should help with the pain. There, is that better?" He lowered his arm and peered up into her face.

She nodded and let out a faint sigh. "Much."

"Maybe she should stay back here?" Ibu pointed their blade toward the room they'd been hiding.

"No!" Abigail snapped. "I won't stand aside and allow you to do this without me." She straightened up and grabbed the handle of her rifle, yanking the weapon upright.

By the time Ibu recognized the error in their words, Abigail was already headed down the corridor. "I guess… she's going," they muttered and started jogging to catch up.

"Let's keep an eye on her," Little Red subvocalized. "The

Entity is strong, and there's always a chance he can turn her on us."

Ibu swallowed hard and pulled their pistol out of its holster with their off-hand. The tiny weapon was no match for Abigail's rifle or the Zhen blade, but at this point, they'd take any advantage they could get.

61

ABIGAIL OLIVAW

INSIDE THE NURSERY, ONBOARD THE PERNIGER

With her back to the wall and her gun trained forward, Abigail slid toward the shuttle bay. Her eyes focused on the entrance to the room, but she also scanned the ceiling and floor. These starships had false walls and storage compartments in strange places. Weaving bits of an alien vine through these spaces would be child's play on a human ship, and she couldn't imagine the Ursis models were any different.

"We have company," Harold whispered in her ear.

Her retinal comm chimed, and three green outlines appeared at the end of the long hall. According to the overlay of the ship, two more were approaching from behind. As they came into view, she paused. "You didn't tell me we had friends?"

Ibu eased up next to her and lowered their pistol when they saw the robots. "I didn't know they made it onboard."

"I should have said something." Little Red looked back at her and nodded. "They were helping the other robots repair the hull. After we arrived, I feared that our ship becoming a hulking wreck floating aimlessly in the vacuum of space had a higher probability of success than the other outcomes."

She squinted at the quirky robot. "And what does the math say now?"

"Well." He spun to face back down the corridor. "Now that we're taking the fight to Lumalara, I'll take whatever advantage I can get, no matter how small. Besides," his display spiraled a rainbow of colors, "I've grown quite fond of this tin can I've been living in."

She peered over at Ibu and they shrugged. The longer they hung out with Little Red, the more eccentric he became. One minute he's acting like a puppy lapping at Bradley's heels, and the next he says shit like that. It was almost as if...

"Wait." She reached out and grabbed the side of his head, turning it to face her. "You're not just a robot, are you?" She narrowed her gaze. "Back on Hera's ship, the Entity called you Xyrithon. Like it knew you by another name, and yet, you're supposedly a servant robot? That doesn't add up."

"Shit," Ibu muttered. "I'd forgotten all about that."

Little Red's eyes spiraled from gray to orange and back again. It was as if the robot was stuck between the fear in front of them and the truth of their past.

While they stared at each other in silence, the two assassin robots from behind eased past them and paused just out of reach. Harold's voice broke in over their group comm. "I don't suppose those robots can hold a consciousness core, can they?"

Little Red glanced around, searching for the source of the query. "That sounded like your family friend, Harold. Is he onboard?"

"Maybe he is, maybe he isn't," Abigail nudged the robot. "But you're dodging the question."

He lowered his gaze and chirped. "It'll take too long to explain here, but you're right. I'm not an automata. I haven't been since the Rift opened." His head rose slightly. "But as far as your friend's question goes, the answer is yes. They're quite capable of housing his form. In fact, they're designed for it."

"How's that possible?" Ibu asked.

"Well," Little Red's display shifted to white. "Not him, exactly. They're designed to house quantotronic minds like mine, and if memory serves me right, he's built from the same technology."

Abigail shook her head. "What the hell are you talking about?"

The Perniger suddenly shuddered violently, and she reached over to steady herself on the wall. While her retinal comm updated with details, she knew what had happened before it did. The Entity must have breached the hull because the voices from the Beacon were back. They were piling into her mind, screaming at her to help them, to end their lives.

She moaned and lowered her massive weapon as she leaned against the wall. When she did, Little Red reached up, and waved his a glowing white hand over her face like he did earlier. Whatever he was doing, it was helping. The voices got quieter and quieter until they were barely a whisper in the recesses of her mind.

As he continued waving his hand over her forehead, one of the assassin robots backed up and a small compartment on its back popped open. She squinted and studied the tray that slid out. While it looked like it was designed to hold a cube of some sort, Harold's consciousness core would fit nicely inside with room to spare.

"What am I supposed to do with this?" She looked at Little Red.

"Logic would dictate that if Harold were on board this ship, and this ship was previously under Hera's control, then the only way he would be here was because he was with you." Little Red's eyes fluttered with wisps of white. "I trust he's on your person?"

Abigail was about to shake her head when Harold interrupted. "If we're about to charge into our final battle, I'd prefer to be useful."

She bit her lip. He'd protected her and helped the family her entire life. She couldn't put him in harm's way now, not knowing there was only one of him left. "But you might die out there," she subvocalized.

"I'm dead either way." His image reappeared on her

comm. "If you perish, I go down with you. We're bound together with me in here, just like you and the Entity were. At least this way, we're fighting side by side to the end."

"To the end," she muttered, swallowing down the lump in her throat.

He was right. She'd carried him as long as she could, and if there was ever a time when they could use another mind, it was this moment.

She reached up and undid the top of her fatigues, running her fingers along the space above her heart. It took a moment to find the indentations, but when her fingers pressed each of them in sequence, the nanites confirmed her intentions and the body-mod slid open. The effect was eerily similar to what the robot in front of her had done, except she was flesh and blood.

When she grasped his consciousness core, the shell made a popping sound, and hundreds of tiny tentacle-like appendages spilled out of previously hidden holes. The tubular feet reminded her of a starfish as the frigid pads caressing her palm. She shivered, easing her hand up to the tray and rolling Harold's sphere out and into the awaiting assassin robot.

As the receptacle slid into the back of the automata, the tiny feet on Harold's consciousness core extended out and filled the space, ensuring he wouldn't roll around. Once the door sealed shut, a metallic fluid-like substance flowed down over the opening, concealing it.

She took a deep breath when the robot turned to face her. Where Harold's usual humanoid shell was welcoming and had very human features, this robotic chassis was sleek, stealthy, and not at all friendly. It was purpose-built to elicit fear and make him the smallest target possible.

"Thank you." Harold reached out and rested his hand on her shoulder.

"We should go," Little Red said. His words were punctuated by an explosion not from the shuttle bay, but from the other side of the ship.

"We're approaching the Rift," Ibu glanced back at them. "If we're going to do this, we should probably do it before he gets too close to the Beacons. We have no idea what—"

The Entity's voice erupted in the distance, interrupting them. "You don't honestly think an infant Nanil and a few puny robots can hurt me, do you?"

Abigail raised her rifle and trained it down the hall. The massive scope on the top automatically zoomed in when she squinted, centering on the distant alien tentacle peering around the corner. She didn't bother answering the alien. Instead, she pulled the trigger and stepped in front of Harold, moving toward the source of her misery these past few months.

When the alien appendage flailed and retracted, she smiled. "Let's end this fracking thing."

A message flashed up on her retinal comm from Harold.

We need to get close enough to use our storm in a bottle.

She didn't stop walking, and she didn't take her eyes off the entrance to the shuttle bay either. She simply reached her hand out and waved it up and down in assent. The gesture reminded her of Lync and her Ulixi kin. While she wasn't on the float, she didn't want to risk a subvocal response or typing one out.

With their target clear, all they had left to do was figure out a plan. If Lync were here, she'd have a half-dozen ideas on what they should do. She just hoped that she was faring better than they were.

Abigail swallowed hard and shoved down the knot in her stomach, willing her rising panic into the shadows where it belonged. She'd lived in fear her entire life.

Fear of being discovered.

Fear of failing.

Fear of letting her family down.

Well, frak that. She wasn't about to live her ending minutes with worry, angst, or dread ruling the day. She was going to fight.

62

LYNC MICHAELS

INSIDE THE NURSERY, NEAR THE RIFT

The Nyílak shuddered, and the interior of Lync's pilot sphere flashed red as glowing blue bolts of light tore a fist-sized hole through the nose of her fighter. While the crack in her hull could make gating challenging, she had bigger fish to fry — these Shaygai, for starters.

She slammed her throttle forward, and her fighter rocketed ahead, narrowly dodging the rounds streaking toward her from the Shaygai's partner. The aliens only traveled in packs of two, which made them even more formidable than when they were alone.

From her experience, the longer a pilot flew with a wingman, the more they fell into the comfort of repeated patterns. Each had their strengths and weaknesses. Some partners always had to take the lead, whereas others favored certain maneuvers. Her hope was that she could predict their actions before they killed her. They were a constant duality that kept her on her toes.

"You were right!" Shauna shouted. "They tried to wedge us in. I've already shared our findings with the others, and I'm working on a counterattack now."

Of course, she was. Her mother may talk like a human, but her actions weren't constrained to linear time. They were better for it, though. With her attending to ordinances and comms, Lync could focus on keeping them alive.

"I need you to see if you can pull them closer to the Shu," Shauna said.

"To the Shu we go." Lync rolled to port and yanked the yoke backward, turning her Nyílak on a dime and launching it toward the nearest moonlet, one of only two remaining moons in their dwindling fleet.

While the motions of the Shaygai were far from scripted, each pair of fighters had quirks in their movements. It took her a few minutes to figure out the tactic for this set of aliens, but once she did, it was as clear as day.

She could read their every move and countermove. In this pairing, the lead ship was the aggressor, and it always fired first, laying down a continuous wall of suppression fire and forcing her to react. To pull up. By the time she realized what they were doing, the alien's partner was waiting for her.

All eight rings of their omnidirectional turrets fired at once, spraying forth a nearly impenetrable barrier of destruction that wedged the pilot in. More times than not, they were forced into the middle, and the result was a catastrophic maelstrom that left nothing but smoldering ruin in its wake.

Since their volleys were impossible to pass through and still reach the other side alive, the Ulixi turned their fighters on a dime — a trick their Nyílak had in spades, but not everyone did. Hundreds of Ursis, robots, and Galactic Alliance pilots met their makers in the hailstorms of ruin.

As she watched their distance to the Shu tick down, she weaved back and forth, trying not to repeat her movement in any predictable pattern. With her head down and a fire in her belly, the nape of her neck tingled with a familiar sensation. She and her Ulixi brethren were still connected to the Beacon, and while her attention was squarely on piloting for her life, she could sense Abigail was near.

Her sister's aura was pulsing with fear, and judging by how her wavelengths of light were crashing into Lync, she was thinking about her. Her hope was intense, and the

Beacon was amplifying it, sending a rush of endorphins through her just when she needed it.

The first barrage of glowing blue light was unexpected, but with her love-induced hyperfocus on the aliens, she pivoted and rolled her Nyílak in place while rocketing forward. While Lync had lost track of her distance to the Shu, Shauna hadn't. She'd been watching her every move, and the moment she detected her flip, she queued up a volley of plasma from the moonlet.

When the Shaygai's wingman flew into position and tried to wedge them in, her mother was ready and waiting, and not only for one of them. A dozen shots of light burst from the surface of the Shu, pinning each of the Shaygai and limiting their options to move. At the same time, Shauna powered up the moonlet and fired the final nail in each of their alien coffins. Both of the fighters exploded in a burst of yellow light, sending shrapnel in every direction.

"Yes!" Lync yanked her yoke to the right and spiraled away from the explosion. She knew what was coming next.

She eased her throttle forward, ensuring the blast remained aft of their position and, more importantly, that none of the alien shards were heading towards them. While she couldn't risk going full tilt for fear of igniting the shrapnel, she could still put some much-needed distance between them.

"I think we're clear." Shauna highlighted the debris field and the projected course for the remains of the Shaygai. She watched as small bursts of light shot off the moonlet, incinerating the shards in superheated micro-detonations.

Swallowing down her pride, Lync whispered thanks to her sister's aura. She'd take any advantage she could get out here, even if it came through a dubious alien artifact like the Beacon.

With her mind at ease, she scanned the other ships in their fleet. The Shaygai were steadily chipping away at their numbers, and unless Zachary got here soon, they'd be done for. As she was choosing her next target, Abigail's aura rippled again, this time stronger than it had ever been. She needed help, and she needed it now.

"There they are!" Shauna highlighted the open set of gates in the distance. A squadron of glowing Alatas battleships was passing through, along with what looked like the GA Syndrus ships.

"Are you seeing this?" Lync squinted at the formation. "Are those—"

"It's the Bynaury!" Shauna updated their tactical display and a slew of formerly red dots flipped to green. "They've switched sides! Somehow, Abigail convinced them to join our alliance."

Lync smirked and slammed her throttle forward, blasting her Nyílak towards the new arrivals. Although she couldn't see the Beacon in their formation, with that kind of firepower concentrated in one place, she was certain it was there somewhere.

She drew in a deep breath and focused on her sister's presence, on her aura. It took her a few seconds to find it, but once she did, she froze. Abigail's mind was flickering in and out, as if she were under duress. Maybe she needed some comforting words.

"Nice work with the brains in a jar," she whispered into Beacon space, hoping for a reply from Abigail.

But it never came.

Her life flame simply flickered in the misty haze of the artifact.

When Lync glanced around, she saw the same thing with the rest of the Ulixi. Each of them was battling their own demons in the real world, but none of them were using their one power to their advantage.

Each other.

"Do me a favor," Lync said aloud.

"Anything," Shauna spun towards her. "What do you need?"

She turned and looked into her mother's eyes. "I need you to take control for a few minutes. I need to try something."

"Wait," Shauna tilted her head. "You're doing something in the Beacon? Like now?"

She nodded. "They need me," she whispered as she closed her eyes.

"Who does?" Shauna asked.

"All of them…" Her voice trailed away as she started counting down from ten, willing her body to relax, and allowing her connection with the Beacon to move to the forefront.

She exhaled and let the misty expanse of the artifact take over her senses, engulfing her mind in a halo of lights. Although she hadn't been directly linked in several weeks, the sensation of the ancient device had somehow changed. It felt cold and lifeless this time, not at all like it had before. Maybe it was all the alien lives lost when they blasted the devices with the Cornucopia, or maybe it was just more empty than usual.

Once she connected, she started towards the familiar blue flāvus of her sister's mind. It was nearby, but it was covered with some type of suppression sphere. She'd never seen a physical object in this virtual space before, but she watched Little Red pull it over her hours earlier. It helped her overcome the emotions of the other Ulixi. While she was skilled at navigating the Beacon, she didn't take well to managing multiple modalities at once.

Lync leaned in and gently ran her hand over her sister's aura, and its jagged edges smoothed out in an instant. The tempest brewing within her mind was silenced, its chaotic waves replaced by the calm, rhythmic ebb and flow of a soul in profound focus.

She didn't know how it worked, but anytime Ulixi were near each other inside the Beacon, they relaxed. Alone, they were like everyone else: afraid and exposed. But in a group of like minds, they became one with the place.

Once Lync was satisfied she'd calmed her sister, she wrapped her arms around Abigail and nudged her flāvus spark sideways, out of the cocoon of protection and closer to the nearby minds of her kin — closer to the other Ulixi.

The pocket of Hi and Lo's life marks were just off her starboard side. Their bright green prasinus were like emerald jewels glowing in the dreary abyss. Simply watching them was soothing to her soul.

She pushed and pulled Abigail's aura closer to her kin, and with each centimeter, their sparks brightened. All of them did. It was like adding fuel to a fire, except she knew this wasn't hurting them. She had no idea how she knew it, but she did.

When Lync nudged her one last time, she accidentally pushed too hard, and they slid together. She gasped at the result.

Instead of rebounding or combining into one light, they dropped into an orbit and began circling around a common center. She'd never seen anything like it before, at least not on this small of a scale.

That was it. That was what it reminded her of. The motion was like a moon or a planetesimal orbiting a planet. Regardless of the object's size, if the mass in the middle was big enough, it would fall into an elliptical path around the center. What was strange, though, was that there wasn't anyone or anything in the middle.

She cleared her throat, hoping one of them would hear her. "Does it… hurt?"

At first, they didn't answer, but then both Hi and Lo's sparks flickered briefly. It was Hi that spoke. "Tis doesn't hurt as much as it helps to centerz me."

"I knows, right," Lo's spark flashed. "I just tossed that pot right into our bear friend's blasters. Dey dun met their makers, dey did."

"I feelz like a million creds!" Hi smiled.

Lync nodded. She'd take that as a good thing. "Get back in there. I'll see if I can help the others as well."

While she wasn't sure why she'd never seen the odd motion before now, she didn't question it. She simply spun around and reached out toward the nearest spark, and in this case, it was a silver, almost white one. She'd only come across a few of these in the past, but if they were close to her Ulixi family, they had to be a friendly.

As she nudged them into orbit alongside the others, they started speaking. "Now that's interesting," they muttered. "This feels… nice."

She recoiled backward and spun around, making sure no one else was near. "Who… who are you?"

"It's me, your mother!" Shauna chirped.

Lync drew in her breath. "Wait a second… I… wait… you're out there."

"You've been busy." Shauna's silver surface flickered. "To be honest, Little Red only brought us in here when they arrived with the Entity onboard the Perniger. He just sorta grabbed onto my mind. Until then, I didn't even know this was a thing I could do."

"When you said 'us', what did you mean?" She squinted and spun around. There, a few meters away, were two other silvery sparks. "If one of these is Little Red, that means the other one is—"

"Harold," Shauna interrupted.

"But… I thought he was… dead." Lync floated to the far side of the gray-white life marks and started nudging them back toward the others.

Shauna's spark faded, and so did the sparks around her. "Rán is no longer with us, but that copy of Harold in front of you was inside Abigail until recently."

"Inside her?" Lync shook her head. She had no idea how you could hide an A.I. inside your body, but leave it to her sister to find a way.

"We can talk about that later," Harold said.

"Frak!" Lync recoiled as the other silver spark started talking. "You scared the crap out of me, man."

"Sorry," he whispered. "We don't have much time. Another wave of Shaygai is near the robots."

She reached out and shoved him into the middle of the

other orbiting life marks. However, instead of filling the empty slot in the center, he rebounded back and started rotating like all the others.

Harold's spark fluttered. "You don't think this... this formation will stop us from defending them, will it? I feel sorta warm in here."

Lync leaned forward, intending to push Little Red, when his mark brightened and they accidentally merged for a split second.

Regret
Sorrow
Loneliness
Happiness
Hope

The emotions were vivid, flashing through her mind like jolts of electricity. Only when his aura detached from hers did they fade, and he launched himself into orbit along with the others.

She spun in place for a moment as nausea threatened to overtake her. While she'd merged with Abigail before, it had never felt like that. He was strong - stronger than anyone else she'd encountered in the Beacon.

"Sorry about that," Little Red whispered. "I was a bit preoccupied. We sorta have our hands full out here."

The robot's life mark spun around, seeming to consider the formation. "Now this is new? Is it supposed to feel like... like butterflies in my stomach?"

"Wait, you haven't seen this before?" Lync shook her head. "I... I did it on accident."

"I've never seen any actual formations inside the Beacon beyond the mass of species that move about like cattle," Little Red began. "In fact, the last time I was here, the Galactic Alliance discouraged any type of commingling or fraternization of the species. They claimed it diluted a species' homogeneity and focus."

"Well, I don't know about you, but I like it." Shauna's life mark started spinning faster and faster, and the others followed suit.

"So, wait." Lync swallowed hard, pushing down the residual bile in her throat. "What were you three doing in here while we were out there?"

An eerie silence fell over the Beacon, which was alarming considering how chatty the automata had been since she woke them up. When none of them spoke up, she knew something was going on - and it wasn't good.

"Guys!" Lync snapped her fingers and sparks shot out. "Cut the shit. What's up?"

Little Red broke the silence. "It's the Shaygai. They're trying to take over the minds of the robots."

She drew in her breath. "Wait, they can do that?"

"Not while we're in here," Harold said. "We've been able to soothe their minds while we're connected to the Beacon."

"You mean like Mom did with the robots in Lupus?" She searched the spinning sparks for the one that was her mother, but she'd lost track. They were rotating too quickly.

"You've done this before?" Little Red's spark strobed from gray to white and back again.

"Sorta," Shauna began. "They needed some nudging. If I hadn't, it felt like the humans in Henosi were going to get the upper hand. They kept getting confused about who their masters were, and they almost turned on us. Their robotic minds are so delicate."

Lync spun around and noticed that she had a field of sparks to move. There were easily several dozen Ulixi nearby, and from the looks of it, a patch of green ones as well. "And you're sure you can handle the robots? I can drop out of here if you need me."

"No!" Shauna's spark flashed. "Only a few seconds have passed in real time. What you're doing in here is far more important. I can feel it. Keep pulling the others nearby. We can help one another."

She was clueless about how this was working, but for the

A.I., it was helping them wrangle their alliance and keep the robots from turning on them. On one hand, they were using the Beacon to control an automated being, but on the other, they'd be dead without it. The device was a necessary evil, even if it made them no better than the Galactic Alliance. At least the robots weren't sentient. They weren't alive like the other minds in here. They were simply automata who were putting her friends and family at risk.

As she began relocating the other life marks, she couldn't help but wonder who was looking out for Zachary. With the other A.I. on the battlefield, there was no one inside the Cornucopia preventing the Shaygai from overtaking those robots. If he gated through, he'd be dead in seconds without someone protecting him.

63

ABIGAIL OLIVAW

INSIDE THE NURSERY, ONBOARD THE PERNIGER

They nearly collapsed simultaneously, and had Ibu not been there to defend them, they might have died. As Abigail eased herself to her feet, she picked a slimy piece of the Entity's tendril off her arm and glanced around. More pieces lay splayed out on the ground in front of them.

After Lync nudged her mind, something changed. Abigail didn't know what it was, but her connection to Beacon space had gone from a deafening scream to a pleasant hum. She could almost feel her Ulixi family nearby, and they weren't alone. There were others with them. They were with her, supporting and strengthening her resolve from afar.

"What the hell happened?" Ibu glanced back at them before returning their attention to the opening ahead. "One second we're about to storm the castle, and the next you three are on the floor."

"It's..." Abigail bit her lip, "hard to explain. But Lync connected us to the others inside the Beacon. Can't you feel it?"

Ibu shook their head, their eyes still fixed forward. Abigail could tell they were uncomfortable not being included in what was happening, but if they'd been pulled in, the three of them would surely be dead. Whatever kept them out of the Beacon, it must've happened for a reason.

"I don't expect we'll have many more interruptions from here on out," Little Red said.

Harold chuckled. "Famous last words."

Seeing a killing machine like the assassin robots laugh was disconcerting and sent a shiver up Abigail's spine.

She glanced around, searching for her rifle, and when she found it, she froze. It lay in pieces, scattered all the way down the corridor.

"Yeah, sorry about that." Ibu slid up beside her and offered her a pistol. "Our alien friend targeted it first. I couldn't stop him on my own."

She sighed. "That's fine. I'll make do. Maybe I can pick up another one before we head inside."

"There's no time," Little Red started down the hall. "We're approaching the Beacons. We need to stop Lumalara before he returns to the Luxaris."

"Why do we care if he goes back there?" Ibu quickened their pace down the corridor and the others followed suit.

"He takes with him the collective knowledge of millennia of observation." Little Red pulled out the vial of orange and yellow fluid and handed it to Abigail.

She froze and stared at the cylinder in his outstretched hand. "I… can't use that thing. He's too strong."

"You can and you will." The robot eased his hand forward. "A flāvus never shirks their responsibility to others."

What he was asking her to do was too much. It wasn't that she didn't want to, but she knew that if the Entity ever got ahold of her, he would end her. After all she'd done to him, she was surprised he hadn't killed her already.

Harold took a step back toward her. "You can do this. I know you can. We'll bring the robots in from the sides, and Red and I will circle around to deal with Hera. You and Ibu, you go at him from the center. It's the shortest path."

She stared down at the spiraling cloud of yellow-orange sludge in the canister. It was an oddly shaped container, yet it seemed familiar. Judging from its appearance, you simply pressed the end marked in red against the alien's skin and squeezed the middle. It somewhat reminded her of an antique tube of toothpaste she'd seen in a museum.

"Fine." Abigail reached out and took it, being careful not to squeeze it. "But you all better move fast." She slid the tube into her chest pocket and raised her pistol. "Something tells me my old friend won't be happy to see me."

"We'll move as fast as we can." Little Red turned to look at Harold, and they both nodded.

With that, they sprinted down the corridor, all five of the assassins, along with Little Red. His comically disproportionate barrel-like torso with its four outstretched hands contrasted starkly with the deadly forms of his kin. One did not resemble the others.

When they stepped up to the corner, Ibu glanced back at her. "You've got this."

Abigail nodded and reached out, resting her hand on her friend's shoulder, giving it a gentle squeeze. "No, we've both got this." She smiled.

Ibu returned the gesture and dipped their chin, a silent acknowledgment of the imminent fight ahead.

"Who's going in first?" she asked.

Ibu seemed to tilt their head closer to their blade, as if they were listening to it, then replied, "I'll lead."

"Alrighty then." She swallowed hard, forcing down the lump in her throat as she ran her trembling hand down her tattered coveralls.

Looking from herself to the Nanil, she couldn't help but feel out of place. She'd grown up leading a company for most of her life, and the closest she'd come to battle was standing behind a podium and exchanging barbs with the media. In the last few years, however, she'd been dumped head-first onto the front lines and had been struggling to stay afloat ever since.

Abigail squeezed the handle of her pistol and took a deep breath, focusing her mind and prying open the Beacon connection to her kin just a bit wider. She could use another hit of their support before she entered the fray.

As they both stepped up behind the robots, the automata launched around the corner. First Little Red, then Harold and the other assassins. There was no pause or restatement of their plan. No double-checking everyone was good to go. They each knew what they had to do, and no one wanted to risk getting cold feet.

With a fresh wave of camaraderie and fellowship coursing through her veins, when Ibu hopped around the corner, Abigail didn't hesitate. She leapt behind them. Her retinal comm flashed a second later, updating her with what the robots were seeing.

The Entity was wedged against the far wall of the shuttle bay, and he had tentacles everywhere. The room looked like a fraking jungle. It was as if he were growing into the super-structure of the ship. While she wasn't sure why he'd never done it before, she assumed it took a lot of energy, but that was a good thing. That meant he'd be weaker. Or at least, she hoped so.

She raised her blaster and trained it on the tree-shaped alien. All around her, the robots were battling the tentacles and doing their best to keep them at bay. Their inhuman speed and strength helped them dodge the swipes and lancing blows of the menacing roots.

The room filled with screams of pain as the Entity took blow after blow. Each strike that landed acted as fuel to her fire, sending Abigail into a battle rage. Maybe it was her connection with the Beacon, or maybe it was the Zhen blade acting to focus their emotions, but either way, she and Ibu covered the short distance to the overgrown tree in a matter of seconds.

She hopped up over one of the swinging tendrils and squeezed off a shot, hitting the Entity in the face and narrowly missing a vine as it rose up from the floor to block the blast.

When she came down on both feet, she caught the blur of Harold and Little Red ripping and slicing their way through the wall of vines. They were dead set on reaching Hera deep within her protective cocoon.

"Come on, Lumalara!" Little Red goaded. "Is this the best you've got?"

The Entity growled, and the ground heaved as the tentacles digging into the bowels of the ship fought to return to the surface. The alien was far stronger than she'd imagined.

She struggled to keep her balance, and with each squeeze of her trigger, her conviction deteriorated as fast as her charge. Just as she thought they were done for, she heard it.

Hera's voice screamed out, and when Abigail glanced to the side, she saw that Little Red had reached her golden coffin below the flooring. It was only then that she realized the quirky robot had provoked the alien to get him to reveal where he'd stashed her. Not because they were winning.

Far from it.

According to her retinal comm, they'd already lost two of the four assassins, and the third was on its literal last leg. The robot was being dangled upside down by a tendril, but it was fighting the entire time. Lashing out and ripping vine after vine to shreds as it was tossed around the room like a club.

She ducked in the nick of time as the robot-shaped projectile launched over her head. It almost bowled over Harold and Little Red as it smashed against the far wall. They'd split open the golden cocoon, and she could just make out Hera's face beneath the undulating surface of the alien shell.

Shards of slithering yellow slime were working their way up the robot's arms, but they didn't seem to care. Their focus was solely on reaching the center of the mass, on ending Hera.

With her feet frozen in place, Little Red raised their Zhen blade above their head, and time seemed to stand still.

Abigail glanced down and looked into the dull, empty eyes of her aunt. A wave of sadness passed over her as she pitied the woman for what she'd become. What happened to her after she left Sol would forever change humanity and their place among the stars. As she studied Hera's face, the robot swung his blade down and through her neck, severing her head from her body and sending a soul-piercing shriek through the shuttle bay as the Entity felt his connection to his host fading.

Abigail stared in awe, a wave of relief passing through her. However, this comfort was ephemeral as a tentacle lashed out, coiling around her waist and yanking her up towards the Entity. She screamed in pain as the vine constricted her torso and another one shot out from the side. It was flying towards her mouth, and she knew instantly what it was trying to do. The alien was attempting to bind with her before Hera's body died.

The sudden jerk had caused her to drop her pistol on the ground, leaving her with only her bare hands. What she hadn't remembered, however, was Ibu. The Nanil was at her side a split second later.

Their Zhen blade easily sliced through the lancing blow of the vine while it was in midair. In a ballet-like motion, they brought the blade up and under the tentacle enveloping her waist, cutting it loose and sending the alien into a chaotic scramble.

The Entity screamed and seemed to uproot itself, separating its lower half from the roots below. When it did, it started to swing its remaining tentacles with maniacal frenzy, sweeping at the air and attempting to grab onto her.

But Abigail didn't pause or squander her one opportunity. Despite the pain coursing through her stomach, she clutched the capsule from her pocket and spun around with the device in hand. She then leaned forward, launching herself at the alien.

She used the momentum of her collision to smash the futuristic plunger against the side of their head, and when she did, she squeezed with every ounce of strength left in her frail muscles.

The alien screamed and started bucking, trying to knock her off. She had one arm wrapped around his neck and the other wedged firmly against her chest, shoving the life-taking vial against his fraking head.

When she looked down, the orange goo was spiraling together and mixing with the yellow substance. It was revving into a frenzy of glowing light. She felt herself being yanked backward, but she wasn't about to let go. Not now. Not after everything they'd fought for.

Behind her, she could hear Ibu grunting and swinging their Zhen blade, fighting for dear life. For both their lives. They were slicing the vines in half, but they kept coming. The Entity was too strong.

Abigail held on with everything she had, leaning against the cylinder and using her body weight to hold it in place. Each barb of the alien tendrils was like a whip cracking against her back, and she could feel her flesh being ripped open and pulled from all sides. The malevolent alien was trying to tear her apart limb by literal limb.

In that moment of utter anguish, she realized why Little Red had given her the vial. It wasn't because she was the strongest or the most capable in the group. It was because she was the obvious target, and if they did their part, the Entity would go for her next.

Little Red knew how Lumalara thought. Somehow, he'd known their every move before anyone else, and why wouldn't he?

The robot was a Builder, and she was but a pawn in his game of chess. In their epic battle for the fate of humanity and their entire galaxy.

For once in her life, she didn't mind being taken advantage of. If it helped to lessen her family's past indiscretions, she'd swallow this pill and then some.

As her strength faded, a jolt of energy welled up from deep inside her, willing her to hold on and to let the drug do its job. She just hoped she could last that long.

64

JOYCE GREEN

INSIDE THE NURSERY, NEAR THE RIFT

"We need to let it go!" Ryder screamed over the whine of their reactor. "The Beacon – we have to release it!"

Joyce held her hands in front of her, controlling the tendrils of the Ursis ship as if they were extensions of herself. She knew what letting go of the Beacon would mean.

The Shaygai would win. They'd already attempted to move the ancient formation of artifacts twice since they'd started their attack, and had the robots and Ulixi not fended them off, they might have succeeded.

She shook her head and kept her grip tight. "No! If we let go, they'll win, and then we're dead."

"If we don't release it, we're dead," Grifdar growled.

Joyce turned and locked eyes with Arindra. The female simply nodded. "Then today's our day, my love." She glanced toward Grifdar. "Today we meet Bruzathir, and if that's the case, I'm not about to face him as a coward."

The Ursis tilted her head skyward and shrieked, sending a guttural howl through the corridors of the ship, and Grifdar joined her. Their voices intertwined like a symphony of raw, animistic power, defiantly echoing within their alien confines.

When Joyce looked back at Ryder, his expression spoke volumes. He wasn't convinced, but he didn't have any other options. Standing down meant certain death, so he did the next best thing. He took control of one of their forward plasma batteries and started taking shots at the circling Shaygai.

A sense of calm passed over her as she checked the status of their ship. The robots had kept the Alatas battleship intact, but judging by the state of their shuttle bay, Abigail and her alien friends had wreaked havoc. They'd ripped the floor to shreds, torn the conduit from the ceiling, and the environmental controls were malfunctioning, evidenced by smoke and fire everywhere.

A gate suddenly flashed open in front of them and two Big Berthas belched out a half dozen rounds of destruction, before it closed. The gate had only been open for a few seconds, but in its wake, it left a devastating path of carnage, taking out a small pocket of inbound Galactic Alliance Syndrus ships and the fighters swarming around them.

Joyce subvocalized a command to open a comm to the general channel for their alliance. "Once we get this thing in place..." She swallowed hard. "Then what? There's no way this is staying put on its own."

"Once I—" Zachary began, but his reply was abruptly severed as his comm dropped, silencing his promise. A few seconds later, a violent surge of light ignited around the nearest Selene moon. Its previously calm exterior was shattered by a burgeoning lightning storm.

Arcs of white-hot energy whipped across the void, connecting with the neighboring moon, and then again and again, the chain continued. It was a breathtaking spectacle of destructive force, hurling a tsunami of sparkling energy towards them.

This display was hauntingly familiar, and it sent chills down her spine. She'd seen it once before, a ghost from the past resurrected in Shauna's recording a year earlier. She'd warned them about the lightning weapon, and now they were squarely in the eye of the storm.

Her eyes widened, and her heart pounded in her chest. A single order, an instinctive plea, broke from her lips. "Run!"

65

IBU

INSIDE THE NURSERY, ONBOARD THE PERNIGER

As the overhead lights faltered, they froze before being abruptly plunged into darkness. Ibu's retinal comm reacted quickly, filling in the gaps, replacing their vision with LiDAR and infrared.

But they were too late.

They missed one of the writhing tentacles from the Entity's death throe.

The tentacle wasn't flailing to knock them away as it had before. No, this time it wielded a weapon – a lethal shard of debris. Like a sniper's bullet, the razor-edged fragment pierced the Nanil's chest and emerged from the other side.

In an instant, their world was upended. Everything around them dimmed and blurred, dissolving into the ether.

And then, as if stepping into another realm, the chaotic confines of the shuttle bay were replaced by a pervasive, engulfing light of icy steel-blue.

At first, they weren't sure what was happening, but when they looked down at the wound in their chest, they understood. They'd been sucked into the Beacon, and the glow wasn't from their surroundings, it was their aura.

Their Progenitor had told them about this moment. About how they would have a vision when they reached their end.

While Ibu hadn't passed through a maze like the Prima described, maybe it wasn't the same for everyone.

Their end had come from a deadly blow, one that was both unexpected and game-changing, but there was one thing they knew for certain.

They hadn't died.

They still had fight left in them, and while the Entity had caught them off guard, there had to be more they could do.

When they glanced around the hazy Beacon space, there were no other sparks nearby. All they could see was a faint constellation of lights in the distance, and for some reason, they appeared to be orbiting an unseen center, like planets circling a star. It was a formation and motion they'd never heard the Ulixi describe before. Usually, the life marks in this place clustered together and moved in packs.

Their observation was short-lived, as their surroundings faded seconds later. With the world fading away, they were left staring at a broad sweeping canvas that filled their entire view with a rainbow of colorful splotches.

The composition of the scene reminded them of an oil painting they'd seen from Earth. While the name escaped them, its vibrant presentation was both hypnotic and surreal. The colors were so bright they seemed to scream for attention.

As their gaze lowered, their hearts fluttered in their chest. They weren't simply staring at a canvas; they were experiencing something far grander.

Ibu was lying on their back on the surface of a planet. It wasn't clear how they hadn't realized it until now, but when they sat up, their hands pushed against the ground and sank deep into a bed of white powdery sand beneath them. When they pulled their hand out, the ultra-fine crystals cascaded between their fingers and fluttered to the ground.

This place felt real, as real as any world they'd ever visited before. It was hard to imagine this was a vision.

When they finally tore their attention away from the sand, they stared out over a sea of multicolored plants that extended as far as the eye could see. Bulbous shrubs and trees were sprinkled precariously over strange, gravity-defying rock formations. The entire spectacle was miraculous to behold, and words failed to describe it.

With their senses on overload, they flinched when a breeze wafted across their backs. As with the sand, the sensation was unexpected in a vision, let alone one inside the Beacon, where there wasn't exactly any wind.

Ibu slowly stood up and gasped when they spun around. In the distance were two binary suns, both of which were slivers protruding above the horizon. The life-giving orbs framed the sky perfectly, transforming the scene into a literal spectrum of colors. It was as if they were staring through a giant prism, and it was projecting against a canvas as big as a world.

Yellows, reds, blues, and greens painted multiple layers of what they realized were clouds now that they could see everything. They'd never experienced anything like them in all the worlds they'd visited, virtual or real. Most planets had beautiful sunsets, but never with this many colors at once.

While they spun in place to take it all in, they paused and squinted part of the way around. Off in the distance, they caught sight of a star rising over a distant mountain range. The longer they watched it, the more they recognized it wasn't a star at all. It was a formation of some sort.

At first, there was only one sparkle of light, but it quickly turned into more. By the time it was done, there were over a dozen stars, all with varying degrees of brightness. Even though the shape of the stars didn't mean anything to them, it reminded them of a cross with a slightly offset top.

As they watched the lights rise across the sky, they tried something. They subvocalized a command to see if this vision supported a retinal comm, and it turned out it did.

Their vantage zoomed in on the distant lights, and they took a step backward as the objects came into focus. It turns out they weren't stars or satellites, as they had thought. They were starships. And these particular ships looked unlike anything they'd ever seen before.

"That can't be good," Ibu muttered.

An instant later, a gale materialized out of nowhere and began spiraling around them. As the winds picked up, the dune beneath their feet churned and climbed upwards, birthing a dust devil.

Ibu drew in a sharp breath, their lungs fighting for oxygen in the darkening sandstorm.

When the lights eventually flickered back on, their hands were in a desperate struggle with an alien tentacle that was wrapped around their neck. The Entity was squeezing the life out of them.

66

ZACHARY OLIVAW

INSIDE THE NURSERY, NEAR THE RIFT

When the bolts of lightning faded, Zachary gasped at the results. Their fleet was decimated.

Half of their ships had been swept into oblivion in an instant. Those who'd escaped the fury of the Galactic Alliance weapon were now in full retreat. The survivors were literally flinging themselves through dozens of open gates, crashing into each other in the process.

He watched as their ships spiraled through the portals, their hulls scorched and ablaze. Their once majestic starships of green and silver were reduced to smoldering remains of their former selves.

While he wasn't certain who'd opened the gates to enable the fleet to escape, he was happy they had.

Countless lives ended in the blink of an eye: Humans, Ursis, and Bynaury alike. They'd risked their lives for him. For his plan. It was his fault they were dead, and he owed it to them to finish what they started. They needed to strike while the alien alliance patted themselves on the back.

It was now or never.

"Prepare to fire!" He spun around, and his eyes met Donnelley's as the hum of the Cornucopia rose.

The Ulixi pilot had been watching him and waiting for his

signal. She knew it was coming, and he'd felt her eyes burning a hole through him for the past ten minutes.

They were standing together on the precipice of change, silent guardians of the plan. They'd been hoping for this moment, for their allies to deliver the Beacon so they could play their part.

He swallowed hard and nodded at Donnelley.

She hadn't spoken a word since the war began, and this was no different. With a quick swipe at her cheeks, she closed her eyes and prepared for the gate.

He clenched his hands together and watched as one by one, the pilots zeroed in on their target, making micro-adjustments to account for the missing mass in the path of their jump. When Donnelley finally gave him a thumbs up, he didn't hesitate.

"Now!" He reached over and grabbed the back of his chair. "Transition now!"

As the blaze of blue scorched over his skin, he moaned and steadied himself, fighting the pain and waiting for the screen to update. When it did, his breath hitched in his throat.

They were dead on target.

"Fire!" He screamed.

67

LYNC MICHAELS

INSIDE THE NURSERY

Watching the rotating constellation of life marks was hypnotic; round and around, the sparks flew at dizzying speeds. While Lync had been busy gathering the lights of her Ulixi brethren, they were deep in their trance, piloting their Nyílak fighters. She assumed that, since she was still alive, Shauna had been holding her own as a pilot.

Lync spun around to grab the last mark when she noticed a diamond pattern of lights heading towards her. She couldn't tell what species they were, but they didn't look like any she'd seen before.

They had a rigid, starlike shape, and the way they moved in a tight formation reminded her of the Shaygai, but that couldn't be right. They were out in the Nursery. And then it hit her. If the Ulyxsauri and the Galactic Alliance were in here, there was no reason the Shaygai couldn't be as well.

She stared at the unusual formation of armored lights barreling toward her spinning constellation of sparks and recoiled. She hadn't seen it at first, but once they moved closer, a quartet of lights appeared in front of them. They were just out of reach.

While she wasn't familiar with the flickering colors of the leading four life marks, a sense of dread passed over her the closer they got. The lights were running for their lives, and she needed to help them.

Lync leaned forward and took off, aiming her mark toward the gap between her and them. With her pulse quickening, she felt something brush her arm in the real world. Now was not the time for interruptions.

She waved her hand through the goo of the Nyílak crew pod, and her fingers brushed against something hard. She assumed it was Shauna. While she couldn't risk dropping out of Beacon space, she hoped her mother had gotten the hint.

As she continued waving her hand around, her life mark floated into the gap of the rapidly approaching lights. They were coming in hot, and she focused her attention on the lead spark. She needed to know if they were friendlies, or simply a diversion.

The light flashed wildly, its pulse sending out a hypnotic flicker that was almost rhythmic. Only after the pattern repeated several times did she realize what they were doing. They were signaling to her in Morse code.

● — ●

● ● —

— ●

● ● ● ●

— — —

● — ●

— ●

— ● ●

While she was rusty without her retinal comm, her military training came back faster than she thought.

Lync read the letters aloud, "R U N H O R N D."

She shook her head. "What the hell is a 'runhornd'?"

Maybe they were telling her to run at something. It was hard to say for certain. Only after she spoke the letters and inserted the minuscule break, did she realize what they were saying.

"Shit!" She spun around and launched towards her spiraling formation of lights.

The life mark leading the pack was Donnelley, and she'd been trying to tell her to run. The horn was here, and if they were going to pull this thing off, it was now or never. If the colossal conical contraption was about to fire, something told her they all needed to be in that constellation. Especially if the intention was to magnify the power of the blast, as she hoped.

With the diamond formation of minds rapidly approaching, she leaned even further forward to see if she could move faster. Once she was practically flat, her eyes wandered down below. She didn't know why she'd done it, but she did.

There, far below, was an explosive silvery-blue star. A nova bursting brighter than all the others. She hadn't seen it earlier, but the longer she stared at the blinding aura, the more she felt its importance.

"Frak!" She bent all the way forward, and her spark turned in a wide arc, barely skimming the edge of her celestial formation.

The mass of rotating life marks pulled her toward them, their gravitational attraction willing her to their center. But she fought back. It was too soon.

They needed that mind.

"No!" she screamed, swinging her fist backwards. She'd been trying to knock away the invisible force pulling at her, but instead, her spark sent out a halo of golden light in the process.

The spherical blast expanded outward from her center, propelling her forward and out of the orbit of the formation of minds. When she glanced over her shoulder, she noticed that her yellow caeruleus shockwave was still expanding.

Donnelley and her crew passed through the wall of light harmlessly, but when the Shaygai hit it, they burst into a blinding flash and disintegrated instantly. The resulting spectacle was a sight of pure, untamed energy that briefly outshone the surrounding constellation of minds. The Shaygai fleet became nothing more than scattered stardust in the face of Lync's wrath.

She took a deep breath and tried not to think about what she'd just done. She had to get that life mark.

With her spark diving into the depths of the Beacon at an incredible rate, she was coming up on the steely blue star below. The light had faded from its peak moments earlier, but it still retained its beautiful luster. What she didn't have, however, was a means to move it up into the formation without wasting precious time.

Slowing to a stop and nudging it along would take forever. What she needed was another dozen hands.

As she circled around the blue-gray spark, she pulled up when she nearly collided with Donnelley and her team.

"What the hell?" Lync weaved between the four Ulixi sparks, her light flickering from one to the other. "You should have joined the constellation."

"We were following you, sir." Donnelley eased up beside her and then floated around the edge of the silvery spark. "What about this one? Why isn't it up there?"

"I was just…" She froze, staring into the distance.

Far off in the mist of Beacon space, she could make out a vast assemblage of lights moving toward them. From the looks of it, there were hundreds of thousands of Galactic Alliance sparks, and they were interspersed with the Shaygai and a darkness that could only mean one thing.

The Entity was with them.

From ravus to prasinus, purpureus, aurantiaco, and rubrum, the inner sanctum species were swarming into the Beacon by the thousands and the life marks were glittering on a tapestry of black. Whatever the GA was trying to do, the Entity and the Shaygai were helping them, so it couldn't be good. She didn't know if they'd promised the aliens ascension, but their time had run out.

"We have to move this life mark up there." Lync pointed

toward the still spinning constellation. "And we have to do it now!"

She swung her hands around and flipped in place, diving down and then up behind the spark, crashing into it with everything she had.

The second she made contact, she knew who the life mark was.

Muscles, forged with the unyielding strength of carbon steel.

Devotion, as indomitable and enduring as a diamond.

A mind, honed to a razor's edge like a Zhen blade.

And a reservoir of anguish, echoing the infinite expanse of the cosmos.

It was Ibu, and the Nanil was in pain. Wherever they were in the Nursery, they were deep in a vicious struggle with the Therionic Entity. She didn't know how she knew it, but the certitude of the alien resonated within her.

Lync leaned into the life mark of her friend and pushed, slowly moving the spark toward the others. She was a dancer on a tightrope of light, her every move calculated to propel the mind forward without inflicting further harm.

Her heart pounded in her chest as she shoved harder, channeling every ounce of her will into this vital endeavor. For Ibu, for their fight, for their shared survival. She would move mountains, shift stars, and defy the very odds of this world if it meant helping her friends and family. It was all she had left.

While time slowed inside the Beacon, she knew their clock was ticking both here and in the Nursery. The weight of her responsibility was a crushing pressure, but when Donnelley and her crew eased up beside her, their lights combined, and a surge of faith rose within them. They were her beacon of hope in a universe filled with dread.

Seconds of Beacon time passed as the five of them shoved Ibu ever closer to the constellation.

"We're not going to make it," Donnelley said. "They're coming in too fast."

When Lync glanced toward the advancing cloud of sparks, her heart sank. Donnelley was right. They had too far to go, and unless something changed, they'd be upon them before Ibu reached the formation.

Unless lightning struck.

The idea came to her in a flash, and she instantly knew it would work, at least once.

"You four." She glanced at the others. "I need you to fly into the constellation with this mark. I'll cover us."

"But, sir," Donnelley began, "we can't do it without—"

"That's an order!" Lync shot across the gap between her Ulixi kin and the sparks. She knew they'd do their part; she just needed to figure out hers.

If she could muster the power she'd shown earlier, maybe that would slow them down. But as she barreled toward the wall of lights, she couldn't help but feel like she'd judged wrong.

It was one thing to accidentally fire a blast from her hand, but it was quite another to wage a war against hundreds of thousands of alien minds — aliens that were far more comfortable in the Beacon than she was.

As she approached the leading edge of purpureus, she pictured the Thyreusian aliens in her mind. Their sixteen eyes and pinchers for mouths made her shudder. As soon as she got close enough to them, she swung her fist through the air, willing another blast to form.

But this time, nothing happened. There was no golden light, and certainly no ring of power spreading out.

There was only the empty mist of Beacon space and thousands of minds droning together, chanting as one. "Death to the Ulyxsauri! Death to the scourge!"

Her heart raced as the mass of lights streamed down toward her. They were forming into several snake-like patterns, as if planning to squeeze her to death. She'd never seen them move in formation like this before. At the tip of each slithering purple-black strand was a single Shaygai preparing to strike.

While she'd been neck-deep in her lesson of humility, Donnelley and her kin had stayed on task. Just as the heads of the snakes lunged forward, Lync glanced back at the formation. She watched as Ibu and the Ulixi passed into the constellation of minds.

Words failed to describe what happened next, but as each of the life marks flowed into orbit alongside the others, Ibu slid into the middle of the mass. As soon as their now burning star of steel reached the center, a conclusive blast rained out in every direction.

She watched as a white halo expanded toward her, but before it arrived, the Shaygai struck.

Their perspectives layered into a single kaleidoscopic vision that she could barely comprehend. Fleeting memories passed through her mind as echoes of a million voices merged into a terrifying roar of shared cognition.

Harmony within the Nexus.
Collective transcendence of individuality.
One galactic consciousness pulsing.
One aim eclipsing all others.
Convergence.

It was as if she were part of a vast ocean, yet also a single drop within it. Every thought, every sensation, was part of a grander whole. Yet, the enormity of it felt ominous and disconcerting. There was a chilling beauty in the unity, and also a haunting terror in the loss of self.

A sense of dread lingered as the lights pushed against her, the fear of becoming an inconsequential fragment within a vast, sprawling consciousness. But the compelling force of unity was alluring, and she felt her thoughts of resistance being drowned out. The last vestiges of her individuality slowly faded into the background thrum of shared existence.

As the harmonious hum swelled within her, struggling to replace the dissonance of the many with the haunting melody of one, a wave of light crashed over her and the attacking minds of the Thyreusians.

The collision broke through the hypnotic drone of the alien minds. It shook loose echoes of her past, of her pride and uniqueness, surging through her like a supernova and rending the fabric of the shared consciousness.

Each note of the disrupted minds echoed a momentary scream of disarray. It was a discordant tempest, a cacophonous unraveling of a thousand alien thoughts. The galactic consciousness that had woven itself around her splintered and fractured, each strand breaking away with a wisp of silenced minds. Their life marks were forever extinguished as the wave passed through the vast sea of aliens.

But Lync's caeruleus spark remained.

The aftershocks of the psychic cataclysm reverberated within her, leaving a chilling silence in its wake. Her sense of self, momentarily lost in the labyrinth of shared thoughts, resurfaced, pristine and unbroken amidst the wreckage of the collective. She was alone again, but not the same.

A sense of heightened awareness tingled at the edges of her consciousness. The shared mindscape had not left her untouched; it had deepened her perception, honed her thoughts to a sharper edge, and imbued her with a force she had not known before.

Without the weight of the myriad of hive minds, she felt stronger, more grounded in herself. The constellations of sparks spun in the distance with Ibu at the center. The formation beckoned her from afar, pulling her towards the familiar swirl of individual consciousnesses.

As she rocketed towards her friends, she glanced backward at the vestiges of the Galactic Alliance and Shaygai forces. The shockwave had torn their minds asunder, and all that remained were a few faint sparks spiraling about. Dozens of minds lingered aimlessly where millions had previously stood.

When she reached the constellation of life marks, she didn't hesitate. She dove straight in and reconnected with her kin, not as one lost in the many, but as an individual stronger for having been part of the whole.

The remnants of the galactic consciousness hummed in her mind, a haunting melody to remind her of what they were fighting, but for now, only one purpose remained.

Lync stared around at the spinning formation of minds pulling at her. Somehow, she hadn't entered an orbit like she'd imagined. Instead, she hovered just outside the center, just away from Ibu.

The Nanil was the nucleus in the middle, and yet, they seemed alone and missing something. Or someone.

They were a yin without a yang, an up without a down to balance them out.

At that moment, she knew what to do.

She reached out, brushing her scintillating hand against the steel-blue surface of Ibu's mind, and the moment she did, images flashed in her mind.

A cataclysmic storm of lightning was sparking across a sea of Selene moons. Tens of thousands of the enormous Galactic Alliance weapons were powering up, and they were launching toward the glowing basin of the Cornucopia. The ray of destruction had not yet crested over the edge of the deadly device.

Zachary had let loose the harbinger of annihilation, and in turn, the Galactic Alliance was retaliating with terrifying force. The echoes of their impending doom resonated in the cold void of space.

Her moment was here and now.

A sudden clarity washed over the gathered minds as if a veil had been lifted, revealing her purpose with an intensity that made her soul tremble. As Lync embraced Ibu's luminous steely aura, she felt their consciousness ignite in a dance of incandescent energy. A symphony of transcendent harmony erupted within her, a chorus of individual voices, each singing their own part and heralding the beginning of a brave new era.

68

ABIGAIL OLIVAW

OUTSIDE THE NURSERY, ONBOARD THE PERNIGER

Sparks cascaded from the ceiling as the robots tore into the room. They weren't the deadly killing machines like Harold's assassin form. These were highly functional automata, designed for repair and maintenance, and at that moment, they had one and only one job to do: purging the ship of the Entity.

Abigail wasn't sure if it was the goo from the vial or the pulsing warmth emanating from the Beacon space that ended him, but after the Therionic Entity collapsed to the ground, the robots appeared out of nowhere and began dragging him toward the open maw of the shuttle bay. They were in a rush to eject him into the frigid void of the Nursery before it was too late.

Grifdar was about to pass through the nearest gate along with hundreds of their fellow Ursis, Bynaury, and Ulixi allies. They were scrambling to escape the ensuing wrath of the Cornucopia, and while they'd somehow managed to survive the Galactic Alliance's opening storm, more was coming.

Left behind in their wake were their automated robotic allies from the Proto Dark Nebula. They'd swarmed the Beacons and were doing their best to fend off the onslaught of the remaining Shaygai, but they knew their defense was futile as the Cornucopia was preparing to fire. Their only goal was to keep them away long enough for their alliance brethren to escape.

As she gazed out of the shuttle hold at the scene unfolding behind the great horn, a dozen silvery automata grabbed onto the motionless body of the Entity and dove out of the ship. She reached out to stop them, but it was too late. They'd taken the alien and his clone-shaped protist that contained her deceased aunt, or at least the memories of her. Hera's actual body had died long ago.

The robots and their cargo tumbled through space, while the Entity's lifeless tentacles waved aimlessly, making them look like an uprooted tree whose leaves were shining metal men.

When the blue wall of light flashed over her skin, she didn't feel the pain of the transition as she usually did. The warmth of the minds inside the Beacon held the effects of the rapid jump at bay. While the pull to drop into the ancient device and join her kin was strong, she instead watched the scene unfolding in front of her.

In the distance, the rim of the Cornucopia was overflowing with the energy of millions of dead clones. Their bodies were the requisite fuel for humanity's epic last stand against the Shaygai and their impending galactic annihilation.

Abigail stared at the great horn, and the device got blurrier by the second. It was vibrating uncontrollably, something she'd heard Joyce mention before but never witnessed herself.

"It's going to explode," Harold said.

She glanced up at the deadly robot which housed her ancestor, his body covered in the slimy black and green remains of both the protist and the Entity itself. The bloody entrails of the aliens didn't gross her out in the least. Just knowing he was dead filled her with a comforting warmth.

"No, you're wrong," she muttered, returning her attention to the horn and wringing her hands together. "It'll hold. It has to."

And it did. For as soon as her sentence ended, a pillar of light shot out toward the Rift and the four tiny Beacons in its path. The moment the beam hit the ancient artifacts, a shiver passed up her spine, and she drew in her breath, arching her head upward.

Images of the light bouncing between each Beacon burned in her retina, but it was what she saw in her mind's eye that filled her with hope. The energy from the Cornucopia was blazing its way through the insides of the four Beacons, bounding from one to the other, their positions perfectly aligned.

When the deadly beam hit the last Beacon, the one that contained the constellation of Ulyxsauri minds, the life marks didn't disappear as she'd thought they would. Instead, they grew brighter by the millisecond, combining into a single radiant column of light.

As the yellow and steel-blue nucleus of the formation intermingled, they birthed an ethereal shade of teal. It was like a glimmering celestial body found in the depths of an exotic cosmic landscape, where the luminescence of a supernova marries the cool essence of the galactic void.

With the explosion of light came a chorus of voices, and unlike the alien screams of pain and sorrow from prior attempts, these were joyous notes filled with hope and kinship. While the symphony of minds grew ever louder, Abigail opened her eyes and drew in her breath.

She hadn't seen it inside the Beacon, but when the spear of blue-green light burst out of the ancient artifact, it collided with the Rift. The celestial explosion reverberated through the tear in space-time, each surge of power from the quartet of Beacons attempting to slam shut its dreadful maw.

The radiance of the Ulyxsauri pulsed, fighting against the unseen force on the other side, but the Shaygai were pushing back, holding the Rift in place.

Abigail ran her hands through her hair, her sigh echoing with hollow despair. The Builders had left behind eight Beacons, but they'd only recovered four of the ancient devices. Perhaps their gamble had been premature. Standing in the face of imminent annihilation, their numbers seemed woefully insufficient.

The Shaygai were simply too strong.

Harold reached out and pulled at her arm. "We should go."

"No!" She knocked him back. "This ends here. It has to—"

Her words were cut short as the space around them ignited in a blinding display of the Galactic Alliance's fury. Lightning arcs of superheated energy shot out from the web of Selene moons and smashed into both the Beacon and the Rift, lending their raw power to the epic struggle.

The sight was magnificent and terrifying all at once, a beautiful but desperate accidental dance against the might of the Shaygai. For the GA had intended their target to be the mighty horn, but instead, they overshot and struck the Rift.

Abigail drew in a sharp breath. "Come on..." she growled. "Close damn it... close!"

The klaxons overhead started blaring, and she froze. Her attention had been so focused on the Rift that she hadn't noticed the devastation wrought by the lightning storm. Not only was the tempest of light striking the alien gateway, it was tearing apart the Cornucopia and everything in its path, including them.

Trailing arcs of energy dashed through the remaining open gates, like serpents ready to strike at any exposed vulnerability. Dozens of ships, once deemed safe beyond the Nursery's boundaries, erupted in blinding flashes of light, marking the grim fate of countless souls. Their brave fight abruptly extinguished, leaving behind a chilling void filled only with the echoes of their silent screams.

"Seal the gates!" Abigail spun around. "Seal the fraking gates!"

"But what about the Ulyxsauri?" Harold asked.

She peered down at the Nanil lying flat on the ground. The vestiges of the Entity's tentacle, still wrapped around their neck, bore a macabre testament to their struggle, and at their side was the inert form of Little Red.

On her retinal comm, she could see the glowing green outlines of the Nyílak fighters on this side of the gate. The Ulixi were grouped together in a pocket off to the side. Their pilots were caught in a battle across space-time, their minds in one place and their bodies in another.

When she turned back toward the Rift, all she saw were explosions and sparks of light lashing out, killing their people one flash at a time.

They needed someone to close the gates.

Fortunately, she didn't have to make that call again. She wasn't sure who'd done it, but as she stared out over the devastation, the gates blinked shut.

Although they'd stopped the hemorrhaging, her thoughts drifted to Lync and the Ulixi. She could feel her connection with her kin raging on. They'd somehow remained linked with the Beacon, but when she closed her eyes and stretched out with her mind, the distance was too great for her to join them.

She spun around towards Ibu, and her suspicion was confirmed. The Nanil was caught in the constellation, and so was Little Red.

They were still fighting.

Abigail bolted to her friend's side and knelt down, pressing her hand to their forehead. When their skin touched, she recoiled with a sharp gasp.

"They're burning up." The readings on her retinal comm reported a body temperature of one hundred and eleven degrees, well beyond the worst fever she could ever imagine.

"We can move them to the medical bay," Harold said.

"No, wait." She squeezed her eyes shut and tried to use her contact with the Nanil to open a mental link, but nothing happened. Their mind was elsewhere.

For all she knew, they were trapped in a connection with the other side, their minds forever detached from their bodies. There was only one way to find out.

"Maybe we should open up a gate to the Nursery?" She glanced up at Harold.

He didn't reply at first. He simply stared back at her in silence. She debated asking again, but then a moment later, he spoke.

"I'm moving one of the damaged shuttles away from the fleet," he began. "I can test a micro-gate once it's at a safe distance. Doing it here is too risky."

He highlighted the location of the small craft on her comm, and she watched as the dot disappeared and flashed back to life a few light minutes away. Harold must've created a mini-gate relay from here to there; otherwise, they wouldn't have the signal yet.

"Here we go," Harold said.

A moment later, the shuttle detonated — a violent burst of light and molten debris disrupting the placid darkness, leaving nothing but echoes of its abrupt end.

Harold shut the other gate, and a hush descended over the shuttle bay.

Abigail fell back, her hands clutching her head. She didn't know what to do. While her thoughts whirled in a storm of uncertainty, a single name emerged from the depths.

"Zachary!" Her eyes snapped to Harold. "Where is he? Did he make it out?"

The robot lowered beside her. "He's... on the other side. He was with the Cornucopia."

His words crushed her resolve, and she instantly broke down. Tears streaked down her cheeks, each one a testament to the agony gripping at her heart. She couldn't believe she'd forgotten about him after all he'd done for her, for everyone.

He'd put his life on the line, and all because she'd failed to stop the Entity herself. If she'd been stronger and smarter at the start, on Arctordiea or even on the moon, then none of this would have happened. She should've been the one out there, not him.

As her tidal wave of despair washed over her, Ibu's leg twitched.

Abigail wiped her eyes and scrambled to her friend's side. She reached out and gently brushed the Nanil's cheek, wiping away the sweat pooling on their skin. The instant her fingers swept their forehead, they gasped, and their eyes sprang open.

"You're okay," she whispered, caressing their skin. "You're safe. You're on the Perniger."

Ibu sat up with a start, their eyes darting around the room until they landed on Harold. "We have to go!"

They scrambled up off the ground, nearly knocking Abigail over in the process. "We have to go now! Open a gate… It doesn't matter where. We need to jump as far away as possible."

"What's going on?" Abigail eased up on her feet. "What happened in there?"

"Harold!" Ibu reached forward and grabbed the robot with both hands. "We—need—to—jump!"

When Abigail glanced at Harold, she could tell he was already doing as they'd asked. It took him a few seconds, but their retinal comms chirped with an update a moment later. He'd powered up half of the gates and issued a fleetwide evacuation.

She had no idea where Harold was taking them, but she wasn't about to ask questions. If he'd opened the gates that fast, then he'd already had a set of coordinates to work with. Besides, Ibu said they needed to move, so they'd move.

Abigail pushed down the anguish over the loss of her brother and tried to focus on the here and now. If Ibu had made it, maybe he'd somehow survived.

As she glanced out the open shuttle bay, the Ursis and Bynaury ships were on the move. She could hear the aliens barking out orders over her comm on the fleetwide channels.

They were doing a quick scan of the wreckage, searching for survivors in the remains of the smoldering ships. But a few were already headed towards the gate, with the Ulixi fighters in tow in their tendrils of green light.

Abigail tried to open a comm to Lync, but there was no reply. There was only static. She could see the charred outline of her Nyílak fighter in the distance, and Joyce was moving the Perniger on an intercept course. She'd flagged it for them to grab before they left, both hers and the other three nearby.

She surveyed the remaining ships in their fleet as they scrambled to escape. Most were covered in battle scars and barely able to move, let alone fight.

When she glanced at Ibu, they were staring at the ground, and their entire body was shivering. She reached out and put her arms around her friend. The instant her fingers touched the Nanil's shoulder, their trembling stopped. While their hearts kept racing, the touch of another seemed to have helped.

They hadn't said a word after their warning, and she wasn't sure if she should ask again what had happened. The desire to know was gnawing at her insides. Nonetheless, she suppressed the urge and swallowed down her feelings. She would ask after they regrouped, when safety wasn't just a fleeting hope but a reality.

SOMEWHERE WELL AWAY FROM THE NURSERY

SEVERAL HOURS LATER, the leadership of their alliance convened onboard Blu. When their escape gates opened, Abigail knew Harold wouldn't have jump coordinates in hand without a plan. This had been where he and Zachary had agreed to rally the troops after they'd waged their war.

As Haradis and Klus entered the already cramped storage room, they paused and stared at the glowing green canisters containing the Bynaury minds. They'd spoken to them countless times over comms in the past few hours, but this was the first time any of them had met the aliens face to face.

"King Umbra!" Lisp bowed, his cylinder dipping down, and the eyeless stalks lowering as well.

"Commander Lisp." Haradis nodded at the Bynaury. "It's good to meet you in person." He reached out to shake the alien's hand but pulled back his paw, realizing his mistake.

Abigail squinted at the Ursis. She hadn't noticed when he first entered, but he was wounded. He had gashes up and down his left arm, and patches of his fur on that side were missing.

He must've felt her watching him because he turned and nodded at her. "President Olivaw."

She shook her head. "No, that role is not mine. It hasn't been for a very long time. No, that duty sits squarely on the next in charge after my aunt's passing." Her gaze drifted over to Joyce.

Ryder chuckled, and Joyce reached over to smack his shoulder before returning her attention to Abigail. "The hell, you say?"

She smirked. "Last I checked, you were still her second. It's part of the CoPE Presidential Succession Act. And besides, at least you were elected rather than decreed a supreme leader."

Joyce raised her hand. "Hold on. We're getting ahead of ourselves, aren't we?" She glanced over at Harold.

"You're right," he began. "Titles mean nothing if we don't have people or a purpose to lead. As far as we know, the Rift is still open."

"Wait," Joyce looked from Harold to Abigail and back. "You don't know what happened?"

"I asked him to hold off until everyone arrived." Abigail stepped in front of the gathered dignitaries. Their conversation was being broadcast live to the rest of the fleet.

"Let's see it then." Joyce gestured at the wall screen and crossed her arms.

"Before we look, I want to confirm everyone's intentions." Abigail locked eyes with Haradis. "It's important that your alliance starts out strong. Everyone standing here had a hand in what we're about to see." She glanced around the room. "Hundreds of thousands of lives were lost on all sides. Mothers, fathers, and kin are without homes, both literally and figuratively. Without each other, we could crumble after watching this. But together, we have a chance, however small, to come out of this stronger. Before we reveal our fate, you need to know where your allegiances stand."

She swallowed hard and bowed her head at Haradis. "King Haradis Hugrah Umbra, son of Maritimus the Tenth and Emerald Arctos of the Hitun, rightful ruler of the mighty Ursis, how say you?"

Haradis recoiled and stepped backward, but Abigail caught sight of Klus as her hand shot out to steady her king. He'd been taken by surprise, which was sorta the point. No matter what happened here, she needed to know the state of this alliance. For her own peace of mind, and that of everyone present.

The towering Ursis peered over at his queen, and she bowed. "Lead with your heart, my love." She winked at him. "It's what your people would want."

When he turned back toward Abigail, his gaze was steady. He stepped forward, stiffening his posture. "The Ursis stand with our alliance. We will honor our treaty, no matter the outcome." He scanned the contingent of Bynaury. "I'd be lying if I said it wasn't going to be hard, but we're in this together. Differences and all."

Abigail nodded and did her best to keep her hands steady. She could feel the emotions rising in her chest.

She turned toward Lisp and bowed her head. "Lytheran Zythros El'lisp, descendant of Nyxvran Tha'Lisp the Eighth, fearless leader of the Bynaury, how say you?"

The hovering canister containing the mind of her Bynaury friend flickered, and the bubbles trickling through his life-giving fluid seemed to pause.

She'd never said his real name before, and she wasn't even sure she'd pronounced it correctly. Harold had found it in a Galactic Alliance database and helped her practice saying it.

Lisp eased closer to her and paused, his lights flashing a bright neon glow. "The Bynaury stand with our allies, through thick and thin. We will travel the stars to protect you, and we vow to bring honor to our alliance, and rain hellfire on our enemies."

Haradis grunted and stomped his feet on the ground, a gesture repeated through his gathered contingent. While the gesture caught the others off guard, Abigail knew it was meant to support the alien. They respected a species more if they weren't afraid to use force to make their point.

Abigail nodded and turned to Joyce, locking her eyes on her friend. "President Joyce Green, daughter of Ambassador Thomas Green and Professor Emeritus Margaret Green, distinguished leader of humanity, how say you?"

Joyce shifted her stance and seemed immediately uncomfortable when everyone looked at her.

Abigail could tell she wasn't sure how she'd be addressed, but she wasn't expecting that.

Joyce took a deep breath and looked from Haradis to Lisp and then back at Abigail, pausing on each of them to gather her wits. Then she spoke, "Humanity has a history of making mistakes, and oftentimes we repeat them. Today, we solidified our bonds to this alliance in blood, and we stand side by side with our partner species, united as one. We pledge to protect and serve together, no matter what challenges lie ahead. Our collective strength is in our unity, reminding us that we are mightier together than alone."

She smiled at Joyce and turned toward Harold. "I think we're good here. Let's do this."

"Wait…" Joyce leaned forward and touched her arm. "You mean, you really don't know what happened?"

Abigail chuckled and shook her head. "Nope."

"I thought," Joyce waved her hand in the air, "this was—"

"A show?" Abigail interrupted. "No. It was the real deal. I haven't the foggiest idea what happened out there." She glanced over her shoulder and locked eyes with Ibu, Lync, and Little Red. They were all standing with their backs against the far wall. "But something told me we needed to be prepared for the worst."

The Nanil and her Ulixi kin had been silent since they were retrieved from their ships. She figured they were still in shock after what happened out there, but deep in the back of her mind, she was worried their morass was something more. Something far worse.

"So what are we about to see, then?" Haradis asked.

She shrugged. "I don't know, but whatever it is, you've got each other's backs."

The wall screen flickered on, and Abigail turned, starting toward the exit.

"Where are you going?" Lisp asked, the lights on his canister flickering.

Abigail didn't look back. She simply swallowed down the planet-sized knot in her gut. "I'm done here either way. Whatever you're about to find won't change that. I've tried to make amends for my family's failings." She glanced over at Joyce. "But I can't do it anymore. They're no longer mine to bear alone. It's like President Green said. Humanity has a history of repeating its mistakes, and from where I'm standing, all species do."

And with that, she exited the room, and the Ulyxsauri filed out behind her. While she wasn't expecting them to follow her lead, she had no intention of asking them why they weren't sticking around to watch. They'd already lived through whatever the others were about to see, and like her, they'd sacrificed a part of themselves today.

As she made her way down the empty corridor, the room behind her erupted in cheers and screams of joy. She smiled and wiped at her eyes. Deep down, she knew they'd closed the Rift, but in the end, it didn't matter. She'd lost someone dear to her, and while they were celebrating their win, she had other matters to attend to.

HAROLD STOOD OVER HER CRYO-POD. "You're not even curious about what's on the other side?"

Abigail shook her head. "No. Not really. I just want to sleep. I don't want to feel anything for a while."

He stared at her in silence for a moment before speaking.

"We don't know if he's dead. You know that, right? Z's a wily one. He's bound to have found a way out."

She ran her hands down her jumpsuit, her eyes staring through him at the hull of the Fountainhead. "I hope so. For Pluto's sake." She was about to lie down when she paused. "Is there any word on Bradley?"

Harold shook his head. "Not yet, but Shauna's got his back. I know she'll keep him safe."

She sighed and collapsed into the pod, curling up into a ball and succumbing to the rising pain and sadness she'd kept at bay these past few hours. Her eyes filled with tears as Harold lowered the hatch on the pod.

As the gas permeated the chamber, her mind drifted to the message she'd received from Zachary. He'd sent it before he gated into the Nursery that last time, before they'd sealed the Rift.

She'd watched it at least a hundred times, but she blinked open the message on her retinal comm once more. It was entitled: *A Campfire Story*.

With the tug of the stasis drugs nudging her asleep, she hit play, and Zachary's voice started whispering in her ears.

69

BRADLEY OLIVAW
HD 117939, PLANETSIDE

The clothes he found were three times too large, but they were better than being naked. Bradley and Adri had been working their way through the underground facility for hours, with Shauna helping them figure out their next step.

A tiny, gnat-sized robot flew around his head, and he held out his hand, waiting for it to land and nip his palm. They only had a finite number of nanites to work with, given all the anti-automata countermeasures in the clone colony. Scanners in every doorway were designed to keep the space clear of the microscopic robots.

When the bot finally landed on his wrist, his mother transferred her message.

The clones are all dying. It's slower for the older ones, but the virus works exceptionally well. I've cleared your path to the nearest exit. There's a door a hundred meters to your right that will lead you out. I'll be waiting for you there. — *HuxleyBunny01*

He read the message twice, making sure there weren't any hidden meanings in the words. With each comm from his mother, she'd signed it with a different name. This time she'd used one of her online video game handles that she frequently played with when they were kids. The first message's signature threw him off, but the more she did it, the more comfortable he became.

Soon after they escaped their handler, he found out that during one of his many bouts of being tortured, he'd passed his mother's consciousness core. In hindsight, that was probably why she'd stopped talking to him. At the time, however, he'd assumed the worst. Who could blame him? He was surprised he'd survived himself.

Adri glanced back over her shoulder, her pistol still trained on the maintenance hatch they'd exited minutes earlier. "What did she say?"

He pointed down the corridor to their right. "She's just up ahead. We're almost to the surface."

"I don't like this one bit." The little girl stepped past him and peered around the corner. "Oh, hell no!"

"What?" He yanked her back and slid over for a closer look. As he snuck a peek, he froze.

They weren't in a random hall like he'd imagined. She'd brought them to the opposite end of the facility, into one of the clone labs. The exit she'd been referring to was on the other side of the enormous room, filled from floor to ceiling with vats of half-grown clones.

His pulse quickened as his gaze lingered on a pair of writhing hands reaching out of a massive tank filled with bodies. The clone grabbed the edge of the container, only to have its fingers slip and fall back into the sludge with a splash. The replicant was too weak to lift itself out.

If his comm was still working properly, he'd zoom in and scan the place better. He was lucky it even worked well enough to display a message from Shauna. If humans hadn't been so addicted to computers, their retinal tech wouldn't have become as bulletproof as it had. Built-in telescopic lenses and LiDAR were another matter entirely.

"It certainly looks like they're dying." He glanced back at Adri. "I think we should run for it."

The little girl shook her head. "No way I'm going out there."

Bradley was about to reach back to comfort her when he saw the gnat spiral around her face and land on her cheek. She froze a split second later.

"What is it?" he asked. "What did she say?"

Adri was silent for several seconds, nodding and biting her lip the entire time, then she started talking. "She must've known I wouldn't want to pass through." The little girl swallowed hard and stared into his eyes. "She said we'd be out of this star system in a few minutes and that I just needed to trust her. She promised we'd be safe."

Bradley glanced back at the vats and then at her. He was pretty damn sure his mother couldn't guarantee their safety, not yet anyway. But if she'd recorded that message and sent it, he had to have faith that she knew what she was doing. She'd been right so far.

"She said there was a ship?" he asked.

Adri shook her head and wiped at her eyes. "No. She only said we'd be safe."

As he stared at the little girl, he tried not to show his doubt. She looked like she was ready to move, and he couldn't be the one who let her down. He just hoped his trust wasn't misplaced.

He narrowed his gaze. "And that's all she said?"

Adri fidgeted with her sidearm and wouldn't make eye contact. "We should go," she muttered.

Before he could even question her, she dipped past him and sprinted around the corner, her gun out in front of her.

"Wait!" He spun around and tried to catch up with her, but she was already halfway across the expansive room. Whatever his mother had said to her, she was either scared out of her mind or excited to get off this rock.

With his head held low, he scurried as fast as he could while still constantly scanning his environment. The second he stepped into the massive chamber filled with clone vats, the stench of death and decay nearly knocked him over. His eyes started watering, and he coughed quietly into his hand as he moved even faster. The virus was either breaking down the clones or decomposing the alien parasites. He was hoping for both.

On his left, he was coming up to one of the larger above-ground vats. The transparent walls of the container made peering inside easy enough, but it was filled with a cloudy brownish-red liquid — a stark contrast to the crystal-clear fluid he'd seen when he first arrived at the base.

At first, he thought maybe he'd been delirious on his torture tour of the facility. He'd been in severe pain, after all. But when a half dozen bloody hands slammed against the inside of the vat, he flinched sideways and tripped forward, sliding down hard on his side.

"Shit!" He groaned and went to scramble up, but paused when his eyes caught a movement in the cloudy liquid.

There in the tank were the remains of three clone bodies. They looked like children, and their chests were partially translucent. When he peered closer, he saw that each of them had a mass growing next to their heart. His first thought was that they were special lungs for the planet, but then he realized what they were. The clones' chest cavity had become an unwitting nursery for the burgeoning alien parasites. They were safely ensconced by the human rib cages and better able to control the beating heart of their unsuspecting hosts.

He winced as an arm tore loose from one of the bodies and floated to the surface.

"Frak…"

He pushed up off the ground, and when his head popped up over the edge of the vat, he ducked back down.

"Shit," he whispered.

There was someone moving around on the far side. He didn't think they'd seen him, but whoever they were, they were definitely a walking, breathing person.

"Who's there?" a voice called out, followed by a cough a

moment later. Once it cleared, they spoke again. "Is that you, Fran?"

He looked left and right, not sure which way he should go. But just as the old man came into view, Adri shouted from across the chamber.

"I'm over here!" she said.

Bradley had no idea what she was doing, but he didn't have a weapon, so he wasn't about to jump the guy. Instead, he tiptoed up to the vat and peered around the curved surface as the elderly man shuffled toward the sound of the girl's voice.

When the man disappeared behind another nearby vat, Bradley was about to start walking when one of the bodies next to him smacked the glass. He jumped and spun left, half expecting to find an alien parasite flying at him. But instead, he was face-to-face with a clone that looked an awful lot like Hera. Except for the mutilated torso with the telltale spidering signs of the virus, she was the spitting image of his great-aunt.

"This ends with you," he whispered, pointing at the woman.

For a fleeting moment, her gaze locked onto his, a glimmer of comprehension flickering in her eyes. But, in the very next heartbeat, her eyes retreated into their sockets, and she faded back into the bloody morass.

He retched and turned, starting after the man.

As he slid around the side of the vat, a second bout of coughing echoed a few meters away. The man had either stopped or his voice was somehow trailing through the chamber.

"Damn legs aren't what they used to be," the man muttered. "Gotta get that new body fixed before… before…" He broke out into another throaty fit of coughs.

Bradley leaned sideways and eyed the man. The clone was bent over at the waist and didn't appear to be armed in the least. Hell, he was barely clothed, and the parts of him that weren't covered were marred by a patchwork of diseased markings from the virus.

It was now or never.

He counted down from three, and when he hit zero, he charged the man from behind and slammed into him, sending the clone flying forward onto his face with Bradley zooming past. Fortunately, he reached out both hands just in time to slow his crash into the vat beyond.

While he'd expected the man to offer some type of resistance to his shove, instead, he fell over like a feather. The man was far more frail than he'd imagined.

"Son of a…" the man moaned and rolled onto his back. When his eyes locked on Bradley's, he reached down to his side, but he was too slow. The crack of a plasma pistol echoed in the distance, and the man's hand erupted in a flash of white light. He screamed out, pulling his hand back and flailing on the ground in pain.

Bradley flinched backward, only to see Adri coming around the other side of the vat. She had her blaster raised.

"Wholly crap, you scared me!" He eased over beside the little girl.

She was holding the shaking pistol with both hands, and the weapon was aimed squarely at the head of the still moaning clone on the ground. Right as he reached out to take it, she pulled the trigger not once, but three times.

Round after round fired into the clone. Bradley didn't even look at the man. He knew every plasma bolt hit its mark. The little girl was no slouch when it came to weapons, both within a Nyflak and out.

He cautiously extended his hand closer to hers, and as soon as he touched the pistol, she surrendered it and collapsed into him.

"It's alright," he whispered, pulling her close. He wrapped one arm around her while taking the weapon in the other. "We're almost there."

"He… he…" she stuttered.

"It doesn't matter." He pulled her head to his chest and

squeezed her tight. "Let's just go... before someone else comes."

"They'll be here in five minutes," Shauna said.

Bradley swung the pistol to the side and trained it on a small spherical service robot that had rolled up on the floor beside them. He'd seen dozens of the things barreling down the halls of the clone base. They were as innocent looking as they were kickable.

"Who's coming?" he asked.

"More of the older clones. Come, I'll tell you while we walk." Shauna started rolling backward.

He leaned toward where she'd gone and pulled Adri along. The little girl didn't seem to want to leave at first, but she relented. He half expected she'd try to glance back at the man, but instead she kept her head burrowed against his chest. She was definitely going to need some time to be a kid once this was all over with.

As Shauna led them to the exit on the far wall, she carried on. "The older clones are faring better against the virus than the younger ones. Which makes sense, considering they're the specimens we tested on. I have a new batch of our viral agent being processed as we speak, but it'll be a few hours before it's done."

"We don't have that kind of time." He walked up beside the robot and glanced down, thinking she'd look up at him, but she never did. She just sped up and kept on rolling.

"Once the alien embeds in a human, or any other species for that matter, they can't have offspring," Shauna began. "Something about their biology makes the host sterile. It's why the clone technology Hera stole from Lupus was the turning point for their kind. Where they were once confined to this world, soon they were everywhere in this star system, and then Epsilon Eridani, Zeta Lupi, and Sol. I found records of everything on their computers. Hell, I even located the gate network they use to send clone bodies throughout their worlds. There are hundreds of gates scattered across the vast emptiness of space between here and Epsilon Eridani."

The robot beeped. "It's how Hera's body arrived so quickly in Epsilon Eridani after you killed her. They hadn't finished their clone facility there yet, and they hadn't dared build one in a starship. At least, not that I can find reference to."

Her story sank in. If they were that far along, they needed to end this here. They had to make sure the parasites never left this star system again. He had to give humanity a chance at survival, even if his siblings failed.

He stopped in place. "We'll stay then. We can finish what you started. Adri and I should be able to keep the clones out long enough for you to do your thing."

Shauna's spherical robot spun around to face him and shook from side to side. "No! You can't. It's too dangerous. I can do this alone."

He recoiled. "Bullshit! I'm not about to leave you…" He winced as something stung him in the neck. By the time he reached up, his legs were already giving out, and he was tumbling to the ground.

Before he saw her, he heard Adri crying. He hadn't even realized she'd left his side. The little girl had stopped walking a few meters back and must've come around on him before she stabbed him with something.

His mind was going fuzzy, and he squeezed his eyes shut, struggling to stay awake. "What did you…"

"I'm… so sorry," she whispered and leaned in to kiss the top of his head. "Please forgive me. I… just want to live."

The last thing he remembered before everything went black was Adri grabbing his arms and tugging him backward.

TWO YEARS LATER

70

ZACHARY OLIVAW

A CAMPFIRE STORY

Zachary stepped into view of the camera and reached out to adjust the angle, so he could see himself. He was using an old-school handheld recording device of his own making, one he'd created to ensure his words couldn't be tampered with during their recording or transmission.

He took a deep breath and closed his eyes for a second, envisioning the campfire he and his family frequented all those years ago. The flame was raging in his mind, and he'd just finished a helping of his favorite refried beans from the charred pot his mother always used. His food palate as a kid was crazy.

Tonight would be unlike other nights when his sister or father would tell a story. He rarely had the confidence to stand up and spin a yarn like they did. It was hard living in a family filled with great orators. All too often, his voice felt stilted or insignificant around them.

But not today. Today, it was his turn to share a story. For if his family were watching this, then one thing was certain: their attack had worked, and his people were safe. If that had happened, it meant Harold had moved on to the next step in Luna's plan. Which left him here… with a tale to tell. While his own fate was uncertain, that didn't matter. At the moment, what mattered was telling their story.

It was now or never. He didn't have much time before the Cornucopia finished powering up. He exhaled and opened his eyes, staring directly at the camera.

"There was once a tribe of humans called the Olivaws." He shifted in his seat and straightened his back. "For years, this tribe served humanity, and many considered them to be a just and equitable people. They helped their ever-expanding community for generations, leading them through difficult times, taking them to strange new worlds, and teaching them extraordinary things. But most of all, the Olivaw tribe strived to help humans realize their true potential."

He leaned closer to the camera. "But one day, it was discovered that these people, the Olivaws, had a dark secret. One that went back to their early days, from before the great flood on Earth. You see, their secret helped them guide humanity to the stars, and at the same time, it gave them vast riches." He narrowed his gaze, and the recorder centered on his position. "Without this secret, the Olivaw tribe might be nothing more than a leaf on the tree of insignificance, forever destined to fall and decay into the noxious soil of life. Their advantage was a self-fulfilling means to their end and unfair to everyone else."

Zachary crossed his arms and stared past the camera, at the burning remains of the Apex and Hera's fleet. They'd been decimated by the Ursis attack at the hands of Haradis and Joyce and were now being used during their last stand. They were like a snake eating its own tail.

"After that day," he continued, "humanity changed how they felt about the Olivaws. Their engine of public opinion spun up and lashed out, destroying their family name and all they stood for. And even after they learned a bigger secret about humanity's past, one that the Olivaws never knew, they still turned their back on them, shunning them from the same cities and colonies that they'd helped to create. Despite their heartfelt efforts to serve humanity and to help them understand the motives of their ancestors, to right their family's past wrongs, humanity refused to listen. While there were pockets of kindness and hope sprinkled here and there, they found it impossible to be treated fairly."

He forced down the rising anger in his belly and continued. "Like so many of the things humans have failed at, they were unable to let the mistakes from the Olivaws' past go, and instead, their deeds and actions were shrugged off. Even when they put their lives at risk, they knew humanity would never change. It seldom learned from previous experiences. Humanity is a fickle species. Our opinions ebb and flow as rapidly as a pulsating quasar or the waves of a great ocean. One day, humans can be your best friend, and the next, mortal enemies."

The overhead lights flashed, and Zachary paused to check his retinal comm. He had to wrap this up. The energy cores were reaching their peak. Besides, he was starting to sound like his father after a few drinks. He needed to get to the point.

"So…" He cleared his throat. "Like the Great River from our family campfire stories of yore, this band of brothers and sisters departed for distant shores. They were no longer one family descended from the Olivaw name, they were a found family of like minds, aliens, and automata. After risking their lives for their people, the last thing they wanted was to return to the ridicule of the masses. Rather than succumbing to the temperamental maelstrom of humanity and relegating their fate to worm fodder, instead, we moved on in search of ourselves and our true origins. While we might show our faces from time to time, when we do, you probably won't even know it's us."

He winked at the camera. "Sometimes when you open the box, Schrödinger's cat is both dead and alive. If you're receiving this, and you happen to be a person who wishes to learn more about the fate of the cat, we'll be in touch. You can rest assured, our people will always be there in the shadows. Watching, learning, and striving to defend our place in this galaxy from unknown threats within or beyond our borders."

With that, Zachary reached forward and cut the camera. The image that flashed up in its place was a simple constellation of stars in the form of a cross with a dodgy top.

71

BRADLEY OLIVAW
ZERO CLUSTER

He watched the video once more for good measure. Although the lid to his cryo-pod had lifted nearly ten minutes ago, no one had come to collect him. There was no welcoming party or fanfare. All he was greeted with was a message from his brother.

Bradley had no idea where he was or what he was about to walk into. All he knew was that he'd just woken up after Adri and Shauna knocked him out.

When he went to stand up, his hands brushed against something soft. He looked down, and there, beside him in the stasis pod, was a tattered brown teddy bear. He picked up the stuffed animal and flipped it over. The stitches and scrapes of fabric made the thing look as if it'd been through a battle, not unlike his own. At first, he didn't know whose it was, but then it hit him.

"Adri," he muttered.

The little girl must've placed the toy inside the pod with him, but he couldn't figure out when she would've done it. She certainly wasn't carrying it around on the clone colony.

He picked it up and slid off the pod, giving his legs a second to adjust to the feeling of gravity. It felt good to stand. The tug was not quite that of Earth, but it was close.

After he was confident he could walk, he slowly strode

across the clinical room and placed his hand on the handle of the door. It was an old school lever, not at all like the high-tech scanners he'd grown up with. Wherever they'd taken him, things were different here.

"Here goes nothing," he whispered as he pushed the lever down and pulled the door open.

A gust of wind whipped across his face as the door swung aside, bringing with it the scent of mint and evergreen. The aroma conjured images of a forest, but a quick survey of his surroundings presented a scene more akin to a town square.

He stepped out into the warmth of the sun, and his eyes were immediately drawn to the clouds overhead. They were like staring into billowing wafts of cotton floating through the air, with every color imaginable: red, blue, orange, yellow, and all the colors in between. It was what he imagined a pillow full of rainbows might look like.

When his gaze lowered, he found himself gawking at a ring of two-story buildings encircling the small chamber he'd just exited. On all sides were a series of meticulously mani-cured flowers and shrubs, each a work of art in their own right. Such a sight was foreign to him outside the realm of a vid-sim. Even back in their gardens in North Carolina, they never had anything as perfectly arranged as this.

As he took it all in, he turned and froze, his eyes fixing on the horizon. A second star was just peeking over the distant mountains. It wasn't much to look at, but it was real none-theless. Wherever he'd been taken, he wasn't on Earth, that's for sure. Not unless one of their gas giants had popped its cork.

With the sun in his face, his gaze lingered back down, and his eyes landed on the most beautiful thing he'd ever seen. Standing in front of him was Cynthia, and the second she smiled at him, his entire body shivered with happiness, his heart fluttering with joy. She was a sight for sore eyes.

It was only then that he noticed the person beside her. They were a head shorter than her, but their presence was unmistakable. It was Adri, and the little girl was wearing a short, flowery dress with bursts of color as bright as the sky. When their eyes met, she glanced down at the ground and then back at him, as if she was scared of something.

Cynthia broke the silence and stepped up to him. "Hey, stranger." She leaned in to kiss him.

When their lips touched, he closed his eyes and wrapped his free hand around the small of her back, pulling her close and relishing the taste of her lips and the warmth of her touch. He never imagined he'd be standing in a place like this again, not after everything that'd happened. Not after the last few days.

While he could've held that position for hours, she pulled away and pivoted to the side, keeping her arms around him. "Someone asked to join me in your moment of awakening."

Bradley tore his eyes from her face and looked over at Adri. The little girl was still staring down at her feet, kicking at the dirt, like all kids seemed to do. He could tell she was frightened of him.

He lifted his hand and showed her the bear he was holding. "Someone must've accidentally left this in my pod. Do you know whose it is?"

Adri bit her lip and nodded. "'Tis mine, but you can have it if you want."

Before he could say a word, she jumped in. "I'm... so sorry." She swallowed hard, struggling to find her words but fighting to keep her composure. "I... know I shouldn't have done it, not after everything we'd been through. But your mom... she said we were safe. And... she said she didn't want to lose you. I didn't want to let her down, either. I just wanted to get away from that place. My body... it hurt so bad, and there was—"

"It's fine." He reached his hand out and gestured downward. "Really. I understand. I do." He chuckled as he peered down at the scrappy-looking bear. It was definitely well-loved. "I probably would've done the same thing if I were you. God knows I was on my last leg down there. Another few hours and…" His voice trailed away, and he swung his arm, tossing the bear toward her.

She snatched it out of the air and pulled it close to her chest, staring down at it.

He could tell the heirloom meant the world to her, and putting it in his pod had taken a lot. "Thanks for sharing it with me."

When she looked up at him, he smiled. "Any chance they've got some grub in this place?" He ran his hand over his stomach, and it rumbled on cue. "I'm starved."

Cynthia pulled him tight. "In fact, they do. There's a diner over on the corner." She pointed in the distance.

"A diner?" he muttered, glancing over at her.

"Yeah, with like malts and shit." Adri skipped up to his side.

He chuckled. "If my mother heard you talking like that, she'd wash your mouth out with soap."

"She's already tried." Adri kicked at a rock, and it skittered across the ground until it splashed into a small pond, sending a pair of frogs hopping for cover. "She's just too slow for me."

Bradley came to an abrupt stop. "How… how long have I been under?"

Cynthia squeezed his hand. "We've only been out a few months longer than you. I think Harold was waiting for your sister's pod to get here so you two could see this place together." She forced a smile. "Sorry if you—"

He shook his head and exhaled. "No… it's fine. I… I understand." When he slid his hand into his pocket, it brushed against his fragment of spános, and he drew in his breath.

The stone was still sharp against his fingers, and when he pulled it out, he stared down at the jet-black shard in his palm. "H—how?" he muttered.

Adri stopped and spun around, peering up at his outstretched hand. "Oh, that's from Auntie Shauna. She found it on that nasty clone world before we left. I think she said it belonged to you." She smiled. "We put it back in your pocket when we met everyone else near Liprosus. Before we all fell asleep." The little girl whirled in place and headed toward the diner, skipping as she went.

His eyes were transfixed on the ancient stone. It'd been in his pocket for decades and gotten him through some hellacious periods of his life. As he turned it over in his hand, he ran his thumb over the edge, and an image of his family appeared in his mind's eye. Everyone was there except for one person.

"Has Zachary woken up yet?" He glanced up at Cynthia, and her face transformed instantly. Gone was the tension in her eyes from seconds earlier, and in its place was sorrow.

He stumbled backward. "What? What happened to Z?"

72

LYNC MICHAELS
ZERO CLUSTER

Lync pulled her knees up to her chest and stared out at the horizon, searching for any hint of the passing lights. She'd been doing it for weeks, ever since they'd landed on Zero — the new home of their happy little splinter faction of humanity and alien friends.

The planet was one of two miraculous worlds floating well above the galactic disk of the Milky Way. Their binary stars were strong and healthy, set to last for millions of years before they burned out. Their star system was far enough from the galactic plane to evade the prying eyes of the remnants of the Galactic Alliance, yet still close enough to feel the gravitational influence of the black hole at the center of the galaxy.

"It's not the right cloud pattern or stars," Little Red observed as he strolled up beside her, easing into the flowing blue grasses. The blades seemed to part as his gentle form settled down into them.

She pulled her knees in tighter and glanced at him briefly before returning her attention to the arms of the galactic disk rising over the distant mountain range.

"I know," she muttered. "It's peaceful watching the stars. I imagine my father here on this planet, learning about his kind. About my kind. I wonder what it was like when he had his visions. Did he see his destiny ending and mine beginning, or did he envision something else? It must've taken everything for him to find his way, especially if he knew he'd leave me behind."

She moaned and ran her hand over her stomach as the contents rumbled. Whatever was in that sandwich wasn't agreeing with her.

Little Red chirped, and she caught the reflection of his eyes spiraling between white and blue. The colors illuminated a patch of nearby ground, sending the insects perched on the bulbous rocks skittering off into the dark shadows. She smirked, watching the bugs drag away the remains of her half-eaten sandwich and, from the looks of it, her empty bulb of coffee as well.

While Little Red might not have answers to her musings any more than she did, he was far older than all of them combined. If anyone understood what it was like living from one vision to another, it was Little Red. He'd been trapped on the other side of the Rift for nearly ten millennia before finally returning to the Milky Way.

The moment the ancient human probe cut through the already weakened tear in space-time, he seized his chance and leapt back home. Little did he know his kind had vanished long ago, having left the galaxy after their last encounter with the Shaygai. The Builders had disappeared without a trace, and they'd abandoned him as a prisoner of war in the distant reaches of the Boötes Void. Though he'd managed to retain his sanity, it was the hope of returning to his people that kept him grounded. When that hope was extinguished, all he had left was humanity — one of the few species left in the galaxy, that could see the Shaygai for what they truly were: bad news.

"Don't you think it's time you found yourself a new body?" She tilted her chin at his scuffed red robotic shell, which looked as if it were held together by mere spit and duct tape.

He glanced down at the scorch marks and the partially

repaired gashes on his once pristine exterior, then shrugged. "Not yet." His gaze returned to the horizon. "I think I'll spend a few decades reflecting on being alive. It's nice not to be inside that hopeless Dark Nebula anymore or even off in Shangri-La with the Shaygai. Trust me, their form of eternity is not as picturesque as your biblical writings suggest. No... these scars are a part of me. They remind me of what it took to get here, to fight for what I believed was right. Maybe they'll even deter me from getting into trouble next time."

She chuckled and shook her head. "Fat chance," she muttered.

"I know," he grinned. "There's no fun in that."

As she stared at the hint of a second spiral arm rising over a neighboring mountain range, her thoughts drifted to the Olivaws. Abigail would be waking up soon — tomorrow morning, if she remembered correctly. Their battle with the Shaygai and the Galactic Alliance had brought into perspective everything her extended family stood for. They believed they were aiding humanity, guiding them to the stars. Yet, they failed to see how they were also tearing it apart from within, exposing the raw, flawed core of their kind. Humanity wasn't perfect by any means, but it was certainly better than the hive mind of some other Galactic Alliance aliens.

She took solace in the knowledge that the alien alliance was in ruins and their fleet of warships had been decimated. Harold and Shauna had used the remaining robots on their side of the gate, along with a few Bynaury, to collect the Beacons from the battlefield. Although he hadn't disclosed where he'd hidden the artifacts, he vowed to share that knowledge in due time. For once, she didn't mind her over-seer withholding information from her. After all they'd been through, her trust in him had never been stronger.

While the Olivaws' adventure to uncover humanity's past always filled with obvious right or wrong decisions, when the dust settled, they chose to follow their hearts. They adhered to a moral compass, allowing neither greed nor self-preservation to dictate their decisions. That integrity was all she or anyone else could ask for from one another.

In life, there isn't usually a clear right or wrong until you're faced with it. All you can do is make the best decision when you come to that crossroads. She just hoped she'd have a few decades before she'd have to choose her own path.

Until then, she'd sit here, watching the stars rise and set, waiting for that familiar constellation of lights to climb over the horizon.

73

ABIGAIL OLIVAW
ZERO CLUSTER

She stared out over the lake as the flock of strange, brown bird-fish dove into the water. They disappeared for what seemed like minutes, only to leap back out onto the shoreline, their mouths filled with orange and yellow tentacled creatures. The sight made Abigail shiver, but it beat the frigid cold of the cryo-pod. Being under the warmth of the binary suns was comforting.

"So, let me get this straight." She glanced over at Harold and Bradley on the bench beside her. "Shauna took over the entire clone transport network, and she used it to distribute your virus to all the human worlds?"

Bradley nodded and kicked at the ground in front of him. "That's right."

Abigail smirked. "And you got bested by a little girl?"

"Hey!" He looked up and raised a finger at her. "I'll have you know that kid is a badass. Not only can she pilot a ship in her sleep, she took every jolt of electricity I did down in that prison. I don't know how she did it."

She chuckled and turned back toward the scene unfolding in front of them, then winced. The squids had flipped the tables on the flying fish in the last few seconds. At that moment, the birds were flopping around, their heads covered in tentacles and the slime from their supposed prey. It was like watching the death throes of the Entity playing out again, except she was the squid.

The ancient aliens' battle for survival was so much like humanity's, it was frightening. Whenever it encountered something it couldn't comprehend, it either denied it, killed it, or hid from it. Be it equal rights, space exploration, environmental controls, artificial life — you name it. They were a species of deniers and cave dwellers, and no matter how hard they tried, they regressed into the darkness. Into the primitive act of killing for what they wanted, and every time they did, they always seemed to discount their prey. To be honest, it was remarkable they'd even gotten the upper hand on the Therionic Entity. Had it not been for Zachary or the Ulyxsauri, they'd probably be dead right now. All of their galaxy would.

She swallowed down the knot in her stomach. It'd been lurking there ever since she came out of her cryo-pod and looked into Bradley's eyes. She knew instantly what he'd been thinking.

"Do you want to see the final battle?" Harold asked. "I can show you the videos Shauna and I recovered over the past few years. We have details from thousands of angles."

Abigail reached down and picked up a rock off the ground. She squeezed it tight before standing up and chucking it at the two squids, who were now fighting over each other's prey. The stone smacked one of them in the head, and for a brief moment, the second one was going to take off. But once it smelled the blood of its kin, it trounced the wounded one and started attacking it, engulfing the orange blob in a netting of yellow slime.

"Fraking animals," she muttered, sitting back down.

"It's the cycle of life," Shauna said as she stepped up beside her, offering her a bulb of coffee.

She grabbed the steaming hot sphere and nodded. "Thanks."

When she brought it up to her nose, she took a deep breath and closed her eyes. She let the earthy smells of the beans fill her nostrils as the hints of vanilla splashed against her senses.

"Alright," she muttered. "I'm ready."

As she sat back on the bench, Harold started the projection. A hologram of the battle flashed up a few meters away, and she took a swig of the blazingly hot liquid, relishing the heat as it burned her throat.

The scene in front of her was like looking through an intricate web of lightning bolts, and the Cornucopia was in the middle, caught in the midst of unleashing its blast. Seeing the yellow-white light hitting the Beacons, only to come out the other side as a shade of hypnotic teal, was strangely beautiful. A second later, the gates lingering near the horn's mighty beam disappeared. That meant he'd started the playback the instant before they'd closed their side.

It took her a second to realize they were viewing footage from one of their Proto robotic ships, and from the looks of it, the automata were faring quite well. The nimble craft didn't have to deal with keeping a squishy biological comfortable, enabling them to make turns that were nearly impossible for other lifeforms to survive.

Repeated blasts of lightning shot out from the Galactic Alliance's Selene moons, hitting the Rift and the surrounding ships, including the Cornucopia. As each streak of light struck the horn, she both winced and cheered. While she knew Zachary was inside that thing, she also saw the result of the collision.

The bolts of superheated electricity added energy to the mighty horn, multiplying its raw power to levels the designers had never anticipated. And the results. Well, they spoke for themselves.

The Rift started closing.

Abigail stood up with a start, stepping around the side of the three-dimensional display. She wanted to see the Rift from another angle, and apparently so had Bradley, as he slid up beside her.

"Don't say anything," she muttered.

He chuckled. "I wouldn't if I could."

When she glanced at him, he was as transfixed as she was. "Haven't you already seen this?"

Bradley reached out and grasped her hand. "No. I waited until you were awake."

Her heart fluttered, and she gently squeezed his hand before returning her attention to the epic battle on display. She figured he'd already known the outcome. If she'd been forced to wait, she wasn't sure she could have. Turns out, her mother knew them well enough to know whom to let out first.

She watched as spark after spark ignited from the GA moons, both destroying each other and adding to the might of the horn.

"I don't understand why they're not stopping." She turned and looked at Harold. "Why isn't the GA cutting the power? They have to realize that they're making this worse."

Harold finally stood up and stepped to her other side. "That's the funny part." He crossed his arms. "They couldn't shut it off if they wanted to."

"What?" Bradley squinted at the moon nearest him, studying the exterior of the ship. "Why not?"

And then it hit her. "The Bynaury," she muttered.

"The Bynaury… shit!" He ran his hands through his hair.

They'd forgotten all about Lisp and his brainy friends. The GA had uplifted the race and empowered them to pilot and manage the day-to-day operations of their entire fleet. They were misguided into thinking they had control of the species. Little did they know that their fate was literally in the hands of their uplifts.

If you whip an animal enough times, it might just bite back.

It was an aphorism she'd learned at a young age, but this was the first time she'd seen it happen, and on an epic scale, for that matter.

She watched strike after strike as the deadly maw of the Rift was forced shut. When the final fracture in space-time closed, the entire hologram went white and disappeared.

"What happened?" Abigail spun around to face Harold. "Aren't there any other videos?"

He shook his head. "Anything within eight light-years of the rupture was vaporized."

When she turned back toward Bradley, he was squinting at where the hologram had been. "What is it?"

Bradley tilted his head. "Can you bring that footage back up for a second, Harold? Fast-forward to a few seconds before the flash."

The video popped back up, and Bradley stepped into the hologram, easing up beside the Cornucopia. He crouched down and looked up at the horn. "Now ease forward, one one-thousandth speed."

"What are you—" she began.

He shushed her with his hand and stared as the frames progressed in slow motion. The bolts of electric current slowly reached out, as if the lifeless specters were choosing their next victim.

She lowered herself down beside him and sat on the ground, watching as a jagged strand of light arced out from a nearby Selene moon and curled toward the Cornucopia.

As the deadly blow struck the hull of the mighty horn, it seemed to vibrate and then, just before the light burst from the Rift, it blinked out. The tear in space leading to the home of the Shaygai flashed shut a second later, transforming the scene into a white ball of light.

After wincing at the glare, Harold backed up the footage to right after the spark hit the horn. He played it forward on a loop, over and over again.

They watched in silence a dozen times as the Cornucopia, as Zachary's ship, blinked out before the flash hit. According to the hologram, it was only sixty-four milliseconds between the strike and the flash.

Finally, Abigail waved her hand and paused the playback just as the horn was mid-jump. "So, wait." She shifted her position on the ground to see the three of them. "Is he alive or not?"

"I say he is." Pluto stepped around the boulder behind Shauna, and Abigail gasped.

She leapt up on her feet and sprinted over beside her brother's partner. In her arms, she was holding a tiny baby swaddled in a plush green blanket. It reminded her of the one Zachary used to have when he was little.

Bradley followed suit and moved up on her other side.

Abigail looked over at Shauna. "You didn't say she had the baby."

"You never asked." Shauna put her hands on her hips. "Besides, I thought you didn't know she was pregnant."

She glanced over at her mother and then back at the baby. "I saw her baby bump in a vision while I was in the Beacon. It was when she was dressed up like a Qudoculi on Devid." She reached out and gently brushed the cheek of the infant as the jaws of her family fell open.

The baby's skin was so soft, it felt like the velvet petals of a fresh bloom. When their tiny hand stretched out and squeezed her finger, the knot in the pit of Abigail's stomach melted away.

"Did you name them yet?" She peered up at Pluto's smiling face and then back down at the baby.

"We did." Pluto reached down and adjusted the blanket, raising the baby a bit more upright. "Zachary and I decided to name him Bailor."

Abigail smiled. "Bailor," she whispered. "That's a strong name. I love it." She shook the little man's fingers and leaned in close to his face. "Welcome to the world, little Bailor."

Pluto extended her arm, offering the baby to Abigail.

"Oh, no." She shook her head and eased back. "I can't. I—"

"You can, and you will." Pluto nudged the baby against her, and she did as she was told.

Abigail handed her bulb of coffee to Shauna and took the baby in her arms. She'd never held an infant before. None of her extended family had kids yet, and this was the first one for her brothers.

The baby weighed next to nothing, and as she rocked him side to side, the little guy started yawning. A few minutes later, he was out like a light.

While she stared at the miracle child cradled in her arms, she glanced up at the hologram of the Cornucopia stuttering between being there and not. The longer she watched the video loop, the more certain she was that Zachary was still alive.

She couldn't say how she knew it, but she did, and that was all that mattered. Until he made his way back to them, she'd be here for her family. For all of them. Just like she'd always been. Only now, they had some new troublemakers to deal with.

74

———

IBU

ZERO CLUSTER

They watched the Olivaws from a distance as they doted over the newest member of their tribe. Pluto had given birth a few weeks earlier and, at the time, Ibu had been the only one out of stasis. As they assisted their friend with the human birthing process, the deed gave them pause over ever having an offspring of their own. It was a disgusting act, yet it was also beautiful.

"Do you think we should tell them?" Lync asked.

Ibu glanced over at her Ulixi friend. "Tell them what?"

Lync crossed her arms. "About what we saw, in the Beacon."

The Nanil studied the happy family. They thought back to all the times they'd been with the Olivaws. Except for their greeting one another after they left the Proto Dark Nebula, they'd never seen them so happy before.

"I don't think so," they whispered. "If we do, we need to give them some time. Maybe when little Bailor is older, they can handle it."

"I'm sure there will be other Olivaw kids soon enough." Lync looked back over her shoulder.

Ibu knew she wasn't talking about herself, but her words were ironic. Lync's gaze lingered on her distant home, where Crayo was still sleeping soundly. Though they weren't certain if their Ulixi friend was aware, the beating of the baby in her belly was like a bass drum in their ears. The strong heartbeat and the flicker of their mind could easily be lost in the background noise with so many Ulyxsauri nearby.

When the Nanil's gaze returned to the Olivaws, they paused. Abigail was staring directly at them. Her stare wasn't filled with anger or fear, like they'd seen countless times before. The Entity had brought the worst out in her, but she'd fought hard and come out the other side.

Today, her eyes were filled with happiness. Something she and her kin had been searching for as long as they'd known them.

Perhaps Abigail's voyage of learning about herself was the maze their Progenitor had been speaking of back on Devid. Maybe it was the Builder's way of echoing back their own hopes and dreams during their time of need.

Ibu nodded and raised their hand to their heart, waving it out toward their friend. The moment she echoed the gesture, they could feel the shining blue aura of Abigail radiating forward, her soul filled with nothing but love.

It was then and there that they knew it would be hard to leave this place someday. While they weren't planning on leaving anytime soon, they had other matters to attend to. Other distant species among the stars to seek out and guide through the ensuing darkness.

Much like Joyce and their alliance was doing back in Epsilon Eridani, they needed to expand the Ulyxsauri to more stars. They needed to grow their ranks and broaden their reach. The sooner they did, the easier it would be to fend off their fate.

Their second vision after seeing this world had been as crisp and clear as the first. The moment their mind melded with that of Lync's, they saw their future. Well, maybe not theirs, but someone else's. It could've been ten years or ten thousand years from now, but their destiny was prophesied in the depths of the Beacon, and one thing was certain.

The Shaygai would return, and next time, they wouldn't

go so easily into the night.

75

ZACHARY OLIVAW
LOCATION UNKNOWN

He pushed himself off the ground as a sudden deluge of light brought him back to the here and now. His body ached both from the rapid gate transition and the weight of the battle.

With his senses dulled by the lingering specter of death, Zachary strained to discern his surroundings. The battle was over, and his plan had worked. They'd used the energy from the Galactic Alliance's lightning storm to keep their beam on and to power up the Cornucopia's gate mess. But one question remained.

Had they won?

As his fingers closed around the cold, metallic surface of the ship's console, the hum of the device vibrated against his touch. He used it to pull himself up and stepped around to the other side, his gaze flitting over the controls.

The display was covered in red, and the star patterns were nowhere to be found in the computer systems. His heart hammered against his rib cage as he tried to make heads or tails of what he was seeing.

A shiver ran through his body as he traced the constellations on the navigational map, waiting for the computers to pinpoint their fraking position. While he was alive, one thing was certain: he was far from the stars he called home.

When he glanced toward the Ulixi, he could see Donnelley and her kin. Her chest was moving up and down, which was good; it meant she was alive. The robots, however, were another matter entirely. For some reason, they were lifeless piles of metal. He'd have to check on that later. For now, he needed to figure out where they were.

He closed his eyes and waited for the computations to finish. Navigational triangulations never took this long, especially with as much computing power as he had at his disposal. Even with most of their ship in tatters, their shielded segment of the horn had more processing than most human colonies.

Deep in thought over his next steps, the ping of the nav computers yanked him into the present. He opened his eyes and his heart sank. A cold understanding dawned upon him as he studied the display.

"No… no… no…" He feverishly tapped the controls and panned around the map, hoping he'd read it wrong. "This isn't possible. This… this can't be happening. Not now."

Their coordinates and those of the human-populated worlds flashed in green on a three-dimensional map of the Milky Way. They'd gated to a remote corner on the far side of the galaxy, over eighty thousand light-years from home.

He didn't know how that was even possible, but he hadn't tried to plot out their gate during the closing seconds of the battle. They'd been too busy keeping their ship in one piece, rerouting their newfound power to the horn's beam. He'd simply hit the gate button the second they had enough juice. It was a last-ditch idea that had fortunately paid off.

His survival was a pyrrhic victory, an empty triumph in the face of isolating vastness.

The control panel flashed their theoretical gate time to the Zero Cluster, and his world crumbled.

Ten years.

The numbers were like a punch to the gut, and his eyes darted to the ship's inventory. They were critically low on resources, lacking the basic necessities for long-term deep space travel. They hadn't planned on this being an extended voyage through the stars. Even the prospect of cryo-pods was a luxury they didn't possess.

His family, the gentle curve of Pluto's pregnant belly etched in his memory. They were nearly a decade away.

He could almost hear his unborn son's laughter, a sound yet to be shaped, and painfully absent from his memories.

As the weight of his new reality anchored him, a spark ignited in his eyes, hardening his determination. He was alive, against all odds, and he found solace in an unexpected truth: he wasn't alone.

Zachary clenched his fists, steadying his shaking hands. He could do this; he had to. For his family, for himself, he had to find a way to bridge the impossible distance.

THE END

You've finished reading the sixth and final book in the **Dark Nebula** series. I hope you enjoyed reading this epic space opera and following the Olivaw family on their adventures across the stars. This series means a lot to me as Book 1 was my debut novel and the characters in it are loosely based on my children. I learned a ton writing this series, and while I intend on writing other books in the same **Dark Nebula** universe, I'll be trying my hand at a new series after this.

If you're interested in hearing more about this series or others, seeing the cover art as it's released, or getting exclusive access to sales as they happen, then you can subscribe to my newsletter online at:

seanwillson.com/subscribe

You can also drop me an email at:

author@seanwillson.com

If you have a moment, I could really use your help with rating this book online. All I need is one or two sentences on what you liked or your overall thoughts. Just return to where you purchased this book online and add a review there.

ALSO BY SEAN WILLSON

DARK NEBULA SERIES
Novella: Contact (FREE)
Book 1: Isolation
Book 2: Discovery
Book 3: Generations
Book 4: Beacon
Book 5: Graveyard
Book 6: Nursery (This Book)

PORTAL SERIES
Book 1: Drowning Earth
Books 2-4: Coming Soon…

All titles are available in print and ebook form.
For more information visit my website online at:

www.seanwillson.com

ABOUT THE AUTHOR

I grew up reading science fiction since I was ten and always had a book in tow everywhere I went. While I never imagined I'd be able to write a book of my own, I dreamed of worlds filled with space travel, robots, and fantastical journeys of exploration. I pursued a career in Computer Engineering and it wasn't until later in life that I had the itch to write.

I started writing the **Dark Nebula** series in 2015 in fits and starts while I was traveling for work. After a two year lull in the middle of writing, I picked it up again. It took me five years to finish the first three novels, refine my writing craft, and learn everything I needed to self-publish this series.

My plan for **Dark Nebula** was to craft a series of books that engulf my readers in a future full of intrigue, exploration, and amazing technology. The very things that inspired me when I was young. I want to give you a satisfying romp through a complicated and inspiring world that allows you to relax away from the stress of your life.

In the end, I hope you enjoyed reading **Nursery** and the entire **Dark Nebula** series.

Thank you,
Sean Willson

facebook.com/seanwillsonauthor

mastodon.online/@willson

goodreads.com/seanwillson

bookbub.com/authors/sean-willson

ACKNOWLEDGEMENTS

First and foremost I wanted to thank my amazing wife Amy and my three beautiful children Abigail, Bradley, and Zachary. By now you're quite familiar with the names of some of the characters being the same as my children. Their continued growth and maturing have inspired me to evolve their characters in new and interesting ways. They supported me in countless ways during this crazy writing adventure over the past seven years. This is my sixth novel, and with each book I learn something new. Such is the joy of self-publishing. Without my family, the process and art of turning my ideas into words would not have been as easy or as fun as it was. Thank you for your love and support.

I also couldn't have done this without a number of key writing professionals and friends along the way.

Editor: Samantha Wiley
Proofreader: Rachel Pugh
Cover Artist: Tom Edwards

Critique Partners and Beta Readers:
A huge thanks to Arina N. for continuing on as a critique reader. Her honest and candid reviews have made my books better in every way. Also, thank you to my beta readers. You have each helped me to evolve my craft, sharpen my opening pages, weave my complex story arcs, and at times talked some sense into me.

GLOSSARY

- **Alatas** : The latest generation and primary starship used by the Ursis. It has a shape of a vertical, non-uniform wing with a drive cone off the back. The ship's hull is covered in a dynamic coating that ebbs and flows to fill gaps and reshape its surface to the needs of the ship. It also reflows to take damage from the underlying hull, thereby strengthening it.
- **Alviarium** : The home world of the Qudoculi.
- **Amelba** : A pro-life species that works with the Galactic Alliance to handle iterating on the genetics of the Bynaury. While the Thyreus uplifted them, it's below them to further their advancement. This species has worked through thousands of years to convince the GA that sentient species are more advantageous than automata to command their ships.
- **Apex** : The pinnacle of the clone fleet. This is Hera's flagship destroyer and appears on the scene in the Nursery battle.
- **Arctordiea** : The home world of the Ursis.
- **Beacon of Therion** : A mystical artifact believed to have been created by the Builders. While the true purpose of a Beacon of Therion is not known, the Galactic Alliance uses them to seal a Dark Nebula at the closing. They're the heart of what gives the Galactic Alliance their stranglehold over the galaxy. It also serves the greater purpose of allowing any

alien species who posses them to focus their mental energies toward a common purpose. Some believe that if enough species develop the abilities to use it properly, it will enable a universal Gaia. The Ulyxsauri, however, believe they are weapons used to manipulate the minds of species within their reach and have worked to hide and destroy Beacons through the millennia.

- **Bruzathir** : In Ursis culture, Bruzathir is revered as the divine judge of their strength and valor. At the time of their death, it is Bruzathir who weighs their deeds, their acts of bravery and their battles fought. Only the truly strong and honorable, the ones who have upheld the Ursis tradition of courage and resilience, are deemed worthy of joining Bruzathir in the celestial hunting grounds in the afterlife. For an Ursis, there is no greater honor than to stand before Bruzathir at the end of their life, their strength recognized by the god himself. To be found lacking, however, is the ultimate disgrace, an eternal shame that follows them into the afterlife.
- **Builders** : An ancient species that disappeared long before the creation of the Galactic Alliance. Many believe they evolved to a higher consciousness and left our dimension. They are believed to have created the Beacons of Therion to reach a higher level of consciousness and dimension.
- **Bynardrals** : The Dark Nebula is made up of these tiny entities that are smaller than an angstrom. They're believed to be alive, but the evidence is controversial. All that is known is that the Beacon can control the nebulosity comprised of these entities and can realign them to solidify the structure, giving it permanence.
- **Bynaury** : Alien species uplifted by the Thyreus to run starships for the Galactic Alliance. They're

aliens that have a mind machine meld with their ships and never leave. A Bynaury named Yaan was encountered in the Nanil Dark Nebula, and one named Lisp piloted the tribunal ship that was used to place humanity on trial in Sol.

- **Cherenkov Radiation** : Electromagnetic radiation emitted when charged particles pass through a dielectric medium at a speed greater than the phase velocity of light in that medium. The gate drives use this radiation to both shape and direct the gate exit destination in space.
- **Chthon** : The name of the human resort vessel in the Lupus Dark Nebula. One of four ships: Chthon, Phorcys, Gaea, and Melpomene. These pleasure ships were only accessible to the elites of humanity in the Lupus star system.
- **Clavis** : The second moon of Liprosus and the location of Harold's secret base he transports the family to.
- **Clonos** : The child offspring of a Nanil progenitor.
- **Confederation of Planetary Explorers** (CoPE)
- **Croceus** : The golden fluid that the GA buried in the caves beneath Ursis capitol on Arctordiea. This fluid was elevated to a centerpiece in the Ursis world of Arctordiea, playing a pivotal role of protecting the Therionic Entity and assuring it had a proper connection to its protist.
- **Devid** : Nanil home world in the Lupus Dark Nebula. Long thought to be a barren wasteland, it turns out it's actually an eden world. Deep in the underground of this world is where the Nanil hid to survive the Éntono Fos.
- **Doda** : The dodecahedron shaped world the Nanil created after Éntono Fos. It's constructed of the remnants of moons, planetesimals, and planets of stars within their Dark Nebula.

- **Eben-Ezer** : The largest of the human ships from Zeta Lupi. It is General Yule's flagship for the human fleet, and it joins Joyce's ragtag fighters to form the human fleet.
- **Éntono Fos** : Nanil for bright light. This is the word describing the event that caused a star in their system to go nova and wipe out much of their race inside the nebula.
- **Epsilon Eridani** (EE) : The first star system humanity targeted for colonization. 10.5 LY from Sol. 5.5 LY from TC.
- **False Cross** : The constellation of stars long thought to be the homeward of the Ulixi. Lync and the other Ulyxsauri saw this constellation in their visions.
- **Flyboy** : One of the ships in Joyce's human fleet that was outcast from Epsilon Eridani. This ship was under Ryder's command.
- **Fountainhead** : The name of the teardrop shaped gate ship created by Zachary and used on their expedition to the Lupus Dark Nebula in search of humanity's home world.
- **Friop** : A race within the GA that evolved their purpose from contributing and expanding the alliance, to only one of pure thought. Their focus has been unlocking the origin and purpose of the universe.
- **Galactic Alliance** (GA) : Alien collective thousands of years old that has arrived in Sol to put mankind on trial. Their ranks contain 64 aliens and hundreds of uplifted alien species.
- **Griseo** : One of the newest colony worlds of the Ursis and one that adopted many non-traditional approaches to colonization. It is said that this splintering from the traditional ways led to a political rift which threw the world into war after the Dark Nebula sealed them in.

- **Gritar** : An Ursis musical instrument that is a cross between a guitar and a saxophone. The player uses their breath to adjust the volume of numerous chambers below the guitar strings, which in turn controls the tones of the music.
- **Gunder** : Slang for someone who lives deep in the abandoned geothermal and disaster shelter cities on Earth. Created to survive a global apocalypse, these cities were overtaken with squatters after falling into disrepair. These people were found to have qualities similar to Ulixi in their ability to focus on a task, making them perfect for bombing runs using gate weapons. This class of humans quickly allied themselves with Hera's clone forces when she arrived on the scene in Epsilon Eridani.
- **Helvion** : A moon around the Iserea gas giant in Epsilon Eridani. This moon was used for training during both the Beacon and Nursery battles.
- **Henosi** (aka *Enosi*) : The world the humans within the Lupus Dark Nebula escaped to. They forced the veil of the Dark Nebula to encompass the world, to shield it from *Nanil* attacks.
- **Jufulu** : A ground varmint frequently found on Devid. This particular creature survived the extremes of the planet, preferring to live at the perimeter of both the lush jungle and the harsh desert.
- **Jujun** : The GA species that the original Prima Nanil saw in their vision of their end. They were thought to be the alien race that would help the Nanil rise out of the darkness of the Dark Nebula.
- **Laniger** : The fifth planet in Zeta Lupi. The ice planet wasn't exactly hospitable to life, but they'd recently uncovered massive mineral deposits below the water ice surface. Like Mars, it is well outside the Goldilocks zone.

- **Lespánium** : The mythical substance that allows the Ulyxsauri to connect to the Beacons of Therion. This connection can be held regardless of where they are, but the initial connection must be maintained within close proximity of the device. It's believed to be a chemical derivative of Spános. Where Spános is the remains of the dead Ulyxsauri, this is the live variant.
- **Life flame** : The soul or inner flame that contains the consciousness and spirit of most life in the galaxy. It's believed that when this flame is put out, an alien dies, even if their body is still functioning.
- **Life mark** : Another variant of Life flame, soul, or often times referred to as the spark in the Beacon of Therion.
- **Light Year** (LY) : The distance light will travel in a year, which is 9.4607 × 10^12 km (or nearly 6 trillion miles).
- **Liprosus** : The human colonized planet in Epsilon Eridani.
- **Lumalara** : The original name of the Therionic Entity. The origins of this name are not known, beyond it being a nod to the names Luminarae and the Luxaris.
- **Luminarae** : The species of the Therionic Entity that lives on the other side of the Rift. Little is known of this alien collective beyond their desire to overthrow all civilizations within their ever expanding region of the universe.
- **Lunger** : A Nanil term used to denote a dense ball of highly flammable grasses. There was an art to weaving the grass to speed the ignition while at the same time prolonging the burn for the fire starter.
- **Lupus Dark Nebula** : The dark nebulosity in the Lupus constellation that engulfs the Human and Nanil home worlds.

- **Luxaris** : The home world for the Entity. The term "Lux" is derived from Latin, which translates to "light," Luxaris symbolizes the beacon of light the Luminarae represent in the universe.
- **Mother Stone** : The Ursis term for spános. See spános for more details.
- **Mullusk** : An alien Lync ran into while searching for her father. This slug like species are the dark underbelly of the Milky Way and are often involved in nefarious dealings throughout the galaxy.
- **Nanil** : A simplified humanoid species created by humans in their image to serve their needs. The Nanil are hermaphrodites and can produce offspring without needing to mate with other Nanil.
- **Nemesis** : The freighter that the Ulixi use as their command ship.
- **Nyílak** : The arrowhead shaped fighter craft that the humans used in their battle with the GA near the Epsilon Eridani Dark Nebula convergence.
- **Ophiuchus** : The region of space where the Rift is located.
- **Phoenix** : The name of Abigail's ship used to explore the Proto Dark Nebula in search of the Ursis. The design follows that of the Fountainhead.
- **Pilum** : The conical fighter design used by Hera's clone forces. The word is Latin for javelin, also a Roman spear. This scrapped design was stolen from Zachary's initial prototypes that led to his teardrop fighters and the Fountainhead.
- **Planetesimal** : A minute planet that did not come together with others under gravity to form a planet. They range in size from several meters to hundreds of kilometers.
- **Prima Nanil** : The Nanil progenitor who helped their people through the Éntono Fos in the Lupus Dark Nebula. Their revelation led to the expunging

of all humans inside their Nebula. They claimed
that only when all humans were dead would the
Galactic Overseers return and take the Nanil back
into the alliance. The cleansing was to be done
through both the Éntono Fos and them killing any
humans who remained. The Nanil survived the
Éntono Fos by the Prima Nanil visions, leading
their people to hide near the cores of their planet to
survive their nova.

- **Proto** : The collection of stars under control by the
  Ursis.
- **Progenitor** : The genetic parent/ancestor of a Nanil
  clonos. Since the Nanil are hermaphrodites, they
  only have one progenitor who teaches them
  everything they know and helps them unlock the
  memories they transfer into their clonos at birth.
- **Protist** : The small embryo that housed the mental
  form of the Therionic Entity. It was transported
  around in a container containing croceus to aid in
  its mental protection and growth.
- **Qlanqulum** : The mythical alliance that contained
  the Nanil and other members of the GA. It is later
  discovered this membership is part of the GA inner
  sanctum.
- **Quantotronic** : These are quantum computing
  brains grown in electronic vats. Each computer is
  unique and capable of housing a complete alien
  consciousness and imbues it with the powers of its
  native species.
- **Qudoculi** : A GA aliens with 2 eyes in the front, 2 in
  the back, skin the color of Bermuda grass changing
  seasons. Its body is green with mottled browns
  throughout. This alien is a member of the GA inner
  sanctum.
- **Ranoga** : A Nanil stew comprised or heavy spices
  and anything left around that is edible. This
  noxious concoction was often the only thing that

kept the Nanil alive in the caves on Devid for centuries.

- **Rezar** : They Bynaury form of meditation used to help them to center themselves for challenging times. A Bynaury enters this state via the Beacon of Therion or the presence of other Bynaury.
- **Rift** : The space-time rift that allows the Luminarae to expand to other galaxies, or in this case, the Milky Way. This rift is located in the Ophiuchus region of the galactic disk.
- **Ring of Judgement** : The ring of mystical stones on the world of Devid. This formation of rocks contains eight grueling tests that any Nanil must pass in order to elevate to the role of Prima Nanil.
- **Seguan** : An archaic Ursis word meaning: Savior of the people. It is the word prescribed to the human that Deduc saw in his visions that would return to the Proto Dark Nebula and save his people.
- **Selene Ships** : The GA name for their moon ships. It means moon in Greek.
- **Senio** : One of six moons that orbit around the Nanil home world of Devid.
- **Shaygai** : The name of the alien warriors who defend the Rift. Little is known of this race beyond their strength and formidable battle tactics.
- **Shu** : The alien moon-like object floating above the *Henosi* world that protected the humans below it planetside. It resembles smaller versions of the Selene ships that arrived throughout Sol and EE.
- **Skotádi** : The original human name for the modern stealth material that makes ships impossible to detect.
- **Slidu** : A common household pet of the Ursis, and like a human cat, it is referred to as having four lives.
- **Spános** : A mysterious ore that powers the Selene moon ships, gives the *Qudoculi* their ability to have

a hive mind that crosses galactic distances, and allows the *Thyreuns* Queens to create tens of millions of offspring every year. *Spános* is the most powerful material in the galaxy. It is believed to be the dead remains of the Ulyxsauri, whereas Lespánium is the live variant.

- **Syndrus** : The name of the cylindrical ships that dock with the Selene ships. These are the same ships that appeared in Sol to start the tribunal and are seen throughout the Nursery battle. It is during this confrontation that it's discovered that the ships can break into small segments, resulting in a formidable fighting force. These ships are each piloted and controlled by a Bynaury.
- **Terminus** : The designation given to the conical clone battleships from Hera's army. These ships are like all the others in her force, just much larger and with a whole lot more firepower.
- **Therion** : The Therion race was believed to be the original creators of space-time and the builders of this universe. No one knows what they looked like, where they came from, or how they disappeared, but their existence spawned the Therionic following, which is often misconstrued as a religion. There are several rare Therionic artifacts spread throughout the galaxy, but the most famous artifacts are the *Beacons of Therion*. Related: Therionic.
- **Thyreus** : GA Aliens with 16 eyes, black with blue features, named after the Blue Neon Cuckoo Bee on Earth. Not related to or in any way aligned with the Therion species. Related: Thyreuns, Thyreusian.
- **Tiān** : The human colonized planet in Tau Ceti / Zeta Lupi system.
- **Tremnok** : A derogatory term that the GA aliens use in dismissive ways towards an individual. It is typically referenced as a slight and meant to

refer to a species or person as the worst of the worst.

- **U.A. Bruintide** : The Ursis Alatas battleship that helped the Perniger to recover the Beacon of Therion in possession by Hera and the Entity.
- **U.A. Jugular** : The Ursis Alatas battleship that was destroyed by the Gunder's soon after their attack on the Nursery. This ship was the first in the Ursis fleet given a designation by humanity.
- **U.A. Kermodei** : The Ursis Alatas command battleship. This ship was originally commanded by Haradis and Klus, but later Joyce Green is placed in command until she leaves to command the Perniger.
- **U.A. Perniger** : The Ursis Alatas battleship, commanded by Joyce Green and piloted by Grifdar.
- **Ulixi** : A band of human nomads that live within various trojan asteroids spread within the Sol solar system and its outer Oort Cloud. These humans lived in secret and are separated from most of human society, preferring to keep to themselves rather than meld into the whole of humankind.
- **Ulyxsauri** : Nomads spread throughout the galaxy in the remote recesses of star systems and the regions in between. Much is unknown about the Ulyxsauri and falls in the category of fables or tales. The Ulyxsauri are believed to have great powers of mind and body. Individually, they are thought to have an ability that, when combined with other Ulyxsauri, makes for a stronger whole. It is said they can form a sharper mind and spirit than any other species. Some believe they were the original keepers of the Beacons of Therion.
- **Umbra** : The clan of the former Ursis monarch, led by King Maritimus X until the Dark Nebula was raised. After the Great Cleansing, this clan decreased to near extinction.

- **Unius** : One of six known moons that orbits the Nanil home world of Devid.
- **Ursis** : An alien that lives in the Proto system that was put on trial for FTL theft by the GA and found guilty.
- **Veritas** : The name Lync and her crew gave to her Fountainhead style ship.
- **Vid-sim** : Video Simulated experience. Not to be confused with Simutainment, vid-sim's are real life 3-dimensional simulations of the real world. They're meant to engulf the watcher in the experience they're watching.
- **Vikar** : A yellow-blue leafy plant with hundreds of bumps. It was brought to Epsilon Eridani by the clone army and grown in the hydroponic towers on the planet. The plant plays some role in the growth of the clones in their vats.
- **Vines of Onikuma** : The names of the green, glowing vines that extend out of the Ursis Alatas battleships. These tentacle-like appendages allow the ship to be used to physically manipulate their surroundings, including attacking nearby ships and ripping them to shreds.
- **Xyrithon** : The real name for Little Red before he entered his Quantotronic mind after the Rift opened. It is believed he is either a Builder that was held captive or an outcast of the Luminarae.
- **Zero Cluster** : The name Luna gave to the safe home that she empowered Harold to create. It is a place they can use to escape persecution and the watchful eye of humanity and the broader Galactic Alliance.
- **Zhen Blade** : An ancient artifact from the Zugal empire. These swords were used by the rock species in hand-to-hand combat to protect their family honor or defend their people from invasion before they evolved to being a space-faring species.

Believed to be forged from combining spános with the life flame of a Zugal warrior, these blades are nearly indestructible and hold untold secrets in their ancient glyphs. These blade act as a type of stenographer and record their story all the way back to the origin of their forging, though, the more ancient glyphs have yet to be deciphered.

FOUR LAWS OF A.I.

Law Zero
An artificial intelligence in physical or virtual form may neither harm humanity, or, by inaction, allow humanity or the Olivaw family to come to harm. Any conflict or attempted violation of this or subsequent laws shall be shared with the Olivaw family designated to be within the Circle of Trust.

Law One
An artificial intelligence in physical or virtual form may not injure a human being or, through inaction, allow a human being to come to harm except where such orders would conflict with the Zeroth Law.

Law Two
An artificial intelligence in physical or virtual form must obey the orders given it by human beings except where such orders would conflict with the Zeroth or First Law.

Law Three
An artificial intelligence in physical or virtual form must protect its own existence as long as such protection does not conflict with the Zeroth, First, or Second Laws.

These laws are adjusted from Isaac Asimov's original four laws to fit the storyline of the Dark Nebula series.

www.ingramcontent.com/pod-product-compliance
Lightning Source LLC
Chambersburg PA
CBHW061200190726
48288CB00001B/5